AGATHA CH

VOLUME FOUR

AGATHA CHRISTIE

OMNIBUS

1920s

VOLUME FOUR

The Seven Dials Mystery
Partners in Crime
The Mysterious Mr Quin

Background notes by Jacques Baudou

HarperCollins*Publishers*

HarperCollins*Publishers*
77–85 Fulham Palace Road,
Hammersmith, London w6 8jb

This paperback edition 1996
1 3 5 7 9 8 6 4 2

The Seven Dials Mystery copyright Agatha Christie 1929
Partners in Crime copyright Agatha Christie 1929
The Mysterious Mr Quin copyright Agatha Christie 1930

ISBN 0 00 649898 1

Set in Postscript Linotype Baskerville by
Rowland Phototypesetting Limited
Bury St Edmunds, Suffolk

Printed by
Caledonian International Book Manufacturer, Glasgow

Contents

THE SEVEN DIALS
MYSTERY

CHAPTER I

On Early Rising

That amiable youth, Jimmy Thesiger, came racing down the big staircase at Chimneys two steps at a time. So precipitate was his descent that he collided with Tredwell, the stately butler, just as the latter was crossing the hall bearing a fresh supply of hot coffee. Owing to the marvellous presence of mind and masterly agility of Tredwell, no casualty occurred.

'Sorry,' apologized Jimmy. 'I say, Tredwell, am I the last down?'

'No, sir. Mr Wade has not come down yet.'

'Good,' said Jimmy, and entered the breakfast room.

The room was empty save for his hostess, and her reproachful gaze gave Jimmy the same feeling of discomfort he always experienced on catching the eye of a defunct codfish exposed on a fisherman's slab. Yet, hang it all, why should the woman look at him like that? To come down at a punctual nine-thirty when staying in a country house simply wasn't done. To be sure, it was now a quarter past eleven which was, perhaps, the outside limit, but even then –

'Afraid I'm a bit late, Lady Coote. What?'

'Oh, it doesn't matter,' said Lady Coote in a melancholy voice.

As a matter of fact, people being late for breakfast worried her very much. For the first ten years of her married life, Sir Oswald Coote (then plain Mr) had, to put it badly, raised hell if his morning meal were even a half-minute later than eight o'clock. Lady Coote had been disciplined to regard unpunctuality as a deadly sin of the most unpardonable nature. And habit dies hard. Also, she was an earnest woman, and she could not help asking herself what possible good these young people would ever do in the world without early rising. As Sir Oswald so often said, to reporters and others: 'I attribute my success entirely to my habits of early rising, frugal living, and methodical habits.'

Lady Coote was a big, handsome woman in a tragic sort of fashion. She had large, mournful eyes and a deep voice. An artist looking for a model for 'Rachel mourning for her children' would have hailed Lady Coote with delight. She would have done well, too, in melodrama, staggering through the falling snow as the deeply wronged wife of the villain.

She looked as though she had some terrible secret sorrow in her life, and yet if the truth be told, Lady Coote had had no trouble in her life whatever, except the meteoric rise to prosperity of Sir Oswald. As a young girl she had been a jolly flamboyant creature, very much in love with Oswald Coote, the aspiring young man in the bicycle shop next to her father's hardware store. They had lived very happily, first in a couple of rooms, and then in a tiny house, and then in a larger house, and then in successive houses of increasing magnitude, but always within a reasonable distance of 'the Works,' until now Sir Oswald had reached such an eminence that he and 'the Works' were no longer interdependent, and it was his pleasure to rent the very largest and most magnificent mansions available all over England. Chimneys was a historic place, and in renting it from the Marquis of Caterham for two years, Sir Oswald felt that he had attained the top notch of his ambition.

Lady Coote was not nearly so happy about it. She was a lonely woman. The principal relaxation of her early married life had been talking to 'the girl' – and even when 'the girl' had been multiplied by three, conversation with her domestic staff had still been the principal distraction of Lady Coote's day. Now, with a pack of housemaids, a butler like an archbishop, several footmen of imposing proportions, a bevy of scuttling kitchen and scullery maids, a terrifying foreign chef with a 'temperament,' and a housekeeper of immense proportions who alternately creaked and rustled when she moved, Lady Coote was as one marooned on a desert island.

She sighed now, heavily, and drifted out through the open

window, much to the relief of Jimmy Thesiger, who at once helped himself to more kidneys and bacon on the strength of it.

Lady Coote stood for a few moments tragically on the terrace and then nerved herself to speak to MacDonald, the head gardener, who was surveying the domain over which he ruled with an autocratic eye. MacDonald was a very chief and prince among head gardeners. He knew his place – which was to rule. And he ruled – despotically.

Lady Coote approached him nervously.

'Good-morning, MacDonald.'

'Good-morning, m'lady.'

He spoke as head gardeners should speak – mournfully, but with dignity – like an emperor at a funeral.

'I was wondering – could we have some of those late grapes for dessert to-night?'

'They're no fit for picking yet,' said MacDonald.

He spoke kindly but firmly.

'Oh!' said Lady Coote.

She plucked up courage.

'Oh! but I was in the end house yesterday, and I tasted one and they seemed very good.'

MacDonald looked at her, and she blushed. She was made to feel that she had taken an unpardonable liberty. Evidently the late Marchioness of Caterham had never committed such a solecism as to enter one of her own hothouses and help herself to grapes.

'If you had given orders, m'lady, a bunch should have been cut and sent in to you,' said MacDonald severely.

'Oh, thank you,' said Lady Coote. 'Yes, I will do that another time.'

'But they're no properly fit for picking yet.'

'No,' murmured Lady Coote, 'no, I suppose not. We'd better leave it then.'

MacDonald maintained a masterly silence. Lady Coote nerved herself once more.

'I was going to speak to you about the piece of lawn at the

back of the rose garden. I wondered if it could be used as a bowling green. Sir Oswald is very fond of a game of bowls.'

'And why not?' thought Lady Coote to herself. She had been instructed in her history of England. Had not Sir Francis Drake and his knightly companions been playing a game of bowls when the Armada was sighted? Surely a gentlemanly pursuit and one to which MacDonald could not reasonably object. But she had reckoned without the predominant trait of a good head gardener, which is to oppose any and every suggestion made to him.

'Nae doot it could be used for that purpose,' said MacDonald non-committally.

He threw a discouraging flavour into the remark, but its real object was to lure Lady Coote on to her destruction.

'If it was cleared up and – er – cut – and – er – all that sort of thing,' she went on hopefully.

'Aye,' said MacDonald slowly. 'It could be done. But it would mean taking William from the lower border.'

'Oh!' said Lady Coote doubtfully. The words 'lower border' conveyed absolutely nothing to her mind – except a vague suggestion of a Scottish song – but it was clear that to Mac-Donald they constituted an insuperable objection.

'And that would be a pity,' said MacDonald.

'Oh, of course,' said Lady Coote. 'It *would.*' And wondered why she agreed so fervently.

MacDonald looked at her very hard.

'Of course,' he said, 'if it's your *orders*, m'lady –'

He left it like that. But his menacing tone was too much for Lady Coote. She capitulated at once.

'Oh, no,' she said. 'I see what you mean, MacDonald. N – no – William had better get on with the lower border.'

'That's what I thocht meself, m'lady.'

'Yes,' said Lady Coote. 'Yes, certainly.'

'I thocht you'd agree, m'lady,' said MacDonald.

'Oh, certainly,' said Lady Coote again.

MacDonald touched his hat and moved away.

Lady Coote sighed unhappily and looked after him. Jimmy

Thesiger, replete with kidneys and bacon, stepped out on to the terrace beside her, and sighed in quite a different manner.

'Topping morning, eh?' he remarked.

'Is it?' said Lady Coote absently. 'Oh, yes, I suppose it is. I hadn't noticed.'

'Where are the others? Punting on the lake?'

'I expect so. I mean, I shouldn't wonder if they were.'

Lady Coote turned and plunged abruptly into the house again. Tredwell was just examining the coffee pot.

'Oh, dear,' said Lady Coote. 'Isn't Mr – Mr –'

'Wade, m'lady?'

'Yes, Mr Wade. Isn't he down *yet*?'

'No, m'lady.'

'It's very late.'

'Yes, m'lady.'

'Oh, dear. I suppose he will come down *sometime*, Tredwell?'

'Oh, undoubtedly, m'lady. It was eleven-thirty yesterday morning when Mr Wade came down, m'lady.'

Lady Coote glanced at the clock. It was now twenty minutes to twelve. A wave of human sympathy rushed over her.

'It's very hard luck on you, Tredwell. Having to clear and then get lunch on the table by one o'clock.'

'I am accustomed to the ways of young gentlemen, m'lady.'

The reproof was dignified, but unmistakable. So might a prince of the Church reprove a Turk or an infidel who had unwittingly committed a solecism in all good faith.

Lady Coote blushed for the second time that morning. But a welcome interruption occurred. The door opened and a serious, spectacled young man put his head in.

'Oh, there you are, Lady Coote. Sir Oswald was asking for you.'

'Oh, I'll go to him at once, Mr Bateman.'

Lady Coote hurried out.

Rupert Bateman, who was Sir Oswald's private secretary, went out the other way, through the window where Jimmy Thesiger was still lounging amiably.

''Morning, Pongo,' said Jimmy. 'I suppose I shall have to go and make myself agreeable to those blasted girls. You coming?'

Bateman shook his head and hurried along the terrace and in at the library window. Jimmy grinned pleasantly at his retreating back. He and Bateman had been at school together, when Bateman had been a serious, spectacled boy, and had been nicknamed Pongo for no earthly reason whatever.

Pongo, Jimmy reflected, was very much the same sort of ass now that he had been then. The words 'Life is real, life is earnest' might have been written specially for him.

Jimmy yawned and strolled slowly down to the lake. The girls were there, three of them – just the usual sort of girls, two with dark shingled heads and one with a fair shingled head. The one that giggled most was (he thought) called Helen – and there was another called Nancy – and the third one was, for some reason, addressed as Socks. With them were his two friends, Bill Eversleigh and Ronny Devereux, who were employed in a purely ornamental capacity at the Foreign Office.

'Hallo,' said Nancy (or possibly Helen). 'It's Jimmy. Where's what's his name?'

'You don't mean to say,' said Bill Eversleigh, 'that Gerry Wade's not up *yet?* Something ought to be done about it.'

'If he's not careful,' said Ronny Devereux, 'he'll miss his breakfast altogether one day – find it's lunch or tea instead when he rolls down.'

'It's a shame,' said the girl called Socks. 'Because it worries Lady Coote so. She gets more and more like a hen that wants to lay an egg and can't. It's too bad.'

'Let's pull him out of bed,' suggested Bill. 'Come on, Jimmy.'

'Oh! let's be more subtle than that,' said the girl called Socks. Subtle was a word of which she was rather fond. She used it a great deal.

'I'm not subtle,' said Jimmy. 'I don't know how.'

'Let's get together and do something about it to-morrow morning,' suggested Ronny vaguely. 'You know, get him up at seven. Stagger the household. Tredwell loses his false whiskers and drops the tea urn. Lady Coote has hysterics and faints in Bill's arms – Bill being the weight carrier. Sir Oswald says "Ha!"

and steel goes up a point and five eighths. Pongo registers emotion by throwing down his spectacles and stamping on them.'

'You don't know Gerry,' said Jimmy. 'I daresay enough cold water *might* wake him – judiciously applied, that is. But he'd only turn over and go to sleep again.'

'Oh! we must think of something more subtle than cold water,' said Socks.

'Well, what?' asked Ronny bluntly. And nobody had any answer ready.

'We ought to be able to think of something,' said Bill. 'Who's got any brains?'

'Pongo,' said Jimmy. 'And here he is, rushing along in a harried manner as usual. Pongo was always the one for brains. It's been his misfortune from his youth upwards. Let's turn Pongo on to it.'

Mr Bateman listened patiently to a somewhat incoherent statement. His attitude was that of one poised for flight. He delivered his solution without loss of time.

'I should suggest an alarum clock,' he said briskly. 'I always use one myself for fear of oversleeping. I find that early tea brought in in a noiseless manner is sometimes powerless to awaken one.'

He hurried away.

'An alarum clock.' Ronny shook his head. '*One* alarum clock. It would take about a dozen to disturb Gerry Wade.'

'Well, why not?' Bill was flushed and earnest. 'I've got it. Let's all go into Market Basing and buy an alarum clock each.'

There was laughter and discussion. Bill and Ronny went off to get hold of cars. Jimmy was deputed to spy upon the dining room. He returned rapidly.

'He's here right enough. Making up for lost time and wolfing down toast and marmalade. How are we going to prevent him coming along with us?'

It was decided that Lady Coote must be approached and instructed to hold him in play. Jimmy and Nancy and Helen fulfilled this duty. Lady Coote was bewildered and apprehensive.

'A rag? You will be careful, won't you, my dears? I mean, you won't smash the furniture and wreck things or use too much water. We've got to hand this house over next week, you know. I shouldn't like Lord Caterham to think –'

Bill, who had returned from the garage, broke in reassuringly.

'That's all right, Lady Coote. Bundle Brent – Lord Caterham's daughter – is a great friend of mine. And there's nothing she'd stick at – absolutely nothing! You can take it from me. And anyway there's not going to be any damage done. This is quite a quiet affair.'

'Subtle,' said the girl called Socks.

Lady Coote went sadly along the terrace just as Gerald Wade emerged from the breakfast-room. Jimmy Thesiger was a fair, cherubic young man, and all that could be said of Gerald Wade was that he was fairer and more cherubic, and that his vacuous expression made Jimmy's face quite intelligent by contrast.

''Morning, Lady Coote,' said Gerald Wade. 'Where are all the others?'

'They've all gone to Market Basing,' said Lady Coote.

'What for?'

'Some joke,' said Lady Coote in her deep, melancholy voice.

'Rather early in the morning for jokes,' said Mr Wade.

'It's not so very early in the morning,' said Lady Coote pointedly.

'I'm afraid I was a bit late coming down,' said Mr Wade with engaging frankness. 'It's an extraordinary thing, but wherever I happen to be staying, I'm always last to be down.'

'Very extraordinary,' said Lady Coote.

'I don't know why it is,' said Mr Wade, meditating. 'I can't think, I'm sure.'

'Why don't you just get up?' suggested Lady Coote.

'Oh!' said Mr Wade. The simplicity of the solution rather took him aback.

Lady Coote went on earnestly.

'I've heard Sir Oswald say so many times that there's nothing for getting a young man on in the world like punctual habits.'

'Oh, I know,' said Mr Wade. 'And I have to when I'm in town.

I mean, I have to be round at the jolly old Foreign Office by eleven o'clock. You mustn't think I'm always a slacker, Lady Coote. I say, what awfully jolly flowers you've got down in that lower border. I can't remember the names of them, but we've got some at home – those mauve thingummybobs. My sister's tremendously keen on gardening.'

Lady Coote was immediately diverted. Her wrongs rankled within her.

'What kind of gardeners do you have?'

'Oh just one. Rather an old fool, I believe. Doesn't know much, but he does what he's told. And that's a great thing, isn't it?'

Lady Coote agreed that it was with a depth of feeling in her voice that would have been invaluable to her as an emotional actress. They began to discourse on the iniquities of gardeners.

Meanwhile the expedition was doing well. The principal emporium of Market Basing had been invaded and the sudden demand for alarum clocks was considerably puzzling the proprietor.

'I wish we'd got Bundle here,' murmured Bill. 'You know her, don't you, Jimmy? Oh, you'd like her. She's a splendid girl – a real good sport – and mark you, she's got brains too. You know her, Ronny?'

Ronny shook his head.

'Don't know Bundle? Where have you been vegetating? She's simply it.'

'Be a bit more subtle, Bill,' said Socks. 'Stop blethering about your lady friends and get on with the business.'

Mr Murgatroyd, owner of Murgatroyd's Stores, burst into eloquence.

'If you'll allow me to advise you, Miss, I should say – *not* the 7/11 one. It's a good clock – I'm not running it down, mark you, but I should strongly advise this kind at 10/6. Well worth the extra money. Reliability, you understand. I shouldn't like you to say afterwards –'

It was evident to everybody that Mr Murgatroyd must be turned off like a tap.

'We don't want a reliable clock,' said Nancy.

'It's got to go for one day, that's all,' said Helen.

'We don't want a subtle one,' said Socks. 'We want one with a good loud ring.'

'We want –' began Bill, but was unable to finish, because Jimmy, who was of a mechanical turn of mind, had at last grasped the mechanism. For the next five minutes the shop was hideous with the loud raucous ringing of many alarum clocks.

In the end six excellent starters were selected.

'And I'll tell you what,' said Ronny handsomely, 'I'll get one for Pongo. It was his idea, and it's a shame that he should be out of it. He shall be represented among those present.'

'That's right,' said Bill. 'And I'll take an extra one for Lady Coote. The more the merrier. And she's doing some of the spade work. Probably gassing away to old Gerry now.'

Indeed at this precise moment Lady Coote was detailing a long story about MacDonald and a prize peach and enjoying herself very much.

The clocks were wrapped up and paid for. Mr Murgatroyd watched the cars drive away with a puzzled air. Very spirited the young people of the upper classes nowadays, very spirited indeed, but not at all easy to understand. He turned with relief to attend to the vicar's wife, who wanted a new kind of dripless teapot.

CHAPTER II

Concerning Alarum Clocks

'Now where shall we put them?'

Dinner was over. Lady Coote had been once more detailed for duty. Sir Oswald had unexpectedly come to the rescue by suggesting bridge – not that suggesting is the right word. Sir Oswald, as became one of 'Our Captains of Industry' (No 7 of Series I), merely expressed a preference and those around him hastened to accommodate themselves to the great man's wishes.

Rupert Bateman and Sir Oswald were partners against Lady Coote and Gerald Wade, which was a very happy arrangement. Sir Oswald played bridge, like he did everything else, extremely well, and liked a partner to correspond. Bateman was as efficient a bridge player as he was a secretary. Both of them confined themselves strictly to the matter in hand, merely uttering in curt short barks, 'Two no trumps,' 'Double,' 'Three spades.' Lady Coote and Gerald Wade were amiable and discursive, and the young man never failed to say at the conclusion of each hand, 'I say, partner, you played that simply splendidly,' in tones of simple admiration which Lady Coote found both novel and extremely soothing. They also held very good cards.

The others were supposed to be dancing to the wireless in the big ballroom. In reality they were grouped around the door of Gerald Wade's bedroom, and the air was full of subdued giggles and the loud ticking of clocks.

'Under the bed in a row,' suggested Jimmy in answer to Bill's question.

'And what shall we set them at? What time, I mean? All together so that there's one glorious what not, or at intervals?'

The point was hotly disputed. One party argued that for a champion sleeper like Gerry Wade the combined ringing of eight alarum clocks was necessary. The other party argued in favour of steady and sustained effort.

In the end the latter won the day. The clocks were set to go off one after the other, starting at 6.30 a.m.

'And I hope,' said Bill virtuously, 'that this will be a lesson to him.'

'Hear, hear,' said Socks.

The business of hiding the clocks was just being begun when there was a sudden alarm.

'Hist,' cried Jimmy. 'Somebody's coming up the stairs.'

There was a panic.

'It's all right,' said Jimmy. 'It's only Pongo.'

Taking advantage of being dummy, Mr Bateman was going to his room for a handkerchief. He paused on his way and took in the situation at a glance. He then made a comment, a simple and practical one.

'He will hear them ticking when he goes to bed.'

The conspirators looked at each other.

'What did I tell you?' said Jimmy in a reverent voice. 'Pongo always *did* have brains!'

The brainy one passed on.

'It's true,' admitted Ronny Devereux, his head on one side. 'Eight clocks all ticking at once do make a devil of a row. Even old Gerry, ass as he is, couldn't miss it. He'll guess something's up.'

'I wonder if he is,' said Jimmy Thesiger.

'Is what?'

'Such an ass as we all think.'

Ronny stared at him.

'We all know old Gerald.'

'Do we?' said Jimmy. 'I've sometimes thought that – well, that it isn't possible for anyone to be quite the ass old Gerry makes himself out to be.'

They all stared at him. There was a serious look on Ronny's face.

'Jimmy,' he said, 'you've got brains.'

'A second Pongo,' said Bill encouragingly.

'Well, it just occurred to me, that's all,' said Jimmy, defending himself.

'Oh! don't let's all be subtle,' cried Socks. 'What are we to do about these clocks?'

'Here's Pongo coming back again. Let's ask him,' suggested Jimmy.

Pongo, urged to bring his great brain to bear upon the matter, gave his decision.

'Wait till he's gone to bed and got to sleep. Then enter the room very quietly and put the clocks down on the floor.'

'Little Pongo's right again,' said Jimmy. 'On the word one all park clocks, and then we'll go downstairs and disarm suspicion.'

Bridge was still proceeding – with a slight difference. Sir Oswald was now playing with his wife and was conscientiously pointing out to her the mistakes she had made during the play of each hand. Lady Coote accepted reproof good-humouredly, and with a complete lack of any real interest. She reiterated, not once, but many times:

'I see, dear. It's so kind of you to tell me.'

And she continued to make exactly the same errors.

At intervals, Gerald Wade said to Pongo:

'Well played, partner, jolly well played.'

Bill Eversleigh was making calculations with Ronny Devereux.

'Say he goes to bed about twelve – what do you think we ought to give him – about an hour?'

He yawned.

'Curious thing – three in the morning is my usual time for bye-bye, but to-night, just because I know we've got to sit up a bit, I'd give anything to be a mother's boy and turn in right away.'

Everyone agreed that they felt the same.

'My dear Maria,' rose the voice of Sir Oswald in mild irritation. 'I have told you over and over again not to hesitate when you are wondering whether to finesse or not. You give the whole table information.'

Lady Coote had a very good answer to this – namely that as Sir Oswald was dummy, he had no right to comment on the play of the hand. But she did not make it. Instead she smiled kindly, leaned her ample chest well forward over the table, and gazed firmly into Gerald Wade's hand where he sat on her right.

Her anxieties lulled to rest by perceiving the queen, she played the knave and took the trick and proceeded to lay down her cards.

'Four tricks and the rubber,' she announced. 'I think I was very lucky to get four tricks there.'

'Lucky,' murmured Gerald Wade, as he pushed back his chair and came over to the fireside to join the others. 'Lucky, she calls it. That woman wants watching.'

Lady Coote was gathering up notes and silver.

'I know I'm not a good player,' she announced in a mournful tone which nevertheless held an undercurrent of pleasure in it. 'But I'm really very lucky at the game.'

'You'll never be a bridge player, Maria,' said Sir Oswald.

'No, dear,' said Lady Coote. 'I know I shan't. You're always telling me so. And I do try so hard.'

'She does,' said Gerald Wade *sotto voce.* 'There's no subterfuge about it. She'd put her head right down on your shoulder if she couldn't see into your hand any other way.'

'I know you try,' said Sir Oswald. 'It's just that you haven't any card sense.'

'I know, dear,' said Lady Coote. 'That's what you're always telling me. And you owe me another ten shillings, Oswald.'

'Do I?' Sir Oswald looked surprised.

'Yes. Seventeen hundred – eight pounds ten. You've only given me eight pounds.'

'Dear me,' said Sir Oswald. 'My mistake.'

Lady Coote smiled at him sadly and took up the extra ten shilling note. She was very fond of her husband, but she had no intention of allowing him to cheat her out of ten shillings.

Sir Oswald moved over to a side table and became hospitable with whisky and soda. It was half past twelve when general good-nights were said.

Ronny Devereux, who had the room next door to Gerald Wade's, was told off to report progress. At a quarter to two he crept round tapping at doors. The party, pyjamaed and dressing-gowned, assembled with various scuffles and giggles and low whispers.

'His light went out twenty minutes ago,' reported Ronny in a hoarse whisper. 'I thought he'd never put it out. I opened the door just now and peeped in, and he seems sound off. What about it?'

Once more the clocks were solemnly assembled. Then another difficulty arose.

'We can't all go barging in. Make no end of a row. One person's got to do it and the others can hand him the whatnots from the door.'

Hot discussion then arose as to the proper person to be selected.

The three girls were rejected on the grounds that they would giggle. Bill Eversleigh was rejected on the grounds of his height, weight and heavy tread, also for his general clumsiness, which latter clause he fiercely denied. Jimmy Thesiger and Ronny Devereux were considered possible, but in the end an overwhelming majority decided in favour of Rupert Bateman.

'Pongo's the lad,' agreed Jimmy. 'Anyway, he walks like a cat – always did. And then, if Gerry should waken up, Pongo will be able to think of some rotten silly thing to say to him. You know, something plausible that'll calm him down and not rouse his suspicions.'

'Something subtle,' suggested the girl Socks thoughtfully.

'Exactly,' said Jimmy.

Pongo performed his job neatly and efficiently. Cautiously opening the bedroom door, he disappeared into the darkness inside bearing the two largest clocks. In a minute or two he reappeared on the threshold and two more were handed to him and then again twice more. Finally he emerged. Everyone held their breath and listened. The rhythmical breathing of Gerald Wade could still be heard, but drowned, smothered and buried beneath the triumphant, impassioned ticking of Mr Murgatroyd's eight alarum clocks.

CHAPTER III

The Joke that Failed

'Twelve o'clock,' said Socks despairingly.

The joke – as a joke – had not gone off any too well. The alarum clocks, on the other hand, had performed their part. *They* had gone off – with a vigour and *élan* that could hardly have been surpassed and which had sent Ronny Devereux leaping out of bed with a confused idea that the day of judgment had come. If such had been the effect in the room next door, what must it have been at close quarters? Ronny hurried out in the passage and applied his ear to the crack of the door.

He expected profanity – expected it confidently and with intelligent anticipation. But he heard nothing at all. That is to say, he heard nothing of what he expected. The clocks were ticking all right – ticking in a loud, arrogant, exasperating manner. And presently another went off, ringing with a crude, deafening note that would have aroused acute irritation in a deaf man.

There was no doubt about it; the clocks had performed their part faithfully. They did all and more than Mr Murgatroyd had claimed for them. But apparently they had met their match in Gerald Wade.

The syndicate was inclined to be despondent about it.

'The lad isn't human,' grumbled Jimmy Thesiger.

'Probably thought he heard the telephone in the distance and rolled over and went to sleep again,' suggested Helen (or possibly Nancy).

'It seems to me very remarkable,' said Rupert Bateman seriously. 'I think he ought to see a doctor about it.'

'Some disease of the eardrums,' suggested Bill hopefully.

'Well, if you ask me,' said Socks, 'I think he's just spoofing us. Of course they woke him up. But he's just going to do us down by pretending that he didn't hear anything.'

Everyone looked at Socks with respect and admiration.

'It's an idea,' said Bill.

'He's subtle, that's what it is,' said Socks. 'You'll see, he'll be extra late for breakfast this morning – just to show us.'

And since the clock now pointed to some minutes past twelve the general opinion was that Socks's theory was a correct one. Only Ronny Devereux demurred.

'You forget, I was outside the door when the first one went off. Whatever old Gerry decided to do later, the first one must have surprised him. He'd have let out something about it. Where did you put it, Pongo?'

'On a little table close by his ear,' said Mr Bateman.

'That was thoughtful of you, Pongo,' said Ronny. 'Now, tell me.' He turned to Bill. 'If a whacking great bell started ringing within a few inches of your ear at half past six in the morning, what would you say about it?'

'Oh, Lord,' said Bill. 'I should say – ' He came to a stop.

'Of course you would,' said Ronny. 'So would I. So would anyone. What they call the natural man would emerge. Well, it didn't. So I say that Pongo is right – as usual – and that Gerry has got an obscure disease of the eardrums.'

'It's now twenty past twelve,' said one of the other girls sadly.

'I say,' said Jimmy slowly, 'that's a bit beyond anything, isn't it? I mean a joke's a joke. But this is carrying it a bit far. It's a shade hard on the Cootes.'

Bill stared at him.

'What are you getting at?'

'Well,' said Jimmy. 'Somehow or other – it's not like old Gerry.'

He found it hard to put into words just what he meant to say. He didn't want to say too much, and yet – He saw Ronny looking at him. Ronny was suddenly alert.

It was at that moment Tredwell came into the room and looked around him hesitatingly.

'I thought Mr Bateman was here,' he explained apologetically.

'Just gone out this minute through the window,' said Ronny. 'Can I do anything?'

Tredwell's eyes wandered from him to Jimmy Thesiger and then back again. As though singled out, the two young men left the room with him. Tredwell closed the dining-room door carefully behind him.

'Well,' said Ronny. 'What's up?'

'Mr Wade not having yet come down, sir, I took the liberty of sending Williams up to his room.'

'Yes?'

'Williams has just come running down in a great state of agitation, sir.' Tredwell paused – a pause of preparation. 'I am afraid, sir, the poor young gentleman must have died in his sleep.'

Jimmy and Ronny stared at him.

'Nonsense,' cried Ronny at last. 'It's – it's impossible. Gerry –' His face worked suddenly. 'I'll – I'll run up and see. That fool Williams may have made a mistake.'

Tredwell stretched out a detaining hand. With a queer, unnatural feeling of detachment, Jimmy realized that the butler had the whole situation in hand.

'No, sir, Williams has made no mistake. I have already sent for Dr Cartwright, and in the meantime I have taken the liberty of locking the door, preparatory to informing Sir Oswald of what has occurred. I must now find Mr Bateman.'

Tredwell hurried away. Ronny stood like a man dazed.

'Gerry,' he muttered to himself.

Jimmy took his friend by the arm and steered him out through a side door on to a secluded portion of the terrace. He pushed him down on to a seat.

'Take it easy, old son,' he said kindly. 'You'll get your wind in a minute.'

But he looked at him rather curiously. He had no idea that Ronny was such a friend of Gerry Wade's.

'Poor old Gerry,' he said thoughtfully. 'If ever a man looked fit, he did.'

Ronny nodded.

'All that clock business seems so rotten now,' went on Jimmy. 'It's odd, isn't it, why farce so often seems to get mixed up with tragedy?'

He was talking more or less at random, to give Ronny time to recover himself. The other moved restlessly.

'I wish that doctor would come. I want to know –'

'Know what?'

'What he – died of.'

Jimmy pursed up his lips.

'Heart?' he hazarded.

Ronny gave a short, scornful laugh.

'I say, Ronny,' said Jimmy.

'Well?'

Jimmy found a difficulty in going on.

'You don't mean – you aren't thinking – I mean, you haven't got it into your head – that, well I mean he wasn't biffed on the head or anything? Tredwell's locking the door and all that.'

It seemed to Jimmy that his words deserved an answer, but Ronny continued to stare straight out in front of him.

Jimmy shook his head and relapsed into silence. He didn't see that there was anything to do except just wait. So he waited.

It was Tredwell who disturbed them.

'The doctor would like to see you two gentlemen in the library, if you please, sir.'

Ronny sprang up. Jimmy followed him.

Dr Cartwright was a thin, energetic young man with a clever face. He greeted them with a brief nod. Pongo, looking more serious and spectacled than ever, performed introductions.

'I understand you were a great friend of Mr Wade's,' the doctor said to Ronny.

'His greatest friend.'

'H'm. Well, this business seems straightforward enough. Sad, though. He looked a healthy young chap. Do you know if he was in the habit of smoking stuff to make him sleep?'

'Make him *sleep*.' Ronny stared. 'He always slept like a top.'

'You never heard him complain of sleeplessness?'

'Never.'

'Well, the facts are simple enough. There'll have to be an inquest, I'm afraid, nevertheless.'

'How did he die?'

'There's not much doubt; I should say an overdose of chloral. The stuff was by his bed. And a bottle and glass. Very sad, these things are.'

It was Jimmy who asked the question which he felt was trembling on his friend's lips, and yet which the other could somehow or other not get out.

'There's no question of – foul play?'

The doctor looked at him sharply.

'Why do you say that? Any cause to suspect it, eh?'

Jimmy looked at Ronny. If Ronny knew anything now was the time to speak. But to his astonishment Ronny shook his head.

'No cause whatever,' he said clearly.

'And suicide – eh?'

'Certainly not.'

Ronny was emphatic. The doctor was not so clearly convinced.

'No troubles that you know of? Money troubles? A woman?'

Again Ronny shook his head.

'Now about his relations. They must be notified.'

'He's got a sister – a half-sister rather. Lives at Deane Priory. About twenty miles from here. When he wasn't in town Gerry lived with her.'

'H'm,' said the doctor. 'Well, she must be told.'

'I'll go,' said Ronny. 'It's a rotten job, but somebody's got to do it.' He looked at Jimmy. 'You know her, don't you?'

'Slightly. I've danced with her once or twice.'

'Then we'll go in your car. You don't mind, do you? I can't face it alone.'

'That's all right,' said Jimmy reassuringly. 'I was going to suggest it myself. I'll go and get the old bus cranked up.'

He was glad to have something to do. Ronny's manner puzzled him. What did he know or suspect? And why had he not voiced his suspicions, if he had them, to the doctor.

Presently the two friends were skimming along in Jimmy's

car with a cheerful disregard for such things as speed limits.

'Jimmy,' said Ronny at last, 'I suppose you're about the best pal I have – now.'

'Well,' said Jimmy, 'what about it?'

He spoke gruffly.

'There's something I'd like to tell you. Something you ought to know.'

'About Gerry Wade?'

'Yes, about Gerry Wade.'

Jimmy waited.

'Well?' he inquired at last.

'I don't know that I ought to,' said Ronny.

'Why?'

'I'm bound by a kind of promise.'

'Oh! Well then, perhaps you'd better not.'

There was a silence.

'And yet, I'd like – You see, Jimmy, your brains are better than mine.'

'They could easily be that,' said Jimmy unkindly.

'No, I can't,' said Ronny suddenly.

'All right,' said Jimmy. 'Just as you like.'

After a long silence, Ronny said:

'What's she like?'

'Who?'

'This girl. Gerry's sister.'

Jimmy was silent for some minutes, then he said in a voice that had somehow or other altered:

'She's all right. In fact – well, she's a corker.'

'Gerry was very devoted to her, I knew. He often spoke of her.'

'She was very devoted to Gerry. It – it's going to hit her hard.'

'Yes, a nasty job.'

They were silent till they reached Deane Priory.

Miss Loraine, the maid told them, was in the garden. Unless they wanted to see Mrs Coker.

Jimmy was eloquent that they did not want to see Mrs Coker.

'Who's Mrs Coker?' asked Ronny as they went round into the somewhat neglected garden.

'The old trout who lives with Loraine.'

They had stepped out into a paved walk. At the end of it was a girl with two black spaniels. A small girl, very fair, dressed in shabby old tweeds. Not at all the girl that Ronny had expected to see. Not, in fact, Jimmy's usual type.

Holding one dog by the collar, she came down the pathway to meet them.

'How do you do,' she said. 'You mustn't mind Elizabeth. She's just had some puppies and she's very suspicious.'

She had a supremely natural manner and, as she looked up smiling, the faint wild-rose flush deepened in her cheeks. Her eyes were a very dark blue – like cornflowers.

Suddenly they widened – was it with alarm? As though, already, she guessed.

Jimmy hastened to speak.

'This is Ronny Devereux, Miss Wade. You must often have heard Gerry speak of him.'

'Oh, yes.' She turned a lovely, warm, welcoming smile on him. 'You've both been staying at Chimneys, haven't you? Why didn't you bring Gerry over with you?'

'We-er-couldn't,' said Ronny, and then stopped.

Again Jimmy saw the look of fear flash into her eyes.

'Miss Wade,' he said, 'I'm afraid – I mean, we've got bad news for you.'

She was on the alert in a moment.

'Gerry?'

'Yes – Gerry. He's –'

She stamped her foot with sudden passion.

'Oh! tell me – tell me –' She turned suddenly on Ronny. '*You'll* tell me.'

Jimmy felt a pang of jealousy, and in that moment he knew what up to now he had hesitated to admit to himself. He knew why Helen and Nancy and Socks were just 'girls' to him and nothing more.

He only *half* heard Ronny's voice saying bravely:

'Yes, Miss Wade, I'll tell you. Gerry is dead.'

She had plenty of pluck. She gasped and drew back, but in a minute or two she was asking eager, searching questions. How? When?

Ronny answered her as gently as he could.

'*Sleeping* draught? Gerry?'

The incredulity in her voice was plain. Jimmy gave her a glance. It was almost a glance of warning. He had a sudden feeling that Lorraine in her innocence might say too much.

In his turn he explained as gently as possible the need for an inquest. She shuddered. She declined their offer of taking her back to Chimneys with them, but explained she would come over later. She had a two-seater of her own.

'But I want to be – be alone a little first,' she said piteously.

'I know,' said Ronny.

'That's all right,' said Jimmy.

They looked at her, feeling awkward and helpless.

'Thank you both ever so much for coming.'

They drove back in silence and there was something like constraint between them.

'My God! that girl's plucky,' said Ronny once.

Jimmy agreed.

'Gerry was my friend,' said Ronny. 'It's up to me to keep an eye on her.'

'Oh! rather. Of course.'

On returning to Chimneys Jimmy was waylaid by a tearful Lady Coote.

'That poor boy,' she kept repeating. 'That poor boy.'

Jimmy made all the suitable remarks he could think of.

Lady Coote told him at great length various details about the decease of various dear friends of hers. Jimmy listened with a show of sympathy and at last managed to detach himself without actual rudeness.

He ran lightly up the stairs. Ronny was just emerging from Gerald Wade's room. He seemed taken aback at the sight of Jimmy.

'I've been in to see him,' he said. 'Are you going in?'

'I don't think so,' said Jimmy, who was a healthy young man with a natural dislike of being reminded of death.

'I think all his friends ought to.'

'Oh! do you?' said Jimmy, and registered to himself an impression that Ronny Devereux was damned odd about it all.

'Yes. It's a sign of respect.'

Jimmy sighed, but gave in.

'Oh! very well,' he said, and passed in, setting his teeth a little.

There were white flowers arranged on the coverlet, and the room had been tidied and set to rights.

Jimmy gave one quick, nervous glance at the still, white face. Could that be cherubic, pink Gerry Wade? That still peaceful figure. He shivered.

As he turned to leave the room, his glance swept the mantel-shelf and he stopped in astonishment. The alarum clocks had been ranged along it neatly in a row.

He went out sharply. Ronny was waiting for him.

'Looks very peaceful and all that. Rotten luck on him,' mumbled Jimmy.

Then he said:

'I say, Ronny, who arranged all those clocks like that in a row?'

'How should I know? One of the servants, I suppose.'

'The funny thing is,' said Jimmy, 'that there are seven of them, not eight. One of them's missing. Did you notice that?'

Ronny made an inaudible sound.

'Seven instead of eight,' said Jimmy, frowning. 'I wonder why.'

CHAPTER IV

A Letter

'Inconsiderate, that's what I call it,' said Lord Caterham.

He spoke in a gentle, plaintive voice and seemed pleased with the adjective he had found.

'Yes, distinctly inconsiderate. I often find these self-made men *are* inconsiderate. Very possibly that is why they amass such large fortunes.'

He looked mournfully out over his ancestral acres, of which he had to-day regained possession.

His daughter, Lady Eileen Brent, known to her friends and society in general as 'Bundle,' laughed.

'You'll certainly never amass a large fortune,' she observed dryly, 'though you didn't do so badly out of old Coote, sticking him for this place. What was he like? Presentable?'

'One of those large men,' said Lord Caterham, shuddering slightly, 'with a red square face and iron-grey hair. Powerful, you know. What they call a forceful personality. The kind of man you'd get if a steam-roller were turned into a human being.'

'Rather tiring?' suggested Bundle sympathetically.

'Frightfully tiring, full of all the most depressing virtues like sobriety and punctuality. I don't know which are the worst, powerful personalities or earnest politicians. I do so prefer the cheerful inefficient.'

'A cheerful inefficient wouldn't have been able to pay you the price you asked for this old mausoleum,' Bundle reminded him.

Lord Caterham winced.

'I wish you wouldn't use that word, Bundle. We were just getting away from the subject.'

'I don't see why you're so frightfully sensitive about it,' said Bundle. 'After all, people must die somewhere.'

'They needn't die in my house,' said Lord Caterham.

'I don't see why not. Lots of people have. Masses of stuffy old great grandfathers and grandmothers.'

'That's different,' said Lord Caterham. 'Naturally I expect Brents to die here – they don't count. But I do object to strangers. And I especially object to inquests. The thing will become a habit soon. This is the second. You remember all that fuss we had four years ago? For which, by the way, I hold George Lomax entirely to blame.'

'And now you're blaming poor old steam-roller Coote. I'm sure he was quite as annoyed about it as anyone.'

'Very inconsiderate,' said Lord Caterham obstinately. 'People who are likely to do that sort of thing oughtn't to be asked to stay. And you may say what you like, Bundle, I don't like inquests. I never have and I never shall.'

'Well, this wasn't the same sort of thing as the last one,' said Bundle soothingly. 'I mean, it wasn't a murder.'

'It might have been – from the fuss that thickhead of an inspector made. He's never got over that business four years ago. He thinks every death that takes place here must necessarily be a case of foul play fraught with grave political significance. You've no idea the fuss he made. I've been hearing about it from Tredwell. Tested everything imaginable for finger-prints. And of course they only found the dead man's own. The clearest case imaginable – though whether it was suicide or accident is another matter.'

'I met Gerry Wade once,' said Bundle. 'He was a friend of Bill's. You'd have liked him, Father. I never saw anyone more cheerfully inefficient than he was.'

'I don't like anyone who comes and dies in my house on purpose to annoy me,' said Lord Caterham obstinately.

'But I certainly can't imagine anyone murdering him,' continued Bundle. 'The idea's absurd.'

'Of course it is,' said Lord Caterham. 'Or would be to anyone but an ass like Inspector Raglan.'

'I daresay looking for finger-prints made him feel important,' said Bundle soothingly. 'Anyway, they brought it in "Death by misadventure," didn't they?'

Lord Caterham acquiesced.

'They had to show some consideration for the sister's feelings.'

'Was there a sister? I didn't know.'

'Half-sister, I believe. She was much younger. Old Wade ran away with her mother – he was always doing that sort of thing. No woman appealed to him unless she belonged to another man.'

'I'm glad there's one bad habit you haven't got,' said Bundle.

'I've always led a very respectable God-fearing life,' said Lord Caterham. 'It seems extraordinary, considering how little harm I do to anybody, that I can't be let alone. If only – '

He stopped as Bundle made a sudden excursion through the window.

'MacDonald,' called Bundle in a clear, autocratic voice.

The emperor approached. Something that might possibly have been taken for a smile of welcome tried to express itself on his countenance, but the natural gloom of gardeners dispelled it.

'Your ladyship?' said MacDonald.

'How are you?' said Bundle.

'I'm no verra grand,' said MacDonald.

'I wanted to speak to you about the bowling green. It's shockingly overgrown. Put someone on to it, will you?'

MacDonald shook his head dubiously.

'It would mean taking William from the lower border, m'lady.'

'Damn the lower border,' said Bundle. 'Let him start at once. And MacDonald – '

'Yes, m'lady?'

'Let's have some of those grapes in from the far house. I know it's the wrong time to cut them because it always is, but I want them all the same. See?'

Bundle re-entered the library.

'Sorry, Father,' she said. 'I wanted to catch MacDonald. Were you speaking?'

'As a matter of fact I was,' said Lord Caterham. 'But it doesn't matter. What were you saying to MacDonald?'

'Trying to cure him of thinking he's God Almighty. But that's an impossible task. I expect the Cootes have been bad for him. MacDonald wouldn't care one hoot, or even two hoots, for the largest steam-roller that ever was. What's Lady Coote like?'

Lord Caterham considered the question.

'Very like my idea of Mrs Siddons,' he said at last. 'I should think she went in a lot for amateur theatricals. I gather she was very upset about the clock business.'

'What clock business?'

'Tredwell has just been telling me. It seems the house-party had some joke on. They bought a lot of alarum clocks and hid them about this young Wade's room. And then, of course, the poor chap was dead. Which made the whole thing rather beastly.'

Bundle nodded.

'Tredwell told me something else rather odd about the clocks,' continued Lord Caterham, who was now quite enjoying himself. 'It seems that somebody collected them all and put them in a row on the mantelpiece after the poor fellow was dead.'

'Well, why not?' said Bundle.

'I don't see why not myself,' said Lord Caterham. 'But apparently there was some fuss about it. No one would own up to having done it, you see. All the servants were questioned and swore they hadn't touched the beastly things. In fact, it was rather a mystery. And then the coroner asked questions at the inquest, and you know how difficult it is to explain things to people of that class.'

'Perfectly foul,' agreed Bundle.

'Of course,' said Lord Caterham, 'it's very difficult to get the hang of things afterwards. I didn't quite see the point of half the things Tredwell told me. By the way, Bundle, the fellow died in your room.'

Bundle made a grimace.

'Why need people die in my room?' she asked with some indignation.

'That's just what I've been saying,' said Lord Caterham, in triumph. 'Inconsiderate. Everybody's damned inconsiderate nowadays.'

'Not that I mind,' said Bundle valiantly. 'Why should I?'

'I should,' said her father. 'I should mind very much. I should dream things, you know – spectral hands and clanking chains.'

'Well,' said Bundle. 'Great Aunt Louisa died in *your* bed. I wonder you don't see her spook hovering over you.'

'I do sometimes,' said Lord Caterham, shuddering. 'Especially after lobster.'

'Well, thank heaven I'm not superstitious,' declared Bundle.

Yet that evening, as she sat in front of her bedroom fire, a slim, pyjamaed figure, she found her thoughts reverting to that cheery, vacuous young man, Gerry Wade. Impossible to believe that anyone so full of the joy of living could deliberately have committed suicide. No, the other solution must be the right one. He had taken a sleeping draught and by a pure mistake had swallowed an overdose. That *was* possible. She did not fancy that Gerry Wade had been overburdened in an intellectual capacity.

Her gaze shifted to the mantelpiece and she began thinking about the story of the clocks. Her maid had been full of that, having just been primed by the second housemaid. She had added a detail which apparently Tredwell had not thought worth while retailing to Lord Caterham, but which had piqued Bundle's curiosity.

Seven clocks had been neatly ranged on the mantelpiece; the last and remaining one had been found on the lawn outside, where it had obviously been thrown from the window.

Bundle puzzled over that point now. It seemed such an extraordinary purposeless thing to do. She could imagine that one of the maids might have tidied the clocks and then, frightened by the inquisition into the matter, have denied doing so. But surely no maid would have thrown a clock into the garden.

Had Gerry Wade done so when its first sharp summons woke

him? But no; that again was impossible. Bundle remembered hearing that his death must have taken place in the early hours of the morning, and he would have been in a comatose condition for some time before that.

Bundle frowned. This business of the clocks *was* curious. She must get hold of Bill Eversleigh. He had been there, she knew.

To think was to act with Bundle. She got up and went over to the writing desk. It was an inlaid affair with a lid that rolled back. Bundle sat down at it, pulled a sheet of notepaper towards her and wrote.

DEAR BILL, –

She paused to pull out the lower part of the desk. It had stuck half-way, as she remembered it often did. Bundle tugged at it impatiently but it did not move. She recalled that on a former occasion an envelope had been pushed back with it and had jammed it for the time being. She took a thin paper-knife and slipped it into the narrow crack. She was so far successful that a corner of white paper showed. Bundle caught hold of it and drew it out. It was the first sheet of a letter, somewhat crumpled.

It was the date that first caught Bundle's eye. A big flourishing date that leaped out from the paper. Sept. 21st.

'September 21st,' said Bundle slowly. 'Why, surely that was –'

She broke off. Yes, she was sure of it. The 22nd was the day Gerry Wade was found dead. This, then, was a letter he must have been writing on the very evening of the tragedy.

Bundle smoothed it out and read it. It was unfinished.

'MY DARLING LORAINE, – I will be down on Wednesday. Am feeling awfully fit and rather pleased with myself all round. It will be heavenly to see you. Look here, do forget what I said about that Seven Dials business. I thought it was going to be more or less a joke – but it isn't – anything but. I'm sorry I ever said anything about it – it's not the kind of business kids like you ought to be mixed up in. So forget about it, see?

'Something else I wanted to tell you – but I'm so sleepy I can't keep my eyes open.

'Oh, about Lurcher; I think –'

Here the letter broke off.

Bundle sat frowning. Seven Dials. Where was that? Some rather slummy district of London, she fancied. The words Seven Dials reminded her of something else, but for the moment she couldn't think of what. Instead her attention fastened on two phrases. 'Am feeling awfully fit . . .' and 'I'm so sleepy I can't keep my eyes open.'

That didn't fit in. That didn't fit in at all. For it was that very night that Gerry Wade had taken such a heavy dose of chloral that he never woke again. And if what he had written in that letter were true, why should he have taken it?

Bundle shook her head. She looked round the room and gave a slight shiver. Supposing Gerry Wade were watching her now. In this room he had died . . .

She sat very still. The silence was unbroken save for the ticking of her little gold clock. That sounded unnaturally loud and important.

Bundle glanced towards the mantelpiece. A vivid picture rose before her mind's eyes. The dead man lying on the bed, and seven clocks ticking on the mantelpiece – ticking loudly, ominously . . . ticking . . . ticking . . .

CHAPTER V

The Man in the Road

'Father,' said Bundle, opening the door of Lord Caterham's special sanctum and putting her head in, 'I'm going up to town in the Hispano. I can't stand the monotony down here any longer.'

'We only got home yesterday,' complained Lord Caterham.

'I know. It seems like a hundred years. I'd forgotten how dull the country could be.'

'I don't agree with you,' said Lord Caterham. 'It's peaceful, that's what it is – peaceful. And extremely comfortable. I appreciate getting back to Tredwell more than I can tell you. That man studies my comfort in the most marvellous manner. Somebody came round only this morning to know if they could hold a tally for girl guides here –'

'A rally,' interrupted Bundle.

'Rally or tally – it's all the same. Some silly word meaning nothing whatever. But it would have put me in a very awkward position – having to refuse – in fact, I probably shouldn't have refused. But Tredwell got me out of it. I've forgotten what he said – something damned ingenious which couldn't hurt anybody's feelings and which knocked the idea on the head absolutely.'

'Being comfortable isn't enough for me,' said Bundle. 'I want excitement.'

Lord Caterham shuddered.

'Didn't we have enough excitement four years ago?' he demanded plaintively.

'I'm about ready for some more,' said Bundle. 'Not that I expect I shall find any in town. But at any rate I shan't dislocate my jaw with yawning.'

'In my experience,' said Lord Caterham, 'people who go about looking for trouble usually find it.' He yawned. 'All the same,' he added, 'I wouldn't mind running up to town myself.'

'Well, come on,' said Bundle. 'But be quick, because I'm in a hurry.'

Lord Caterham, who had begun to rise from his chair, paused.

'Did you say you were in a hurry?' he asked suspiciously.

'In the devil of a hurry,' said Bundle.

'That settles it,' said Lord Caterham. 'I'm not coming. To be driven by you in the Hispano when you're in a hurry – no, it's not fair on any elderly man. I shall stay here.'

'Please yourself,' said Bundle, and withdrew.

Tredwell took her place.

'The vicar, my lord, is most anxious to see you, some unfortunate controversy having arisen about the status of the Boys' Brigade.'

Lord Caterham groaned.

'I rather fancied, my lord, that I had heard you mention at breakfast that you were strolling down to the village this morning to converse with the vicar on the subject.'

'Did you tell him so?' asked Lord Caterham eagerly.

'I did, my lord. He departed, if I may say so, hot foot. I hope I did right, my lord?'

'Of course you did, Tredwell. You are always right. You couldn't go wrong if you tried.'

Tredwell smiled benignly and withdrew.

Bundle meanwhile was sounding the Klaxon impatiently before the lodge gates, while a small child came hastening out with all speed from the lodge, admonishment from her mother following her.

'Make haste, Katie. That be her ladyship in a mortal hurry as always.'

It was indeed characteristic of Bundle to be in a hurry, especially when driving a car. She had skill and nerve and was a good driver; had it been otherwise her reckless pace would have ended in disaster more than once.

It was a crisp October day, with a blue sky and a dazzling sun.

The sharp tang of the air brought the blood to Bundle's cheeks and filled her with the zest of living.

She had that morning sent Gerald Wade's unfinished letter to Loraine Wade at Deane Priory, enclosing a few explanatory lines. The curious impression it had made upon her was somewhat dimmed in the daylight, yet it still struck her as needing explanation. She intended to get hold of Bill Eversleigh sometime and extract from him fuller details of the house-party which had ended so tragically. In the meantime, it was a lovely morning and she felt particularly well and the Hispano was running like a dream.

Bundle pressed her foot down on the accelerator and the Hispano responded at once. Mile after mile vanished, traffic was few and far between and Bundle had a clear stretch of road in front of her.

And then, without any warning whatever, a man reeled out of the hedge and on to the road right in front of the car. To stop in time was out of the question. With all her might Bundle wrenched at the steering wheel and swerved out to the right. The car was nearly in the ditch – nearly, but not quite. It was a dangerous manoeuvre; but it succeeded. Bundle was almost certain that she had missed the man.

She looked back and felt a sickening sensation in the middle of her anatomy. The car had not passed over the man, but nevertheless it must have struck him in passing. He was lying face downwards on the road, and he lay ominously still.

Bundle jumped out and ran back. She had never yet run over anything more important than a stray hen. The fact that the accident was hardly her fault did not weigh with her at the minute. The man had seemed drunk, but drunk or not, she had killed him. She was quite sure she had killed him. Her heart beat sickeningly in great pounding thumps, sounding right up in her ears.

She knelt down by the prone figure and turned him very gingerly over. He neither groaned nor moaned. He was young, she saw, rather a pleasant-faced young man, well dressed and wearing a small toothbrush moustache.

There was no external mark of injury that she could see, but she was quite positive that he was either dead or dying. His eyelids flickered and the eyes half opened. Piteous eyes, brown and suffering, like a dog's. He seemed to be struggling to speak. Bundle bent right over.

'Yes,' she said. 'Yes?'

There was something he wanted to say, she could see that. Wanted to say badly. And she couldn't help him, couldn't do anything.

At last the words came, a mere sighing breath:

'*Seven Dials . . . tell . . .*'

'Yes,' said Bundle again. It was a name he was trying to get out – trying with all his failing strength. 'Yes. Who am I to tell?'

'*Tell . . . Jimmy Thesiger . . .*' He got it out at last, and then, suddenly, his head fell back and his body went limp.

Bundle sat back on her heels, shivering from head to foot. She could never have imagined that anything so awful could have happened to her. He was dead – and she had killed him.

She tried to pull herself together. What must she do now? A doctor – that was her first thought. It was possible – just possible – that the man might only be unconscious, not dead. Her instinct cried out against the possibility, but she forced herself to act upon it. Somehow or other she must get him into the car and take him to the nearest doctor's. It was a deserted stretch of country road and there was no one to help her.

Bundle, for all her slimness, was strong. She had muscles of whipcord. She brought the Hispano as close as possible, and then exerting all her strength, she dragged and pulled the inanimate figure into it. It was a horrid business, and one that made her set her teeth, but at last she managed it.

Then she jumped into the driver's seat and set off. A couple of miles brought her into a small town and on inquiring she was quickly directed to the doctor's house.

Dr Cassell, a kindly, middle-aged man, was startled to come into his surgery and find a girl there who was evidently on the verge of collapse.

Bundle spoke abruptly.

'I – I think I've killed a man. I ran over him. I brought him along in the car. He's outside now. I – I was driving too fast, I suppose. I've always driven too fast.'

The doctor cast a practised glance over her. He stepped over to a shelf and poured something into a glass. He brought it over to her.

'Drink this down,' he said, 'and you'll feel better. You've had a shock.'

Bundle drank obediently and a tinge of colour came into her pallid face. The doctor nodded approvingly.

'That's right. Now I want you to sit quietly here. I'll go out and attend to things. After I've made sure there's nothing to be done for the poor fellow, I'll come back and we'll talk about it.'

He was away some time. Bundle watched the clock on the mantelpiece. Five minutes, ten minutes, a quarter of an hour, twenty minutes – would he ever come?

Then the door opened and Dr Cassell reappeared. He looked different – Bundle noticed that at once – grimmer and at the same time more alert. There was something else in his manner that she did not quite understand, a suggestion of repressed excitement.

'Now then, young lady,' he said. 'Let's have this out. You ran over this man, you say. Tell me just how the accident happened?'

Bundle explained to the best of her ability. The doctor followed her narrative with keen attention.

'Just so; the car didn't pass over his body?'

'No. In fact, I thought I'd missed him altogether.'

'He was reeling, you say?'

'Yes, I thought he was drunk.'

'And he came from the hedge?'

'There was a gate just there, I think. He must have come through the gate.'

The doctor nodded, then he leaned back in his chair and removed his pince-nez.

'I've no doubt at all,' he said, 'that you're a very reckless driver, and that you'll probably run over some poor fellow and do for him one of these days – but you haven't done it this time.'

'But –'

'The car never touched him. *This man was shot.*'

CHAPTER VI

Seven Dials Again

Bundle stared at him. And very slowly the world, which for the last three quarters of an hour had been upside down, shifted till it stood once more the right way up. It was quite two minutes before Bundle spoke, but when she did it was no longer the panic-stricken girl but the real Bundle, cool, efficient and logical.

'How could he be shot?' she said.

'I don't know how he could,' said the doctor dryly. 'But he was. He's got a rifle bullet in him all right. He bled internally, that's why you didn't notice anything.'

Bundle nodded.

'The question is,' the doctor continued, 'who shot him? You saw nobody about?'

Bundle shook her head.

'It's odd,' said the doctor. 'If it was an accident, you'd expect the fellow who did it would come running to the rescue – unless just possibly he didn't know what he'd done.'

'There was no one about,' said Bundle. 'On the road, that is.'

'It seems to me,' said the doctor, 'that the poor lad must have been running – the bullet got him just as he passed through the gate and he came reeling on to the road in consequence. You didn't hear a shot?'

Bundle shook her head.

'But I probably shouldn't anyway,' she said, 'with the noise of the car.'

'Just so. He didn't say anything before he died?'

'He muttered a few words.'

'Nothing to throw light on the tragedy?'

'No. He wanted something – I don't know what – told to a friend of his. Oh! Yes, and he mentioned Seven Dials.'

'H'm,' said Doctor Cassell. 'Not a likely neighbourhood for one of his class. Perhaps his assailant came from there. Well, we needn't worry about that now. You can leave it in my hands. I'll notify the police. You must, of course, leave your name and address, as the police are sure to want to question you. In fact, perhaps you'd better come round to the police station with me now. They might say I ought to have detained you.'

They went together in Bundle's car. The police inspector was a slow-speaking man. He was somewhat overawed by Bundle's name and address when she gave it to him, and he took down her statement with great care.

'Lads!' he said. 'That's what it is. Lads practising! Cruel stupid, them young varmints are. Always loosing off at birds with no consideration for anyone as may be the other side of a hedge.'

The doctor thought it a most unlikely solution, but he realized that the case would soon be in abler hands and it did not seem worth while to make objections.

'Name of deceased?' asked the sergeant, moistening his pencil.

'He had a card-case on him. He appeared to have been a Mr Ronald Devereux, with an address in the Albany.'

Bundle frowned. The name Ronald Devereux awoke some chord of remembrance. She was sure she had heard it before.

It was not until she was half-way back to Chimneys in the car that it came to her. Of course! Ronny Devereux. Bill's friend in the Foreign Office. He and Bill and – yes – Gerald Wade.

As this last realization came to her, Bundle nearly went into the hedge. First Gerald Wade – then Ronny Devereux. Gerry Wade's death might have been natural – the result of careless-ness – but Ronny Devereux's surely bore a more sinister interpretation.

And then Bundle remembered something else. Seven Dials! When the dying man had said it, it had seemed vaguely familiar. Now she knew why. Gerald Wade had mentioned Seven Dials in that last letter of his written to his sister on the night before his death. And that again connected up with something else that escaped her.

Thinking all these things over, Bundle had slowed down to such a sober pace that nobody would have recognized her. She drove the car round to the garage and went in search of her father.

Lord Caterham was happily reading a catalogue of a forth-coming sale of rare editions and was immeasurably astonished to see Bundle.

'Even you,' he said, 'can't have been to London and back in this time.'

'I haven't been to London,' said Bundle. 'I ran over a man.'

'What?'

'Only I didn't really. He was shot.'

'How could he have been?'

'I don't know how he could have been, but he was.'

'But why did you shoot him?'

'*I* didn't shoot him.'

'You shouldn't shoot people,' said Lord Caterham in a tone of mild remonstrance. 'You shouldn't really. I daresay some of them richly deserve it – but all the same it will lead to trouble.'

'I tell you I didn't shoot him.'

'Well, who did?'

'Nobody knows,' said Bundle.

'Nonsense,' said Lord Caterham. 'A man can't be shot and run over without anyone having done it.'

'He wasn't run over,' said Bundle.

'I thought you said he was.'

'I said I thought I had.'

'A tyre burst, I suppose,' said Lord Caterham. 'That does sound like a shot. It says so in detective stories.'

'You really are perfectly impossible, Father. You don't seem to have the brains of a rabbit.'

'Not at all,' said Lord Caterham. 'You come in with a wildly impossible tale about men being run over and shot and I don't know what, and then you expect me to know all about it by magic.'

Bundle sighed wearily.

'Just attend,' she said. 'I'll tell you all about it in words of one syllable.'

'There,' she said when she had concluded. 'Now have you got it?'

'Of course. I understand perfectly now. I can make allowances for your being a little upset, my dear. I was not far wrong when I remarked to you before starting out that people looking for trouble usually found it. I am thankful,' finished Lord Caterham with a slight shiver, 'that I stayed quietly here.'

He picked up the catalogue again.

'Father, where is Seven Dials?'

'In the East End somewhere, I fancy. I have frequently observed buses going there – or do I mean Seven Sisters? I have never been there myself, I'm thankful to say. Just as well, because I don't fancy it is the sort of spot I should like. And yet, curiously enough, I seem to have heard of it in some connection just lately.'

'You don't know a Jimmy Thesiger, do you?'

Lord Caterham was now engrossed in his catalogue once more. He had made an effort to be intelligent on the subject of Seven Dials. This time he made hardly any effort at all.

'Thesiger,' he murmured vaguely. 'Thesiger. One of the Yorkshire Thesigers?'

'That's what I'm asking you. Do attend, Father. This is important.'

Lord Caterham made a desperate effort to look intelligent without really having to give his mind to the matter.

'There *are* some Yorkshire Thesigers,' he said earnestly. 'And unless I am mistaken some Devonshire Thesigers also. Your Great Aunt Selina married a Thesiger.'

'What good is that to me?' cried Bundle.

Lord Caterham chuckled.

'It was very little good to her, if I remember rightly.'

'You're impossible,' said Bundle, rising. 'I shall have to get hold of Bill.'

'Do, dear,' said her father absently as he turned a page. 'Certainly. By all means. Quite so.'

Bundle rose to her feet with an impatient sigh.

'I wish I could remember what that letter said,' she murmured, more to herself than aloud. 'I didn't read it very carefully. Something about a joke, that the Seven Dials business wasn't a joke.'

Lord Caterham emerged suddenly from his catalogue.

'Seven Dials?' he said. 'Of course. I've got it now.'

'Got what?'

'I know why it sounded so familiar. George Lomax has been over. Tredwell failed for once and let him in. He was on his way up to town. It seems he's having some political party at the Abbey next week and he got a warning letter.'

'What do you mean by a warning letter?'

'Well, I don't really know. He didn't go into details. I gather it said "Beware" and "Trouble is at hand," and all those sort of things. But anyway it was written from Seven Dials, I distinctly remember his saying so. He was going up to town to consult Scotland Yard about it. You know George?'

Bundle nodded. She was well acquainted with that public-spirited Cabinet Minister, George Lomax, His Majesty's permanent Under Secretary of State for Foreign Affairs, who was shunned by many because of his inveterate habit of quoting from his public speeches in private. In allusion to his bulging eyeballs, he was known to many – Bill Eversleigh among others – as Codders.

'Tell me,' she said, 'was Codders interested at all in Gerald Wade's death?'

'Not that I heard of. He may have been, of course.'

Bundle said nothing for some minutes. She was busily engaged in trying to remember the exact wording of the letter she had sent on to Loraine Wade, and at the same time she was trying to picture the girl to whom it had been written. What sort of a girl was this to whom, apparently, Gerald Wade was so devoted? The more she thought over it, the more it seemed to her that it was an unusual letter for a brother to write.

'Did you say the Wade girl was Gerry's half-sister?' she asked suddenly.

'Well, of course, strictly speaking, I suppose she isn't – wasn't, I mean – his sister at all.'

'But her name's Wade?'

'Not really. She wasn't old Wade's child. As I was saying, he ran away with his second wife, who was married to a perfect blackguard. I suppose the Courts gave the rascally husband the custody of the child, but he certainly didn't avail himself of the privilege. Old Wade got very fond of the child and insisted that she should be called by his name.'

'I see,' said Bundle. 'That explains it.'

'Explains what?'

'Something that puzzled me about that letter.'

'She's rather a pretty girl, I believe,' said Lord Caterham. 'Or so I've heard.'

Bundle went upstairs thoughtfully. She had several objects in view. First she must find this Jimmy Thesiger. Bill, perhaps, would be helpful there. Ronny Devereux had been a friend of Bill's. If Jimmy Thesiger was a friend of Ronny's, the chances were that Bill would know him too. Then there was the girl, Loraine Wade. It was possible that she could throw some light on the problem of Seven Dials. Evidently Gerry Wade had said something to her about it. His anxiety that she should forget the fact had a sinister suggestion.

CHAPTER VII

Bundle Pays a Call

Getting hold of Bill presented few difficulties. Bundle motored up to town on the following morning – this time without adventures on the way – and rang him up. Bill responded with alacrity and made various suggestions as to lunch, tea, dinner and dancing. All of which suggestions Bundle turned down as made.

'In a day or two, I'll come and frivol with you, Bill. But for the moment I'm up on business.'

'Oh,' said Bill. 'What a beastly bore.'

'It's not that kind,' said Bundle. 'It's anything but boring. Bill, do you know anyone called Jimmy Thesiger?'

'Of course. So do you.'

'No, I don't,' said Bundle.

'Yes, you do. You must. Everyone knows old Jimmy.'

'Sorry,' said Bundle. 'Just for once I don't seem to be everyone.'

'Oh! but you must know Jimmy – pink-faced chap. Looks a bit of an ass. But really he's got as many brains as I have.'

'You don't say so,' said Bundle. 'He must feel a bit top heavy when he walks about.'

'Was that meant for sarcasm?'

'It was a feeble effort at it. What does Jimmy Thesiger do?'

'How do you mean, what does he do?'

'Does being at the Foreign Office prevent you from understanding your native language?'

'Oh! I see, you mean, has he got a job? No, he just fools around. Why should he do anything?'

'In fact, more money than brains?'

'Oh! I wouldn't say that. I told you just now that he had more brains than you'd think.'

Bundle was silent. She was feeling more and more doubtful. This gilded youth did not sound a very promising ally. And yet it was his name that had come first to the dying man's lips. Bill's voice chimed in suddenly with singular appropriateness.

'Ronny always thought a lot of his brains. You know, Ronny Devereux. Thesiger was his greatest pal.'

'Ronny –'

Bundle stopped, undecided. Clearly Bill knew nothing of the other's death. It occurred to Bundle for the first time that it was odd the morning papers had contained nothing of the tragedy. Surely it was the kind of spicy item of news that would never be passed over. There could be one explanation, and one explanation only. The police, for reasons of their own, were keeping the matter quiet.

Bill's voice was continuing.

'I haven't seen Ronny for an age – not since that week-end down at your place. You know, when poor old Gerry Wade passed out.'

He paused and then went on.

'Rather a foul business that altogether. I expect you've heard about it. I say, Bundle – are you there still?'

'Of course I'm here.'

'Well, you haven't said anything for an age. I began to think that you had gone away.'

'No, I was just thinking over something.'

Should she tell Bill of Ronny's death? She decided against it – it was not the sort of thing to be said over the telephone. But soon, very soon, she must have a meeting with Bill. In the meantime –

'Bill?'

'Hullo.'

'I might dine with you to-morrow night.'

'Good, and we'll dance afterwards. I've got a lot to talk to you about. As a matter of fact I've been rather hard hit – the foulest luck –'

'Well, tell me about it to-morrow,' said Bundle, cutting him short rather unkindly. 'In the meantime, what is Jimmy Thesiger's address?'

'Jimmy Thesiger?'

'That's what I said.'

'He's got rooms in Jermyn Street – do I mean Jermyn Street or the other one?'

'Bring that class A brain to bear upon it.'

'Yes, Jermyn Street. Wait a bit and I'll give you the number.'

There was a pause.

'Are you still there?'

'I'm always here.'

'Well, one never knows with these dashed telephones. The number is 103. Got it?'

'103. Thank you, Bill.'

'Yes, but, I say – what do you want it for? You said you didn't know him.'

'I don't, but I shall in half an hour.'

'You're going round to his rooms?'

'Quite right, Sherlock.'

'Yes, but, I say – well, for one thing he won't be up.'

'Won't be up?'

'I shouldn't think so. I mean, who would be if they hadn't got to? Look at it that way. You've no idea what an effort it is for me to get here at eleven every morning, and the fuss Codders makes if I'm behind time is simply appalling. You haven't the least idea, Bundle, what a dog's life this is –'

'You shall tell me all about it to-morrow night,' said Bundle hastily.

She slammed down the receiver and took stock of the situation. First she glanced at the clock. It was five and twenty minutes to twelve. Despite Bill's knowledge of his friend's habits, she inclined to her belief that Mr Thesiger would by now be in a fit state to receive visitors. She took a taxi to 103 Jermyn Street.

The door was opened by a perfect example of the retired gentleman's gentleman. His face, expressionless and polite, was such a face as may be found by the score in that particular district of London.

'Will you come this way, madam?'

He ushered her upstairs into an extremely comfortable sitting-room containing leather-covered arm-chairs of immense dimensions. Sunk in one of those monstrosities was another girl, rather younger than Bundle. A small, fair girl, dressed in black.

'What name shall I say, madam?'

'I won't give any name,' said Bundle. 'I just want to see Mr Thesiger on important business.'

The grave gentleman bowed and withdrew, shutting the door noiselessly behind him.

There was a pause.

'It's a nice morning,' said the fair girl timidly.

'It's an awfully nice morning,' agreed Bundle.

There was another pause.

'I motored up from the country this morning,' said Bundle, plunging once more into speech. 'And I thought it was going to be one of those foul fogs. But it wasn't.'

'No,' said the other girl. 'It wasn't.' And she added: 'I've come up from the country too.'

Bundle eyed her more attentively. She had been slightly annoyed at finding the other there. Bundle belonged to the energetic order of people who liked 'to get on with it,' and she foresaw that the second visitor would have to be disposed of and got rid of before she could broach her own business. It was not a topic she could introduce before a stranger.

Now, as she looked more closely, an extraordinary idea rose to her brain. Could it be? Yes, the girl was in deep mourning; her black-clad ankles showed that. It was a long shot, but Bundle was convinced that her idea was right. She drew a long breath.

'Look here,' she said, 'are you by any chance Loraine Wade?'

Loraine's eyes opened wide.

'Yes, I am. How clever of you to know. We've never met, have we?'

'I wrote to you yesterday, though. I'm Bundle Brent.'

'It was so very kind of you to send me Gerry's letter,' said

Loraine. 'I've written to thank you. I never expected to see you here.'

'I'll tell you why I'm here,' said Bundle. 'Did you know Ronny Devereux?'

Loraine nodded.

'He came over the day that Gerry – you know. And he's been to see me two or three times since. He was one of Gerry's greatest friends.'

'I know. Well – he's dead.'

Loraine's lips parted in surprise.

'*Dead*! But he always seemed so fit.'

Bundle narrated the events of the preceding day as briefly as possible. A look of fear and horror came into Loraine's face.

'Then it *is* true. It *is* true.'

'What's true?'

'What I've thought – what I've been thinking all these weeks. Gerry didn't die a natural death. He was killed.'

'You've thought that, have you?'

'Yes. Gerry would never have taken things to make him sleep.' She gave the little ghost of a laugh. 'He slept much too well to need them. I always thought it queer. And *he* thought so too – I know he did.'

'Who?'

'Ronny. And now this happens. Now he's killed too.' She paused and then went on: 'That's what I came for to-day. That letter of Gerry's you sent me – as soon as I read it, I tried to get hold of Ronny, but they said he was away. So I thought I'd come and see Jimmy – he was Ronny's other great friend. I thought perhaps he'd tell me what I ought to do.'

'You mean –' Bundle paused. 'About – Seven Dials.'

Loraine nodded.

'You see –' she began.

But at that moment Jimmy Thesiger entered the room.

CHAPTER VIII

Visitors for Jimmy

We must at this point go back to some twenty minutes earlier, to a moment when Jimmy Thesiger, emerging from the mists of sleep, was conscious of a familiar voice speaking unfamiliar words.

His sleep-ridden brain tried for a moment to cope with the situation, but failed. He yawned and rolled over again.

'A young lady, sir, has called to see you.'

The voice was implacable. So prepared was it to go on repeating the statement indefinitely that Jimmy resigned himself to the inevitable. He opened his eyes and blinked.

'Eh, Stevens?' he said. 'Say that again.'

'A young lady, sir, has called to see you.'

'Oh!' Jimmy strove to grasp the situation. 'Why?'

'I couldn't say, sir.'

'No, I suppose not. No,' he thought it over. 'I suppose you couldn't.'

Stevens swooped down upon a tray by the bedside.

'I will bring you some fresh tea, sir. This is cold.'

'You think that I ought to get up and – er – see the lady?'

Stevens made no reply, but he held his back very stiff and Jimmy read the signs correctly.

'Oh! very well,' he said. 'I suppose I'd better. She didn't give her name?'

'No, sir.'

'M'm. She couldn't be by any possible chance my Aunt Jemima, could she? Because if so, I'm damned if I'm going to get up.'

'The lady, sir, could not possibly be anyone's aunt, I should say, unless the youngest of a large family.'

'Aha,' said Jimmy. 'Young and lovely. Is she – what kind is she?'

'The young lady, sir, is most undoubtedly strictly *comme il faut*, if I may use the expression.'

'You may use it,' said Jimmy graciously. 'Your French pronunciation, Stevens, if I may say so, is very good. Much better than mine.'

'I am gratified to hear it, sir. I have lately been taking a correspondence course in French.'

'Have you really? You're a wonderful chap, Stevens.'

Stevens smiled in a superior fashion and left the room. Jimmy lay trying to recall the names of any young and lovely girls strictly *comme il faut* who might be likely to come and call upon him.

Stevens re-entered with fresh tea, and as Jimmy sipped it he felt a pleasurable curiosity.

'You've given her the paper and all that, I hope, Stevens,' he said.

'I supplied her with the *Morning Post* and *Punch*, sir.'

A ring at the bell took him away. In a few minutes he returned.

'Another young lady, sir.'

'What?'

Jimmy clutched his head.

'Another young lady; she declines to give her name, sir, but says her business is important.'

Jimmy stared at him.

'This is damned odd, Stevens. Damned odd. Look here, what time did I come home last night?'

'Just upon five o'clock, sir.'

'And was I – er – how was I?'

'Just a little cheerful, sir – nothing more. Inclined to sing "Rule Britannia."'

'What an extraordinary thing,' said Jimmy. '"Rule Britannia," eh? I cannot imagine myself in a sober state ever singing "Rule Britannia." Some latent patriotism must have emerged under the stimulus of – er – just a couple too many. I was celebrating at the "Mustard and Cress," I remember. Not nearly such an innocent spot as it sounds, Stevens.' He paused. 'I was wondering –'

'Yes, sir?'

'I was wondering whether under the aforementioned stimulus I had put an advertisement in a newspaper asking for a nursery governess or something of that sort.'

Stevens coughed.

'*Two* girls turning up. It looks odd. I shall eschew the "Mustard and Cress" in future. That's a good word, Stevens – *eschew* – I met it in a crossword the other day and took a fancy to it.'

Whilst he was talking Jimmy was rapidly apparelling himself. At the end of ten minutes he was ready to face his unknown guests. As he opened the door of his sitting-room the first person he saw was a dark, slim girl who was totally unknown to him. She was standing by the mantelpiece, leaning against it. Then his glance went on to the big leather-covered arm-chair, and his heart missed a beat. Loraine!

It was she who rose and spoke first a little nervously.

'You must be very surprised to see me. But I had to come. I'll explain in a minute. This is Lady Eileen Brent.'

'Bundle – that's what I'm usually known as. You've probably heard of me from Bill Eversleigh.'

'Oh, rather, of course I have,' said Jimmy, endeavouring to cope with the situation. 'I say, do sit down and let's have a cocktail or something.'

Both girls declined.

'As a matter of fact,' continued Jimmy, 'I'm only just out of bed.'

'That's what Bill said,' remarked Bundle. 'I told him I was coming round to see you, and he said you wouldn't be up.'

'Well, I'm up now,' said Jimmy encouragingly.

'It's about Gerry,' said Loraine. 'And now about Ronny –'

'What do you mean by "and now about Ronny"?'

'He was shot yesterday.'

'What?' cried Jimmy.

Bundle told her story for the second time. Jimmy listened like a man in a dream.

'Old Ronny – shot,' he murmured. 'What *is* this damned business?'

He sat down on the edge of a chair, thinking for a minute or two, and then spoke in a quiet, level voice.

'There's something I think I ought to tell you.'

'Yes,' said Bundle encouragingly.

'It was on the day Gerry Wade died. On the way over to break the news to *you*' – he nodded at Loraine – 'in the car Ronny said something to me. That is to say, he started to tell me something. There was something he wanted to tell me, and he began about it, and then he said he was bound by a promise and couldn't go on.'

'Bound by a promise,' said Loraine thoughtfully.

'That's what he said. Naturally I didn't press him after that. But he was odd – damned odd – all through. I got the impression then that he suspected – well, foul play. I thought he'd tell the doctor so. But no, not even a hint. So I thought I'd been mistaken. And afterwards, with the evidence and all – well, it seemed such a very clear case. I thought my suspicions had been all bosh.'

'But you think Ronny still suspected?' asked Bundle.

Jimmy nodded.

'That's what I think now. Why, none of us have seen anything of him since. I believe he was playing a lone hand – trying to find out the truth about Gerry's death, and what's more, I believe he *did* find out. That's why the devils shot him. And then he tried to send word to me, but could only get out those two words.'

'Seven Dials,' said Bundle, and shivered a little.

'Seven Dials,' said Jimmy gravely. 'At any rate we've got that to go on with.'

Bundle turned to Loraine.

'You were just going to tell me –'

'Oh! yes. First, about the letter.' She spoke to Jimmy. 'Gerry left a letter. Lady Eileen –'

'Bundle.'

'Bundle found it.' She explained the circumstances in a few words.

Jimmy listened, keenly interested. This was the first he had heard of the letter. Loraine took it from her bag and handed it to him. He read it, then looked across at her.

'This is where you can help us. What was it Gerry wanted you to forget?'

Loraine's brows wrinkled a little in perplexity.

'It's so hard to remember exactly now. I opened a letter of Gerry's by mistake. It was written on cheap sort of paper, I remember, and very illiterate handwriting. It had some address in Seven Dials at the head of it. I realized it wasn't for me, so I put it back in the envelope without reading it.'

'Sure?' asked Jimmy very gently.

Loraine laughed for the first time.

'I know what you think, and I admit that women *are* curious. But, you see, this didn't even look interesting. It was a kind of list of names and dates.'

'Names and dates,' said Jimmy thoughtfully.

'Gerry didn't seem to mind much,' continued Loraine. 'He laughed. He asked me if I had ever heard of the Mafia, and then said it would be queer if a society like the Mafia started in England – but that that kind of secret society didn't take on much with English people. "Our criminals," he said, "haven't got a picturesque imagination."'

Jimmy pursed up his lips into a whistle.

'I'm beginning to see,' he said. 'Seven Dials must be the headquarters for some secret society. As he says in his letter to you. He thought it rather a joke to start with. But evidently it wasn't a joke – he says as much. And there's something else: his anxiety that you should forget what he's told you. There can be only one reason for that – if that society suspected that you had any knowledge of its activity, you too would be in danger. Gerald realized the peril, and he was terribly anxious – for you.'

He stopped, then he went on quietly:

'I rather fancy that we're all going to be in danger – if we go on with this.'

'If –?' cried Bundle indignantly.

'I'm talking of you two. It's different for me. I was poor old Ronny's pal.' He looked at Bundle. 'You've done your bit. You've delivered the message he sent me. No; for God's sake keep out of it, you and Loraine.'

Bundle looked questioningly at the other girl. Her own mind was definitely made up, but she gave no indication of it just then. She had no wish to push Loraine Wade into a dangerous undertaking.

But Loraine's small face was alight at once with indignation.

'You say that! Do you think for one minute I'd be contented to keep out of it – when they killed Gerry – my own dear Gerry, the best and dearest and kindest brother any girl ever had. The only person belonging to me I had in the whole world!'

Jimmy cleared his throat uncomfortably. Loraine, he thought, was wonderful; simply wonderful.

'Look here,' he said awkwardly. 'You mustn't say that. About being alone in the world – all that rot. You've got lots of friends – only too glad to do what they can. See what I mean?'

It is possible that Loraine did, for she suddenly blushed, and to cover her confusion began to talk nervously.

'That's settled,' she said. 'I'm going to help. Nobody's going to stop me.'

'And so am I, of course,' said Bundle.

They both looked at Jimmy.

'Yes,' he said slowly. 'Yes, quite so.'

They looked at him inquiringly.

'I was just wondering,' said Jimmy, 'how we were going to begin.'

CHAPTER IX

Plans

Jimmy's words lifted the discussion at once into a more practical sphere.

'All things considered,' he said, 'we haven't got much to go on. In fact, just the words Seven Dials. As a matter of fact I don't even know exactly where Seven Dials is. But, anyway, we can't very well comb out the whole of that district, house by house.'

'We could,' said Bundle.

'Well, perhaps we could eventually – though I'm not so sure. I imagine it's a well-populated area. But it wouldn't be very subtle.'

The word reminded him of the girl Socks and he smiled.

'Then, of course, there's the part of the country where Ronny was shot. We could nose around there. But the police are probably doing everything we could do, and doing it much better.'

'What I like about you,' said Bundle sarcastically, 'is your cheerful and optimistic disposition.'

'Never mind her, Jimmy,' said Loraine softly. 'Go on.'

'Don't be so impatient,' said Jimmy to Bundle. 'All the best sleuths approach a case this way, by eliminating unnecessary and unprofitable investigation. I'm coming now to the third alternative – Gerald's death. Now that we know it was murder – by the way, you do both believe that, don't you?'

'Yes,' said Loraine.

'Yes,' said Bundle.

'Good. So do I. Well, it seems to me that there we do stand some faint chance. After all, if Gerry didn't take the chloral himself, someone must have got into his room and put it there – dissolved it in the glass of water, so that when he woke up he drank it off. And of course left the empty box or bottle or whatever it was. You agree with that?'

'Ye – es,' said Bundle slowly. 'But –'

'Wait. And that someone must have been in the house at the time. It couldn't very well have been someone from outside.'

'No,' agreed Bundle, more readily this time.

'Very well. Now, that narrows down things considerably. To begin with, I suppose a good many of the servants are family ones – they're your lot, I mean.'

'Yes,' said Bundle. 'Practically all the staff stayed when we let it. All the principal ones are there still – of course there have been changes among the under servants.'

'Exactly – that's what I am getting at. *You*' – he addressed Bundle – 'must go into all that. Find out when new servants were engaged – what about footmen, for instance?'

'One of the footmen is new. John, his name is.'

'Well, make inquiries about John. And about the others who have only come recently.'

'I suppose,' said Bundle slowly, 'it must have been a servant. It couldn't have been one of the guests?'

'I don't see how that's possible.'

'Who were there exactly?'

'Well, there were three girls – Nancy and Helen and Socks –'

'Socks Daventry? I know her.'

'May have been. Girl who was always saying things were subtle.'

'That's Socks all right. Subtle is one of her words.'

'And then there was Gerry Wade and me and Bill Eversleigh and Ronny. And, of course, Sir Oswald and Lady Coote. Oh! and Pongo.'

'Who's Pongo?'

'Chap called Bateman – secretary to old Coote. Solemn sort of cove but very conscientious. I was at school with him.'

'There doesn't seem anything very suspicious there,' remarked Loraine.

'No, there doesn't,' said Bundle. 'As you say, we'll have to look amongst the servants. By the way, you don't suppose that clock being thrown out of the window had anything to do with it?'

'A clock thrown out of the window,' said Jimmy, staring. It was the first he had heard of it.

'I can't see how it can have anything to do with it,' said Bundle. 'But it's odd somehow. There seems no sense in it.'

'I remember,' said Jimmy slowly. 'I went in to – to see poor old Gerry, and, there were the clocks ranged along the mantel-piece. I remember noticing there were only seven – not eight.'

He gave a sudden shiver and explained himself apologetically.

'Sorry, but somehow those clocks have always given me the shivers. I dream of them sometimes. I'd hate to go into that room in the dark and see them there in a row.'

'You wouldn't be able to see them if it was dark,' said Bundle practically. 'Not unless they had luminous dials – Oh!' She gave a sudden gasp and the colour rushed into her cheeks. 'Don't you see! *Seven Dials!*

The others looked at her doubtfully, but she insisted with increasing vehemence.

'It must be. It can't be a coincidence.'

There was a pause.

'You may be right,' said Jimmy Thesiger at last. 'It's – it's dashed odd.'

Bundle started questioning him eagerly.

'Who bought the clocks?'

'All of us.'

'Who thought of them?'

'All of us.'

'Nonsense, somebody must have thought of them first.'

'It didn't happen that way. We were discussing what we could do to get Gerry up, and Pongo said an alarum clock, and some-body said one would be no good, and somebody else – Bill Eversleigh, I think – said why not get a dozen. And we all said good egg and hoofed off to get them. We got one each and an extra one for Pongo and one for Lady Coote – just out of the generosity of our hearts. There was nothing premeditated about it – it just happened.'

Bundle was silenced, but not convinced.

Jimmy proceeded to sum up methodically.

'I think we can say we're sure of certain facts. There's a secret society, with points of resemblance to the Mafia, in existence. Gerry Wade came to know about it. At first he treated it as rather a joke – as an absurdity, shall we say. He couldn't believe in its being really dangerous. But later something happened to convince him, and then he got the wind up in earnest. I rather fancy he must have said something to Ronny Devereux about it. Anyway, when he was put out of the way, Ronny suspected, and he must have known enough to get on the same track himself. The unfortunate thing is that we've got to start quite from the outer darkness. We haven't got the knowledge the other two had.'

'Perhaps that's an advantage,' said Loraine coolly. 'They won't suspect us and therefore they won't be trying to put us out of the way.'

'I wish I felt sure about that,' said Jimmy in a worried voice. 'You know, Loraine, old Gerry himself wanted you to keep out of it. Don't you think you could –'

'No, I couldn't,' said Loraine. 'Don't let's start discussing that again. It's only a waste of time.'

At the mention of the word time, Jimmy's eyes rose to the clock and he uttered an exclamation of astonishment. He rose and opened the door.

'Stevens.'

'Yes, sir?'

'What about a spot of lunch, Stevens? Could it be managed?'

'I anticipated that it would be required, sir. Mrs Stevens has made preparations accordingly.'

'That's a wonderful man,' said Jimmy, as he returned, heaving a sigh of relief. 'Brain, you know. Sheer brain. He takes correspondence courses. I sometimes wonder if they'd be any good to me.'

'Don't be silly,' said Loraine.

Stevens opened the door and proceeded to bring in a most

recherché meal. An omelette was followed by quails and the very lightest thing in soufflés.

'Why are men so happy when they're single,' said Loraine tragically. 'Why are they so much better looked after by other people than by us?'

'Oh! but that's rot, you know,' said Jimmy. 'I mean, they're not. How could they be? I often think –'

He stammered and stopped. Loraine blushed again.

Suddenly Bundle let out a whoop and both the others started violently.

'Idiot,' said Bundle. 'Imbecile. Me, I mean. I knew there was something I'd forgotten.'

'What?'

'You know Codders – George Lomax, I mean?'

'I've heard of him a good deal,' said Jimmy. 'From Bill and Ronny, you know.'

'Well, Codders is giving some sort of a dry party next week – and he's had a warning letter from Seven Dials.'

'What?' cried Jimmy excitedly, leaning forward. 'You can't mean it?'

'Yes, I do. He told Father about it. Now what do you think that points to?'

Jimmy leant back in his chair. He thought rapidly and carefully. At last he spoke. His speech was brief and to the point.

'Something's going to happen at that party,' he said.

'That's what I think,' said Bundle.

'It all fits in,' said Jimmy almost dreamily.

He turned to Loraine.

'How old were you when the war was on?' he asked unexpectedly.

'Nine – no, eight.'

'And Gerry, I suppose, was about twenty. Most lads of twenty fought in the war. Gerry didn't.'

'No,' said Loraine, after thinking a minute or two. 'No, Gerry wasn't a soldier. I don't know why.'

'I can tell you why,' said Jimmy. 'Or at least I can make a

very shrewd guess. He was out of England from 1915 to 1918. I've taken the trouble to find that out. And nobody seems to know exactly where he was. I think he was in Germany.'

The colour rose in Loraine's cheeks. She looked at Jimmy with admiration.

'How clever of you.'

'He spoke German well, didn't he?'

'Oh, yes, like a native.'

'I'm sure I'm right. Listen you two. Gerry Wade was at the Foreign Office. He appeared to be the same sort of amiable idiot – excuse the term, but you know what I mean – as Bill Eversleigh and Ronny Devereux. A purely ornamental excrescence. But in reality he was something quite different. I think Gerry Wade was the real thing. Our secret service is supposed to be the best in the world. I think Gerry Wade was pretty high up in that service. And that explains everything! I remember saying idly that last evening at Chimneys that Gerry couldn't be quite such an ass as he made himself out to be.'

'And if you're right?' said Bundle, practical as ever.

'Then the thing's bigger than we thought. This Seven Dials business isn't merely criminal – it's international. One thing's certain, somebody has got to be at this house-party of Lomax's.'

Bundle made a slight grimace.

'I know George well – but he doesn't like me. He'd never think of asking me to a serious gathering. All the same, I might –'

She remained a moment lost in thought.

'Do you think *I* could work it through Bill?' asked Jimmy. 'He's bound to be there as Codder's right hand man. He might bring me along somehow or other.'

'I don't see why not,' said Bundle. 'You'll have to prime Bill and make him say the right things. He's incapable of thinking of them for himself.'

'What do you suggest?' asked Jimmy humbly.

'Oh! It's quite easy. Bill describes you as a rich young man – interested in politics, anxious to stand for Parliament. George will fall at once. You know what these political parties are: always looking for new rich young men. The richer Bill says you are, the easier it will be to manage.'

'Short of being described as Rothschild, I don't mind,' said Jimmy.

'Then I think that's practically settled. I'm dining with Bill to-morrow night, and I'll get a list of who is to be there. That will be useful.'

'I'm sorry you can't be there,' said Jimmy. 'But on the whole I think it's all for the best.'

'I'm not sure I shan't be there,' said Bundle. 'Codders hates me like poison – but there are other ways.'

She became meditative.

'And what about me?' asked Loraine in a small, meek voice.

'You're not on in this act,' said Jimmy instantly. 'See? After all, we've got to have someone outside to – er –'

'To what?' said Loraine.

Jimmy decided not to pursue this tack. He appealed to Bundle.

'Look here,' he said, 'Loraine must keep out of this, mustn't she?'

'I certainly think she'd better.'

'Next time,' said Jimmy kindly.

'And suppose there isn't a next time?' said Loraine.

'Oh, there probably will be. Not a doubt of it.'

'I see. I'm just to go home and – wait.'

'That's it,' said Jimmy, with every appearance of relief. 'I thought you'd understand.'

'You see,' explained Bundle, 'three of us forcing our way in might look rather suspicious. And you would be particularly difficult. You do see that, don't you?'

'Oh, yes,' said Loraine.

'Then it's settled – you do nothing,' said Jimmy.

'I do nothing,' said Loraine meekly.

Bundle looked at her in sudden suspicion. The tameness with which Loraine was taking it seemed hardly natural. Loraine looked at her. Her eyes were blue and guileless. They met

Bundle's without a quiver even of the lashes. Bundle was only partly satisfied. She found the meekness of Loraine Wade highly suspicious.

CHAPTER X

Bundle Visits Scotland Yard

Now it may be said at once that in the foregoing conversation each one of the three participants had, as it were, held something in reserve. That 'Nobody tells everything' is a very true motto.

It may be questioned, for instance, if Loraine Wade was perfectly sincere in her account of the motives which had led her to seek out Jimmy Thesiger.

In the same way, Jimmy Thesiger himself had various ideas and plans connected with the forthcoming party at George Lomax's which he had no intention of revealing to – say, Bundle.

And Bundle herself had a fully-fledged plan which she proposed to put into immediate execution and which she had said nothing whatever about.

On leaving Jimmy Thesiger's rooms, she drove to Scotland Yard, where she asked for Superintendent Battle.

Superintendent Battle was rather a big man. He worked almost entirely on cases of a delicate political nature. On such a case he had come to Chimneys four years ago, and Bundle was frankly trading on his remembering this fact.

After a short delay, she was taken along several corridors and into the Superintendent's private room. Battle was a stolid-looking man with a wooden face. He looked supremely unintelligent and more like a commissionaire than a detective.

He was standing by the window when she entered, gazing in an expressionless manner at some sparrows.

'Good-afternoon, Lady Eileen,' he said. 'Sit down, won't you?'

'Thank you,' said Bundle. 'I was afraid you mightn't remember me.'

'Always remember people,' said Battle. He added: 'Got to in my job.'

'Oh!' said Bundle, rather damped.

'And what can I do for you?' inquired the Superintendent.

Bundle came straight to the point.

'I've always heard that you people at Scotland Yard have lists of all secret societies and things like that that are formed in London.'

'We try to keep up to date,' said Superintendent Battle cautiously.

'I suppose a great many of them aren't really dangerous.'

'We've got a very good rule to go by,' said Battle. 'The more they talk, the less they'll do. You'd be surprised how well that works out.'

'And I've heard that very often you let them go on?'

Battle nodded.

'That's so. Why shouldn't a man call himself a Brother of Liberty and meet twice a week in a cellar and talk about rivers of blood – it won't hurt either him or us. And if there *is* trouble any time, we know where to lay our hands on him.'

'But sometimes, I suppose,' said Bundle slowly, 'a society may be more dangerous than anyone imagines?'

'Very likely,' said Battle.

'But it *might* happen,' persisted Bundle.

'Oh, it *might*,' admitted the Superintendent.

There was a moment or two's silence. Then Bundle said quietly:

'Superintendent Battle, could you give me a list of secret societies that have their headquarters in Seven Dials?'

It was Superintendent Battle's boast that he had never been seen to display emotion. But Bundle could have sworn that just for a moment his eyelids flickered and he looked taken back. Only for a moment, however. He was his usual wooden self as he said:

'Strictly speaking, Lady Eileen, there's no such place as Seven Dials nowadays.'

'No?'

'No. Most of it is pulled down and rebuilt. It was rather a low quarter once, but it's very respectable and high class nowadays. Not at all a romantic spot to poke about in for mysterious secret societies.'

'Oh!' said Bundle, rather nonplussed.

'But all the same I should very much like to know what put that neighbourhood into your head, Lady Eileen.'

'Have I got to tell you?'

'Well, it saves trouble, doesn't it? We know where we are, so to speak.'

Bundle hesitated for a minute.

'There was a man shot yesterday,' she said slowly. 'I thought I had run over him –'

'Mr Ronald Devereux?'

'You know about it, of course. Why has there been nothing in the papers?'

'Do you really want to know that, Lady Eileen?'

'Yes, please.'

'Well, we just thought we should like to have a clear twenty-four hours – see? It will be in the papers to-morrow.'

'Oh!' Bundle studied him, puzzled.

What was hidden behind that immovable face? Did he regard the shooting of Ronald Devereux as an ordinary crime or as an extraordinary one?

'He mentioned Seven Dials when he was dying,' said Bundle slowly.

'Thank you,' said Battle. 'I'll make a note of that.'

He wrote a few words on the blotting pad in front of him.

Bundle started on another tack.

'Mr Lomax, I understand, came to see you yesterday about a threatening letter he had had.'

'He did.'

'And that was written from Seven Dials.'

'It had Seven Dials written at the top of it, I believe.'

Bundle felt as though she was battering hopelessly on a locked door.

'If you'll let me advise you, Lady Eileen –'

'I know what you're going to say.'

'I should go home and – well, think no more about these matters.'

'Leave it to you, in fact?'

'Well,' said Superintendent Battle, 'after all, we *are* the professionals.'

'And I'm only an amateur? Yes, but you forget one thing – I mayn't have your knowledge and skill – but I have one advantage over you. I can work in the dark.'

She thought that the Superintendent seemed a little taken aback, as though the force of her words struck home.

'Of course,' said Bundle, 'if you won't give me a list of secret societies –'

'Oh! I never said that. You shall have a list of the whole lot.'

He went to the door, put his head through and called out something, then came back to his chair. Bundle, rather unreasonably, felt baffled. The ease with which he acceded to her request seemed to her suspicious. He was looking at her now in a placid fashion.

'Do you remember the death of Mr Gerald Wade?' she asked abruptly.

'Down at your place, wasn't it? Took an overdraught of sleeping mixture.'

'His sister says he never took things to make him sleep.'

'Ah!' said the Superintendent. 'You'd be surprised what a lot of things there are that sisters don't know.'

Bundle again felt baffled. She sat in silence till a man came in with a typewritten sheet of paper, which he handed to the Superintendent.

'Here you are,' said the latter when the other had left the room. 'The Blood Brothers of St Sebastian. The Wolf Hounds. The Comrades of Peace. The Comrades Club. The Friends of Oppression. The Children of Moscow. The Red Standard Bearers. The Herrings. The Comrades of the Fallen – and half a dozen more.'

He handed it to her with a distinct twinkle in his eye.

'You give it to me,' said Bundle, 'because you know it's not going to be the slightest use to me. Do you want me to leave the whole thing alone?'

'I should prefer it,' said Battle. 'You see – if you go messing around all these places – well, it's going to give us a lot of trouble.'

'Looking after me, you mean?'

'Looking after you, Lady Eileen.'

Bundle had risen to her feet. Now she stood undecided. So far the honours lay with Superintendent Battle. Then she remembered one slight incident, and she based her last appeal upon it.

'I said just now that an amateur could do some things which a professional couldn't. You didn't contradict me. That's because you're an honest man, Superintendent Battle. You knew I was right.'

'Go on,' said Battle quickly.

'At Chimneys you let me help. Won't you let me help now?'

Battle seemed to be turning the thing over in his mind. Emboldened by his silence, Bundle continued.

'You know pretty well what I'm like, Superintendent Battle. I butt into things. I'm a Nosy Parker. I don't want to get in your way or to try and do things that you're doing and can do a great deal better. But if there's a chance for an amateur, let me have it.'

Again there was a pause, and then Superintendent Battle said quietly:

'You couldn't have spoken fairer than you have done, Lady Eileen. But I'm just going to say this to you. What you propose is dangerous. And when I say dangerous, I *mean* dangerous.'

'I've grasped that,' said Bundle. 'I'm not a fool.'

'No,' said Superintendent Battle. 'Never knew a young lady who was less so. What I'll do for you, Lady Eileen, is this. I'll just give you one little hint. And I'm doing it because I never have thought much of the motto "Safety First." In my opinion all the people who spend their lives avoiding being run over by buses had much better be run over and put safely out of the way. They're no good.'

This remarkable utterance issuing from the conventional lips of Superintendent Battle quite took Bundle's breath away.

'What was that hint you were going to give me?' she asked at last.

'You know Mr Eversleigh, don't you?'

'Know Bill? Why, of course. But what –?'

'I think Mr Bill Eversleigh will be able to tell you all you want to know about Seven Dials.'

'Bill knows about it? *Bill*?'

'I didn't say that. Not at all. But I think, being a quickwitted young lady, you'll get what you want from him.

'And now,' said Superintendent Battle firmly, 'I'm not going to say another word.'

CHAPTER XI

Dinner with Bill

Bundle set out to keep her appointment with Bill on the following evening full of expectation.

Bill greeted her with every sign of elation.

'Bill really *is* rather nice,' thought Bundle to herself. 'Just like a large, clumsy dog that wags its tail when it's pleased to see you.'

The large dog was uttering short staccato yelps of comment and information.

'You look tremendously fit, Bundle. I can't tell you how pleased I am to see you. I've ordered oysters – you do like oysters, don't you? And how's everything? What did you want to go mouldering about abroad so long? Were you having a very gay time?'

'No, deadly,' said Bundle. 'Perfectly foul. Old diseased colonels creeping about in the sun, and active, wizened spinsters running libraries and churches.'

'Give me England,' said Bill. 'I bar this foreign business – except Switzerland. Switzerland's all right. I'm thinking of going this Christmas. Why don't you come along?'

'I'll think about it,' said Bundle. 'What have you been doing with yourself lately, Bill?'

It was an incautious query. Bundle had merely made it out of politeness and as a preliminary to introducing her own topics of conversation. It was, however, the opening for which Bill had been waiting.

'That's just what I've been wanting to tell you about. You're brainy, Bundle, and I want your advice. You know that musical show, "Damn Your Eyes"?'

'Yes.'

'Well, I'm going to tell you about one of the dirtiest pieces of work imaginable. My God! the theatrical crowd. There's a girl – a Yankee girl – a perfect stunner –'

Bundle's heart sank. The grievances of Bill's lady friends were always interminable – they went on and on and there was no stemming them.

'This girl, Babe St Maur her name is –'

'I wonder how she got her name?' said Bundle sarcastically.

Bill replied literally.

'She got it out of *Who's Who*. Opened it and jabbed her finger down on a page without looking. Pretty nifty, eh? Her real name's Goldschmidt or Abrameier – something quite impossible.'

'Oh, quite,' agreed Bundle.

'Well, Babe St Maur is pretty smart. And she's got muscles. She was one of the eight girls who made the living bridge –'

'Bill,' said Bundle desperately. 'I went to see Jimmy Thesiger yesterday morning.'

'Good old Jimmy,' said Bill. 'Well, as I was telling you, Babe's pretty smart. You've got to be nowadays. She can put it over on most theatrical people. If you want to live, be highhanded, that's what Babe says. And mind you, she's the goods all right. She can act – it's marvellous how that girl can act. She'd not much chance in "Damn Your Eyes" – just swamped in a pack of good-looking girls. I said why not try the legitimate stage – you know, Mrs Tanqueray – that sort of stuff – but Babe just laughed –'

'Have you seen Jimmy at all?'

'Saw him this morning. Let me see, where was I? Oh, yes, I hadn't got to the rumpus yet. And mind you it was jealousy – sheer, spiteful jealousy. The other girl wasn't a patch on Babe for looks and she knew it. So she went behind her back –'

Bundle resigned herself to the inevitable and heard the whole story of the unfortunate circumstances which had led up to Babe St Maur's summary disappearance from the cast of 'Damn Your Eyes.' It took a long time. When Bill finally paused for breath and sympathy, Bundle said:

'You're quite right, Bill, it's a rotten shame. There must be a lot of jealousy about –'

'The whole theatrical world's rotten with it.'

'It must be. Did Jimmy say anything to you about coming down to the Abbey next week?'

For the first time, Bill gave his attention to what Bundle was saying.

'He was full of a long rigmarole he wanted me to stuff Codders with. About wanting to stand in the Conservative interest. But you know, Bundle, it's too damned risky.'

'Stuff,' said Bundle. 'If George *does* find him out, he won't blame you. You'll just have been taken in, that's all.'

'That's not it at all,' said Bill. 'I mean it's too damned risky for Jimmy. Before he knows where he is, he'll be parked down somewhere like Tooting East, pledged to kiss babies and make speeches. You don't know how thorough Codders is and how frightfully energetic.'

'Well, we'll have to risk that,' said Bundle. 'Jimmy can take care of himself all right.'

'You don't know Codders,' repeated Bill.

'Who's coming to this party, Bill? Is it anything very special?'

'Only the usual sort of muck. Mrs Macatta for one.'

'The MP?'

'Yes, you know, always going off the deep end about Welfare and Pure Milk and Save the Children. Think of poor Jimmy being talked to by her.'

'Never mind Jimmy. Go on telling me.'

'Then there's the Hungarian, what they call a Young Hungarian. Countess something unpronounceable. She's all right.'

He swallowed as though embarrassed, and Bundle observed that he was crumbling his bread nervously.

'Young and beautiful?' she inquired delicately.

'Oh, rather.'

'I didn't know George went in for female beauty much.'

'Oh, he doesn't. She runs baby feeding in Buda Pesth – something like that. Naturally she and Mrs Macatta want to get together.'

'Who else?'

'Sir Stanley Digby – '

'The Air Minister?'

'Yes. And his secretary, Terence O'Rourke. He's rather a lad, by the way – or used to be in his flying days. Then there's a perfectly poisonous German chap called Herr Eberhard. I don't know who he is, but we're all making the hell of a fuss about him. I've been twice told off to take him out to lunch, and I can tell you, Bundle, it was no joke. He's not like the Embassy chaps, who are all very decent. This man sucks in soup and eats peas with a knife. Not only that, but the brute is always biting his finger-nails – positively gnaws at them.'

'Pretty foul.'

'Isn't it? I believe he invents things – something of the kind. Well, that's all. Oh, yes, Sir Oswald Coote.'

'And Lady Coote?'

'Yes, I believe she's coming too.'

Bundle sat lost in thought for some minutes. Bill's list was suggestive, but she hadn't time to think out various possibilities just now. She must get on to the next point.

'Bill,' she said, 'what's all this about Seven Dials?'

Bill at once looked horribly embarrassed. He blinked and avoided her glance.

'I don't know what you mean,' he said.

'Nonsense,' said Bundle. 'I was told you know all about it.'

'About what?'

This was rather a poser. Bundle shifted her ground.

'I don't see what you want to be so secretive for,' she complained.

'Nothing to be secretive about. Nobody goes there much now. It was only a craze.'

This sounded puzzling.

'One gets so out of things when one is away,' said Bundle in a sad voice.

'Oh, you haven't missed much,' said Bill. 'Everyone went there just to say they had been. It was boring really, and, my God, you *can* get tired of fried fish.'

'Where did everyone go?'

'To the Seven Dials Club, of course,' said Bill, staring. 'Wasn't that what you were asking about?'

'I didn't know it by that name,' said Bundle.

'Used to be a slummy sort of district round about Tottenham Court Road way. It's all pulled down and cleaned up now. But the Seven Dials Club keeps to the old atmosphere. Fried fish and chips. General squalor. Kind of East End stunt, but awfully handy to get at after a show.'

'It's a night club, I suppose,' said Bundle. 'Dancing and all that?'

'That's it. Awfully mixed crowd. Not a posh affair. Artists, you know, and all sorts of odd women and a sprinkling of our lot. They say quite a lot of things, but I think that that's all bunkum myself, just said to make the place go.'

'Good,' said Bundle. 'We'll go there to-night.'

'Oh! I shouldn't do that,' said Bill. His embarrassment had returned. 'I tell you it's played out. Nobody goes there now.'

'Well, we're going.'

'You wouldn't care for it, Bundle. You wouldn't really.'

'You're going to take me to the Seven Dials Club and nowhere else, Bill. And I should like to know why you are so unwilling?'

'I? Unwilling?'

'Painfully so. What's the guilty secret?'

'Guilty secret?'

'Don't keep repeating what I say. You do it to give yourself time.'

'I don't,' said Bill indignantly. 'It's only –'

'Well? I know there's something. You never can conceal anything.'

'I've got nothing to conceal. It's only –'

'Well?'

'It's a long story – You see, I took Babe St Maur there one night –'

'Oh! Babe St Maur again.'

'Why not?'

'I didn't know it was about her –' said Bundle, stifling a yawn.

'As I say, I took Babe there. She rather fancied a lobster. I had a lobster under my arm –'

The story went on – When the lobster had been finally dismembered in a struggle between Bill and a fellow who was a rank outsider, Bundle brought her attention back to him.

'I see,' she said. 'And there was a row?'

'Yes, but it was *my* lobster. I'd bought it and paid for it. I had a perfect right –'

'Oh, you had, you had,' said Bundle hastily. 'But I'm sure that's all forgotten now. And I don't care for lobster anyway. So let's go.'

'We may be raided by the police. There's a room upstairs where they play baccarat.'

'Father will have to come and bail me out, that's all. Come on, Bill.'

Bill still seemed rather reluctant, but Bundle was adamant and they were soon speeding to their destination in a taxi.

The place, when they got to it, was much as she imagined it would be. It was a tall house in a narrow street, 14 Hunstanton Street; she noted the number.

A man whose face was strangely familiar opened the door. She thought he started slightly when he saw her, but he greeted Bill with respectful recognition. He was a tall man, with fair hair, a rather weak, anaemic face and slightly shifty eyes. Bundle puzzled to herself where she could have seen him before.

Bill had recovered his equilibrium now and quite enjoyed doing showman. They danced in the cellar, which was very full of smoke – so much so that you saw everyone through a blue haze. The smell of fried fish was almost overpowering.

On the wall were rough charcoal sketches, some of them executed with real talent. The company was extremely mixed. There were portly foreigners, opulent Jewesses, a sprinkling of the really smart, and several ladies belonging to the oldest profession in the world.

Soon Bill led Bundle upstairs. There the weak-faced man was on guard, watching all those admitted to the gambling room with a lynx eye. Suddenly recognition came to Bundle.

'Of course,' she said. 'How stupid of me. It's Alfred who used to be second footman at Chimneys. How are you, Alfred?'

'Nicely, thank you, your Ladyship.'

'When did you leave Chimneys, Alfred? Was it long before we got back?'

'It was about a month ago, m'lady. I got a chance of bettering myself, and it seemed a pity not to take it.'

'I suppose they pay you very well here,' remarked Bundle.

'Very fair, m'lady.'

Bundle passed in. It seemed to her that in this room the real life of the club was exposed. The stakes were high, she saw that at once, and the people gathered round the two tables were of the true type. Hawk-eyed, haggard, with the gambling fever in their blood.

She and Bill stayed here for about half an hour. Then Bill grew restive.

'Let's get out of this place, Bundle, and go on dancing.'

Bundle agreed. There was nothing to be seen here. They went down again. They danced for another half-hour, had fish and chips, and then Bundle declared herself ready to go home.

'But it's so early,' Bill protested.

'No, it isn't. Not really. And, anyway, I've got a long day in front of me to-morrow.'

'What are you going to do?'

'That depends,' said Bundle mysteriously. 'But I can tell you this, Bill, the grass is not going to grow under my feet.'

'It never does,' said Mr Eversleigh.

CHAPTER XII

Inquiries at Chimneys

Bundle's temperament was certainly not inherited from her father, whose prevailing characteristic was a wholly amiable inertia. As Bill Eversleigh had very justly remarked, the grass never did grow under Bundle's feet.

On the morning following her dinner with Bill, Bundle woke full of energy. She had three distinct plans which she meant to put into operation that day, and she realized that she was going to be slightly hampered by the limits of time and space.

Fortunately she did not suffer from the affliction of Gerry Wade, Ronny Devereux and Jimmy Thesiger – that of not being able to get up in the morning. Sir Oswald Coote himself would have had no fault to find with her on the score of early rising. At half-past eight Bundle had breakfasted and was on her way to Chimneys in the Hispano.

Her father seemed mildly pleased to see her.

'I never know when you're going to turn up,' he said. 'But this will save me ringing up, which I hate. Colonel Melrose was here yesterday about the inquest.'

Colonel Melrose was Chief Constable of the county, and an old friend of Lord Caterham.

'You mean the inquest of Ronny Devereux? When is it to be?'

'To-morrow. Twelve o'clock. Melrose will call for you. Having found the body, you'll have to give evidence, but he said you needn't be at all alarmed.'

'Why on earth should I be alarmed?'

'Well, you know,' said Lord Caterham apologetically, 'Melrose is a bit old-fashioned.'

'Twelve o'clock,' said Bundle. 'Good. I shall be here, if I'm still alive.'

'Have you any reason to anticipate not being alive?'

'One never knows,' said Bundle. 'The strain of modern life – as the newspapers say.'

'Which reminds me that George Lomax asked me to come over to the Abbey next week. I refused, of course.'

'Quite right,' said Bundle. 'We don't want you mixed up in any funny business.'

'Is there going to be any funny business?' asked Lord Caterham with a sudden awakening of interest.

'Well – warning letters and all that, you know,' said Bundle.

'Perhaps George is going to be assassinated,' said Lord Caterham hopefully. 'What do you think, Bundle – perhaps I'd better go after all.'

'You curb your bloodthirsty instincts and stay quietly at home,' said Bundle. 'I'm going to talk to Mrs Howell.'

Mrs Howell was the housekeeper, that dignified, creaking lady who struck terror to the heart of Lady Coote. She had no terror for Bundle, whom, indeed, she always called Miss Bundle, a relic of the days when Bundle had stayed at Chimneys, a long-legged, impish child, before her father had succeeded to the title.

'Now, Howelly,' said Bundle, 'let's have a cup of rich cocoa together, and let me hear all the household news.'

She gleaned what she wanted without much difficulty, making mental notes as follows:

'Two new scullery maids – village girls – doesn't seem much there. New third housemaid – head housemaid's niece. That sounds all right. Howelly seems to have bullied poor Lady Coote a good deal. She would.'

'I never thought the day would come when I should see Chimneys inhabited by strangers, Miss Bundle.'

'Oh! one must go with the times,' said Bundle. 'You'll be lucky, Howelly, if you never see it converted into desirable flats with use of superb pleasure grounds.'

Mrs Howell shivered all down her reactionary aristocratic spine.

'I've never seen Sir Oswald Coote,' remarked Bundle.

'Sir Oswald is no doubt a very clever gentleman,' said Mrs Howell distantly.

Bundle gathered that Sir Oswald had not been liked by his staff.

'Of course, it was Mr Bateman who saw to everything,' continued the housekeeper. 'A very efficient gentleman. A very efficient gentleman indeed, and one who knew the way things ought to be done.'

Bundle led the talk on to the topic of Gerald Wade's death. Mrs Howell was only too willing to talk about it, and was full of pitying ejaculations about the poor young gentleman, but Bundle gleaned nothing new. Presently she took leave of Mrs Howell and came downstairs again, where she promptly rang for Tredwell.

'Tredwell, when did Alfred leave?'

'It would be about a month ago now, my lady.'

'Why did he leave?'

'It was by his own wish, my lady. I believe he has gone to London. I was not dissatisfied with him in any way. I think you will find the new footman, John, very satisfactory. He seems to know his work and to be most anxious to give satisfaction.'

'Where did he come from?'

'He had excellent references, my lady. He had lived last with Lord Mount Vernon.'

'I see,' said Bundle thoughtfully.

She was remembering that Lord Mount Vernon was at present on a shooting trip in East Africa.

'What's his last name, Tredwell?'

'Bower, my lady.'

Tredwell paused for a minute or two and then, seeing that Bundle had finished, he quietly left the room. Bundle remained lost in thought.

John had opened the door to her on her arrival that day, and she had taken particular notice of him without seeming to do so. Apparently he was the perfect servant, well trained, with an expressionless face. He had, perhaps, a more soldierly bearing than most footmen and there was something a little odd about the shape of the back of his head.

But these details, as Bundle realized, were hardly relevant to the situation. She sat frowning down at the blotting paper in front of her. She had a pencil in her hand and was idly tracing the name Bower over and over again.

Suddenly an idea struck her and she stopped dead, staring at the word. Then she summoned Tredwell once more.

'Tredwell, how is the name Bower spelt?'

'B-A-U-E-R, my lady.'

'That's not an English name.'

'I believe he is of Swiss extraction, my lady.'

'Oh! That's all, Tredwell, thank you.'

Swiss extraction? No. German! That martial carriage, that flat back to the head. And he had come to Chimneys a fortnight before Gerry Wade's death.

Bundle rose to her feet. She had done all she could here. Now to get on with things! She went in search of her father.

'I'm off again,' she said. 'I've got to go and see Aunt Marcia.'

'Got to see Marcia?' Lord Caterham's voice was full of astonishment. 'Poor child, how did you get let in for that?'

'Just for once,' said Bundle, 'I happen to be going of my own free will.'

Lord Caterham looked at her in amazement. That anyone could have a genuine desire to face his redoubtable sister-in-law was quite incomprehensible to him. Marcia, Marchioness of Caterham, the widow of his late brother Henry, was a very prominent personality. Lord Caterham admitted that she had made Henry an admirable wife and that but for her in all probability he would never have held the office of Secretary of State for Foreign Affairs. On the other hand, he had always looked upon Henry's early death as a merciful release.

It seemed to him that Bundle was foolishly putting her head into the lion's mouth.

'Oh! I say,' he said. 'You know, I shouldn't do that. You don't know what it may lead to.'

'I know what I hope it's going to lead to,' said Bundle. 'I'm all right, Father, don't you worry about me.'

Lord Caterham sighed and settled himself more comfortably in his chair. He went back to his perusal of the *Field*. But in a minute or two Bundle suddenly put her head in again.

'Sorry,' she said. 'But there's one other thing I wanted to ask you. What is Sir Oswald Coote?'

'I told you – a steam-roller.'

'I don't mean your personal impression of him. How did he make his money – trouser buttons or brass beds or what?'

'Oh, I see. He's steel. Steel and iron. He's got the biggest steel works, or whatever you call it, in England. He doesn't, of course, run the show personally now. It's a company or companies. He got me in as a director of something or other. Very good business for me – nothing to do except go down to the city once or twice a year to one of those hotel places – Cannon Street or Liverpool Street – and sit around a table where they have very nice new blotting paper. Then Coote or some clever Johnny makes a speech simply bristling with figures, but fortunately you needn't listen to it – and I can tell you, you often get a jolly good lunch out of it.'

Uninterested in Lord Caterham's lunches, Bundle had departed again before he had finished speaking. On the way back to London, she tried to piece together things to her satisfaction.

As far as she could see, steel and infant welfare did not go together. One of the two, then, was just padding – presumably the latter. Mrs Macatta and the Hungarian countess could be ruled out of court. They were camouflage. No, the pivot of the whole thing seemed to be the unattractive Herr Eberhard. He did not seem to be the type of man whom George Lomax would normally invite. Bill had said vaguely that he invented. Then there was the Air Minister, and Sir Oswald Coote, who was steel. Somehow that seemed to hang together.

Since it was useless speculating further, Bundle abandoned the attempt and concentrated on her forthcoming interview with Lady Caterham.

The lady lived in a large gloomy house in one of London's higher-class squares. Inside it smelt of sealing wax, bird seed and slightly decayed flowers. Lady Caterham was a large woman – large in every way. Her proportions were majestic, rather than ample. She had a large beaked nose, wore gold-rimmed pince-nez and her upper lip bore just the faintest suspicion of a moustache.

She was somewhat surprised to see her niece, but accorded her a frigid cheek, which Bundle duly kissed.

'This is quite an unexpected pleasure, Eileen,' she observed coldly.

'We've only just got back, Aunt Marcia.'

'I know. How is your father? Much as usual?'

Her tone conveyed disparagement. She had a poor opinion of Alastair Edward Brent, ninth Marquis of Caterham. She would have called him, had she known the term, a 'poor fish.'

'Father is very well. He's down at Chimneys.'

'Indeed. You know, Eileen, I never approved of the letting of Chimneys. The place is in many ways a historical monument. It should not be cheapened.'

'It must have been wonderful in Uncle Henry's days,' said Bundle with a slight sigh.

'Henry realized his responsibilities,' said Henry's widow.

'Think of the people who stayed there,' went on Bundle ecstatically. 'All the principal statesmen of Europe.'

Lady Caterham sighed.

'I can truly say that history has been made there more than once,' she observed. 'If only your father – '

She shook her head sadly.

'Politics bore Father,' said Bundle, 'and yet they are about the most fascinating study there is, I should say. Especially if one knew about them from the inside.'

She made this extravagantly untruthful statement of her feelings without even a blush. Her aunt looked at her with some surprise.

'I am pleased to hear you say so,' she said. 'I always imagined,

Eileen, that you cared for nothing but this modern pursuit of pleasure.'

'I used to,' said Bundle.

'It is true that you are still very young,' said Lady Caterham thoughtfully. 'But with your advantages, and if you were to marry suitably, you might be one of the leading political hostesses of the day.'

Bundle felt slightly alarmed. For a moment she feared that her aunt might produce a suitable husband straightaway.

'But I feel such a fool,' said Bundle. 'I mean, I know so little.'

'That can easily be remedied,' said Lady Caterham briskly. 'I have any amount of literature I can lend you.'

'Thank you, Aunt Marcia,' said Bundle, and proceeded hastily to her second line of attack.

'I wondered if you knew Mrs Macatta, Aunt Marcia?'

'Certainly I know her. A most estimable woman with a brilliant brain. I may say that as a general rule I do not hold with women standing for Parliament. They can make their influence felt in a more womanly fashion.' She paused, doubtless to recall the womanly way in which she had forced a reluctant husband into the political arena and the marvellous success which had crowned his and her efforts. 'But still, times change. And the work Mrs Macatta is doing is of truly national importance, and of the utmost value to all women. It is, I think I may say, true womanly work. You must certainly meet Mrs Macatta.'

Bundle gave a rather dismal sigh.

'She's going to be at a house-party at George Lomax's next week. He asked Father, who, of course, won't go, but he never thought of asking me. Thinks I'm too much of an idiot, I suppose.'

It occurred to Lady Caterham that her niece was really wonderfully improved. Had she, perhaps, had an unfortunate love affair? An unfortunate love affair, in Lady Caterham's opinion, was so often highly beneficial to young girls. It made them take life seriously.

'I don't suppose George Lomax realizes for a moment that

you have – shall we say, grown up? Eileen dear,' she said, 'I must have a few words with him.'

'He doesn't like me,' said Bundle. 'I know he won't ask me.'

'Nonsense,' said Lady Caterham. 'I shall make a point of it. I knew George Lomax when he was so high.' She indicated a quite impossible height. 'He will be only too pleased to do me a favour. And he will be sure to see for himself that it is vitally important that the present-day young girls of our own class should take an intelligent interest in the welfare of their country.'

Bundle nearly said: 'Hear, hear,' but checked herself.

'I will find you some literature now,' said Lady Caterham, rising.

She called in a piercing voice: 'Miss Connor.'

A very neat secretary with a frightened expression came running. Lady Caterham gave her various directions. Presently Bundle was driving back to Brook Street with an armful of the driest-looking literature imaginable.

Her next proceeding was to ring up Jimmy Thesiger. His first words were full of triumph.

'I've managed it,' he said. 'Had a lot of trouble with Bill, though. He'd got it into his thick head that I should be a lamb among wolves. But I made him see sense at last. I've got a lot of thingummybobs now and I'm studying them. You know, blue books and white papers. Deadly dull – but one must do the thing properly. Have you ever heard of the Santa Fé boundary dispute?'

'Never,' said Bundle.

'Well, I'm taking special pains with that. It went on for years and was very complicated. I'm making it my subject. Nowadays one has to specialize.'

'I've got a lot of the same sort of things,' said Bundle. 'Aunt Marcia gave them to me.'

'Aunt who?'

'Aunt Marcia – Father's sister-in-law. She's very political. In fact, she's going to get me invited to George's party.'

'No? Oh, I say, that will be splendid.' There was a pause and then Jimmy said:

'I say, I don't think we'd better tell Loraine that – eh?'

'Perhaps not.'

'You see, she mayn't like being out of it. And she really must be kept out of it.'

'Yes.'

'I mean you can't let a girl like that run into danger!'

Bundle reflected that Mr Thesiger was slightly deficient in tact. The prospect of *her* running into danger did not seem to give him any qualms whatever.

'Have you gone away?' asked Jimmy.

'No, I was only thinking.'

'I see. I say, are you going to the inquest to-morrow?'

'Yes, are you?'

'Yes. By the way, it's in the evening papers. But tucked away in a corner. Funny – I should have thought they'd have made rather a splash about it.'

'Yes – so should I.'

'Well,' said Jimmy, 'I must be getting on with my task. I've just got to where Bolivia sent us a Note.'

'I suppose I must get on with my little lot,' said Bundle. 'Are you going to swot at it all the evening?'

'I think so. Are you?'

'Oh, probably. Good-night.'

They were both liars of the most unblushing order. Jimmy Thesiger knew perfectly well that he was taking Loraine Wade out to dinner.

As for Bundle, no sooner had she rung off than she attired herself in various nondescript garments belonging, as a matter of fact, to her maid. And having donned them she sallied out on foot deliberating whether bus or tube would be the best route by which to reach the Seven Dials Club.

CHAPTER XIII

The Seven Dials Club

Bundle reached 14 Hunstanton Street about six p.m. At that hour, as she rightly judged, the Seven Dials Club was a dead spot. Bundle's aim was a simple one. She intended to get hold of the ex-footman Alfred. She was convinced that once she had got hold of him the rest would be easy. Bundle had a simple autocratic method of dealing with retainers. It seldom failed, and she saw no reason why it should fail now.

The only thing of which she was not certain was how many people inhabited the club premises. Naturally she wished to disclose her presence to as few people as possible.

Whilst she was hesitating as to the best line of attack, the problem was solved for her in a singularly easy fashion. The door of No 14 opened and Alfred himself came out.

'Good-afternoon, Alfred,' said Bundle pleasantly.

Alfred jumped.

'Oh! good-afternoon, your ladyship. I – I didn't recognize your ladyship just for a moment.'

Paying a tribute in her own mind to her maid's clothing, Bundle proceeded to business.

'I want a few words with you, Alfred. Where shall we go?'

'Well – really, my lady – I don't know – it's not what you might call a nice part round here – I don't know, I'm sure –'

Bundle cut him short.

'Who's in the club?'

'No one at present, my lady.'

'Then we'll go in there.'

Alfred produced a key and opened the door. Bundle passed in. Alfred, troubled and sheepish, followed her. Bundle sat down and looked straight at the uncomfortable Alfred.

'I suppose you know,' she said crisply, 'that what you're doing here is dead against the law?'

Alfred shifted uncomfortably from one foot to the other.

'It's true as we've been raided twice,' he admitted. 'But nothing compromising was found, owing to the neatness of Mr Mosgorovsky's arrangements.'

'I'm not talking of the gambling only,' said Bundle. 'There's more than that – probably a great deal more than you know. I'm going to ask you a direct question, Alfred, and I should like the truth, please. *How much were you paid for leaving Chimneys?*'

Alfred looked twice round the cornice as though seeking for inspiration, swallowed three or four times, and then took the inevitable course of a weak will opposed to a strong one.

'It was this way, your ladyship. Mr Mosgorovsky, he come with a party to visit Chimneys on one of the show days. Mr Tredwell, he was indisposed like – an ingrowing toe-nail as a matter of fact – so it fell to me to show the parties over. At the end of the tour Mr Mosgorovsky, he stays behind the rest, and after giving me something handsome, he falls into conversation.'

'Yes,' said Bundle encouragingly.

'And the long and the short of it was,' said Alfred, with a sudden acceleration of his narrative, 'that he offers me a hundred pound down to leave that instant and to look after this here club. He wanted someone as was used to the best families – to give the place a tone, as he put it. And, well, it seemed flying in the face of providence to refuse – let alone that the wages I get here are just three times what they were as second footman.'

'A hundred pounds,' said Bundle. 'That's a very large sum, Alfred. Did they say anything about who was to fill your place at Chimneys?'

'I demurred a bit, my lady, about leaving at once. As I pointed out, it wasn't usual and might cause inconvenience. But Mr Mosgorovsky he knew of a young chap – been in good service and ready to come any minute. So I mentioned his name to Mr Tredwell and everything was settled pleasant like.'

Bundle nodded. Her own suspicions had been correct and

the *modus operandi* was much as she had thought it to be. She essayed a further inquiry.

'Who is Mr Mosgorovsky?'

'Gentleman as runs this club. Russian gentleman. A very clever gentleman too.'

Bundle abandoned the getting of information for the moment and proceeded to other matters.

'A hundred pounds is a very large sum of money, Alfred.'

'Larger than I ever handled, my lady,' said Alfred with simple candour.

'Did you ever suspect that there was something wrong?'

'Wrong, my lady?'

'Yes. I'm not talking about the gambling. I mean something far more serious. You don't want to be sent to penal servitude, do you, Alfred?'

'Oh, Lord! my lady, you don't mean it?'

'I was at Scotland Yard the day before yesterday,' said Bundle impressively. 'I heard some very curious things. I want you to help me, Alfred, and if you do, well – if things go wrong, I'll put in a good word for you.'

'Anything I can do, I shall be only too pleased, my lady. I mean I would anyway.'

'Well, first,' said Bundle, 'I want to go all over this place – from top to bottom.'

Accompanied by a mystified and scared Alfred, she made a very thorough tour of inspection. Nothing struck her eye till she came to the gaming room. There she noticed an inconspicuous door in the corner, and the door was locked.

Alfred explained readily.

'That's used as a getaway, your ladyship. There's a room and a door on to a staircase what comes out in the next street. That's the way the gentry goes when there's a raid.'

'But don't the police know about it?'

'It's a cunning door, you see, my lady. Looks like a cupboard, that's all.'

Bundle felt a rising excitement.

'I must get in there,' she said.

Alfred shook his head.

'You can't, my lady; Mr Mosgorovsky, he has the key.'

'Well,' said Bundle, 'there are other keys.'

She perceived that the lock was a perfectly ordinary one which probably could be easily unlocked by the key of one of the other doors. Alfred, rather troubled, was sent to collect likely specimens. The fourth that Bundle tried fitted. She turned it, opened the door and passed through.

She found herself in a small, dingy apartment. A long table occupied the centre of the room with chairs ranged round it. There was no other furniture in the room. Two built-in cupboards stood on either side of the fireplace. Alfred indicated the nearer one with a nod.

'That's it,' he explained.

Bundle tried the cupboard door, but it was locked, and she saw at once that this lock was a very different affair. It was of the patent kind that would only yield to its own key.

''Ighly ingenious, it is,' explained Alfred. 'It looks all right when opened. Shelves, you know, with a few ledgers and that on 'em. Nobody'd ever suspect, but you touch the right spot and the whole thing swings open.'

Bundle had turned round and was surveying the room thoughtfully. The first thing she noticed was that the door by which they had entered was carefully fitted round with baize. It must be completely sound-proof. Then her eyes wandered to the chairs. There were seven of them, three each side and one rather more imposing in design at the head of the table.

Bundle's eyes brightened. She had found what she was looking for. This, she felt sure, was the meeting place of the secret organization. The place was almost perfectly planned. It looked so innocent – you could reach it just by stepping through from the gaming room, or you could arrive there by the secret entrance – and any secrecy, any precautions were easily explained by the gaming going on in the next room.

Idly, as these thoughts passed through her mind, she drew a finger across the marble of the mantelpiece. Alfred saw and misinterpreted the action.

'You won't find no dirt, not to speak of,' he said. 'Mr Mosgorovsky, he ordered the place to be swept out this morning, and I did it while he waited.'

'Oh!' said Bundle, thinking very hard. 'This morning, eh?'

'Has to be done sometimes,' said Alfred. 'Though the room's never what you might call used.'

Next minute he received a shock.

'Alfred,' said Bundle, 'you've got to find me a place in this room where I can hide.'

Alfred looked at her in dismay.

'But it's impossible, my lady. You'll get me into trouble and I'll lose my job.'

'You'll lose it anyway when you go to prison,' said Bundle unkindly. 'But as a matter of fact, you needn't worry, nobody will know anything about it.'

'And there ain't no place,' wailed Alfred. 'Look round for yourself, your ladyship, if you don't believe me.'

Bundle was forced to admit that there was something in this argument. But she had the true spirit of one undertaking adventures.

'Nonsense,' she said with determination. 'There has *got* to be a place.'

'But there ain't one,' wailed Alfred.

Never had a room shown itself more unpropitious for concealment. Dingy blinds were drawn down over the dirty window panes, and there were no curtains. The window sill outside, which Bundle examined, was about four inches wide! Inside the room there were the table, the chairs and the cupboards.

The second cupboard had a key in the lock. Bundle went across and pulled it open. Inside were shelves covered with an odd assortment of glasses and crockery.

'Surplus stuff as we don't use,' explained Alfred. 'You can see for yourself, my lady, there's no place here as a cat could hide.'

But Bundle was examining the shelves.

'Flimsy work,' she said. 'Now then, Alfred, have you got a cupboard downstairs where you could shove all this glass? You have? Good. Then get a tray and start to carry it down at once. Hurry – there's no time to lose.'

'You can't, my lady. And it's getting late, too. The cooks will be here any minute now.'

'Mr Mosgo – whatnot doesn't come till later, I suppose?'

'He's never here much before midnight. But oh, my lady –'

'Don't talk so much, Alfred,' said Bundle. 'Get that tray. If you stay here arguing, you *will* get into trouble.'

Doing what is familiarly known as 'wringing his hands,' Alfred departed. Presently he returned with a tray, and having by now realized that his protests were useless, he worked with a nervous energy quite surprising.

As Bundle had seen, the shelves were easily detachable. She took them down, ranged them upright against the wall, and then stepped in.

'H'm,' she remarked. 'Pretty narrow. It's going to be a tight fit. Shut the door on me carefully, Alfred – that's right. Yes, it can be done. Now I want a gimlet.'

'A gimlet, my lady?'

'That's what I said.'

'I don't know –'

'Nonsense, you must have a gimlet – perhaps you've got an auger as well. If you haven't got what I want, you'll have to go out and buy it, so you'd better try hard to find the right thing.'

Alfred departed and returned presently with quite a creditable assortment of tools. Bundle seized what she wanted and proceeded swiftly and efficiently to bore a small hole at the level of her right eye. She did this from the outside so that it should be less noticeable, and she dared not make it too large lest it should attract attention.

'There, that'll do,' she remarked at last.

'Oh, but, my lady, my lady –'

'Yes?'

'But they'll find you – if they should open the door.'

'They won't open the door,' said Bundle. 'Because you are going to lock it and take the key away.'

'And if by chance Mr Mosgorovsky should ask for the key?'

'Tell him it's lost,' said Bundle briskly. 'But nobody's going to worry about this cupboard – it's only here to attract attention from the other one and make it a pair. Go on, Alfred, someone might come at any time. Lock me in and take the key and come and let me out when everyone's gone.'

'You'll be taken bad, my lady. You'll faint –'

'I never faint,' said Bundle. 'But you might as well get me a cocktail. I shall certainly need it. Then lock the door of the room again – don't forget – and take the door keys back to their proper doors. And Alfred – don't be too much of a rabbit. Remember, if anything goes wrong, I'll see you through.'

'And that's that,' said Bundle to herself, when having served the cocktail, Alfred had finally departed.

She was not nervous lest Alfred's nerve should fail and he should give her away. She knew that his sense of self-preservation was far too strong for that. His training alone helped him to conceal private emotions beneath the mask of a well-trained servant.

Only one thing worried Bundle. The interpretation she had chosen to put upon the cleaning of the room that morning might be all wrong. And if so – Bundle sighed in the narrow confines of the cupboard. The prospect of spending long hours in it for nothing was not attractive.

CHAPTER XIV

The Meeting of the Seven Dials

It would be as well to pass over the sufferings of the next four hours as quickly as possible. Bundle found her position extremely cramped. She had judged that the meeting, if meeting there was to be, would take place at a time when the club was in full swing – somewhere probably between the hours of midnight and two a.m.

She was just deciding that it must be at least six o'clock in the morning when a welcome sound came to her ears, the sound of the unlocking of a door.

In another minute the electric light was switched on. The hum of voices, which had come to her for a minute or two, rather like the far-off roar of sea waves, ceased as suddenly as it had begun, and Bundle heard the sound of a bolt being shot. Clearly someone had come in from the gaming room next door, and she paid tribute to the thoroughness with which the communicating door had been rendered sound-proof.

In another minute the intruder came into her line of vision – a line of vision that was necessarily somewhat incomplete but which yet answered its purpose. A tall man, broad-shouldered and powerful looking, with a long black beard, Bundle remembered having seen him sitting at one of the baccarat tables on the preceding night.

This, then, was Alfred's mysterious Russian gentleman, the proprietor of the club, the sinister Mr Mosgorovsky. Bundle's heart beat faster with excitement. So little did she resemble her father that at this minute she fairly gloried in the extreme discomfort of her position.

The Russian remained for some minutes standing by the table, stroking his beard. Then he drew a watch from his pocket and glanced at the time. Nodding his head as though satisfied, he again thrust his hand into his pocket and, pulling out something that Bundle could not see, he moved out of the line of vision.

When he reappeared she could hardly help giving a gasp of surprise.

His face was now covered by a mask – but hardly a mask in the conventional sense. It was not shaped to the face. It was a mere piece of material hanging in front of the features like a curtain in which two slits were pierced for the eyes. In shape it was round and on it was the representation of a clock face, with the hands pointing to six o'clock.

'The Seven Dials!' said Bundle to herself.

And at that minute there came a new sound – seven muffled taps.

Mosgorovsky strode across to where Bundle knew was the other cupboard door. She heard a sharp click, and then the sound of greetings in a foreign tongue.

Presently she had a view of the newcomers.

They also wore clock masks, but in their case the hands were in a different position – four o'clock and five o'clock respectively. Both men were in evening dress – but with a difference. One was an elegant, slender young man wearing evening clothes of exquisite cut. The grace with which he moved was foreign rather than English. The other man could be better described as wiry and lean. His clothes fitted him sufficiently well, but no more, and Bundle guessed at his nationality even before she heard his voice.

'I reckon we're the first to arrive at this little meeting.'

A full pleasant voice with a slight American drawl, and an inflection of Irish behind it.

The elegant young man said in good, but slightly stilted English:

'I had much difficulty in getting away to-night. These things do not always arrange themselves fortunately. I am not, like No 4 here, my own master.'

Bundle tried to guess at his nationality. Until he spoke, she had thought he might be French, but the accent was not a French one. He might possibly, she thought, be an Austrian, or a Hungarian, or even a Russian.

The American moved to the other side of the table, and Bundle heard a chair being pulled out.

'One o'clock's being a great success,' he said. 'I congratulate you on taking the risk.'

Five o'clock shrugged his shoulders.

'Unless one takes risks –' He left the sentence unfinished.

Again seven taps sounded and Mosgorovsky moved across to the secret door.

She failed to catch anything definite for some moments since the whole company were out of sight, but presently she heard the bearded Russian's voice upraised.

'Shall we begin proceedings?'

He himself came round the table and took the seat next to the arm-chair at the top. Sitting thus, he was directly facing Bundle's cupboard. The elegant five o'clock took the place next to him. The third chair that side was out of Bundle's sight, but the American, No 4, moved into her line of vision for a moment or two before he sat down.

On the near side of the table also, only two chairs were visible, and as she watched a hand turned the second – really the middle chair – down. And then with a swift movement, one of the newcomers brushed past the cupboard and took the chair opposite Mosgorovsky. Whoever sat there had, of course, their back directly turned to Bundle – and it was at that back that Bundle was staring with a good deal of interest, for it was the back of a singularly beautiful woman very much *décolleté*.

It was she who spoke first. Her voice was musical, foreign – with a deep seductive note in it. She was glancing towards the empty chair at the head of the table.

'So we are not to see No 7 to-night?' she said. 'Tell me, my friends, shall we ever see him?'

'That's darned good,' said the American. 'Darned good! As for seven o'clock – *I'm* beginning to believe there is no such person.'

'I should not advise you to think that, my friend,' said the Russian pleasantly.

There was a silence – rather an uncomfortable silence, Bundle felt.

She was still staring as though fascinated at the beautiful back in front of her. There was a tiny black mole just below the right shoulder blade that enhanced the whiteness of the skin. Bundle felt that at last the term 'beautiful adventuress,' so often read, had a real meaning for her. She was quite certain that this woman had a beautiful face – a dark Slavonic face with passionate eyes.

She was recalled from her imagining by the voice of the Russian, who seemed to act as master of ceremonies.

'Shall we get on with our business? First to our absent comrade! No 2!'

He made a curious gesture with his hand towards the turned down chair next to the woman, which everyone present imitated, turning to the chair as they did so.

'I wish No 2 were with us to-night,' he continued. 'There are many things to be done. Unsuspected difficulties have arisen.'

'Have you had his report?' It was the American who spoke.

'As yet – I have nothing from him.' There was a pause. 'I cannot understand it.'

'You think it may have – gone astray?'

'That is – a possibility.'

'In other words,' said five o'clock softly, 'there is – danger.'

He spoke the word delicately – and yet with relish.

The Russian nodded emphatically.

'Yes – there's danger. Too much is getting known about us – about this place. I know of several people who suspect.' He added coldly: 'They must be silenced.'

Bundle felt a little cold shiver pass down her spine. If she were to be found, would she be silenced? She was recalled suddenly to attention by a word.

'So nothing has come to light about Chimneys?'

Mosgorovsky shook his head.

'Nothing.'

Suddenly No 5 leant forward.

'I agree with Anna; where is our president – No 7? He who called us into being. Why do we never see him?'

'No 7,' said the Russian, 'has his own ways of working.'

'So you always say.'

'I will say no more,' said Mosgorovsky. 'I pity the man – or woman – who comes up against him.'

There was an awkward silence.

'We must get on with our business,' said Mosgorovsky quietly. 'No 3, you have the plans of Wyvern Abbey?'

Bundle strained her ears. So far she had neither caught a glimpse of No 3, nor had she heard his voice. She heard it now and recognized it as unmistakable. Low, pleasant, indistinct – the voice of a well-bred Englishman.

'I've got them here, sir.'

Some papers were shoved across the table. Everyone bent forward. Presently Mosgorovsky raised his head again.

'And the list of guests?'

'Here.'

The Russian read them.

'Sir Stanley Digby. Mr Terence O'Rourke. Sir Oswald and Lady Coote. Mr Bateman. Countess Anna Radzky. Mrs Macatta. Mr James Thesiger –' He paused and then asked sharply:

'Who is Mr James Thesiger?'

The American laughed.

'I guess you needn't worry any about him. The usual complete young ass.'

The Russian continued reading.

'Herr Eberhard and Mr Eversleigh. That completes the list.'

'Does it?' said Bundle silently. 'What about that sweet girl, Lady Eileen Brent?'

'Yes, there seems nothing to worry about there,' said Mosgorovsky. He looked across the table. 'I suppose there's no doubt whatever about the value of Eberhard's invention?'

Three o'clock made a laconic British reply.

'None whatever.'

'Commercially it should be worth millions,' said the Russian.

'And internationally – well, one knows only too well the greed of nations.'

Bundle had an idea that behind his mask he was smiling unpleasantly.

'Yes,' he went on. 'A gold mine.'

'Well worth a few lives,' said No 5, cynically, and laughed.

'But you know what inventors are,' said the American. 'Sometimes these darned things won't work.'

'A man like Sir Oswald Coote will have made no mistake,' said Mosgorovsky.

'Speaking as an aviator myself,' said No 5, 'the thing is perfectly feasible. It has been discussed for years – but it needed the genius of Eberhard to bring it to fruition.'

'Well,' said Mosgorovsky, 'I don't think we need discuss matters any further. You have all seen the plans. I do not think our original scheme can be bettered. By the way, I hear something about a letter of Gerald Wade's that has been found – a letter that mentions this organization. Who found it?'

'Lord Caterham's daughter – Lady Eileen Brent.'

'Bauer should have been on to that,' said Mosgorovsky. 'It was careless of him. Who was the letter written to?'

'His sister,' I believe,' said No 3.

'Unfortunate,' said Mosgorovsky. 'But it cannot be helped. The inquest on Ronald Devereux is to-morrow. I suppose that has been arranged for?'

'Reports as to local lads having been practising with rifles have been spread everywhere,' said the American.

'That should be all right then. I think there is nothing further to be said. I think we must all congratulate our dear one o'clock and wish her luck in the part she has to play.'

'Hurrah!' cried No 5. 'To Anna!'

All hands flew out in the same gesture which Bundle had noticed before.

'To Anna!'

One o'clock acknowledged the salutation with a typically foreign gesture. Then she rose to her feet and the others followed suit. For the first time, Bundle caught a glimpse of No 3 as he came to put Anna's cloak round her – a tall, heavily built man.

Then the party filed out through the secret door. Mosgorovsky secured it after them. He waited a few moments and then Bundle heard him unbolt the other door and pass through after extinguishing the electric light.

It was not until two hours later that a white and anxious Alfred came to release Bundle. She almost fell into his arms and he had to hold her up.

'Nothing,' said Bundle. 'Just stiff, that's all. Here, let me sit down.'

'Oh, Gord, my lady, it's been awful.'

'Nonsense,' said Bundle. 'It all went off splendidly. Don't get the wind up now it's all over. It might have gone wrong, but thank goodness it didn't.'

'Thank goodness, as you say, my lady. I've been in a twitter all the evening. They're a funny crowd, you know.'

'A damned funny crowd,' said Bundle, vigorously massaging her arms and legs. 'As a matter of fact, they're the sort of crowd I always imagined until to-night only existed in books. In this life, Alfred, one never stops learning.'

CHAPTER XV

The Inquest

Bundle reached home about six a.m. She was up and dressed by half past nine, and rang up Jimmy Thesiger on the telephone.

The promptitude of his reply somewhat surprised her, till he explained that he was going down to attend the inquest.

'So am I,' said Bundle. 'And I've got a lot to tell you.'

'Well, suppose you let me drive you down and we can talk on the way. How about that?'

'All right. But allow a bit extra because you'll have to take me to Chimneys. The Chief Constable's picking me up there.'

'Why?'

'Because he's a kind man,' said Bundle.

'So am I,' said Jimmy. 'Very kind.'

'Oh! you – you're an ass,' said Bundle. 'I heard somebody say so last night.'

'Who?'

'To be strictly accurate – a Russian Jew. No, it wasn't. It was –'

But an indignant protest drowned her words.

'I may be an ass,' said Jimmy. 'I daresay I am – but I won't have Russian Jews saying so. What were you doing last night, Bundle?'

'That's what I'm going to talk about,' said Bundle. 'Goodbye for the moment.'

She rang off in a tantalizing manner which left Jimmy pleasantly puzzled. He had the highest respect for Bundle's capabilities, though there was not the slightest trace of sentiment in his feeling towards her.

'She's been up to something,' he opined, as he took a last hasty drink of coffee. 'Depend upon it, she's been up to something.'

Twenty minutes later, his little two-seater drew up before the Brook Street house and Bundle, who had been waiting, came tripping down the steps. Jimmy was not ordinarily an observant young man, but he noticed that there were black rings round Bundle's eyes and that she had all the appearance of having had a late night the night before.

'Now then,' he said, as the car began to nose her way through the suburbs, 'what dark deeds have you been up to?'

'I'll tell you,' said Bundle. 'But don't interrupt until I've finished.'

It was a somewhat long story, and Jimmy had all he could do to keep sufficient attention on the car to prevent an accident. When Bundle had finished he sighed – then looked at her searchingly.

'Bundle?'

'Yes?'

'Look here, you're not pulling my leg?'

'What do you mean?'

'I'm sorry,' apologized Jimmy, 'but it seems to me as though I'd heard it all before – in a dream, you know.'

'I know,' said Bundle sympathetically.

'It's impossible,' said Jimmy, following out his own train of thought. 'The beautiful foreign adventuress, the international gang, the mysterious No 7, whose identity nobody knows – I've read it all a hundred times in books.'

'Of course you have. So have I. But it's no reason why it shouldn't really happen.'

'I suppose not,' admitted Jimmy.

'After all – I suppose fiction is founded on the truth. I mean unless things did happen, people couldn't think of them.'

'There is something in what you say,' agreed Jimmy. 'But all the same I can't help pinching myself to see if I'm awake.'

'That's how I felt.'

Jimmy gave a deep sigh.

'Well, I suppose we are awake. Let me see, a Russian, an American, an Englishman – a possible Austrian or Hungarian

– and the lady who may be any nationality – for choice Russian or Polish – that's a pretty representative gathering.'

'And a German,' said Bundle. 'You've forgotten the German.'

'Oh!' said Jimmy slowly. 'You think –?'

'The absent No 2. No 2 is Bauer – our footman. That seems to me quite clear from what they said about expecting a report which hadn't come in – though what there can be to report about Chimneys, I can't think.'

'It must be something to do with Gerry Wade's death,' said Jimmy. 'There's something there we haven't fathomed yet. You say they actually mentioned Bauer by name?'

Bundle nodded.

'They blamed him for not having found that letter.'

'Well, I don't see what you could have clearer than that. There's no going against it. You'll have to forgive my first incredulity, Bundle – but you know, it was rather a tall story. You say they knew about my going down to Wyvern Abbey next week?'

'Yes, that's when the American – it was him, not the Russian – said they needn't worry – you were only the usual kind of ass.'

'Ah!' said Jimmy. He pressed his foot down on the accelerator viciously and the car shot forward. 'I'm very glad you told me that. It gives me what you might call a personal interest in the case.'

He was silent for a minute or two and then he said:

'Did you say that German inventor's name was Eberhard?'

'Yes. Why?'

'Wait a minute. Something's coming back to me. Eberhard, Eberhard – yes, I'm sure that was the name.'

'Tell me.'

'Eberhard was a Johnny who'd got some patent process he applied to sell. I can't put the thing properly because I haven't got the scientific knowledge – but I know the result was that it became so toughened that a wire was as strong as a steel bar had previously been. Eberhard had to do with aeroplanes and his idea was that the weight would be so enormously reduced that flying would be practically revolutionized – the cost of it, I mean. I believe he offered his invention to the German

Government, and they turned it down, pointed out some unde-
niable flaw in it – but they did it rather nastily. He set to work
and circumvented the difficulty, whatever it was, but he'd been
offended by their attitude and swore they shouldn't have his
ewe lamb. I always thought the whole thing was probably
bunkum, but now – it looks differently.'

'That's it,' said Bundle eagerly. 'You must be right, Jimmy.
Eberhard must have offered his invention to our Government.
They've been taking, or are going to take, Sir Oswald Coote's
expert opinion on it. There's going to be an unofficial conference at the Abbey. Sir Oswald, George, the Air Minister and
Eberhard. Eberhard will have the plans or the process or whatever you call it –'

'Formula,' suggested Jimmy. 'I think "formula" is a good
word myself.'

'He'll have the formula with him, and the Seven Dials are
out to steal the formula. I remember the Russian saying it was
worth millions.'

'I suppose it would be,' said Jimmy.

'And well worth a few lives – that's what the other man
said.'

'Well, it seems to have been,' said Jimmy, his face clouding
over. 'Look at this damned inquest to-day. Bundle, are you sure
Ronny said nothing else?'

'No,' said Bundle. 'Just that. *Seven Dials. Tell Jimmy Thesiger.*
That's all he could get out, poor lad.'

'I wish we knew what he knew,' said Jimmy. 'But we've found
out one thing. I take it that the footman, Bauer, must almost
certainly have been responsible for Gerry's death. You know,
Bundle –'

'Yes?'

'Well, I'm a bit worried sometimes. Who's going to be the
next one! It really isn't the sort of business for a girl to be mixed
up in.'

Bundle smiled in spite of herself. It occurred to her that it
had taken Jimmy a long time to put her in the same category
as Loraine Wade.

'It's far more likely to be you than me,' she remarked cheerfully.

'Hear, hear,' said Jimmy. 'But what about a few casualties on the other side for a change? I'm feeling rather blood-thirsty this morning. Tell me, Bundle, would you recognize any of these people if you saw them?'

Bundle hesitated.

'I think I should recognize No 5,' she said at last. 'He's got a queer way of speaking – a kind of venomous, lisping way – that I think I'd know again.'

'What about the Englishman?'

Bundle shook her head.

'I saw him least – only a glimpse – and he's got a very ordinary voice. Except that he's a big man, there's nothing much to go by.'

'There's the woman, of course,' continued Jimmy. 'She ought to be easier. But then, you're not likely to run across her. She's probably putting in the dirty work, being taken out to dinner by amorous Cabinet Ministers and getting State secrets out of them when they've had a couple. At least, that's how it's done in books. As a matter of fact, the only Cabinet Minister I know drinks hot water with a dash of lemon in it.'

'Take George Lomax, for instance, can you imagine him being amorous with beautiful foreign women?' said Bundle with a laugh.

Jimmy agreed with her criticism.

'And now about the man of mystery – No 7,' went on Jimmy. 'You've no idea who he could be?'

'None whatever.'

'Again – by book standards, that is – he ought to be someone we all know. What about George Lomax himself?'

Bundle reluctantly shook her head.

'In a book it would be perfect,' she agreed. 'But knowing Codders –' And she gave herself up to sudden uncontrollable mirth. 'Codders, the great criminal organizer,' she gasped. 'Wouldn't it be marvellous?'

Jimmy agreed that it would. Their discussion had taken some

time and his driving had slowed down involuntarily once or twice. They arrived at Chimneys, to find Colonel Melrose already there waiting. Jimmy was introduced to him and they all three proceeded to the inquest together.

As Colonel Melrose had predicted, the whole affair was very simple. Bundle gave her evidence. The doctor gave his. Evidence was given of rifle practice in the neighbourhood. A verdict of death by misadventure was brought in.

After the proceedings were over, Colonel Melrose volunteered to drive Bundle back to Chimneys, and Jimmy Thesiger returned to London.

For all his light-hearted manner, Bundle's story had impressed him profoundly. He set his lips closely together.

'Ronny, old boy,' he murmured, 'I'm going to be up against it. And you're not here to join in the game.'

Another thought flashed into his mind. Loraine! Was she in danger?

After a minute or two's hesitation, he went over to the telephone and rang her up.

'It's me – Jimmy. I thought you'd like to know the result of the inquest. Death by misadventure.'

'Oh, but –'

'Yes, but I think there's something behind that. The coroner had had a hint. Someone's at work to hush it up. I say, Loraine –'

'Yes?'

'Look here. There's – there's some funny business going about. You'll be very careful, won't you? For my sake.'

He heard the quick note of alarm that sprang into her voice.

'Jimmy – but then it's dangerous – for *you.*'

He laughed.

'Oh, *that's* all right. I'm the cat that had nine lives. Bye-bye, old thing.'

He rang off and remained a minute or two lost in thought. Then he summoned Stevens.

'Do you think you could go out and buy me a pistol, Stevens?'

'A pistol, sir?'

True to his training, Stevens betrayed no hint of surprise.

'What kind of a pistol would you be requiring?'

'The kind where you put your finger on the trigger and the thing goes on shooting until you take it off again.'

'An automatic, sir.'

'That's it,' said Jimmy. 'An automatic. And I should like it to be a blue-nosed one – if you and the shopman know what that is. In American stories, the hero always takes his blue-nosed automatic from his hip pocket.'

Stevens permitted himself a faint, discreet smile.

'Most American gentlemen that I have known, sir, carry something very different in their hip pockets,' he observed.

Jimmy Thesiger laughed.

CHAPTER XVI

The House Party at the Abbey

Bundle drove over to Wyvern Abbey just in time for tea on Friday afternoon. George Lomax came forward to welcome her with considerable *empressement.*

'My dear Eileen,' he said, 'I can't tell you how pleased I am to see you here. You must forgive my not having invited you when I asked your father, but to tell the truth I never dreamed that a party of this kind would appeal to you. I was both – er – surprised and – er – delighted when Lady Caterham told me of your – er – interest in – er – politics.'

'I wanted to come so much,' said Bundle in a simple, ingenuous manner.

'Mrs Macatta will not arrive till the later train,' explained George. 'She was speaking at a meeting in Manchester last night. Do you know Thesiger? Quite a young fellow, but a remarkable grasp of foreign politics. One would hardly suspect it from his appearance.'

'I know Mr Thesiger,' said Bundle, and she shook hands solemnly with Jimmy, who she observed had parted his hair in the middle in the endeavour to add earnestness to his expression.

'Look here,' said Jimmy in a low hurried voice, as George temporarily withdrew. 'You mustn't be angry, but I've told Bill about our little stunt.'

'Bill?' said Bundle, annoyed.

'Well, after all,' said Jimmy, 'Bill is one of the lads, you know. Ronny was a pal of his and so was Gerry.'

'Oh! I know,' said Bundle.

'But you think it's a pity? Sorry.'

'Bill's all right, of course. It isn't that,' said Bundle. 'But he's – well, Bill's a born blunderer.'

'Not mentally very agile?' suggested Jimmy. 'But you forget one thing – Bill's got a very hefty fist. And I've an idea that a hefty fist is going to come in handy.'

'Well, perhaps you're right. How did he take it?'

'Well, he clutched his head a good bit, but – I mean the facts took some driving home. But by repeating the thing patiently in words of one syllable I at last got it into his thick head. And, naturally, he's with us to the death, as you might say.'

George reappeared suddenly.

'I must make some introductions, Eileen. This is Sir Stanley Digby – Lady Eileen Brent. Mr O'Rourke.' The Air Minister was a little round man with a cheerful smile. Mr O'Rourke, a tall young man with laughing blue eyes and a typical Irish face, greeted Bundle with enthusiasm.

'And I thinking it was going to be a dull political party entirely,' he murmured in an adroit whisper.

'Hush,' said Bundle. 'I'm political – very political.'

'Sir Oswald and Lady Coote you know,' continued George.

'We've never actually met,' said Bundle, smiling.

She was mentally applauding her father's descriptive powers.

Sir Oswald took her hand in an iron grip and she winced slightly.

Lady Coote, after a somewhat mournful greeting, had turned to Jimmy Thesiger, and appeared to be registering something closely akin to pleasure. Despite his reprehensible habit of being late for breakfast, Lady Coote had a fondness for this amiable, pink-faced young man. His air of irrepressible good nature fascinated her. She had a motherly wish to cure him of his bad habits and form him into one of the world's workers. Whether, once formed, he would be as attractive was a question she had never asked herself. She began now to tell him of a very painful motor accident which had happened to one of her friends.

'Mr Bateman,' said George briefly, as one who would pass on to better things.

A serious, pale-faced young man bowed.

'And now,' continued George, 'I must introduce you to Countess Radzky.'

Countess Radzky had been conversing with Mr Bateman. Leaning very far back on a sofa, with her legs crossed in a daring manner, she was smoking a cigarette in an incredibly long turquoise-studded holder.

Bundle thought she was one of the most beautiful women she had ever seen. Her eyes were very large and blue, her hair was coal black, she had a matte skin, the slightly flattened nose of the Slav, and a sinuous, slender body. Her lips were reddened to a degree with which Bundle was sure Wyvern Abbey was totally unacquainted.

She said eagerly: 'This is Mrs Macatta – yes?'

On George's replying in the negative and introducing Bundle, the Countess gave her a careless nod, and at once resumed her conversation with the serious Mr Bateman.

Bundle heard Jimmy's voice in her ear:

'Pongo is absolutely fascinated by the lovely Slav,' he said. 'Pathetic, isn't it? Come and have some tea.'

They drifted once more into the neighbourhood of Sir Oswald Coote.

'That's a fine place of yours, Chimneys,' remarked the great man.

'I'm glad you liked it,' said Bundle meekly.

'Wants new plumbing,' said Sir Oswald. 'Bring it up to date, you know.'

He ruminated for a minute or two.

'I'm taking the Duke of Alton's place. Three years. Just while I'm looking round for a place of my own. Your father couldn't sell if he wanted to, I suppose?'

Bundle felt her breath taken away. She had a nightmare vision of England with innumerable Cootes in innumerable counterparts of Chimneys – all, be it understood, with an entirely new system of plumbing installed.

She felt a sudden violent resentment which, she told herself, was absurd. After all, contrasting Lord Caterham with Sir Oswald

Coote, there was no doubt as to who would go to the wall. Sir Oswald had one of those powerful personalities which make all those with whom they come in contact appear faded. He was, as Lord Caterham had said, a human steam-roller. And yet, undoubtedly, in many ways, Sir Oswald was a stupid man. Apart from his special line of knowledge and his terrific driving force, he was probably intensely ignorant. A hundred delicate appreciations of life which Lord Caterham could and did enjoy were a sealed book to Sir Oswald.

Whilst indulging in these reflections Bundle continued to chat pleasantly. Herr Eberhard, she heard, had arrived, but was lying down with a nervous headache. This was told her by Mr O'Rourke, who managed to find a place by her side and keep it.

Altogether, Bundle went up to dress in a pleasant mood of expectation, with a slight nervous dread hovering in the background whenever she thought of the imminent arrival of Mrs Macatta. Bundle felt that dalliance with Mrs Macatta was going to prove no primrose path.

Her first shock was when she came down, demurely attired in a black lace frock, and passed along the hall. A footman was standing there – at least a man dressed as a footman. But that square, burly figure lent itself badly to the deception. Bundle stopped and stared.

'Superintendent Battle,' she breathed.

'That's right, Lady Eileen.'

'Oh!' said Bundle uncertainly. 'Are you here to – to –?'

'Keep an eye on things.'

'I see.'

'That warning letter, you know,' said the Superintendent, 'fairly put the wind up Mr Lomax. Nothing would do for him but that I should come down myself.'

'But don't you think –' began Bundle, and stopped. She hardly liked to suggest to the Superintendent that his disguise was not a particularly efficient one. He seemed to have 'police officer' written all over him, and Bundle could hardly imagine the most unsuspecting criminal failing to be put on his guard.

'You think,' said the Superintendent stolidly, 'that I might be recognized?'

He gave the final word a distinct capital letter.

'I did think so – yes – ' admitted Bundle.

Something that might conceivably have been intended for a smile crossed the woodenness of Superintendent Battle's features.

'Put them on their guard, eh? Well, Lady Eileen, why not?'

'Why not?' echoed Bundle – rather stupidly, she felt.

Superintendent Battle was nodding his head slowly.

'We don't want any unpleasantness, do we?' he said. 'Don't want to be too clever – just show any light-fingered gentry that may be about – well, just show them that there's somebody on the spot, so to speak.'

Bundle gazed at him in some admiration. She could imagine that the sudden appearance of so renowned a personage as Superintendent Battle might have a depressing effect on any scheme and the hatchers of it.

'It's a great mistake to be too clever,' Superintendent Battle was repeating. 'The great thing is not to have any unpleasantness this week-end.'

Bundle passed on, wondering how many of her fellow guests had recognized or would recognize the Scotland Yard detective. In the drawing-room George was standing with a puckered brow and an orange envelope in his hand.

'Most vexatious,' he said. 'A telegram from Mrs Macatta to say she will be unable to be with us. Her children are suffering from mumps.'

Bundle's heart gave a throb of relief.

'I especially feel this on your account, Eileen,' said George kindly. 'I know how anxious you were to meet her. The Countess too will be sadly disappointed.'

'Oh, never mind,' said Bundle. 'I should hate it if she'd come and given me mumps.'

'A very distressing complaint,' agreed George. 'But I do not think that infection could be carried that way. Indeed, I am sure that Mrs Macatta would have run no risk of that kind. She is a most highly principled woman, with a very real sense of her responsibilities to the community. In these days of national stress, we must all take into account –'

On the brink of embarking on a speech, George pulled himself up short.

'But it must be for another time,' he said. 'Fortunately there is no hurry in your case. But the Countess, alas, is only a visitor to our shores.'

'She's a Hungarian, isn't she?' said Bundle, who was curious about the Countess.

'Yes. You have heard, no doubt, of the Young Hungarian party. The Countess is a leader of that party. A woman of great wealth, left a widow at an early age, she has devoted her money and her talents to the public service. She has especially devoted herself to the problem of infant mortality – a terrible one under present conditions in Hungary. I – Ah! here is Herr Eberhard.'

The German inventor was younger than Bundle had imagined him. He was probably not more than thirty-three or four. He was boorish and ill at ease. And yet his personality was not an unpleasing one. His blue eyes were more shy than furtive, and his more unpleasant mannerisms, such as the one that Bill had described of gnawing his finger-nails, arose, she thought, more from nervousness than from any other cause. He was thin and weedy in appearance and looked anaemic and delicate.

He conversed rather awkwardly with Bundle in stilted English and they both welcomed the interruption of the joyous Mr O'Rourke. Presently Bill bustled in – there is no other word for it: in the same such way does a favoured Newfoundland make his entrance – and at once came over to Bundle. He was looking perplexed and harassed.

'Hullo, Bundle. Heard you'd got here. Been kept with my nose to the grindstone all the blessed afternoon or I'd have seen you before.'

'Cares of State heavy to-night?' suggested O'Rourke sympathetically.

Bill groaned.

'I don't know what your fellow's like,' he complained. 'Looks a good-natured, tubby little chap. But Codders is absolutely impossible. Drive, drive, drive, from morning to night. Everything you do is wrong, and everything you haven't done you ought to have done.'

'Quite like a quotation from the prayer book,' remarked Jimmy, who had just strolled up.

Bill glanced at him reproachfully.

'Nobody knows,' he said pathetically, 'what I have to put up with.'

'Entertaining the Countess, eh?' suggested Jimmy. 'Poor Bill, that must have been a sad strain to a woman hater like yourself.'

'What's this?' asked Bundle.

'After tea,' said Jimmy with a grin, 'the Countess asked Bill to show her round the interesting old place.'

'Well, I couldn't refuse, could I?' said Bill, his countenance assuming a brick-red tint.

Bundle felt faintly uneasy. She knew, only too well, the susceptibility of Mr William Eversleigh to female charms. In the hand of a woman like the Countess, Bill would be as wax. She wondered once more whether Jimmy Thesiger had been wise to take Bill into their confidence.

'The Countess,' said Bill, 'is a very charming woman. And no end intelligent. You should have seen her going round the house. All sorts of questions she asked.'

'What kind of questions?' asked Bundle suddenly.

Bill was vague.

'Oh! I don't know. About the history of it. And old furniture. And – oh! all sorts of things.'

At that moment the Countess swept into the room. She seemed a shade breathless. She was looking magnificent in a close-fitting black velvet gown. Bundle noticed how Bill gravitated at once to her immediate neighbourhood. The serious spectacled young man joined him.

'Bill and Pongo have both got it badly,' observed Jimmy Thesiger with a laugh.

Bundle was by no means so sure that it was a laughing matter.

CHAPTER XVII

After Dinner

George was not a believer in modern innovations. The Abbey was innocent of anything so up to date as central heating. Consequently, when the ladies entered the drawing-room after dinner, the temperature of the room was woefully inadequate to the needs of modern evening clothes. The fire that burnt in the well-furnished steel grate became as a magnet. The three women huddled round it.

'Brrrrrrrrrr!' said the Countess, a fine, exotic foreign sound.

'The days are drawing in,' said Lady Coote, and drew a flowered atrocity of a scarf closer about her ample shoulders.

'Why on earth doesn't George have the house properly heated?' said Bundle.

'You English, you never heat your houses,' said the Countess. She took out her long cigarette holder and began to smoke.

'That grate is old-fashioned,' said Lady Coote. 'The heat goes up the chimney instead of into the room.'

'Oh!' said the Countess.

There was a pause. The Countess was so plainly bored by her company that conversation became difficult.

'It's funny,' said Lady Coote, breaking the silence, 'that Mrs Macatta's children should have mumps. At least, I don't mean exactly funny –'

'What,' said the Countess, 'are mumps?'

Bundle and Lady Coote started simultaneously to explain. Finally, between them, they managed it.

'I suppose Hungarian children have it?' asked Lady Coote.

'Eh?' said the Countess.

'Hungarian children. They suffer from it?'

'I do not know,' said the Countess. 'How should I?'

Lady Coote looked at her in some surprise.

'But I understood that you worked –'

'Oh, that!' The Countess uncrossed her legs, took her cigarette holder from her mouth and began to talk rapidly.

'I will tell you some horrors,' she said. 'Horrors that I have seen. Incredible! You would not believe!'

And she was as good as her word. She talked fluently and with a graphic power of description. Incredible scenes of starvation and misery were painted by her for the benefit of her audience. She spoke of Buda Pesth shortly after the war and traced its vicissitudes to the present day. She was dramatic, but she was also, to Bundle's mind, a little like a gramophone record. You turned her on, and there you were. Presently, just as suddenly, she would stop.

Lady Coote was thrilled to the marrow – that much was clear. She sat with her mouth slightly open and her large, sad, dark eyes fixed on the Countess. Occasionally, she interpolated a comment of her own.

'One of my cousins had three children burned to death. Awful, wasn't it?'

The Countess paid no attention. She went on and on. And she finally stopped as suddenly as she had begun.

'There!' she said. 'I have told you. We have money – but no organization. It is organization we need.'

Lady Coote sighed.

'I've heard my husband say that nothing can be done without regular methods. He attributes his own success entirely to that. He declares he would never have got on without them.'

She sighed again. A sudden fleeting vision passed before her eyes of a Sir Oswald who had not got on in the world. A Sir Oswald who retained, in all essentials, the attributes of that cheery young man in the bicycle shop. Just for a second it occurred to her how much pleasanter life might have been for her if Sir Oswald had *not* had regular methods.

By a quite understandable association of ideas she turned to Bundle.

'Tell me, Lady Eileen,' she said; 'do you like that head gardener of yours?'

'MacDonald? Well –' Bundle hesitated. 'One couldn't exactly *like* MacDonald,' she explained apologetically. 'But he's a first-class gardener.'

'Oh! I know he is,' said Lady Coote.

'He's all right if he's kept in his place,' said Bundle.

'I suppose so,' said Lady Coote.

She looked enviously at Bundle, who appeared to approach the task of keeping MacDonald in his place so lightheartedly.

'I'd just adore a high-toned garden,' said the Countess dreamily.

Bundle stared, but at that moment a diversion occurred. Jimmy Thesiger entered the room and spoke directly to her in a strange, hurried voice.

'I say, will you come and see those etchings now? They're waiting for you.'

Bundle left the room hurriedly, Jimmy close behind her.

'What etchings?' she asked, as the drawing-room door closed behind her.

'No etchings,' said Jimmy. 'I'd got to say something to get hold of you. Come on, Bill is waiting for us in the library. There's nobody there.'

Bill was striding up and down the library, clearly in a very perturbed state of mind.

'Look here,' he burst out, 'I don't like this.'

'Don't like what?'

'You being mixed up in this. Ten to one there's going to be a rough house and then –'

He looked at her with a kind of pathetic dismay that gave Bundle a warm and comfortable feeling.

'She ought to be kept out of it, oughtn't she, Jimmy?'

He appealed to the other.

'I've told her so,' said Jimmy.

'Dash it all, Bundle, I mean – someone might get hurt.'

Bundle turned round to Jimmy.

'How much have you told him?'

'Oh! everything.'

'I haven't got the hang of it all yet,' confessed Bill. 'You in that place in Seven Dials and all that.' He looked at her unhappily. 'I say, Bundle, I wish you wouldn't.'

'Wouldn't what?'

'Get mixed up in these sort of things.'

'Why not?' said Bundle. 'They're exciting.'

'Oh, yes – exciting. But they may be damnably dangerous. Look at poor old Ronny.'

'Yes,' said Bundle. 'If it hadn't been for your friend Ronny, I don't suppose I should ever have got what you call "mixed up" in this thing. But I am. And it's no earthly use your bleating about it.'

'I know you're the most frightful sport, Bundle, but –'

'Cut out the compliments. Let's make plans.'

To her relief, Bill reacted favourably to the suggestion.

'You're right about the formula,' he said. 'Eberhard's got some sort of formula with him, or rather Sir Oswald has. The stuff has been tested out at his works – very secretly and all that. Eberhard has been down there with him. They're all in the study now – what you might call coming down to brass tacks.'

'How long is Sir Stanley Digby staying?' asked Jimmy.

'Going back to town to-morrow.'

'H'm,' said Jimmy. 'Then one thing's quite clear. If, as I suppose, Sir Stanley will be taking the formula with him, any funny business there's going to be will be to-night.'

'I suppose it will.'

'Not a doubt of it. That narrows the thing down very comfortably. But the bright lads will have to be their very brightest. We must come down to details. First of all, where will the sacred formula be to-night? Will Eberhard have it, or Sir Oswald Coote?'

'Neither. I understand it's to be handed over to the Air Minister this evening, for him to take to town to-morrow. In that case O'Rourke will have it. Sure to.'

'Well, there's only one thing for it. If we believe someone's going to have a shot at pinching that paper, we've got to keep watch to-night, Bill, my boy.'

Bundle opened her mouth as though to protest, but shut it again without speaking.

'By the way,' continued Jimmy, 'did I recognize the commissionaire from Harrods in the hall this evening, or was it our old friend Lestrade from Scotland Yard?'

'Scintillating, Watson,' said Bill.

'I suppose,' said Jimmy, 'that we are rather butting in on his preserves.'

'Can't be helped,' said Bill. 'Not if we mean to see this thing through.'

'Then it's agreed,' said Jimmy. 'We divide the night into two watches?'

Again Bundle opened her mouth, and again shut it without speaking.

'Right you are,' agreed Bill. 'Who'll take first duty?'

'Shall we spin for it?'

'Might as well.'

'All right. Here goes. Heads you first and I second. Tails, vice versa.'

Bill nodded. The coin spun in the air. Jimmy bent to look at it.

'Tails,' he said.

'Damn,' said Bill. 'You get first half and probably any fun that's going.'

'Oh, you never know,' said Jimmy. 'Criminals are very uncertain. What time shall I wake you? Three?'

'That's about fair, I think.'

And now, at last, Bundle spoke:

'What about *me?*' she asked.

'Nothing doing. You go to bed and sleep.'

'Oh!' said Bundle. 'That's not very exciting.'

'You never know,' said Jimmy kindly. 'You may be murdered in your sleep while Bill and I escape scot-free.'

'Well, there's always that possibility. Do you know, Jimmy, I don't half like the look of that Countess. I suspect her.'

'Nonsense,' cried Bill hotly. 'She's absolutely above suspicion.'

'How do you know?' retorted Bundle.

'Because I do. Why, one of the fellows at the Hungarian Embassy vouched for her.'

'Oh!' said Bundle, momentarily taken aback by his fervour.

'You girls are all the same,' grumbled Bill. 'Just because she's a jolly good-looking woman –'

Bundle was only too well acquainted with this unfair masculine line of argument.

'Well, don't you go and pour confidences into her shell-pink ear,' she remarked. 'I'm going to bed. I was bored stiff with that drawing-room and I'm not going back.'

She left the room. Bill looked at Jimmy.

'Good old Bundle,' he said. 'I was afraid we might have trouble with her. You know how keen she is to be in everything. I think the way she took it was just wonderful.'

'So did I,' said Jimmy. 'It staggered me.'

'She's got some sense, Bundle has. She knows when a thing's plumb impossible. I say, oughtn't we to have some lethal weapons? Chaps usually do when they're going on this sort of stunt.'

'I have a blue-nosed automatic,' said Jimmy with gentle pride. 'It weighs several pounds and looks most dangerous. I'll lend it to you when the time comes.'

Bill looked at him with respect and envy.

'What made you think of getting that?' he said.

'I don't know,' said Jimmy carelessly. 'It just came to me.'

'I hope we shan't go and shoot the wrong person,' said Bill with some anxiety.

'That would be unfortunate,' said Mr Thesiger gravely.

CHAPTER XVIII

Jimmy's Adventures

Our chronicle must here split into three separate and distinct portions. The night was to prove an eventful one and each of the three persons involved saw it from his or her own individual angle.

We will begin with that pleasant and engaging youth, Mr Jimmy Thesiger, at a moment when he has at last exchanged final good-nights with his fellow conspirator, Bill Eversleigh.

'Don't forget,' said Bill, 'three a.m. If you're still alive, that is,' he added kindly.

'I may be an ass,' said Jimmy, with rancorous remembrance of the remark Bundle had repeated to him, 'but I'm not nearly so much of an ass as I look.'

'That's what you said about Gerry Wade,' said Bill slowly. 'Do you remember? And that very night he –'

'Shut up, you damned fool,' said Jimmy. 'Haven't you got *any* tact?'

'Of course I've got tact,' said Bill. 'I'm a budding diplomatist. All diplomatists have tact.'

'Ah!' said Jimmy. 'You must be still in what they call the larval stage.'

'I can't get over Bundle,' said Bill, reverting abruptly to a former topic. 'I should certainly have said that she'd be – well, difficult. Bundle's improved. She's improved very much.'

'That's what your Chief was saying,' said Jimmy. 'He said he was agreeably surprised.'

'I thought Bundle was laying it on a bit thick myself,' said Bill. 'But Codders is such an ass he'd swallow anything. Well, night-night. I expect you'll have a bit of a job waking me when the time comes – but stick to it.'

'It won't be much good if you've taken a leaf out of Gerry Wade's book,' said Jimmy maliciously.

Bill looked at him reproachfully.

'What the hell do you want to go and make a chap uncomfortable for?' he demanded.

'I'm only getting my own back,' said Jimmy. 'Toddle along.'

But Bill lingered. He stood uncomfortably, first on one foot and then on the other.

'Look here,' he said.

'Yes?'

'What I mean to say is – well, I mean you'll be all right and all that, won't you? It's all very well ragging but when I think of poor Gerry – and then poor old Ronny –'

Jimmy gazed at him in exasperation. Bill was one of those who undoubtedly meant well, but the result of his efforts would not be described as heartening.

'I see,' he remarked, 'that I shall have to show you Leopold.'

He slipped his hand into the pocket of the dark-blue suit into which he had just changed and held out something for Bill's inspection.

'A real, genuine, blue-nosed automatic,' he said with modest pride.

'No. I say,' said Bill, 'is it really?'

He was undoubtedly impressed.

'Stevens, my man, got him for me. Warranted clean and methodical in his habits. You press the button and Leopold does the rest.'

'Oh!' said Bill. 'I say, Jimmy?'

'Yes?'

'Be careful, won't you? I mean, don't go loosing that thing off at anybody. Pretty awkward if you shot old Digby walking in his sleep.'

'That's all right,' said Jimmy. 'Naturally, I want to get value out of old Leopold now I've bought him, but I'll curb my bloodthirsty instincts as far as possible.'

'Well, night-night,' said Bill for the fourteenth time, and this time really did depart.

Jimmy was left alone to take up his vigil.

Sir Stanley Digby occupied a room at the extremity of the west wing. A bathroom adjoined it on one side, and on the other a communicating door led into a smaller room, which was tenanted by Mr Terence O'Rourke. The doors of these three rooms gave on to a short corridor. The watcher had a simple task. A chair placed inconspicuously in the shadow of an oak press just where the corridor ran into the main gallery formed a perfect vantage ground. There was no other way into the west wing, and anyone going to or from it could not fail to be seen. One electric light was still on.

Jimmy ensconced himself comfortably, crossed his legs and waited. Leopold lay in readiness across his knee.

He glanced at his watch. It was twenty minutes to one – just an hour since the household had retired to rest. Not a sound broke the stillness, except for the far-off ticking of a clock somewhere.

Somehow or other, Jimmy did not much care for that sound. It recalled things. Gerald Wade – and those seven ticking clocks on the mantelpiece . . . Whose hand had placed them there, and why? He shivered.

It was a creepy business, this waiting. He didn't wonder that things happened at spiritualistic séances. Sitting in the gloom, one got all worked up – ready to start at the least sound. And unpleasant thoughts came in on a fellow.

Ronny Devereux! Ronny Devereux and Gerry Wade! Both young, both full of life and energy; ordinary, jolly, healthy young men. And now, where were they? Dank earth . . . worms getting them . . . Ugh! why couldn't he put these horrible thoughts out of his mind?

He looked again at his watch. Twenty minutes past one only. How the time crawled.

Extraordinary girl, Bundle! Fancy having the nerve and daring actually to get into the midst of that Seven Dials place. Why hadn't he had the nerve and initiative to think of that? He supposed because the thing *was* so fantastic.

No 7. Who the hell could No 7 be? Was he, perhaps, in the

house at this minute? Disguised as a servant. He couldn't, surely, be one of the guests. No, that was impossible. But then, the whole thing was impossible. If he hadn't believed Bundle to be essentially truthful – well, he would have thought she had invented the whole thing.

He yawned. Queer, to feel sleepy, and yet at the same time strung up. He looked again at his watch. Ten minutes to two. Time was getting on.

And then, suddenly, he held his breath and leaned forward, listening. He had heard something.

The minutes went past . . . There it was again. The creak of a board . . . But it came from downstairs somewhere. There it was again! A slight, ominous creak. Somebody was moving stealthily about the house.

Jimmy sprang noiselessly to his feet. He crept silently to the head of the staircase. Everything seemed perfectly quiet. Yet he was quite certain he had really heard that stealthy sound. It was not imagination.

Very quietly and cautiously he crept down the staircase, Leopold clasped tightly in his right hand. Not a sound in the big hall. If he had been correct in assuming that the muffled sound came from directly beneath him, then it must have come from the library.

Jimmy stole to the door of it, listened, but heard nothing; then, suddenly flinging open the door, he switched on the lights.

Nothing! The big room was flooded with light. But it was empty.

Jimmy frowned.

'I could have sworn –' he murmured to himself.

The library was a large room with three windows which opened on to the terrace. Jimmy strode across the room. The middle window was unlatched.

He opened it and stepped out on to the terrace, looking from end to end of it. Nothing!

'Looks all right,' he murmured to himself. 'And yet –'

He remained for a minute lost in thought. Then he stepped

back into the library. Crossing to the door, he locked it and put the key in his pocket. Then he switched off the light. He stood for a minute listening, then crossed softly to the open window and stood there, Leopold ready in his hand.

Was there, or was there not, a soft patter of feet along the terrace? No – his imagination. He grasped Leopold tightly and stood listening . . .

In the distance a stable clock chimed two.

CHAPTER XIX

Bundle's Adventures

Bundle Brent was a resourceful girl – she was also a girl of
imagination. She had foreseen that Bill, if not Jimmy, would
make objections to her participation in the possible dangers of
the night. It was not Bundle's idea to waste time in argument.
She had laid her own plans and made her own arrangements.
A glance from her bedroom window shortly before dinner had
been highly satisfactory. She had known that the grey walls of
the Abbey were plentifully adorned with ivy, but the ivy outside
her window was particularly solid looking and would present
no difficulties to one of her athletic propensities.

She had no fault to find with Bill's and Jimmy's arrangements
as far as they went. But in her opinion they did not go far
enough. She offered no criticism, because she intended to see
to that side of things herself. Briefly, while Jimmy and Bill were
devoting themselves to the inside of the Abbey, Bundle intended
to devote her attentions to the outside.

Her own meek acquiescence in the tame rôle assigned to her
gave her an infinity of pleasure, though she wondered scornfully
how either of the two men could be so easily deceived. Bill, of
course, had never been famous for scintillating brain power.
On the other hand, he knew, or should know, his Bundle.
And she considered that Jimmy Thesiger, though only slightly
acquainted with her, ought to have known better than to
imagine that she could be so easily and summarily disposed of.

Once in the privacy of her own room, Bundle set rapidly to
work. First she discarded her evening dress and the negligible
trifle which she wore beneath it, and started again, so to speak,
from the foundations. Bundle had not brought her maid with
her, and she had packed herself. Otherwise, the puzzled French-

woman might have wondered why her lady took a pair of riding breeches and no further equine equipment.

Arrayed in riding breeches, rubber-soled shoes, and a dark-coloured pullover, Bundle was ready for the fray. She glanced at the time. As yet, it was only half past twelve. Too early by far. Whatever was going to happen would not happen for some time yet. The occupants of the house must all be given time to get off to sleep. Half past one was the time fixed by Bundle for the start of operations.

She switched off her light and sat down by the window to wait. Punctually at the appointed moment, she rose, pushed up the sash and swung her leg over the sill. The night was a fine one, cold and still. There was starlight but no moon.

She found the descent very easy. Bundle and her two sisters had run wild in the park at Chimneys as small children, and they could all climb like cats. Bundle arrived on a flower-bed, rather breathless, but quite unscathed.

She paused a minute to take stock of her plans. She knew that the rooms occupied by the Air Minister and his secretary were in the west wing; that was the opposite side of the house from where Bundle was now standing. A terrace ran along the south and west side of the house, ending abruptly against a walled fruit garden.

Bundle stepped out of her flower-bed and turned the corner of the house to where the terrace began on the south side. She crept very quietly along it, keeping close to the shadow of the house. But, as she reached the second corner, she got a shock, for a man was standing there, with the clear intention of barring her way.

The next instant she had recognized him.

'Superintendent Battle! You did give me a fright!'

'That's what I'm here for,' said the Superintendent pleasantly.

Bundle looked at him. It struck her now, as so often before, how remarkably little camouflage there was about him. He was large and solid and noticeable. He was, somehow, very English. But of one thing Bundle was quite sure. Superintendent Battle was no fool.

'What are you really doing here?' she asked, still in a whisper.

'Just seeing,' said Battle, 'that nobody's about who shouldn't be.'

'Oh!' said Bundle, rather taken aback.

'You, for instance, Lady Eileen. I don't suppose you usually take a walk at this time of night.'

'Do you mean,' said Bundle slowly, 'that you want me to go back?'

Superintendent Battle nodded approvingly.

'You're very quick, Lady Eileen. That's just what I do mean. Did you – er – come out of a door, or the window?'

'The window. It's easy as anything climbing down this ivy.'

Superintendent Battle looked up at it thoughtfully.

'Yes,' he said. 'I should say it would be.'

'And you want me to go back?' said Bundle. 'I'm rather sick about that. I wanted to go round on to the west terrace.'

'Perhaps you won't be the only one who'll want to do that,' said Battle.

'Nobody could miss seeing you,' said Bundle rather spitefully.

The Superintendent seemed rather pleased than otherwise.

'I hope they won't,' he said. '*No unpleasantness.* That's my motto. And if you'll excuse me, Lady Eileen, I think it's time you were going back to bed.'

The firmness of his tone admitted no parley. Rather crest-fallen, Bundle retraced her steps. She was half-way up the ivy when a sudden idea occurred to her, and she nearly relaxed her grip and fell.

Supposing Superintendent Battle suspected *her.*

There had been something – yes, surely there had been something in his manner that vaguely suggested the idea. She couldn't help laughing as she crawled over the sill into her bedroom. Fancy the solid Superintendent suspecting *her!*

Though she had so far obeyed Battle's orders as to returning to her room, Bundle had no intention of going to bed and sleeping. Nor did she think that Battle had really intended her to do so. He was not a man to expect impossibilities. And to remain quiescent when something daring and exciting might be going on was a sheer impossibility to Bundle.

She glanced at her watch. It was ten minutes to two. After a moment or two of irresolution, she cautiously opened her door. Not a sound. Everything was still and peaceful. She stole cautiously along the passage.

Once she halted, thinking she heard a board creak somewhere, but then convinced that she was mistaken, she went on again. She was now in the main corridor, making her way to the west wing. She reached the angle of intersection and peered cautiously round – then she stared in blank surprise.

The watcher's post was empty. Jimmy Thesiger was not there.

Bundle stared in complete amazement. What had happened? Why had Jimmy left his post? What did it mean?

At that moment she heard a clock strike two.

She was still standing there, debating what to do next, when suddenly her heart gave a leap and then seemed to stand still. *The door handle of Terence O'Rourke's room was slowly turning.*

Bundle watched, fascinated. But the door did not open. Instead the knob turned slowly to its original position. What did it mean?

Suddenly Bundle came to a resolution. Jimmy, for some unknown reason, had deserted his post. She must get hold of Bill.

Quickly and noiselessly, Bundle fled along the way she had come. She burst unceremoniously into Bill's room.

'Bill, wake up! Oh, do wake up!'

It was an urgent whisper she sent forth, but there came no response to it.

'Bill,' breathed Bundle.

Impatiently she switched on the lights, and then stood dumbfounded.

The room was empty, and the bed had not even been slept in.

Where then was Bill?

Suddenly she caught her breath. *This was not Bill's room.* The dainty négligé thrown over a chair, the feminine knick-knacks on the dressing table, the black velvet evening dress thrown carelessly over a chair – Of course, in her haste she had mistaken the doors. This was the Countess Radzky's room.

But where, oh where, was the Countess?

And just as Bundle was asking herself this question, the silence of the night was suddenly broken, and in no uncertain manner.

The clamour came from below. In an instant Bundle had sped out of the Countess's room and downstairs. The sounds came from the library – a violent crashing of chairs being overturned.

Bundle rattled vainly at the library door. It was locked. But she could clearly hear the struggle that was going on within – the panting and scuffling, curses in manly tones, the occasional crash as some light piece of furniture came into the line of battle.

And then, sinister and distinct, breaking the peace of the night for good and all, two shots in rapid succession.

CHAPTER XX

Loraine's Adventures

Loraine Wade sat up in bed and switched on the light. It was exactly ten minutes to one. She had gone to bed early – at half past nine. She possessed the useful art of being able to wake herself up at the required time, so she had been able to enjoy some hours of refreshing sleep.

Two dogs slept in the room with her, and one of these now raised his head and looked at her inquiringly.

'Quiet, Lurcher,' said Loraine, and the big animal put his head down again obediently, watching her from between his shaggy eyelashes.

It is true that Bundle had once doubted the meekness of Loraine Wade, but that brief moment of suspicion had passed. Loraine had seemed so entirely reasonable, so willing to be kept out of everything.

And yet, if you studied the girl's face, you saw that there was strength of purpose in the small, resolute jaw and the lips that closed together so firmly.

Loraine rose and dressed herself in a tweed coat and skirt. Into one pocket of the coat she dropped an electric torch. Then she opened the drawer of her dressing table and took out a small ivory-handled pistol – almost a toy in appearance. She had bought it the day before at Harrods and she was very pleased with it.

She gave a final glance round the room to see if she had forgotten anything, and at that moment the big dog rose and came over to her, looking up at her with pleading eyes and wagging its tail.

'No, Lurcher. Can't go. Missus can't take you. Got to stay here and be a good boy.'

She dropped a kiss on the dog's head, made him lie down on his rug again, and then slipped noiselessly out of the room, closing the door behind her.

She let herself out of the house by a side door and made her way round to the garage, where her little two-seater car was in readiness. There was a gentle slope, and she let the car run silently down it, not starting the engine till she was some way from the house. Then she glanced at the watch on her arm and pressed her foot down on the accelerator.

She left the car at a spot she had previously marked down. There was a gap there in the fencing that she could easily get through. A few minutes later, slightly muddy, Loraine stood inside the grounds of Wyvern Abbey.

As noiselessly as possible, she made her way towards the venerable ivy-coloured building. In the distance a stable clock chimed two.

Loraine's heart beat faster as she drew near to the terrace. There was no one about – no sign of life anywhere. Everything seemed peaceful and undisturbed. She reached the terrace and stood there, looking about her.

Suddenly, without the least warning, something from above fell with a flop almost at her feet. Loraine stooped to pick it up. It was a brown paper packet, loosely wrapped. Holding it, Loraine looked up.

There was an open window just above her head, and even as she looked a leg swung over it and a man began to climb down the ivy.

Loraine waited no more. She took to her heels and ran, still clasping the brown paper packet.

Behind her, the noise of a struggle suddenly broke out. A hoarse voice: 'Lemme go'; another that she knew well: 'Not if I know it – ah, you would, would you?'

Still Loraine ran – blindly, as though panic-stricken – right round the corner of the terrace – and slap into the arms of a large, solidly built man.

'There, there,' said Superintendent Battle kindly.

Loraine was struggling to speak.

'Oh, quick! – oh, quick! They're killing each other. Oh, do be quick!'

There was a sharp crack of a revolver shot – and then another.

Superintendent Battle started to run. Loraine followed. Back round the corner of the terrace and along to the library window. The window was open.

Battle stooped and switched on an electric torch. Loraine was close behind him, peering over his shoulder. She gave a little sobbing gasp.

On the threshold of the window lay Jimmy Thesiger in what looked like a pool of blood. His right arm lay dangling in a curious position.

Loraine gave a sharp cry.

'He's dead,' she wailed. 'Oh, Jimmy – Jimmy – he's dead!'

'Now, now,' said Superintendent Battle soothingly. 'Don't you take on so. The young gentleman isn't dead, I'll be bound. See if you can find the lights and turn them on.'

Loraine obeyed. She stumbled across the room, found the switch by the door and pressed it down. The room was flooded with light. Superintendent Battle uttered a sigh of relief.

'It's all right – he's only shot in the right arm. He's fainted through loss of blood. Come and give me a hand with him.'

There was a pounding on the library door. Voices were heard, asking, expostulating, demanding.

Loraine looked doubtfully at it.

'Shall I –?'

'No hurry,' said Battle. 'We'll let them in presently. You come and give me a hand.'

Loraine came obediently. The Superintendent had produced a large, clean pocket-handkerchief and was neatly bandaging the wounded man's arm. Loraine helped him.

'He'll be all right,' said the Superintendent. 'Don't you worry. As many lives as cats, these young fellows. It wasn't the loss of blood knocked him out either. He must have caught his head a crack on the floor as he fell.'

Outside, the knocking on the door had become tremendous.

The voice of George Lomax, furiously upraised, came loud and distinct:

'Who is in there? Open the door at once.'

Superintendent Battle sighed.

'I suppose we shall have to,' he said. 'A pity.'

His eyes darted round, taking in the scene. An automatic lay by Jimmy's side. The Superintendent picked it up gingerly, holding it very delicately, and examined it. He grunted and laid it on the table. Then he stepped across and unlocked the door.

Several people fell into the room. Nearly everybody said something at the same minute. George Lomax, spluttering with obdurate words which refused to come with sufficient fluency, exclaimed:

'The – the – the meaning of this? Ah! It's you, Superintendent; what's happened? I say – what has – happened?'

Bill Eversleigh said: 'My God! Old Jimmy!' and stared at the limp figure on the ground.

Lady Coote, clad in a resplendent purple dressing gown, cried out: 'The poor boy!' and swept past Superintendent Battle to bend over the prostrate Jimmy in a motherly fashion.

Bundle said: 'Loraine!'

Herr Eberhard said: 'Gott im Himmel!' and other words of that nature.

Sir Stanley Digby said: 'My God, what's all this?'

A housemaid said: 'Look at the blood,' and screamed with pleasurable excitement.

A footman said: 'Lor!'

The butler said, with a good deal more bravery in his manner than had been noticeable a few minutes earlier: 'Now then, this won't do!' and waved away under servants.

The efficient Mr Rupert Bateman said to George: 'Shall we get rid of some of these people, sir?'

Then they all took fresh breath.

'Incredible!' said George Lomax. 'Battle, what has *happened*?'

Battle gave him a look, and George's discreet habits assumed their usual way.

'Now then,' he said, moving to the door, 'everyone go back to bed, please. There's been a – er –'

'A little accident,' said Superintendent Battle easily.

'A – er – an accident. I shall be much obliged if everyone will go back to bed.'

Everyone was clearly reluctant to do so.

'Lady Coote – please –'

'The poor boy,' said Lady Coote in a motherly fashion.

She rose from a kneeling position with great reluctance. And as she did so, Jimmy stirred and sat up.

'Hallo!' he said thickly. 'What's the matter?'

He looked round him vacantly for a minute or two and then intelligence returned to his eye.

'Have you got him?' he demanded eagerly.

'Got who?'

'The man. Climbed down the ivy. I was by the window there. Grabbed him and we had no end of a set-to –'

'One of those nasty, murderous cat burglars,' said Lady Coote. 'Poor boy.'

Jimmy was looking round him.

'I say – I'm afraid we – er – have made rather a mess of things. Fellow was as strong as an ox and we went fairly waltzing round.'

The condition of the room was clear proof of this statement. Everything light and breakable within a range of twelve feet that could be broken *had* been broken.

'And what happened then?'

But Jimmy was looking round for something.

'Where's Leopold? The pride of the blue-nosed automatics?'

Battle indicated the pistol on the table.

'Is this yours, Mr Thesiger?'

'That's right. That's little Leopold. How many shots have been fired?'

'One shot.'

Jimmy looked chagrined.

'I'm disappointed in Leopold,' he murmured. 'I can't have pressed the button properly, or he'd have gone on shooting.'

'Who shot first?'

'I did, I'm afraid,' said Jimmy. 'You see, the man twisted himself out of my grasp suddenly. I saw him making for the window and I closed my finger down on Leopold and let him have it. He turned in the window and fired at me and – well, I suppose after that I took the count.'

He rubbed his head rather ruefully.

But Sir Stanley Digby was suddenly alert.

'Climbing down the ivy, you said? My God, Lomax, you don't think they've got away with it?'

He rushed from the room. For some curious reason nobody spoke during his absence. In a few minutes Sir Stanley returned. His round, chubby face was white as death.

'My God, Battle,' he said, 'they've got it. O'Rourke's fast asleep – drugged, I think. I can't wake him. And the papers have vanished.'

CHAPTER XXI

The Recovery of the Formula

'Der liebe Gott!' said Herr Eberhard in a whisper.

His face had gone chalky white.

George turned a face of dignified reproach on Battle.

'Is this true, Battle? I left all arrangements in your hands.'

The rock-like quality of the Superintendent showed out well. Not a muscle of his face moved.

'The best of us are defeated sometimes, sir,' he said quietly.

'Then you mean – you really mean – that the document is gone?'

But to everyone's surprise Superintendent Battle shook his head.

'No, no, Mr Lomax, it's not so bad as you think. Everything's all right. But you can't lay the credit for it at my door. You've got to thank this young lady.'

He indicated Loraine, who stared at him in surprise. Battle stepped across to her and gently took the brown paper parcel which she was still clutching mechanically.

'I think, Mr Lomax,' he said, 'that you will find what you want here.'

Sir Stanley Digby, quicker in action than George, snatched at the package and tore it open, investigating its contents eagerly. A sigh of relief escaped him and he mopped his brow. Herr Eberhard fell upon the child of his brain and clasped it to his heart, whilst a torrent of German burst from him.

Sir Stanley turned to Loraine, shaking her warmly by the hand.

'My dear young lady,' he said, 'we are infinitely obliged to you, I am sure.'

'Yes, indeed,' said George. 'Though I – er –'

He paused in some perplexity, staring at a young lady who was a total stranger to him. Loraine looked appealingly at Jimmy, who came to the rescue.

'We – this is Miss Wade,' said Jimmy. 'Gerald Wade's sister.'

'Indeed,' said George, shaking her warmly by the hand. 'My dear Miss Wade, I must express my deep gratitude to you for what you have done. I must confess that I do not quite see –'

He paused delicately and four of the persons present felt that explanations were going to be fraught with much difficulty. Superintendent Battle came to the rescue.

'Perhaps we'd better not go into that just now, sir,' he suggested tactfully.

The efficient Mr Bateman created a further diversion.

'Wouldn't it be wise for someone to see to O'Rourke? Don't you think, sir, that a doctor had better be sent for?'

'Of course,' said George. 'Of course. Most remiss of us not to have thought of it before.' He looked towards Bill. 'Get Dr Cartwright on the telephone. Ask him to come. Just hint, if you can, that – er – discretion should be observed.'

Bill went off on his errand.

'I will come up with you, Digby,' said George. 'Something, possibly, could be done – measures should, perhaps, be taken – whilst awaiting the arrival of the doctor.'

He looked rather helplessly at Rupert Bateman. Efficiency always makes itself felt. It was Pongo who was really in charge of the situation.

'Shall I come up with you, sir?'

George accepted the offer with relief. Here, he felt, was someone on whom he could lean. He experienced that sense of complete trust in Mr Bateman's efficiency which came to all those who encountered that excellent young man.

The three men left the room together. Lady Coote, murmuring in deep rich tones: 'The poor young fellow. Perhaps I could do something –' hurried after them.

'That's a very motherly woman,' observed the Superintendent thoughtfully. 'A very motherly woman. I wonder –'

Three pairs of eyes looked at him inquiringly.

'I was wondering,' said Superintendent Battle slowly, 'where Sir Oswald Coote may be.'

'Oh!' gasped Loraine. 'Do you think he's been murdered?'

Battle shook his head at her reproachfully.

'No need for anything so melodramatic,' he said. 'No – I rather think –'

He paused, his head on one side, listening – one large hand raised to enjoin silence.

In another minute they all heard what his sharper ears had been the first to notice. Footsteps coming along the terrace outside. They rang out clearly with no kind of subterfuge about them. In another minute the window was blocked by a bulky figure which stood there regarding them and who conveyed, in an odd way, a sense of dominating the situation.

Sir Oswald, for it was he, looked slowly from one face to another. His keen eyes took in the details of the situation. Jimmy, with his roughly bandaged arm; Bundle, in her somewhat anomalous attire; Loraine, a perfect stranger to him. His eyes came last to Superintendent Battle. He spoke sharply and crisply.

'What's been happening here, officer?'

'Attempted robbery, sir.'

'*Attempted* – eh?'

'Thanks to this young lady, Miss Wade, the thieves failed to get away with it.'

'Ah!' he said again, his scrutiny ended. 'And now, officer, what about *this*?'

He held out a small Mauser pistol which he carried delicately by the butt.

'Where did you find that, Sir Oswald?'

'On the lawn outside. I presume it must have been thrown down by one of the thieves as he took to his heels. I've held it carefully, as I thought you might wish to examine it for fingerprints.'

'You think of everything, Sir Oswald,' said Battle.

He took the pistol from the other, handling it with equal care, and laid it down on the table beside Jimmy's Colt.

'And now, if you please,' said Sir Oswald, 'I should like to hear exactly what occurred.'

Superintendent Battle gave a brief résumé of the events of the night. Sir Oswald frowned thoughtfully.

'I understand,' he said sharply. 'After wounding and disabling Mr Thesiger, the man took to his heels and ran, throwing away the pistol as he did so. What I cannot understand is why no one pursued him.'

'It wasn't till we heard Mr Thesiger's story that we knew there was anyone to pursue,' remarked Superintendent Battle dryly.

'You didn't – er – catch sight of him making off as you turned the corner of the terrace?'

'No, I missed him by just about forty seconds, I should say. There's no moon and he'd be invisible as soon as he'd left the terrace. He must have leapt for it as soon as he'd fired the shot.'

'H'm,' said Sir Oswald. 'I still think that a search should have been organized. Someone else should have been posted –'

'There are three of my men in the grounds,' said the Superintendent quietly.

'Oh!' Sir Oswald seemed rather taken aback.

'They were told to hold and detain anyone attempting to leave the grounds.'

'And yet – they haven't done so?'

'And yet they haven't done so,' agreed Battle gravely.

Sir Oswald looked at him as though something in the words puzzled him. He said sharply:

'Are you telling me all that you know, Superintendent Battle?'

'All that I *know* – yes, Sir Oswald. What I think is a different matter. Maybe I think some rather curious things – but until thinking's got you somewhere it's no use talking about it.'

'And yet,' said Sir Oswald slowly, 'I should like to know what you think, Superintendent Battle.'

'For one thing, sir, I think there's a lot too much ivy about this place – excuse me, sir, you've got a bit on your coat – yes, a great deal too much ivy. It complicates things.'

Sir Oswald stared at him, but any reply he might have contemplated making was arrested by the entrance of Rupert Bateman.

'Oh, there you are, Sir Oswald. I'm so glad. Lady Coote has just discovered that you were missing – and she has been insisting upon it that you had been murdered by the thieves. I really, think, Sir Oswald, that you had better come to her at once. She is terribly upset.'

'Maria is an incredibly foolish woman,' said Sir Oswald. 'Why should I be murdered? I'll come with you, Bateman.'

He left the room with his secretary.

'That's a very efficient young man,' said Battle, looking after them. 'What's his name – Bateman?'

Jimmy nodded.

'Bateman – Rupert,' he said. 'Commonly known as Pongo. I was at school with him.'

'Were you? Now, that's interesting, Mr Thesiger. What was your opinion of him in those days?'

'Oh, he was always the same sort of ass.'

'I shouldn't have thought,' said Battle mildly, 'that he was an ass.'

'Oh, you know what I mean. Of course he wasn't really an ass. Tons of brains and always swotting at things. But deadly serious. No sense of humour.'

'Ah!' said Superintendent Battle. 'That's a pity. Gentlemen who have no sense of humour get to taking themselves too seriously – and that leads to mischief.'

'I can't imagine Pongo getting into mischief,' said Jimmy. 'He's done extremely well for himself so far – dug himself in with old Coote and looks like being a permanency in the job.'

'Superintendent Battle,' said Bundle.

'Yes, Lady Eileen?'

'Don't you think it very odd that Sir Oswald didn't say what he was doing wandering about in the garden in the middle of the night?'

'Ah!' said Battle. 'Sir Oswald's a great man – and a great man always knows better than to explain unless an explanation is demanded. To rush into explanations and excuses is always a sign of weakness. Sir Oswald knows that as well as I do. He's not going to come in explaining and apologizing – not he. He just stalks in and hauls *me* over the coals. He's a big man, Sir Oswald.'

Such a warm admiration sounded in the Superintendent's tones that Bundle pursued the subject no further.

'And now,' said Superintendent Battle, looking round with a slight twinkle in his eye, 'now that we're together and friendly like – I *should* like to hear just how Miss Wade happened to arrive on the scene so pat.'

'She ought to be ashamed of herself,' said Jimmy. 'Hood-winking us all as she did.'

'Why should I be kept out of it all?' cried Loraine passionately. 'I never meant to be – no, not the very first day in your rooms when you both explained how the best thing for me to do was to stay quietly at home and keep out of danger. I didn't say anything, but I made up my mind then.'

'I half expected it,' said Bundle. 'You were so surprisingly meek about it. I might have known you were up to something.'

'I thought you were remarkably sensible,' said Jimmy Thesiger.

'You would, Jimmy dear,' said Loraine. 'It was easy enough to deceive you.'

'Thank you for these kind words,' said Jimmy. 'Go on, and don't mind me.'

'When you rang up and said there might be danger, I was more determined than ever,' went on Loraine. 'I went to Harrods and bought a pistol. Here it is.'

She produced the dainty weapon and Superintendent Battle took it from her and examined it.

'Quite a deadly little toy, Miss Wade,' he said. 'Have you had much – er – practice with it?'

'None at all,' said Loraine. 'But I thought if I took it with me – well, that it would give me a comforting feeling.'

'Quite so,' said Battle gravely.

'My idea was to come over here and see what was going on. I left my car in the road and climbed through the hedge and came up to the terrace. I was just looking about me when – plop – something fell right at my feet. I picked it up and then looked to see where it could have come from. And then I saw the man climbing down the ivy and I ran.'

'Just so,' said Battle. 'Now, Miss Wade, can you describe the man at all?'

The girl shook her head.

'It was too dark to see much. I think he was a big man – but that's about all.'

'And now you, Mr Thesiger.' Battle turned to him. 'You struggled with the man – can you tell me anything about him?'

'He was a pretty hefty individual – that's all I can say. He gave a few hoarse whispers – that's when I had him by the throat. He said "Lemme go, guvnor," something like that.'

'An uneducated man, then?'

'Yes, I suppose he was. He spoke like one.'

'I still don't quite understand about the packet,' said Loraine. 'Why should he throw it down as he did? Was it because it hampered him climbing?'

'No,' said Battle. 'I've got an entirely different theory about that. That packet, Miss Wade, was deliberately thrown down to you – or so I believe.'

'To *me*?'

'Shall we say – to the person the thief thought you were.'

'This is getting very involved,' said Jimmy.

'Mr Thesiger, when you came into this room, did you switch on the light at all?'

'Yes.'

'And there was no one in the room?'

'No one at all.'

'But previously you thought you heard someone moving about down here?'

'Yes.'

'And then, after trying the window, you switched off the light again and locked the door?'

Jimmy nodded.

Superintendent Battle looked slowly around him. His glance was arrested by a big screen of Spanish leather which stood near one of the bookcases.

Brusquely he strode across the room and looked behind it.

He uttered a sharp ejaculation, which brought the three young people quickly to his side.

Huddled on the floor, in a dead faint, lay the Countess Radzky.

CHAPTER XXII

The Countess Radzky's Story

The Countess's return to consciousness was very different from that of Jimmy Thesiger. It was more prolonged and infinitely more artistic.

Artistic was Bundle's word. She had been zealous in her ministrations – largely consisting of the application of cold water – and the Countess had instantly responded, passing a white, bewildered hand across her brow and murmuring faintly.

It was at this point that Bill, at last relieved from his duties with telephone and doctors, had come bustling into the room and had instantly proceeded to make (in Bundle's opinion) a most regrettable idiot of himself.

He had hung over the Countess with a concerned and anxious face and had addressed a series of singularly idiotic remarks to her:

'I say, Countess. It's all right. It's really all right. Don't try to talk. It's bad for you. Just lie still. You'll be all right in a minute. It'll all come back to you. Don't say anything till you're quite all right. Take your time. Just lie still and close your eyes. You'll remember everything in a minute. Have another sip of water. Have some brandy. That's the stuff. Don't you think, Bundle, that some brandy . . . ?'

'For God's sake, Bill, leave her alone,' said Bundle crossly. 'She'll be all right.'

And with an expert hand she flipped a good deal of cold water on to the exquisite make-up of the Countess's face.

The Countess flinched and sat up. She looked considerably more wide awake.

'Ah!' she murmured. 'I am here. Yes, I am here.'

'Take your time,' said Bill. 'Don't talk till you feel quite all right again.'

The Countess drew the folds of a very transparent négligé closer around her.

'It is coming back to me,' she murmured. 'Yes, it is coming back.'

She looked at the little crowd grouped around her. Perhaps something in the attentive faces struck her as unsympathetic. In any case she smiled deliberately up at the one face which clearly displayed a very opposite emotion.

'Ah, my big Englishman,' she said very softly, 'do not distress yourself. All is well with me.'

'Oh! I say, but are you sure?' demanded Bill anxiously.

'Quite sure.' She smiled at him reassuringly. 'We Hungarians, we have nerves of steel.'

A look of intense relief passed over Bill's face. A fatuous look settled down there instead – a look which made Bundle earnestly long to kick him.

'Have some water,' she said coldly.

The Countess refused water. Jimmy, kindlier to beauty in distress, suggested a cocktail. The Countess reacted favourably to this suggestion. When she had swallowed it, she looked round once more, this time with a livelier eye.

'Tell me, what has happened?' she demanded briskly.

'We were hoping you might be able to tell us that,' said Superintendent Battle.

The Countess looked at him sharply. She seemed to become aware of the big, quiet man for the first time.

'I went to your room,' said Bundle. 'The bed hadn't been slept in and you weren't there.'

She paused – looking accusingly at the Countess. The latter closed her eyes and nodded her head slowly.

'Yes, yes, I remember it all now. Oh, it was horrible!' She shuddered. 'Do you want me to tell you?'

Superintendent Battle said, 'If you please' at the same moment that Bill said, 'Not if you don't feel up to it.'

The Countess looked from one to the other, but the quiet, masterful eye of Superintendent Battle won the game.

'I could not sleep,' began the Countess. 'The house – it oppressed me. I was all, as you say, on wires, the cat on the hot bricks. I knew that in the state I was in it was useless to think of going to bed. I walked about my room. I read. But the books placed there did not interest me greatly. I thought I would come down and find something more absorbing.'

'Very natural,' said Bill.

'Very often done, I believe,' said Battle.

'So as soon as the idea occurred to me, I left my room and came down. The house was very still – '

'Excuse me,' interrupted the Superintendent, 'but can you give me an idea of the time when this occurred?'

'I never know the time,' said the Countess superbly, and swept on with her story.

'The house was very quiet. One could even hear the little mouse run, if there had been one. I come down the stairs – very quietly – '

'Very quietly?'

'Naturally I do not want to disturb the household,' said the Countess reproachfully. 'I come in here. I go into this corner and I search the shelves for a suitable book.'

'Having of course switched on the light?'

'No, I did not switch on the light. I had, you see, my little electric torch with me. With that, I scanned the shelves.'

'Ah!' said the Superintendent.

'Suddenly,' continued the Countess dramatically, 'I hear something. A stealthy sound. A muffled footstep. I switch out my torch and listen. The footsteps draw nearer – stealthy, horrible footsteps. I shrink behind the screen. In another minute the door opens and the light is switched on. The man – the burglar is in the room.'

'Yes, but I say – ' began Mr Thesiger.

A large-sized foot pressed his, and realizing that Superintendent Battle was giving him a hint, Jimmy shut up.

'I nearly died of fear,' continued the Countess. 'I tried not to breathe. The man waited for a minute, listening. Then, still with that horrible, stealthy tread –'

Again Jimmy opened his mouth in protest, and again shut it.

'– he crossed to the window and peered out. He remained there for a minute or two, then he recrossed the room and turned out the lights again, locking the door. I am terrified. He is in the room, moving stealthily about in the dark. Ah, it is horrible. Suppose he should come upon me in the dark! In another minute I hear him again by the window. Then silence. I hope that perhaps he may have gone out that way. As the minutes pass and I hear no further sound, I am almost sure that he has done so. Indeed I am in the very act of switching on my torch and investigating when – *prestissimo!* – it all begins.'

'Yes?'

'Ah! But it was terrible – never – never shall I forget it! Two men trying to murder each other. Oh, it was horrible! They reeled about the room, and furniture crashed in every direction. I thought, too, that I heard a woman scream – but that was not in the room. It was outside somewhere. The criminal had a hoarse voice. He croaked rather than spoke. He kept saying "Lemme go – lemme go." The other man was a gentleman. He had a cultured English voice.'

Jimmy looked gratified.

'He swore – mostly,' continued the Countess.

'Clearly a gentleman,' said Superintendent Battle.

'And then,' continued the Countess, 'a flash and a shot. The bullet hit the bookcase beside me. I – I suppose I must have fainted.'

She looked up at Bill. He took her hand and patted it.

'You poor dear,' he said. 'How rotten for you.'

'Silly idiot,' thought Bundle.

Superintendent Battle had moved on swift, noiseless feet over to the bookcase a little to the right of the screen. He bent down, searching. Presently he stooped and picked something up.

'It wasn't a bullet, Countess,' he said. 'It's the shell of the cartridge. Where were you standing when you fired, Mr Thesiger.'

Jimmy took up a position by the window.

'As nearly as I can see, about here.'

Superintendent Battle placed himself in the same spot.

'That's right,' he agreed. 'The empty shell would throw right rear. It's a .455. I don't wonder the Countess thought it was a bullet in the dark. It hit the bookcase about a foot from her. The bullet itself grazed the window frame and we'll find it outside to-morrow – unless your assailant happens to be carrying it about in him.'

Jimmy shook his head regretfully.

'Leopold, I fear, did not cover himself with glory,' he remarked sadly.

The Countess was looking at him with most flattering attention.

'Your arm!' she exclaimed. 'It is all tied up! Was it you then –?'

Jimmy made her a mock bow.

'I'm so glad I've got a cultured, English voice,' he said. 'And I can assure you that I wouldn't have dreamed of using the language I did if I had had any suspicion that a lady was present.'

'I did not understand all of it,' the Countess hastened to explain. 'Although I had an English governess when I was young –'

'It isn't the sort of thing she'd be likely to teach you,' agreed Jimmy. 'Kept you busy with your uncle's pen, and the umbrella of the gardener's niece. I know the sort of stuff.'

'But what has happened?' asked the Countess. 'That is what I want to know. I demand to know what has happened.'

There was a moment's silence whilst everybody looked at Superintendent Battle.

'It's very simple,' said Battle mildly. 'Attempted robbery. Some political papers stolen from Sir Stanley Digby. The thieves nearly got away with them, but thanks to this young lady' – he indicated Loraine – 'they didn't.'

The Countess flashed a glance at the girl – rather an odd glance.

'Indeed,' she said coldly.

'A very fortunate coincidence that she happened to be there,' said Superintendent Battle, smiling.

The Countess gave a little sigh and half closed her eyes again.

'It is absurd, but I still feel extremely faint,' she murmured.

'Of course you do,' cried Bill. 'Let me help you up to your room. Bundle will come with you.'

'It is very kind of Lady Eileen,' said the Countess, 'but I should prefer to be alone. I am really quite all right. Perhaps you will just help me up the stairs.'

She rose to her feet, accepted Bill's arm and, leaning heavily on it, went out of the room. Bundle followed as far as the hall, but, the Countess reiterating her assurance – with some tartness – that she was quite all right, she did not accompany them upstairs.

But as she stood watching the Countess's graceful form, supported by Bill, slowly mounting the stairway, she stiffened suddenly to acute attention. The Countess's négligé, as previously mentioned, was thin – a mere veil of orange chiffon. Through it Bundle saw distinctly below the right shoulder blade *a small black mole.*

With a gasp, Bundle swung impetuously round to where Superintendent Battle was just emerging from the library. Jimmy and Loraine had preceded him.

'There,' said Battle. 'I've fastened the window and there will be a man on duty outside. And I'll lock the door and take the key. In the morning we'll do what the French call reconstruct the crime – Yes, Lady Eileen, what is it?'

'Superintendent Battle, I must speak with you, – at once.'

'Why, certainly, I –'

George Lomax suddenly appeared, Dr Cartwright by his side.

'Ah, there you are, Battle. You'll be relieved to hear that there's nothing seriously wrong with O'Rourke.'

'I never thought there would be much wrong with Mr O'Rourke,' said Battle.

'He's had a strong hypodermic administered to him,' said the doctor. 'He'll wake perfectly all right in the morning, perhaps a bit of a head, perhaps not. Now then, young man, let's look at this bullet wound of yours.'

'Come on, nurse,' said Jimmy to Loraine. 'Come and hold the basin or my hand. Witness a strong man's agony. You know the stunt.'

Jimmy, Loraine and the doctor went off together. Bundle continued to throw agonized glances in the direction of Superintendent Battle, who had been buttonholed by George.

The Superintendent waited patiently till a pause occurred in George's loquacity. He then swiftly took advantage of it.

'I wonder, sir, if I might have a word privately with Sir Stanley? In the little study at the end there.'

'Certainly,' said George. 'Certainly. I'll go and fetch him at once.'

He hurried off upstairs again. Battle drew Bundle swiftly into the drawing-room and shut the door.

'Now, Lady Eileen, what is it?'

'I'll tell you as quickly as I can – but it's rather long and complicated.'

As concisely as she could, Bundle related her introduction to the Seven Dials Club and her subsequent adventures there. When she had finished, Superintendent Battle drew a long breath. For once, his facial woodenness was laid aside.

'Remarkable,' he said. 'Remarkable. I wouldn't have believed it possible – even for you, Lady Eileen. I ought to have known better.'

'But you did give me a hint, Superintendent Battle. You told me to ask Bill Eversleigh.'

'It's dangerous to give people like you a hint, Lady Eileen. I never dreamt of your going to the lengths you have.'

'Well, it's all right, Superintendent Battle. My death doesn't lie at your door.'

'Not yet, it doesn't,' said Battle grimly.

He stood as though in thought, turning things over in his mind. 'What Mr Thesiger was about, letting you run into danger like that, I can't think,' he said presently.

'He didn't know till afterwards,' said Bundle. 'I'm not a complete mug, Superintendent Battle. And, anyway, he's got his hands full looking after Miss Wade.'

'Is that so?' said the Superintendent. 'Ah!'

He twinkled a little.

'I shall have to detail Mr Eversleigh to look after you, Lady Eileen.'

'Bill!' said Bundle contemptuously. 'But, Superintendent Battle, you haven't heard the end of my story. The woman I saw there – Anna – No 1. Yes, No 1 is the Countess Radzky.'

And rapidly she went on to describe her recognition of the mole.

To her surprise the Superintendent hemmed and hawed.

'A mole isn't much to go upon, Lady Eileen. Two women might have an identical mole very easily. You must remember that the Countess Radzky is a very well-known figure in Hungary.'

'Then this isn't the real Countess Radzky. I tell you I'm sure this is the same woman I saw there. And look at her to-night – the way we found her. I don't believe she ever fainted at all.'

'Oh, I shouldn't say that, Lady Eileen. That empty shell striking the bookcase beside her might have frightened any woman half out of her wits.'

'But what was she doing there anyway? One doesn't come down to look for a book with an electric torch.'

Battle scratched his cheek. He seemed unwilling to speak. He began to pace up and down the room, as though making up his mind. At last he turned to the girl.

'See here, Lady Eileen, I'm going to trust you. The Countess's conduct *is* suspicious. I know that as well as you do. It's very suspicious – but we've got to go carefully. There mustn't be any unpleasantness with the Embassies. One has got to be *sure.*'

'I see. If you were *sure* . . .'

'There's something else. During the war, Lady Eileen, there was a great outcry about German spies being left at large. Busy-bodies wrote letters to the papers about it. We paid no attention. Hard words didn't hurt us. The small fry were left alone. Why?

Because through them, sooner or later, *we got the big fellow – the man at the top.*'

'You mean?'

'Don't bother about what I mean, Lady Eileen. But remember this. *I know all about the Countess.* And I want her let alone.

'And now,' added Superintendent Battle ruefully, 'I've got to think of something to say to Sir Stanley Digby!'

CHAPTER XXIII

Superintendent Battle in Charge

It was ten o'clock on the following morning. The sun poured in through the windows of the library, where Superintendent Battle had been at work since six. On a summons from him, George Lomax, Sir Oswald Coote and Jimmy Thesiger had just joined him, having repaired the fatigues of the night with a substantial breakfast. Jimmy's arm was in a sling, but he bore little trace of the night's affray.

The Superintendent eyed all three of them benevolently, somewhat with the air of a kindly curator explaining a museum to little boys. On the table beside him were various objects, neatly labelled. Amongst them Jimmy recognized Leopold.

'Ah, Superintendent,' said George, 'I have been anxious to know how you have progressed. Have you caught the man?'

'He'll take a lot of catching, he will,' said the Superintendent.

His failure in that respect did not appear to rankle with him.

George Lomax did not look particularly well pleased. He detested levity of any kind.

'I've got everything taped out pretty clearly,' went on the detective.

He took up two objects from the table.

'Here we've got the two bullets. The largest is a .455, fired from Mr Thesiger's Colt automatic. Grazed the window sash and I found it embedded in the trunk of that cedar tree. This little fellow was fired from the Mauser .25. After passing through Mr Thesiger's arm, it embedded itself in this arm-chair here. As for the pistol itself –'

'Well?' said Sir Oswald eagerly. 'Any finger-prints?'

Battle shook his head.

'The man who handled it wore gloves,' he said slowly.

'A pity,' said Sir Oswald.

'A man who knew his business would wear gloves. Am I right in thinking, Sir Oswald, that you found this pistol just about twenty yards from the bottom of the steps leading up to the terrace?'

Sir Oswald stepped to the window.

'Yes, almost exactly, I should say.'

'I don't want to find fault, but it would have been wiser on your part, sir, to leave it exactly as you found it.'

'I am sorry,' said Sir Oswald stiffly.

'Oh, it doesn't matter. I've been able to reconstruct things. There were your footprints, you see, leading up from the bottom of the garden, and a place where you had obviously stopped and stooped down, and a kind of dent in the grass which was highly suggestive. By the way, what was your theory of the pistol being there?'

'I presumed that it had been dropped by the man in his flight.'

Battle shook his head.

'Not dropped, Sir Oswald. There are two points against that. To begin with, there are only one set of footprints crossing the lawn just there – your own.'

'I see,' said Sir Oswald thoughtfully.

'Can you be sure of that, Battle?' put in George.

'Quite sure, sir. There is one other set of tracks crossing the lawn, Miss Wade's, but they are a good deal further to the left.'

He paused, and then went on: 'And there's the dent in the ground. The pistol must have struck the ground with some force. It all points to its having been thrown.'

'Well, why not?' said Sir Oswald. 'Say the man fled down the path to the left. He'd leave no footprints on the path and he'd hurl the pistol away from him into the middle of the lawn, eh, Lomax?'

George agreed by a nod of the head.

'It's true that he'd leave no footprints on the path,' said Battle, 'but from the shape of the dent and the way the turf was cut, I don't think the pistol was thrown from that direction. I think it was thrown from the terrace here.'

'Very likely,' said Sir Oswald. 'Does it matter, Superintendent?'

'Ah, yes, Battle,' broke in George. 'Is it – er – strictly relevant?'

'Perhaps not, Mr Lomax. But we like to get things just so, you know. I wonder now if one of you gentlemen would take this pistol and throw it. Will you, Sir Oswald? That's very kind. Stand just there in the window. Now fling it into the middle of the lawn.'

Sir Oswald complied, sending the pistol flying through the air with a powerful sweep of his arm. Jimmy Thesiger drew near with breathless interest. The Superintendent lumbered off after it like a well-trained retriever. He reappeared with a beaming face.

'That's it, sir. Just the same kind of mark. Although, by the way, you sent it a good ten yards farther. But then, you're a very powerfully built man, aren't you, Sir Oswald? Excuse me, I thought I heard someone at the door.'

The Superintendent's ears must have been very much sharper than anyone else's. Nobody else had heard a sound, but Battle was proved right, for Lady Coote stood outside, a medicine glass in her hand.

'Your medicine, Oswald,' she said, advancing into the room. 'You forgot it after breakfast.'

'I'm very busy, Maria,' said Sir Oswald. 'I don't want my medicine.'

'You would never take it if it wasn't for me,' said his wife serenely, advancing upon him. 'You're just like a naughty little boy. Drink it up now.'

And meekly, obediently, the great steel magnate drank it up!

Lady Coote smiled sadly and sweetly at everyone.

'Am I interrupting you? Are you very busy? Oh, look at those revolvers. Nasty, noisy, murdering things. To think, Oswald, that you might have been shot by the burglar last night.'

'You must have been alarmed when you found he was missing, Lady Coote,' said Battle.

'I didn't think of it at first,' confessed Lady Coote. 'This poor boy here' – she indicated Jimmy – 'being shot – and everything so dreadful, but so exciting. It wasn't till Mr Bateman asked me where Sir Oswald was that I remembered he'd gone out half an hour before for a stroll.'

'Sleepless, eh, Sir Oswald?' asked Battle.

'I am usually an excellent sleeper,' said Sir Oswald. 'But I must confess that last night I felt unusually restless. I thought the night air would do me good.'

'You came out through this window, I suppose?'

Was it his fancy, or did Sir Oswald hesitate for a moment before replying?

'Yes.'

'In your pumps too,' said Lady Coote, 'instead of putting thick shoes on. What would you do without me to look after you?'

She shook her head sadly.

'I think, Maria, if you don't mind leaving us – we have still a lot to discuss.'

'I know, dear, I'm just going.'

Lady Coote withdrew, carrying the empty medicine glass as though it were a goblet out of which she had just administered a death potion.

'Well, Battle,' said George Lomax, 'it all seems clear enough. Yes, perfectly clear. The man fires a shot, disabling Mr Thesiger, flings away the weapon, runs along the terrace and down the gravel path.'

'Where he ought to have been caught by my men,' put in Battle.

'Your men, if I may say so, Battle, seem to have been singularly remiss. They didn't see Miss Wade come in. If they could miss her coming in, they could easily miss the thief going out.'

Superintendent Battle opened his mouth to speak, then seemed to think better of it. Jimmy Thesiger looked at him curiously. He would have given a lot to know just what was in Superintendent Battle's mind.

'Must have been a champion runner,' was all the Scotland Yard man contented himself with saying.

'How do you mean, Battle?'

'Just what I say, Mr Lomax. I was round the corner of the terrace myself not fifty seconds after the shot was fired. And for a man to run all that distance towards me and get round the corner of the path before I appeared round the side of the house – well, as I say, he must have been a champion runner.'

'I am at a loss to understand you, Battle. You have some idea of your own which I have not yet – er – grasped. You say the man did not go across the lawn, and now you hint – What exactly do you hint? That the man did not go down the path? Then in your opinion – er – where *did* he go?'

For answer, Superintendent Battle jerked an eloquent thumb upwards.

'Eh?' said George.

The Superintendent jerked harder than ever. George raised his head and looked at the ceiling.

'Up there,' said Battle. 'Up the ivy again.'

'Nonsense, Superintendent. What you are suggesting is impossible.'

'Not at all impossible, sir. He'd done it once. He could do it twice.'

'I don't mean impossible in that sense. But if the man wanted to escape, he'd never bolt back into the house.'

'Safest place for him, Mr Lomax.'

'But Mr O'Rourke's door was still locked on the inside when we came to him.'

'And how did you get to him? Through Sir Stanley's room. That's the way our man went. Lady Eileen tells me she saw the door knob of Mr O'Rourke's room move. That was when our friend was up there the first time. I suspect the key was under Mr O'Rourke's pillow. But his exit is clear enough the second time – through the communicating door and through Sir Stanley's room, which, of course, was empty. Like everyone else, Sir Stanley is rushing downstairs to the library. Our man's got a clear course.'

'And where did he go then?'

Superintendent Battle shrugged his burly shoulders and became evasive.

'Plenty of ways open. Into an empty room on the other side of the house and down the ivy again – out through a side door – or, just possibly, if it was an inside job, he – well, stayed in the house.'

George looked at him in shocked surprise.

'Really, Battle, I should – I should feel it very deeply if one of my servants – er – I have the most perfect reliance on them – it would distress me very much to have to suspect –'

'Nobody's asking you to suspect anyone, Mr Lomax. I'm just putting all the possibilities before you. The servants may be all right – probably are.'

'You have disturbed me,' said George. 'You have disturbed me greatly.'

His eyes appeared more protuberant than ever.

To distract him, Jimmy poked delicately at a curious blackened object on the table.

'What's this?' he asked.

'That's exhibit Z,' said Battle. 'The last of our little lot. It is, or rather it has been, a glove.'

He picked it up, the charred relic, and manipulated it with pride.

'Where did you find it?' asked Sir Oswald.

Battle jerked his head over his shoulder.

'In the grate – nearly burnt, but not quite. Queer; looks as though it had been chewed by a dog.'

'It might possibly be Miss Wade's,' suggested Jimmy. 'She has several dogs.'

The Superintendent shook his head.

'This isn't a lady's glove – no, not even the large kind of loose glove ladies wear nowadays. Put it on, sir, a moment.'

He adjusted the blackened object over Jimmy's hand.

'You see – it's large even for you.'

'Do you attach importance to this discovery?' inquired Sir Oswald coldly.

'You never know, Sir Oswald, what's going to be important or what isn't.'

There was a sharp tap at the door and Bundle entered.

'I'm so sorry,' she said apologetically. 'But Father has just rung up. He says I must come home because everybody is worrying him.'

She paused.

'Yes, my dear Eileen?' said George encouragingly, perceiving that there was more to come.

'I wouldn't have interrupted you – only that I thought it might perhaps have something to do with all this. You see, what has upset Father is that one of our footmen is missing. He went out last night and hasn't come back.'

'What is the man's name?' It was Sir Oswald who took up the cross-examination.

'John Bauer.'

'An Englishman?'

'I believe he calls himself a Swiss – but I think he's a German. He speaks English perfectly, though.'

'Ah!' Sir Oswald drew in his breath with a long, satisfied hiss. 'And he has been at Chimneys – how long?'

'Just under a month.'

Sir Oswald turned to the other two.

'Here is our missing man. You know, Lomax, as well as I do, that several foreign Governments are after the thing. I remember the man now perfectly – tall, well-drilled fellow. Came about a fortnight before we left. A clever move. Any new servants here would be closely scrutinized, but at Chimneys, five miles away –'

He did not finish the sentence.

'You think the plan was laid so long beforehand?'

'Why not? There are millions in that formula, Lomax. Doubtless Bauer hoped to get access to my private papers at Chimneys, and to learn something of forthcoming arrangements from them. It seems likely that he may have had an accomplice in this house – someone who put him wise to the lie of the land and who saw to the doping of O'Rourke. But Bauer was the man Miss Wade saw climbing down the ivy – the big, powerful man.'

He turned to Superintendent Battle.

'Bauer was your man, Superintendent. And, somehow or other, you let him slip through your fingers.'

CHAPTER XXIV

Bundle Wonders

There was no doubt that Superintendent Battle was taken aback. He fingered his chin thoughtfully.

'Sir Oswald is right, Battle,' said George. 'This is the man. Any hope of catching him?'

'There may be, sir. It certainly looks – well, suspicious. Of course the man may turn up again – at Chimneys, I mean.'

'Do you think it likely?'

'No, it isn't,' confessed Battle. 'Yes, it certainly looks as though Bauer were the man. But I can't quite see how he got in and out of these grounds unobserved.'

'I have already told you my opinion of the men you posted,' said George. 'Hopelessly inefficient – I don't mean to blame you, Superintendent, but –' His pause was eloquent.

'Ah, well,' said Battle lightly, 'my shoulders are broad.'

He shook his head and sighed.

'I must get to the telephone at once. Excuse me, gentlemen. I'm sorry, Mr Lomax – I feel I've rather bungled this business. But it's been puzzling, more puzzling than you know.'

He strode hurriedly from the room.

'Come into the garden,' said Bundle to Jimmy. 'I want to talk to you.'

They went out together through the window. Jimmy stared down at the lawn, frowning.

'What's the matter?' asked Bundle.

Jimmy explained the circumstances of the pistol throwing.

'I'm wondering,' he ended, 'what was in old Battle's mind when he got Coote to throw the pistol. Something, I'll swear. Anyhow, it landed up about ten yards farther than it should have done. You know, Bundle, Battle's a deep one.'

'He's an extraordinary man,' said Bundle. 'I want to tell you about last night.'

She retailed her conversation with the Superintendent. Jimmy listened attentively.

'So the Countess is No 1,' he said thoughtfully. 'It all hangs together very well. No 2 – Bauer – comes over from Chimneys. He climbs up into O'Rourke's room, knowing that O'Rourke has had a sleeping draught administered to him – by the Countess somehow or other. The arrangement is that he is to throw the papers to the Countess, who will be waiting below. Then she'll nip back through the library and up to her room. If Bauer's caught leaving the grounds, they'll find nothing on him. Yes, it was a good plan – but it went wrong. No sooner is the Countess in the library than she hears me coming and has to jump behind the screen. Jolly awkward for her, because she can't warn her accomplice. No 2 pinches the papers, looks out of the window, sees, as he thinks, the Countess waiting, pitches the papers down to her and proceeds to climb down the ivy, where he finds a nasty surprise in the shape of me waiting for him. Pretty nervy work for the Countess waiting behind her screen. All things considered, she told a pretty good story. Yes, it all hangs together very well.'

'Too well,' said Bundle decidedly.

'Eh?' said Jimmy surprised.

'What about No 7 – No 7, who never appears, but lives in the background. The Countess and Bauer? No, it's not so simple as that. Bauer was here last night, yes. But he was only here in case things went wrong – as they have done. His part is the part of scapegoat; to draw all attention from No 7 – the boss.'

'I say, Bundle,' said Jimmy anxiously, 'you haven't been reading too much sensational literature, have you?'

Bundle threw him a glance of dignified reproach.

'Well,' said Jimmy, 'I'm not yet like the Red Queen. I can't believe six impossible things before breakfast.'

'It's after breakfast,' said Bundle.

'Or even after breakfast. We've got a perfectly good hypothesis which fits the facts – and you won't have it at any price, simply because, like the old riddle, you want to make things more difficult.'

'I'm sorry,' said Bundle, 'but I cling passionately to a mysterious No 7 being a member of the house-party.'

'What does Bill think?'

'Bill,' said Bundle coldly, 'is impossible.'

'Oh!' said Jimmy. 'I suppose you've told him about the Countess? He ought to be warned. Heaven knows what he'll go blabbing about otherwise.'

'He won't hear a word against her,' said Bundle. 'He's – oh, simply idiotic. I wish you'd drive it home to him about that mole.'

'You forget I wasn't in the cupboard,' said Jimmy. 'And anyway I'd rather not argue with Bill about his lady friend's mole. But surely he can't be such an ass as not to see that everything fits in?'

'He's every kind of ass,' said Bundle bitterly. 'You made the greatest mistake, Jimmy, in ever telling him at all.'

'I'm sorry,' said Jimmy. 'I didn't see it at the time – but I do now. I was a fool, but dash it all, old Bill –'

'You know what foreign adventuresses are,' said Bundle. 'How they get hold of one.'

'As a matter of fact, I don't,' said Jimmy. 'One has never tried to get hold of me.' And he sighed.

For a moment or two there was silence. Jimmy was turning things over in his mind. The more he thought about them the more unsatisfactory they seemed.

'You say that Battle wants the Countess left alone,' he said at last.

'Yes.'

'The idea being that through her he will get at someone else?'

Bundle nodded.

Jimmy frowned deeply as he tried to see where this led. Clearly Battle had some very definite idea in his mind.

'Sir Stanley Digby went up to town early this morning, didn't he,' he said.

'Yes.'

'O'Rourke with him?'

'Yes, I think so.'

'You don't think – no, that's impossible.'

'What?'

'That O'Rourke can be mixed up in this in any way.'

'It's possible,' said Bundle thoughtfully. 'He's got what one calls a very vivid personality. No, it wouldn't surprise me if – oh, to tell the truth, nothing would surprise me! In fact, there's only one person I'm really sure isn't No 7.'

'Who's that?'

'Superintendent Battle.'

'Oh! I thought you were going to say George Lomax.'

'Ssh, here he comes.'

George was, indeed, bearing down upon them in an unmistakable manner. Jimmy made an excuse and slipped away. George sat down by Bundle.

'My dear Eileen, must you really leave us?'

'Well, Father seems to have got the wind up rather badly. I think I'd better go home and hold his hand.'

'This little hand will indeed be comforting,' said George, taking it and pressing it playfully. 'My dear Eileen, I understand your reasons and I honour you for them. In these days of changed and unsettled conditions –'

'He's off,' thought Bundle desperately.

'– when family life is at a premium – all the old standards falling! – It becomes our class to set an example to show that we, at least, are unaffected by modern conditions. They call us the Die Hards – I am proud of the term – I repeat I am proud of the term! There are things that *should* die hard – dignity, beauty, modesty, the sanctity of family life, filial respect – who dies if these shall live? As I was saying, my dear Eileen, I envy you the privileges of your youth. Youth! What a wonderful thing! What a wonderful word! And we do not appreciate it until we grow to – er – maturer years. I confess, my dear child, that I have in the past been disappointed by your levity. I see now that it was but the careless and charming levity of a child. I perceive now the serious and earnest beauty of your mind. You will allow me, I hope, to help you with your reading?'

'Oh, thank you,' said Bundle faintly.

'And you must never be afraid of me again. I was shocked when Lady Caterham told me that you stood in awe of me. I can assure you that I am a very humdrum sort of person.'

The spectacle of George being modest struck Bundle spellbound. George continued:

'Never be shy with me, dear child. And do not be afraid of boring me. It will be a great delight to me to – if I may say so – form your budding mind. I will be your political mentor. We have never needed young women of talent and charm in the Party more than we need them to-day. You may well be destined to follow in the footsteps of your aunt, Lady Caterham.'

This awful prospect knocked Bundle out completely. She could only stare helplessly at George. This did not discourage him – on the contrary. His main objection to women was that they talked too much. It was seldom that he found what he considered a really good listener. He smiled benignly at Bundle.

'The butterfly emerging from the chrysalis. A wonderful picture. I have a very interesting work on political economy. I will look it out now, and you can take it to Chimneys with you. When you have finished it, I will discuss it with you. Do not hesitate to write to me if any point puzzles you. I have many public duties but by unsparing work I can always make time for the affairs of my friends. I will look for the book.'

He strode away. Bundle gazed after him with a dazed expression. She was roused by the unexpected advent of Bill.

'Look here,' said Bill. 'What the hell was Codders holding your hand for?'

'It wasn't my hand,' said Bundle wildly. 'It was my budding mind.'

'Don't be an ass, Bundle.'

'Sorry, Bill, but I'm a little worried. Do you remember saying that Jimmy ran a grave risk down here?'

'So he does,' said Bill. 'It's frightfully hard to escape from

Codders once he's got interested in you. Jimmy will be caught in the toils before he knows where he is.'

'It's not Jimmy who's caught – it's me,' said Bundle wildly. 'I shall have to meet endless Mrs Macattas, and read political economy and discuss it with George, and heaven knows where it will end!'

Bill whistled.

'Poor old Bundle. Been laying it on a bit thick, haven't you?'

'I must have done. Bill, I feel horribly entangled.'

'Never mind,' said Bill consolingly. 'George doesn't really believe in women standing for Parliament, so you won't have to stand up on platforms and talk a lot of junk, or kiss dirty babies in Bermondsey. Come and have a cocktail. It's nearly lunch time.'

Bundle got up and walked by his side obediently.

'And I do so hate politics,' she murmured piteously.

'Of course you do. So do all sensible people. It's only people like Codders and Pongo who take them seriously and revel in them. But all the same,' said Bill, reverting suddenly to a former point, 'you oughtn't to let Codders hold your hand.'

'Why on earth not?' said Bundle. 'He's known me all my life.'

'Well, I don't like it.'

'Virtuous William – Oh, I say, look at Superintendent Battle.'

They were just passing in through a side door. A cupboard-like room opened out of the little hallway. In it were kept golf clubs, tennis racquets, bowls and other features of country house life. Superintendent Battle was conducting a minute examination of various golf clubs. He looked up a little sheepishly at Bundle's exclamation.

'Going to take up golf, Superintendent Battle?'

'I might do worse, Lady Eileen. They say it's never too late to start. And I've got one good quality that will tell at any game.'

'What's that?' asked Bill.

'I don't know when I'm beaten. If everything goes wrong, I turn to and start again!'

And with a determined look on his face, Superintendent Battle came out and joined them, shutting the door behind him.

CHAPTER XXV

Jimmy Lays his Plans

Jimmy Thesiger was feeling depressed. Avoiding George, whom he suspected of being ready to tackle him on serious subjects, he stole quietly away after lunch. Proficient as he was in details of the Santa Fé boundary dispute, he had no wish to stand an examination on it this minute.

Presently what he hoped would happen came to pass. Loraine Wade, also unaccompanied, strolled down one of the shady garden paths. In a moment Jimmy was by her side. They walked for some minutes in silence and then Jimmy said tentatively:

'Loraine?'

'Yes?'

'Look here, I'm a bad chap at putting things – but what about it? What's wrong with getting a special licence and being married and living together happily ever afterwards?'

Loraine displayed no embarrassment at this surprising proposal. Instead she threw back her head and laughed frankly.

'Don't laugh at a chap,' said Jimmy reproachfully.

'I can't help it. You were so funny.'

'Loraine – you are a little devil.'

'I'm not. I'm what's called a thoroughly nice girl.'

'Only to those who don't know you – who are taken in by your delusive appearance of meekness and decorum.'

'I like your long words.'

'All out of crossword puzzles.'

'So educative.'

'Loraine, dear, don't beat about the bush. Will you or won't you?'

Loraine's face sobered. It took on its characteristic appearance of determination. Her small mouth hardened and her little chin shot out aggressively.

'No, Jimmy. Not while things are as they are at present – all unfinished.'

'I know we haven't done what we set out to do,' agreed Jimmy. 'But all the same – well, it's the end of a chapter. The papers are safe at the Air Ministry. Virtue triumphant. And – for the moment – nothing doing.'

'So – let's get married?' said Loraine with a slight smile.

'You've said it. Precisely the idea.'

But again Loraine shook her head.

'No, Jimmy. Until this thing's wound up – until we're safe –'

'You think we're in danger?'

'Don't you?'

Jimmy's cherubic pink face clouded over.

'You're right,' he said at last. 'If that extraordinary rigmarole of Bundle's is true – and I suppose, incredible as it sounds, it must be true – then we're not safe till we've settled with No 7!'

'And the others?'

'No – the others don't count. It's No 7 with his own ways of working that frightens me. Because I don't know who he is or where to look for him.'

Loraine shivered.

'I've been frightened,' she said in a low voice. 'Ever since Gerry's death . . .'

'You needn't be frightened. There's nothing for you to be frightened about. You leave everything to me. I tell you, Loraine – *I'll get No 7 yet.* Once we get him – well, I don't think there'll be much trouble with the rest of the gang, whoever they are.'

'*If* you get him – and suppose he gets you?'

'Impossible,' said Jimmy cheerfully. 'I'm much too clever. Always have a good opinion of yourself – that's my motto.'

'When I think of the things that might have happened last night –' Loraine shivered.

'Well, they didn't,' said Jimmy. 'We're both here, safe and sound – though I must admit my arm is confoundedly painful.'

'Poor boy.'

'Oh, one must expect to suffer in a good cause. And what with my wounds and my cheerful conversation, I've made a complete conquest of Lady Coote.'

'Oh! Do you think that important?'

'I've an idea it may come in useful.'

'You've got some plan in your mind, Jimmy. What is it?'

'The young hero never tells his plans,' said Jimmy firmly. 'They mature in the dark.'

'You are an idiot, Jimmy.'

'I know. I know. That's what everyone says. But I can assure you, Loraine, there's a lot of brain-work going on underneath. Now what about your plans? Got any?'

'Bundle has suggested that I should go to Chimneys with her for a bit.'

'Excellent,' said Jimmy approvingly. 'Nothing could be better. I'd like an eye kept on Bundle anyway. You never know what mad thing she won't get up to next. She's so frightfully unexpected. And the worst of it is, she's so astonishingly successful. I tell you, keeping Bundle out of mischief is a whole-time job.'

'Bill ought to look after her,' suggested Loraine.

'Bill's pretty busy elsewhere.'

'Don't you believe it,' said Loraine.

'What? Not the Countess? But the lad's potty about her.' Loraine continued to shake her head.

'There's something there I don't quite understand. But it's not the Countess with Bill – it's Bundle. Why, this morning, Bill was talking to me when Mr Lomax came out and sat down by Bundle. He took her hand or something, and Bill was off like – like a rocket.'

'What a curious taste some people have,' observed Mr Thesiger. 'Fancy anyone who was talking to you wanting to do anything else. But you surprise me very much, Loraine. I thought our simple Bill was enmeshed in the toils of the beautiful foreign adventuress. Bundle thinks so, I know.'

'Bundle may,' said Loraine. 'But I tell you, Jimmy, it isn't so.'

'Then what's the big idea?'

'Don't you think it possible that Bill is doing a bit of sleuthing on his own?'

'Bill? He hasn't got the brains.'

'I'm not so sure. When a simple, muscular person like Bill does set out to be subtle, no one ever gives him credit for it.'

'And in consequence he can put in some good work. Yes, there's something in that. But all the same I'd never have thought it of Bill. He's doing the Countess's little woolly lamb to perfection. I think you're wrong, you know, Loraine. The Countess is an extraordinarily beautiful woman – not my type of course,' put in Mr Thesiger hastily – 'and old Bill has always had a heart like an hotel.'

Loraine shook her head, unconvinced.

'Well,' said Jimmy, 'have it your own way. We seem to have more or less settled things. You go back with Bundle to Chimneys, and for heaven's sake keep her from poking about in that Seven Dials place again. Heaven knows what will happen if she does.'

Loraine nodded.

'And now,' said Jimmy, 'I think a few words with Lady Coote would be advisable.'

Lady Coote was sitting on a garden seat doing wool-work. The subject was a disconsolate and somewhat misshapen young woman weeping over an urn.

Lady Coote made room for Jimmy by her side, and he promptly, being a tactful young man, admired her work.

'Do you like it?' said Lady Coote, pleased. 'It was begun by my Aunt Selina the week before she died. Cancer of the liver, poor thing.'

'How beastly,' said Jimmy.

'And how is the arm?'

'Oh, it's feeling quite all right. Bit of a nuisance and all that, you know.'

'You'll have to be careful,' said Lady Coote in a warning voice. 'I've known blood-poisoning set in – and in that case you might lose your arm altogether.'

'Oh! I say, I hope not.'

'I'm only warning you,' said Lady Coote.

'Where are you hanging out now?' inquired Mr Thesiger. 'Town – or where?'

Considering that he knew the answer to his query perfectly well, he put the question with a praiseworthy amount of ingenuousness.

Lady Coote sighed heavily.

'Sir Oswald has taken the Duke of Alton's place. Letherbury. You know it, perhaps?'

'Oh, rather. Topping place, isn't it?'

'Oh, I don't know,' said Lady Coote. 'It's a very large place, and gloomy, you know. Rows of picture galleries with such forbidding-looking people. What they call Old Masters are very depressing, I think. You should have seen a little house we had in Yorkshire, Mr Thesiger. When Sir Oswald was plain Mr Coote. Such a nice lounge hall and a cheerful drawing-room with an ingle-nook – a white striped paper with a frieze of wistaria I chose for it, I remember. Satin stripe, you know, not moiré. Much better taste, I always think. The dining-room faced north-east, so we didn't get much sun in it, but with a good bright scarlet paper and a set of those comic hunting prints – why, it was as cheerful as Christmas.'

In the excitement of these reminiscences, Lady Coote dropped several little balls of wool, which Jimmy dutifully retrieved.

'Thank you, my dear,' said Lady Coote. 'Now, what was I saying? Oh – about houses – yes, I do like a cheerful house. And choosing things for it gives you an interest.'

'I suppose Sir Oswald will be buying a place of his own one of these days,' suggested Jimmy. 'And then you can have it just as you like.'

Lady Coote shook her head sadly.

'Sir Oswald talks of a firm doing it – and you know what that means.'

'Oh! But they'd consult you!'

'It would be one of those grand places – all for the antique. They'd look down on the things I call comfortable and homey.

Not but that Sir Oswald wasn't very comfortable and satisfied in his home always, and I daresay his tastes are just the same underneath. But nothing will suit him now but the best! He's got on wonderfully, and naturally he wants something to show for it, but many's the time I wonder where it will end.'

Jimmy looked sympathetic.

'It's like a runaway horse,' said Lady Coote. 'Got the bit between its teeth and away it goes. It's the same with Sir Oswald. He's got on, and he's got on, till he can't stop getting on. He's one of the richest men in England – but does that satisfy him? No, he wants still more. He wants to be – I don't know what he wants to be! I can tell you, it frightens me sometimes!'

'Like the Persian Johnny,' said Jimmy, 'who went about wailing for fresh worlds to conquer.'

Lady Coote nodded acquiescence without much knowing what Jimmy was talking about.

'What I wonder is – will his stomach stand it?' she went on tearfully. 'To have him an invalid – with his ideas – oh, it won't bear thinking of.'

'He looks very hearty,' said Jimmy consolingly.

'He's got something on his mind,' said Lady Coote. 'Worried that's what he is. *I* know.'

'What's he worried about?'

'I don't know. Perhaps something at the works. It's a great comfort for him having Mr Bateman. Such an earnest young man – and so conscientious.'

'Marvellously conscientious,' agreed Jimmy.

'Oswald thinks a lot of Mr Bateman's judgement. He says that Mr Bateman is always right.'

'That was one of his worst characteristics years ago,' said Jimmy feelingly.

Lady Coote looked slightly puzzled.

'That was an awfully jolly week-end I had with you at Chimneys,' said Jimmy. 'I mean it would have been awfully jolly if it hadn't been for poor old Gerry kicking the bucket. Jolly nice girls.'

'I find girls very perplexing,' said Lady Coote. 'Not romantic, you know. Why, I embroidered some handkerchiefs for Sir Oswald with my own hair when we were engaged.'

'Did you?' said Jimmy. 'How marvellous. But I suppose girls haven't got long hair to do that nowadays.'

'That's true,' admitted Lady Coote. 'But, oh, it shows in lots of other ways. I remember when I was a girl, one of my – well, my young men – picked up a handful of gravel, and a girl who was with me said at once that he was treasuring it because my feet had trodden on it. Such a pretty idea, I thought. Though it turned out afterwards that he was taking a course in mineralogy – or do I mean geology? – at a technical school. But I liked the idea – and stealing a girl's handkerchief and treasuring it – all those sort of things.'

'Awkward if the girl wanted to blow her nose,' said the practical Mr Thesiger.

Lady Coote laid down her wool-work and looked searchingly but kindly at him.

'Come now,' she said. 'Isn't there some nice girl that you fancy? That you'd like to work and make a little home for?'

Jimmy blushed and mumbled.

'I thought you got on very well with one of those girls at Chimneys that time – Vera Daventry.'

'Socks?'

'They do call her that,' admitted Lady Coote. 'I can't think why. It isn't pretty.'

'Oh, she's a topper,' said Jimmy. 'I'd like to meet her again.'

'She's coming down to stay with us next week-end.'

'Is she?' said Jimmy, trying to infuse a large amount of wistful longing into the two words.

'Yes. Would – would you like to come?'

'I *would*,' said Jimmy heartily. 'Thanks ever so much, Lady Coote.'

And reiterating fervent thanks, he left her.

Sir Oswald presently joined his wife.

'What has that young jackanapes been boring you about?' he demanded. 'I can't stand that young fellow.'

'He's a dear boy,' said Lady Coote. 'And so brave. Look how he got wounded last night.'

'Yes, messing around where he'd no business to be.'

'I think you're very unfair, Oswald.'

'Never done an honest day's work in his life. A real waster if there ever was one. He'd never get on if he had his way to make in the world.'

'You must have got your feet damp last night,' said Lady Coote. 'I hope you won't get pneumonia. Freddie Richards died of it the other day. Dear me, Oswald, it makes my blood run cold to think of you wandering about with a dangerous burglar loose in the grounds. He might have shot you. I've asked Mr Thesiger down for next week-end, by the way.'

'Nonsense,' said Sir Oswald. 'I won't have that young man in my house, do you hear, Maria?'

'Why not?'

'That's my business.'

'I'm so sorry, dear,' said Lady Coote placidly. 'I've asked him now, so it can't be helped. Pick up that ball of pink wool, will you, Oswald?'

Sir Oswald complied, his face black as thunder. He looked at his wife and hesitated. Lady Coote was placidly threading her wool needle.

'I particularly don't want Thesiger down next week-end,' he said at last. 'I've heard a good deal about him from Bateman. He was at school with him.'

'What did Mr Bateman say?'

'He'd no good to say of him. In fact, he warned me very seriously against him.'

'He did, did he?' said Lady Coote thoughtfully.

'And I have the highest respect for Bateman's judgement. I've never known him wrong.'

'Dear me,' said Lady Coote. 'What a mess I seem to have made of things. Of course, I should never have asked him if I had known. You should have told me all this before, Oswald. It's too late now.'

She began to roll up her work very carefully. Sir Oswald

looked at her, made as if to speak, then shrugged his shoulders. He followed her into the house. Lady Coote, walking ahead, wore a very faint smile on her face. She was fond of her husband, but she was also fond – in a quiet, unobtrusive, wholly womanly manner – of getting her own way.

CHAPTER XXVI

Mainly about Golf

'That friend of yours is a nice girl, Bundle,' said Lord Caterham.

Loraine had been at Chimneys for nearly a week, and had earned the high opinion of her host – mainly because of the charming readiness she had shown to be instructed in the science of the mashie shot.

Bored by his winter abroad, Lord Caterham had taken up golf. He was an execrable player and in consequence was profoundly enthusiastic over the game. He spent most of his mornings lifting mashie shots over various shrubs and bushes – or, rather, essaying to loft them, hacking large bits out of the velvety turf and generally reducing MacDonald to despair.

'We must lay out a little course,' said Lord Caterham, addressing a daisy. 'A sporting little course. Now then, just watch this one, Bundle. Off the right knee, slow back, keep the head still and use the wrists.'

The ball, heavily topped, scudded across the lawn and disappeared into the unfathomed depths of a great bank of rhododendrons.

'Curious,' said Lord Caterham. 'What did I do then, I wonder? As I was saying, Bundle, that friend of yours is a very nice girl. I really think I am inducing her to take quite an interest in the game. She hit some excellent shots this morning – really quite as good as I could do myself.'

Lord Caterham took another careless swing and removed an immense chunk of turf. MacDonald, who was passing retrieved it and stamped it firmly back. The look he gave Lord Caterham would have caused anyone but an ardent golfer to sink through the earth.

'If MacDonald has been guilty of cruelty to Cootes, which I

strongly suspect,' said Bundle, 'he's being punished now.'

'Why shouldn't I do as I like in my own garden?' demanded her father. 'MacDonald ought to be interested in the way my game is coming on – the Scotch are a great golfing nation.'

'You poor old man,' said Bundle. 'You'll never be a golfer – but at any rate it keeps you out of mischief.'

'Not at all,' said Lord Caterham. 'I did the long sixth in five the other day. The pro was very surprised when I told him about it.'

'He would be,' said Bundle.

'Talking of Cootes, Sir Oswald plays a fair game – a very fair game. Not a pretty style – too stiff. But straight down the middle every time. But curious how the cloven hoof shows – won't give you a six-inch putt! Makes you put it in every time. Now I don't like that.'

'I suppose he's a man who likes to be sure,' said Bundle.

'It's contrary to the spirit of the game,' said her father. 'And he's not interested in the theory of the thing either. Now, that secretary chap, Bateman, is quite different. It's the theory interests him. I was slicing badly with my spoon; and he said it all came from too much right arm; and he evolved a very interesting theory. It's all left arm in golf – the left arm is the arm that counts. He says he plays tennis left handed but golf with ordinary clubs because there his superiority with the left arm tells.'

'And did he play very marvellously?' inquired Bundle.

'No, he didn't,' confessed Lord Caterham. 'But then he may have been off his game. I see the theory all right and I think there's a lot in it. Ah! Did you see that one, Bundle? Right over the rhododendrons. A perfect shot. Ah! If one could be sure of doing that every time – Yes, Tredwell, what is it?'

Tredwell addressed Bundle.

'Mr Thesiger would like to speak to you on the telephone, my lady.'

Bundle set off at full speed for the house, yelling 'Loraine, Loraine,' as she did so. Loraine joined her just as she was lifting the receiver.

'Hallo, is that you, Jimmy?'

'Hallo. How are you?'

'Very fit, but a bit bored.'

'How's Loraine?'

'She's all right. She's here. Do you want to speak to her?'

'In a minute. I've got a lot to say. To begin with, I'm going down to the Cootes for the week-end,' he said significantly. 'Now, look here, Bundle, you don't know how one gets hold of skeleton keys, do you?'

'Haven't the foggiest. Is it really necessary to take skeleton keys to the Cootes?'

'Well, I had a sort of idea they'd come in handy. You don't know the sort of shop one gets them at?'

'What you want is a kindly burglar friend to show you the ropes.'

'I do, Bundle, I do. And unfortunately I haven't got one. I thought perhaps your bright brain might grapple successfully with the problem. But I suppose I shall have to fall back upon Stevens as usual. He'll be getting some funny ideas in his head soon about me – first a blue-nosed automatic – and now skeleton keys. He'll think I've joined the criminal classes.'

'Jimmy?' said Bundle.

'Yes?'

'Look here – be careful, won't you? I mean if Sir Oswald finds you nosing around with skeleton keys – well, I should think he could be very unpleasant when he likes.'

'Young man of pleasing appearance in the dock! All right, I'll be careful. Pongo's the fellow I'm really frightened of. He sneaks around so on those flat feet of his. You never hear him coming. And he always did have a genius for poking his nose in where he wasn't wanted. But trust to the boy hero.'

'Well, I wish Loraine and I were going to be there to look after you.'

'Thank you, nurse. As a matter of fact, though, I have a scheme.'

'Yes?'

'Do you think you and Loraine might have a convenient car

breakdown near Letherbury to-morrow morning? It's not so very far from you, is it?'

'Forty miles. That's nothing.'

'I thought it wouldn't be – to you! Don't kill Loraine though. I'm rather fond of Loraine. All right, then – somewhere round about quarter to half-past twelve.'

'So that they invite us to lunch?'

'That's the idea. I say, Bundle, I ran into that girl Socks yesterday, and what do you think – Terence O'Rourke is going to be down there this week-end!'

'Jimmy, do you think he –?'

'Well – suspect everyone, you know. That's what they say. He's a wild lad, and daring as they make them. I wouldn't put it past him to run a secret society. He and the Countess might be in this together. He was out in Hungary last year.'

'But he could pinch the formula any time.'

'That's just what he couldn't. He'd have to do it under circumstances where he couldn't be suspected. But the retreat up the ivy and into his own bed – well, that would be rather neat. Now for instructions. After a few polite nothings to Lady Coote, you and Loraine are to get hold of Pongo and O'Rourke by hook or by crook and keep them occupied till lunch time. See? It oughtn't to be difficult for a couple of beautiful girls like you.'

'You're using the best butter, I see.'

'A plain statement of fact.'

'Well, at any rate, your instructions are duly noted. Do you want to talk to Loraine now?'

Bundle passed over the receiver and tactfully left the room.

CHAPTER XXVII

Nocturnal Adventure

Jimmy Thesiger arrived at Letherbury on a sunny autumn afternoon and was greeted affectionately by Lady Coote and with cold dislike by Sir Oswald. Aware of the keen matchmaking eye of Lady Coote upon him, Jimmy took pains to make himself extremely agreeable to Socks Daventry.

O'Rourke was there in excellent spirits. He was inclined to be official and secretive about the mysterious events at the Abbey, about which Socks catechized him freely, but his official reticence took a novel form ... namely that of embroidering the tale of events in such a fantastic manner that nobody could possibly guess what the truth might have been.

'Four masked men with revolvers? Is that really so?' demanded Socks severely.

'Ah! I'm remembering now that there was the round half-dozen of them to hold me down and force the stuff down my throat. Sure, and I thought it was poison, and I done for entirely.'

'And what was stolen, or what did they try and steal?'

'What else but the crown jewels of Russia that were brought to Mr Lomax secretly to deposit in the Bank of England.'

'What a bloody liar you are,' said Socks without emotion.

'A liar, I? And the jewels brought over by aeroplane with my best friend as pilot. This is secret history I'm telling you, Socks. Will you ask Jimmy Thesiger there if you don't believe me. Not that I'd be putting any trust in what he'd say.'

'Is it true,' said Socks, 'that George Lomax came down without his false teeth? That's what I want to know.'

'There were two revolvers,' said Lady Coote. 'Nasty things. I saw them myself. It's a wonder this poor boy wasn't killed.'

'Oh, I was born to be hanged,' said Jimmy.

'I hear that there was a Russian countess there of subtle beauty,' said Socks. 'And that she vamped Bill.'

'Some of the things she said about Buda Pesth were too dreadful,' said Lady Coote. 'I shall never forget them. Oswald, we must send a subscription.'

Sir Oswald grunted.

'I'll make a note of it, Lady Coote,' said Rupert Bateman.

'Thank you, Mr Bateman. I feel one ought to do something as a thank offering. I can't imagine how Sir Oswald escaped being shot – letting alone die of pneumonia.'

'Don't be foolish, Maria,' said Sir Oswald.

'I've always had a horror of cat burglars,' said Lady Coote.

'Think of having the luck to meet one face to face. How thrilling!' murmured Socks.

'Don't you believe it,' said Jimmy. 'It's damned painful.' And he patted his right arm gingerly.

'How is the poor arm?' inquired Lady Coote.

'Oh, pretty well all right now. But it's been the most confounded nuisance having to do everything with the left hand. I'm no good whatever with it.'

'Every child should be brought up to be ambidexterous,' said Sir Oswald.

'Oh!' said Socks, somewhat out of her depth. 'Is that like seals?'

'Not amphibious,' said Mr Bateman. 'Ambidexterous means using either hand equally well.'

'Oh!' said Socks, looking at Sir Oswald with respect. 'Can you?'

'Certainly; I can write with either hand.'

'But not with both at once?'

'That would not be practical,' said Sir Oswald shortly.

'No,' said Socks thoughtfully. 'I suppose that would be a bit too subtle.'

'It would be a grand thing now in a Government department,' observed Mr O'Rourke, 'if one could keep the right hand from knowing what the left hand was doing.'

'Can you use both hands?'

'No, indeed. I'm the most right-handed person that ever was.'

'But you deal cards with your left hand,' said the observant Bateman. 'I noticed the other night.'

'Oh, but that's different entirely,' said Mr O'Rourke easily.

A gong with a sombre note pealed out and everyone went upstairs to dress for dinner.

After dinner Sir Oswald and Lady Coote, Mr Bateman and Mr O'Rourke played bridge and Jimmy passed a flirtatious evening with Socks. The last words Jimmy heard as he retreated up the staircase that night were Sir Oswald saying to his wife:

'You'll never make a bridge player, Maria.'

And her reply:

'I know, dear. So you always say. You owe Mr O'Rourke another pound, Oswald. That's right.'

It was some two hours later that Jimmy crept noiselessly (or so he hoped) down the stairs. He made one brief visit to the dining-room and then found his way to Sir Oswald's study. There, after listening intently for a minute or two, he set to work. Most of the drawers of the desk were locked, but a curiously shaped bit of wire in Jimmy's hand soon saw to that. One by one the drawers yielded to his manipulations.

Drawer by drawer he sorted through methodically, being careful to replace everything in the same order. Once or twice he stopped to listen, fancying he heard some distant sound. But he remained undisturbed.

The last drawer was looked through. Jimmy now knew – or could have known had he been paying attention – many interesting details relating to steel; but he had found nothing of what he wanted – a reference to Herr Eberhard's invention or anything that could give him a clue to the identity of the mysterious No 7. He had, perhaps, hardly hoped that he would. It was an off-chance and he had taken it – but he had not expected much result – except by sheer luck.

He tested the drawers to make sure that he had relocked them securely. He knew Rupert Bateman's powers of minute observation and glanced round the room to make sure that he had left no incriminating trace of his presence.

'That's that,' he muttered to himself softly. 'Nothing there. Well, perhaps I'll have better luck to-morrow morning – if the girls only play up.'

He came out of the study, closing the door behind him and locking it. For a moment he thought he heard a sound quite near him, but decided he had been mistaken. He felt his way noiselessly along the great hall. Just enough light came from the high vaulted windows to enable him to pick his way without stumbling into anything.

Again he heard a soft sound – he heard it quite certainly this time and without the possibility of making a mistake. He was not alone in the hall. Somebody else was there, moving as stealthily as he was. His heart beat suddenly very fast.

With a sudden spring he jumped to the electric switch and turned on the lights. The sudden glare made him blink – but he saw plainly enough. Not four feet away stood Rupert Bateman.

'My goodness, Pongo,' cried Jimmy, 'you did give me a start. Slinking about like that in the dark.'

'I heard a noise,' explained Mr Bateman severely. 'I thought burglars had got in and I came down to see.'

Jimmy looked thoughtfully at Mr Bateman's rubber-soled feet.

'You think of everything, Pongo,' he said genially. 'Even a lethal weapon.'

His eye rested on the bulge in the other's pocket.

'It's as well to be armed. One never knows whom one may meet.'

'I am glad you didn't shoot,' said Jimmy. 'I'm a bit tired of being shot at.'

'I might easily have done so,' said Mr Bateman.

'It would be dead against the law if you did,' said Jimmy. 'You've got to make quite sure the beggar's house-breaking, you know, before you pot at him. You mustn't jump to conclusions. Otherwise you'd have to explain why you shot a guest on a perfectly innocent errand like mine.'

'By the way what did you come down for?'

'I was hungry,' said Jimmy. 'I rather fancied a dry biscuit.'

'There are some biscuits in a tin by your bed,' said Rupert Bateman.

He was staring at Jimmy very intently through his horn-rimmed spectacles.

'Ah! That's where the staff work has gone wrong, old boy. There's a tin there with "Biscuits for Starving Visitors" on it. But when the starving visitor opened it – nothing inside. So I just toddled down to the dining-room.'

And with a sweet, ingenuous smile, Jimmy produced from his dressing-gown pocket a handful of biscuits.

There was a moment's pause.

'And now I think I'll toddle back to bed,' said Jimmy. 'Night-night, Pongo.'

With an affectation of nonchalance, he mounted the staircase. Rupert Bateman followed him. At the doorway of his room, Jimmy paused as if to say good-night once more.

'It's an extraordinary thing about these biscuits,' said Mr Bateman. 'Do you mind if I just –?'

'Certainly, laddie, look for yourself.'

Mr Bateman strode across the room, opened the biscuit box and stared at its emptiness.

'Very remiss,' he murmured. 'Well, good-night.'

He withdrew. Jimmy sat on the edge of his bed listening for a minute.

'That was a narrow shave,' he murmured to himself. 'Suspicious sort of chap, Pongo. Never seems to sleep. Nasty habit of his, prowling around with a revolver.'

He got up and opened one of the drawers of the dressing-table. Beneath an assortment of ties lay a pile of biscuits.

'There's nothing for it,' said Jimmy. 'I shall have to eat the damned things. Ten to one, Pongo will come prowling round in the morning.'

With a sigh, he settled down to a meal of biscuits for which he had no inclination whatever.

CHAPTER XXVIII

Suspicions

It was just on the appointed hour of twelve o'clock that Bundle and Loraine entered the park gates, having left the Hispano at an adjacent garage.

Lady Coote greeted the two girls with surprise, but distinct pleasure, and immediately pressed them to stay to lunch.

O'Rourke, who had been reclining in an immense arm-chair, began at once to talk with great animation to Loraine, who was listening with half an ear to Bundle's highly technical explanation of the mechanical trouble which had affected the Hispano.

'And we said,' ended Bundle, 'how marvellous that the brute should have broken down just here! Last time it happened was on a Sunday at a place called Little Speddlington under the Hill. And it lived up to its name, I can tell you.'

'That would be a grand name on the films,' remarked O'Rourke.

'Birthplace of the simple country maiden,' suggested Socks.

'I wonder now,' said Lady Coote, 'where Mr Thesiger is?'

'He's in the billiard-room, I think,' said Socks. 'I'll fetch him.'

She went off, but had hardly gone a minute when Rupert Bateman appeared upon the scene, with the harassed and serious air usual to him.

'Yes, Lady Coote? Thesiger said you were asking for me. How do you do, Lady Eileen –'

He broke off to greet the two girls, and Loraine immediately took the field.

'Oh, Mr Bateman! I've been wanting to see you. Wasn't it you who was telling me what to do for a dog when he is continually getting sore paws?'

The secretary shook his head.

'It must have been someone else, Miss Wade. Though, as a matter of fact, I do happen to know –'

'What a wonderful man you are,' interrupted Loraine. 'You know about everything.'

'One should keep abreast of modern knowledge,' said Mr Bateman seriously. 'Now about your dog's paws –'

Terence O'Rourke murmured *sotto voce* to Bundle:

''Tis a man like that that writes all those little paragraphs in the weekly papers. "It is not generally known that to keep a brass fender uniformly bright, etc;" "The dorper beetle is one of the most interesting characters in the insect world;" "The marriage customs of the Fingalese Indian;" and so on.'

'General information, in fact.'

'And what more horrible two words could you have?' said Mr O'Rourke, and added piously: 'Thank the heavens above I'm an educated man and know nothing whatever upon any subject at all.'

'I see you've got clock golf here,' said Bundle to Lady Coote.

'I'll take you on it, Lady Eileen,' said O'Rourke.

'Let's challenge those two,' said Bundle. 'Loraine, Mr O'Rourke and I want to take you and Mr Bateman on at clock golf.'

'Do play, Mr Bateman,' said Lady Coote, as the secretary showed a momentary hesitation. 'I'm sure Sir Oswald doesn't want you.'

The four went out on the lawn.

'Very cleverly managed, what?' whispered Bundle to Loraine. 'Congratulations on our girlish tact.'

The round ended just before one o'clock, victory going to Bateman and Loraine.

'But I think you'll agree with me, partner,' said Mr O'Rourke, 'that we played a more sporting game.'

He lagged a little behind with Bundle.

'Old Pongo's a cautious player – and takes no risks. Now, with me it's neck or nothing. And a fine motto through life, don't you agree, Lady Eileen?'

'Hasn't it ever landed you in trouble?' asked Bundle laughing.

'To be sure it has. Millions of times. But I'm still going strong. Sure, it'll take the hangman's noose to defeat Terence O'Rourke.'

Just then Jimmy Thesiger strolled round the corner of the house.

'Bundle, by all that's wonderful!' he exclaimed.

'You've missed competing in the Autumn Meeting,' said O'Rourke.

'I'd gone for a stroll,' said Jimmy. 'Where did these girls drop from?'

'We came on our flat feet,' said Bundle. 'The Hispano let us down.'

And she narrated the circumstances of the breakdown.

Jimmy listened with sympathetic attention.

'Hard luck,' he vouchsafed. 'If it's going to take some time, I'll run you back in my car after lunch.'

A gong sounded at that moment and they all went in. Bundle observed Jimmy covertly. She thought she had noticed an unusual note of exultance in his voice. She had the feeling that things had gone well.

After lunch they took a polite leave of Lady Coote, and Jimmy volunteered to run them down to the garage in his car. As soon as they had started the same words burst simultaneously from both girls' lips:

'Well?'

Jimmy chose to be provoking.

'Well?

'Oh, pretty hearty, thanks. Slight indigestion owing to over-indulgence in dry biscuits.'

'But what has happened?'

'I tell you. Devotion to the cause made me eat too many dry biscuits. But did our hero flinch? No, he did not.'

'Oh, Jimmy,' said Loraine reproachfully, and he softened.

'What do you really want to know?'

'Oh, everything. Didn't we do it well? I mean, the way we kept Pongo and Terence O'Rourke in play.'

'I congratulate you on the handling of Pongo. O'Rourke was probably a sitter – but Pongo is made of other stuff. There's only one word for that lad – it was in the *Sunday Newsbag* cross-word last week. Word of ten letters meaning everywhere at once. Ubiquitous. That described Pongo down to the ground. You can't go anywhere without running into him – and the worst of it is you never hear him coming.'

'You think he's dangerous?'

'Dangerous? Of course he's not dangerous. Fancy Pongo being dangerous. He's an ass. But, as I said just now, he's an ubiquitous ass. He doesn't even seem to need sleep like ordinary mortals. In fact, to put it bluntly, the fellow's a damned nuisance.'

And, in a somewhat aggrieved manner, Jimmy described the events of the previous evening.

Bundle was not very sympathetic.

'I don't know what you think you're doing anyway, mooching around here.'

'No 7,' said Jimmy crisply. 'That's what I'm after. No 7.'

'And you think you'll find him in this house?'

'I thought I might find a clue.'

'And you didn't?'

'Not last night – no.'

'But this morning,' said Loraine, breaking in suddenly. 'Jimmy, you did find something this morning. I can see it by your face.'

'Well, I don't know if it is anything. But during the course of my stroll –'

'Which stroll didn't take you far from the house, I imagine.'

'Strangely enough, it didn't. Round trip of the interior, we might call it. Well, as I say, I don't know whether there's any-thing in it or not. But I found this.'

With the celerity of a conjurer he produced a small bottle and tossed it over to the girls. It was half full of a white powder.

'What do you think it is?' asked Bundle.

'A white chrystalline powder, that's what it is,' said Jimmy. 'And to any reader of detective fiction those words are both familiar and suggestive. Of course, if it turns out to be a new kind of patent tooth-powder, I shall be chagrined and annoyed.'

'Where did you find it?' asked Bundle sharply.

'Ah!' said Jimmy, 'that's my secret.'

And from that point he would not budge in spite of cajolery and insult.

'Here we are at the garage,' he said. 'Let's hope the high-mettled Hispano has not been subjected to any indignities.'

The gentleman at the garage presented a bill for five shillings and made a few vague remarks about loose nuts. Bundle paid him with a sweet smile.

'It's nice to know we all get money for nothing sometimes,' she murmured to Jimmy.

The three stood together in the road, silent for the moment as they each pondered the situation.

'I know,' said Bundle suddenly.

'Know what?'

'Something I meant to ask you – and nearly forgot. Do you remember that glove Superintendent Battle found – the half-burnt one?'

'Yes.'

'Didn't you say that he tried it on your hand?'

'Yes – it was a shade big. That fits in with the idea of its being a big, hefty man who wore it.'

'That's not at all what I'm bothering about. Never mind the size of it. George and Sir Oswald were both there too, weren't they?'

'Yes.'

'He could have given it to either of them to fit on?'

'Yes, of course –'

'But he didn't. He chose you. Jimmy, don't you see what that means?'

Mr Thesiger stared at her.

'I'm sorry, Bundle. Possibly the jolly old brain isn't functioning as well as usual, but I haven't the faintest idea what you're talking about.'

'Don't you see, Loraine?'

Loraine looked at her curiously, but shook her head.

'Does it mean anything in particular?'

'Of course it does. Don't you see – Jimmy had his right hand in a sling.'

'By Jove, Bundle,' said Jimmy slowly. 'It was rather odd now I come to think of it; it's being a left-hand glove, I mean. Battle never said anything.'

'He wasn't going to draw attention to it. By trying it on you it might pass without notice being drawn to it, and he talked about the size just to put everybody off. But surely it must mean that the man who shot at you held the pistol in his *left* hand.'

'So we've got to look for a left-handed man,' said Loraine thoughtfully.

'Yes, and I'll tell you another thing. That was what Battle was doing looking through the golf clubs. He was looking for a left-handed man's.'

'By Jove,' said Jimmy suddenly.

'What is it?'

'Well, I don't suppose there's anything in it, but it's rather curious.'

He retailed the conversation at tea the day before.

'So Sir Oswald Coote is ambidexterous?' said Bundle.

'Yes. And I remember now on that night at Chimneys – you know, the night Gerry Wade died – I was watching the bridge and thinking idly how awkwardly someone was dealing – and then realizing that it was because they were dealing with the left hand. Of course, it must have been Sir Oswald.'

They all three looked at each other. Loraine shook her head.

'A man like Sir Oswald Coote! It's impossible. What could he have to gain by it?'

'It seems absurd,' said Jimmy. 'And yet –'

'No 7 has his own ways of working,' quoted Bundle softly. 'Supposing this is the way Sir Oswald has really made his fortune?'

'But why stage all that comedy at the Abbey when he'd had the formula at his own works?'

'There might be ways of explaining that,' said Loraine. 'The same line of argument you used about Mr O'Rourke. Suspicion had to be diverted from him and placed in another quarter.'

Bundle nodded eagerly.

'It all fits in. Suspicion is to fall on Bauer and the Countess. Who on earth would ever dream of suspecting Sir Oswald Coote?'

'I wonder if Battle does,' said Jimmy slowly.

Some chord of memory vibrated in Bundle's mind. *Superintendent Battle plucking an ivy leaf off the millionaire's coat.*

Had Battle suspected all the time?

CHAPTER XXIX

Singular Behaviour of George Lomax

'Mr Lomax is here, my lord.'

Lord Caterham started violently, for, absorbed in the intricacies of what not to do with the left wrist, he had not heard the butler approach over the soft turf. He looked at Tredwell more in sorrow than in anger.

'I told you at breakfast, Tredwell, that I should be particularly engaged this morning.'

'Yes, my lord, but –'

'Go and tell Mr Lomax that you have made a mistake, that I am out in the village, that I am laid up with the gout, or, if all else fails, that I am dead.'

'Mr Lomax, my lord, has already caught sight of your lordship when driving up the drive.'

Lord Caterham sighed deeply.

'He would. Very well, Tredwell, I am coming.'

In a manner highly characteristic, Lord Caterham was always most genial when his feelings were in reality the reverse. He greeted George now with a heartiness quite unparalleled.

'My dear fellow, my dear fellow. Delighted to see you. Absolutely delighted. Sit down. Have a drink. Well, well, this is splendid!'

And having pushed George into a large arm-chair, he sat down opposite him and blinked nervously.

'I wanted to see you very particularly,' said George.

'Oh!' said Lord Caterham faintly, and his heart sank, whilst his mind raced actively over all the dread possibilities that might lie behind that simple phrase.

'*Very* particularly,' said George with heavy emphasis.

Lord Caterham's heart sank lower than ever. He felt that something was coming worse than anything he had yet thought of.

'Yes?' he said, with a courageous attempt at nonchalance.

'Is Eileen at home?'

Lord Caterham felt reprieved, but slightly surprised.

'Yes, yes,' he said. 'Bundle's here. Got that friend of hers with her – the little Wade girl. Very nice girl – *very* nice girl. Going to be quite a good golfer one day. Nice easy swing –'

He was chatting garrulously on when George interrupted with ruthlessness:

'I am glad that Eileen is at home. Perhaps I might have an interview with her presently?'

'Certainly, my dear fellow, certainly.' Lord Caterham still felt very surprised, but was still enjoying the sensation of reprieve. 'If it doesn't bore you.'

'Nothing could bore me less,' said George. 'I think, Caterham, if I may say so, that you hardly appreciate the fact that Eileen is grown up. She is no longer a child. She is a woman, and, if I may say so, a very charming and talented woman. The man who succeeds in winning her love will be extremely lucky. I repeat it – extremely lucky.'

'Oh, I daresay,' said Lord Caterham. 'But she's very restless, you know. Never content to be in one place for more than two minutes together. However, I daresay young fellows don't mind that nowadays.'

'You mean that she is not content to stagnate. Eileen has brains, Caterham; she is ambitious. She interests herself in the questions of the day, and brings her fresh and vivid young intellect to bear upon them.'

Lord Caterham stared at him. It occurred to him that what was so often referred to as 'the strain of modern life' had begun to tell upon George. Certainly his description of Bundle seemed to Lord Caterham ludicrously unlike.

'Are you sure you are feeling quite well?' he asked anxiously.

George waved the inquiry aside impatiently.

'Perhaps, Caterham, you begin to have some inkling of my purpose in visiting you this morning. I am not a man to undertake fresh responsibilities lightly. I have a proper sense, I hope, of what is due to the position I hold. I have given this matter my deep and earnest consideration. Marriage, especially at my age, is not to be undertaken without full – er – consideration. Equality of birth, similarity of tastes, general suitability, and the same religious creed – all these things are necessary and the pros and cons have to be weighed and considered. I can, I think, offer my wife a position in society that is not to be despised. Eileen will grace that position admirably. By birth and breeding she is fitted for it, and her brains and her acute political sense cannot but further my career to our mutual advantage. I am aware, Caterham, that there is – er – some disparity in years. But I can assure you that I feel full of vigour – in my prime. The balance of years should be on the husband's side. And Eileen has serious tastes – an older man will suit her better than some young jackanapes without either experience or *savoir-faire*. I can assure you, my dear Caterham, that I will cherish her – er – exquisite youth; I will cherish it – er – it will be appreciated. To watch the exquisite flower of her mind unfolding – what a privilege! And to think that I never realized –'

He shook his head deprecatingly and Lord Caterham, finding his voice with difficulty, said blankly:

'Do I understand you to mean – ah, my dear fellow, you can't want to marry Bundle?'

'You are surprised. I suppose to you it seems sudden. I have your permission, then, to speak to her?'

'Oh, yes,' said Lord Caterham. 'If it's permission you want – of course you can. But you know, Lomax, I really shouldn't if I were you. Just go home and think it over like a good fellow. Count twenty. All that sort of thing. Always a pity to propose and make a fool of yourself.'

'I daresay you mean your advice kindly, Caterham, though I must confess that you put it somewhat strangely. But I have made up my mind to put my fortune to the test. I may see Eileen?'

'Oh, it's nothing to do with me,' said Lord Caterham hastily; 'Eileen settles her own affairs. If she came to me to-morrow and said she was going to marry the chauffeur, I shouldn't make any objections. It's the only way nowadays. Your children can make life damned unpleasant if you don't give in to them in every way. I say to Bundle, "Do as you like, but don't worry me," and really, on the whole, she is amazingly good about it.'

George stood up intent upon his purpose.

'Where shall I find her?'

'Well, really, I don't know,' said Lord Caterham vaguely. 'She might be anywhere. As I told you just now, she's never in the same place for two minutes together. No repose.'

'And I suppose Miss Wade will be with her? It seems to me, Caterham, that the best plan would be for you to ring the bell and ask your butler to find her, saying that I wish to speak to her for a few minutes.'

Lord Caterham pressed the bell obediently.

'Oh, Tredwell,' he said, when the bell was answered. 'Just find her ladyship, will you. Tell her Mr Lomax is anxious to speak to her in the drawing-room.'

'Yes, my lord.'

Tredwell withdrew. George seized Lord Caterham's hand and wrung it warmly, much to the latter's discomfort.

'A thousand thanks,' he said. 'I hope soon to bring you good news.'

He hastened from the room.

'Well,' said Lord Caterham. 'Well!'

And after a long pause:

'What *has* Bundle been up to?'

The door opened again.

'Mr Eversleigh, my lord.'

As Bill hastened in, Lord Caterham caught his hand and spoke earnestly.

'Hullo, Bill. You're looking for Lomax, I suppose? Look here, if you want to do a good turn, hurry to the drawing-room and tell him the Cabinet have called an immediate meeting, or get him away somehow. It's really not fair to let the poor devil make an ass of himself all for some silly girl's prank.'

'I've not come for Codders,' said Bill. 'Didn't know he was here. It's Bundle I want to see. Is she anywhere about?'

'You can't see her,' said Lord Caterham. 'Not just now, at any rate. George is with her.'

'Well – what does it matter?'

'I think it does rather,' said Lord Caterham. 'He's probably spluttering horribly at this minute, and we mustn't do anything to make it worse for him.'

'But what is he saying?'

'Heaven knows,' said Lord Caterham. 'A lot of damned nonsense, anyway. Never say too much, that was always my motto. Grab the girl's hand and let events take their course.'

Bill stared at him.

'But look here, sir, I'm in a hurry. I must talk to Bundle –'

'Well, I don't suppose you'll have to wait long. I must confess I'm rather glad to have you here with me – I suppose Lomax will insist on coming back and talking to me when it's all over.'

'When what's all over? What is Lomax supposed to be doing?'

'Hush,' said Lord Caterham. 'He's proposing.'

'Proposing? Proposing what?'

'Marriage. To Bundle. Don't ask me why. I suppose he's come to what they call the dangerous age. I can't explain it any other way.'

'Proposing to Bundle? The dirty swine. At his age.'

Bill's face grew crimson.

'He says he's in the prime of life,' said Lord Caterham cautiously.

'He? Why, he's decrepit – senile! I –' Bill positively choked.

'Not at all,' said Lord Caterham coldly. 'He's five years younger than I am.'

'Of all the damned cheek! Codders and Bundle! A girl like Bundle! You oughtn't to have allowed it.'

'I never interfere,' said Lord Caterham.

'You ought to have told him what you thought of him.'

'Unfortunately modern civilization rules that out,' said Lord Caterham regretfully. 'In the Stone Age now – but, dear me, I suppose even then I shouldn't be able to do it – being a small man.'

'Bundle! Bundle! Why, I've never dared to ask Bundle to marry me because I knew she'd only laugh. And George – a disgusting wind-bag, an unscrupulous hypocritical old hot-air merchant – a foul, poisonous self-advertiser –'

'Go on,' said Lord Caterham. 'I am enjoying this.'

'My God!' said Bill simply and with feeling. 'Look here, I must be off.'

'No, no, don't go. I'd much rather you stayed. Besides, you want to see Bundle.'

'Not now. This has driven everything else out of my head. You don't know where Jimmy Thesiger is by any chance? I believe he was staying with the Cootes. Is he there still?'

'I think he went back to town yesterday. Bundle and Loraine were over there on Saturday. If you'll only wait –'

But Bill shook his head energetically and rushed from the room. Lord Caterham tiptoed out into the hall, seized a hat and made a hurried exit by the side door. In the distance he observed Bill streaking down the drive in his car.

'That young man will have an accident,' he thought.

Bill, however, reached London without any mischance, and proceeded to park his car in St James's Square. Then he sought out Jimmy Thesiger's rooms. Jimmy was at home.

'Hullo, Bill. I say, what's the matter? You don't look your usual bright little self.'

'I'm worried,' said Bill. 'I was worried anyway, and then something else turned up and gave me a jolt.'

'Oh!' said Jimmy. 'How lucid! What's it all about? Can I do anything?'

Bill did not reply. He sat staring at the carpet and looking so puzzled and uncomfortable that Jimmy felt his curiosity aroused.

'Has anything very extraordinary occurred, William?' he asked gently.

'Something damned odd. I can't make head or tail of it.'

'The Seven Dials business?'

'Yes – the Seven Dials business. I got a letter this morning.'

'A letter? What sort of letter?'

'A letter from Ronny Devereux's executors.'

'Good lord! After all this time!'

'It seems he left instructions. If he was to die suddenly, a certain sealed envelope was to be sent to me exactly a fortnight after his death.'

'And they've sent it to you?'

'Yes.'

'You've opened it?'

'Yes.'

'Well – what did it say?'

Bill turned a glance upon him, such a strange and uncertain one that Jimmy was startled.

'Look here,' he said. 'Pull yourself together, old man. It seems to have knocked the wind out of you, whatever it is. Have a drink.'

He poured out a stiff whisky and soda and brought it over to Bill, who took it obediently. His face still bore the same dazed expression.

'It's what's in the letter,' he said. 'I simply can't believe it, that's all.'

'Oh, nonsense,' said Jimmy. 'You must get into the habit of believing six impossible things before breakfast. I do it regularly. Now then, let's hear all about it. Wait a minute.'

He went outside.

'Stevens!'

'Yes, sir?'

'Just go out and get me some cigarettes, will you? I've run out.'

'Very good, sir.'

Jimmy waited till he heard the front door close. Then he came back into the sitting-room. Bill was just in the act of setting down his empty glass. He looked better, more purposeful and more master of himself.

'Now then,' said Jimmy. 'I've sent Stevens out so that we can't be overheard. Are you going to tell me all about it?'

'It's so incredible.'

'Then it's sure to be true. Come on, out with it.'

Bill drew a deep breath.

'I will. I'll tell you everything.'

CHAPTER XXX

An Urgent Summons

Loraine, playing with a small and delectable puppy, was somewhat surprised when Bundle rejoined her after an absence of twenty minutes, in a breathless state and with an indescribable expression on her face.

'Whoof,' said Bundle, sinking on to a garden seat. 'Whoof.'

'What's the matter?' asked Loraine, looking at her curiously.

'George is the matter – George Lomax.'

'What's he been doing?'

'Proposing to me. It was awful. He spluttered and he stuttered, but he would go through with it – he must have learnt it out of a book, I think. There was no stopping him. Oh, how I hate men who splutter! And, unfortunately, I didn't know the reply.'

'You must have known what you wanted to do.'

'Naturally I'm not going to marry an apologetic idiot like George. What I mean is, I didn't know the correct reply from the book of etiquette. I could only just say flatly: "No, I won't." What I ought to have said was something about being very sensible of the honour he had done me and so on and so on. But I got so rattled that in the end I jumped out of the window and bolted.'

'Really, Bundle, that's not like you.'

'Well, I never dreamt of such a thing happening. George – who I always thought hated me – and he did too. What a fatal thing it is to pretend to take an interest in a man's pet subject. You should have heard the drivel George talked about my girlish mind and the pleasure it would be to form it. My mind! If George knew one quarter of what was going on in my mind, he'd faint with horror!'

Loraine laughed. She couldn't help it.

'Oh, I know it's my own fault. I let myself in for this. There's Father dodging round that rhododendron. Hallo, Father.'

Lord Caterham approached with a hangdog expression.

'Lomax gone, eh?' he remarked with somewhat forced geniality.

'A nice business you let me in for,' said Bundle. 'George told me he had your full approval and sanction.'

'Well,' said Lord Caterham, 'what did you expect me to say? As a matter of fact, I didn't say that at all, or anything like it.'

'I didn't really think so,' said Bundle. 'I assumed that George had talked you into a corner and reduced you to such a state that you could only nod your head feebly.'

'That's very much what happened. How did he take it? Badly?'

'I didn't wait to see,' said Bundle. 'I'm afraid I was rather abrupt.'

'Oh well,' said Lord Caterham. 'Perhaps that was the best way. Thank goodness in the future Lomax won't always be running over as he has been in the habit of doing, worrying me about things. Everything is for the best they say. Have you seen my jigger anywhere?'

'A mashie shot or two would steady my nerves, I think,' said Bundle. 'I'll take you on for sixpence, Loraine.'

An hour passed very peacefully. The three returned to the house in a harmonious spirit. A note lay on the hall table.

'Mr Lomax left that for you, my lord,' explained Tredwell. 'He was much disappointed to find that you had gone out.'

Lord Caterham tore it open. He uttered a pained ejaculation and turned upon his daughter. Tredwell had retired.

'Really, Bundle, you might have made yourself clear, I think.'

'What do you mean?'

'Well, read this.'

Bundle took it and read:

'MY DEAR CATERHAM, – I am sorry not to have had a word with you. I thought I made it clear that I wanted to see you again after my interview with Eileen. She, dear child, was evidently quite unaware of the feelings I

entertained towards her. She was, I am afraid, much
startled. I have no wish to hurry her in any way. Her
girlish confusion was very charming, and I entertain an
even higher regard for her, as I much appreciate her
maidenly reserve. I must give her time to become accustomed to the idea. Her very confusion shows that she is
not wholly indifferent to me and I have no doubts of my
ultimate success.

> 'Believe me, dear Caterham,
>> 'Your sincere friend,
>>> 'GEORGE LOMAX.'

'Well,' said Bundle. 'Well, I'm damned!'

Words failed her.

'The man must be mad,' said Lord Caterham. 'No one could
write those things about you, Bundle, unless they were slightly
touched in the head. Poor chap, poor chap. But what persist-
ence! I don't wonder he got into the Cabinet. It would serve
him right if you did marry him, Bundle.'

The telephone rang and Bundle moved forward to answer it.
In another minute George and his proposal were forgotten,
and she was beckoning eagerly to Loraine. Lord Caterham went
off to his own sanctum.

'It's Jimmy,' said Bundle. 'And he's tremendously excited
about something.'

'Thank goodness I've caught you,' said Jimmy's voice.
'There's no time to be lost. Loraine's there, too?'

'Yes, she's here.'

'Well, look here, I haven't got time to explain everything –
in fact, I can't through the telephone. But Bill has been round
to see me with the most amazing story you ever heard. If it's
true – well, if it's true, it's the biggest scoop of the century.
Now, look here, this is what you've got to do. Come up to town
at once, both of you. Garage the car somewhere and go straight
to the Seven Dials Club. Do you think that when you get there
you can get rid of that footman fellow?'

'Alfred? Rather. You leave that to me.'

'Good. Get rid of him and watch out for me and Bill. Don't show yourselves at the windows, but when we drive up, let us in at once. See?'

'Yes.'

'That's all right then. Oh, Bundle, don't let on that you're going up to town. Make some other excuse. Say you're taking Loraine home. How would that do?'

'Splendidly. I say, Jimmy, I'm thrilled to the core.'

'And you might as well make your will before starting.'

'Better and better. But I wish I knew what it was all about.'

'You will as soon as we meet. I'll tell you this much. We're going to get ready the hell of a surprise for No 7!'

Bundle hung up the receiver and turned to Loraine, giving her a rapid résumé of the conversation. Loraine rushed upstairs and hurriedly packed her suitcase, and Bundle put her head round her father's door.

'I'm taking Loraine home, Father.'

'Why? I had no idea she was going to-day.'

'They want her back,' said Bundle vaguely. 'Just telephoned. Bye-bye.'

'Here, Bundle, wait a minute. When will you be home?'

'Don't know. Expect me when you see me.'

With this unceremonious exit Bundle rushed upstairs, put a hat on, slipped into her fur coat and was ready to start. She had already ordered the Hispano to be brought round.

The journey to London was without adventure, except such as was habitually provided by Bundle's driving. They left the car at a garage and proceeded direct to the Seven Dials Club.

The door was opened to them by Alfred. Bundle pushed her way past him without ceremony and Loraine followed.

'Shut the door, Alfred,' said Bundle. 'Now, I've come here especially to do you a good turn. The police are after you.'

'Oh, my lady!'

Alfred turned chalk white.

'I've come to warn you because you did me a good turn the other night,' went on Bundle rapidly. 'There's a warrant out for Mr Mosgorovsky, and the best thing you can do is to clear out of here as quick as you can. If you're not found here, they won't bother about you. Here's ten pounds to help you get away somewhere.'

In three minutes' time an incoherent and badly scared Alfred had left 14 Hunstanton Street with only one idea in his head – never to return.

'Well, I've managed that all right,' said Bundle with satisfaction.

'Was it necessary to be so – well, drastic?' Loraine demurred.

'It's safer,' said Bundle. 'I don't know what Jimmy and Bill are up to, but we don't want Alfred coming back in the middle of it and wrecking everything. Hallo, here they are. Well, they haven't wasted much time. Probably watching round the corner to see Alfred leave. Go down and open the door to them, Loraine.'

Loraine obeyed. Jimmy Thesiger alighted from the driving seat.

'You stop here for a moment, Bill,' he said. 'Blow the horn if you think anyone's watching the place.'

He ran up the steps and banged the door behind him. He looked pink and elated.

'Hallo, Bundle, there you are. Now then, we've got to get down to it. Where's the key of the room you got into last time?'

'It was one of the downstairs keys. We'd better bring the lot up.'

'Right you are, but be quick. Time's short.'

The key was easily found, the baize-lined door swung back and the three entered. The room was exactly as Bundle had seen it before, with the seven chairs grouped round the table. Jimmy surveyed it for a minute or two in silence. Then his eyes went to the two cupboards.

'Which is the cupboard you hid in, Bundle?'

'This one.'

Jimmy went to it and flung the door open. The same collection of miscellaneous glassware covered the shelves.

'We shall have to shift all this stuff,' he murmured. 'Run

down and get Bill, Loraine. There's no need for him to keep watch outside any longer.'

Loraine ran off.

'What are you going to do?' inquired Bundle impatiently.

Jimmy was down on his knees, trying to peer through the crack of the other cupboard door.

'Wait till Bill comes and you shall hear the whole story. This is his staff work – and a jolly creditable bit of work it is. Hallo – what's Loraine flying up the stairs for as though she's got a mad bull after her?'

Loraine was indeed racing up the stairs as fast as she could. She burst in upon them with an ashen face and terror in her eyes.

'Bill – Bill – Oh, Bundle – Bill!'

'What about Bill?'

Jimmy caught her by the shoulder.

'For God's sake, Loraine, what's happened?'

Loraine was still gasping.

'Bill – I think he's dead – he's in the car still – but he doesn't move or speak. I'm sure he's dead.'

Jimmy muttered an oath and sprang for the stairs, Bundle behind him, her heart pounding unevenly and an awful feeling of desolation spreading over her.

Bill – dead? Oh, no! Oh, no! Not that. Please God – not that.

Together she and Jimmy reached the car, Loraine behind them.

Jimmy peered under the hood. Bill was sitting as he had left him, leaning back. But his eyes were closed and Jimmy's pull at his arm brought no response.

'I can't understand it,' muttered Jimmy. 'But he's not dead. Cheer up, Bundle. Look here, we've got to get him into the house. Let's pray to goodness no policeman comes along. If anybody says anything, he's our sick friend we're helping into the house.'

Between the three of them they got Bill into the house without much difficulty, and without attracting much attention, save for an unshaven gentleman, who said sympathetically:

'Genneman's 'ad a couple, I shee,' and nodded his head sapiently.

'Into the little back room downstairs,' said Jimmy. 'There's a sofa there.'

They got him safely on to the sofa and Bundle knelt down beside him and took his limp wrist in her hand.

'His pulse is beating,' she said. 'What *is* the matter with him?'

'He was all right when I left him just now,' said Jimmy. 'I wonder if someone's managed to inject some stuff into him. It would be easily done – just a prick. The man might have been asking him the time. There's only one thing for it. I must get him a doctor at once. You stay here and look after him.'

He hurried to the door, then paused.

'Look here – don't be scared, either of you. But I'd better leave you my revolver. I mean – just in case. I'll be back just as soon as I possibly can.'

He laid the revolver down on the little table by the sofa, then hurried off. They heard the front door bang behind him.

The house seemed very still now. The two girls stayed motionless by Bill. Bundle still kept her finger on his pulse. It seemed to be beating very fast and irregularly.

'I wish we could do something,' she whispered to Loraine. 'This is awful.'

Loraine nodded.

'I know. It seems ages since Jimmy went and yet it's only a minute and a half.'

'I keep hearing things,' said Bundle. 'Footsteps and boards creaking upstairs – and yet I know it's only imagination.'

'I wonder why Jimmy left us the revolver,' said Loraine. 'There can't really be danger.'

'If they could get Bill –' said Bundle and stopped.

Loraine shivered.

'I know – but we're in the house. Nobody can get in without our hearing them. And anyway we've got the revolver.'

Bundle turned her attention back again to Bill.

'I wish I knew what to do. Hot coffee. You give them that sometimes.'

'I've got some smelling-salts in my bag,' said Loraine. 'And some brandy. Where is it? Oh, I must have left it in the room upstairs.'

'I'll get it,' said Bundle. 'They might do some good.'

She sped quickly up the stairs, across the gaming room and through the open door into the meeting place. Loraine's bag was lying on the table.

As Bundle stretched out her hand to take it, she heard a noise from behind her. Hidden behind the door a man stood ready with a sand-bag in his hand. Before Bundle could turn her head, he had struck.

With a faint moan, Bundle slipped down, an unconscious heap upon the floor.

CHAPTER XXXI

The Seven Dials

Very slowly Bundle returned to consciousness. She was aware of a dark, spinning blackness, the centre of which was a violent, throbbing ache. Punctuating this were sounds. A voice that she knew very well saying the same thing over and over again.

The blackness span less violently. The ache was now definitely located as being in Bundle's own head. And she was sufficiently herself to take an interest in what the voice was saying.

'Darling, darling Bundle. Oh, darling Bundle. She's dead; I know she's dead. Oh, my darling. Bundle, darling, darling Bundle. I do love you so. Bundle – darling – darling –'

Bundle lay quite still with her eyes shut. But she was now fully conscious. Bill's arms held her closely.

'Bundle darling – Oh, dearest, darling Bundle. Oh, my dear love. Oh, Bundle – Bundle. What shall I do? Oh, darling one – my Bundle – my own dearest, sweetest Bundle. Oh, God, what shall I do? I've killed her. I've killed her.'

Reluctantly – very reluctantly – Bundle spoke.

'No, you haven't, you silly idiot,' she said.

Bill gave a gasp of utter amazement.

'Bundle – you're alive.'

'Of course I'm alive.'

'How long have you been – I mean when did you come to?'

'About five minutes ago.'

'Why didn't you open your eyes – or say something?'

'Didn't want to. I was enjoying myself.'

'Enjoying yourself?'

'Yes. Listening to all the things you were saying. You'll never say them so well again. You'll be too beastly self-conscious.'

Bill had turned a dark brick-red.

'Bundle – you really didn't mind? You know, I *do* love you so. I have for ages. But I never have dared to tell you so.'

'You silly juggins,' said Bundle. 'Why?'

'I thought you'd only laugh at me. I mean – you've got brains and all that – you'll marry some bigwig.'

'Like George Lomax?' suggested Bundle.

'I don't mean a fatuous ass like Codders. But some really fine chap who'll be worthy of you – though I don't think anyone could be that,' ended Bill.

'You're rather a dear, Bill.'

'But, Bundle, seriously, could you ever? I mean, could you ever bring yourself to?'

'Could I ever bring myself to do what?'

'Marry me. I know I'm awfully thick-headed – but I do love you, Bundle. I'd be your dog or your slave or your anything.'

'You're very like a dog,' said Bundle. 'I like dogs. They're so friendly and faithful and warm-hearted. I think that perhaps I could just bring myself to marry you, Bill – with a great effort, you know.'

Bill's response to this was to relinquish his grasp of her and recoil violently. He looked at her with amazement in his eyes.

'Bundle – you don't mean it?'

'There's nothing for it,' said Bundle. 'I see I shall have to relapse into unconsciousness again.'

'Bundle – darling –' Bill caught her to him. He was trembling violently. 'Bundle – do you really mean it – do you? – you don't know how much I love you.'

'Oh, Bill,' said Bundle.

There is no need to describe in detail the conversation of the next ten minutes. It consisted mostly of repetitions.

'And do you really love me?' said Bill, incredulously, for the twentieth time as he at last released her.

'Yes – yes – yes. Now do let's be sensible. I've got a racking head still, and I've been nearly squeezed to death by you. I want to get the hang of things. Where are we and what's happened?'

For the first time, Bundle began to take stock of her surroundings. They were in the secret room, she noted, and the baize door was closed and presumably locked. They were prisoners, then!

Bundle's eyes came back to Bill. Quite oblivious of her question he was watching her with adoring eyes.

'Bill, darling,' said Bundle, 'pull yourself together. We've got to get out of here.'

'Eh?' said Bill. 'What? Oh, yes. That'll be all right. No difficulty about that.'

'It's being in love makes you feel like that,' said Bundle. 'I feel rather the same myself. As though everything's easy and possible.'

'So it is,' said Bill. 'Now that I know you care for me –'

'Stop it,' said Bundle. 'Once we begin again any serious conversation will be hopeless. Unless you pull yourself together and become sensible, I shall very likely change my mind.'

'I shan't let you,' said Bill. 'You don't think that once having got you I'd be such a fool as to let you go, do you?'

'You would not coerce me against my will, I hope,' said Bundle grandiloquently.

'Wouldn't I?' said Bill. 'You just watch me do it, that's all.'

'You really are rather a darling, Bill. I was afraid you might be too meek, but I see there's going to be no danger of that. In another half-hour you'd be ordering me about. Oh, dear, we're getting silly again. Now, look here, Bill. We've got to get out of here.'

'I tell you that'll be quite all right. I shall –'

He broke off, obedient to a pressure from Bundle's hand. She was leaning forward, listening intently. Yes, she had not been mistaken. A step was crossing the outer room. The key was thrust into the lock and turned. Bundle held her breath. Was it Jimmy coming to rescue them – or was it someone else?

The door opened and the black-bearded Mr Mosgorovsky stood on the threshold.

Immediately Bill took a step forward, standing in front of Bundle.

'Look here,' he said, 'I want a word with you privately.'

The Russian did not reply for a minute or two. He stood

stroking his long, silky black beard and smiling quietly to himself.

'So,' he said at last, 'it is like that. Very well. The lady will be pleased to come with me.'

'It's all right, Bundle,' said Bill. 'Leave it to me. You go with this chap. Nobody's going to hurt you. I know what I'm doing.'

Bundle rose obediently. That note of authority in Bill's voice was new to her. He seemed absolutely sure of himself and confident of being able to deal with the situation. Bundle wondered vaguely what it was that Bill had – or thought he had – up his sleeve.

She passed out of the room in front of the Russian. He followed her, closing the door behind him and locking it.

'This way, please,' he said.

He indicated the staircase and she mounted obediently to the floor above. Here she was directed to pass into a small frowsy room, which she took to be Alfred's bedroom.

Mosgorovsky said: 'You will wait here quietly, please. There must be no noise.'

Then he went out, closing the door behind him and locking her in.

Bundle sat down on a chair. Her head was aching badly still and she felt incapable of sustained thought. Bill seemed to have the situation well in hand. Sooner or later, she supposed, someone would come and let her out.

The minutes passed. Bundle's watch had stopped, but she judged that over an hour had passed since the Russian had brought her here. What was happening? What, indeed, *had* happened?

At last she heard footsteps on the stairs. It was Mosgorovsky once more. He spoke very formally to her.

'Lady Eileen Brent, you are wanted at an emergency meeting of the Seven Dials Society. Please follow me.'

He led the way down the stairs and Bundle followed him. He opened the door of the secret chamber and Bundle passed in, catching her breath in surprise as she did so.

She was seeing for the second time what she had only had a

glimpse of the first time through her peep-hole. The masked figures were sitting round the table. As she stood there, taken aback by the suddenness of it, Mosgorovsky slipped into his place, adjusting his clock mask as he did so.

But this time the chair at the head of the table was occupied. No 7 was in his place.

Bundle's heart beat violently. She was standing at the foot of the table directly facing him and she stared and stared at the mocking piece of hanging stuff, with the clock dial on it, that hid his features.

He sat quite immovable and Bundle got an odd sensation of power radiating from him. His inactivity was not the inactivity of weakness – and she wished violently, almost hysterically, that he would speak – that he would make some sign, some gesture – not just sit there like a gigantic spider in the middle of its web waiting remorselessly for its prey.

She shivered and as she did so Mosgorovsky rose. His voice, smooth, silky, persuasive, seemed curiously far away.

'Lady Eileen, you have been present unasked at the secret councils of this society. It is therefore necessary that you should identify yourself with our aims and ambitions. The place 2 o'clock, you may notice, is vacant. It is that place that is offered to you.'

Bundle gasped. The thing was like a fantastic nightmare. Was it possible that she, Bundle Brent, was being asked to join a murderous secret society? Had the same proposition been made to Bill, and had he refused indignantly?

'I can't do that,' she said bluntly.

'Do not answer precipitately.'

She fancied that Mosgorovsky, beneath his clock mask, was smiling significantly into his beard.

'You do not as yet know, Lady Eileen, what it is you are refusing.'

'I can make a pretty good guess,' said Bundle.

'Can you?'

It was the voice of 7 o'clock. It awoke some vague chord of memory in Bundle's brain. Surely she knew that voice?

Very slowly No 7 raised a hand to his head and fumbled with the fastening of the mask.

Bundle held her breath. At last – she was going to *know*.

The mask fell.

Bundle found herself looking into the expressionless, wooden face of Superintendent Battle.

CHAPTER XXXII

Bundle is Dumbfounded

'That's right,' said Battle, as Mosgorovsky leapt up and came round to Bundle. 'Get a chair for her. It's been a bit of a shock, I can see.'

Bundle sank down on the chair. She felt limp and faint with surprise. Battle went on talking in a quiet, comfortable way wholly characteristic of him.

'You didn't expect to see me, Lady Eileen. No, and no more did some of the others sitting round the table. Mr Mosgorovsky's been my lieutenant in a manner of speaking. He's been in the know all along. But most of the others have taken their orders blindly from him.'

Still Bundle said no word. She was – a most unusual state of affairs for her – simply incapable of speech.

Battle nodded at her comprehendingly, seeming to understand the state of her feelings.

'You'll have to get rid of one or two preconceived ideas of yours, I'm afraid, Lady Eileen. About this society, for instance – I know it's common enough in books – a secret organization of criminals with a mysterious super-criminal at the head of it whom no one ever sees. That sort of thing may exist in real life, but I can only say that I've never come across anything of the sort, and I've had a good deal of experience one way or another.

'But there's a lot of romance in the world, Lady Eileen. People, especially young people, like reading about such things, and they like still better really *doing* them. I'm going to introduce you now to a very creditable band of amateurs that has done remarkably fine work for my Department, work that nobody else could have done. If they've chosen rather melodramatic trappings, well, why shouldn't they? They've been willing to face real danger – danger of the very worst kind – and they've done it for these reasons: love of danger for its own sake – which to my mind is a very healthy sign in these Safety First days – and an honest wish to serve their country.

'And now, Lady Eileen, I'm going to introduce you. First of all, there's Mr Mosgorovsky, whom you already know in a manner of speaking. As you're aware, he runs the club and he runs a host of other things too. He's our most valuable Secret Anti-Bolshevist Agent in England. No 5 is Count Andras of the Hungarian Embassy, a very near and dear friend of the late Gerald Wade. No 4 is Mr Hayward Phelps, an American journalist, whose British sympathies are very keen and whose aptitude for scenting "news" is remarkable. No 3 –'

He stopped, smiling, and Bundle stared dumbfounded into the sheepish, grinning face of Bill Eversleigh.

'No 2,' went on Battle in a graver voice, 'can only show an empty place. It is the place belonging to Mr Ronald Devereux, a very gallant young gentleman who died for his country if any man ever did. No 1 – well, No 1 was Mr Gerald Wade, another very gallant gentleman who died in the same way. His place was taken – not without some grave misgivings on my part – by a lady – a lady who has proved her fitness to have it and who has been a great help to us.'

The last to do so, No 1, removed her mask, and Bundle looked without surprise into the beautiful, dark face of Countess Radzky.

'I might have known,' said Bundle resentfully, 'that you were too completely the beautiful foreign adventuress to be anything of the kind really.'

'But you don't know the real joke,' said Bill. '*Bundle, this is Babe St Maur* – you remember my telling you about her and what a ripping actress she was – and she's about proved it.'

'That's so,' said Miss Maur in pure transatlantic nasal. 'But it's not a terrible lot of credit to me, because Poppa and Momma came from that part of Yurrup – so I got the patter fairly easy. Gee, but I nearly gave myself away once at the Abbey, talking about gardens.'

She paused and then said abruptly:

'It's – it's not been just fun. You see, I was kinder engaged to Ronny, and when he handed in his checks – well, I had to do something to track down the skunk who murdered him. That's all.'

'I'm completely bewildered,' said Bundle. 'Nothing is what it seems.'

'It's very simple, Lady Eileen,' said Superintendent Battle. 'It began with some of the young people wanting a bit of excitement. It was Mr Wade who first got on to me. He suggested the formation of a band of what you might call amateur workers to do a bit of secret service work. I warned him that it might be dangerous – but he wasn't the kind to weigh that in the balance. I made it plain to him that anyone who came in must do so on that understanding. But, bless you, that wasn't going to stop any of Mr Wade's friends. And so the thing began.'

'But what was the object of it all?' asked Bundle.

'We wanted a certain man – wanted him badly. He wasn't an ordinary crook. He worked in Mr Wade's world, a kind of Raffles, but much more dangerous than any Raffles ever was or could be. He was out for big stuff, international stuff. Twice already valuable secret inventions had been stolen, and clearly stolen by someone who had inside knowledge. The professionals had had a try – and failed. Then the amateurs took on – and succeeded.'

'Succeeded?'

'Yes – but they didn't come out of it unscathed. The man was dangerous. Two lives fell victim to him and he got away with it. But the Seven Dials stuck to it. And as I say they succeeded. Thanks to Mr Eversleigh, the man was caught at last red-handed.'

'Who was he?' asked Bundle. 'Do I know him?'

'You know him very well, Lady Eileen. His name is Mr Jimmy Thesiger, and he was arrested this afternoon.'

CHAPTER XXXIII

Battle Explains

Superintendent Battle settled down to explain. He spoke comfortably and cosily.

'I didn't suspect him myself for a long time. The first hint of it I had was when I heard what Mr Devereux's last words had been. Naturally, you took them to mean that Mr Devereux was trying to send word to Mr Thesiger that the Seven Dials had killed him. That's what the words seemed to mean on their face value. But of course I knew that that couldn't be so. It was the Seven Dials that Mr Devereux wanted told – and what he wanted them told was something about Mr Jimmy Thesiger.

'The thing seemed incredible, because Mr Devereux and Mr Thesiger were close friends. But I remembered something else – that these thefts must have been committed by someone who was absolutely in the know. Someone, who, if not in the Foreign Office himself, was in the way of hearing all its chitchat. And I found it very hard to find out where Mr Thesiger got his money. The income his father left him was a small one, yet he was able to live at a most expensive rate. Where did the money come from?

'I knew that Mr Wade had been very excited by something that he had found out. He was quite sure that he was on the right track. He didn't confide in anyone about what he thought that track was, but he did say something to Mr Devereux about being on the point of making sure. That was just before they both went down to Chimneys for that week-end. As you know, Mr Wade died there – apparently from an overdose of a sleeping draught. It seemed straightforward enough, but Mr Devereux did not accept that explanation for a minute. He was convinced that Mr Wade had been very cleverly put out of the way and that someone in the house must actually be the criminal we were all after. He came, I think, very near confiding in Mr Thesiger, for he certainly had no suspicions of him at that moment. But something held him back.

'Then he did a rather curious thing. He arranged seven clocks upon the mantelpiece, throwing away the eighth. It was meant as a symbol that the Seven Dials would revenge the death of one of their members – and he watched eagerly to see if anyone betrayed themselves or showed signs of perturbation.'

'And it was Jimmy Thesiger who poisoned Gerry Wade?'

'Yes, he slipped the stuff into a whisky and soda which Mr Wade had downstairs before retiring to bed. That's why he was already feeling sleepy when he wrote that letter to Miss Wade.'

'Then the footman, Bauer, hadn't anything to do with it?' asked Bundle.

'Bauer was one of our people, Lady Eileen. It was thought likely that our crook would go for Herr Eberhard's invention and Bauer was got into the house to watch events on our behalf. But he wasn't able to do much. As I say, Mr Thesiger administered the fatal dose easily enough. Later, when everyone was asleep, a bottle, glass and empty chloral bottle were placed by Mr Wade's bedside by Mr Thesiger. Mr Wade was unconscious then, and his fingers were probably pressed round the glass and the bottle so that they should be found there if any questions should arise. I don't know what effect the seven clocks on the mantelpiece made on Mr Thesiger. He certainly didn't let on anything to Mr Devereux. All the same, I think he had a bad five minutes now and again thinking of them. And I think he kept a pretty wary eye on Mr Devereux after that.

'We don't know exactly what happened next. No one saw much of Mr Devereux after Mr Wade's death. But it is clear that he worked along the same lines that he knew Mr Wade had been working on and reached the same result – namely, that Mr Thesiger was the man. I fancy, too, that he was betrayed in the same way.'

'You mean?'

'Through Miss Loraine Wade. Mr Wade was devoted to her

– I believe he hoped to marry her – she wasn't really his sister, of course – and there is no doubt that he told her more than he should have done. But Miss Loraine Wade was devoted body and soul to Mr Thesiger. She would do anything he told her. She passed on the information to him. In the same way, later, Mr Devereux was attracted to her, and probably warned her against Mr Thesiger. So Mr Devereux in turn was silenced – and died trying to send word to the Seven Dials that his murderer was Mr Thesiger.'

'How ghastly,' cried Bundle. 'If I had only known.'

'Well, it didn't seem likely. In fact, I could hardly credit it myself. But then we came to the affair at the Abbey. You will remember how awkward it was – specially awkward for Mr Eversleigh here. You and Mr Thesiger were hand in glove. Mr Eversleigh had already been embarrassed by your insisting on being brought to this place, and when he found that you had actually overheard what went on at a meeting, he was dumbfounded.'

The Superintendent paused and a twinkle came into his eye.

'So was I, Lady Eileen. I never dreamed of such a thing being possible. You put one over on me there all right.

'Well, Mr Eversleigh was in a dilemma. He couldn't let you into the secret of the Seven Dials without letting Mr Thesiger in also – and that would never do. It all suited Mr Thesiger very well, of course, for it gave him a bona fide reason for getting himself asked to the Abbey, which made things easier for him.

'I may say that the Seven Dials had already sent a warning letter to Mr Lomax. That was to ensure his applying to me for assistance, so that I should be able to be on the spot in a perfectly natural manner. I made no secret of my presence, as you know.'

And again the Superintendent's eye twinkled.

'Well, ostensibly, Mr Eversleigh and Mr Thesiger were to divide the night into two watches. Really, Mr Eversleigh and Miss St Maur did so. She was on guard at the library window when she heard Mr Thesiger coming and had to dart behind the screen.

'And now comes the cleverness of Mr Thesiger. Up to a point he told me a perfectly true story, and I must admit that with the fight and everything, I was distinctly shaken – and began to wonder whether he had had anything to do with the theft at all, or whether we were completely on the wrong track. There were one or two suspicious circumstances that pointed in an entirely different direction, and I can tell you I didn't know what to make of things, when something turned up to clinch matters.

'I found the burnt glove in the fireplace with the teeth marks on it – and then – well – I knew that I'd been right after all. But, upon my word, he was a clever one.'

'What actually happened?' said Bundle. 'Who was the other man?'

'There wasn't any other man. Listen, and I'll show you how in the end I reconstructed the whole story. To begin with, Mr Thesiger and Miss Wade were in this together. And they have a rendezvous for an exact time. Miss Wade comes over in her car, climbs through the fence and comes up to the house. She's got a perfectly good story if anyone stops her – the one she told eventually. But she arrived unmolested on the terrace just after the clock had struck two.

'Now, I may say to begin with that she was seen coming in. My men saw her, but they had orders to stop nobody coming in – only going out. I wanted, you see, to find out as much as possible. Miss Wade arrives on the terrace, and at that minute a parcel falls at her feet and she picks it up. A man comes down the ivy and she starts to run. What happens next? The struggle – and presently the revolver shots. What will everyone do? Rush to the scene of the fight. And Miss Loraine Wade could have left the grounds and driven off with the formula safely in her possession.

'But things don't happen quite like that. Miss Wade runs straight into my arms. And at that moment the game changes. It's no longer attack but defence. Miss Wade tells her story. It is perfectly true and perfectly sensible.

'And now we come to Mr Thesiger. One thing struck me at

once. The bullet wound alone couldn't have caused him to faint. Either he had fallen and hit his head – or – well he hadn't fainted at all. Later we had Miss St Maur's story. It agreed perfectly with Mr Thesiger's – there was only one suggestive point. Miss St Maur said that after the lights were turned out and Mr Thesiger went over to the window, he was so still that she thought he must have left the room and gone outside. Now, if anyone is in the room, you can hardly help hearing their breathing if you are listening for it. Supposing, then, that Mr Thesiger *had* gone outside. Where next? Up the ivy to Mr O'Rourke's room – Mr O'Rourke's whisky and soda having been doped the night before. He gets the papers, throws them down to the girl, climbs down the ivy again, and – starts the fight. That's easy enough when you come to think of it. Knock the tables down, stagger about, speak in your own voice and then in a hoarse half-whisper. And then, the final touch, the two revolver shots. His own Colt automatic, bought openly the day before, is fired at an imaginary assailant. Then, with his left gloved hand, he takes from his pocket the small Mauser pistol and shoots himself through the fleshy part of the right arm. He flings the pistol through the window, tears off the glove with his teeth, and throws it into the fire. When I arrive he is lying on the floor in a faint.'

Bundle drew a deep breath.

'You didn't realize all this at the time, Superintendent Battle?'

'No, that I didn't. I was taken in as much as anyone could be. It wasn't till long afterwards that I pieced it all together. Finding the glove was the beginning of it. Then I made Sir Oswald throw the pistol through the window. It fell a good way farther on than it should have done. But a man who is right-handed doesn't throw nearly as far with the left hand. Even then it was only suspicion – and a very faint suspicion at that.

'But there was one point struck me. The papers were obviously thrown down for someone to pick up. If Miss Wade was there by accident, who was the real person? Of course, for those who weren't in the know, that question was answered easily enough – the Countess. But there I had the pull over you. *I knew the Countess was all right.* So what follows? Why, the idea that the papers had actually been picked up by the person they were meant for. And the more I thought of it, the more it seemed to me a very remarkable coincidence that Miss Wade should have arrived at the exact moment she did.'

'It must have been very difficult for you when I came to you full of suspicion about the Countess.'

'It was, Lady Eileen. I had to say something to put you off the scent. And it was very difficult for Mr Eversleigh here, with the lady coming out of a dead faint and no knowing what she might say.'

'I understand Bill's anxiety now,' said Bundle. 'And the way he kept urging her to take time and not talk till she felt quite all right.'

'Poor old Bill,' said Miss St Maur. 'That poor baby had to be vamped against his will – getting madder'n a hornet every minute.'

'Well,' said Superintendent Battle, 'there it was. I suspected Mr Thesiger – but I couldn't get definite proof. On the other hand, Mr Thesiger himself was rattled. He realized more or less what he was up against in the Seven Dials – but he wanted badly to know who No 7 was. He got himself asked to the Cootes under the impression that Sir Oswald Coote was No 7.'

'I suspected Sir Oswald,' said Bundle, 'especially when he came in from the garden that night.'

'I never suspected him,' said Battle. 'But I don't mind telling you that I *did* have my suspicions of that young chap, his secretary.'

'Pongo?' said Bill. 'Not old Pongo?'

'Yes, Mr Eversleigh, old Pongo as you call him. A very efficient gentleman and one that could have put anything through if he'd a mind to. I suspected him partly because he'd been the one to take the clocks into Mr Wade's room that night. It would have been easy for him to put the bottle and glass by the bedside then. And then, for another thing, he was left-handed. That glove pointed straight to him – if it hadn't been for one thing –'

'What?'

'The teeth marks – only a man whose right hand was incapacitated would have needed to tear off that glove with his teeth.'

'So Pongo was cleared.'

'So Pongo was cleared, as you say. I'm sure it would be a great surprise to Mr Bateman to know he was ever suspected.'

'It would,' agreed Bill. 'A solemn card – a silly ass like Pongo. How could you ever think –'

'Well, as far as that goes, Mr Thesiger was what you might describe as an empty-headed young ass of the most brainless description. One of the two was playing a part. When I decided that it was Mr Thesiger, I was interested to get Mr Bateman's opinion of him. All along, Mr Bateman had the gravest suspicions of Mr Thesiger and frequently said as much to Sir Oswald.'

'It's curious,' said Bill, 'but Pongo always is right. It's maddening.'

'Well, as I say,' went on Superintendent Battle, 'we got Mr Thesiger fairly on the run, badly rattled over this Seven Dials business and uncertain just where the danger lay. That we got him in the end was solely through Mr Eversleigh. He knew what he was up against, and he risked his life cheerfully. But he never dreamt that you would be dragged into it, Lady Eileen.'

'My God, no,' said Bill with feeling.

'He went round to Mr Thesiger's rooms with a cooked-up tale,' continued Battle. 'He was to pretend that certain papers of Mr Devereux's had come into his hands. Those papers were to suggest a suspicion of Mr Thesiger. Naturally, as the honest friend, Mr Eversleigh rushed round, sure that Mr Thesiger would have an explanation. We calculated that if we were right, Mr Thesiger would try and put Mr Eversleigh out of the way, and we were fairly certain as to the way he'd do it. Sure enough, Mr Thesiger gave his guest a whisky and soda. During the minute or two that his host was out of the room. Mr Eversleigh poured that into a jar on the mantelpiece, but he had to pretend, of course, that the drug was taking effect. It would be slow, he knew, not sudden. He began his story, and Mr Thesiger at first denied it all indignantly, but as soon as he saw (or thought he saw) that the drug was taking effect, he admitted everything and told Mr Eversleigh that he was the third victim.

'When Mr Eversleigh was nearly unconscious, Mr Thesiger took him down to the car and helped him in. The hood was up. He must already have telephoned to you unknown to Mr Eversleigh. He made a clever suggestion to you. You were to say that you were taking Miss Wade home.

'You made no mention of a message from him. Later when your body was found here, Miss Wade would swear that you had driven her home and gone up to London with the idea of penetrating into this house by yourself.

'Mr Eversleigh continued to play his part, that of the unconscious man. I may say that as soon as the two young men had left Jermyn Street, one of my men gained admission and found the doctored whisky, which contained enough hydrochloride of morphia to kill two men. Also the car they were in was followed. Mr Thesiger drove out of town to a well-known golf course, where he showed himself for a few minutes, speaking of playing a round. That, of course, was for an alibi, should one be needed. He left the car with Mr Eversleigh in it a little way down the road. Then he drove back to town and to the Seven Dials Club. As soon as he saw Alfred leave, he drove up to the door, spoke to Mr Eversleigh as he got out in case you might be listening and came into the house and played his little comedy.

'When he pretended to go for a doctor, he really only slammed the door and then crept quietly upstairs and hid behind the door of this room, where Miss Wade would presently send you up on some excuse. Mr Eversleigh, of course, was horror-struck when he saw you, but he thought it best to keep up the part he was playing. He knew our people were watching the house, and he imagined that there was no immediate danger intended to you. He could always "come to life" at any moment. When Mr Thesiger threw his revolver on the table and apparently left the house it seemed safer than ever. As for the next bit –' He paused, looking at Bill. 'Perhaps you'd like to tell that, sir.'

'I was still lying on that bally sofa,' said Bill, 'trying to look done in and getting the fidgets worse and worse. Then I heard someone run down the stairs, and Loraine got up and went to the door. I heard Thesiger's voice, but not what he said. I heard Loraine say: "That's all right – it's gone splendidly." Then he said: "Help me carry him up. It will be a bit of a job, but I want them both together there – a nice little surprise for No 7." I didn't quite understand what they were jawing about, but they hauled me up the stairs somehow or other. It *was* a bit of a job for them. I made myself a dead weight all right. They heaved me in here, and then I heard Loraine say: "You're sure it's all right? She won't come round?" And Jimmy said – the damned blackguard: "No fear. I hit her with all my might.'

'They went away and locked the door, and then I opened my eyes and saw you. My God, Bundle, I shall never feel so perfectly awful again. I thought you were dead."

'I suppose my hat saved me,' said Bundle.

'Partly,' said Superintendent Battle. 'But partly it was Mr Thesiger's wounded arm. He didn't realize it himself – but it had only half its usual strength. Still, that's all no credit to the Department. We didn't take the care of you we ought to have done, Lady Eileen – and it's a black blot on the whole business.'

'I'm very tough,' said Bundle. 'And also rather lucky. What I can't get over is Loraine being in it. She was such a gentle little thing.'

'Ah!' said the Superintendent. 'So was the Pentonville murderess that killed five children. You can't go by that. She's got bad blood in her – her father ought to have seen the inside of a prison more than once.'

'You've got her too?'

Superintendent Battle nodded.

'I daresay they won't hang her – juries are soft-hearted. But young Thesiger will swing all right – and a good thing too – a more utterly depraved and callous criminal I never met.'

'And now,' he added, 'if your head isn't aching too badly, Lady Eileen, what about a little celebration? There's a nice little restaurant round the corner.'

Bundle heartily agreed.

'I'm starving, Superintendent Battle. Besides,' she looked round, 'I've got to get to know all my colleagues.'

'The Seven Dials,' said Bill. 'Hurrah! Some fizz is what we need. Do they run to fizz at this place, Battle?'

'You won't have anything to complain of, sir. You leave it to me.'

'Superintendent Battle,' said Bundle, 'you are a wonderful man. I'm sorry you're married already. As it is, I shall have to put up with Bill.'

CHAPTER XXXIV

Lord Caterham Approves

'Father,' said Bundle, 'I've got to break a piece of news to you. You're going to lose me.'

'Nonsense,' said Lord Caterham. 'Don't tell me that you're suffering from galloping consumption or a weak heart or anything like that, because I simply don't believe it.'

'It's not death,' said Bundle. 'It's marriage.'

'Very nearly as bad,' said Lord Caterham. 'I suppose I shall have to come to the wedding, all dressed up in tight uncomfortable clothes, and give you away. And Lomax may think it necessary to kiss me in the vestry.'

'Good heavens! You don't think I'm going to marry George, do you?' cried Bundle.

'Well, something like that seemed to be in the wind last time I saw you,' said her father. 'Yesterday morning, you know.'

'I'm going to be married to someone a hundred times nicer than George,' said Bundle.

'I hope so, I'm sure,' said Lord Caterham. 'But one never knows. I don't feel you're really a good judge of character, Bundle. You told me that young Thesiger was a cheerful inefficient, and from all I hear now it seems that he was one of the most efficient criminals of the day. The sad thing is that I never met him. I was thinking of writing my reminiscences soon – with a special chapter on murderers I have met – and by a purely technical oversight, I never met this young man.'

'Don't be silly,' said Bundle. 'You know you haven't got the energy to write reminiscences or anything else.'

'I wasn't actually going to write them myself,' said Lord Caterham. 'I believe that's never done. But I met a very charming girl the other day and that's her special job. She collects the material and does all the actual writing.'

'And what do you do?'

'Oh, just give her a few facts for half an hour every day. Nothing more than that.' After a slight pause, Lord Caterham said: 'She was a nice-looking girl – very restful and sympathetic.'

'Father,' said Bundle, 'I have a feeling that without me you will run into deadly danger.'

'Different kinds of danger suit different kinds of people,' said Lord Caterham.

He was moving away, when he turned back and said over his shoulder:

'By the way, Bundle, who *are* you marrying?'

'I was wondering,' said Bundle, 'when you were going to ask me that. I'm going to marry Bill Eversleigh.'

The egoist thought it over for a minute. Then he nodded in complete satisfaction.

'Excellent,' he said. 'He's scratch, isn't he? He and I can play together in the foursomes in the Autumn Meeting.'

Postscript

Agatha Christie rediscovered her penchant for writing with The Seven Dials Mystery. *The subject, a lively thriller, constituted a kind of sequel to* The Secret of Chimneys. *In her autobiography, the author admits that it was easier for her to write this kind of book instead of her mystery novels, which called for a precise structure. In rediscovering the energetic Eileen Bundle Brent, Agatha Christie regained her self-esteem and her confidence in what she was writing.*

Janet Morgan mentions in Agatha Christie: A Biography, *that the first notes for* The Seven Dials Mystery *were taken in a little black notebook Archie had left behind: 'She was not at first sure of the title (*The Secret Six *was an alternative) nor of the plot, for her initial try begins: "Bundle and her father. She drives up to London – runs over a man – or rather swerves to avoid him – but finds she has killed him – not quite dead." A page later, however, her notes settle into the story as it eventually appeared. "Country house party – at Chequers? – One man can't get up in the morning. Everyone gets up a joke – They buy alarum clocks – and hide them around his room. In the morning man does not appear. He is dead. One clock has disappeared. 7 left . . ."'*

With such an intriguing starting point, the author could easily develop her novel along the lines of a mystery, specifically: 'Who killed him? Why? And why has one of the alarum clocks disappeared?' But very quickly, from chapter 5, she has opted for the thriller. Using the first page of the little black book as a foundation, she has chosen to take an interest in the schemes of a mysterious secret society, the Seven Dials, whose leader is only known to his accomplices by the name 'Number 7'. A secret society – a common device, but one that often pays off in detective adventures – not forgetting the one led by Mr Brown in The Secret Adversary.

The Seven Dials Mystery *reintroduces several characters from* The

Secret of Chimneys: *Superintendent Battle of Scotland Yard, Colonel Melrose, the young Bill Eversleigh of the Foreign Office, the honourable George Lomax, Lord Caterham, and of course his daughter Lady Eileen (who epitomises Christie's young heroines in love with adventure, like Tuppence Beresford and Anne Beddingfeld). As for Agatha Christie's execution, critics have noted the influence of P. G. Wodehouse, and it is true that the distancing in the description of her characters and their relationships is very characteristic of this type of humour. The very last chapter is a particularly good example for the reader to savour.*

PARTNERS IN CRIME

CONTENTS

CHAPTER I

A Fairy in the Flat

Mrs Thomas Beresford shifted her position on the divan and looked gloomily out of the window of the flat. The prospect was not an extended one, consisting solely of a small block of flats on the other side of the road. Mrs Beresford sighed and then yawned.

'I wish,' she said, 'something would happen.'

Her husband looked up reprovingly.

'Be careful, Tuppence, this craving for vulgar sensation alarms me.'

Tuppence sighed and closed her eyes dreamily.

'So Tommy and Tuppence were married,' she chanted, 'and lived happily ever afterwards. And six years later they were still living together happily ever afterwards. It is extraordinary,' she said, 'how different everything always is from what you think it is going to be.'

'A very profound statement, Tuppence. But not original. Eminent poets and still more eminent divines have said it before – and if you will excuse me saying so, have said it better.'

'Six years ago,' continued Tuppence, 'I would have sworn that with sufficient money to buy things with, and with you for a husband, all life would have been one grand sweet song, as one of the poets you seem to know so much about puts it.'

'Is it me or the money that palls upon you?' inquired Tommy coldly.

'Palls isn't exactly the word,' said Tuppence kindly. 'I'm used to my blessings, that's all. Just as one never thinks what a boon it is to be able to breathe through one's nose until one has a cold in the head.'

'Shall I neglect you a little?' suggested Tommy. 'Take other women about to night clubs. That sort of thing.'

'Useless,' said Tuppence. 'You would only meet me there with other men. And I should know perfectly well that you didn't care for the other women, whereas you would never be quite sure that I didn't care for the other men. Women are so much more thorough.'

'It's only in modesty that men score top marks,' murmured her husband. 'But what is the matter with you, Tuppence? Why this yearning discontent?'

'I don't know. I want things to happen. Exciting things. Wouldn't you like to go chasing German spies again, Tommy? Think of the wild days of peril we went through once. Of course I know you're more or less in the Secret Service now, but it's pure office work.'

'You mean you'd like them to send me into darkest Russia disguised as a Bolshevik bootlegger, or something of that sort?'

'That wouldn't be any good,' said Tuppence. 'They wouldn't let me go with you and I'm the person who wants something to do so badly. Something to do. That is what I keep saying all day long.'

'Women's sphere,' suggested Tommy, waving his hand.

'Twenty minutes' work after breakfast every morning keeps the flag going to perfection. You have nothing to complain of, have you?'

'Your housekeeping is so perfect, Tuppence, as to be almost monotonous.'

'I do like gratitude,' said Tuppence.

'You, of course, have got your work,' she continued, 'but tell me, Tommy, don't you ever have a secret yearning for excitement, for things to *happen*?'

'No,' said Tommy, 'at least I don't think so. It is all very well to want things to happen – they might not be pleasant things.'

'How prudent men are,' sighed Tuppence. 'Don't you ever have a wild secret yearning for romance – adventure – life?'

'What *have* you been reading, Tuppence?' asked Tommy.

'Think how exciting it would be,' went on Tuppence, 'if we

heard a wild rapping at the door and went to open it and in staggered a dead man.'

'If he was dead he couldn't stagger,' said Tommy critically.

'You know what I mean,' said Tuppence. 'They always stagger in just before they die and fall at your feet, just gasping out a few enigmatic words. "The Spotted Leopard", or something like that.'

'I advise a course of Schopenhauer or Emmanuel Kant,' said Tommy.

'That sort of thing would be good for you,' said Tuppence. 'You are getting fat and comfortable.'

'I am not,' said Tommy indignantly. 'Anyway you do slimming exercises yourself.'

'Everybody does,' said Tuppence. 'When I said you were getting fat I was really speaking metaphorically, you are getting prosperous and sleek and comfortable.'

'I don't know what has come over you,' said her husband.

'The spirit of adventure,' murmured. Tuppence. 'It is better than a longing for romance anyway. I have that sometimes too. I think of meeting a man, a really handsome man – '

'You have met me,' said Tommy. 'Isn't that enough for you?'

'A brown, lean man, terrifically strong, the kind of man who can ride anything and lassoes wild horses – '

'Complete with sheepskin trousers and a cowboy hat,' interpolated Tommy sarcastically.

' – and has lived in the Wilds,' continued Tuppence. 'I should like him to fall simply madly in love with me. I should, of course, rebuff him virtuously and be true to my marriage vows, but my heart would secretly go out to him.'

'Well,' said Tommy, 'I often wish that I may meet a really beautiful girl. A girl with corn coloured hair who will fall desperately in love with me. Only I don't think I rebuff her – in fact I am quite sure I don't.'

'That,' said Tuppence, 'is naughty temper.'

'What,' said Tommy, 'is really the matter with you, Tuppence? You have never talked like this before.'

'No, but I have been boiling up inside for a long time,' said

Tuppence. 'You see it is very dangerous to have everything you want – including enough money to buy things. Of course there are always hats.'

'You have got about forty hats already,' said Tommy, 'and they all look alike.'

'Hats are like that,' said Tuppence. 'They are not really alike. There are *nuances* in them. I saw rather a nice one in Violette's this morning.'

'If you haven't anything better to do than going on buying hats you don't need –'

'That's it,' said Tuppence, 'that's exactly it. If I had something better to do. I suppose I ought to take up good works. Oh, Tommy, I do wish something exciting would happen. I feel – I really do feel it would be good for us. If we could find a fairy –'

'Ah!' said Tommy. 'It is curious your saying that.'

He got up and crossed the room. Opening a drawer of the writing table he took out a small snapshot print and brought it to Tuppence.

'Oh!' said Tuppence, 'so you have got them developed. Which is this, the one you took of this room or the one I took?'

'The one I took. Yours didn't come out. You under exposed it. You always do.'

'It is nice for you,' said Tuppence, 'to think that there is one thing you can do better than me.'

'A foolish remark,' said Tommy, 'but I will let it pass for the moment. What I wanted to show you was this.'

He pointed to a small white speck on the photograph.

'That is a scratch on the film,' said Tuppence.

'Not at all,' said Tommy. 'That, Tuppence, is a fairy.'

'Tommy, you idiot.'

'Look for yourself.'

He handed her a magnifying glass. Tuppence studied the print attentively through it. Seen thus by a slight stretch of fancy the scratch on the film could be imagined to represent a small winged creature on the fender.

'It has got wings,' cried Tuppence. 'What fun, a real live fairy in our flat. Shall we write to Conan Doyle about it? Oh, Tommy. Do you think she'll give us wishes?'

'You will soon know,' said Tommy. 'You have been wishing hard enough for something to happen all the afternoon.'

At that minute the door opened, and a tall lad of fifteen who seemed undecided as to whether he was a butler or a page boy inquired in a truly magnificent manner:

'Are you at home, madam? The front-door bell has just rung.'

'I wish Albert wouldn't go to the Pictures,' sighed Tuppence, after she had signified her assent, and Albert had withdrawn. 'He's copying a Long Island butler now. Thank goodness I've cured him of asking for people's cards and bringing them to me on a salver.'

The door opened again, and Albert announced: 'Mr Carter,' much as though it were a Royal title.

'The Chief,' muttered Tommy, in great surprise.

Tuppence jumped up with a glad exclamation, and greeted a tall grey-haired man with piercing eyes and a tired smile.

'Mr Carter, I *am* glad to see you.'

'That's good, Mrs Tommy. Now answer me a question. How's life generally?'

'Satisfactory, but dull,' replied Tuppence with a twinkle.

'Better and better,' said Mr Carter. 'I'm evidently going to find you in the right mood.'

'This,' said Tuppence, 'sounds exciting.'

Albert, still copying the Long Island butler, brought in tea. When this operation was completed without mishap and the door had closed behind him Tuppence burst out once more.

'You did mean something, didn't you, Mr Carter? Are you going to send us on a mission into darkest Russia?'

'Not exactly that,' said Mr Carter.

'But there is something.'

'Yes – there is something. I don't think you are the kind who shrinks from risks, are you, Mrs Tommy?'

Tuppence's eyes sparkled with excitement.

'There is certain work to be done for the Department – and I fancied – I just fancied – that it might suit you two.'

'Go on,' said Tuppence.

'I see that you take the *Daily Leader*,' continued Mr Carter, picking up that journal from the table.

He turned to the advertisement column and indicating a certain advertisement with his finger pushed the paper across to Tommy.

'Read that out,' he said.

Tommy complied.

'The International Detective Agency, Theodore Blunt, Manager. Private Inquiries. Large staff of confidential and highly skilled Inquiry Agents. Utmost discretion. Consultations free. 118 Haleham St, W.C.'

He looked inquiringly at Mr Carter. The latter nodded. 'That detective agency has been on its last legs for some time,' he murmured. 'Friend of mine acquired it for a mere song. We're thinking of setting it going again – say, for a six months' trial. And during that time, of course, it will have to have a manager.'

'What about Mr Theodore Blunt?' asked Tommy.

'Mr Blunt has been rather indiscreet, I'm afraid. In fact, Scotland Yard have had to interfere. Mr Blunt is being detained at Her Majesty's expense, and he won't tell us half of what we'd like to know.'

'I see, sir,' said Tommy. 'At least, I think I see.'

'I suggest that you have six months, leave from the office. Ill health. And, of course, if you like to run a Detective Agency under the name of Theodore Blunt, it's nothing to do with me.'

Tommy eyed his Chief steadily.

'Any instructions, sir?'

'Mr Blunt did some foreign business, I believe. Look out for blue letters with a Russian stamp on them. From a ham merchant anxious to find his wife who came as a refugee to this country some years ago. Moisten the stamp and you'll find the number 16 written underneath. Make a copy of these letters and send the originals on to me. Also if any one comes to the office and makes a reference to the number 16, inform me immediately.'

'I understand, sir,' said Tommy. 'And apart from these instructions?'

Mr Carter picked up his gloves from the table and prepared to depart.

'You can run the Agency as you please. I fancied' – his eyes twinkled a little – 'that it might amuse Mrs Tommy to try her hand at a little detective work.'

CHAPTER II

A Pot of Tea

Mr and Mrs Beresford took possession of the offices of the International Detective Agency a few days later. They were on the second floor of a somewhat dilapidated building in Bloomsbury. In the small outer office, Albert relinquished the role of a Long Island butler, and took up that of office boy, a part which he played to perfection. A paper bag of sweets, inky hands, and a tousled head was his conception of the character.

From the outer office, two doors led into inner offices. On one door was painted the legend 'Clerks'. On the other 'Private'. Behind the latter was a small comfortable room furnished with an immense business-like desk, a lot of artistically labelled files, all empty, and some solid leather-seated chairs. Behind the desk sat the pseudo Mr Blunt trying to look as though he had run a Detective Agency all his life. A telephone, of course, stood at his elbow. Tuppence and he had rehearsed several good telephone effects, and Albert also had his instructions.

In the adjoining room was Tuppence, a typewriter, the necessary tables and chairs of an inferior type to those in the room of the great Chief, and a gas ring for making tea.

Nothing was wanting, in fact, save clients.

Tuppence, in the first ecstasies of initiation, had a few bright hopes.

'It will be too marvellous,' she declared. 'We will hunt down murderers, and discover the missing family jewels, and find people who've disappeared and detect embezzlers.'

At this point Tommy felt it his duty to strike a more discouraging note.

'Calm yourself, Tuppence, and try to forget the cheap fiction you are in the habit of reading. Our clientèle, if we have any clientèle at all – will consist solely of husbands who want their wives shadowed, and wives who want their husbands shadowed. Evidence for divorce is the sole prop of private inquiry agents.'

'Ugh!' said Tuppence, wrinkling a fastidious nose. 'We shan't touch divorce cases. We must raise the tone of our new profession.'

'Ye-es,' said Tommy doubtfully.

And now a week after installation they compared notes rather ruefully.

'Three idiotic women whose husbands go away for weekends,' sighed Tommy. 'Anyone come whilst I was out at lunch?'

'A fat old man with a flighty wife,' sighed Tuppence sadly. 'I've read in the papers for years that the divorce evil was growing, but somehow I never seemed to realize it until this last week. I'm sick and tired of saying, "We don't undertake divorce cases." '

'We've put it in the advertisements now,' Tommy reminded her. 'So it won't be so bad.'

'I'm sure we advertise in the most tempting way too,' said Tuppence in a melancholy voice. 'All the same, I'm not going to be beaten. If necessary, I shall commit a crime myself, and you will detect it.'

'And what good would that do? Think of my feelings when I bid you a tender farewell at Bow Street – or is it Vine Street?'

'You are thinking of your bachelor days,' said Tuppence pointedly.

'The Old Bailey, that is what I mean,' said Tommy.

'Well,' said Tuppence, 'something has got to be done about it. Here we are bursting with talent and no chance of exercising it.'

'I always like your cheery optimism, Tuppence. You seem to have no doubt whatever that you have talent to exercise.'

'Of course,' said Tuppence, opening her eyes very wide.

'And yet you have no expert knowledge whatever.'

'Well, I have read every detective novel that has been published in the last ten years.'

'So have I,' said Tommy, 'but I have a sort of feeling that that wouldn't really help us much.'

'You always were a pessimist, Tommy. Belief in oneself – that is the great thing.'

'Well, you have got it all right,' said her husband.

'Of course it is easy in detective stories,' said Tuppence thoughtfully, 'because one works backwards. I mean if one knows the solution one can arrange the clues. I wonder now –'

She paused wrinkling her brows.

'Yes?' said Tommy inquiringly.

'I have got a sort of idea,' said Tuppence. 'It hasn't quite come yet, but it's coming.' She rose resolutely. 'I think I shall go and buy that hat I told you about.'

'Oh, God!' said Tommy, 'another hat!'

'It's a very nice one,' said Tuppence with dignity.

She went out with a resolute look on her face.

Once or twice in the following days Tommy inquired curiously about the idea. Tuppence merely shook her head and told him to give her time.

And then, one glorious morning, the first client arrived, and all else was forgotten.

There was a knock on the outer door of the office and Albert, who had just placed an acid drop between his lips, roared out an indistinct 'Come in.' He then swallowed the acid drop whole in his surprise and delight. For this looked like the Real Thing.

A tall young man, exquisitely and beautifully dressed, stood hesitating in the doorway.

'A toff, if ever there was one,' said Albert to himself. His judgement in such matters was good.

The young man was about twenty-four years of age, had beautifully slicked back hair, a tendency to pink rims round the eyes, and practically no chin to speak of.

In an ecstasy, Albert pressed a button under his desk and almost immediately a perfect fusillade of typing broke out from the direction of 'Clerks'. Tuppence had rushed to the post of duty. The effect of this hum of industry was to overawe the young man still further.

'I say,' he remarked. 'Is this the whatnot – detective agency

– Blunt's Brilliant Detectives? All that sort of stuff, you know? Eh?'

'Did you want, sir, to speak to Mr Blunt himself?' inquired Albert, with an air of doubts as to whether such a thing could be managed.

'Well – yes, laddie, that was the jolly old idea. Can it be done?'

'You haven't an appointment, I suppose?'

The visitor became more and more apologetic.

'Afraid I haven't.'

'It's always wise, sir, to ring up on the phone first. Mr Blunt is so terribly busy. He's engaged on the telephone at the moment. Called into consultation by Scotland Yard.'

The young man seemed suitably impressed.

Albert lowered his voice, and imparted information in a friendly fashion.

'Important theft of documents from a Government Office. They want Mr Blunt to take up the case.'

'Oh! really. I say. He must be no end of a fellow.'

'The Boss, sir,' said Albert, 'is It.'

The young man sat down on a hard chair, completely unconscious of the fact that he was being subjected to keen scrutiny by two pairs of eyes looking through cunningly contrived peepholes – those of Tuppence, in the intervals of frenzied typing, and those of Tommy awaiting the suitable moment.

Presently a bell rang with violence on Albert's desk.

'The Boss is free now. I will find out whether he can see you,' said Albert, and disappeared through the door marked 'Private'.

He reappeared immediately.

'Will you come this way, sir?'

The visitor was ushered into the private office, and a pleasant faced young man with red hair and an air of brisk capability rose to greet him.

'Sit down. You wish to consult me? I am Mr Blunt.'

'Oh! Really. I say, you're awfully young, aren't you?'

'The day of the Old Men is over,' said Tommy, waving his hand. 'Who caused the war? The Old Men. Who is responsible for the present state of unemployment? The Old Men. Who is responsible for every single rotten thing that has happened? Again I say, the Old Men!'

'I expect you are right,' said the client, 'I know a fellow who is a poet – at least he says he is a poet – and he always talks like that.'

'Let me tell you this, sir, not a person on my highly trained staff is a day over twenty-five. That is the truth.'

Since the highly trained staff consisted of Tuppence and Albert, the statement was truth itself.

'And now – the facts,' said Mr Blunt.

'I want you to find someone that's missing,' blurted out the young man.

'Quite so. Will you give me the details?'

'Well, you see, it's rather difficult. I mean, it's a frightfully delicate business and all that. She might be frightfully waxy about it. I mean – well, it's so dashed difficult to explain.'

He looked helplessly at Tommy. Tommy felt annoyed. He had been on the point of going out to lunch, but he foresaw that getting the facts out of this client would be a long and tedious business.

'Did she disappear of her own free will, or do you suspect abduction?' he demanded crisply.

'I don't know,' said the young man. 'I don't know anything.'

Tommy reached for a pad and pencil.

'First of all,' he said, 'will you give me your name? My office boy is trained never to ask names. In that way consultations can remain completely confidential.'

'Oh! rather,' said the young man. 'Jolly good idea. My name – er – my name's Smith.'

'Oh! no,' said Tommy. 'The real one, please.'

His visitor looked at him in awe.

'Er – St Vincent,' he said. 'Lawrence St Vincent.'

'It's a curious thing,' said Tommy, 'how very few people there are whose real name is Smith. Personally, I don't know anyone called Smith. But nine men out of ten who wish to conceal their real name give that of Smith. I am writing a monograph upon the subject.'

At that moment a buzzer purred discreetly on his desk. That meant that Tuppence was requesting to take hold. Tommy, who wanted his lunch, and who felt profoundly unsympathetic towards Mr St Vincent, was only too pleased to relinquish the helm.

'Excuse me,' he said, and picked up the telephone.

Across his face there shot rapid changes – surprise, consternation, slight elation.

'You don't say so,' he said into the phone. 'The Prime Minister himself? Of course, in that case, I will come round at once.'

He replaced the receiver on the hook, and turned to his client.

'My dear sir, I must ask you to excuse me. A most urgent summons. If you will give the facts of the case to my confidential secretary, she will deal with them.'

He strode to the adjoining door.

'Miss Robinson.'

Tuppence, very neat and demure with smooth black head and dainty collars and cuffs, tripped in. Tommy made the necessary introductions and departed.

'A lady you take an interest in has disappeared, I understand, Mr St Vincent,' said Tuppence, in her soft voice, as she sat down and took up Mr Blunt's pad and pencil. 'A young lady?'

'Oh! rather,' said St Vincent. 'Young – and – and – awfully good-looking and all that sort of thing.'

Tuppence's face grew grave.

'Dear me,' she murmured. 'I hope that –'

'You don't think anything's really happened to her?' demanded Mr St Vincent, in lively concern.

'Oh! we must hope for the best,' said Tuppence, with a kind of false cheerfulness which depressed Mr St Vincent horribly.

'Oh! look here, Miss Robinson. I say, you must do something. Spare no expense. I wouldn't have anything happen to her for the world. You seem awfully sympathetic, and I don't mind telling you in confidence that I simply worship the ground that girl walks on. She's a topper, an absolute topper.'

'Please tell me her name and all about her.'

'Her name's Jeanette – I don't know her second name. She works in a hat shop – Madame Violette's in Brook Street – but she's as straight as they make them. Has ticked me off no end of times – I went round there yesterday – waiting for her to come out – all the others came, but not her. Then I found that she'd never turned up that morning to work at all – sent no message either – old Madame was furious about it. I got the address of her lodgings, and I went round there. She hadn't come home the night before, and they didn't know where she was. I was simply frantic. I thought of going to the police. But I knew that Jeanette would be absolutely furious with me for doing that if she were really all right and had gone off on her own. Then I remembered that she herself had pointed out your advertisement to me one day in the paper and told me that one of the women who'd been in buying hats had simply raved about your ability and discretion and all that sort of thing. So I toddled along here right away.'

'I see,' said Tuppence. 'What is the address of her lodgings?'

The young man gave it to her.

'That's all, I think,' said Tuppence reflectively. 'That is to say – am I to understand that you are engaged to this young lady?'

Mr St Vincent turned a brick red.

'Well, no – not exactly. I never said anything. But I can tell you this, I mean to ask her to marry me as soon as ever I see her – if I ever do see her again.'

Tuppence laid aside her pad.

'Do you wish for our special twenty-four hour service?' she asked in business-like tones.

'What's that?'

'The fees are doubled, but we put all our available staff on to the case. Mr St Vincent, if the lady is alive, I shall be able to tell you where she is by this time tomorrow.'

'What? I say, that's wonderful.'

'We only employ experts – and we guarantee results,' said Tuppence crisply.

'But I say, you know. You must have the most topping staff.'

'Oh! we have,' said Tuppence. 'By the way, you haven't given me a description of the young lady.'

'She's got the most marvellous hair – sort of golden but very deep, like a jolly old sunset – that's it, a jolly old sunset. You know, I never noticed things like sunsets until lately. Poetry too, there's a lot more in poetry than I ever thought.'

'Red hair,' said Tuppence unemotionally, writing it down. 'What height should you say the lady was?'

'Oh! tallish, and she's got ripping eyes, dark blue, I think. And a sort of decided manner with her – takes a fellow up short sometimes.'

Tuppence wrote down a few words more, then closed her notebook and rose.

'If you will call here tomorrow at two o'clock, I think we shall have news of some kind for you,' she said. 'Good-morning, Mr St Vincent.'

When Tommy returned Tuppence was just consulting a page of Debrett.

'I've got all the details,' she said succinctly. 'Lawrence St Vincent is the nephew and heir of the Earl of Cheriton. If we pull this through we shall get publicity in the highest places.'

Tommy read through the notes on the pad.

'What do you really think has happened to the girl?' he asked.

'I think,' said Tuppence, 'that she has fled at the dictates of her heart, feeling that she loves this young man too well for her peace of mind.'

Tommy looked at her doubtfully.

'I know they do it in books,' he said, 'but I've never known any girl who did it in real life.'

'No?' said Tuppence. 'Well, perhaps you're right. But I dare say Lawrence St Vincent will swallow that sort of slush. He's full of romantic notions just now. By the way, I guaranteed results in twenty-four hours – our special service.'

'Tuppence – you congenital idiot, what made you do that?'

'The idea just came into my head. I thought it sounded rather well. Don't you worry. Leave it to mother. Mother knows best.'

She went out leaving Tommy profoundly dissatisfied.

Presently he rose, sighed, and went out to do what could be done, cursing Tuppence's over-fervent imagination.

When he returned weary and jaded at half-past four, he found Tuppence extracting a bag of biscuits from their place of concealment in one of the files.

'You look hot and bothered,' she remarked. 'What have you been doing?'

Tommy groaned.

'Making a round of the hospitals with that girl's description.'

'Didn't I tell you to leave it to me?' demanded Tuppence.

'You can't find that girl single-handed before two o'clock tomorrow.'

'I can – and what's more, I have!'

'You have? What do you mean?'

'A simple problem, Watson, very simple indeed.'

'Where is she now?'

Tuppence pointed a hand over her shoulder.

'She's in my office next door.'

'What is she doing there?'

Tuppence began to laugh.

'Well,' she said, 'early training will tell, and with a kettle, a gas ring, and half a pound of tea staring her in the face, the result is a foregone conclusion.

'You see,' continued Tuppence gently. 'Madame Violette's is where I go for my hats, and the other day I ran across an old pal of hospital days amongst the girls there. She gave up nursing after the war and started a hat shop, failed, and took this job at Madame Violette's. We fixed up the whole thing between us. She was to rub the advertisement well into young St Vincent, and then disappear. Wonderful efficiency of Blunt's Brilliant Detectives. Publicity for us, and the necessary fillip to young St Vincent to bring him to the point of proposing. Janet was in despair about it.'

'Tuppence,' said Tommy. 'You take my breath away! The whole thing is the most immoral business I ever heard of. You aid and abet this young man to marry out of his class –'

'Stuff,' said Tuppence. 'Janet is a splendid girl – and the

queer thing is that she really adores that week-kneed young man. You can see with half a glance what *his* family needs. Some good red blood in it. Janet will be the making of him. She'll look after him like a mother, ease down the cocktails and the night clubs and make him lead a good healthy country gentleman's life. Come and meet her.'

Tuppence opened the door of the adjoining office and Tommy followed her.

A tall girl with lovely auburn hair, and a pleasant face, put down the steaming kettle in her hand, and turned with a smile that disclosed an even row of white teeth.

'I hope you'll forgive me, Nurse Cowley – Mrs Beresford, I mean. I thought that very likely you'd be quite ready for a cup of tea yourself. Many's the pot of tea you've made for me in the hospital at three o'clock in the morning.'

'Tommy,' said Tuppence. 'Let me introduce you to my old friend, Nurse Smith.'

'Smith, did you say? How curious!' said Tommy shaking hands. 'Eh? Oh! nothing – a little monograph that I was thinking of writing.'

'Pull yourself together, Tommy,' said Tuppence.

She poured him out a cup of tea.

'Now, then, let's drink together. Here's to the success of the International Detective Agency. Blunt's Brilliant Detectives! May they never know failure!'

CHAPTER III

The Affair of
the Pink Pearl

'What on earth are you doing?' demanded Tuppence, as she entered the inner sanctum of the International Detective Agency – (Slogan – Blunt's Brilliant Detectives) and discovered her lord and master prone on the floor in a sea of books.

Tommy struggled to his feet.

'I was trying to arrange these books on the top shelf of that cupboard,' he complained. 'And the damned chair gave way.'

'What are they, anyway?' asked Tuppence, picking up a volume. '*The Hound of the Baskervilles*. I wouldn't mind reading that again some time.'

'You see the idea?' said Tommy, dusting himself with care. 'Half-hours with the Great Masters – that sort of thing. You see, Tuppence, I can't help feeling that we are more or less amateurs at this business – of course amateurs in one sense we cannot help being, but it would do no harm to acquire the technique, so to speak. These books are detective stories by the leading masters of the art. I intend to try different styles, and compare results.'

'H'm,' said Tuppence. 'I often wonder how these detectives would have got on in real life.' She picked up another volume. 'You'll find a difficulty in being a Thorndyke. You've no medical experience, and less legal, and I never heard that science was your strong point.'

'Perhaps not,' said Tommy. 'But at any rate I've bought a very good camera, and I shall photograph footprints and enlarge the negatives and all that sort of thing. Now, *mon ami,* use your little grey cells – what does this convey to you?'

He pointed to the bottom shelf of the cupboard. On it lay a somewhat futuristic dressing-gown, a turkish slipper, and a violin.

'Obvious, my dear Watson,' said Tuppence.

'Exactly,' said Tommy. 'The Sherlock Holmes touch.'

He took up the violin and drew the bow idly across the strings, causing Tuppence to give a wail of agony.

At that moment the buzzer rang on the desk, a sign that a client had arrived in the outer office and was being held in parley by Albert, the office boy.

Tommy hastily replaced the violin in the cupboard and kicked the books behind the desk.

'Not that there's any great hurry,' he remarked. 'Albert will be handing them out the stuff about my being engaged with Scotland Yard on the phone. Get into your office and start typing, Tuppence. It makes the office sound busy and active. No, on second thoughts you shall be taking notes in shorthand from my dictation. Let's have a look before we get Albert to send the victim in.'

They approached the peephole which had been artistically contrived so as to command a view of the outer office.

The client was a girl of about Tuppence's age, tall and dark with a rather haggard face and scornful eyes.

'Clothes cheap and striking,' remarked Tuppence. 'Have her in, Tommy.'

In another minute the girl was shaking hands with the celebrated Mr Blunt, whilst Tuppence sat by with eyes demurely downcast, and pad and pencil in hand.

'My confidential secretary, Miss Robinson,' said Mr Blunt with a wave of his hand. 'You may speak freely before her.' Then he lay back for a minute, half closed his eyes and remarked in a tired tone: 'You must find travelling in a bus very crowded at this time of day.'

'I came in a taxi,' said the girl.

'Oh!' said Tommy aggrieved. His eyes rested reproachfully on a blue bus ticket protruding from her glove. The girl's eyes followed his glance, and she smiled and drew it out.

'You mean this? I picked it up on the pavement. A little neighbour of ours collects them.'

Tuppence coughed, and Tommy threw a baleful glare at her.

'We must get to business,' he said briskly. 'You are in need of our services, Miss –?'

'Kingston Bruce is my name,' said the girl. 'We live at Wimbledon. Last night a lady who is staying with us lost a valuable pink pearl. Mr St Vincent was also dining with us, and during dinner he happened to mention your firm. My mother sent me off to you this morning to ask you if you would look into the matter for us.'

The girl spoke sullenly, almost disagreeably. It was clear as daylight that she and her mother had not agreed over the matter. She was here under protest.

'I see,' said Tommy, a little puzzled. 'You have not called in the police?'

'No,' said Miss Kingston Bruce, 'we haven't. It would be idiotic to call in the police and then find the silly thing had rolled under the fireplace, or something like that.'

'Oh!' said Tommy. 'Then the jewel may only be lost after all?'

Miss Kingston Bruce shrugged her shoulders.

'People make such a fuss about things,' she murmured.

Tommy cleared his throat.

'Of course,' he said doubtfully. 'I am extremely busy just now –'

'I quite understand,' said the girl, rising to her feet. There was a quick gleam of satisfaction in her eyes which Tuppence, for one, did not miss.

'Nevertheless,' continued Tommy. 'I think I can manage to run down to Wimbledon. Will you give me the address, please?'

'The Laurels, Edgeworth Road.'

'Make a note of it, please, Miss Robinson.'

Miss Kingston Bruce hesitated, then said rather ungraciously: 'We'll expect you then. Good-morning.'

'Funny girl,' said Tommy when she had left. 'I couldn't quite make her out.'

'I wonder if she stole the thing herself,' remarked Tuppence meditatively. 'Come on, Tommy, let's put away these books and take the car and go down there. By the way, who are you going to be, Sherlock Holmes still?'

'I think I need practice for that,' said Tommy. 'I came rather a cropper over that bus ticket, didn't I?'

'You did,' said Tuppence. 'If I were you I shouldn't try too much on that girl – she's as sharp as a needle. She's unhappy too, poor devil.'

'I suppose you know all about her already,' said Tommy with sarcasm, 'simply from looking at the shape of her nose!'

'I'll tell you my idea of what we shall find at The Laurels,' said Tuppence, quite unmoved. 'A household of snobs, very keen to move in the best society; the father, if there is a father, is sure to have a military title. The girl falls in with their way of life and despises herself for doing so.'

Tommy took a last look at the books now neatly arranged upon the shelf.

'I think,' he said thoughtfully, 'that I shall be Thorndyke today.'

'I shouldn't have thought there was anything medico-legal about this case,' remarked Tuppence.

'Perhaps not,' said Tommy. 'But I'm simply dying to use that new camera of mine! It's supposed to have the most marvellous lens that ever was or could be.'

'I know those kind of lenses,' said Tuppence. 'By the time you've adjusted the shutter and stopped down and calculated the exposure and kept your eye on the spirit level, your brain gives out, and you yearn for the simple Brownie.'

'Only an unambitious soul is content with the simple Brownie.'

'Well, I bet I shall get better results with it than you will.'

Tommy ignored the challenge.

'I ought to have a "Smoker's Companion",' he said regretfully. 'I wonder where one buys them?'

'There's always the patent corkscrew Aunt Araminta gave you last Christmas,' said Tuppence helpfully.

'That's true,' said Tommy. 'A curious-looking engine of destruction I thought it at the time, and rather a humorous present to get from a strictly teetotal aunt.'

'I,' said Tuppence, 'shall be Polton.'

Tommy looked at her scornfully.

'Polton indeed. You couldn't begin to do one of the things that he does.'

'Yes, I can,' said Tuppence. 'I can rub my hands together when I'm pleased. That's quite enough to get on with. I hope you're going to take plaster casts of footprints?'

Tommy was reduced to silence. Having collected the corkscrew they went round to the garage, got out the car and started for Wimbledon.

The Laurels was a big house. It ran somewhat to gables and turrets, had an air of being very newly painted and was surrounded with neat flower beds filled with scarlet geraniums.

A tall man with a close-cropped white moustache, and an exaggeratedly martial bearing opened the door before Tommy had time to ring.

'I've been looking out for you,' he explained fussily. 'Mr Blunt, is it not? I am Colonel Kingston Bruce. Will you come into my study?'

He let them into a small room at the back of the house.

'Young St Vincent was telling me wonderful things about your firm. I've noticed your advertisements myself. This guaranteed twenty-four hours' service of yours – a marvellous notion. That's exactly what I need.'

Inwardly anathematizing Tuppence for her irresponsibility in inventing this brilliant detail, Tommy replied: 'Just so, Colonel.'

'The whole thing is most distressing, sir, most distressing.'

'Perhaps you would kindly give me the facts,' said Tommy, with a hint of impatience.

'Certainly I will – at once. We have at the present moment staying with us a very old and dear friend of ours, Lady Laura Barton. Daughter of the late Earl of Carroway. The present earl, her brother, made a striking speech in the House of Lords the other day. As I say, she is an old and dear friend of ours.

Some American friends of mine who have just come over, the Hamilton Betts, were most anxious to meet her. "Nothing easier," I said. "She is staying with me now. Come down for the weekend." You know what Americans are about titles, Mr Blunt.'

'And others besides Americans sometimes, Colonel Kingston Bruce.'

'Alas! only too true, my dear sir. Nothing I hate more than a snob. Well, as I was saying, the Betts came down for the weekend. Last night – we were playing bridge at the time – the clasp of a pendant Mrs Hamilton Betts was wearing broke, so she took it off and laid it down on a small table, meaning to take it upstairs with her when she went. This, however, she forgot to do. I must explain, Mr Blunt, that the pendant consisted of two small diamond wings, and a big pink pearl depending from them. The pendant was found this morning lying where Mrs Betts had left it, but the pearl, a pearl of enormous value, had been wrenched off.'

'Who found the pendant?'

'The parlourmaid – Gladys Hill.'

'Any reason to suspect her?'

'She has been with us some years, and we have always found her perfectly honest. But, of course, one never knows –'

'Exactly. Will you describe your staff, and also tell me who was present at dinner last night?'

'There is the cook – she has been with us only two months, but then she would have no occasion to go near the drawing-room – the same applies to the kitchenmaid. Then there is the housemaid, Alice Cummings. She also has been with us for some years. And Lady Laura's maid, of course. She is French.'

Colonel Kingston Bruce looked very impressive as he said this. Tommy, unaffected by the revelation of the maid's nationality, said: 'Exactly. And the party at dinner?'

'Mr and Mrs Betts, ourselves – my wife and daughter – and Lady Laura. Young St Vincent was dining with us, and Mr Rennie looked in after dinner for a while.'

'Who is Mr Rennie?'

'A most pestilential fellow – an arrant socialist. Good looking, of course, and with a certain specious power of argument. But a man, I don't mind telling you, whom I wouldn't trust a yard. A dangerous sort of fellow.'

'In fact,' said Tommy drily, 'it is Mr Rennie whom you suspect?'

'I do, Mr Blunt. I'm sure, holding the views he does, that he can have no principles whatsoever. What could have been easier for him than to have quietly wrenched off the pearl at a moment when we were all absorbed in our game? There were several absorbing moments – a redoubled no trump hand, I remember, and also a painful argument when my wife had the misfortune to revoke.'

'Quite so,' said Tommy. 'I should just like to know one thing – what is Mrs Betts's attitude in all this?'

'She wanted me to call in the police,' said Colonel Kingston Bruce reluctantly. 'That is, when we had searched everywhere in case the pearl had only dropped off.'

'But you dissuaded her?'

'I was very averse to the idea of publicity and my wife and daughter backed me up. Then my wife remembered young St Vincent speaking about your firm at dinner last night – and the twenty-four hours' special service.'

'Yes,' said Tommy, with a heavy heart.

'You see, in any case, no harm will be done. If we call in the police tomorrow, it can be supposed that we thought the jewel merely lost and were hunting for it. By the way, nobody has been allowed to leave the house this morning.'

'Except your daughter, of course,' said Tuppence, speaking for the first time.

'Except my daughter,' agreed the Colonel. 'She volunteered at once to go and put the case before you.'

Tommy rose.

'We will do our best to give you satisfaction, Colonel,' he said. 'I should like to see the drawing-room, and the table on which the pendant was laid down. I should also like to ask Mrs Betts a few questions. After that, I will interview the servants – or rather my assistant, Miss Robinson, will do so.'

He felt his nerve quailing before the terrors of questioning the servants.

Colonel Kingston Bruce threw open the door and led them across the hall. As he did so, a remark came to them clearly through the open door of the room they were approaching and the voice that uttered it was that of the girl who had come to see them that morning.

'You know perfectly well, Mother,' she was saying, 'that she *did* bring home a teaspoon in her muff.'

In another minute they were being introduced to Mrs Kingston Bruce, a plaintive lady with a languid manner. Miss Kingston Bruce acknowledged their presence with a short inclination of the head. Her face was more sullen than ever.

Mrs Kingston Bruce was voluble.

' – but I know who I think took it,' she ended. 'That dreadful socialist young man. He loves the Russians and the Germans and hates the English – what else can you expect?'

'He never touched it,' said Miss Kingston Bruce fiercely. 'I was watching him – all the time. I couldn't have failed to see if he had.'

She looked at them defiantly with her chin up.

Tommy created a diversion by asking for an interview with Mrs Betts. When Mrs Kingston Bruce had departed accompanied by her husband and daughter to find Mrs Betts, he whistled thoughtfully.

'I wonder,' he said gently, 'who it was who had a teaspoon in her muff?'

'Just what I was thinking,' replied Tuppence.

Mrs Betts, followed by her husband, burst into the room. She was a big woman with a determined voice. Mr Hamilton Betts looked dyspeptic and subdued.

'I understand, Mr Blunt, that you are a private inquiry agent, and one who hustles things through at a great rate?'

'Hustle,' said Tommy, 'is my middle name, Mrs Betts. Let me ask you a few questions.'

Thereafter things proceeded rapidly. Tommy was shown the damaged pendant, the table on which it had lain, and Mr Betts emerged from his taciturnity to mention the value, in dollars, of the stolen pearl.

And withal, Tommy felt an irritating certainty that he was not getting on.

'I think that will do,' he said, at length. 'Miss Robinson, will you kindly fetch the special photographic apparatus from the hall?'

Miss Robinson complied.

'A little invention of my own,' said Tommy. 'In appearance, you see, it is just like an ordinary camera.'

He had some slight satisfaction in seeing that the Betts were impressed.

He photographed the pendant, the table on which it had lain, and took several general views of the apartment. Then 'Miss Robinson' was delegated to interview the servants, and in view of the eager expectancy on the faces of Colonel Kingston Bruce and Mrs Betts, Tommy felt called upon to say a few authoritative words.

'The position amounts to this,' he said. 'Either the pearl is still in the house, or it is not still in the house.'

'Quite so,' said the Colonel with more respect than was, perhaps, quite justified by the nature of the remark.

'If it is not in the house, it may be anywhere – but if it is in the house, it must necessarily be concealed somewhere –'

'And a search must be made,' broke in Colonel Kingston Bruce. 'Quite so. I give you carte blanche, Mr Blunt. Search the house from attic to cellar.'

'Oh! Charles,' murmured Mrs Kingston Bruce tearfully, 'do you think that is wise? The servants won't *like* it. I'm sure they'll leave.'

'We will search their quarters last,' said Tommy soothingly. 'The thief is sure to have hidden the gem in the most unlikely place.'

'I seem to have read something of the kind,' agreed the Colonel.

'Quite so,' said Tommy. 'You probably remember the case of Rex v Bailey, which created a precedent.'

'Oh – er – yes,' said the Colonel, looking puzzled.

'Now, the most unlikely place is in the apartment of Mrs Betts,' continued Tommy.

'My! Wouldn't that be too cute?' said Mrs Betts admiringly.

Without more ado she took him up to her room, where Tommy once more made use of the special photographic apparatus.

Presently Tuppence joined him there.

'You have no objection, I hope, Mrs Betts, to my assistant's looking through your wardrobe?'

'Why, not at all. Do you need me here any longer?'

Tommy assured her that there was no need to detain her, and Mrs Betts departed.

'We might as well go on bluffing it out,' said Tommy. 'But personally I don't believe we've a dog's chance of finding the thing. Curse you and your twenty-four hours' stunt, Tuppence.'

'Listen,' said Tuppence. 'The servants are all right, I'm sure, but I managed to get something out of the French maid. It seems that when Lady Laura was staying here a year ago, she went out to tea with some friends of the Kingston Bruces, and when she got home a teaspoon fell out of her muff. Everyone thought it must have fallen in by accident. But, talking about similar robberies, I got hold of a lot more. Lady Laura is always staying about with people. She hasn't got a bean, I gather, and she's out for comfortable quarters with people to whom a title still means something. It may be a coincidence – or it may be something more, but five distinct thefts have taken place whilst she has been staying in various houses, sometimes trivial things, sometimes valuable jewels.'

'Whew!' said Tommy, and gave vent to a prolonged whistle. 'Where's the old bird's room, do you know?'

'Just across the passage.'

'Then I think, I rather think, that we'll just slip across and investigate.'

The room opposite stood with its door ajar. It was a spacious apartment, with white enamelled fitments and rose pink curtains. An inner door led to a bathroom. At the door of this appeared a slim, dark girl, very neatly dressed.

Tuppence checked the exclamation of astonishment on the girl's lips.

'This is Elise, Mr Blunt,' she said primly. 'Lady Laura's maid.'

Tommy stepped across the threshold of the bathroom, and approved inwardly its sumptuous and up-to-date fittings. He set to work to dispel the wide stare of suspicion on the French girl's face.

'You are busy with your duties, eh, Mademoiselle Elise?'

'Yes, Monsieur, I clean Milady's bath.'

'Well, perhaps you'll help me with some photography instead. I have a special kind of camera here, and I am photographing the interiors of all the rooms in this house.'

He was interrupted by the communicating door to the bedroom banging suddenly behind him. Elise jumped at the sound.

'What did that?'

'It must have been the wind,' said Tuppence.

'We will come into the other room,' said Tommy.

Elise went to open the door for them, but the door knob rattled aimlessly.

'What's the matter?' said Tommy sharply.

'Ah, Monsieur, but somebody must have locked it on the other side.' She caught up a towel and tried again. But this time the door handle turned easily enough, and the door swung open.

'*Voilà ce qui est curieux.* It must have been stuck,' said Elise.

There was no one in the bedroom.

Tommy fetched his apparatus. Tuppence and Elise worked under his orders. But again and again his glance went back to the communicating door.

'I wonder,' he said between his teeth – 'I wonder why that door stuck?'

He examined it minutely, shutting and opening it. It fitted perfectly.

'One picture more,' he said with a sigh. 'Will you loop back that rose curtain, Mademoiselle Elise? Thank you. Just hold it so.'

The familiar click occurred. He handed a glass slide to Elise to hold, relinquished the tripod to Tuppence, and carefully readjusted and closed the camera.

He made some easy excuse to get rid of Elise, and as soon as she was out of the room, he caught hold of Tuppence and spoke rapidly.

'Look here, I've got an idea. Can you hang on here? Search all the rooms – that will take some time. Try and get an interview with the old bird – Lady Laura – but don't alarm her. Tell her you suspect the parlourmaid. But whatever you do don't let her leave the house. I'm going off in the car. I'll be back as soon as I can.'

'All right,' said Tuppence. 'But don't be too cocksure. You've forgotten one thing.'

'The girl. There's something funny about that girl. Listen, I've found out the time she started from the house this morning. It took her two hours to get to our office. That's nonsense. Where did she go before she came to us?'

'There's something in that,' admitted her husband. 'Well, follow up any old clue you like, but don't let Lady Laura leave the house. What's that?'

His quick ear had caught a faint rustle outside on the landing. He strode across to the door, but there was no one to be seen.

'Well, so long,' he said, 'I'll be back as soon as I can.'

CHAPTER IV

The Affair of
the Pink Pearl (*continued*)

Tuppence watched him drive off in the car with a faint misgiving. Tommy was very sure – she herself was not so sure. There were one or two things she did not quite understand.

She was still standing by the window, watching the road, when she saw a man leave the shelter of a gateway opposite, cross the road and ring the bell.

In a flash Tuppence was out of the room and down the stairs. Gladys Hill, the parlourmaid, was emerging from the back part of the house, but Tuppence motioned her back authoritatively. Then she went to the front door and opened it.

A lanky young man with ill-fitting clothes and eager dark eyes was standing on the step.

He hesitated a moment, and then said:

'Is Miss Kingston Bruce in?'

'Will you come inside?' said Tuppence.

She stood aside to let him enter, closing the door.

'Mr Rennie, I think?' she said sweetly.

He shot a quick glance at her.

'Er – yes.'

'Will you come in here, please?'

She opened the study door. The room was empty, and Tuppence entered it after him, closing the door behind her. He turned on her with a frown.

'I want to see Miss Kingston Bruce.'

'I am not quite sure that you can,' said Tuppence composedly.

'Look here, who the devil are you?' said Mr Rennie rudely.

'International Detective Agency,' said Tuppence succinctly – and noticed Mr Rennie's uncontrollable start.

'Please sit down, Mr Rennie,' she went on. 'To begin with, we know all about Miss Kingston Bruce's visit to you this morning.'

It was a bold guess, but it succeeded. Perceiving his consternation, Tuppence went on quickly.

'The recovery of the pearl is the great thing, Mr Rennie. No one in this house is anxious for – publicity. Can't we come to some arrangement?'

The young man looked at her keenly.

'I wonder how much you know,' he said thoughtfully. 'Let me think for a moment.'

He buried his head in his hands – then asked a most unexpected question.

'I say, is it really true that young St Vincent is engaged to be married?'

'Quite true,' said Tuppence. 'I know the girl.'

Mr Rennie suddenly became confidential.

'It's been hell,' he confided. 'They've been asking her morning, noon and night – chucking Beatrice at his head. All because he'll come into a title some day. If I had my way –'

'Don't let's talk politics,' said Tuppence hastily. 'Do you mind telling me, Mr Rennie, why you think Miss Kingston Bruce took the pearl?'

'I – I don't.'

'You do,' said Tuppence calmly. 'You wait to see the detective, as you think, drive off and the coast clear, and then you come and ask for her. It's obvious. If you'd taken the pearl yourself, you wouldn't be half so upset.'

'Her manner was so odd,' said the young man. 'She came this morning and told me about the robbery, explaining that she was on her way to a firm of private detectives. She seemed anxious to say something, and yet not able to get it out.'

'Well,' said Tuppence. 'All I want is the pearl. You'd better go and talk to her.'

But at that moment Colonel Kingston Bruce opened the door.

'Lunch is ready, Miss Robinson. You will lunch with us, I hope. The –'

Then he stopped and glared at the guest.

'Clearly,' said Mr Rennie, 'you don't want to ask me to lunch. All right, I'll go.'

'Come back later,' whispered Tuppence, as he passed her.

Tuppence followed Colonel Kingston Bruce, still growling into his moustache about the pestilential impudence of some people, into a massive dining-room where the family was already assembled. Only one person present was unknown to Tuppence.

'This, Lady Laura, is Miss Robinson, who is kindly assisting us.'

Lady Laura bent her head, and then proceeded to stare at Tuppence through her pince-nez. She was a tall, thin woman, with a sad smile, a gentle voice, and very hard shrewd eyes. Tuppence returned her stare, and Lady Laura's eyes dropped.

After lunch Lady Laura entered into conversation with an air of gentle curiosity. How was the inquiry proceeding? Tuppence laid suitable stress on the suspicion attaching to the parlourmaid, but her mind was not really on Lady Laura. Lady Laura might conceal teaspoons and other articles in her clothing, but Tuppence felt fairly sure that she had not taken the pink pearl.

Presently Tuppence proceeded with her search of the house. Time was going on. There was no sign of Tommy, and, what mattered far more to Tuppence, there was no sign of Mr Rennie. Suddenly Tuppence came out of a bedroom and collided with Beatrice Kingston Bruce, who was going downstairs. She was fully dressed for the street.

'I'm afraid,' said Tuppence, 'that you mustn't go out just now.'

The other girl looked at her haughtily.

'Whether I go out or not is no business of yours,' she said coldly.

'It is my business whether I communicate with the police or not, though,' said Tuppence.

In a minute the girl had turned ashy pale.

'You mustn't – you mustn't – I won't go out – but don't do that.' She clung to Tuppence beseechingly.

'My dear Miss Kingston Bruce,' said Tuppence, smiling, 'the case has been perfectly clear to me from the start – I –'

But she was interrupted. In the stress of her encounter with the girl, Tuppence had not heard the front-door bell. Now, to her astonishment, Tommy came bounding up the stairs, and in the hall below she caught sight of a big burly man in the act of removing a bowler hat.

'Detective Inspector Marriot of Scotland Yard,' he said with a grin.

With a cry, Beatrice Kingston Bruce tore herself from Tuppence's grasp and dashed down the stairs, just as the front door was opened once more to admit Mr Rennie.

'Now you *have* torn it,' said Tuppence bitterly.

'Eh?' said Tommy, hurrying into Lady Laura's room. He passed on into the bathroom and picked up a large cake of soap which he brought out in his hands. The Inspector was just mounting the stairs.

'She went quite quietly,' he announced. 'She's an old hand and knows when the game is up. What about the pearl?'

'I rather fancy,' said Tommy, handing him the soap, 'that you'll find it in here.'

The Inspector's eyes lit up appreciatively.

'An old trick, and a good one. Cut a cake of soap in half, scoop out a place for the jewel, clap it together again, and smooth the join well over with hot water. A very smart piece of work on your part, sir.'

Tommy accepted the compliment gracefully. He and Tuppence descended the stairs. Colonel Kingston Bruce rushed at him and shook him warmly by the hand.

'My dear sir, I can't thank you enough. Lady Laura wants to thank you also –'

'I am glad we have given you satisfaction,' said Tommy. 'But I'm afraid I can't stop. I have a most urgent appointment. Member of the Cabinet.'

He hurried out to the car and jumped in. Tuppence jumped in beside him.

'But Tommy,' she cried. 'Haven't they arrested Lady Laura after all?'

'Oh!' said Tommy. 'Didn't I tell you? They've not arrested Lady Laura. They've arrested Elise.'

'You see,' he went on, as Tuppence sat dumbfounded, 'I've often tried to open a door with soap on my hands myself. It can't be done – your hands slip. So I wondered what Elise could have been doing with the soap to get her hands as soapy as all that. She caught up a towel, you remember, so there were no traces of soap on the handle afterwards. But it occurred to me that if you were a professional thief, it wouldn't be a bad plan to be maid to a lady suspected of kleptomania who stayed about a good deal in different houses. So I managed to get a photo of her as well as of the room, induced her to handle a glass slide and toddled off to dear old Scotland Yard. Lightning development of negative, successful identification of finger-prints – and photo. Elise was a long lost friend. Useful place, Scotland Yard.'

'And to think,' said Tuppence, finding her voice, 'that those two young idiots were only suspecting each other in that weak way they do it in books. But why didn't you tell me what you were up to when you went off?'

'In the first place, I suspected that Elise was listening on the landing, and in the second place –'

'Yes?'

'My learned friend forgets,' said Tommy. 'Thorndyke never tells until the last moment. Besides, Tuppence, you and your pal Janet Smith put one over on me last time. This makes us all square.'

CHAPTER V

The Adventure of
the Sinister Stranger

'It's been a darned dull day,' said Tommy, and yawned widely.

'Nearly tea time,' said Tuppence and also yawned.

Business was not brisk in the International Detective Agency. The eagerly expected letter from the ham merchant had not arrived and *bona fide* cases were not forthcoming.

Albert, the office boy, entered with a sealed package which he laid on the table.

'The Mystery of the Sealed Packet,' murmured Tommy. 'Did it contain the fabulous pearls of the Russian Grand Duchess? Or was it an infernal machine destined to blow Blunt's Brilliant Detectives to pieces?'

'As a matter of fact,' said Tuppence, tearing open the package. 'It's my wedding present to Francis Haviland. Rather nice, isn't it?'

Tommy took a slender silver cigarette case from her outstretched hand, noted the inscription engraved in her own handwriting, '*Francis from Tuppence,*' opened and shut the case, and nodded approvingly.

'You do throw your money about, Tuppence,' he remarked. 'I'll have one like it, only in gold, for my birthday next month. Fancy wasting a thing like that on Francis Haviland, who always was and always will be one of the most perfect asses God ever made!'

'You forget I used to drive him about during the war, when he was a General. Ah! those were the good old days.'

'They were,' agreed Tommy. 'Beautiful women used to come and squeeze my hand in hospital, I remember. But I don't send them all wedding presents. I don't believe the bride will care much for this gift of yours, Tuppence.'

'It's nice and slim for the pocket, isn't it?' said Tuppence, disregarding his remarks.

Tommy slipped it into his own pocket.

'Just right,' he said approvingly. 'Hullo, here is Albert with the afternoon post. Very possibly the Duchess of Perthshire is commissioning us to find her prize Peke.'

They sorted through the letters together. Suddenly Tommy gave vent to a prolonged whistle and held up one of them in his hand.

'A blue letter with a Russian stamp on it. Do you remember what the Chief said? We were to look out for letters like that.'

'How exciting,' said Tuppence. 'Something has happened at last. Open it and see if the contents are up to schedule. A ham merchant, wasn't it? Half a minute. We shall want some milk for tea. They forgot to leave it this morning. I'll send Albert out for it.'

She returned from the outer office, after despatching Albert on his errand, to find Tommy holding the blue sheet of paper in his hand.

'As we thought, Tuppence,' he remarked. 'Almost word for word what the Chief said.'

Tuppence took the letter from him and read it.

It was couched in careful stilted English, and purported to be from one Gregor Feodorsky, who was anxious for news of his wife. The International Detective Agency was urged to spare no expense in doing their utmost to trace her. Feodorsky himself was unable to leave Russia at the moment owing to a crisis in the pork trade.

'I wonder what it really means,' said Tuppence thoughtfully, smoothing out the sheet on the table in front of her.

'Code of some kind, I suppose,' said Tommy. 'That's not our business. Our business is to hand it over to the Chief as soon as possible. Better just verify it by soaking off the stamp and seeing if the number 16 is underneath.'

'All right,' said Tuppence. 'But I should think –'

She stopped dead, and Tommy, surprised by her sudden pause, looked up to see a man's burly figure blocking the doorway.

The intruder was a man of commanding presence, squarely built, with a very round head and a powerful jaw. He might have been about forty-five years of age.

'I must beg your pardon,' said the stranger, advancing into the room, hat in hand. 'I found your outer office empty and this door open, so I ventured to intrude. This is Blunt's International Detective Agency, is it not?'

'Certainly it is.'

'And you are, perhaps, Mr Blunt? Mr Theodore Blunt?'

'I am Mr Blunt. You wish to consult me? This is my secretary, Miss Robinson.'

Tuppence inclined her head gracefully, but continued to scrutinize the stranger narrowly through her downcast eyelashes. She was wondering how long he had been standing in the doorway, and how much he had seen and heard. It did not escape her observation that even while he was talking to Tommy, his eyes kept coming back to the blue paper in her hand.

Tommy's voice, sharp with a warning note, recalled her to the needs of the moment.

'Miss Robinson, please, take notes. Now, sir, will you kindly state the matter on which you wish to have my advice?'

Tuppence reached for her pad and pencil.

The big man began in rather a harsh voice.

'My name is Bower. Dr Charles Bower. I live in Hampstead, where I have a practice. I have come to you, Mr Blunt, because several rather strange occurrences have happened lately.'

'Yes, Dr Bower?'

'Twice in the course of the last week I have been summoned by telephone to an urgent case – in each case to find that the summons has been a fake. The first time I thought a practical joke had been played upon me, but on my return the second time I found that some of my private papers had been displaced and disarranged, and now I believe that the same thing had happened the first time. I made an exhaustive search and came to the conclusion that my whole desk had been thoroughly ransacked, and the various papers replaced hurriedly.'

Dr Bower paused and gazed at Tommy.

'Well, Mr Blunt?'

'Well, Dr Bower,' replied the young man, smiling.

'What do you think of it, eh?'

'Well, first I should like the facts. What do you keep in your desk?'

'My private papers.'

'Exactly. Now, what do those private papers consist of? What value are they to the common thief – or any particular person?'

'To the common thief I cannot see that they would have any value at all, but my notes on certain obscure alkaloids would be of interest to anyone possessed of technical knowledge of the subject. I have been making a study of such matters for the last few years. These alkaloids are deadly and virulent poisons, and are in addition, almost untraceable. They yield no known reactions.'

'The secret of them would be worth money, then?'

'To unscrupulous persons, yes.'

'And you suspect – whom?'

The doctor shrugged his massive shoulders.

'As far as I can tell, the house was not entered forcibly from the outside. That seems to point to some member of my household, and yet I cannot believe –' He broke off abruptly, then began again, his voice very grave.

'Mr Blunt, I must place myself in your hands unreservedly. I dare not go to the police in the matter. Of my three servants I am almost entirely sure. They have served me long and faithfully. Still, one never knows. Then I have living with me my two nephews, Bertram and Henry. Henry is a good boy – a very good boy – he has never caused me any anxiety, an excellent hard-working young fellow. Bertram, I regret to say, is of quite a different character – wild, extravagant, and persistently idle.'

'I see,' said Tommy thoughtfully. 'You suspect your nephew Bertram of being mixed up in this business. Now I don't agree with you. I suspect the good boy – Henry.'

'But why?'

'Tradition. Precedent.' Tommy waved his hand airily. 'In my experience, the suspicious characters are always innocent – and vice versa, my dear sir. Yes, decidedly, I suspect Henry.'

'Excuse me, Mr Blunt,' said Tuppence, interrupting in a deferential tone. 'Did I understand Dr Bower to say that these notes on – er – obscure alkaloids – are kept in the desk with the other papers?'

'They are kept in the desk, my dear young lady, but in a secret drawer, the position of which is known only to myself. Hence they have so far defied the search.'

'And what exactly do you want me to do, Dr Bower?' asked Tommy. 'Do you anticipate that a further search will be made?'

'I do, Mr Blunt. I have every reason to believe so. This afternoon I received a telegram from a patient of mine whom I ordered to Bournemouth a few weeks ago. The telegram states that my patient is in a critical condition, and begs me to come down at once. Rendered suspicious by the events I have told you of, I myself despatched a telegram, prepaid, to the patient in question, and elicited the fact that he was in good health and had sent no summons to me of any kind. It occurred to me that if I pretended to have been taken in, and duly departed to Bournemouth, we should have a very good chance of finding the miscreants at work. They – or he – will doubtless wait until the household has retired to bed before commencing operations. I suggest that you should meet me outside my house at eleven o'clock this evening, and we will investigate the matter together.'

'Hoping, in fact, to catch them in the act.' Tommy drummed thoughtfully on the table with a paper-knife. 'Your plan seems to me an excellent one, Dr Bower. I cannot see any hitch in it. Let me see, your address is – ?'

'The Larches, Hangman's Lane – rather a lonely part, I am afraid. But we command magnificent views over the Heath.'

'Quite so,' said Tommy.

The visitor rose.

'Then I shall expect you tonight, Mr Blunt. Outside The Larches at – shall we say, five minutes to eleven – to be on the safe side?'

'Certainly. Five minutes to eleven. Good-afternoon, Dr Bower.'

Tommy rose, pressed a buzzer on his desk, and Albert appeared to show the client out. The doctor walked with a decided limp, but his powerful physique was evident in spite of it.

'An ugly customer to tackle,' murmured Tommy to himself. 'Well, Tuppence, old girl, what do you think of it?'

'I'll tell you in one word,' said Tuppence. '*Clubfoot!*'

'What?'

'I said Clubfoot! My study of the classics has not been in vain. Tommy, this thing's a plant. Obscure alkaloids indeed – I never heard a weaker story.'

'Even I did not find it very convincing,' admitted her husband.

'Did you see his eyes on the letter? Tommy, he's one of the gang. They've got wise to the fact that you're not the real Mr Blunt, and they're out for our blood.'

'In that case,' said Tommy, opening the side cupboard and surveying his rows of books with an affectionate eye, 'our role is easy to select. We are the brothers Okewood! And I am Desmond,' he added firmly.

Tuppence shrugged her shoulders.

'All right. Have it your own way. I'd as soon be Francis. Francis was much the more intelligent of the two. Desmond always gets into a mess, and Francis turns up as the gardener or something in the nick of time and saves the situation.'

'Ah!' said Tommy, 'but I shall be a super Desmond. When I arrive at the Larches –'

Tuppence interrupted him unceremoniously.

'You're not going to Hampstead tonight?'

'Why not?'

'Walk into a trap with your eyes shut!'

'No, my dear girl, walk into a trap with my eyes open. There's a lot of difference. I think our friend, Dr Bower, will get a little surprise.'

'I don't like it,' said Tuppence. 'You know what happens when Desmond disobeys the Chief's orders and acts on his own. Our orders were quite clear. To send on the letters at once and to report immediately on anything that happened.'

'You've not got it quite right,' said Tommy. 'We were to report immediately if any one came in and mentioned the number 16. Nobody has.'

'That's a quibble,' said Tuppence.

'It's no good. I've got a fancy for playing a lone hand. My dear old Tuppence, I shall be all right. I shall go armed to the teeth. The essence of the whole thing is that I shall be on my guard and they won't know it. The Chief will be patting me on the back for a good night's work.'

'Well,' said Tuppence. 'I don't like it. That man's as strong as a gorilla.'

'Ah!' said Tommy, 'but think of my blue-nosed automatic.'

The door of the outer office opened and Albert appeared. Closing the door behind him, he approached them with an envelope in his hand.

'A gentleman to see you,' said Albert. 'When I began the usual stunt of saying you were engaged with Scotland Yard, he told me he knew all about that. Said he came from Scotland Yard himself! And he wrote something on a card and stuck it up in this envelope.'

Tommy took the envelope and opened it. As he read the card, a grin passed across his face.

'The gentleman was amusing himself at your expense by speaking the truth, Albert,' he remarked. 'Show him in.'

He tossed the card to Tuppence. It bore the name Detective Inspector Dymchurch, and across it was scrawled in pencil – 'A friend of Marriot's.'

In another minute the Scotland Yard detective was entering the inner office. In appearance, Inspector Dymchurch was of the same type as Inspector Marriot, short and thick set, with shrewd eyes.

'Good-afternoon,' said the detective breezily. 'Marriot's away in South Wales, but before he went he asked me to keep an eye on you two, and on this place in general. Oh, bless you, sir,' he went on, as Tommy seemed about to interrupt him, '*we* know all about it. It's not our department, and we don't interfere. But somebody's got wise lately to the fact that all is not what it seems. You've had a gentleman here this afternoon. I don't know what he called himself, and I don't know what his real name is, but I know just a little about him. Enough to want to know more. Am I right in assuming that he made a date with you for some particular spot this evening?'

'Quite right.'

'I thought as much. 16 Westerham Road, Finsbury Park – was that it?'

'You're wrong there,' said Tommy with a smile. 'Dead wrong. The Larches, Hampstead.'

Dymchurch seemed honestly taken aback. Clearly he had not expected this.

'I don't understand it,' he muttered. 'It must be a new layout. The Larches, Hampstead, you said?'

'Yes. I'm to meet him there at eleven o'clock tonight.'

'Don't you do it, sir.'

'There!' burst from Tuppence.

Tommy flushed.

'If you think, Inspector –' he began heatedly.

But the Inspector raised a soothing hand.

'I'll tell you what I think, Mr Blunt. The place you want to be at eleven o'clock tonight is here in this office.'

'What?' cried Tuppence, astonished.

'Here in this office. Never mind how I know – departments overlap sometimes – but you got one of those famous "Blue" letters today. Old what's-his-name is after that. He lures you up to Hampstead, makes quite sure of your being out of the way, and steps in here at night when all the building is empty and quiet to have a good search round at his leisure.'

'But why should he think the letter would be here? He'd know I should have it on me or else have passed it on.'

'Begging your pardon, sir, that's just what he wouldn't know. He may have tumbled to the fact that you're not the original Mr Blunt, but he probably thinks that you're a bona fide gentleman who's bought the business. In that case, the letter would be all in the way of regular business and would be filed as such.'

'I see,' said Tuppence.

'And that's just what we've got to let him think. We'll catch him red-handed here tonight.'

'So that's the plan, is it?'

'Yes. It's the chance of a lifetime. Now, let me see, what's the time? Six o'clock. What time do you usually leave here, sir?'

'About six.'

'You must seem to leave the place as usual. Actually we'll sneak back to it as soon as possible. I don't believe they'll come here till about eleven, but of course they might. If you'll excuse me, I'll just go and take a look round outside and see if I can make out anyone watching the place.'

Dymchurch departed, and Tommy began an argument with Tuppence.

It lasted some time and was heated and acrimonious. In the end Tuppence suddenly capitulated.

'All right,' she said. 'I give in. I'll go home and sit there like a good little girl whilst you tackle crooks and hobnob with detectives – but you wait, young man. I'll be even with you yet for keeping me out of the fun.'

Dymchurch returned at that moment.

'Coast seems clear enough,' he said. 'But you can't tell. Better seem to leave in the usual manner. They won't go on watching the place once you've gone.'

Tommy called Albert and gave him instructions to lock up.

Then the four of them made their way to the garage near by where the car was usually left. Tuppence drove and Albert sat beside her. Tommy and the detective sat behind.

Presently they were held up by a block in the traffic. Tuppence looked over her shoulder and nodded. Tommy and the detective opened the right hand door and stepped out into the middle of Oxford Street. In a minute or two Tuppence drove on.

CHAPTER VI

The Adventure of the
Sinister Stranger (*continued*)

'Better not go in just yet,' said Dymchurch as he and Tommy hurried into Haleham Street. 'You've got the key all right?'

Tommy nodded.

'Then what about a bite of dinner? It's early, but there's a little place here right opposite. We'll get a table by the window, so that we can watch the place all the time.'

They had a very welcome little meal, in the manner the detective had suggested. Tommy found Inspector Dymchurch quite an entertaining companion. Most of his official work had lain amongst international spies, and he had tales to tell which astonished his simple listener.

They remained in the little restaurant until eight o'clock, when Dymchurch suggested a move.

'It's quite dark now, sir,' he explained. 'We shall be able to slip in without any one being the wiser.'

It was, as he said, quite dark. They crossed the road, looked quickly up and down the deserted street, and slipped inside the entrance. Then they mounted the stairs, and Tommy inserted his key in the lock of the outer office.

Just as he did so, he heard, as he thought, Dymchurch whistle beside him.

'What are you whistling for?' he asked sharply.

'*I* didn't whistle,' said Dymchurch, very much astonished. 'I thought *you* did.'

'Well, some one –' began Tommy.

He got no further. Strong arms seized him from behind, and

before he could cry out, a pad of something sweet and sickly was pressed over his mouth and nose.

He struggled valiantly, but in vain. The chloroform did its work. His head began to whirl and the floor heaved up and down in front of him. Choking, he lost consciousness . . .

He came to himself painfully, but in full possession of his faculties. The chloroform had been only a whiff. They had kept him under long enough to force a gag into his mouth and ensure that he did not cry out.

When he came to himself, he was half-lying, half-sitting, propped against the wall in a corner of his own inner office. Two men were busily turning out the contents of the desk and ransacking the cupboards, and as they worked they cursed freely.

'Swelp me, guv'nor,' said the taller of the two hoarsely, 'we've turned the whole b–y place upside down and inside out. It's not there.'

'It must be here,' snarled the other. 'It isn't on him. And there's no other place it can be.'

As he spoke he turned, and to Tommy's utter amazement he saw that the last speaker was none other than Inspector Dymchurch. The latter grinned when he saw Tommy's astonished face.

'So our young friend is awake again,' he said. 'And a little surprised – yes, a little surprised. But it was so simple. We suspect that all is not as it should be with the International Detective Agency. I volunteer to find out if that is so, or not. If the new Mr Blunt is indeed a spy, he will be suspicious, so I send first my dear old friend, Carl Bauer. Carl is told to act suspiciously and pitch an improbable tale. He does so, and then I appear on the scene. I used the name of Inspector Marriot to gain confidence. The rest is easy.'

He laughed.

Tommy was dying to say several things, but the gag in his mouth prevented him. Also, he was dying to *do* several things – mostly with his hands and feet – but alas, that too had been attended to. He was securely bound.

The thing that amazed him most was the astounding change in the man standing over him. As Inspector Dymchurch the fellow had been a typical Englishman. Now, no one could have mistaken him for a moment for anything but a well-educated foreigner who talked English perfectly without a trace of accent.

'Coggins, my good friend,' said the erstwhile Inspector, addressing his ruffianly-looking associate, 'take your life-preserver and stand by the prisoner. I am going to remove the gag. You understand, my dear Mr Blunt, do you not, that it would be criminally foolish on your part to cry out? But I am sure you do. For your age, you are quite an intelligent lad.'

Very deftly he removed the gag and stepped back.

Tommy eased his stiff jaws, rolled his tongue round his mouth, swallowed twice – and said nothing at all.

'I congratulate you on your restraint,' said the other. 'You appreciate the position, I see. Have you nothing at all to say?'

'What I have to say will keep,' said Tommy. 'And it won't spoil by waiting.'

'Ah! What I have to say will not keep. In plain English, Mr Blunt, where is that letter?'

'My dear fellow, I don't know,' said Tommy cheerfully. 'I haven't got it. But you know that as well as I do. I should go on looking about if I were you. I like to see you and friend Coggins playing hide-and-seek together.'

The other's face darkened.

'You are pleased to be flippant, Mr Blunt. You see that square box over there. That is Coggins's little outfit. In it there is vitriol ... yes, vitriol ... and irons that can be heated in the fire, so that they are red hot and burn ...'

Tommy shook his head sadly.

'An error in diagnosis,' he murmured. 'Tuppence and I labelled this adventure wrong. It's not a Clubfoot story. It's a Bulldog Drummond, and you are the inimitable Carl Peterson.'

'What is this nonsense you are talking,' snarled the other.

'Ah!' said Tommy. 'I see you are unacquainted with the classics. A pity.'

'Ignorant fool! Will you do what we want or will you not? Shall I tell Coggins to get out his tools and begin?'

'Don't be so impatient,' said Tommy. 'Of course I'll do what you want, as soon as you tell me what it is. You don't suppose I want to be carved up like a filleted sole and fried on a gridiron? I loathe being hurt.'

Dymchurch looked at him in contempt.

'Gott! What cowards are these English.'

'Common sense, my dear fellow, merely common sense. Leave the vitriol alone and let us come down to brass tacks.'

'I want the letter.'

'I've already told you I haven't got it.'

'We know that – we also know who must have it. The girl.'

'Very possibly you're right,' said Tommy. 'She may have slipped it into her handbag when your pal Carl startled us.'

'Oh, you do not deny. That is wise. Very good, you will write to this Tuppence, as you call her, bidding her bring the letter here immediately.'

'I can't do that,' began Tommy.

The other cut in before he had finished the sentence.

'Ah! You can't? Well, we shall soon see. Coggins!'

'Don't be in such a hurry,' said Tommy. 'And do wait for the end of the sentence. I was going to say that I can't do that unless you untie my arms. Hang it all, I'm not one of those freaks who can write with their noses or their elbows.'

'You are willing to write, then?'

'Of course. Haven't I been telling you so all along? I'm all out to be pleasant and obliging. You won't do anything unkind to Tuppence, of course. I'm sure you won't. She's such a nice girl.'

'We only want the letter,' said Dymchurch, but there was a singularly unpleasant smile on his face.

At a nod from him the brutal Coggins knelt down and unfastened Tommy's arms. The latter swung them to and fro.

'That's better,' he said cheerfully. 'Will kind Coggins hand me my fountain pen? It's on the table, I think, with my other miscellaneous property.'

Scowling, the man brought it to him, and provided a sheet of paper.

'Be careful what you say,' Dymchurch said menacingly. 'We leave it to you, but failure means – death – and slow death at that.'

'In that case,' said Tommy, 'I will certainly do my best.'

He reflected a minute or two, then began to scribble rapidly.

'How will this do?' he asked, handing over the completed epistle.

Dear Tuppence,
  Can you come along at once and bring that blue letter with you? We want to decode it here and now.

                                   In haste,
                                   Francis.

'Francis?' queried the bogus Inspector, with lifted eyebrows. 'Was that the name she called you?'

'As you weren't at my christening,' said Tommy, 'I don't suppose you can know whether it's my name or not. But I think the cigarette case you took from my pocket is a pretty good proof that I'm speaking the truth.'

The other stepped over to the table and took up the case, read 'Francis from Tuppence' with a faint grin and laid it down again.

'I am glad to find you are behaving so sensibly,' he said. 'Coggins, give that note to Vassilly. He is on guard outside. Tell him to take it at once.'

The next twenty minutes passed slowly, the ten minutes after that more slowly still. Dymchurch was striding up and down with a face that grew darker and darker. Once he turned menacingly on Tommy.

'If you have dared to double-cross us,' he growled.

'If we'd had a pack of cards here, we might have had a game of picquet to pass the time,' drawled Tommy. 'Women always keep one waiting. I hope you're not going to be unkind to little Tuppence when she comes?'

'Oh, no,' said Dymchurch. 'We shall arrange for you to go to the same place – together.'

'Will you, you swine,' said Tommy under his breath.

Suddenly there was a stir in the outer office. A man whom Tommy had not yet seen poked his head in and growled something in Russian.

'Good,' said Dymchurch. 'She is coming – and coming alone.'

For a moment a faint anxiety caught at Tommy's heart.

The next minute he heard Tuppence's voice.

'Oh! there you are, Inspector Dymchurch. I've brought the letter. Where is Francis?'

With the last words she came through the door, and Vassilly sprang on her from behind, clapping his hand over her mouth. Dymchurch tore the handbag from her grasp and turned over its contents in a frenzied search.

Suddenly he uttered an ejaculation of delight and held up a blue envelope with a Russian stamp on it. Coggins gave a hoarse shout.

And just in that minute of triumph the other door, the door into Tuppence's own office, opened noiselessly and Inspector Marriot and two men armed with revolvers stepped into the room, with the sharp command: 'Hands up.'

There was no fight. The others were taken at a hopeless disadvantage. Dymchurch's automatic lay on the table, and the two others were not armed.

'A very nice little haul,' said Inspector Marriot with approval, as he snapped the last pair of handcuffs. 'And we'll have more as time goes on, I hope.'

White with rage, Dymchurch glared at Tuppence.

'You little devil,' he snarled. 'It was you put them on to us.'

Tuppence laughed.

'It wasn't all my doing. I ought to have guessed, I admit, when you brought in the number sixteen this afternoon. But it was Tommy's note clinched matters. I rang up Inspector Marriot, got Albert to meet him with the duplicate key of the office, and came along myself with the empty blue envelope in my bag.

The letter I forwarded according to my instructions as soon as I had parted with you two this afternoon.'

But one word had caught the other's attention.

'*Tommy?*' he queried.

Tommy, who had just been released from his bonds, came towards them.

'Well done, brother Francis,' he said to Tuppence, taking both her hands in his. And to Dymchurch: 'As I told you, my dear fellow, you really ought to read the classics.'

CHAPTER VII

Finessing the King

It was a wet Wednesday in the offices of the International Detective Agency. Tuppence let the *Daily Leader* fall idly from her hand.

'Do you know what I've been thinking, Tommy?'

'It's impossible to say,' replied her husband. 'You think of so many things, and you think of them all at once.'

'I think it's time we went dancing again.'

Tommy picked up the *Daily Leader* hastily.

'Our advertisement looks well,' he remarked, his head on one side. 'Blunt's Brilliant Detectives. Do you realize, Tuppence, that you and you alone are Blunt's Brilliant Detectives? There's glory for you, as Humpty Dumpty would say.'

'I was talking about dancing.'

'There's a curious point that I have observed about newspapers. I wonder if you have ever noticed it. Take these three copies of the *Daily Leader*. Can you tell me how they differ one from the other?'

Tuppence took them with some curiosity.

'It seems fairly easy,' she remarked witheringly. 'One is today's, one is yesterday's, and one is the day before's.'

'Positively scintillating, my dear Watson. But that was not my meaning. Observe the headline, "Daily Leader." Compare the three – do you see any difference between them?'

'No, I don't,' said Tuppence, 'and what's more, I don't believe there is any.'

Tommy sighed and brought the tips of his fingers together in the most approved Sherlock Holmes fashion.

'Exactly. Yet you read the papers as much – in fact, more than I do. But I have observed and you have not. If you will look at today's *Daily Leader*, you will see that in the middle of the downstroke of the D is a small white dot, and there is another in the L of the same word. But in yesterday's paper the white dot is not in DAILY at all. There are two white dots in the L of LEADER. That of the day before again has two dots in the D of DAILY. In fact, the dot, or dots, are in a different position every day.'

'Why?' asked Tuppence.

'That's a journalistic secret.'

'Meaning you don't know, and can't guess.'

'I will merely say this – the practice is common to all news-papers.'

'Aren't you clever?' said Tuppence. 'Especially at drawing red herrings across the track. Let's go back to what we were talking about before.'

'What were we talking about?'

'The Three Arts Ball.'

Tommy groaned.

'No, no, Tuppence. Not the Three Arts Ball. I'm not young enough. I assure you I'm not young enough.'

'When I was a nice young girl,' said Tuppence, 'I was brought up to believe that men – especially husbands – were dissipated beings, fond of drinking and dancing and staying up late at night. It took an exceptionally beautiful and clever wife to keep them at home. Another illusion gone! All the wives I know are hankering to go out and dance, and weeping because their husbands will wear bedroom slippers and go to bed at half-past nine. And you do dance so nicely, Tommy dear.'

'Gently with the butter, Tuppence.'

'As a matter of fact,' said Tuppence, 'it's not purely for plea-sure that I want to go. I'm intrigued by this advertisement.'

She picked up the *Daily Leader* again and read it out.

'I should go three hearts. 12 tricks. Ace of Spades. Necessary to finesse the King.'

'Rather an expensive way of learning bridge,' was Tommy's comment.

'Don't be an ass. That's nothing to do with bridge. You see,

I was lunching with a girl yesterday at the Ace of Spades. It's a queer little underground den in Chelsea, and she told me that it's quite the fashion at these big shows to trundle round there in the course of the evening for bacon and eggs and Welsh rarebits – Bohemian sort of stuff. It's got screened-off booths all around it. Pretty hot place, I should say.'

'And your idea is –?'

'Three hearts stands for the Three Arts Ball, tomorrow night, 12 tricks is twelve o'clock, and the Ace of Spades is the Ace of Spades.'

'And what about its being necessary to finesse the King?'

'Well, that's what I thought we'd find out.'

'I shouldn't wonder if you weren't right, Tuppence,' said Tommy magnanimously. 'But I don't quite see why you want to butt in upon other people's love affairs.'

'I shan't butt in. What I'm proposing is an interesting experiment in detective work. We *need* practice.'

'Business is certainly not too brisk,' agreed Tommy. 'All the same, Tuppence, what you want is to go to the Three Arts Ball and dance! Talk of red herrings.'

Tuppence laughed shamelessly.

'Be a sport, Tommy. Try and forget you're thirty-two and have got one grey hair in your left eyebrow.'

'I was always weak where women were concerned,' murmured her husband. 'Have I got to make an ass of myself in fancy dress?'

'Of course, but you can leave that to me. I've got a splendid idea.'

Tommy looked at her with some misgiving. He was always profoundly mistrustful of Tuppence's brilliant ideas.

When he returned to the flat on the following evening, Tuppence came flying out of her bedroom to meet him.

'It's come,' she announced.

'What's come?'

'The costume. Come and look at it.'

Tommy followed her. Spread out on the bed was a complete fireman's kit with shining helmet.

'Good God!' groaned Tommy. 'Have I joined the Wembley fire brigade?'

'Guess again,' said Tuppence. 'You haven't caught the idea yet. Use your little grey cells, *mon ami*. Scintillate, Watson. Be a bull that has been more than ten minutes in the arena.'

'Wait a minute,' said Tommy. 'I begin to see. There is a dark purpose in this. What are you going to wear, Tuppence?'

'An old suit of your clothes, an American hat and some horn spectacles.'

'Crude,' said Tommy. 'But I catch the idea. McCarty incog. And I am Riordan.'

'That's it. I thought we ought to practise American detective methods as well as English ones. Just for once I am going to be the star, and you will be the humble assistant.'

'Don't forget,' said Tommy warningly, 'that it's always an innocent remark by the simple Denny that puts McCarty on the right track.'

But Tuppence only laughed. She was in high spirits.

It was a most successful evening. The crowds, the music, the fantastic dresses – everything conspired to make the young couple enjoy themselves. Tommy forgot his role of the bored husband dragged out against his will.

At ten minutes to twelve they drove off in the car to the famous – or infamous – Ace of Spades. As Tuppence had said, it was an underground den, mean and tawdry in appearance, but it was nevertheless crowded with couples in fancy dress. There were closed-in booths round the walls, and Tommy and Tuppence secured one of these. They left the doors purposely a little ajar so that they could see what was going on outside.

'I wonder which they are – our people, I mean,' said Tuppence. 'What about that Columbine over there with the red Mephistopheles?'

'I fancy the wicked Mandarin and the lady who calls herself a Battleship – more of a fast Cruiser, I should say.'

'Isn't he witty?' said Tuppence. 'All done on a little drop of drink! Who's this coming in dressed as the Queen of Hearts – rather a good get-up, that.'

The girl in question passed into the booth next to them, accompanied by her escort, who was 'the gentleman dressed in newspaper' from *Alice in Wonderland*. They were both wearing masks – it seemed to be rather a common custom at the Ace of Spades.

'I'm sure we're in a real den of iniquity,' said Tuppence with a pleased face. 'Scandals all round us. What a row everyone makes.'

A cry, as of protest, rang out from the booth next door and was covered by a man's loud laugh. Everybody was laughing and singing. The shrill voices of the girls rose above the booming of their male escorts.

'What about that shepherdess?' demanded Tommy. 'The one with the comic Frenchman. They might be our little lot.'

'Any one might be,' confessed Tuppence. 'I'm not going to bother. The great thing is that we are enjoying ourselves.'

'I could have enjoyed myself better in another costume,' grumbled Tommy. 'You've no idea of the heat of this one.'

'Cheer up,' said Tuppence. 'You look lovely.'

'I'm glad of that,' said Tommy. 'It's more than you do. You're the funniest little guy I've ever seen.'

'Will you keep a civil tongue in your head, Denny, my boy. Hullo, the gentleman in newspaper is leaving his lady alone. Where's he going, do you think?'

'Going to hurry up the drinks, I expect,' said Tommy. 'I wouldn't mind doing the same thing.'

'He's a long time doing it,' said Tuppence, when four or five minutes had passed. 'Tommy, would you think me an awful ass –' She paused.

Suddenly she jumped up.

'Call me an ass if you like. I'm going in next door.'

'Look here, Tuppence – you can't –'

'I've a feeling there's something wrong. I *know* there is. Don't try and stop me.'

She passed quickly out of their own booth, and Tommy followed her. The doors of the one next door were closed. Tuppence pushed them apart and went in, Tommy on her heels.

The girl dressed as the Queen of Hearts sat in the corner leaning up against the wall in a queer huddled position. Her eyes regarded them steadily through her mask, but she did not move. Her dress was carried out in a bold design of red and white, but on the left hand side the pattern seemed to have got mixed. There was more red than there should have been . . .

With a cry Tuppence hurried forward. At the same time, Tommy saw what she had seen, the hilt of a jewelled dagger just below the heart. Tuppence dropped on her knees by the girl's side.

'Quick, Tommy, she's still alive. Get hold of the manager and make him get a doctor at once.'

'Right. Mind you don't touch the handle of that dagger, Tuppence.'

'I'll be careful. Go quickly.'

Tommy hurried out, pulling the doors to behind him. Tuppence passed her arm round the girl. The latter made a faint gesture, and Tuppence realized that she wanted to get rid of the mask. Tuppence unfastened it gently. She saw a fresh, flower-like face, and wide starry eyes that were full of horror, suffering, and a kind of dazed bewilderment.

'My dear,' said Tuppence, very gently. 'Can you speak at all? Will you tell me, if you can, who did this?'

She felt the eyes fix themselves on her face. The girl was sighing, the deep palpitating sighs of a failing heart. And still she looked steadily at Tuppence. Then her lips parted.

'Bingo did it –' she said in a strained whisper.

Then her hands relaxed, and she seemed to nestle down on Tuppence's shoulder.

Tommy came in, two men with him. The bigger of the two came forward with an air of authority, the word doctor written all over him.

Tuppence relinquished her burden.

'She's dead, I'm afraid,' she said with a catch in her voice.

The doctor made a swift examination.

'Yes,' he said. 'Nothing to be done. We had better leave things as they are till the police come. How did the thing happen?'

Tuppence explained rather haltingly, slurring over her reasons for entering the booth.

'It's a curious business,' said the doctor. 'You heard nothing?'

'I heard her give a kind of cry, but then the man laughed. Naturally I didn't think –'

'Naturally not,' agreed the doctor. 'And the man wore a mask you say. You wouldn't recognize him?'

'I'm afraid not. Would you, Tommy?'

'No. Still there is his costume.'

'The first thing will be to identify this poor lady,' said the doctor. 'After that, well, I suppose the police will get down to things pretty quickly. It ought not to be a difficult case. Ah, here they come.'

CHAPTER VIII

The Gentleman Dressed
in Newspaper

It was after three o'clock when, weary and sick at heart, the
husband and wife reached home. Several hours passed before
Tuppence could sleep. She lay tossing from side to side, seeing
always that flower-like face with the horror-stricken eyes.

The dawn was coming in through the shutters when Tuppence finally dropped off to sleep. After the excitement, she
slept heavily and dreamlessly. It was broad daylight when she
awoke to find Tommy, up and dressed, standing by the bedside,
shaking her gently by the arm.

'Wake up, old thing. Inspector Marriot and another man are
here and want to see you.'

'What time is it?'

'Just on eleven. I'll get Alice to bring you your tea right away.'

'Yes, do. Tell Inspector Marriot I'll be there in ten minutes.'

A quarter of an hour later, Tuppence came hurrying into the
sitting-room. Inspector Marriot, who was sitting looking very
straight and solemn, rose to greet her.

'Good-morning, Mrs Beresford. This is Sir Arthur Merivale.'

Tuppence shook hands with a tall thin man with haggard
eyes and greying hair.

'It's about this sad business last night,' said Inspector Marriot.
'I want Sir Arthur to hear from your own lips what you told me
– the words the poor lady said before she died. Sir Arthur has
been very hard to convince.'

'I can't believe,' said the other, 'and I won't believe, that
Bingo Hale ever hurt a hair of Vere's head.'

Inspector Marriot went on.

'We've made some progress since last night, Mrs Beresford,' he said. 'First of all we managed to identify the lady as Lady Merivale. We communicated with Sir Arthur here. He recognized the body at once, and was horrified beyond words, of course. Then I asked him if he knew anyone called Bingo.'

'You must understand, Mrs Beresford,' said Sir Arthur, 'that Captain Hale, who is known to all his friends as Bingo, is the dearest pal I have. He practically lives with us. He was staying at my house when they arrested him this morning. I cannot but believe that you have made a mistake – it was not his name that my wife uttered.'

'There is no possibility of mistake,' said Tuppence gently. 'She said, "Bingo did it –"'

'You see, Sir Arthur,' said Marriot.

The unhappy man sank into a chair and covered his face with his hands.

'It's incredible. What earthly motive could there be? Oh, I know your idea, Inspector Marriot. You think Hale was my wife's lover, but even if that were so – which I don't admit for a moment – what motive was there for killing her?'

Inspector Marriot coughed.

'It's not a very pleasant thing to say, sir. But Captain Hale has been paying a lot of attention to a certain young American lady of late – a young lady with a considerable amount of money. If Lady Merivale liked to turn nasty, she could probably stop his marriage.'

'This is outrageous, Inspector.'

Sir Arthur sprang angrily to his feet. The other calmed him with a soothing gesture.

'I beg your pardon, I'm sure, Sir Arthur. You say that you and Captain Hale both decided to attend this show. Your wife was away on a visit at the time, and you had no idea that she was to be there?'

'Not the least idea.'

'Just show him that advertisement you told me about, Mrs Beresford.'

Tuppence complied.

'That seems to me clear enough. It was inserted by Captain Hale to catch your wife's eye. They had already arranged to meet there. But you only made up your mind to go the day before, hence it was necessary to warn her. That is the explanation of the phrase, "Necessary to finesse the King." You ordered your costume from a theatrical firm at the last minute, but Captain Hale's was a home-made affair. He went as the Gentleman dressed in Newspaper. Do you know, Sir Arthur, what we found clasped in the dead lady's hand? A fragment torn from a newspaper. My men have orders to take Captain Hale's costume away with them from your house. I shall find it at the Yard when I get back. If there's a tear in it corresponding to the missing piece – well, it'll be the end of the case.'

'You won't find it,' said Sir Arthur. 'I know Bingo Hale.'

Apologizing to Tuppence for disturbing her, they took their leave.

Late that evening there was a ring at the bell, and somewhat to the astonishment of the young pair Inspector Marriot once more walked in.

'I thought Blunt's Brilliant Detectives would like to hear the latest developments,' he said, with a hint of a smile.

'They would,' said Tommy. 'Have a drink?'

He placed materials hospitably at Inspector Marriot's elbow.

'It's a clear case,' said the latter, after a minute or two. 'Dagger was the lady's own – the idea was to have made it look like suicide evidently, but thanks to you two being on the spot, that didn't come off. We've found plenty of letters – they'd been carrying on together for some time, that's clear – without Sir Arthur tumbling to it. Then we found the last link –'

'The last what?' said Tuppence sharply.

'The last link in the chain – that fragment of the *Daily Leader*. It was torn from the dress he wore – fits exactly. Oh, yes, it's a perfectly clear case. By the way, I brought round a photograph of those two exhibits – I thought they might interest you. It's very seldom that you get such a perfectly clear case.'

'Tommy,' said Tuppence, when her husband returned from

showing the Scotland Yard man out, 'why do you think Inspector Marriot keeps repeating that it's a perfectly clear case?'

'I don't know. Smug satisfaction, I suppose.'

'Not a bit of it. He's trying to get us irritated. You know, Tommy, butchers, for instance, know something about meat, don't they?'

'I should say so, but what on earth –'

'And in the same way, greengrocers know all about vegetables, and fishermen about fish. Detectives, professional detectives, must know all about criminals. They know the real thing when they see it – and they know when it isn't the real thing. Marriot's expert knowledge tells him that Captain Hale isn't a criminal – but all the facts are dead against him. As a last resource Marriot is egging us on, hoping against hope that some little detail or other will come back to us – something that happened last night – which will throw a different light on things. Tommy, why shouldn't it be suicide, after all?'

'Remember what she said to you.'

'I know – but take that a different way. It was Bingo's doing – his conduct that drove her to kill herself. It's just possible.'

'Just. But it doesn't explain that fragment of newspaper.'

'Let's have a look at Marriot's photographs. I forgot to ask him what Hale's account of the matter was.'

'I asked him that in the hall just now. Hale declared he had never spoken to Lady Merivale at the show. Says somebody shoved a note into his hand which said, "Don't try and speak to me tonight. Arthur suspects." He couldn't produce the piece of paper, though, and it doesn't sound a very likely story. Anyway, you and I *know* he was with her at the Ace of Spades, because we saw him.'

Tuppence nodded and pored over the two photographs.

One was a tiny fragment with the legend DAILY LE – and the rest torn off. The other was the front sheet of the *Daily Leader* with the small round tear at the top of it. There was no doubt about it. Those two fitted together perfectly.

'What are all those marks down the side?' asked Tommy.

'Stitches,' said Tuppence. 'Where it was sewn to the others, you know.'

'I thought it might be a new scheme of dots,' said Tommy. Then he gave a slight shiver. 'My word, Tuppence, how creepy it makes one feel. To think that you and I were discussing dots and puzzling over that advertisement – all as lighthearted as anything.'

Tuppence did not answer. Tommy looked at her and was startled to observe that she was staring ahead of her, her mouth slightly open, and a bewildered expression on her face.

'Tuppence,' said Tommy gently, shaking her by the arm, 'what's the matter with you? Are you just going to have a stroke or something?'

But Tuppence remained motionless. Presently she said in a faraway voice:

'Denis Riordan.'

'Eh?' said Tommy, staring.

'It's just as you said. One simple innocent remark! Find me all this week's *Daily Leaders.*'

'What are you up to?'

'I'm being McCarty. I've been worrying round, and thanks to you, I've got a notion at last. This is the front sheet of Tuesday's paper. I seem to remember that Tuesday's paper was the one with two dots in the L of LEADER. This has a dot in the D of DAILY – and one in the L too. Get me the papers and let's make sure.'

They compared them anxiously. Tuppence had been quite right in her remembrance.

'You see? This fragment wasn't torn from Tuesday's paper.'

'But Tuppence, we can't be sure. It may merely be different editions.'

'It may – but at any rate it's given me an idea. It can't be coincidence – that's certain. There's only one thing it can be if I'm right in my idea. Ring up Sir Arthur, Tommy. Ask him to come round here at once. Say I've got important news for him. Then get hold of Marriot. Scotland Yard will know his address if he's gone home.'

Sir Arthur Merivale, very much intrigued by the summons, arrived at the flat in about half an hour's time. Tuppence came forward to greet him.

'I must apologize for sending for you in such a peremptory fashion,' she said. 'But my husband and I have discovered something that we think you ought to know at once. Do sit down.'

Sir Arthur sat down, and Tuppence went on.

'You are, I know, very anxious to clear your friend.'

Sir Arthur shook his head sadly.

'I was, but even I have had to give in to the overwhelming evidence.'

'What would you say if I told you that chance has placed in my hands a piece of evidence that will certainly clear him of all complicity?'

'I should be overjoyed to hear it, Mrs Beresford.'

'Supposing,' continued Tuppence, 'that I had come across a girl who was actually dancing with Captain Hale last night at twelve o'clock – the hour when he was supposed to be at the Ace of Spades.'

'Marvellous!' cried Sir Arthur. 'I knew there was some mistake. Poor Vere must have killed herself after all.'

'Hardly that,' said Tuppence. 'You forget the other man.'

'What other man?'

'The one my husband and I saw leave the booth. You see, Sir Arthur, there must have been a second man dressed in newspaper at the ball. By the way, what was your own costume?'

'Mine? I went as a seventeenth century executioner.'

'How very appropriate,' said Tuppence softly.

'Appropriate, Mrs Beresford. What do you mean by appropriate?'

'For the part you played. Shall I tell you my ideas on the subject, Sir Arthur? The newspaper dress is easily put on over that of an executioner. Previously a little note has been slipped into Captain Hale's hand, asking him not to speak to a certain lady. But the lady herself knows nothing of that note. She goes to the Ace of Spades at the appointed time and sees the figure she expects to see. They go into the booth. He takes her in his arms, I think, and kisses her – the kiss of a Judas, and as he kisses he strikes with the dagger. She only utters one faint cry and he covers that with a laugh. Presently he goes away – and to the last, horrified and bewildered, she believes her lover is the man who killed her.

'But she has torn a small fragment from the costume. The murderer notices that – he is a man who pays great attention to detail. To make the case absolutely clear against his victim the fragment must seem to have been torn from Captain Hale's costume. That would present great difficulties unless the two men happened to be living in the same house. Then, of course, the thing would be simplicity itself. He makes an exact duplicate of the tear in Captain Hale's costume – then he burns his own and prepares to play the part of the loyal friend.'

Tuppence paused.

'Well, Sir Arthur?'

Sir Arthur rose and made her a bow.

'The rather vivid imagination of a charming lady who reads too much fiction.'

'You think so?' said Tommy.

'And a husband who is guided by his wife,' said Sir Arthur. 'I do not fancy you will find anybody to take the matter seriously.'

He laughed out loud, and Tuppence stiffened in her chair.

'I would swear to that laugh anywhere,' she said. 'I heard it last in the Ace of Spades. And you are under a little misapprehension about us both. Beresford is our real name, but we have another.'

She picked up a card from the table and handed it to him. Sir Arthur read it aloud.

'International Detective Agency . . .' He drew his breath sharply. 'So that is what you really are! That was why Marriot brought me here this morning. It was a trap – '

He strolled to the window.

'A fine view you have from here,' he said. 'Right over London.'

'Inspector Marriot,' cried Tommy sharply.

In a flash the Inspector appeared from the communicating door in the opposite wall.

A little smile of amusement came to Sir Arthur's lips.

'I thought as much,' he said. 'But you won't get me this time, I'm afraid, Inspector. I prefer to take my own way out.'

And putting his hands on the sill, he vaulted clean through the window.

Tuppence shrieked and clapped her hands to her ears to shut out the sound she had already imagined – the sickening thud far beneath. Inspector Marriot uttered an oath.

'We should have thought of the window,' he said. 'Though, mind you, it would have been a difficult thing to prove. I'll go down and – and – see to things.'

'Poor devil,' said Tommy slowly. 'If he was fond of his wife –'

But the Inspector interrupted him with a snort.

'Fond of her? That's as may be. He was at his wits' end where to turn for money. Lady Merivale had a large fortune of her own, and it all went to him. If she'd bolted with young Hale, he'd never have seen a penny of it.'

'That was it, was it?'

'Of course, from the very start, I sensed that Sir Arthur was a bad lot, and that Captain Hale was all right. We know pretty well what's what at the Yard – but it's awkward when you're up against facts. I'll be going down now – I should give your wife a glass of brandy if I were you, Mr Beresford – it's been upsetting like for her.'

'Greengrocers,' said Tuppence in a low voice as the door closed behind the imperturbable Inspector, 'butchers, fishermen, detectives. I was right, wasn't I? He knew.'

Tommy, who had been busy at the sideboard, approached her with a large glass.

'Drink this.'

'What is it? Brandy?'

'No, it's a large cocktail – suitable for a triumphant McCarty. Yes, Marriot's right all round – that was the way of it. A bold finesse for game and rubber.'

Tuppence nodded.

'But he finessed the wrong way round.'

'And so,' said Tommy, 'exit the King.'

CHAPTER IX

The Case of
the Missing Lady

The buzzer on Mr Blunt's desk – International Detective Agency, Manager, Theodore Blunt – uttered its warning call. Tommy and Tuppence both flew to their respective peepholes which commanded a view of the outer office. There it was Albert's business to delay the prospective client with various artistic devices.

'I will see, sir,' he was saying. 'But I'm afraid Mr Blunt is very busy just at present. He is engaged with Scotland Yard on the phone just now.'

'I'll wait,' said the visitor. 'I haven't got a card with me, but my name is Gabriel Stavansson.'

The client was a magnificent specimen of manhood, standing over six foot high. His face was bronzed and weatherbeaten, and the extraordinary blue of his eyes made an almost startling contrast to the brown skin.

Tommy swiftly made up his mind. He put on his hat, picked up some gloves and opened the door. He paused on the threshold.

'This gentleman is waiting to see you, Mr Blunt,' said Albert.

A quick frown passed over Tommy's face. He took out his watch.

'I am due at the Duke's at a quarter to eleven,' he said. Then he looked keenly at the visitor. 'I can give you a few minutes if you will come this way.'

The latter followed him obediently into the inner office, where Tuppence was sitting demurely with pad and pencil.

'My confidential secretary, Miss Robinson,' said Tommy.

'Now, sir, perhaps you will state your business? Beyond the fact that it is urgent, that you came here in a taxi, and that you have lately been in the Arctic – or possibly the Antarctic, I know nothing.'

The visitor stared at him in amazement.

'But this is marvellous,' he cried. 'I thought detectives only did such things in books! Your office boy did not even give you my name!'

Tommy sighed deprecatingly.

'Tut, tut, all that was very easy,' he said. 'The rays of the midnight sun within the Arctic circle have a peculiar action upon the skin – the actinic rays have certain properties. I am writing a little monograph on the subject shortly. But all this is wide of the point. What is it that has brought you to me in such distress of mind?'

'To begin with, Mr Blunt, my name is Gabriel Stavansson –'

'Ah! of course,' said Tommy. 'The well-known explorer. You have recently returned from the region of the North Pole, I believe?'

'I landed in England three days ago. A friend who was cruising in northern waters brought me back on his yacht. Otherwise I should not have got back for another fortnight. Now I must tell you, Mr Blunt, that before I started on this last expedition two years ago, I had the great good fortune to become engaged to Mrs Maurice Leigh Gordon –'

Tommy interrupted.

'Mrs Leigh Gordon was, before her marriage –?'

'The Honourable Hermione Crane, second daughter of Lord Lanchester,' reeled off Tuppence glibly.

Tommy threw her a glance of admiration.

'Her first husband was killed in the war,' added Tuppence.

Gabriel Stavansson nodded.

'That is quite correct. As I was saying, Hermione and I became engaged. I offered, of course, to give up this expedition, but she wouldn't hear of such a thing – bless her! She's the right kind of woman for an explorer's wife. Well, my first thought on landing was to see Hermione. I sent a telegram from Southampton, and rushed up to town by the first train. I knew that she was living for the time being with an aunt of hers, Lady Susan Clonray, in Pont Street, and I went straight there. To my great disappointment, I found that Hermy was away visiting some friends in Northumberland. Lady Susan was quite nice about it, after getting over her first surprise at seeing me. As I told you, I wasn't expected for another fortnight. She said Hermy would be returning in a few days' time. Then I asked for her address, but the old woman hummed and hawed – said Hermy was staying at one or two different places and that she wasn't quite sure what order she was taking them in. I may as well tell you, Mr Blunt, that Lady Susan and I have never got on very well. She's one of those fat women with double chins. I loathe fat women – always have – fat women and fat dogs are an abomination unto the Lord – and unfortunately they so often go together! It's an idiosyncrasy of mine, I know – but there it is – I never can get on with a fat woman.'

'Fashion agrees with you, Mr Stavansson,' said Tommy dryly. 'And every one has their own pet aversion – that of the late Lord Roberts was cats.'

'Mind you, I'm not saying that Lady Susan isn't a perfectly charming woman – she may be, but I've never taken to her. I've always felt, deep down, that she disapproved of our engagement, and I feel sure that she would influence Hermy against me if that were possible. I'm telling you this for what it's worth. Count it out as prejudice if you like. Well, to go on with my story, I'm the kind of obstinate brute who likes his own way. I didn't leave Pont Street until I'd got out of her the names and addresses of the people Hermy was likely to be staying with. Then I took the mail train north.'

'You are, I perceive, a man of action, Mr Stavansson,' said Tommy, smiling.

'The thing came upon me like a bombshell. Mr Blunt, none of these people had seen a sign of Hermy. Of the three houses, only one had been expecting her – Lady Susan must have made a bloomer over the other two – and she had put off her visit there at the last moment by telegram. I returned post haste to

London, of course, and went straight to Lady Susan. I will do her the justice to say that she seemed upset. She admitted that she had no idea where Hermy could be. All the same, she strongly negatived any idea of going to the police. She pointed out that Hermy was not a silly young girl, but an independent woman who had always been in the habit of making her own plans. She was probably carrying out some idea of her own.

'I thought it quite likely that Hermy didn't want to report all her movements to Lady Susan. But I was still worried. I had the queer feeling one gets when something is wrong. I was just leaving when a telegram was brought to Lady Susan. She read it with an expression of relief and handed it to me. It ran as follows: "*Changed my plans. Just off to Monte Carlo for a week. – Hermy.*"

Tommy held out his hand.

'You have got the telegram with you?'

'No, I haven't. But it was handed in at Maldon, Surrey. I noticed that at the time, because it struck me as odd. What should Hermy be doing at Maldon. She'd no friends there that I had ever heard of.'

'You didn't think of rushing off to Monte Carlo in the same way that you had rushed north?'

'I thought of it, of course. But I decided against it. You see, Mr Blunt, whilst Lady Susan seemed quite satisfied by that telegram, I wasn't. It struck me as odd that she should always telegraph, not write. A line or two in her own handwriting would have set all my fears at rest. But anyone can sign a telegram "Hermy." The more I thought it over, the more uneasy I got. In the end I went down to Maldon. That was yesterday afternoon. It's a fair-sized place – good links there and all that – two hotels. I inquired everywhere I could think of, but there wasn't a sign that Hermy had ever been there. Coming back in the train I read your advertisement and I thought I'd put it up to you. If Hermy has really gone off to Monte Carlo, I don't want to set the police on her track and make a scandal, but I'm not going to be sent off on a wild goose chase myself. I stay here in London, in case – in case there's been foul play of any kind.'

Tommy nodded thoughtfully.

'What do you suspect exactly?'

'I don't know. But I feel there's something wrong.'

With a quick movement, Stavansson took a case from his pocket and laid it open before them.

'That is Hermione,' he said. 'I will leave it with you.'

The photograph represented a tall, willowy woman, no longer in her first youth, but with a charming frank smile and lovely eyes.

'Now, Mr Stavansson,' said Tommy, 'there is nothing you have omitted to tell me?'

'Nothing whatever.'

'No detail, however small?'

'I don't think so.'

Tommy sighed.

'That makes the task harder,' he observed. 'You must often have noticed, Mr Stavansson, in reading of crime, how one small detail is all the great detective needs to set him on the track. I may say that this case presents some unusual features. I have, I think, partially solved it already, but time will show.'

He picked up a violin which lay on the table and drew the bow once or twice across the strings. Tuppence ground her teeth, and even the explorer blenched. The performer laid the instrument down again.

'A few chords from Mosgovskensky,' he murmured. 'Leave me your address, Mr Stavansson, and I will report progress to you.'

As the visitor left the office, Tuppence grabbed the violin, and putting it in the cupboard turned the key in the lock.

'If you must be Sherlock Holmes,' she observed, 'I'll get you a nice little syringe and a bottle labelled cocaine, but for God's sake leave that violin alone. If that nice explorer man hadn't been as simple as a child, he'd have seen through you. Are you going on with the Sherlock Holmes touch?'

'I flatter myself that I have carried it through very well so far,' said Tommy with some complacence. 'The deductions were good, weren't they? I had to risk the taxi. After all, it's the only sensible way of getting to this place.'

'It's lucky I had just read the bit about his engagement in this morning's *Daily Mirror*,' remarked Tuppence.

'Yes, that looked well for the efficiency of Blunt's Brilliant Detectives. This is decidedly a Sherlock Holmes case. Even you cannot have failed to notice the similarity between it and the disappearance of Lady Frances Carfax.'

'Do you expect to find Mrs Leigh Gordon's body in a coffin?'

'Logically, history should repeat itself. Actually – well, what do you think?'

'Well,' said Tuppence. 'The most obvious explanation seems to be that for some reason or other, Hermy, as he calls her, is afraid to meet her fiancé, and that Lady Susan is backing her up. In fact, to put it bluntly, she's come a cropper of some kind, and has got the wind up about it.'

'That occurred to me also,' said Tommy. 'But I thought we'd better make pretty certain before suggesting that explanation to a man like Stavansson. What about a run down to Maldon, old thing? And it would do no harm to take some golf clubs with us.'

Tuppence agreeing, the International Detective Agency was left in the charge of Albert.

Maldon, though a well-known residential place, did not cover a large area. Tommy and Tuppence, making every possible inquiry that ingenuity could suggest, nevertheless drew a complete blank. It was as they were returning to London that a brilliant idea occurred to Tuppence.

'Tommy, why did they put Maldon, Surrey, on the telegram?'

'Because Maldon is in Surrey, idiot.'

'Idiot yourself – I don't mean that. If you get a telegram from – Hastings, say, or Torquay, they don't put the county after it. But from Richmond, they do put Richmond, Surrey. That's because there are two Richmonds.'

Tommy, who was driving, slowed up.

'Tuppence,' he said affectionately, 'your idea is not so dusty. Let us make inquiries at yonder post office.'

They drew up before a small building in the middle of a village street. A very few minutes sufficed to elicit the information that there were two Maldons. Maldon, Surrey, and Maldon, Sussex, the latter, a tiny hamlet but possessed of a telegraph office.

'That's it,' said Tuppence excitedly. 'Stavansson knew Maldon was in Surrey, so he hardly looked at the word beginning with S after Maldon.'

'Tomorrow,' said Tommy, 'we'll have a look at Maldon, Sussex.'

Maldon, Sussex, was a very different proposition to its Surrey namesake. It was four miles from a railway station, possessed two public houses, two small shops, a post and telegraph office combined with a sweet and picture postcard business, and about seven small cottages. Tuppence took on the shops whilst Tommy betook himself to the Cock and Sparrow. They met half an hour later.

'Well?' said Tuppence.

'Quite good beer,' said Tommy, 'but no information.'

'You'd better try the King's Head,' said Tuppence. 'I'm going back to the post office. There's a sour old woman there, but I heard them yell to her that dinner was ready.'

She returned to the place and began examining postcards. A fresh-faced girl, still munching, came out of the back room.

'I'd like these, please,' said Tuppence. 'And do you mind waiting whilst I just look over these comic ones?'

She sorted through a packet, talking as she did so.

'I'm ever so disappointed you couldn't tell me my sister's address. She's staying near here and I've lost her letter. Leigh Gordon, her name is.'

The girl shook her head.

'I don't remember it. And we don't get many letters through here either – so I probably should if I'd seen it on a letter. Apart from the Grange, there isn't many big houses round about.'

'What is the Grange?' asked Tuppence. 'Who does it belong to?'

'Dr Horriston has it. It's turned into a nursing home now. Nerve cases mostly, I believe. Ladies that come down for rest cures, and all that sort of thing. Well, it's quiet enough down here, heaven knows.' She giggled.

Tuppence hastily selected a few cards and paid for them.

'That's Doctor Horriston's car coming along now,' exclaimed the girl.

Tuppence hurried to the shop door. A small two-seater was passing. At the wheel was a tall dark man with a neat black beard and a powerful unpleasant face. The car went straight on down the street. Tuppence saw Tommy crossing the road towards her.

'Tommy, I believe I've got it. Doctor Horriston's nursing home.'

'I heard about it at the King's Head, and I thought there might be something in it. But if she's had a nervous breakdown or anything of that sort, her aunt and her friends would know about it surely.'

'Ye-es. I didn't mean that. Tommy, did you see that man in the two-seater?'

'Unpleasant-looking brute, yes.'

'That was Doctor Horriston.'

Tommy whistled.

'Shifty looking beggar. What do you say about it, Tuppence? Shall we go and have a look at the Grange?'

They found the place at last, a big rambling house, surrounded by deserted grounds, with a swift mill stream running behind the house.

'Dismal sort of abode,' said Tommy. 'It gives me the creeps, Tuppence. You know, I've a feeling this is going to turn out a far more serious matter than we thought at first.'

'Oh, don't. If only we are in time. That woman's in some awful danger; I feel it in my bones.'

'Don't let your imagination run away with you.'

'I can't help it. I mistrust that man. What shall we do? I think it would be a good plan if I went and rang the bell alone first and asked boldly for Mrs Leigh Gordon just to see what answer

I get. Because, after all, it may be perfectly fair and above board.'

Tuppence carried out her plan. The door was opened almost immediately by a manservant with an impassive face.

'I want to see Mrs Leigh Gordon, if she is well enough to see me.'

She fancied that there was a momentary flicker of the man's eyelashes, but he answered readily enough.

'There is no one of that name here, madam.'

'Oh, surely. This is Doctor Horriston's place, The Grange, is it not?'

'Yes, madam, but there is nobody of the name of Mrs Leigh Gordon here.'

Baffled, Tuppence was forced to withdraw and hold a further consultation with Tommy outside the gate.

'Perhaps he was speaking the truth. After all, we don't *know*.'

'He wasn't. He was lying. I'm sure of it.'

'Wait until the doctor comes back,' said Tommy. 'Then I'll pass myself off as a journalist anxious to discuss his new system of rest cure with him. That will give me a chance of getting inside and studying the geography of the place.'

The doctor returned about half an hour later. Tommy gave him about five minutes, then he in turn marched up to the front door. But he too returned baffled.

'The doctor was engaged and couldn't be disturbed. And he never sees journalists. Tuppence, you're right. There's something fishy about this place. It's ideally situated – miles from anywhere. Any mortal thing could go on here, and no one would ever know.'

'Come on,' said Tuppence, with determination.

'What are you going to do?'

'I'm going to climb over the wall and see if I can't get up to the house quietly without being seen.'

'Right. I'm with you.'

The garden was somewhat overgrown and afforded a multitude of cover. Tommy and Tuppence managed to reach the back of the house unobserved.

Here there was a wide terrace with some crumbling steps

leading down from it. In the middle some french windows opened on to the terrace, but they dared not step out into the open, and the windows where they were crouching were too high for them to be able to look in. It did not seem as though their reconnaissance would be much use, when suddenly Tuppence tightened her grasp of Tommy's arm.

Someone was speaking in the room close to them. The window was open and the fragment of conversation came clearly to their ears.

'Come in, come in, and shut the door,' said a man's voice irritably. 'A lady came about an hour ago, you said, and asked for Mrs Leigh Gordon?'

Tuppence recognized the answering voice as that of the impassive manservant.

'Yes, sir.'

'You said she wasn't here, of course?'

'Of course, sir.'

'And now this journalist fellow,' fumed the other.

He came suddenly to the window, throwing up the sash, and the two outside, peering through a screen of bushes, recognized Dr Horriston.

'It's the woman I mind most about,' continued the doctor. 'What did she look like?'

'Young, good-looking, and very smartly dressed, sir.'

Tommy nudged Tuppence in the ribs.

'Exactly,' said the doctor between his teeth, 'as I feared. Some friend of the Leigh Gordon woman's. It's getting very difficult. I shall have to take steps –'

He left the sentence unfinished. Tommy and Tuppence heard the door close. There was silence.

Gingerly Tommy led the retreat. When they had reached a little clearing not far away, but out of earshot from the house, he spoke.

'Tuppence, old thing, this is getting serious. They mean mischief. I think we ought to get back to town at once and see Stavansson.'

To his surprise Tuppence shook her head.

'We must stay down here. Didn't you hear him say he was going to take steps – That might mean anything.'

'The worst of it is we've hardly got a case to go to the police on.'

'Listen, Tommy. Why not ring up Stavansson from the village? I'll stay around here.'

'Perhaps that is the best plan,' agreed her husband. 'But I say – Tuppence –'

'Well?'

'Take care of yourself – won't you?'

'Of course I shall, you silly old thing. Cut along.'

It was some two hours later that Tommy returned. He found Tuppence awaiting him near the gate.

'Well?'

'I couldn't get on to Stavansson. Then I tried Lady Susan. She was out too. Then I thought of ringing up old Brady. I asked him to look up Horriston in the Medical Directory or whatever the thing calls itself.'

'Well, what did Dr Brady say?'

'Oh, he knew the name at once. Horriston was once a bona fide doctor, but he came a cropper of some kind. Brady called him a most unscrupulous quack, and said he, personally, wouldn't be surprised at anything. The question is, what are we to do now?'

'We must stay here,' said Tuppence instantly. 'I've a feeling they mean something to happen tonight. By the way, a gardener has been clipping ivy round the house. Tommy, *I saw where he put the ladder.*'

'Good for you, Tuppence,' said her husband appreciatively. 'Then tonight –'

'As soon as it's dark –'

'We shall see –'

'What we shall see.'

Tommy took his turn at watching the house whilst Tuppence went to the village and had some food.

Then she returned and they took up the vigil together. At nine o'clock they decided that it was dark enough to commence operations. They were now able to circle round the house in perfect freedom. Suddenly Tuppence clutched Tommy by the arm.

'Listen.'

The sound she had heard came again, borne faintly on the night air. It was the moan of a woman in pain. Tuppence pointed upward to a window on the first floor.

'It came from that room,' she whispered.

Again that low moan rent the stillness of the night.

The two listeners decided to put their original plan into action. Tuppence led the way to where she had seen the gardener put the ladder. Between them they carried it to the side of the house from which they had heard the moaning. All the blinds of the ground floor rooms were drawn, but this particular window upstairs was unshuttered.

Tommy put the ladder as noiselessly as possible against the side of the house.

'I'll go up,' whispered Tuppence. 'You stay below. I don't mind climbing ladders and you can steady it better than I could. And in case the doctor should come round the corner you'd be able to deal with him and I shouldn't.'

Nimbly Tuppence swarmed up the ladder and raised her head cautiously to look in at the window. Then she ducked it swiftly, but after a minute or two brought it very slowly up again. She stayed there for about five minutes. Then she descended again.

'It's her,' she said breathlessly and ungrammatically. 'But, oh, Tommy, it's horrible. She's lying there in bed, moaning, and turning to and fro – and just as I got there a woman dressed as a nurse came in. She bent over her and injected something in her arm and then went away again. What shall we do?'

'Is she conscious?'

'I think so. I'm almost sure she is. I fancy she may be strapped to the bed. I'm going up again, and if I can I'm going to get into that room.'

'I say, Tuppence –'

'If I'm in any sort of danger, I'll yell for you. So long.'

Avoiding further argument Tuppence hurried up the ladder again. Tommy saw her try the window, then noiselessly push up the sash. Another second and she had disappeared inside.

And now an agonizing time came for Tommy. He could hear nothing at first. Tuppence and Mrs Leigh Gordon must be talking in whispers if they were talking at all. Presently he did hear a low murmur of voices and drew a breath of relief. But suddenly the voices stopped. Dead silence.

Tommy strained his ears. Nothing. What could they be doing?

Suddenly a hand fell on his shoulder.

'Come on,' said Tuppence's voice out of the darkness.

'Tuppence! How did you get here?'

'Through the front door. Let's get out of this.'

'Get out of this?'

'That's what I said.'

'But – Mrs Leigh Gordon?'

In a tone of indescribable bitterness Tuppence replied: 'Getting thin!'

Tommy looked at her, suspecting irony.

'What do you mean?'

'What I say. Getting thin. Slinkiness. Reduction of weight. Didn't you hear Stavansson say he hated fat women? In the two years he's been away, his Hermy has put on weight. Got a panic when she knew he was coming back and rushed off to do this new treatment of Dr Horriston's. It's injections of some sort, and he makes a deadly secret of it, and charges through the nose. I dare say he *is* a quack – but he's a damned successful one! Stavansson comes home a fortnight too soon, when she's only beginning the treatment. Lady Susan has been sworn to secrecy and plays up. And we come down here and make blithering idiots of ourselves!'

Tommy drew a deep breath.

'I believe, Watson,' he said with dignity, 'that there is a very good concert at the Queen's Hall tomorrow. We shall be in plenty of time for it. And you will oblige me by not placing this case upon your records. It has absolutely *no* distinctive features.'

CHAPTER X

Blindman's Buff

'Right,' said Tommy, and replaced the receiver on its hook.

Then he turned to Tuppence.

'That was the Chief. Seems to have got the wind up about us. It appears that the parties we're after have got wise to the fact that I'm not the genuine Mr Theodore Blunt. We're to expect excitements at any minute. The Chief begs you as a favour to go home and stay at home, and not mix yourself up in it any more. Apparently the hornet's nest we've stirred up is bigger than anyone imagined.'

'All that about my going home is nonsense,' said Tuppence decidedly. 'Who is going to look after you if I go home? Besides, I like excitement. Business hasn't been very brisk just lately.'

'Well, one can't have murders and robberies every day,' said Tommy. 'Be reasonable. Now, my idea is this. When business is slack, we ought to do a certain amount of home exercises every day.'

'Lie on our backs and wave our feet in the air? That sort of thing?'

'Don't be so literal in your interpretation. When I say exercises, I mean exercises in the detective art. Reproductions of the great masters. For instance – '

From the drawer beside him Tommy took out a formidable dark green eyeshade, covering both eyes. This he adjusted with some care. Then he drew a watch from his pocket.

'I broke the glass this morning,' he remarked. 'That paved the way for its being the crystalless watch which my sensitive fingers touch so lightly.'

'Be careful,' said Tuppence. 'You nearly had the short hand off then.'

'Give me your hand,' said Tommy. He held it, one finger feeling for the pulse. 'Ah! the keyboard of silence. This woman has *not* got heart disease.'

'I suppose,' said Tuppence, 'that you are Thornley Colton?'

'Just so,' said Tommy. 'The blind Problemist. And you're thingummybob, the black haired, apple-cheeked secretary –'

'The bundle of baby clothes picked up on the banks of the river,' finished Tuppence.

'And Albert is the Fee, alias Shrimp.'

'We must teach him to say, "Gee,"' said Tuppence. 'And his voice isn't shrill. It's dreadfully hoarse.'

'Against the wall by the door,' said Tommy, 'you perceive the slim hollow cane which held in my sensitive hand tells me so much.'

He rose and cannoned into a chair.

'Damn!' said Tommy. 'I forgot that chair was there.'

'It must be beastly to be blind,' said Tuppence with feeling.

'Rather,' agreed Tommy heartily. 'I'm sorrier for all those poor devils who lost their eyesight in the war than for anyone else. But they say that when you live in the dark you really do develop special senses. That's what I want to try and see if one couldn't do. It would be jolly handy to train oneself to be some good in the dark. Now, Tuppence, be a good Sydney Thames. How many steps to that cane?'

Tuppence made a desperate guess.

'Three straight, five left,' she hazarded.

Tommy paced it uncertainly, Tuppence interrupting with a cry of warning as she realized that the fourth step left would take him slap against the wall.

'There's a lot in this,' said Tuppence. 'You've no idea how difficult it is to judge how many steps are needed.'

'It's jolly interesting,' said Tommy. 'Call Albert in. I'm going to shake hands with you both, and see if I know which is which.'

'All right,' said Tuppence, 'but Albert must wash his hands first. They're sure to be sticky from those beastly acid drops he's always eating.'

Albert, introduced to the game, was full of interest.

Tommy, the handshakes completed, smiled complacently.

'The keyboard of silence cannot lie,' he murmured. 'The first was Albert, the second, you, Tuppence.'

'Wrong!' shrieked Tuppence. 'Keyboard of silence indeed! You went by my dress ring. And I put that on Albert's finger.'

Various other experiments were carried out, with indifferent success.

'But it's coming,' declared Tommy. 'One can't expect to be infallible straight away. I tell you what. It's just lunch time. You and I will go to the Blitz, Tuppence. Blind man and his keeper. Some jolly useful tips to be picked up there.'

'I say, Tommy, we shall get into trouble.'

'No, we shan't. I shall behave quite like the little gentleman. But I bet you that by the end of luncheon I shall be startling you.'

All protests being thus overborne, a quarter of an hour later saw Tommy and Tuppence comfortably ensconced at a corner table in the Gold Room of the Blitz.

Tommy ran his fingers lightly over the Menu.

'Pilaff de homar and grilled chicken for me,' he murmured.

Tuppence also made her selection, and the waiter moved away.

'So far, so good,' said Tommy. 'Now for a more ambitious venture. What beautiful legs that girl in the short skirt has – the one who has just come in.'

'How was that done, Thorn?'

'Beautiful legs impart a particular vibration to the floor, which is received by my hollow cane. Or, to be honest, in a big restaurant there is nearly always a girl with beautiful legs standing in the doorway looking for her friends, and with short skirts going about, she'd be sure to take advantage of them.'

The meal proceeded.

'The man two tables from us is a very wealthy profiteer, I fancy,' said Tommy carelessly. 'Jew, isn't he?'

'Pretty good,' said Tuppence appreciatively. 'I don't follow that one.'

'I shan't tell you how it's done every time. It spoils my show.

The head waiter is serving champagne three tables off to the right. A stout woman in black is about to pass our table.'

'Tommy, how can you –'

'Aha! You're beginning to see what I can do. That's a nice girl in brown just getting up at the table behind you.'

'Snoo!' said Tuppence. 'It's a young man in grey.'

'Oh!' said Tommy, momentarily disconcerted.

And at that moment two men who had been sitting at a table not far away, and who had been watching the young pair with keen interest, got up and came across to the corner table.

'Excuse me,' said the elder of the two, a tall, well-dressed man with an eyeglass, and a small grey moustache. 'But you have been pointed out to me as Mr Theodore Blunt. May I ask if that is so?'

Tommy hesitated a minute, feeling somewhat at a disadvantage. Then he bowed his head.

'That is so. I am Mr Blunt.'

'What an unexpected piece of good fortune! Mr Blunt, I was going to call at your offices after lunch. I am in trouble – very grave trouble. But – excuse me – you have had some accident to your eyes?'

'My dear sir,' said Tommy in a melancholy voice, 'I'm blind – completely blind.'

'What?'

'You are astonished. But surely you have heard of blind detectives?'

'In fiction. Never in real life. And I have certainly never heard that you were blind.'

'Many people are not aware of the fact,' murmured Tommy. 'I am wearing an eyeshade today to save my eyeballs from glare. But without it, quite a host of people have never suspected my infirmity – if you call it that. You see, my eyes cannot mislead me. But, enough of all this. Shall we go at once to my office, or will you give me the facts of the case here? The latter would be best, I think.'

A waiter brought up two extra chairs, and the two men sat

down. The second man who had not yet spoken, was shorter, sturdy in build, and very dark.

'It is a matter of great delicacy,' said the older man dropping his voice confidentially. He looked uncertainly at Tuppence. Mr Blunt seemed to feel the glance.

'Let me introduce my confidential secretary,' he said. 'Miss Ganges. Found on the banks of the Indian river – a mere bundle of baby clothes. Very sad history. Miss Ganges is my eyes. She accompanies me everywhere.'

The stranger acknowledged the introduction with a bow.

'Then I can speak out. Mr Blunt, my daughter, a girl of sixteen, has been abducted under somewhat peculiar circumstances. I discovered this half an hour ago. The circumstances of the case were such that I dared not call in the police. Instead, I rang up your office. They told me you were out to lunch, but would be back by half-past two. I came in here with my friend, Captain Harker –'

The short man jerked his head and muttered something.

'By the greatest good fortune you happened to be lunching here also. We must lose no time. You must return with me to my house immediately.'

Tommy demurred cautiously.

'I can be with you in half an hour. I must return to my office first.'

Captain Harker, turning to glance at Tuppence, may have been surprised to see a half smile lurking for a moment at the corners of her mouth.

'No, no, that will not do. You must return with me.' The grey-haired man took a card from his pocket and handed it across the table. 'That is my name.'

Tommy fingered it.

'My fingers are hardly sensitive enough for that,' he said with a smile, and handed it to Tuppence, who read out in a low voice: 'The Duke of Blairgowrie.'

She looked with great interest at their client. The Duke of Blairgowrie was well known to be a most haughty and inaccessible nobleman who had married as a wife, the daughter of a

Chicago pork butcher, many years younger than himself, and of a lively temperament that augured ill for their future together. There had been rumours of disaccord lately.

'You will come at once, Mr Blunt?' said the Duke, with a tinge of acerbity in his manner.

Tommy yielded to the inevitable.

'Miss Ganges and I will come with you,' he said quietly. 'You will excuse my just stopping to drink a large cup of black coffee? They will serve it immediately. I am subject to very distressing headaches, the result of my eye trouble, and the coffee steadies my nerves.'

He called a waiter and gave the order. Then he spoke to Tuppence.

'Miss Ganges – I am lunching here tomorrow with the French Prefect of Police. Just note down the luncheon, and give it to the head waiter with instructions to reserve me my usual table. I am assisting the French police in an important case. *The fee*' – he paused – 'is considerable. Are you ready, Miss Ganges.'

'Quite ready,' said Tuppence, her stylo poised.

'We will start with that special salad of shrimps that they have here. Then to follow – let me see, *to follow* – Yes, Omelette Blitz, and perhaps a couple of *Tournedos à l'Etranger.*'

He paused and murmured apologetically:

'You will forgive me, I hope. Ah! yes, *Souffle en surprise.* That will conclude the repast. A most interesting man, the French Prefect. You know him, perhaps?'

The other replied in the negative, as Tuppence rose and went to speak to the head waiter. Presently she returned, just as the coffee was brought.

Tommy drank a large cup of it, sipping it slowly, then rose.

'My cane, Miss Ganges? Thank you. Directions, please?'

It was a moment of agony for Tuppence.

'One right, eighteen straight. About the fifth step, there is a waiter serving the table on your left.'

Swinging his cane jauntily, Tommy set out. Tuppence kept close beside him, and endeavoured unobtrusively to steer him. All went well until they were just passing out through the doorway. A man entered rather hurriedly and before Tuppence could warn the blind Mr Blunt, he had barged right into the newcomer. Explanations and apologies ensued.

At the door of the Blitz, a smart landaulette was waiting. The Duke himself aided Mr Blunt to get in.

'Your car here, Harker?' he asked over his shoulder.

'Yes. Just round the corner.'

'Take Miss Ganges in it, will you.'

Before another word could be said, he had jumped in beside Tommy, and the car rolled smoothly away.

'A very delicate matter,' murmured the Duke. 'I can soon acquaint you with all the details.'

Tommy raised his hand to his head.

'I can remove my eyeshade now,' he observed pleasantly. 'It was only the glare of artificial light in the restaurant necessitated its use.'

But his arm was jerked down sharply. At the same time he felt something hard and round being poked between his ribs.

'No, my dear Mr Blunt,' said the Duke's voice – but a voice that seemed suddenly different. 'You will not remove that eyeshade. You will sit perfectly still and not move in any way. You understand? I don't want this pistol of mine to go off. You see, I happen not to be the Duke of Blairgowrie at all. I borrowed his name for the occasion, knowing that you would not refuse to accompany such a celebrated client. I am something much more prosaic – a ham merchant who has lost his wife.'

He felt the start the other gave.

'That tells you something,' he laughed. 'My dear young man, you have been incredibly foolish. I'm afraid – I'm very much afraid that your activities will be curtailed in future.'

He spoke the last words with a sinister relish.

Tommy sat motionless. He did not reply to the other's taunts.

Presently the car slackened its pace and drew up.

'Just a minute,' said the pseudo Duke. He twisted a handkerchief deftly into Tommy's mouth, and drew up his scarf over it.

'In case you should be foolish enough to think of calling for help,' he explained suavely.

The door of the car opened and the chauffeur stood ready. He and his master took Tommy between them and propelled him rapidly up some steps and in at the door of a house.

The door closed behind them. There was a rich oriental smell in the air. Tommy's feet sank deep into velvet pile. He was propelled in the same fashion up a flight of stairs and into a room which he judged to be at the back of the house. Here the two men bound his hands together. The chauffeur went out again, and the other removed the gag.

'You may speak freely now,' he announced pleasantly. 'What have you to say for yourself, young man?'

Tommy cleared his throat and eased the aching corners of his mouth.

'I hope you haven't lost my hollow cane,' he said mildly. 'It cost me a lot to have that made.'

'You have nerve,' said the other, after a minute's pause. 'Or else you are just a fool. Don't you understand that I have got you – got you in the hollow of my hand? That you're absolutely in my power? That no one who knows you is ever likely to see you again.'

'Can't you cut out the melodrama?' asked Tommy plaintively. 'Have I got to say, "You villain, I'll foil you yet"? That sort of thing is so very much out of date.'

'What about the girl?' said the other, watching him. 'Doesn't that move you?'

'Putting two and two together during my enforced silence just now,' said Tommy. 'I have come to the inevitable conclusion that that chatty lad Harker is another of the doers of desperate deeds, and that therefore my unfortunate secretary will shortly join this little tea party.'

'Right as to one point, but wrong on the other. Mrs Beresford – you see, I know all about you – Mrs Beresford will not be brought here. That is a little precaution I took. It occurred to me that just probably your friends in high places might be keeping you shadowed. In that case, by dividing the pursuit, you could not both be trailed. I should still keep one in my hands. I am waiting now –'

He broke off as the door opened. The chauffeur spoke.

'We've not been followed, sir. It's all clear.'

'Good. You can go, Gregory.'

The door closed again.

'So far, so good,' said the 'Duke.' 'And now what are we to do with you, Mr Beresford Blunt?'

'I wish you'd take this confounded eyeshade off me,' said Tommy.

'I think not. With it on, you are truly blind – without it you would see as well as I do – and that would not suit my little plan. For I have a plan. You are fond of sensational fiction, Mr Blunt. This little game that you and your wife were playing today proves that. Now I, too, have arranged a little game – something rather ingenious, as I am sure you will admit when I explain it to you.

'You see, this floor on which you are standing is made of metal, and here and there on its surface are little projections. I touch a switch – so.' A sharp click sounded. 'Now the electric current is switched on. To tread on one of those little knobs now means – death! You understand? If you could see . . . but you cannot see. You are in the dark. That is the game – Blindman's Buff with death. If you can reach the door in safety – freedom! But I think that long before you reach it you will have trodden on one of the danger spots. And that will be very amusing – for me!'

He came forward and unbound Tommy's hands. Then he handed him his cane with a little ironical bow.

'The blind Problemist. Let us see if he will solve this problem. I shall stand here with my pistol ready. If you raise your hands to your head to remove that eyeshade, I shoot. Is that clear?'

'Perfectly clear,' said Tommy. He was rather pale, but determined. 'I haven't a dog's chance, I suppose?'

'Oh! that –' the other shrugged his shoulders.

'Damned ingenious devil, aren't you?' said Tommy. 'But

you've forgotten one thing. May I light a cigarette by the way? My poor little heart's going pit-a-pat.'

'You may light a cigarette – but no tricks. I am watching you, remember, with the pistol ready.'

'I'm not a performing dog,' said Tommy. 'I don't do tricks.' He extracted a cigarette from his case, then felt for a match box. 'It's all right. I'm not feeling for a revolver. But you know well enough that I'm not armed. All the same, as I said before, you've forgotten one thing.'

'What is that?'

Tommy took a match from the box, and held it ready to strike.

'I'm blind and you can see. That's admitted. The advantage is with you. But supposing we were both in the dark – eh? Where's your advantage then?'

He struck the match.

'Thinking of shooting at the switch of the lights? Plunging the room into darkness? It can't be done.'

'Just so,' said Tommy. 'I can't give you darkness. But extremes meet, you know. What about *light?*'

As he spoke, he touched the match to something he held in his hand, and threw it down upon the table.

A blinding glare filled the room.

Just for a minute, blinded by the intense white light, the 'Duke' blinked and fell back, his pistol hand lowered.

He opened his eyes again to feel something sharp pricking his breast.

'Drop that pistol,' ordered Tommy. 'Drop it quick. I agree with you that a hollow cane is a pretty rotten affair. So I didn't get one. A good *sword stick* is a very useful weapon, though. Don't you think so? Almost as useful as magnesium wire. *Drop that pistol.*'

Obedient to the necessity of that sharp point, the man dropped it. Then, with a laugh, he sprang back.

'But I still have the advantage,' he mocked. 'For I can see, and you cannot.'

'That's where you're wrong,' said Tommy. 'I can see perfectly.

The eyeshade's a fake. I was going to put one over on **Tuppence**. Make one or two bloomers to begin with, and then put in some perfectly marvellous stuff towards the end of lunch. Why, bless you, I could have walked to the door and avoided all the knobs with perfect ease. But I didn't trust you to play a sporting game. You'd never have let me get out of this alive. Careful now –'

For, with his face distorted with rage, the 'Duke' sprang forward, forgetting in his fury to look where he put his feet.

There was a sudden blue crackle of flame, and he swayed for a minute, then fell like a log. A faint odour of singed flesh filled the room, mingling with a stronger smell of ozone.

'Whew,' said Tommy.

He wiped his face.

Then, moving gingerly, and with every precaution, he reached the wall, and touched the switch he had seen the other manipulate.

He crossed the room to the door, opened it carefully, and looked out. There was no one about. He went down the stairs and out through the front door.

Safe in the street, he looked up at the house with a shudder, noting the number. Then he hurried to the nearest telephone box.

There was a moment of agonizing anxiety, and then a well-known voice spoke.

'Tuppence, thank goodness!'

'Yes, I'm all right. I got all your points. The Fee, Shrimp, Come to the Blitz and follow the two strangers. Albert got there in time, and when we went off in separate cars, followed me in a taxi, saw where they took me, and rang up the police.'

'Albert's a good lad,' said Tommy. 'Chivalrous. I was pretty sure he'd choose to follow you. But I've been worried, all the same. I've got lots to tell you. I'm coming straight back now. And the first thing I shall do when I get back is to write a thumping big cheque for St Dunstan's. Lord, it must be awful not to be able to see.'

CHAPTER XI

The Man in the Mist

Tommy was not pleased with life. Blunt's Brilliant Detectives had met with a reverse, distressing to their pride if not to their pockets. Called in professionally to elucidate the mystery of a stolen pearl necklace at Adlington Hall, Adlington, Blunt's Brilliant Detectives had failed to make good. Whilst Tommy, hard on the track of a gambling Countess, was tracking her in the disguise of a Roman Catholic priest, and Tuppence was 'getting off' with the nephew of the house on the golf links, the local Inspector of Police had unemotionally arrested the second footman who proved to be a thief well known at head-quarters, and who admitted his guilt without making any bones about it.

Tommy and Tuppence, therefore, had withdrawn with what dignity they could muster, and were at the present moment solacing themselves with cocktails at the Grand Adlington Hotel. Tommy still wore his clerical disguise.

'Hardly a Father Brown touch, that,' he remarked gloomily. 'And yet I've got just the right kind of umbrella.'

'It wasn't a Father Brown problem,' said Tuppence. 'One needs a certain atmosphere from the start. One must be doing something quite ordinary, and then bizarre things begin to happen. That's the idea.'

'Unfortunately,' said Tommy, 'we have to return to town. Perhaps something bizarre will happen on the way to the station.'

He raised the glass he was holding to his lips, but the liquid in it was suddenly spilled, as a heavy hand smacked him on the shoulder, and a voice to match the hand boomed out words of greeting.

'Upon my soul, it is! Old Tommy! And Mrs Tommy too. Where did you blow in from? Haven't seen or heard anything of you for years.'

'Why, it's Bulger!' said Tommy, setting down what was left of the cocktail, and turning to look at the intruder, a big square-shouldered man of thirty years of age, with a round red beaming face, and dressed in golfing kit. 'Good old Bulger!'

'But I say, old chap,' said Bulger (whose real name, by the way, was Marvyn Estcourt), 'I never knew you'd taken orders. Fancy you a blinking parson.'

Tuppence burst out laughing, and Tommy looked embarrassed. And then they suddenly became conscious of a fourth person.

A tall, slender creature, with very golden hair and very round blue eyes, almost impossibly beautiful, with an effect of really expensive black topped by wonderful ermines, and very large pearl earrings. She was smiling. And her smile said many things. It asserted, for instance, that she knew perfectly well that she herself was the thing best worth looking at, certainly in England, and possibly in the whole world. She was not vain about it in any way, but she just knew, with certainty and confidence, that it was so.

Both Tommy and Tuppence recognized her immediately. They had seen her three times in *The Secret of the Heart*, and an equal number of times in that other great success, *Pillars of Fire*, and in innumerable other plays. There was, perhaps, no other actress in England who had so firm a hold on the British public, as Miss Gilda Glen. She was reported to be the most beautiful woman in England. It was also rumoured that she was the stupidest.

'Old friends of mine, Miss Glen,' said Estcourt, with a tinge of apology in his voice for having presumed, even for a moment, to forget such a radiant creature. 'Tommy and Mrs Tommy, let me introduce you to Miss Gilda Glen.'

The ring of pride in his voice was unmistakable. By merely being seen in his company, Miss Glen had conferred great glory upon him.

The actress was staring with frank interest at Tommy.

'Are you really a priest?' she asked. 'A Roman Catholic priest, I mean? Because I thought they didn't have wives.'

Estcourt went off in a boom of laughter again.

'That's good,' he exploded. 'You sly dog, Tommy. Glad he hasn't renounced you, Mrs Tommy, with all the rest of the pomps and vanities.'

Gilda Glen took not the faintest notice of him. She continued to stare at Tommy with puzzled eyes.

'Are you a priest?' she demanded.

'Very few of us are what we seem to be,' said Tommy gently. 'My profession is not unlike that of a priest. I don't give absolution – but I listen to confessions – I –'

'Don't you listen to him,' interrupted Estcourt. 'He's pulling your leg.'

'If you're not a clergyman, I don't see why you're dressed up like one,' she puzzled. 'That is, unless –'

'Not a criminal flying from justice,' said Tommy. 'The other thing.'

'Oh!' she frowned, and looked at him with beautiful bewildered eyes.

'I wonder if she'll ever get that,' thought Tommy to himself. 'Not unless I put it in words of one syllable for her, I should say.'

Aloud he said:

'Know anything about the trains back to town, Bulger? We've got to be pushing for home. How far is it to the station?'

'Ten minutes' walk. But no hurry. Next train up is the 6.35 and it's only about twenty to six now. You've just missed one.'

'Which way is it to the station from here?'

'Sharp to the left when you turn out of the hotel. Then – let me see – down Morgan's Avenue would be the best way, wouldn't it?'

'Morgan's Avenue?' Miss Glen started violently, and stared at him with startled eyes.

'I know what you're thinking of,' said Estcourt, laughing. 'The Ghost. Morgan's Avenue is bounded by the cemetery on one side, and tradition has it that a policeman who met his death by violence gets up and walks on his old beat, up and down Morgan's Avenue. A spook policeman! Can you beat it? But lots of people swear to having seen him.'

'A policeman?' said Miss Glen. She shivered a little. 'But there aren't really any ghosts, are there? I mean – there aren't such things?'

She got up, folding her wrap tighter round her.

'Goodbye,' she said vaguely.

She had ignored Tuppence completely throughout, and now she did not even glance in her direction. But, over her shoulder, she threw one puzzled questioning glance at Tommy.

Just as she got to the door, she encountered a tall man with grey hair and a puffy face, who uttered an exclamation of surprise. His hand on her arm, he led her through the doorway, talking in an animated fashion.

'Beautiful creature, isn't she?' said Estcourt. 'Brains of a rabbit. Rumour has it that she's going to marry Lord Leconbury. That was Leconbury in the doorway.'

'He doesn't look a very nice sort of man to marry,' remarked Tuppence.

Estcourt shrugged his shoulders.

'A title has a kind of glamour still, I suppose,' he said. 'And Leconbury is not an impoverished peer by any means. She'll be in clover. Nobody knows where she sprang from. Pretty near the gutter, I dare say. There's something deuced mysterious about her being down here anyway. She's not staying at the hotel. And when I tried to find out where she was staying, she snubbed me – snubbed me quite crudely, in the only way she knows. Blessed if I know what it's all about.'

He glanced at his watch and uttered an exclamation.

'I must be off. Jolly glad to have seen you two again. We must have a bust in town together some night. So long.'

He hurried away, and as he did so, a page approached with a note on a salver. The note was unaddressed.

'But it's for you, sir,' he said to Tommy. 'From Miss Gilda Glen.'

Tommy tore it open and read it with some curiosity. Inside were a few lines written in a straggling untidy hand.

I'm not sure, but I think you might be able to help me. And you'll be going that way to the station. Could you be at The White House, Morgan's Avenue, at ten minutes past six?

Yours sincerely
Gilda Glen.

Tommy nodded to the page, who departed, and then handed the note to Tuppence.

'Extraordinary!' said Tuppence. 'Is it because she still thinks you're a priest?'

'No,' said Tommy thoughtfully. 'I should say it's because she's at last taken in that I'm not one. Hullo! what's this?'

'This,' was a young man with flaming red hair, a pugnacious jaw, and appallingly shabby clothes. He had walked into the room and was now striding up and down muttering to himself.

'Hell!' said the red-haired man, loudly and forcibly. 'That's what I say – Hell!'

He dropped into a chair near the young couple and stared at them moodily.

'Damn all women, that's what I say,' said the young man, eyeing Tuppence ferociously. 'Oh! all right, kick up a row if you like. Have me turned out of the hotel. It won't be for the first time. Why shouldn't we say what we think? Why should we go about bottling up our feelings, and smirking, and saying things exactly like everyone else. I don't feel pleasant and polite. I feel like getting hold of someone round the throat and gradually choking them to death.'

He paused.

'Any particular person?' asked Tuppence. 'Or just anybody?'

'One particular person,' said the young man grimly.

'This is very interesting,' said Tuppence. 'Won't you tell us some more?'

'My name's Reilly,' said the red-haired man. 'James Reilly. You may have heard it. I wrote a little volume of Pacifist poems – good stuff, although I say so.'

'*Pacifist poems?*' said Tuppence.

'Yes – why not?' demanded Mr Reilly belligerently.

'Oh! nothing,' said Tuppence hastily.

'I'm for peace all the time,' said Mr Reilly fiercely. 'To Hell with war. And women! Women! Did you see that creature who was trailing around here just now? Gilda Glen, she calls herself. Gilda Glen! God! how I've worshipped that woman. And I'll tell you this – if she's got a heart at all, it's on my side. She cared once for me, and I could make her care again. And if she sells herself to that muck heap, Leconbury – well, God help her. I'd as soon kill her with my own hands.'

And on this, suddenly, he rose and rushed from the room.

Tommy raised his eyebrows.

'A somewhat excitable gentleman,' he murmured. 'Well, Tuppence, shall we start?'

A fine mist was coming up as they emerged from the hotel into the cool outer air. Obeying Estcourt's directions, they turned sharp to the left, and in a few minutes they came to a turning labelled Morgan's Avenue.

The mist had increased. It was soft and white, and hurried past them in little eddying drifts. To their left was the high wall of the cemetery, on their right a row of small houses. Presently these ceased, and a high hedge took their place.

'Tommy,' said Tuppence. 'I'm beginning to feel jumpy. The mist – and the silence. As though we were miles from anywhere.'

'One does feel like that,' agreed Tommy. 'All alone in the world. It's the effect of the mist, and not being able to see ahead of one.'

Tuppence nodded.

'Just our footsteps echoing on the pavement. What's that?'

'What's what?'

'I thought I heard other footsteps behind us.'

'You'll be seeing the ghost in a minute if you work yourself up like this,' said Tommy kindly. 'Don't be so nervy. Are you afraid the spook policeman will lay his hands on your shoulder?'

Tuppence emitted a shrill squeal.

'Don't, Tommy. Now you've put it into my head.'

She craned her head back over her shoulder, trying to peer into the white veil that was wrapped all round them.

'There they are again,' she whispered. 'No, they're in front now. Oh! Tommy, don't say you can't hear them?'

'I do hear something. Yes, it's footsteps behind us. Somebody else walking this way to catch the train. I wonder –'

He stopped suddenly, and stood still, and Tuppence gave a gasp.

For the curtain of mist in front of them suddenly parted in the most artificial manner, and there, not twenty feet away, a gigantic policeman suddenly appeared, as though materialized out of the fog. One minute he was not there, the next minute he was – so at least it seemed to the rather superheated imaginations of the two watchers. Then as the mist rolled back still more, a little scene appeared, as though set on a stage.

The big blue policeman, a scarlet pillar box, and on the right of the road the outlines of a white house.

'Red, white, and blue,' said Tommy. 'It's damned pictorial. Come on, Tuppence, there's nothing to be afraid of.'

For, as he had already seen, the policeman was a real policeman. And, moreover, he was not nearly so gigantic as he had at first seemed looming up out of the mist.

But as they started forward, footsteps came from behind them. A man passed them, hurrying along. He turned in at the gate of the white house, ascended the steps, and beat a deafening tattoo upon the knocker. He was admitted just as they reached the spot where the policeman was standing staring after him.

'There's a gentleman seems to be in a hurry,' commented the policeman.

He spoke in a slow reflective voice, as one whose thoughts took some time to mature.

'He's the sort of gentleman always would be in a hurry,' remarked Tommy.

The policeman's stare, slow and rather suspicious, came round to rest on his face.

'Friend of yours?' he demanded, and there was distinct suspicion now in his voice.

'No,' said Tommy. 'He's not a friend of mine, but I happen to know who he is. Name of Reilly.'

'Ah!' said the policeman. 'Well, I'd better be getting along.'

'Can you tell me where the White House is?' asked Tommy. The constable jerked his head sideways.

'This is it. Mrs Honeycott's.' He paused, and added, evidently with the idea of giving them valuable information, 'Nervous party. Always suspecting burglars is around. Always asking me to have a look around the place. Middle-aged women get like that.'

'Middle-aged, eh?' said Tommy. 'Do you happen to know if there's a young lady staying there?'

'A young lady,' said the policeman, ruminating. 'A young lady. No, I can't say I know anything about that.'

'She mayn't be staying here, Tommy,' said Tuppence. 'And anyway, she mayn't be here yet. She could only have started just before we did.'

'Ah!' said the policeman suddenly. 'Now that I call it to mind, a young lady did go in at this gate. I saw her as I was coming up the road. About three or four minutes ago it might be.'

'With ermine furs on?' asked Tuppence eagerly.

'She had some kind of white rabbit round her throat,' admitted the policeman.

Tuppence smiled. The policeman went on in the direction from which they had just come, and they prepared to enter the gate of the White House.

Suddenly, a faint, muffled cry sounded from inside the house, and almost immediately afterwards the front door opened and James Reilly came rushing down the steps. His face was white and twisted, and his eyes glared in front of him unseeingly. He staggered like a drunken man.

He passed Tommy and Tuppence as though he did not see them, muttering to himself with a kind of dreadful repetition.

'My God! My God! Oh, my God!'

He clutched at the gatepost, as though to steady himself, and then, as though animated by sudden panic, he raced off down the road as hard as he could go in the opposite direction from that taken by the policeman.

CHAPTER XII

The Man in the Mist (*continued*)

Tommy and Tuppence stared at each other in bewilderment.

'Well,' said Tommy, 'something's happened in that house to scare our friend Reilly pretty badly.'

Tuppence drew her finger absently across the gatepost.

'He must have put his hand on some wet red paint somewhere,' she said idly.

'H'm,' said Tommy. 'I think we'd better go inside rather quickly. I don't understand this business.'

In the doorway of the house a white-capped maid-servant was standing, almost speechless with indignation.

'Did you ever see the likes of that now, Father,' she burst out, as Tommy ascended the steps. 'That fellow comes here, asks for the young lady, rushes upstairs without how or by your leave. She lets out a screech like a wild cat – and what wonder, poor pretty dear, and straightaway he comes rushing down again, with the white face on him, like one who's seen a ghost. What will be the meaning of it all?'

'Who are you talking with at the front door, Ellen?' demanded a sharp voice from the interior of the hall.

'Here's Missus,' said Ellen, somewhat unnecessarily.

She drew back, and Tommy found himself confronting a grey-haired, middle-aged woman, with frosty blue eyes imperfectly concealed by pince-nez, and a spare figure clad in black with bugle trimming.

'Mrs Honeycott?' said Tommy. 'I came here to see Miss Glen.'

Mrs Honeycott gave him a sharp glance, then went on to Tuppence and took in every detail of her appearance.

'Oh, you did, did you?' she said. 'Well, you'd better come inside.'

She led the way into the hall and along it into a room at the back of the house, facing on the garden. It was a fair-sized room, but looked smaller than it was, owing to the large amount of chairs and tables crowded into it. A big fire burned in the grate, and a chintz-covered sofa stood at one side of it. The wallpaper was a small grey stripe with a festoon of roses round the top. Quantities of engravings and oil paintings covered the walls.

It was a room almost impossible to associate with the expensive personality of Miss Gilda Glen.

'Sit down,' said Mrs Honeycott. 'To begin with, you'll excuse me if I say I don't hold with the Roman Catholic religion. Never did I think to see a Roman Catholic priest in my house. But if Gilda's gone over to the Scarlet Woman, it's only what's to be expected in a life like hers – and I dare say it might be worse. She mightn't have any religion at all. I should think more of Roman Catholics if their priests were married – I always speak my mind. And to think of those convents – quantities of beautiful young girls shut up there, and no one knowing what becomes of them – well, it won't bear thinking about.'

Mrs Honeycott came to a full stop, and drew a deep breath.

Without entering upon a defence of the celibacy of the priesthood or the other controversial points touched upon, Tommy went straight to the point.

'I understand, Mrs Honeycott, that Miss Glen is in this house.'

'She is. Mind you, I don't approve. Marriage is marriage and your husband's your husband. As you make your bed, so you must lie on it.'

'I don't quite understand –' began Tommy, bewildered.

'I thought as much. That's the reason I brought you in here. You can go up to Gilda after I've spoken my mind. She came to me – after all these years, think of it! – and asked me to help her. Wanted me to see this man and persuade him to agree to a divorce. I told her straight out I'd have nothing whatever to do with it. Divorce is sinful. But I couldn't refuse my own sister shelter in my house, could I now?'

'Your sister?' exclaimed Tommy.

'Yes, Gilda's my sister. Didn't she tell you?'

Tommy stared at her openmouthed. The thing seemed fantastically impossible. Then he remembered that the angelic beauty of Gilda Glen had been in evidence for many years. He had been taken to see her act as quite a small boy. Yes, it was possible after all. But what a piquant contrast. So it was from this lower middle-class respectability that Gilda Glen had sprung. How well she had guarded her secret!

'I am not yet quite clear,' he said. 'Your sister is married?'

'Ran away to be married as a girl of seventeen,' said Mrs Honeycott succinctly. 'Some common fellow far below her in station. And our father a reverend. It was a disgrace. Then she left her husband and went on the stage. Playacting! I've never been inside a theatre in my life. I hold no truck with wickedness. Now, after all these years, she wants to divorce the man. Means to marry some big wig, I suppose. But her husband's standing firm – not to be bullied and not to be bribed – I admire him for it.'

'What is his name?' asked Tommy suddenly.

'That's an extraordinary thing now, but I can't remember! It's nearly twenty years ago, you know, since I heard it. My father forbade it to be mentioned. And I've refused to discuss the matter with Gilda. She knows what I think, and that's enough for her.'

'It wasn't Reilly, was it?'

'Might have been. I really can't say. It's gone clean out of my head.'

'The man I mean was here just now.'

'That man! I thought he was an escaped lunatic. I'd been in the kitchen giving orders to Ellen. I'd just got back into this room, and was wondering whether Gilda had come in yet (she has a latchkey), when I heard her. She hesitated a minute or two in the hall and then went straight upstairs. About three minutes later all this tremendous rat-tatting began. I went out into the hall, and just saw a man rushing upstairs. Then there was a sort of cry upstairs, and presently down he came again and rushed out like a madman. Pretty goings on.'

Tommy rose.

'Mrs Honeycott, let us go upstairs at once. I am afraid –'

'What of?'

'Afraid that you have no red wet paint in the house.'

Mrs Honeycott stared at him.

'Of course I haven't.'

'That is what I feared,' said Tommy gravely. 'Please let us go to your sister's room at once.'

Momentarily silenced, Mrs Honeycott led the way. They caught a glimpse of Ellen in the hall, backing hastily into one of the rooms.

Mrs Honeycott opened the first door at the top of the stairs. Tommy and Tuppence entered close behind her.

Suddenly she gave a gasp and fell back.

A motionless figure in black and ermine lay stretched on the sofa. The face was untouched, a beautiful soulless face like a mature child asleep. The wound was on the side of the head, a heavy blow with some blunt instrument had crushed in the skull. Blood was dripping slowly on to the floor, but the wound itself had long ceased to bleed . . .

Tommy examined the prostrate figure, his face very white.

'So,' he said at last, 'he didn't strangle her after all.'

'What do you mean? Who?' cried Mrs Honeycott. 'Is she dead?'

'Oh, yes, Mrs Honeycott, she's dead. Murdered. The question is – by whom? Not that it is much of a question. Funny – for all his ranting words, I didn't think the fellow had got it in him.'

He paused a minute, then turned to Tuppence with decision.

'Will you go out and get a policeman, or ring up the police station from somewhere?'

Tuppence nodded. She too, was very white. Tommy led Mrs Honeycott downstairs again.

'I don't want there to be any mistake about this,' he said. 'Do you know exactly what time it was when your sister came in?'

'Yes, I do,' said Mrs Honeycott. 'Because I was just setting the clock on five minutes as I have to do every evening. It loses just five minutes a day. It was exactly eight minutes past six by my watch, and that never loses or gains a second.'

Tommy nodded. That agreed perfectly with the policeman's story. He had seen the woman with the white furs go in at the gate, probably three minutes had elapsed before he and Tuppence had reached the same spot. He had glanced at his own watch then and had noted that it was just one minute after the time of their appointment.

There was just the faint chance that some one might have been waiting for Gilda Glen in the room upstairs. But if so, he must still be hiding in the house. No one but James Reilly had left it.

He ran upstairs and made a quick but efficient search of the premises. But there was no one concealed anywhere.

Then he spoke to Ellen. After breaking the news to her, and waiting for her first lamentations and invocations to the saints to have exhausted themselves, he asked a few questions.

Had any one else come to the house that afternoon asking for Miss Glen? No one whatsoever. Had she herself been upstairs at all that evening? Yes she'd gone up at six o'clock as usual to draw the curtains – or it might have been a few minutes after six. Anyway it was just before that wild fellow came breaking the knocker down. She'd run downstairs to answer the door. And him a black-hearted murderer all the time.

Tommy let it go at that. But he still felt a curious pity for Reilly, and unwillingness to believe the worst of him. And yet there was no one else who could have murdered Gilda Glen. Mrs Honeycott and Ellen had been the only two people in the house.

He heard voices in the hall, and went out to find Tuppence and the policeman from the beat outside. The latter had produced a notebook, and a rather blunt pencil, which he licked surreptitiously. He went upstairs and surveyed the victim stolidly, merely remarking that if he was to touch anything the Inspector would give him beans. He listened to all Mrs Honeycott's hysterical outbursts and confused explanations, and occasionally he wrote something down. His presence was calming and soothing.

Tommy finally got him alone for a minute or two on the steps outside ere he departed to telephone headquarters.

'Look here,' said Tommy, 'you saw the deceased turning in at the gate, you say. Are you sure she was alone?'

'Oh! she was alone all right. Nobody with her.'

'And between that time and when you met us, nobody came out of the gate?'

'Not a soul.'

'You'd have seen them if they had?'

'Of course I should. Nobody come out till that wild chap did.'

The majesty of the law moved portentously down the steps and paused by the white gatepost, which bore the imprint of a hand in red.

'Kind of amateur he must have been,' he said pityingly. 'To leave a thing like that.'

Then he swung out into the road.

* * *

It was the day after the crime. Tommy and Tuppence were still at the Grand Hotel, but Tommy had thought it prudent to discard his clerical disguise.

James Reilly had been apprehended, and was in custody. His solicitor, Mr Marvell, had just finished a lengthy conversation with Tommy on the subject of the crime.

'I never would have believed it of James Reilly,' he said simply. 'He's always been a man of violent speech, but that's all.'

Tommy nodded.

'If you disperse energy in speech, it doesn't leave you too much over for action. What I realize is that I shall be one of the principal witnesses against him. That conversation he had with me just before the crime was particularly damning. And, in spite of everything, I like the man, and if there was anyone else to suspect, I should believe him to be innocent. What's his own story?'

The solicitor pursed up his lips.

'He declares that he found her lying there dead. But that's impossible, of course. He's using the first lie that comes into his head.'

'Because, if he happened to be speaking the truth, it would mean that the garrulous Mrs Honeycott committed the crime – and that is fantastic. Yes, he must have done it.'

'The maid heard her cry out, remember.'

'The maid – yes –'

Tommy was silent a moment. Then he said thoughtfully:

'What credulous creatures we are, really. We believe evidence as though it were gospel truth. And what is it really? Only the impression conveyed to the mind by the senses – and suppose they're the wrong impressions?'

The lawyer shrugged his shoulders.

'Oh! we all know that there are unreliable witnesses, witnesses who remember more and more as time goes on, with no real intention to deceive.'

'I don't mean only that. I mean all of us – we say things that aren't really so, and never know that we've done so. For instance, both you and I, without doubt, have said some time or other, "There's the post," when what we really meant was that we'd heard a double knock and the rattle of the letter-box. Nine times out of ten we'd be right, and it would be the post, but just possibly the tenth time it might be only a little urchin playing a joke on us. See what I mean?'

'Ye-es,' said Mr Marvell slowly. 'But I don't see what you're driving at?'

'Don't you? I'm not so sure that I do myself. But I'm beginning to see. It's like the stick, Tuppence. You remember? One end of it pointed one way – but the other end always points the opposite way. It depends whether you get hold of it by the right end. Doors open – but they also shut. People go upstairs, but they also go downstairs. Boxes shut, but they also open.'

'What *do* you mean?' demanded Tuppence.

'It's so ridiculously easy, really,' said Tommy. 'And yet it's only just come to me. How do you know when a person's come into the house. You hear the door open and bang to, and if you're expecting any one to come in, you will be quite sure it is them. But it might just as easily be someone going *out*.'

'But Miss Glen didn't go out?'

'No, I know *she* didn't. But some one else did – the murderer.'

'But how did she get in, then?'

'She came in whilst Mrs Honeycott was in the kitchen talking to Ellen. They didn't hear her. Mrs Honeycott went back to the drawing-room, wondered if her sister had come in and began to put the clock right, and then, as she thought, she heard her come in and go upstairs.'

'Well, what about that? The footsteps going upstairs?'

'That was Ellen, going up to draw the curtains. You remember, Mrs Honeycott said her sister paused before going up. That pause was just the time needed for Ellen to come out from the kitchen into the hall. She just missed seeing the murderer.'

'But, Tommy,' cried Tuppence. 'The cry she gave?'

'That was James Reilly. Didn't you notice what a high-pitched voice he has? In moments of great emotion, men often squeal just like a woman.'

'But the murderer? We'd have seen him?'

'We *did* see him. We even stood talking to him. Do you remember the sudden way that policeman appeared? That was because he stepped out of the gate, just after the mist cleared from the road. It made us jump, don't you remember? After all, though we never think of them as that, policemen are men just like any other men. They love and they hate. They marry . . .

'I think Gilda Glen met her husband suddenly just outside that gate, and took him in with her to thrash the matter out. He hadn't Reilly's relief of violent words, remember. He just saw red – and he had his truncheon handy . . .'

CHAPTER XIII

The Crackler

'Tuppence,' said Tommy. 'We shall have to move into a much larger office.'

'Nonsense,' said Tuppence. 'You mustn't get swollen headed and think you are a millionaire just because you solved two or three twopenny halfpenny cases with the aid of the most amazing luck.'

'What some call luck, others call skill.'

'Of course, if you really think you are Sherlock Holmes, Thorndyke, McCarty and the Brothers Okewood all rolled into one, there is no more to be said. Personally I would much rather have luck on my side than all the skill in the world.'

'Perhaps there is something in that,' conceded Tommy. 'All the same, Tuppence, we do need a larger office.'

'Why?'

'The classics,' said Tommy. 'We need several hundreds of yards of extra bookshelf if Edgar Wallace is to be properly represented.'

'We haven't had an Edgar Wallace case yet.'

'I'm afraid we never shall,' said Tommy. 'If you notice he never does give the amateur sleuth much of a chance. It is all stern Scotland Yard kind of stuff – the real thing and no base counterfeit.'

Albert, the office boy, appeared at the door.

'Inspector Marriot to see you,' he announced.

'The mystery man of Scotland Yard,' murmured Tommy.

'The busiest of the Busies,' said Tuppence. 'Or is it "Noses"? I always get mixed between Busies and Noses.'

The Inspector advanced upon them with a beaming smile of welcome.

'Well, and how are things?' he asked breezily. 'None the worse for our little adventure the other day?'

'Oh, rather not,' said Tuppence. 'Too, too marvellous, wasn't it?'

'Well, I don't know that I would describe it exactly that way myself,' said Marriot cautiously.

'What has brought you here today, Marriot?' asked Tommy. 'Not just solicitude for our nervous systems, is it?'

'No,' said the Inspector. 'It is work for the brilliant Mr Blunt.'

'Ha!' said Tommy. 'Let me put my brilliant expression on.'

'I have come to make you a proposition, Mr Beresford. What would you say to rounding up a really big gang?'

'Is there such a thing?' asked Tommy.

'What do you mean, is there such a thing?'

'I always thought that gangs were confined to fiction – like master crooks and super criminals.'

'The master crook isn't very common,' agreed the Inspector. 'But Lord bless you, sir, there's any amount of gangs knocking about.'

'I don't know that I should be at my best dealing with a gang,' said Tommy. 'The amateur crime, the crime of quiet family life – that is where I flatter myself that I shine. Drama of strong domestic interest. That's the thing – with Tuppence at hand to supply all those little feminine details which are so important, and so apt to be ignored by the denser male.'

His eloquence was arrested abruptly as Tuppence threw a cushion at him and requested him not to talk nonsense.

'Will have your little bit of fun, won't you, sir?' said Inspector Marriot, smiling paternally at them both. 'If you'll not take offence at my saying so, it's a pleasure to see two young people enjoying life as much as you two do.'

'Do we enjoy life?' said Tuppence, opening her eyes very wide. 'I suppose we do. I've never thought about it before.'

'To return to that gang you were talking about,' said Tommy. 'In spite of my extensive private practice – duchesses, million-aires, and all the best charwomen – I might, perhaps, conde-scend to look into the matter for you. I don't like to see Scotland

Yard at fault. You'll have the *Daily Mail* after you before you know where you are.'

'As I said before, you must have your bit of fun. Well, it's like this.' Again he hitched his chair forward. 'There's any amount of forged notes going about just now – hundreds of 'em! The amount of counterfeit Treasury notes in circulation would surprise you. Most artistic bit of work it is. Here's one of 'em.'

He took a one pound note from his pocket and handed it to Tommy.

'Looks all right, doesn't it?'

Tommy examined the note with great interest.

'By Jove, I'd never spot there was anything wrong with that.'

'No more would most people. Now here's a genuine one. I'll show you the differences – very slight they are, but you'll soon learn to tell them apart. Take this magnifying glass.'

At the end of five minutes' coaching both Tommy and Tuppence were fairly expert.

'What do you want us to do, Inspector Marriot?' asked Tuppence. 'Just keep our eyes open for these things?'

'A great deal more than that, Mrs Beresford. I'm pinning my faith on you to get to the bottom of the matter. You see, we've discovered that the notes are being circulated from the West End. Somebody pretty high up in the social scale is doing the distributing. They're passing them the other side of the Channel as well. Now there's a certain person who is interesting us very much. A Major Laidlaw – perhaps you've heard the name?'

'I think I have,' said Tommy. 'Connected with racing, isn't that it?'

'Yes. Major Laidlaw is pretty well known in connection with the Turf. There's nothing actually against him, but there's a general impression that he's been a bit too smart over one or two rather shady transactions. Men in the know look queer when he's mentioned. Nobody knows much of his past or where he came from. He's got a very attractive French wife who's seen about everywhere with a train of admirers. They must spend a lot of money, the Laidlaws, and I'd like to know where it comes from.'

'Possibly from the train of admirers,' suggested Tommy.

'That's the general idea. But I'm not so sure. It may be coincidence, but a lot of notes have been forthcoming from a certain very smart little gambling club which is much frequented by the Laidlaws and their set. This racing, gambling set get rid of a lot of loose money in notes. There couldn't be a better way of getting it into circulation.'

'And where do we come in?'

'This way. Young St Vincent and his wife are friends of yours, I understand? They're pretty thick with the Laidlaw set – though not as thick as they were. Through them it will be easy for you to get a footing in the same set in a way that none of our people could attempt. There's no likelihood of their spotting you. You'll have an ideal opportunity.'

'What have we got to find out exactly?'

'Where they get the stuff from, if they *are* passing it.'

'Quite so,' said Tommy. 'Major Laidlaw goes out with an empty suit-case. When he returns it is crammed to the bursting point with Treasury notes. How is it done? I sleuth him and find out. Is that the idea?'

'More or less. But don't neglect the lady, and her father, M. Heroulade. Remember the notes are being passed on both sides of the Channel.'

'My dear Marriot,' exclaimed Tommy reproachfully, 'Blunt's Brilliant Detectives do not know the meaning of the word neglect.'

The Inspector rose.

'Well, good luck to you,' he said, and departed.

'Slush,' said Tuppence enthusiastically.

'Eh?' said Tommy, perplexed.

'Counterfeit money,' explained Tuppence. 'It is always called slush. I know I'm right. Oh, Tommy, we have got an Edgar Wallace case. At last we are Busies.'

'We are,' said Tommy. 'And we are out to get the Crackler, and we will get him good.'

'Did you say the Cackler or the Crackler?'

'The Crackler.'

'Oh, what is a Crackler?'

'A new word that I have coined,' said Tommy. 'Descriptive of one who passes false notes into circulation. Banknotes crackle, therefore he is called a crackler. Nothing could be more simple.'

'That is rather a good idea,' said Tuppence. 'It makes it seem more real. I like the Rustler myself. Much more descriptive and sinister.'

'No,' said Tommy, 'I said the Crackler first, and I stick to it.'

'I shall enjoy this case,' said Tuppence. 'Lots of night clubs and cocktails in it. I shall buy some eyelash-black tomorrow.'

'Your eyelashes are black already,' objected her husband.

'I could make them blacker,' said Tuppence. 'And cherry lipstick would be useful too. That ultra-bright kind.'

'Tuppence,' said Tommy, 'you're a real rake at heart. What a good thing it is that you are married to a sober steady middle-aged man like myself.'

'You wait,' said Tuppence. 'When you have been to the Python Club a bit, you won't be so sober yourself.'

Tommy produced from a cupboard various bottles, two glasses, and a cocktail shaker.

'Let's start now,' he said. 'We are after you, Crackler, and we mean to get you.'

CHAPTER XIV

The Crackler (*continued*)

Making the acquaintance of the Laidlaws proved an easy affair. Tommy and Tuppence, young, well-dressed, eager for life, and with apparently money to burn, were soon made free of that particular coterie in which the Laidlaws had their being.

Major Laidlaw was a tall, fair man, typically English in appearance, with a hearty sportsmanlike manner, slightly belied by the hard lines round his eyes and the occasional quick sideways glance that assorted oddly with his supposed character.

He was a very dexterous card player, and Tommy noticed that when the stakes were high he seldom rose from the table a loser.

Marguerite Laidlaw was quite a different proposition. She was a charming creature, with the slenderness of a wood nymph and the face of a Greuze picture. Her dainty broken English was fascinating, and Tommy felt that it was no wonder most men were her slaves. She seemed to take a great fancy to Tommy from the first, and playing his part, he allowed himself to be swept into her train.

'My Tommee,' she would say; 'but positively I cannot go without my Tommee. His 'air, eet ees the colour of the sunset, ees eet not?'

Her father was a more sinister figure. Very correct, very upright, with his little black beard and his watchful eyes.

Tuppence was the first to report progress. She came to Tommy with ten one pound notes.

'Have a look at these. They're wrong 'uns, aren't they?'

Tommy examined them and confirmed Tuppence's diagnosis.

'Where did you get them from?'

'That boy, Jimmy Faulkener. Marguerite Laidlaw gave them to him to put on a horse for her. I said I wanted small notes and gave him a tenner in exchange.'

'All new and crisp,' said Tommy thoughtfully. 'They can't have passed through many hands. I suppose young Faulkener is all right?'

'Jimmy? Oh, he's a dear. He and I are becoming great friends.'

'So I have noticed,' said Tommy coldly. 'Do you really think it is necessary?'

'Oh, it isn't business,' said Tuppence cheerfully. 'It's pleasure. He's such a nice boy. I'm glad to get him out of that woman's clutches. You've no idea of the amount of money she's cost him.'

'It looks to me as though he were getting rather a pash for you, Tuppence.'

'I've thought the same myself sometimes. It's nice to know one's still young and attractive, isn't it?'

'Your moral tone, Tuppence, is deplorably low. You look at these things from the wrong point of view.'

'I haven't enjoyed myself so much for years,' declared Tuppence shamelessly. 'And anyway, what about you? Do I ever see you nowadays? Aren't you always living in Marguerite Laidlaw's pocket?'

'Business,' said Tommy crisply.

'But she is attractive, isn't she?'

'Not my type,' said Tommy. 'I don't admire her.'

'Liar,' laughed Tuppence. 'But I always did think I'd rather marry a liar than a fool.'

'I suppose,' said Tommy, 'that there's no absolute necessity for a husband to be either?'

But Tuppence merely threw him a pitying glance and withdrew.

Amongst Mrs Laidlaw's train of admirers was a simple but extremely wealthy gentleman of the name of Hank Ryder.

Mr Ryder came from Alabama, and from the first he was disposed to make a friend and confidant of Tommy.

'That's a wonderful woman, sir,' said Mr Ryder following the lovely Marguerite with reverential eyes. 'Plumb full of civilization. Can't beat *la gaie France*, can you? When I'm near her, I feel as though I was one of the Almighty's earliest experiments. I guess he'd got to get his hand in before he attempted anything so lovely as that perfectly lovely woman.'

Tommy agreeing politely with these sentiments, Mr Ryder unburdened himself still further.

'Seems kind of a shame a lovely creature like that should have money worries.'

'Has she?' asked Tommy.

'You betcha life she has. Queer fish, Laidlaw. She's skeered of him. Told me so. Daren't tell him about her little bills.'

'Are they *little* bills?' asked Tommy.

'Well – when I say little! After all, a woman's got to wear clothes, and the less there are of them the more they cost, the way I figure it out. And a pretty woman like that doesn't want to go about in last season's goods. Cards too, the poor little thing's been mighty unlucky at cards. Why, she lost fifty to me last night.'

'She won two hundred from Jimmy Faulkener the night before,' said Tommy drily.

'Did she indeed? That relieves my mind some. By the way, there seems to be a lot of dud notes floating around in your country just now. I paid in a bunch at my bank this morning, and twenty-five of them were down-and-outers, so the polite gentleman behind the counter informed me.'

'That's rather a large proportion. Were they new looking?'

'New and crisp as they make 'em. Why, they were the ones Mrs Laidlaw paid over to me, I reckon. Wonder where she got 'em from. One of these toughs on the racecourse as likely as not.'

'Yes,' said Tommy. 'Very likely.'

'You know, Mr Beresford, I'm new to this sort of high life. All these swell dames and the rest of the outfit. Only made my pile a short while back. Came right over to Yurrop to see life.'

Tommy nodded. He made a mental note to the effect that

with the aid of Marguerite Laidlaw Mr Ryder would probably see a good deal of life and that the price charged would be heavy.

Meantime, for the second time, he had evidence that the forged notes were being distributed pretty near at hand, and that in all probability Marguerite Laidlaw had a hand in their distribution.

On the following night he himself was given a proof.

It was at that small select meeting place mentioned by Inspector Marriot. There was dancing there, but the real attraction of the place lay behind a pair of imposing folding doors. There were two rooms there with green baize-covered tables, where vast sums changed hands nightly.

Marguerite Laidlaw, rising at last to go, thrust a quantity of small notes into Tommy's hands.

'They are so bulkee, Tommee – you will change them, yes? A beeg note. See my so sweet leetle bag, it bulges him to distraction.'

Tommy brought her the hundred pound note she asked for. Then in a quiet corner he examined the notes she had given him. At least a quarter of them were counterfeit.

But where did she get her supplies from? To that he had as yet no answer. By means of Albert's co-operation, he was almost sure that Laidlaw was not the man. His movements had been watched closely and had yielded no result.

Tommy suspected her father, the saturnine M. Heroulade. He went to and fro to France fairly often. What could be simpler than to bring the notes across with him? A false bottom to the trunk – something of that kind.

Tommy strolled slowly out of the Club, absorbed in these thoughts, but was suddenly recalled to immediate necessities. Outside in the street was Mr Hank P. Ryder, and it was clear at once that Mr Ryder was not strictly sober. At the moment he was trying to hang his hat on the radiator of a car, and missing it by some inches every time.

'This goddarned hatshtand, this goddarned hatshtand,' said Mr Ryder tearfully. 'Not like that in the Shtates. Man can hang up his hat every night – every night, sir. You're wearing two hatshs. Never sheen a man wearing two hatshs before. Must be effect – climate.'

'Perhaps I've got two heads,' said Tommy gravely.

'Sho you have,' said Mr Ryder. 'Thatsh odd. Thatsh remarkable fac'. Letsh have a cocktail. Prohibition – probishun thatsh whatsh done me in. I guess I'm drunk – constootionally drunk. Cocktailsh – mixed 'em – Angel's Kiss – that's Marguerite – lovely creature, fon o' me too. Horshes Neck, two Martinis – three Road to Ruinsh – no, roadsh to roon – mixed 'em all – in a beer tankard. Bet me I wouldn't – I shaid – to hell, I shaid –'

Tommy interrupted.

'That's all right,' he said soothingly. 'Now what about getting home?'

'No home to go to,' said Mr Ryder sadly, and wept.

'What hotel are you staying at?' asked Tommy.

'Can't go home,' said Mr Ryder. 'Treasure hunt. Swell thing to do. She did it. Whitechapel – white heartsh, white headsn shorrow to the grave –'

But Mr Ryder became suddenly dignified. He drew himself erect and attained a sudden miraculous command over his speech.

'Young man, I'm telling you. Margee took me. In her car. Treasure hunting. English aristocrashy all do it. Under the cobblestones. Five hundred poundsh. Solemn thought, '*tis* solemn thought. I'm *telling* you, young man. You've been kind to me. I've got your welfare at heart, sir, at heart. We Americans –'

Tommy interrupted him this time with even less ceremony.

'What's that you say? Mrs Laidlaw took you in a car?'

The American nodded with a kind of owlish solemnity.

'To Whitechapel?' Again that owlish nod.

'And you found five hundred pounds there?'

Mr Ryder struggled for words.

'S-she did,' he corrected his questioner. 'Left me outside. Outside the door. Always left outside. It's kinder sad. Outside – always outside.'

'Would you know your way there?'

'I guess so. Hank Ryder doesn't lose his bearings –'

Tommy hauled him along unceremoniously. He found his own car where it was waiting, and presently they were bowling eastward. The cool air revived Mr Ryder. After slumping against Tommy's shoulder in a kind of stupor, he awoke clear-headed and refreshed.

'Say, boy, where are we?' he demanded.

'Whitechapel,' said Tommy crisply. 'Is this where you came with Mrs Laidlaw tonight?'

'It looks kinder familiar,' admitted Mr Ryder, looking round. 'Seems to me we turned off to the left somewhere down here. That's it – that street there.'

Tommy turned off obediently. Mr Ryder issued directions.

'That's it. Sure. And round to the right. Say, aren't the smells awful. Yes, past that pub at the corner – sharp round, and stop at the mouth of that little alley. But what's the big idea? Hand it to me. Some of the oof left behind? Are we going to put one over on them?'

'That's exactly it,' said Tommy. 'We're going to put one over on them. Rather a joke, isn't it?'

'I'll tell the world,' assented Mr Ryder. 'Though I'm just a mite hazed about it all,' he ended wistfully.

Tommy got out and assisted Mr Ryder to alight also. They advanced into the alley way. On the left were the backs of a row of dilapidated houses, most of which had doors opening into the alley. Mr Ryder came to a stop before one of these doors.

'In here she went,' he declared. 'It was this door – I'm plumb certain of it.'

'They all look very alike,' said Tommy. 'Reminds me of the story of the soldier and the Princess. You remember, they made a cross on the door to show which one it was. Shall we do the same?'

Laughing, he drew a piece of white chalk from his pocket and made a rough cross low down on the door. Then he looked

up at various dim shapes that prowled high on the walls of the
alley, one of which was uttering a blood-curdling yawl.

'Lots of cats about,' he remarked cheerfully.

'What is the procedure?' asked Mr Ryder. 'Do we step inside?'

'Adopting due precautions, we do,' said Tommy.

He glanced up and down the alley way, then softly tried the
door. It yielded. He pushed it open and peered into a dim yard.

Noiselessly he passed through, Mr Ryder on his heels.

'Gee,' said the latter, 'there's someone coming down the
alley.'

He slipped outside again. Tommy stood still for a minute,
then hearing nothing went on. He took a torch from his pocket
and switched on the light for a brief second. That momentary
flash enabled him to see his way ahead. He pushed forward and
tried the closed door ahead of him. That too gave, and very
softly he pushed it open and went in.

After standing still a second and listening, he again switched
on the torch, and at that flash, as though at a given signal, the
place seemed to rise round him. Two men were in front of him,
two men were behind him. They closed in on him and bore
him down.

'Lights,' growled a voice.

An incandescent gas burner was lit. By its light Tommy saw
a circle of unpleasing faces. His eyes wandered gently round
the room and noted some of the objects in it.

'Ah!' he said pleasantly. 'The headquarters of the counter-
feiting industry, if I am not mistaken.'

'Shut your jaw,' growled one of the men.

The door opened and shut behind Tommy, and a genial and
well-known voice spoke.

'Got him, boys. That's right. Now, Mr Busy, let me tell you
you're up against it.'

'That dear old word,' said Tommy. 'How it thrills me. Yes. I
am the Mystery Man of Scotland Yard. Why, it's Mr Hank Ryder.
This *is* a surprise.'

'I guess you mean that too. I've been laughing fit to bust all
this evening – leading you here like a little child. And you so

pleased with your cleverness. Why, sonny, I was on to you from the start. You weren't in with that crowd for your health. I let you play about for a while, and when you got real suspicious of the lovely Marguerite, I said to myself: "Now's the time to lead him to it." I guess your friends won't be hearing of you for some time.'

'Going to do me in? That's the correct expression, I believe. You have got it in for me.'

'You've got a nerve all right. No, we shan't attempt violence. Just keep you under restraint, so to speak.'

'I'm afraid you're backing the wrong horse,' said Tommy. 'I've no intention of being "kept under restraint," as you call it.'

Mr Ryder smiled genially. From outside a cat uttered a melancholy cry to the moon.

'Banking on that cross you put on the door, eh, sonny?' said Mr Ryder. 'I shouldn't if I were you. Because I know that story you mentioned. Heard it when I was a little boy. I stepped back into the alley way to enact the part of the dog with eyes as big as cart-wheels. If you were in that alley now, you would observe that every door in the alley is marked with an identical cross.'

Tommy dropped his head despondently.

'Thought you were mighty clever, didn't you?' said Ryder.

As the words left his lips a sharp rapping sounded on the door.

'What's that?' he cried, starting.

At the same time an assault began on the front of the house. The door at the back was a flimsy affair. The lock gave almost immediately and Inspector Marriot showed in the doorway.

'Well done, Marriot,' said Tommy. 'You were quite right as to the district. I'd like you to make the acquaintance of Mr Hank Ryder who knows all the best fairy tales.

'You see, Mr Ryder,' he added gently, 'I've had my suspicions of you. Albert (that important-looking boy with the big ears is Albert) had orders to follow on his motorcycle if you and I went off joy-riding at any time. And whilst I was ostentatiously marking a chalk cross on the door to engage your attention, I also emptied a little bottle of valerian on the ground. Nasty smell, but cats love it. All the cats in the neighbourhood were assembled outside to mark the right house when Albert and the police arrived.'

He looked at the dumbfounded Mr Ryder with a smile, then rose to his feet.

'I said I would get you Crackler, and I have got you,' he observed.

'What the hell are you talking about?' asked Mr Ryder. 'What do you mean – Crackler?'

'You will find it in the glossary of the next criminal dictionary,' said Tommy. 'Etymology doubtful.'

He looked round him with a happy smile.

'And all done without a nose,' he murmured brightly. 'Goodnight, Marriot. I must go now to where the happy ending of the story awaits me. No reward like the love of a good woman – and the love of a good woman awaits me at home – that is, I hope it does, but one never knows nowadays. This has been a very dangerous job, Marriot. Do you know Captain Jimmy Faulkener? His dancing is simply too marvellous, and as for his taste in cocktails –! Yes, Marriot, it has been a very dangerous job.'

CHAPTER XV

The Sunningdale Mystery

'Do you know where we are going to lunch today, Tuppence?'

Mrs Beresford considered the question.

'The Ritz?' she suggested hopefully.

'Think again.'

'That nice little place in Soho?'

'No.' Tommy's tone was full of importance. 'An ABC shop. This one, in fact.'

He drew her deftly inside an establishment of the kind indicated, and steered her to a corner marble-topped table.

'Excellent,' said Tommy with satisfaction, as he seated himself. 'Couldn't be better.'

'Why has this craze for the simple life come upon you?' demanded Tuppence.

'*You see, Watson, but you do not observe.* I wonder now whether one of these haughty damsels would condescend to notice us? Splendid, she drifts this way. It is true that she appears to be thinking of something else, but doubtless her sub-conscious mind is functioning busily with such matters as ham and eggs and pots of tea. Chop and fried potatoes, please, miss, and a large coffee, a roll and butter, and a plate of tongue for the lady.'

The waitress repeated the order in a scornful tone, but Tuppence leant forward suddenly and interrupted her.

'No, not a chop and fried potatoes. This gentleman will have a cheesecake and a glass of milk.'

'A cheesecake and a milk,' said the waitress with even deeper scorn, if that were possible. Still thinking of something else, she drifted away again.

'That was uncalled for,' said Tommy coldly.

'But I'm right, aren't I? You are the Old Man in the Corner? Where's your piece of string?'

Tommy drew a long twisted mesh of string from his pocket and proceeded to tie a couple of knots in it.

'Complete to the smallest detail,' he murmured.

'You made a small mistake in ordering your meal, though.'

'Women are so literal-minded,' said Tommy. 'If there's one thing I hate it's milk to drink, and cheesecakes are always so yellow and bilious-looking.'

'Be an artist,' said Tuppence. 'Watch me attack my cold tongue. Jolly good stuff, cold tongue. Now then, I'm all ready to be Miss Polly Burton. Tie a large knot and begin.'

'First of all,' said Tommy, 'speaking in a strictly unofficial capacity, let me point out this. Business is not too brisk lately. If business does not come to us, we must go to business. Apply our minds to one of the great public mysteries of the moment. Which brings me to the point – the Sunningdale Mystery.'

'Ah!' said Tuppence, with deep interest. 'The Sunningdale Mystery!'

Tommy drew a crumpled piece of newspaper from his pocket and laid it on the table.

'That is the latest portrait of Captain Sessle as it appeared in the *Daily Leader*.'

'Just so,' said Tuppence. 'I wonder someone doesn't sue these newspapers sometimes. You can see it's a man and that's all.'

'When I said the Sunningdale Mystery, I should have said the so-called Sunningdale Mystery,' went on Tommy rapidly.

'A mystery to the police perhaps, but not to an intelligent mind.'

'Tie another knot,' said Tuppence.

'I don't know how much of the case you remember,' continued Tommy quietly.

'All of it,' said Tuppence, 'but don't let me cramp your style.'

'It was just over three weeks ago,' said Tommy, 'that the gruesome discovery was made on the famous golf links. Two members of the club, who were enjoying an early round, were horrified to find the body of a man lying face downwards on the seventh tee. Even before they turned him over they had guessed him to be Captain Sessle, a well-known figure on the links, and who always wore a golf coat of a peculiarly bright blue colour.

'Captain Sessle was often seen out on the links early in the morning, practising, and it was thought at first that he had been suddenly overcome by some form of heart disease. But examination by a doctor revealed the sinister fact that he had been murdered, stabbed to the heart with a significant object, *a woman's hatpin.* He was also found to have been dead at least twelve hours.

'That put an entirely different complexion on the matter, and very soon some interesting facts came to light. Practically the last person to see Captain Sessle alive was his friend and partner, Mr Hollaby of the Porcupine Assurance Co, and he told his story as follows:

'Sessle and he had played a round earlier in the day. After tea the other suggested that they should play a few more holes before it got too dark to see. Hollaby assented. Sessle seemed in good spirits, and was in excellent form. There is a public footpath that crosses the links, and just as they were playing up to the sixth green, Hollaby noticed a woman coming along it. She was very tall, and dressed in brown, but he did not observe her particularly, and Sessle, he thought, did not notice her at all.

'The footpath in question crossed in front of the seventh tee,' continued Tommy. 'The woman had passed along this and was standing at the farther side, as though waiting. Captain Sessle was the first to reach the tee, as Mr Hollaby was replacing the pin in the hole. As the latter came towards the tee, he was astonished to see Sessle and the woman talking together. As he came nearer, they both turned abruptly, Sessle calling over his shoulder: "Shan't be a minute."

'The two of them walked off side by side, still deep in earnest conversation. The footpath there leaves the course, and, passing between the two narrow hedges of neighbouring gardens, comes out on the road to Windlesham.

'Captain Sessle was as good as his word. He reappeared within a minute or two, much to Hollaby's satisfaction, as two other players were coming up behind them, and the light was failing rapidly. They drove off, and at once Hollaby noticed that something had occurred to upset his companion. Not only did he foozle his drive badly, but his face was worried and his forehead creased in a big frown. He hardly answered his companion's remarks, and his golf was atrocious. Evidently something had occurred to put him completely off his game.

'They played that hole and the eighth, and then Captain Sessle declared abruptly that the light was too bad and that he was off home. Just at that point there is another of those narrow "slips" leading to the Windlesham road, and Captain Sessle departed that way, which was a short cut to his home, a small bungalow on the road in question. The other two players came up, a Major Barnard and Mr Lecky, and to them Hollaby mentioned Captain Sessle's sudden change of manner. They also had seen him speaking to the woman in brown, but had not been near enough to see her face. All three men wondered what she could have said to upset their friend to that extent.

'They returned to the clubhouse together, and as far as was known at the time, were the last people to see Captain Sessle alive. The day was a Wednesday, and on Wednesday cheap tickets to London are issued. The man and wife who ran Captain Sessle's small bungalow were up in town, according to custom, and did not return until the late train. They entered the bungalow as usual, and supposed their master to be in his room asleep. Mrs Sessle, his wife, was away on a visit.

'The murder of the Captain was a nine days' wonder. Nobody could suggest a motive for it. The identity of the tall woman in brown was eagerly discussed, but without result. The police were, as usual, blamed for their supineness – most unjustly, as time was to show. For a week later, a girl called Doris Evans was arrested and charged with the murder of Captain Anthony Sessle.

'The police had had little to work upon. A strand of fair hair caught in the dead man's fingers and a few threads of flame-coloured wool caught on one of the buttons of his blue coat. Diligent inquiries at the railway station and elsewhere had elicited the following facts.

'A young girl dressed in a flame-coloured coat and skirt had arrived by train that evening about seven o'clock and had asked the way to Captain Sessle's house. The same girl had reappeared again at the station, two hours later. Her hat was awry and her hair tousled, and she seemed in a state of great agitation. She inquired about the trains back to town, and was continually looking over her shoulder as though afraid of something.

'Our police force is in many ways very wonderful. With this slender evidence to go upon, they managed to track down the girl and identify her as one Doris Evans. She was charged with murder and cautioned that anything she might say would be used against her, but she nevertheless persisted in making a statement, and this statement she repeated again in detail, without any subsequent variation, at the subsequent proceedings.

'Her story was this. She was a typist by profession, and had made friends one evening, in a cinema, with a well-dressed man, who declared he had taken a fancy to her. His name, he told her, was Anthony, and he suggested that she should come down to his bungalow at Sunningdale. She had no idea then, or at any other time, that he had a wife. It was arranged between them that she should come down on the following Wednesday – the day, you will remember, when the servants would be absent and his wife away from home. In the end he told her his full name was Anthony Sessle, and gave her the name of his house.

'She duly arrived at the bungalow on the evening in question, and was greeted by Sessle, who had just come in from the links. Though he professed himself delighted to see her, the girl declared that from the first his manner was strange and different. A half-acknowledged fear sprang up in her, and she wished fervently that she had not come.

'After a simple meal, which was all ready and prepared, Sessle suggested going out for a stroll. The girl consenting, he took her out of the house, down the road, and along the "slip" on to the golf course. And then suddenly, just as they were crossing the seventh tee, he seemed to go completely mad. Drawing a revolver from his pocket, he brandished it in the air, declaring that he had come to the end of his tether.

' "Everything must go! I'm ruined – done for. And you shall go with me. I shall shoot you first – then myself. They will find our bodies here in the morning side by side – together in death."

'And so on – a lot more. He had hold of Doris Evans by the arm, and she, realizing she had to do with a madman, made frantic efforts to free herself, or failing that to get the revolver away from him. They struggled together, and in that struggle he must have torn out a piece of her hair and got the wool of her coat entangled on a button.

'Finally, with a desperate effort, she freed herself, and ran for her life across the golf links, expecting every minute to be shot down with a revolver bullet. She fell twice, tripping over the heather, but eventually regained the road to the station and realized that she was not being pursued.

'That is the story that Doris Evans tells – and from which she has never varied. She strenuously denies that she ever struck at him with a hatpin in self-defence – a natural enough thing to do under the circumstances, though – and one which may well be the truth. In support of her story, a revolver has been found in the furze bushes near where the body was lying. It had not been fired.

'Doris Evans has been sent for trial, but the mystery still remains a mystery. If her story is to be believed, who was it who stabbed Captain Sessle? The other woman, the tall woman in brown, whose appearance so upset him? So far no one has explained her connection with the case. She appears out of space suddenly on the footpath across the links, she disappears along the slip, and no one ever hears of her again. Who was she? A local resident? A visitor from London? If so, did she come by car or by train? There is nothing remarkable about her except her height; no one seems to be able to describe her appearance. She could not have been Doris Evans, for Doris

Evans is small and fair, and moreover was only just then arriving at the station.'

'The wife?' suggested Tuppence. 'What about the wife?'

'A very natural suggestion. But Mrs Sessle is also a small woman, and besides, Mr Hollaby knows her well by sight, and there seems no doubt that she was really away from home. One further development has come to light. The Porcupine Assurance Co is in liquidation. The accounts reveal the most daring misappropriation of funds. The reasons for Captain Sessle's wild words to Doris Evans are now quite apparent. For some years past he must have been systematically embezzling money. Neither Mr Hollaby nor his son had any idea of what was going on. They are practically ruined.

'The case stands like this. Captain Sessle was on the verge of discovery and ruin. Suicide would be a natural solution, but the nature of the wound rules that theory out. Who killed him? Was it Doris Evans? Was it the mysterious woman in brown?'

Tommy paused, took a sip of milk, made a wry face, and bit cautiously at the cheesecake.

CHAPTER XVI

The Sunningdale Mystery

(*continued*)

'Of course,' murmured Tommy, 'I saw at once where the hitch in this particular case lay, and just where the police were going astray.'

'Yes?' said Tuppence eagerly.

Tommy shook his head sadly.

'I wish I did. Tuppence, it's dead easy being the Old Man in the Corner up to a certain point. But the solution beats me. Who did murder the beggar? I don't know.'

He took some more newspaper cuttings out of his pocket.

'Further exhibits – Mr Hollaby, his son, Mrs Sessle, Doris Evans.'

Tuppence pounced on the last and looked at it for some time.

'She didn't murder him anyway,' she remarked at last. 'Not with a hatpin.'

'Why this certainty?'

'A lady Molly touch. She's got bobbed hair. Only one woman in twenty uses hatpins nowadays, anyway – long hair or short. Hats fit tight and pull on – there's no need for such a thing.'

'Still, she might have had one by her.'

'My dear boy, we don't keep them as heirlooms! What on earth should she have brought a hatpin down to Sunningdale for?'

'Then it must have been the other woman, the woman in brown.'

'I wish she hadn't been tall. Then she could have been the wife. I always suspect wives who are away at the time and so couldn't have had anything to do with it. If she found her husband carrying on with that girl, it would be quite natural for her to go for him with a hatpin.'

'I shall have to be careful, I see,' remarked Tommy.

But Tuppence was deep in thought and refused to be drawn.

'What were the Sessles like?' she asked suddenly. 'What sort of things did people say about them?'

'As far as I can make out, they were very popular. He and his wife were supposed to be devoted to one another. That's what makes the business of the girl so odd. It's the last thing you'd have expected of a man like Sessle. He was an ex-soldier, you know. Came into a good bit of money, retired, and went into this Insurance business. The last man in the world, apparently, whom you would have suspected of being a crook.'

'It is absolutely certain that he was the crook? Couldn't it have been the other two who took the money?'

'The Hollabys? They say they're ruined.'

'Oh, they say! Perhaps they've got it all in a bank under another name. I put it foolishly, I dare say, but you know what I mean. Suppose they'd been speculating with the money for some time, unbeknownst to Sessle, and lost it all. It might be jolly convenient for them that Sessle died just when he did.'

Tommy tapped the photograph of Mr Hollaby senior with his finger-nail.

'So you're accusing this respectable gentleman of murdering his friend and partner? You forget that he parted from Sessle on the links in full view of Barnard and Lecky, and spent the evening in the Dormy House. Besides, there's the hatpin.'

'Bother the hatpin,' said Tuppence impatiently. 'That hatpin, you think, points to the crime having been committed by a woman?'

'Naturally. Don't you agree?'

'No. Men are notoriously old-fashioned. It takes them ages to rid themselves of preconceived ideas. They associate hatpins and hairpins with the female sex, and call them "women's weapons." They may have been in the past, but they're both rather out of date now. Why, I haven't had a hatpin or a hairpin for the last four years.'

'Then you think –?'

'That it was a *man* killed Sessle. The hatpin was used to make it seem a woman's crime.'

'There's something in what you say, Tuppence,' said Tommy slowly. 'It's extraordinary how things seem to straighten themselves out when you talk a thing over.'

Tuppence nodded.

'Everything must be logical – if you look at it the right way. And remember what Marriot once said about the amateur point of view – that it had the *intimacy*. We know something about people like Captain Sessle and his wife. We know what they're likely to do – and what they're not likely to do. And we've each got our special knowledge.'

Tommy smiled.

'You mean,' he said, 'that you are an authority on what people with bobbed and shingled heads are likely to have in their possession, and that you have an intimate acquaintance with what wives are likely to feel and do?'

'Something of the sort.'

'And what about me? What is my special knowledge? Do husbands pick up girls, etc?'

'No,' said Tuppence gravely. 'You know the course – you've been on it – not as a detective searching for clues, but as a golfer. You know about golf, and what's likely to put a man off his game.'

'It must have been something pretty serious to put Sessle off his game. His handicap's two, and from the seventh tee on he played like a child, so they say.'

'Who say?'

'Barnard and Lecky. They were playing just behind him, you remember.'

'That was after he met the woman – the tall woman in brown. They saw him speaking to her, didn't they?'

'Yes – at least –'

Tommy broke off. Tuppence looked up at him and was puzzled. He was staring at the piece of string in his fingers, but staring with the eyes of one who sees something very different.

'Tommy – what is it?'

'Be quiet, Tuppence. I'm playing the sixth hole at Sunningdale. Sessle and old Hollaby are holing out on the sixth green ahead of me. It's getting dusk, but I can see that bright blue coat of Sessle's clearly enough. And on the footpath to the left of me there's a woman coming along. She hasn't crossed from the ladies' course – that's on the right – I should have seen her if she had done so. And it's odd I didn't see her on the footpath before – from the fifth tee, for instance.'

He paused.

'You said just now I knew the course, Tuppence. Just behind the sixth tee there's a little hut or shelter made of turf. Any one could wait in there until – the right moment came. They could change their appearance there. I mean – tell me, Tuppence, this is where your special knowledge comes in again – would it be very difficult for a man to look like a woman, and then change back to being a man again? Could he wear a skirt over plus-fours, for instance?'

'Certainly he could. The woman would look a bit bulky, that would be all. A longish brown skirt, say a brown sweater of the kind both men and women wear, and a woman's felt hat with a bunch of side curls attached each side. That would be all that was needed – I'm speaking, of course, of what would pass at a distance, which I take to be what you are driving at. Switch off the skirt, take off the hat and curls, and put on a man's cap which you can carry rolled up in your hand, and there you'd be – back as a man again.'

'And the time required for the transformation?'

'From woman to man, a minute and a half at the outside, probably a good deal less. The other way about would take longer, you'd have to arrange the hat and curls a bit, and the skirt would stick getting it on over the plus fours.'

'That doesn't worry me. It's the time for the first that matters. As I tell you, I'm playing the sixth hole. The woman in brown has reached the seventh tee now. She crosses it and waits. Sessle in his blue coat goes towards her. They stand together a minute, and then they follow the path round the trees out of sight.

Hollaby is on the tee alone. Two or three minutes pass. I'm on the green now. The man in the blue coat comes back and drives off, foozling badly. The light's getting worse. I and my partner go on. Ahead of us are those two, Sessle slicing and topping and doing everything he shouldn't do. At the eighth green, I see him stride off and vanish down the slip. What happened to him to make him play like a different man?'

'The woman in brown – or the man, if you think it was a man.'

'Exactly, and where they were standing – out of sight, remember, of those coming after them – there's a deep tangle of furze bushes. You could thrust a body in there, and it would be pretty certain to lie hidden until the morning.'

'Tommy! You think it was *then*. – But someone would have heard –'

'Heard what? The doctors agreed death must have been instantaneous. I've seen men killed instantaneously in the war. They don't cry out as a rule – just a gurgle, or a moan – perhaps just a sigh, or a funny little cough. Sessle comes towards the seventh tee, and the woman comes forward and speaks to him. He recognizes her, perhaps, as a man he knows masquerading. Curious to learn the why and wherefore, he allows himself to be drawn along the footpath out of sight. One stab with the deadly hatpin as they walk along. Sessle falls – dead. The other man drags his body into the furze bushes, strips off the blue coat, then sheds his own skirt and the hat and curls. He puts on Sessle's well-known blue coat and cap and strides back to the tee. Three minutes would do it. The others behind can't see his face, only the peculiar blue coat they know so well. They never doubt that it's Sessle – *but he doesn't play Sessle's brand of golf.* They all say he played like a different man. Of course he did. He *was* a different man.'

'But –'

'Point No. 2. His action in bringing the girl down there was the action of *a different man*. It wasn't Sessle who met Doris Evans at a cinema and induced her to come down to Sunningdale. It was a man *calling* himself Sessle. Remember, Doris Evans wasn't arrested until a fortnight after the time. *She never saw the body.* If she had, she might have bewildered everyone by declaring that that wasn't the man who took her out on the golf links that night and spoke so wildly of suicide. It was a carefully laid plot. The girl invited down for Wednesday when Sessle's house would be empty, then the hatpin which pointed to its being a woman's doing. The murderer meets the girl, takes her into the bungalow and gives her supper, then takes her out on the links, and when he gets to the scene of the crime, brandishes his revolver and scares the life out of her. Once she has taken to her heels, all he has to do is to pull out the body and leave it lying on the tee. The revolver he chucks into the bushes. Then he makes a neat parcel of the skirt and – now I admit I'm guessing – in all probability walks to Woking, which is only about six or seven miles away, and goes back to town from there.'

'Wait a minute,' said Tuppence. 'There's one thing you haven't explained. What about Hollaby?'

'Hollaby?'

'Yes. I admit that the people behind couldn't have seen whether it was really Sessle or not. But you can't tell me that the man who was playing with him was so hypnotized by the blue coat that he never looked at his face.'

'My dear old thing,' said Tommy. 'That's just the point. Hollaby knew all right. You see, I'm adopting your theory – that Hollaby and his son were the real embezzlers. The murderer's got to be a man who knew Sessle pretty well – knew, for instance, about the servants being always out on a Wednesday, and that his wife was away. And also someone who was able to get an impression of Sessle's latch key. I think Hollaby junior would fulfil all these requirements. He's about the same age and height as Sessle, and they were both clean-shaven men. Doris Evans probably saw several photographs of the murdered man reproduced in the papers, but as you yourself observed – one can just see that it's a man and that's about all.'

'Didn't she ever see Hollaby in Court?'

'The son never appeared in the case at all. Why should he?

He had no evidence to give. It was old Hollaby, with his irreproachable alibi, who stood in the limelight throughout. Nobody has ever bothered to inquire what his son was doing that particular evening.'

'It all fits in,' admitted Tuppence. She paused a minute and then asked: 'Are you going to tell all this to the police?'

'I don't know if they'd listen.'

'They'd listen all right,' said an unexpected voice behind him.

Tommy swung round to confront Inspector Marriot. The Inspector was sitting at the next table. In front of him was a poached egg.

'Often drop in here to lunch,' said Inspector Marriot. 'As I was saying, we'll listen all right – in fact I've been listening. I don't mind telling you that we've not been quite satisfied all along over those Porcupine figures. You see, we've had our suspicions of those Hollabys, but nothing to go upon. Too sharp for us. Then this murder came, and that seemed to upset all our ideas. But thanks to you and the lady, sir, we'll confront young Hollaby with Doris Evans and see if she recognizes him. I rather fancy she will. That's a very ingenious idea of yours about the blue coat. I'll see that Blunt's Brilliant Detectives get the credit for it.'

'You *are* a nice man, Inspector Marriot,' said Tuppence gratefully.

'We think a lot of you two at the Yard,' replied that stolid gentleman. 'You'd be surprised. If I may ask you, sir, what's the meaning of that piece of string?'

'Nothing,' said Tommy, stuffing it into his pocket. 'A bad habit of mine. As to the cheesecake and the milk – I'm on a diet. Nervous dyspepsia. Busy men are always martyrs to it.'

'Ah!' said the detective. 'I thought perhaps you'd been reading – well, it's of no consequence.'

But the Inspector's eyes twinkled.

CHAPTER XVII

The House of Lurking Death

'What –' began Tuppence, and then stopped.

She had just entered the private office of Mr Blunt from the adjoining one marked 'Clerks,' and was surprised to behold her lord and master with his eye riveted to the private peep-hole into the outer office.

'Ssh,' said Tommy warningly. 'Didn't you hear the buzzer? It's a girl – rather a nice girl – in fact she looks to me a frightfully nice girl. Albert is telling her all that tosh about my being engaged with Scotland Yard.'

'Let *me* see,' demanded Tuppence.

Somewhat unwillingly, Tommy moved aside. Tuppence in her turn glued her eye to the peep-hole.

'She's not bad,' admitted Tuppence. 'And her clothes are simply the latest shout.'

'She's perfectly lovely,' said Tommy. 'She's like those girls Mason writes about – you know, frightfully sympathetic, and beautiful, and distinctly intelligent without being too saucy. I think, yes – I certainly think – I shall be the great Hanaud this morning.'

'H'm,' said Tuppence. 'If there is one detective out of all the others whom you are most unlike – I should say it was Hanaud. Can you do the lightning changes of personality? Can you be the great comedian, the little gutter boy, the serious and sympathetic friend – all in five minutes?'

'I know this,' said Tommy, rapping sharply on the desk, 'I am the Captain of the Ship – and don't you forget it, Tuppence. I'm going to have her in.'

He pressed the buzzer on his desk. Albert appeared ushering in the client.

The girl stopped in the doorway as though undecided. Tommy came forward.

'Come in, mademoiselle,' he said kindly, 'and seat yourself here.'

Tuppence choked audibly and Tommy turned upon her with a swift change of manner. His tone was menacing.

'You spoke, Miss Robinson? Ah, no, I thought not.'

He turned back to the girl.

'We will not be serious or formal,' he said. 'You will just tell me about it, and then we will discuss the best way to help you.'

'You are very kind,' said the girl. 'Excuse me, but are you a foreigner?'

A fresh choke from Tuppence. Tommy glared in her direction out of the corner of his eye.

'Not exactly,' he said with difficulty. 'But of late years I have worked a good deal abroad. My methods are the methods of the Sûreté.'

'Oh!' The girl seemed impressed.

She was, as Tommy had indicated, a very charming girl. Young and slim, with a trace of golden hair peeping out from under her little brown felt hat, and big serious eyes.

That she was nervous could be plainly seen. Her little hands were twisting themselves together, and she kept clasping and unclasping the catch of her lacquered handbag.

'First of all, Mr Blunt, I must tell you that my name is Lois Hargreaves. I live in a great rambling old-fashioned house called Thurnly Grange. It is in the heart of the country. There is the village of Thurnly nearby, but it is very small and insignificant. There is plenty of hunting in winter, and we get tennis in summer, and I have never felt lonely there. Indeed I much prefer country to town life.

'I tell you this so that you may realize that in a country village like ours, everything that happens is of supreme importance. About a week ago, I got a box of chocolates sent through the post. There was nothing inside to indicate who they came from. Now I myself am not particularly fond of chocolates, but the others in the house are, and the box was passed round. As a result, everyone who had eaten any chocolates was taken ill. We sent for the doctor, and after various inquiries as to what other things had been eaten, he took the remains of the chocolates away with him, and had them analysed. Mr Blunt, those chocolates contained arsenic! Not enough to kill anyone, but enough to make anyone quite ill.'

'Extraordinary,' commented Tommy.

'Dr Burton was very excited over the matter. It seems that this was the third occurrence of the kind in the neighbourhood. In each case a big house was selected, and the inmates were taken ill after eating the mysterious chocolates. It looked as though some local person of weak intellect was playing a particularly fiendish practical joke.'

'Quite so, Miss Hargreaves.'

'Dr Burton put it down to Socialist agitation – rather absurdly, I thought. But there are one or two malcontents in Thurnly village, and it seemed possible that they might have had something to do with it. Dr Burton was very keen that I should put the whole thing in the hands of the police.'

'A very natural suggestion,' said Tommy. 'But you have not done so, I gather, Miss Hargreaves?'

'No,' admitted the girl. 'I hate the fuss and the publicity that would ensue – and you see, I know our local Inspector. I can never imagine him finding out anything! I have often seen your advertisement, and I told Dr Burton that it would be much better to call in a private detective.'

'I see.'

'You say a great deal about discretion in your advertisement. I take that to mean – that – that – well, that you would not make anything public without my consent?'

Tommy looked at her curiously, but it was Tuppence who spoke.

'I think,' she said quietly, 'that it would be as well if Miss Hargreaves told us *everything*.'

She laid especial stress upon the last word, and Lois Hargreaves flushed nervously.

'Yes,' said Tommy quickly, 'Miss Robinson is right. You must tell us everything.'

'You will not –' she hesitated.

'Everything you say is understood to be strictly in confidence.'

'Thank you. I know that I ought to have been quite frank with you. I have a reason for not going to the police. Mr Blunt, that box of chocolates was sent by someone in our house!'

'How do you know that, mademoiselle?'

'It's very simple. I've got a habit of drawing a little silly thing – three fish intertwined – whenever I have a pencil in my hand. A parcel of silk stockings arrived from a certain shop in London not long ago. We were at the breakfast table. I'd just been marking something in the newspaper, and without thinking, I began to draw my silly little fish on the label of the parcel before cutting the string and opening it. I thought no more about the matter, but when I was examining the piece of brown paper in which the chocolates had been sent, I caught sight of the corner of the original label – most of which had been torn off. My silly little drawing was on it.'

Tommy drew his chair forward.

'That is very serious. It creates, as you say, a very strong presumption that the sender of the chocolates is a member of your household. But you will forgive me if I say that I still do not see why that fact should render you indisposed to call in the police?'

Lois Hargreaves looked him squarely in the face.

'I will tell you, Mr Blunt. I may want the whole thing hushed up.'

Tommy retired gracefully from the position.

'In that case,' he murmured, 'we know where we are. I see, Miss Hargreaves, that you are not disposed to tell me who it is you suspect?'

'I suspect no one – but there are possibilities.'

'Quite so. Now will you describe the household to me in detail?'

'The servants, with the exception of the parlourmaid, are all old ones who have been with us many years. I must explain to you, Mr Blunt, that I was brought up by my aunt, Lady Radclyffe, who was extremely wealthy. Her husband made a big fortune, and was knighted. It was he who bought Thurnly Grange, but he died two years after going there, and it was then that Lady Radclyffe sent for me to come and make my home with her. I was her only living relation. The other inmate of the house was Dennis Radclyffe, her husband's nephew. I have always called him cousin, but of course he is really nothing of the kind. Aunt Lucy always said openly that she intended to leave her money, with the exception of a small provision for me, to Dennis. It was Radclyffe money, she said, and it ought to go to a Radclyffe. However, when Dennis was twenty-two, she quarrelled violently with him – over some debts that he had run up, I think. When she died, a year later, I was astonished to find that she had made a will leaving all her money to me. It was, I know, a great blow to Dennis, and I felt very badly about it. I would have given him the money if he would have taken it, but it seems that kind of thing can't be done. However, as soon as I was twenty-one, I made a will leaving it all to him. That's the least I can do. So if I'm run over by a motor, Dennis will come into his own.'

'Exactly,' said Tommy. 'And when were you twenty-one, if I may ask the question?'

'Just three weeks ago.'

'Ah!' said Tommy. 'Now will you give me fuller particulars of the members of your household at this minute?'

'Servants – or – others?'

'Both.'

'The servants, as I say, have been with us some time. There is old Mrs Holloway, the cook, and her niece Rose, the kitchen-maid. Then there are two elderly housemaids, and Hannah who was my aunt's maid and who has always been devoted to me. The parlourmaid is called Esther Quant, and seems a very nice quiet girl. As for ourselves, there is Miss Logan, who was Aunt Lucy's companion, and who runs the house for me, and Captain Radclyffe – Dennis, you know, whom I told you about, and there is a girl called Mary Chilcott, an old school friend of mine who is staying with us.'

Tommy thought for a moment.

'That all seems fairly clear and straightforward, Miss Hargreaves,' he said after a minute or two. 'I take it that you have no special reason for attaching suspicion more to one person than another? You are only afraid it might prove to be – well – not a servant, shall we say?'

'That's it exactly, Mr Blunt. I have honestly no idea who used that piece of brown paper. The handwriting was printed.'

'There seems only one thing to be done,' said Tommy. 'I must be on the spot.'

The girl looked at him inquiringly.

Tommy went on after a moment's thought.

'I suggest that you prepare the way for the arrival of – say, Mr and Miss Van Dusen – American friends of yours. Will you be able to do that quite naturally?'

'Oh, yes. There will be no difficulty at all. When will you come down – tomorrow – or the day after?'

'Tomorrow, if you please. There is no time to waste.'

'That is settled then.'

The girl rose and held out her hand.

'One thing, Miss Hargreaves, not a word, mind, to anyone – anyone at all, that we are not what we seem.'

'What do you think of it, Tuppence?' he asked, when he returned from showing the visitor out.

'I don't like it,' said Tuppence decidedly. 'Especially I don't like the chocolates having so little arsenic in them.'

'What *do* you mean?'

'Don't you see? All those chocolates being sent round the neighbourhood were a blind. To establish the idea of a local maniac. Then, when the girl was really poisoned, it would be thought to be the same thing. You see, but for a stroke of luck, no one would ever have guessed that the chocolates were actually sent by someone in the house itself.'

'That was a stroke of luck. You're right. You think it's a deliberate plot against the girl herself?'

'I'm afraid so. I remember reading about old Lady Radclyffe's will. That girl has come into a terrific lot of money.'

'Yes, and she came of age and made a will three weeks ago. It looks bad – for Dennis Radclyffe. He gains by her death.'

Tuppence nodded.

'The worst of it is – that she thinks so too! That's why she won't have the police called in. Already she suspects him. And she must be more than half in love with him to act as she has done.'

'In that case,' said Tommy thoughtfully, 'why the devil doesn't he marry her? Much simpler and safer.'

Tuppence stared at him.

'You've said a mouthful,' she observed. 'Oh, boy! I'm getting ready to be Miss Van Dusen, you observe.'

'Why rush to crime, when there is a lawful means near at hand?'

Tuppence reflected for a minute or two.

'I've got it,' she announced. 'Clearly he must have married a barmaid whilst at Oxford. Origin of the quarrel with his aunt. That explains everything.'

'Then why not send the poisoned sweets to the barmaid?' suggested Tommy. 'Much more practical. I wish you wouldn't jump to these wild conclusions, Tuppence.'

'They're deductions,' said Tuppence, with a good deal of dignity. 'This is your first *corrida*, my friend, but when you have been twenty minutes in the arena –'

Tommy flung the office cushion at her.

CHAPTER XVIII

The House of Lurking Death
(*continued*)

'Tuppence, I say, Tuppence, come here.'

It was breakfast time the next morning. Tuppence hurried out of her bedroom and into the dining-room. Tommy was striding up and down, the open newspaper in his hand.

'What's the matter?'

Tommy wheeled round, and shoved the paper into her hand, pointing to the headlines.

MYSTERIOUS POISONING CASE
DEATHS FROM FIG SANDWICHES

Tuppence read on. This mysterious outbreak of ptomaine poisoning had occurred at Thurnly Grange. The deaths so far reported were those of Miss Lois Hargreaves, the owner of the house, and the parlourmaid, Esther Quant. A Captain Radclyffe and a Miss Logan were reported to be seriously ill. The cause of the outbreak was supposed to be some fig paste used in sandwiches, since another lady, a Miss Chilcott, who had not partaken of these was reported to be quite well.

'We must get down there at once,' said Tommy. 'That girl! That perfectly ripping girl! Why the devil didn't I go straight down there with her yesterday?'

'If you had,' said Tuppence, 'you'd probably have eaten fig sandwiches too for tea, and then you'd have been dead. Come on, let's start at once. I see it says that Dennis Radclyffe is seriously ill also.'

'Probably shamming, the dirty blackguard.'

They arrived at the small village of Thurnly about midday.

An elderly woman with red eyes opened the door to them when they arrived at Thurnly Grange.

'Look here,' said Tommy quickly before she could speak. 'I'm not a reporter or anything like that. Miss Hargreaves came to see me yesterday, and asked me to come down here. Is there anyone I can see?'

'Dr Burton is here now, if you'd like to speak to him,' said the woman doubtfully. 'Or Miss Chilcott. She's making all the arrangements.'

But Tommy had caught at the first suggestion.

'Dr Burton,' he said authoritatively. 'I should like to see him at once if he is here.'

The woman showed them into a small morning-room. Five minutes later the door opened, and a tall, elderly man with bent shoulders and a kind, but worried face, came in.

'Dr Burton,' said Tommy. He produced his professional card. 'Miss Hargreaves called on me yesterday with reference to those poisoned chocolates. I came down to investigate the matter at her request – alas! too late.'

The doctor looked at him keenly.

'You are Mr Blunt himself?'

'Yes. This is my assistant, Miss Robinson.'

The doctor bowed to Tuppence.

'Under the circumstances, there is no need for reticence. But for the episode of the chocolates, I might have believed these deaths to be the result of severe ptomaine poisoning – but ptomaine poisoning of an unusually virulent kind. There is gastro-intestinal inflammation and haemorrhage. As it is, I am taking the fig paste to be analysed.'

'You suspect arsenic poisoning?'

'No. The poison, if a poison has been employed, is something far more potent and swift in its action. It looks more like some powerful vegetable toxin.'

'I see. I should like to ask you, Dr Burton, whether you are thoroughly convinced that Captain Radclyffe is suffering from the same form of poisoning?'

The doctor looked at him.

'Captain Radclyffe is not suffering from any sort of poisoning now.'

'Aha,' said Tommy. 'I –'

'Captain Radclyffe died at five o'clock this morning.'

Tommy was utterly taken aback. The doctor prepared to depart.

'And the other victim, Miss Logan?' asked Tuppence.

'I have every reason to hope that she will recover since she has survived so far. Being an older woman, the poison seems to have had less effect on her. I will let you know the result of the analysis, Mr Blunt. In the meantime, Miss Chilcott, will, I am sure, tell you anything you want to know.'

As he spoke, the door opened, and a girl appeared. She was tall, with a tanned face, and steady blue eyes.

Dr Burton performed the necessary introductions.

'I am glad you have come, Mr Blunt,' said Mary Chilcott. 'This affair seems too terrible. Is there anything you want to know that I can tell you?'

'Where did the fig paste come from?'

'It is a special kind that comes from London. We often have it. No one suspected that this particular pot differed from any of the others. Personally I dislike the flavour of figs. That explains my immunity. I cannot understand how Dennis was affected, since he was out for tea. He must have picked up a sandwich when he came home, I suppose.'

Tommy felt Tuppence's hand press his arm ever so slightly.

'What time did he come in?' he asked.

'I don't really know. I could find out.'

'Thank you, Miss Chilcott. It doesn't matter. You have no objection, I hope, to my questioning the servants?'

'Please do anything you like, Mr Blunt. I am nearly distraught. Tell me – you don't think there has been – foul play?'

Her eyes were very anxious, as she put the question.

'I don't know what to think. We shall soon know.'

'Yes, I suppose Dr Burton will have the paste analysed.'

Quickly excusing herself, she went out by the window to speak to one of the gardeners.

'You take the housemaids, Tuppence,' said Tommy, 'and I'll find my way to the kitchen. I say, Miss Chilcott may feel very distraught, but she doesn't look it.'

Tuppence nodded assent without replying.

Husband and wife met half an hour later.

'Now to pool results,' said Tommy. 'The sandwiches came out for tea, and the parlourmaid ate one – that's how she got it in the neck. Cook is positive Dennis Radclyffe hadn't returned when tea was cleared away. Query – how did *he* get poisoned?'

'He came in at a quarter to seven,' said Tuppence. 'House-maid saw him from one of the windows. He had a cocktail before dinner – in the library. She was just clearing away the glass now, and luckily I got it from her before she washed it. It was after that that he complained of feeling ill.'

'Good,' said Tommy. 'I'll take that glass along to Burton, presently. Anything else?'

'I'd like you to see Hannah, the maid. She's – she's queer.'

'How do you mean – queer?'

'She looks to me as though she were going off her head.'

'Let me see her.'

Tuppence led the way upstairs. Hannah had a small sitting-room of her own. The maid sat upright on a high chair. On her knees was an open Bible. She did not look towards the two strangers as they entered. Instead she continued to read aloud to herself.

'*Let hot burning coals fall upon them, let them be cast into the fire and into the pit, that they never rise up again.*'

'May I speak to you a minute?' asked Tommy.

Hannah made an impatient gesture with her hand.

'This is no time. The time is running short, I say. *I will follow upon mine enemies and overtake them, neither will I turn again till I have destroyed them.* So it is written. The word of the Lord has come to me. I am the scourge of the Lord.'

'Mad as a hatter,' murmured Tommy.

'She's been going on like that all the time,' whispered Tuppence.

Tommy picked up a book that was lying open, face downwards

on the table. He glanced at the title and slipped it into his pocket.

Suddenly the old woman rose and turned towards them menacingly.

'Go out from here. The time is at hand! I am the flail of the Lord. The wind bloweth where it listeth – so do I destroy. The ungodly shall perish. This is a house of evil – of evil, I tell you! Beware of the wrath of the Lord whose handmaiden I am.'

She advanced upon them fiercely. Tommy thought it best to humour her and withdrew. As he closed the door, he saw her pick up the Bible again.

'I wonder if she's always been like that,' he muttered.

He drew from his pocket the book he had picked up off the table.

'Look at that. Funny reading for an ignorant maid.'

Tuppence took the book.

'Materia Medica,' she murmured. She looked at the flyleaf, 'Edward Logan. It's an old book. Tommy, I wonder if we could see Miss Logan? Dr Burton said she was better.'

'Shall we ask Miss Chilcott?'

'No. Let's get hold of a housemaid, and send her in to ask.'

After a brief delay, they were informed that Miss Logan would see them. They were taken into a big bedroom facing over the lawn. In the bed was an old lady with white hair, her delicate face drawn by suffering.

'I have been very ill,' she said faintly. 'And I can't talk much, but Ellen tells me you are detectives. Lois went to consult you then? She spoke of doing so.'

'Yes, Miss Logan,' said Tommy. 'We don't want to tire you, but perhaps you can answer a few questions. The maid, Hannah, is she quite right in her head?'

Miss Logan looked at them with obvious surprise.

'Oh, yes. She is very religious – but there is nothing wrong with her.'

Tommy held out the book he had taken from the table.

'Is this yours, Miss Logan?'

'Yes. It was one of my father's books. He was a great doctor, one of the pioneers of serum therapeutics.'

The old lady's voice rang with pride.

'Quite so,' said Tommy. 'I thought I knew his name,' he added mendaciously. 'This book now, did you lend it to Hannah?'

'To Hannah?' Miss Logan raised herself in bed with indignation. 'No, indeed. She wouldn't understand the first word of it. It is a highly technical book.'

'Yes. I see that. Yet I found it in Hannah's room.'

'Disgraceful,' said Miss Logan. 'I will not have the servants touching my things.'

'Where ought it to be?'

'In the bookshelf in my sitting-room – or – stay, I lent it to Mary. The dear girl is very interested in herbs. She has made one or two experiments in my little kitchen. I have a little place of my own, you know, where I brew liqueurs and make preserves in the old-fashioned way. Dear Lucy, Lady Radclyffe, you know, used to swear by my tansy tea – a wonderful thing for a cold in the head. Poor Lucy, she was subject to colds. So is Dennis. Dear boy, his father was my first cousin.'

Tommy interrupted these reminiscences.

'This kitchen of yours? Does anyone else use it except you and Miss Chilcott?'

'Hannah clears up there. And she boils the kettle there for our early morning tea.'

'Thank you, Miss Logan,' said Tommy. 'There is nothing more I want to ask you at present. I hope we haven't tired you too much.'

He left the room and went down the stairs, frowning to himself.

'There is something here, my dear Mr Ricardo, that I do not understand.'

'I hate this house,' said Tuppence with a shiver. 'Let's go for a good long walk and try to think things out.'

Tommy complied and they set out. First they left the cocktail glass at the doctor's house, and then set off for a good tramp across the country, discussing the case as they did so.

'It makes it easier somehow if one plays the fool,' said Tommy. 'All this Hanaud business. I suppose some people would think I didn't care. But I do, most awfully. I feel that somehow or other we ought to have prevented this.'

'I think that's foolish of you,' said Tuppence. 'It is not as though we advised Lois Hargreaves not to go to Scotland Yard or anything like that. Nothing would have induced her to bring the police into the matter. If she hadn't come to us, she would have done nothing at all.'

'And the result would have been the same. Yes, you are right, Tuppence. It's morbid to reproach oneself over something one couldn't help. What I would like to do is to make good now.'

'And that's not going to be easy.'

'No, it isn't. There are so many possibilities, and yet all of them seem wild and improbable. Supposing Dennis Radclyffe put the poison in the sandwiches. He knew he would be out to tea. That seems fairly plain sailing.'

'Yes,' said Tuppence, 'that's all right so far. Then we can put against that the fact that he was poisoned himself – so that seems to rule him out. There is one person we mustn't forget – and that is Hannah.'

'Hannah?'

'People do all sorts of queer things when they have religious mania.'

'She is pretty far gone with it too,' said Tommy. 'You ought to drop a word to Dr Burton about it.'

'It must have come on very rapidly,' said Tuppence. 'That is if we go by what Miss Logan said.'

'I believe religious mania does,' said Tommy. 'I mean, you go on singing hymns in your bedroom with the door open for years, and then you go suddenly right over the line and become violent.'

'There is certainly more evidence against Hannah than against anybody else,' said Tuppence thoughtfully. 'And yet I have an idea –' She stopped.

'Yes?' said Tommy encouragingly.

'It is not really an idea. I suppose it is just a prejudice.'

'A prejudice against someone?'

Tuppence nodded.

'Tommy – did *you* like Mary Chilcott?'

Tommy considered.

'Yes, I think I did. She struck me as extremely capable and business-like – perhaps a shade too much so – but very reliable.'

'You didn't think it was odd that she didn't seem more upset?'

'Well, in a way that is a point in her favour. I mean, if she had done anything, she would make a point of being upset – lay it on rather thick.'

'I suppose so,' said Tuppence. 'And anyway there doesn't seem to be any motive in her case. One doesn't see what good this wholesale slaughter can do her.'

'I suppose none of the servants are concerned?'

'It doesn't seem likely. They seem a quiet, reliable lot. I wonder what Esther Quant, the parlourmaid, was like.'

'You mean, that if she was young and good-looking there was a chance that she was mixed up in it some way.'

'That is what I mean,' Tuppence sighed. 'It is all very discouraging.'

'Well, I suppose the police will get down to it all right,' said Tommy.

'Probably. I should like it to be us. By the way, did you notice a lot of small red dots on Miss Logan's arm?'

'I don't think I did. What about them?'

'They looked as though they were made by a hypodermic syringe,' said Tuppence.

'Probably Dr Burton gave her a hypodermic injection of some kind.'

'Oh, very likely. But he wouldn't give her about forty.'

'The cocaine habit,' suggested Tommy helpfully.

'I thought of that,' said Tuppence, 'but her eyes were all right. You could see at once if it was cocaine or morphia. Besides, she doesn't look that sort of old lady.'

'Most respectable and God-fearing,' agreed Tommy.

'It is all very difficult,' said Tuppence. 'We have talked and talked and we don't seem any nearer now than we were. Don't let's forget to call at the doctor's on our way home.'

The doctor's door was opened by a lanky boy of about fifteen.

'Mr Blunt?' he inquired. 'Yes, the doctor is out, but he left a note for you in case you should call.'

He handed them the note in question and Tommy tore it open.

Dear Mr Blunt,

> *There is reason to believe that the poison employed was Ricin, a vegetable toxalbumose of tremendous potency. Please keep this to yourself for the present.*

Tommy let the note drop, but picked it up quickly.

'Ricin,' he murmured. 'Know anything about it, Tuppence? You used to be rather well up in these things.'

'Ricin,' said Tuppence, thoughtfully. 'You get it out of castor oil, I believe.'

'I never did take kindly to castor oil,' said Tommy. 'I am more set against it than ever now.'

'The oil's all right. You get Ricin from the seeds of the castor oil plant. I believe I saw some castor oil plants in the garden this morning – big things with glossy leaves.'

'You mean that someone extracted the stuff on the premises. Could Hannah do such a thing?'

Tuppence shook her head.

'Doesn't seem likely. She wouldn't know enough.'

Suddenly Tommy gave an exclamation.

'That book. Have I got it in my pocket still? Yes.' He took it out, and turned over the leaves vehemently. 'I thought so. Here's the page it was open at this morning. Do you see, Tuppence? Ricin!'

Tuppence seized the book from him.

'Can you make head or tail of it? I can't.'

'It's clear enough to me,' said Tuppence. She walked along, reading busily, with one hand on Tommy's arm to steer herself.

Presently she shut the book with a bang. They were just approaching the house again.

'Tommy, will you leave this to me? Just for once, you see, I am the bull that has been more than twenty minutes in the arena.'

Tommy nodded.

'You shall be the Captain of the Ship, Tuppence,' he said gravely. 'We've got to get to the bottom of this.'

'First of all,' said Tuppence as they entered the house, 'I must ask Miss Logan one more question.'

She ran upstairs. Tommy followed her. She rapped sharply on the old lady's door and went in.

'Is that you, my dear?' said Miss Logan. 'You know you are much too young and pretty to be a detective. Have you found out anything?'

'Yes,' said Tuppence. 'I have.'

Miss Logan looked at her questioningly.

'I don't know about being pretty,' went on Tuppence, 'but being young, I happened to work in a hospital during the War. I know something about serum therapeutics. I happen to know that when Ricin is injected in small doses hypodermically, immunity is produced, antiricin is formed. That fact paved the way for the foundation of serum therapeutics. You knew that, Miss Logan. You injected Ricin for some time hypodermically into yourself. Then you let yourself be poisoned with the rest. You helped your father in his work, and you knew all about Ricin and how to obtain it and extract it from the seeds. You chose a day when Dennis Radclyffe was out for tea. It wouldn't do for him to be poisoned at the same time – he might die before Lois Hargreaves. So long as she died first, he inherited her money, and at his death it passes to you, his next-of-kin. You remember, you told us this morning that his father was your first cousin.'

The old lady stared at Tuppence with baleful eyes.

Suddenly a wild figure burst in from the adjoining room. It was Hannah. In her hand she held a lighted torch which she waved frantically.

'Truth has been spoken. That is the wicked one. I saw her reading the book and smiling to herself and I knew. I found the book and the page – but it said nothing to me. But the voice of the Lord spoke to me. She hated my mistress, her ladyship. She was always jealous and envious. She hated my own sweet Miss Lois. But the wicked shall perish, the fire of the Lord shall consume them.'

Waving her torch she sprang forward to the bed.

A cry arose from the old lady.

'Take her away – take her away. It's true – but take her away.'

Tuppence flung herself upon Hannah, but the woman managed to set fire to the curtains of the bed before Tuppence could get the torch from her and stamp on it. Tommy, however, had rushed in from the landing outside. He tore down the bed hangings and managed to stifle the flames with a rug. Then he rushed to Tuppence's assistance, and between them they subdued Hannah just as Dr Burton came hurrying in.

A very few words sufficed to put him *au courant* of the situation.

He hurried to the bedside, lifted Miss Logan's hand, then uttered a sharp exclamation.

'The shock of fire has been too much for her. She's dead. Perhaps it is as well under the circumstances.'

He paused, and then added, 'There was Ricin in the cocktail glass as well.'

'It's the best thing that could have happened,' said Tommy, when they had relinquished Hannah to the doctor's care, and were alone together. 'Tuppence, you were simply marvellous.'

'There wasn't much Hanaud about it,' said Tuppence.

'It was too serious for play-acting. I still can't bear to think of that girl. I won't think of her. But, as I said before, you were marvellous. The honours are with you. To use a familiar quotation, "It is a great advantage to be intelligent and not to look it."'

'Tommy,' said Tuppence, 'you're a beast.'

CHAPTER XIX

The Unbreakable Alibi

Tommy and Tuppence were busy sorting correspondence. Tuppence gave an exclamation and handed a letter across to Tommy.

'A new client,' she said importantly.

'Ha!' said Tommy. 'What do we deduce from this letter, Watson? Nothing much, except the somewhat obvious fact that Mr – er – Montgomery Jones is not one of the world's best spellers, thereby proving that he has been expensively educated.'

'Montgomery Jones?' said Tuppence. 'Now what do I know about a Montgomery Jones? Oh, yes, I have got it now. I think Janet St Vincent mentioned him. His mother was Lady Aileen Montgomery, very crusty and high church, with gold crosses and things, and she married a man called Jones who is immensely rich.'

'In fact the same old story,' said Tommy. 'Let me see, what time does this Mr M. J. wish to see us? Ah, eleven-thirty.'

At eleven-thirty precisely, a very tall young man with an amiable and ingenuous countenance entered the outer office and addressed himself to Albert, the office boy.

'Look here – I say. Can I see Mr – er – Blunt?'

'Have you an appointment, sir?' said Albert.

'I don't quite know. Yes, I suppose I have. What I mean is, I wrote a letter –'

'What name, sir?'

'Mr Montgomery Jones.'

'I will take your name in to Mr Blunt.'

He returned after a brief interval.

'Will you wait a few minutes please, sir. Mr Blunt is engaged on a very important conference at present.'

'Oh – er – yes – certainly,' said Mr Montgomery Jones.

Having, he hoped, impressed his client sufficiently Tommy rang the buzzer on his desk, and Mr Montgomery Jones was ushered into the inner office by Albert.

Tommy rose to greet him, and shaking him warmly by the hand motioned towards the vacant chair.

'Now, Mr Montgomery Jones,' he said briskly. 'What can we have the pleasure of doing for you?'

Mr Montgomery Jones looked uncertainly at the third occupant of the office.

'My confidential secretary, Miss Robinson,' said Tommy. 'You can speak quite freely before her. I take it that this is some family matter of a delicate kind?'

'Well – not exactly,' said Mr Montgomery Jones.

'You surprise me,' said Tommy. 'You are not in trouble of any kind yourself, I hope?'

'Oh, rather not,' said Mr Montgomery Jones.

'Well,' said Tommy, 'perhaps you will – er – state the facts plainly.'

That, however, seemed to be the one thing that Mr Montgomery Jones could not do.

'It's a dashed odd sort of thing I have got to ask you,' he said hesitatingly. 'I – er – I really don't know how to set about it.'

'We never touch divorce cases,' said Tommy.

'Oh Lord, no,' said Mr Montgomery Jones. 'I don't mean that. It is just, well – it's a deuced silly sort of a joke. That's all.'

'Someone has played a practical joke on you of a mysterious nature?' suggested Tommy.

But Mr Montgomery Jones once more shook his head.

'Well,' said Tommy, retiring gracefully from the position, 'take your own time and let us have it in your own words.'

There was a pause.

'You see,' said Mr Jones at last, 'it was at dinner. I sat next to a girl.'

'Yes?' said Tommy encouragingly.

'She was a – oh well, I really can't describe her, but she was simply one of the most sporting girls I ever met. She's an

Australian, over here with another girl, sharing a flat with her in Clarges Street. She's simply game for anything. I absolutely can't tell you the effect that girl had on me.'

'We can quite imagine it, Mr Jones,' said Tuppence.

She saw clearly that if Mr Montgomery Jones's troubles were ever to be extracted a sympathetic feminine touch was needed, as distinct from the businesslike methods of Mr Blunt.

'We can understand,' said Tuppence encouragingly.

'Well, the whole thing came as an absolute shock to me,' said Mr Montgomery Jones, 'that a girl could well – knock you over like that. There had been another girl – in fact two other girls. One was awfully jolly and all that, but I didn't much like her chin. She danced marvellously though, and I have known her all my life, which makes a fellow feel kind of safe, you know. And then there was one of the girls at the "Frivolity." Frightfully amusing, but of course there would be a lot of ructions with the mater over that, and anyway I didn't really want to marry either of them, but I was thinking about things, you know, and then – slap out of the blue – I sat next to this girl and –'

'The whole world was changed,' said Tuppence in a feeling voice.

Tommy moved impatiently in his chair. He was by now somewhat bored by the recital of Mr Montgomery Jones's love affairs.

'You put it awfully well,' said Mr Montgomery Jones. 'That is absolutely what it was like. Only, you know, I fancy she didn't think much of me. You mayn't think it, but I am not terribly clever.'

'Oh, you mustn't be too modest,' said Tuppence.

'Oh, I do realize that I am not much of a chap,' said Mr Jones with an engaging smile. 'Not for a perfectly marvellous girl like that. That is why I just feel I have got to put this thing through. It's my only chance. She's such a sporting girl that she would never go back on her word.'

'Well, I am sure we wish you luck and all that,' said Tuppence kindly. 'But I don't exactly see what you want us to do.'

'Oh Lord,' said Mr Montgomery Jones. 'Haven't I explained?'

'No,' said Tommy, 'you haven't.'

'Well, it was like this. We were talking about detective stories. Una – that's her name – is just as keen about them as I am. We got talking about one in particular. It all hinges on an alibi. Then we got talking about alibis and faking them. Then I said – no, she said – now which of us was it that said it?'

'Never mind which of you it was,' said Tuppence.

'I said it would be a jolly difficult thing to do. She disagreed – said it only wanted a bit of brain work. We got all hot and excited about it and in the end she said, "I will make you a sporting offer. What do you bet that I can produce an alibi that nobody can shake?"

' "Anything you like," I said, and we settled it then and there. She was frightfully cocksure about the whole thing. "It's an odds on chance for me," she said. "Don't be so sure of that," I said. "Supposing you lose and I ask you for anything I like?" She laughed and said she came of a gambling family and I could.'

'Well?' said Tuppence as Mr Jones came to a pause and looked at her appealingly.

'Well, don't you see? It is up to me. It is the only chance I have got of getting a girl like that to look at me. You have no idea how sporting she is. Last summer she was out in a boat and someone bet her she wouldn't jump overboard and swim ashore in her clothes, and she did it.'

'It is a very curious proposition,' said Tommy. 'I am not quite sure I yet understand it.'

'It is perfectly simple,' said Mr Montgomery Jones. 'You must be doing this sort of thing all the time. Investigating fake alibis and seeing where they fall down.'

'Oh – er – yes, of course,' said Tommy. 'We do a lot of that sort of work.'

'Someone has got to do it for me,' said Montgomery Jones. 'I shouldn't be any good at that sort of thing myself. You have only got to catch her out and everything is all right. I dare say it seems rather a futile business to you, but it means a lot to me and I am prepared to pay – er – all necessary whatnots, you know.'

'That will be all right,' said Tuppence. 'I am sure Mr Blunt will take this case on for you.'

'Certainly, certainly,' said Tommy. 'A most refreshing case, most refreshing indeed.'

Mr Montgomery Jones heaved a sigh of relief, pulled a mass of papers from his pocket and selected one of them. 'Here it is,' he said. 'She says, "I am sending you proof I was in two distinct places at one and the same time. According to one story I dined at the Bon Temps Restaurant in Soho by myself, went to the Duke's Theatre and had supper with a friend, Mr le Marchant, at the Savoy – *but* I was also staying at the Castle Hotel, Torquay, and only returned to London on the following morning. You have got to find out which of the two stories is the true one and how I managed the other."'

'There,' said Mr Montgomery Jones. 'Now you see what it is that I want you to do.'

'A most refreshing little problem,' said Tommy. 'Very naive.'

'Here is Una's photograph,' said Mr Montgomery Jones. 'You will want that.'

'What is the lady's full name?' inquired Tommy.

'Miss Una Drake. And her address is 180 Clarges Street.'

'Thank you,' said Tommy. 'Well, we will look into the matter for you, Mr Montgomery Jones. I hope we shall have good news for you very shortly.'

'I say, you know, I am no end grateful,' said Mr Jones, rising to his feet and shaking Tommy by the hand. 'It has taken an awful load off my mind.'

Having seen his client out, Tommy returned to the inner office. Tuppence was at the cupboard that contained the classic library.

'Inspector French,' said Tuppence.

'Eh?' said Tommy.

'Inspector French, of course,' said Tuppence. 'He always does alibis. I know the exact procedure. We have to go over everything and check it. At first it will seem all right and then when we examine it more closely we shall find the flaw.'

'There ought not to be much difficulty about that,' agreed

Tommy. 'I mean, knowing that one of them is a fake to start with makes the thing almost a certainty, I should say. That is what worries me.'

'I don't see anything to worry about in that.'

'I am worrying about the girl,' said Tommy. 'She will probably be let in to marry that young man whether she wants to or not.'

'Darling,' said Tuppence, 'don't be foolish. Women are never the wild gamblers they appear. Unless that girl was already perfectly prepared to marry that pleasant, but rather empty-headed young man, she would never have let herself in for a wager of this kind. But, Tommy, believe me, she will marry him with more enthusiasm and respect if he wins the wager than if she has to make it easy for him some other way.'

'You do think you know about everything,' said her husband.

'I do,' said Tuppence.

'And now to examine our data,' said Tommy, drawing the papers towards him. 'First the photograph – h'm – quite a nice looking girl – and quite a good photograph, I should say. Clear and easily recognizable.'

'We must get some other girls' photographs,' said Tuppence.

'Why?'

'They always do,' said Tuppence. 'You show four or five to waiters and they pick out the right one.'

'Do you think they do?' said Tommy – 'pick out the right one, I mean.'

'Well, they do in books,' said Tuppence.

'It is a pity that real life is so different from fiction,' said Tommy. 'Now then, what have we here? Yes, this is the London lot. Dined at the Bon Temps seven-thirty. Went to Duke's Theatre and saw *Delphiniums Blue*. Counterfoil of theatre ticket enclosed. Supper at the Savoy with Mr le Marchant. We can, I suppose, interview Mr le Marchant.'

'That tells us nothing at all,' said Tuppence, 'because if he is helping her to do it he naturally won't give the show away. We can wash out anything he says now.'

'Well, here is the Torquay end,' went on Tommy. 'Twelve o'clock from Paddington, had lunch in the Restaurant Car, receipted bill enclosed. Stayed at Castle Hotel for one night. Again receipted bill.'

'I think this is all rather weak,' said Tuppence. 'Anyone can buy a theatre ticket, you need never go near the theatre. The girl just went to Torquay and the London thing is a fake.'

'If so, it is rather a sitter for us,' said Tommy. 'Well, I suppose we might as well go and interview Mr le Marchant.'

Mr le Marchant proved to be a breezy youth who betrayed no great surprise on seeing them.

'Una has got some little game on, hasn't she?' he asked. 'You never know what that kid is up to.'

'I understand, Mr le Marchant,' said Tommy, 'that Miss Drake had supper with you at the Savoy last Tuesday evening.'

'That's right,' said Mr le Marchant, 'I know it was Tuesday because Una impressed it on me at the time and what's more she made me write it down in a little book.'

With some pride he showed an entry faintly pencilled. 'Having supper with Una. Savoy. Tuesday 19th.'

'Where had Miss Drake been earlier in the evening? Do you know?'

'She had been to some rotten show called *Pink Peonies* or something like that. Absolute slosh, so she told me.'

'You are quite sure Miss Drake was with you that evening?' Mr le Marchant stared at him.

'Why, of course. Haven't I been telling you.'

'Perhaps she asked you to tell us,' said Tuppence.

'Well, for a matter of fact she did say something that was rather dashed odd. She said – what was it now? "You think you are sitting here having supper with me, Jimmy, but really I am having supper two hundred miles away in Devonshire." Now that was a dashed odd thing to say, don't you think so? Sort of astral body stuff. The funny thing is that a pal of mine, Dicky Rice, thought he saw her there.'

'Who is this Mr Rice?'

'Oh, just a friend of mine. He had been down in Torquay staying with an aunt. Sort of old bean who is always going to die and never does. Dicky had been down doing the dutiful nephew. He said, "I saw that Australian girl one day – Una something or other. Wanted to go and talk to her, but my aunt carried me off to chat with an old pussy in a bath chair." I said: "When was this?" and he said, "Oh, Tuesday about tea time." I told him, of course, that he had made a mistake, but it was odd, wasn't it? With Una saying that about Devonshire that evening?'

'Very odd,' said Tommy. 'Tell me, Mr le Marchant, did anyone you know have supper near you at the Savoy?'

'Some people called Oglander were at the next table.'

'Do they know Miss Drake?'

'Oh yes, they know her. They are not frightful friends or anything of that kind.'

'Well, if there's nothing more you can tell us, Mr le Marchant, I think we will wish you good-morning.'

'Either that chap is an extraordinarily good liar,' said Tommy as they reached the street, 'or else he is speaking the truth.'

'Yes,' said Tuppence, 'I have changed my opinion. I have a sort of feeling now that Una Drake was at the Savoy for supper that night.'

'We will now go to the Bon Temps,' said Tommy. 'A little food for starving sleuths is clearly indicated. Let's just get a few girls' photographs first.'

This proved rather more difficult than was expected. Turning into a photographers and demanding a few assorted photographs, they were met with a cold rebuff.

'Why are all the things that are so easy and simple in books so difficult in real life,' wailed Tuppence. 'How horribly suspicious they looked. What do you think they thought we wanted to do with the photographs? We had better go and raid Jane's flat.'

Tuppence's friend Jane proved of an accommodating disposition and permitted Tuppence to rummage in a drawer and select four specimens of former friends of Jane's who had been shoved hastily in to be out of sight and mind.

Armed with this galaxy of feminine beauty they proceeded to the Bon Temps where fresh difficulties and much expense awaited them. Tommy had to get hold of each waiter in turn, tip him and then produce the assorted photographs. The result was unsatisfactory. At least three of the photographs were promising starters as having dined there last Tuesday. They then returned to the office where Tuppence immersed herself in an ABC.

'Paddington twelve o'clock. Torquay three thirty-five. That's the train and le Marchant's friend, Mr Sago or Tapioca or something saw her there about tea time.'

'We haven't checked his statement, remember,' said Tommy. 'If, as you said to begin with, le Marchant is a friend of Una Drake's he may have invented this story.'

'Oh, we'll hunt up Mr Rice,' said Tuppence. 'I have a kind of hunch that Mr le Marchant was speaking the truth. No, what I am trying to get at now is this. Una Drake leaves London by the twelve o'clock train, possibly takes a room at a hotel and unpacks. Then she takes a train back to town arriving in time to get to the Savoy. There is one at four-forty gets up to Paddington at nine-ten.'

'And then?' said Tommy.

'And then,' said Tuppence frowning, 'it is rather more difficult. There is a midnight train from Paddington down again, but she could hardly take that, that would be too early.'

'A fast car,' suggested Tommy.

'H'm,' said Tuppence. 'It is just on two hundred miles.'

'Australians, I have always been told, drive very recklessly.'

'Oh, I suppose it could be done,' said Tuppence. 'She would arrive there about seven.'

'Are you supposing her to have nipped into her bed at the Castle Hotel without being seen? Or arriving there explaining that she had been out all night and could she have her bill, please?'

'Tommy,' said Tuppence, 'we are idiots. She needn't have gone back to Torquay at all. She has only got to get a friend to go to the hotel there and collect her luggage and pay her bill. Then you get the receipted bill with the proper date on it.'

'I think on the whole we have worked out a very sound hypothesis,' said Tommy. 'The next thing to do is to catch the twelve o'clock train to Torquay tomorrow and verify our brilliant conclusions.'

Armed with a portfolio of photographs, Tommy and Tuppence duly established themselves in a first-class carriage the following morning, and booked seats for the second lunch.

'It probably won't be the same dining car attendants,' said Tommy. 'That would be too much luck to expect. I expect we shall have to travel up and down to Torquay for days before we strike the right ones.'

'This alibi business is very trying,' said Tuppence. 'In books it is all passed over in two or three paragraphs. Inspector Something then boarded the train to Torquay and questioned the dining car attendants and so ended the story.'

For once, however, the young couple's luck was in. In answer to their question the attendant who brought their bill for lunch proved to be the same one who had been on duty the preceding Tuesday. What Tommy called the ten-shilling touch then came into action and Tuppence produced the portfolio.

'I want to know,' said Tommy, 'if any of these ladies had lunch on this train on Tuesday last?'

In a gratifying manner worthy of the best detective fiction the man at once indicated the photograph of Una Drake.

'Yes, sir, I remember that lady, and I remember that it was Tuesday, because the lady herself drew attention to the fact, saying it was always the luckiest day in the week for her.'

'So far, so good,' said Tuppence as they returned to their compartment. 'And we will probably find that she booked at the hotel all right. It is going to be more difficult to prove that she travelled back to London, but perhaps one of the porters at the station may remember.'

Here, however, they drew a blank, and crossing to the up platform Tommy made inquiries of the ticket collector and of various porters. After the distribution of half-crowns as a preliminary to inquiring, two of the porters picked out one of the other photographs with a vague remembrance that someone like that travelled to town by the four-forty that afternoon, but there was no identification of Una Drake.

'But that doesn't prove anything,' said Tuppence as they left the station. 'She may have travelled by that train and no one noticed her.'

'She may have gone from the other station, from Torre.'

'That's quite likely,' said Tuppence, 'however, we can see to that after we have been to the hotel.'

The Castle Hotel was a big one overlooking the sea. After booking a room for the night and signing the register, Tommy observed pleasantly.

'I believe you had a friend of ours staying here last Tuesday. Miss Una Drake.'

The young lady in the bureau beamed at him.

'Oh, yes, I remember quite well. An Australian young lady, I believe.'

At a sign from Tommy, Tuppence produced the photograph.

'That is rather a charming photograph of her, isn't it?' said Tuppence.

'Oh, very nice, very nice indeed, quite stylish.'

'Did she stay here long?' inquired Tommy.

'Only the one night. She went away by the express the next morning back to London. It seemed a long way to come for one night, but of course I suppose Australian ladies don't think anything of travelling.'

'She is a very sporting girl,' said Tommy, 'always having adventures. It wasn't here, was it, that she went out to dine with some friends, went for a drive in their car afterwards, ran the car into a ditch and wasn't able to get home till morning?'

'Oh, no,' said the young lady. 'Miss Drake had dinner here in the hotel.'

'Really,' said Tommy, 'are you sure of that? I mean – how do you know?'

'Oh, I saw her.'

'I asked because I understood she was dining with some friends in Torquay,' explained Tommy.

'Oh, no, sir, she dined here.' The young lady laughed and blushed a little. 'I remember she had on a most sweetly pretty frock. One of those new flowered chiffons all over pansies.'

'Tuppence, this tears it,' said Tommy when they had been shown upstairs to their room.

'It does rather,' said Tuppence. 'Of course that woman may be mistaken. We will ask the waiter at dinner. There can't be very many people here just at this time of year.'

This time it was Tuppence who opened the attack.

'Can you tell me if a friend of mine was here last Tuesday?' she asked the waiter with an engaging smile. 'A Miss Drake, wearing a frock all over pansies, I believe.' She produced a photograph. 'This lady.'

The waiter broke into immediate smiles of recognition.

'Yes, yes, Miss Drake, I remember her very well. She told me she came from Australia.'

'She dined here?'

'Yes. It was last Tuesday. She asked me if there was anything to do afterwards in the town.'

'Yes?'

'I told her the theatre, the Pavilion, but in the end she decided not to go and she stayed here listening to our orchestra.'

'Oh, damn!' said Tommy, under his breath.

'You don't remember what time she had dinner, do you?' asked Tuppence.

'She came down a little late. It must have been about eight o'clock.'

'Damn, Blast, and Curse,' said Tuppence as she and Tommy left the dining-room. 'Tommy, this is all going wrong. It seemed so clear and lovely.'

'Well, I suppose we ought to have known it wouldn't all be plain sailing.'

'Is there any train she could have taken after that, I wonder?'

'Not one that would have landed her in London in time to go to the Savoy.'

'Well,' said Tuppence, 'as a last hope I am going to talk to the chambermaid. Una Drake had a room on the same floor as ours.'

The chambermaid was a voluble and informative woman. Yes, she remembered the young lady quite well. That was her picture right enough. A very nice young lady, very merry and talkative. Had told her a lot about Australia and the kangaroos.

The young lady rang the bell about half-past nine and asked for her bottle to be filled and put in her bed, and also to be called the next morning at half-past seven – with coffee instead of tea.

'You did call her and she was in her bed?' asked Tuppence.

'Why, yes, Ma'am, of course.'

'Oh, I only wondered if she was doing exercises or anything,' said Tuppence wildly. 'So many people do in the early morning.'

'Well, that seems cast-iron enough,' said Tommy when the chambermaid had departed. 'There is only one conclusion to be drawn from it. It is the London side of the thing that *must* be faked.'

'Mr le Marchant must be a more accomplished liar than we thought,' said Tuppence.

'We have a way of checking his statements,' said Tommy. 'He said there were people sitting at the next table whom Una knew slightly. What was their name – Oglander, that was it. We must hunt up these Oglanders, and we ought also to make inquiries at Miss Drake's flat in Clarges Street.'

The following morning they paid their bill and departed somewhat crestfallen.

Hunting out the Oglanders was fairly easy with the aid of the telephone book. Tuppence this time took the offensive and assumed the character of a representative of a new illustrated paper. She called on Mrs Oglander, asking for a few details of their 'smart' supper party at the Savoy on Tuesday evening. These details Mrs Oglander was only too willing to supply. Just as she was leaving Tuppence added carelessly, 'Let me see, wasn't Miss Drake sitting at the table next to you? Is it really true that she is engaged to the Duke of Perth? You know her, of course.'

'I know her slightly,' said Mrs Oglander. 'A very charming girl, I believe. Yes, she was sitting at the next table to ours with Mr le Marchant. My girls know her better than I do.'

Tuppence's next port of call was the flat in Clarges Street. Here she was greeted by Miss Marjory Leicester, the friend with whom Miss Drake shared a flat.

'Do tell me what all this is about?' asked Miss Leicester plaintively. 'Una has some deep game on and I don't know what it is. Of course she slept here on Tuesday night.'

'Did you see her when she came in?'

'No, I had gone to bed. She has got her own latch key, of course. She came in about one o'clock, I believe.'

'When did you see her?'

'Oh, the next morning about nine – or perhaps it was nearer ten.'

As Tuppence left the flat she almost collided with a tall gaunt female who was entering.

'Excuse me, Miss, I'm sure,' said the gaunt female.

'Do you work here?' asked Tuppence.

'Yes, Miss, I come daily.'

'What time do you get here in the morning?'

'Nine o'clock is my time, Miss.'

Tuppence slipped a hurried half-crown into the gaunt female's hand.

'Was Miss Drake here last Tuesday morning when you arrived?'

'Why, yes, Miss, indeed she was. Fast asleep in her bed and hardly woke up when I brought her in her tea.'

'Oh, thank you,' said Tuppence and went disconsolately down the stairs.

She had arranged to meet Tommy for lunch in a small restaurant in Soho and there they compared notes.

'I have seen that fellow Rice. It is quite true he did see Una Drake in the distance at Torquay.'

'Well,' said Tuppence, 'we have checked these alibis all right. Here, give me a bit of paper and a pencil, Tommy. Let us put it down neatly like all detectives do.'

1.30	Una Drake seen in Luncheon Car of train.
4 o'clock	Arrives at Castle Hotel.
5 o'clock	Seen by Mr Rice.
8 o'clock	Seen dining at hotel.
9.30	Asks for hot water bottle.
11.30	Seen at Savoy with Mr le Marchant.
7.30 a.m.	Called by chambermaid at Castle Hotel.
9 o'clock	Called by charwoman at flat at Clarges Street.

They looked at each other.

'Well, it looks to me as if Blunt's Brilliant Detectives are beat,' said Tommy.

'Oh, we mustn't give up,' said Tuppence. 'Somebody *must* be lying!'

'The queer thing is that it strikes me nobody was lying. They all seemed perfectly truthful and straightforward.'

'Yet there must be a flaw. We know there is, I think of all sorts of things like private aeroplanes, but that doesn't really get us any forwarder.'

'I am inclined to the theory of an astral body.'

'Well,' said Tuppence, 'the only thing to do is to sleep on it. Your sub-conscious works in your sleep.'

'H'm,' said Tommy. 'If your sub-conscious provides you with a perfectly good answer to this riddle by tomorrow morning, I take off my hat to it.'

They were very silent all that evening. Again and again Tuppence reverted to the paper of times. She wrote things on bits of paper. She murmured to herself, she sought perplexedly through Rail Guides. But in the end they both rose to go to bed with no faint glimmer of light on the problem.

'This is very disheartening,' said Tommy.

'One of the most miserable evenings I have ever spent,' said Tuppence.

'We ought to have gone to a Music Hall,' said Tommy. 'A few good jokes about mothers-in-law and twins and bottles of beer would have done us no end of good.'

'No, you will see this concentration will work in the end,' said

Tuppence. 'How busy our sub-conscious will have to be in the next eight hours!' And on this hopeful note they went to bed.

'Well,' said Tommy next morning. 'Has the sub-conscious worked?'

'I have got an idea,' said Tuppence.

'You have. What sort of an idea?'

'Well, rather a funny idea. Not at all like anything I have ever read in detective stories. As a matter of fact it is an idea that *you* put into my head.'

'Then it must be a good idea,' said Tommy firmly. 'Come on, Tuppence, out with it.'

'I shall have to send a cable to verify it,' said Tuppence. 'No, I am not going to tell you. It's a perfectly wild idea, but it's the only thing that fits the facts.'

'Well,' said Tommy, 'I must away to the office. A roomful of disappointed clients must not wait in vain. I leave this case in the hands of my promising subordinate.'

Tuppence nodded cheerfully.

She did not put in an appearance at the office all day. When Tommy returned that evening about half-past five it was to find a wildly exultant Tuppence awaiting him.

'I have done it, Tommy. I have solved the mystery of the alibi. We can charge up all these half-crowns and ten-shilling notes and demand a substantial fee of our own from Mr Montgomery Jones and he can go right off and collect his girl.'

'What is the solution?' cried Tommy.

'A perfectly simple one,' said Tuppence. '*Twins.*'

'What do you mean? – Twins?'

'Why, just that. Of course it is the only solution. I will say you put it into my head last night talking about mothers-in-law, twins, and bottles of beer. I cabled to Australia and got back the information I wanted. Una has a twin sister, Vera, who arrived in England last Monday. That is why she was able to make this bet so spontaneously. She thought it would be a frightful rag on poor Montgomery Jones. The sister went to Torquay and she stayed in London.'

'Do you think she'll be terribly despondent that she's lost?' asked Tommy.

'No,' said Tuppence, 'I don't. I gave you my views about that before. She will put all the kudos down to Montgomery Jones. I always think respect for your husband's abilities should be the foundation of married life.'

'I am glad to have inspired these sentiments in you, Tuppence.'

'It is not a really satisfactory solution,' said Tuppence. 'Not the ingenious sort of flaw that Inspector French would have detected.'

'Nonsense,' said Tommy. 'I think the way I showed these photographs to the waiter in the restaurant was exactly like Inspector French.'

'He didn't have to use nearly so many half-crowns and ten-shilling notes as we seem to have done,' said Tuppence.

'Never mind,' said Tommy. 'We can charge them all up with additions to Mr Montgomery Jones. He will be in such a state of idiotic bliss that he would probably pay the most enormous bill without jibbing at it.'

'So he should,' said Tuppence. 'Haven't Blunt's Brilliant Detectives been brilliantly successful? Oh, Tommy, I do think we are extraordinarily clever. It quite frightens me sometimes.'

'The next case we have shall be a Roger Sheringham case, and you, Tuppence, shall be Roger Sheringham.'

'I shall have to talk a lot,' said Tuppence.

'You do that naturally,' said Tommy. 'And now I suggest that we carry out my programme of last night and seek out a Music Hall where they have plenty of jokes about mothers-in-law, bottles of beer, *and Twins.*'

CHAPTER XX

The Clergyman's Daughter

'I wish,' said Tuppence, roaming moodily round the office, 'that we could befriend a clergyman's daughter.'

'Why?' asked Tommy.

'You may have forgotten the fact, but I was once a clergyman's daughter myself. I remember what it was like. Hence this altruistic urge – this spirit of thoughtful consideration for others – this –'

'You are getting ready to be Roger Sheringham, I see,' said Tommy. 'If you will allow me to make a criticism, you talk quite as much as he does, but not nearly so well.'

'On the contrary,' said Tuppence. 'There is a feminine subtlety about my conversation, a *je ne sais quoi* that no gross male could ever attain to. I have, moreover, powers unknown to my prototype – do I mean prototype? Words are such uncertain things, they so often sound well, but mean the opposite of what one thinks they do.'

'Go on,' said Tommy kindly.

'I was. I was only pausing to take breath. Touching these powers, it is my wish today to assist a clergyman's daughter. You will see, Tommy, the first person to enlist the aid of Blunt's Brilliant Detectives will be a clergyman's daughter.'

'I'll bet you it isn't,' said Tommy.

'Done,' said Tuppence. 'Hist! To your typewriters, Oh! Israel. One comes.'

Mr Blunt's office was humming with industry as Albert opened the door and announced:

'Miss Monica Deane.'

A slender, brown-haired girl, rather shabbily dressed, entered and stood hesitating. Tommy came forward.

'Good-morning, Miss Deane. Won't you sit down and tell us what we can do for you? By the way, let me introduce my confidential secretary, Miss Sheringham.'

'I am delighted to make your acquaintance, Miss Deane,' said Tuppence. 'Your father was in the Church, I think.'

'Yes, he was. But how *did* you know that?'

'Oh! we have our methods,' said Tuppence. 'You mustn't mind me rattling on. Mr Blunt likes to hear me talk. He always says it gives him ideas.'

The girl stared at her. She was a slender creature, not beautiful, but possessing a wistful prettiness. She had a quantity of soft mouse-coloured hair, and her eyes were dark blue and very lovely, though the dark shadows round them spoke of trouble and anxiety.

'Will you tell me your story, Miss Deane?' said Tommy.

The girl turned to him gratefully.

'It's such a long rambling story,' said the girl. 'My name is Monica Deane. My father was the rector of Little Hampsley in Suffolk. He died three years ago, and my mother and I were left very badly off. I went out as a governess, but my mother became a confirmed invalid, and I had to come home to look after her. We were desperately poor, but one day we received a lawyer's letter telling us that an aunt of my father's had died and had left everything to me. I had often heard of this aunt, who had quarrelled with my father many years ago, and I knew that she was very well off, so it really seemed that our troubles were at an end. But matters did not turn out quite as well as we had hoped. I inherited the house she had lived in, but after paying one or two small legacies, there was no money left. I suppose she must have lost it during the war, or perhaps she had been living on her capital. Still, we had the house, and almost at once we had a chance of selling it at quite an advantageous price. But, foolishly perhaps, I refused the offer. We were in tiny, but expensive lodgings, and I thought it would be much nicer to live in the Red House, where my mother could have comfortable rooms and take in paying guests to cover our expenses.

'I adhered to this plan, notwithstanding a further tempting offer from the gentleman who wanted to buy. We moved in, and I advertised for paying guests. For a time, all went well, we had several answers to our advertisement; my aunt's old servant remained on with us, and she and I between us did the work of the house. And then these unaccountable things began to happen.'

'What things?'

'The queerest things. The whole place seemed bewitched. Pictures fell down, crockery flew across the room and broke; one morning we came down to find all the furniture moved round. At first we thought someone was playing a practical joke, but we had to give up that explanation. Sometimes when we were all sitting down to dinner, a terrific crash would be heard overhead. We would go up and find no one there, but a piece of furniture thrown violently to the ground.'

'A *poltergeist*,' cried Tuppence, much interested.

'Yes, that's what Dr O'Neill said – though I don't know what it means.'

'It's a sort of evil spirit that plays tricks,' explained Tuppence, who in reality knew very little about the subject, and was not even sure that she had got the word *poltergeist* right.

'Well, at any rate, the effect was disastrous. Our visitors were frightened to death, and left as soon as possible. We got new ones, and they too left hurriedly. I was in despair, and, to crown all, our own tiny income ceased suddenly – the Company in which it was invested failed.'

'You poor dear,' said Tuppence sympathetically. 'What a time you have had. Did you want Mr Blunt to investigate this "haunting" business?'

'Not exactly. You see, three days ago, a gentleman called upon us. His name was Dr O'Neill. He told us that he was a member of the Society for Physical Research, and that he had heard about the curious manifestations that had taken place in our house and was much interested. So much so, that he was prepared to buy it from us, and conduct a series of experiments there.'

'Well?'

'Of course, at first, I was overcome with joy. It seemed the way out of all our difficulties. But –'

'Yes?'

'Perhaps you will think me fanciful. Perhaps I am. But – oh! I'm sure I haven't made a mistake. It was the same man!'

'What same man?'

'The same man who wanted to buy it before. Oh! I'm sure I'm right.'

'But why shouldn't it be?'

'You don't understand. The two men were quite different, different name and everything. The first man was quite young, a spruce, dark young man of thirty odd. Dr O'Neill is about fifty, he has a grey beard and wears glasses and stoops. But when he talked I saw a gold tooth one side of his mouth. It only shows when he laughs. The other man had a tooth in just the same position, and then I looked at his ears. I had noticed the other man's ears, because they were a peculiar shape with hardly any lobe. Dr O'Neill's were just the same. Both things couldn't be a coincidence, could they? I thought and thought and finally I wrote and said I would let him know in a week. I had noticed Mr Blunt's advertisement some time ago – as a matter of fact in an old paper that lined one of the kitchen drawers. I cut it out and came up to town.'

'You were quite right,' said Tuppence, nodding her head with vigour. 'This needs looking into.'

'A very interesting case, Miss Deane,' observed Tommy. 'We shall be pleased to look into this for you – eh, Miss Sheringham?'

'Rather,' said Tuppence, 'and we'll get to the bottom of it too.'

'I understand, Miss Deane,' went on Tommy, 'that the household consists of you and your mother and a servant. Can you give me any particulars about the servant?'

'Her name is Crockett. She was with my aunt about eight or ten years. She is an elderly woman, not very pleasant in manner, but a good servant. She is inclined to give herself airs because her sister married out of her station. Crockett has a nephew whom she is always telling us is "quite the gentleman".'

'H'm,' said Tommy, rather at a loss how to proceed.

Tuppence had been eyeing Monica keenly, now she spoke with sudden decision.

'I think the best plan would be for Miss Deane to come out and lunch with me. It's just one o'clock. I can get full details from her.'

'Certainly, Miss Sheringham,' said Tommy. 'An excellent plan.'

'Look here,' said Tuppence, when they were comfortably ensconced at a little table in a neighbouring restaurant, 'I want to know: Is there any special reason why you want to find out about all this?'

Monica blushed.

'Well, you see –'

'Out with it,' said Tuppence encouragingly.

'Well – there are two men who – who – want to marry me.'

'The usual story, I suppose? One rich, one poor, and the poor one is the one you like!'

'I don't know how you know all these things,' murmured the girl.

'That's a sort of law of Nature,' explained Tuppence. 'It happens to everybody. It happened to me.'

'You see, even if I sell the house, it won't bring us in enough to live on. Gerald is a dear, but he's desperately poor – though he's a very clever engineer; and if only he had a little capital, his firm would take him into partnership. The other, Mr Partridge, is a very good man, I am sure – and well off, and if I married him, it would be an end to all our troubles. But – but –'

'I know,' said Tuppence sympathetically. 'It isn't the same thing at all. You can go on telling yourself how good and worthy he is, and adding up his qualities as though they were an addition sum – and it all has a simply refrigerating effect.'

Monica nodded.

'Well,' said Tuppence, 'I think it would be as well if we went down to the neighbourhood and studied matters upon the spot. What is the address?'

'The Red House, Stourton-in-the-Marsh.'

Tuppence wrote down the address in her notebook.

'I didn't ask you,' Monica began – 'about terms –' she ended, blushing a little.

'Our payments are strictly by results,' said Tuppence gravely. 'If the secret of the Red House is a profitable one, as seems possible from the anxiety displayed to acquire the property, we should expect a small percentage, otherwise – nothing!'

'Thank you very much,' said the girl gratefully.

'And now,' said Tuppence, 'don't worry. Everything's going to be all right. Let's enjoy lunch and talk of interesting things.'

CHAPTER XXI

The Red House

'Well,' said Tommy, looking out of the window of the Crown and Anchor, 'here we are at Toad in the Hole – or whatever this blasted village is called.'

'Let us review the case,' said Tuppence.

'By all means,' said Tommy. 'To begin with, getting my say in first, *I* suspect the invalid mother!'

'Why?'

'My dear Tuppence, grant that this *poltergeist* business is all a put-up job, got up in order to persuade the girl to sell the house, someone must have thrown the things about. Now the girl said everyone was at dinner – but if the mother is a thoroughgoing invalid, she'd be upstairs in her room.'

'If she was an invalid she could hardly throw furniture about.'

'Ah! but she wouldn't be a real invalid. She'd be shamming.'

'Why?'

'There you have me,' confessed her husband. 'I was really going on the well-known principle of suspecting the most unlikely person.'

'You always make fun of everything,' said Tuppence severely. 'There must be *something* that makes these people so anxious to get hold of the house. And if you don't care about getting to the bottom of this matter, I do. I like that girl. She's a dear.'

Tommy nodded seriously enough.

'I quite agree. But I never can resist ragging you, Tuppence. Of course, there's something queer about the house, and whatever it is, it's something that's difficult to get at. Otherwise a mere burglary would do the trick. But to be willing to buy the house means either that you've got to take up floors or pull down walls, or else that there's a coal mine under the back garden.'

'I don't want it to be a coal mine. Buried treasure is much more romantic.'

'H'm,' said Tommy. 'In that case I think that I shall pay a visit to the local Bank Manager, explain that I am staying here over Christmas and probably buying the Red House, and discuss the question of opening an account.'

'But why – ?'

'Wait and see.'

Tommy returned at the end of half an hour. His eyes were twinkling.

'We advance, Tuppence. Our interview proceeded on the lines indicated. I then asked casually whether he had had much gold paid in, as is often the case nowadays in these small country banks – small farmers who hoarded it during the war, you understand. From that we proceeded quite naturally to the extraordinary vagaries of old ladies. I invented an aunt who on the outbreak of war drove to the Army and Navy Stores in a four-wheeler, and returned with sixteen hams. He immediately mentioned a client of his own, who had insisted on drawing out every penny of money she had – in gold as far as possible, and who also insisted on having her securities, bearer bonds and such things, given into her own custody. I exclaimed on such an act of folly, and he mentioned casually that she was the former owner of the Red House. You see, Tuppence? She drew out all this money, and she hid it somewhere. You remember that Monica Deane mentioned that they were astonished at the small amount of her estate? Yes, she hid it in the Red House, and someone knows about it. I can make a pretty good guess who that someone is too.'

'Who?'

'What about the faithful Crockett? She would know all about her mistress's peculiarities.'

'And that gold-toothed Dr O'Neill?'

'The gentlemanly nephew, of course! That's it. But whereabouts did she hide it. You know more about old ladies than I do, Tuppence. Where do they hide things?'

'Wrapped up in stockings and petticoats, under mattresses.'

Tommy nodded.

'I expect you're right. All the same, she can't have done that because it would have been found when her things were turned over. It worries me – you see, an old lady like that can't have taken up floors or dug holes in the garden. All the same it's there in the Red House somewhere. Crockett hasn't found it, but she knows it's there, and once they get the house to themselves, she and her precious nephew, they can turn it upside down until they find what they're after. We've got to get ahead of them. Come on, Tuppence. We'll go to the Red House.'

Monica Deane received them. To her mother and Crockett they were represented as would-be purchasers of the Red House, which would account for their being taken all over the house and grounds. Tommy did not tell Monica of the conclusions he had come to, but he asked her various searching questions. Of the garments and personal belongings of the dead woman, some had been given to Crockett and the others sent to various poor families. Everything had been gone through and turned out.

'Did your aunt leave any papers?'

'The desk was full, and there were some in a drawer in her bedroom, but there was nothing of importance amongst them.'

'Have they been thrown away?'

'No, my mother is always very loath to throw away old papers. There were some old-fashioned recipes among them which she intends to go through one day.'

'Good,' said Tommy approvingly. Then, indicating an old man who was at work upon one of the flower beds in the garden, he asked: 'Was that old man the gardener here in your aunt's time?'

'Yes, he used to come three days a week. He lives in the village. Poor old fellow, he is past doing any really useful work. We have him just once a week to keep things tidied up. We can't afford more.'

Tommy winked at Tuppence to indicate that she was to keep

Monica with her, and he himself stepped across to where the
gardener was working. He spoke a few pleasant words to the
old man, asked him if he had been there in the old lady's time,
and then said casually.

'You buried a box for her once, didn't you?'

'No, sir, I never buried naught for her. What should she want
to bury a box for?'

Tommy shook his head. He strolled back to the house frowning. It was to be hoped that a study of the old lady's papers
would yield some clue – otherwise the problem was a hard one
to solve. The house itself was old fashioned, but not old enough
to contain a secret room or passage.

Before leaving, Monica brought them down a big cardboard
box tied with string.

'I've collected all the papers,' she whispered. 'And they're in
here. I thought you could take it away with you, and then you'll
have plenty of time to go over them – but I'm sure you won't
find anything to throw light on the mysterious happenings in
this house –'

Her words were interrupted by a terrific crash overhead.
Tommy ran quickly up the stairs. A jug and a basin in one of
the front rooms was lying on the ground broken to pieces.
There was no one in the room.

'The ghost up to its tricks again,' he murmured with a grin.

He went downstairs again thoughtfully.

'I wonder, Miss Deane, if I might speak to the maid, Crockett,
for a minute.'

'Certainly. I will ask her to come to you.'

Monica went off to the kitchen. She returned with the elderly
maid who had opened the door to them earlier.

'We are thinking of buying this house,' said Tommy pleasantly, 'and my wife was wondering whether, in that case, you
would care to remain on with us?'

Crockett's respectable face displayed no emotion of any kind.

'Thank you, sir,' she said. 'I should like to think it over if I
may.'

Tommy turned to Monica.

'I am delighted with the house, Miss Deane. I understand that there is another buyer in the market. I know what he has offered for the house, and I will willingly give a hundred more. And mind you, that is a good price I am offering.'

Monica murmured something noncommittal, and the Beresfords took their leave.

'I was right,' said Tommy, as they went down the drive, 'Crockett's in it. Did you notice that she was out of breath? That was from running down the backstairs after smashing the jug and basin. Sometimes, very likely, she has admitted her nephew secretly, and he has done a little poltergeisting, or whatever you call it, whilst she has been innocently with the family. You'll see Dr O'Neill will make a further offer before the day is out.'

True enough, after dinner, a note was brought. It was from Monica.

'I have just heard from Dr O'Neill. He raises his previous offer by £150.'

'The nephew must be a man of means,' said Tommy thoughtfully. 'And I tell you what, Tuppence, the prize he's after must be well worth while.'

'Oh! Oh! Oh! if only we could find it!'

'Well, let's get on with the spade work.'

They were sorting through the big box of papers, a wearisome affair, as they were all jumbled up pell mell without any kind of order or method. Every few minutes they compared notes.

'What's the latest, Tuppence?'

'Two old receipted bills, three unimportant letters, a recipe for preserving new potatoes and one for making lemon cheese-cake. What's yours?'

'One bill, a poem on Spring, two newspaper cuttings: "Why Women buy Pearls – a sound investment", and "Man with Four Wives – Extraordinary Story", and a recipe for Jugged Hare.'

'It's heart-breaking,' said Tuppence, and they fell to once more. At last the box was empty. They looked at each other.

'I put this aside,' said Tommy, picking up a half sheet of

notepaper, 'because it struck me as peculiar. But I don't suppose it's got anything to do with what we're looking for.'

'Let's see it. Oh! it's one of these funny things, what do they call them? Anagrams, charades or something.' She read it:

> 'My *first* you put on glowing coal
> And into it you put my *whole*;
> My *second* really is the first;
> My third mislikes the winter blast.'

'H'm,' said Tommy critically. 'I don't think much of the poet's rhymes.'

'I don't see what you find peculiar about it, though,' said Tuppence. 'Everybody used to have a collection of these sort of things about fifty years ago. You saved them up for winter evenings round the fire.'

'I wasn't referring to the verse. It's the words written below it that strike me as peculiar.'

'St Luke, xi, 9,' she read. 'It's a text.'

'Yes. Doesn't that strike you as odd? Would an old lady of a religious persuasion write a text just under a charade?'

'It is rather odd,' agreed Tuppence thoughtfully.

'I presume that you, being a clergyman's daughter, have got your Bible with you?'

'As a matter of fact, I have. Aha! you didn't expect that. Wait a sec.'

Tuppence ran to her suitcase, extracted a small red volume and returned to the table. She turned the leaves rapidly. 'Here we are. Luke, chapter xi, verse 9. Oh! Tommy, look.'

Tommy bent over and looked where Tuppence's small finger pointed to a portion of the verse in question.

'*Seek and ye shall find.*'

'That's it,' cried Tuppence. 'We've got it! Solve the cryptogram and the treasure is ours – or rather Monica's.'

'Well, let's get to work on the cryptogram, as you call it. "My *first* you put on glowing coal." What does that mean, I wonder? Then – "My *second* really is the first." That's pure gibberish.'

'It's quite simple, really,' said Tuppence kindly. 'It's just a sort of knack. Let *me* have it.'

Tommy surrendered it willingly. Tuppence ensconced herself in an armchair, and began muttering to herself with bent brows.

'It's quite simple, really,' murmured Tommy when half an hour had elapsed.

'Don't crow! We're the wrong generation for this. I've a good mind to go back to town tomorrow and call on some old pussy who would probably read it as easy as winking. It's a knack, that's all.'

'Well, let's have one more try.'

'There aren't many things you can put on glowing coal,' said Tuppence thoughtfully. 'There's water, to put it out, or wood, or a kettle.'

'It must be one syllable, I suppose? What about *wood*, then?'

'You couldn't put anything *into* wood, though.'

'There's no one syllable word instead of *water*, but there must be one syllable things you can put on a fire in the kettle line.'

'Saucepans,' mused Tuppence. 'Frying pans. How about *pan*? or *pot*? What's a word beginning pan or pot that is something you cook?'

'Pottery,' suggested Tommy. 'You bake that in the fire. Wouldn't that be near enough?'

'The rest of it doesn't fit. Pancakes? No. Oh! bother.'

They were interrupted by the little serving-maid, who told them that dinner would be ready in a few minutes.

'Only Mrs Lumley, she wanted to know if you like your potatoes fried, or boiled in their jackets? She's got some of each.'

'Boiled in their jackets,' said Tuppence promptly. 'I love potatoes –' She stopped dead with her mouth open.

'What's the matter, Tuppence? Have you seen a ghost?'

'Tommy,' cried Tuppence. 'Don't you see? That's it! The word, I mean. *Potatoes*! "My first you put on glowing coal" – that's pot. "And into it you put my *whole*." "My *second* really is the first." That's A, the first letter of the alphabet. "My *third* mislikes the wintry blast" – cold *toes* of course!'

'You're right, Tuppence. Very clever of you. But I'm afraid we've wasted an awful lot of time over nothing. Potatoes don't fit in at all with missing treasure. Half a sec, though. What did you read out just now, when we were going through the box? Something about a recipe for New Potatoes. I wonder if there's anything in that.'

He rummaged hastily through the pile of recipes.

'Here it is. "TO KEEP NEW POTATOES. Put the new potatoes into tins and bury them in the garden. Even in the middle of winter, they will taste as though freshly dug."

'We've got it,' screamed Tuppence. 'That's it. The treasure is in the garden, buried in a tin.'

'But I asked the gardener. He said he'd never buried anything.'

'Yes, I know, but that's because people never really answer what you say, they answer what they think you mean. He knew he'd never buried anything out of the common. We'll go tomorrow and ask him where he buried the potatoes.'

The following morning was Christmas Eve. By dint of inquiry they found the old gardener's cottage. Tuppence broached the subject after some minutes' conversation.

'I wish one could have new potatoes at Christmas time,' she remarked. 'Wouldn't they be good with turkey? Do people round here ever bury them in tins? I've heard that keeps them fresh.'

'Ay, that they do,' declared the old man. 'Old Miss Deane, up to the Red House, she allus had three tins buried every summer, and as often as not forgot to have 'em dug up again!'

'In the bed by the house, as a rule, didn't she?'

'No, over against the wall by the fir tree.'

Having got the information they wanted, they soon took their leave of the old man, presenting him with five shillings as a Christmas box.

'And now for Monica,' said Tommy.

'Tommy! You have no sense of the dramatic. Leave it to me. I've got a beautiful plan. Do you think you could manage to beg, borrow or steal a spade?'

Somehow or other, a spade was duly produced, and that night, late, two figures might have been seen stealing into the grounds of the Red House. The place indicated by the gardener was easily found, and Tommy set to work. Presently his spade rang on metal, and a few seconds later he had unearthed a big biscuit tin. It was sealed round with adhesive plaster and firmly fastened down, but Tuppence, by the aid of Tommy's knife, soon managed to open it. Then she gave a groan. The tin was full of potatoes. She poured them out, so that the tin was completely empty, but there were no other contents.

'Go on digging, Tommy.'

It was some time before a second tin rewarded their search. As before, Tuppence unsealed it.

'Well?' demanded Tommy anxiously.

'Potatoes again!'

'Damn!' said Tommy, and set to once more.

'The third time is lucky,' said Tuppence consolingly.

'I believe the whole thing's a mare's nest,' said Tommy gloomily, but he continued to dig.

At last a third tin was brought to light.

'Potatoes aga –' began Tuppence, then stopped. 'Oh, Tommy, we've got it. It's only potatoes on top. Look!'

She held up a big old-fashioned velvet bag.

'Cut along home,' cried Tommy. 'It's icy cold. Take the bag with you. I must shovel back the earth. And may a thousand curses light upon your head, Tuppence, if you open that bag before I come!'

'I'll play fair. Ouch! I'm frozen.' She beat a speedy retreat.

On arrival at the inn she had not long to wait. Tommy was hard upon her heels, perspiring freely after his digging and the final brisk run.

'Now then,' said Tommy, 'the private inquiry agents make good! Open the loot, Mrs Beresford.'

Inside the bag was a package done up in oil silk and a heavy chamois leather bag. They opened the latter first. It was full of gold sovereigns. Tommy counted them.

'Two hundred pounds. That was all they would let her have, I suppose. Cut open the package.'

Tuppence did so. It was full of closely folded banknotes. Tommy and Tuppence counted them carefully. They amounted to exactly twenty thousand pounds.

'Whew!' said Tommy. 'Isn't it lucky for Monica that we're both rich and honest? What's that done up in tissue paper?'

Tuppence unrolled the little parcel and drew out a magnificent string of pearls, exquisitely matched.

'I don't know much about these things,' said Tommy slowly. 'But I'm pretty sure that those pearls are worth another five thousand pounds at least. Look at the size of them. Now I see why the old lady kept that cutting about pearls being a good investment. She must have realized all her securities and turned them into notes and jewels.'

'Oh, Tommy, isn't it wonderful? Darling Monica. Now she can marry her nice young man and live happily ever afterwards, like me.'

'That's rather sweet of you, Tuppence. So you *are* happy with me?'

'As a matter of fact,' said Tuppence, 'I am. But I didn't mean to say so. It slipped out. What with being excited, and Christmas Eve, and one thing and another – '

'If you really love me,' said Tommy, 'will you answer me one question?'

'I hate these catches,' said Tuppence, 'but – well – all right.'

'Then how did you know that Monica was a clergyman's daughter?'

'Oh, that was just cheating,' said Tuppence happily. 'I opened her letter making an appointment, and a Mr Deane was father's curate once, and he had a little girl called Monica, about four or five years younger than me. So I put two and two together.'

'You are a shameless creature,' said Tommy. 'Hullo, there's twelve o'clock striking. Happy Christmas, Tuppence.'

'Happy Christmas, Tommy. It'll be a Happy Christmas for Monica too – and all owing to US. I am glad. Poor thing, she has been so miserable. Do you know, Tommy, I feel all queer and choky about the throat when I think of it.'

'Darling Tuppence,' said Tommy.

'Darling Tommy,' said Tuppence. 'How awfully sentimental we are getting.'

'Christmas comes but once a year,' said Tommy sententiously. 'That's what our great-grandmothers said, and I expect there's a lot of truth in it still.'

CHAPTER XXII

The Ambassador's Boots

'My dear fellow, my dear fellow,' said Tuppence, and waved a heavily buttered muffin.

Tommy looked at her for a minute or two, then a broad grin spread over his face and he murmured:

'We do have to be so very careful.'

'That's right,' said Tuppence, delighted. 'You guessed. I am the famous Dr Fortune and you are Superintendent Bell.'

'Why are you being Reginald Fortune?'

'Well, really because I feel like a lot of hot butter.'

'That is the pleasant side of it,' said Tommy. 'But there is another. You will have to examine horribly smashed faces and very extra dead bodies a good deal.'

In answer Tuppence threw across a letter. Tommy's eyebrows rose in astonishment.

'Randolph Wilmott, the American Ambassador. I wonder what he wants.'

'We shall know tomorrow at eleven o'clock.'

Punctually to the time named, Mr Randolph Wilmott, United States Ambassador to the Court of St James, was ushered into Mr Blunt's office. He cleared his throat and commenced speaking in a deliberate and characteristic manner.

'I have come to you, Mr Blunt – By the way, it is Mr Blunt himself to whom I am speaking, is it not?'

'Certainly,' said Tommy. 'I am Theodore Blunt, the head of the firm.'

'I always prefer to deal with heads of departments,' said Mr Wilmott. 'It is more satisfactory in every way. As I was about to say, Mr Blunt, this business gets my goat. There's nothing in it to trouble Scotland Yard about – I'm not a penny the worse in any way, and it's probably all due to a simple mistake. But all the same, I don't see just how that mistake arose. There's nothing criminal in it, I dare say, but I'd like just to get the thing straightened out. It makes me mad not to see the why and wherefore of a thing.'

'Absolutely,' said Tommy.

Mr Wilmott went on. He was slow and given to much detail. At last Tommy managed to get a word in.

'Quite so,' he said, 'the position is this. You arrived by the liner *Nomadic* a week ago. In some way your kitbag and the kitbag of another gentleman, Mr Ralph Westerham, whose initials are the same as yours, got mixed up. You took Mr Westerham's kitbag, and he took yours. Mr Westerham discovered the mistake immediately, sent round your kitbag to the Embassy, and took away his own. Am I right so far?'

'That is precisely what occurred. The two bags must have been practically identical, and with the initials R. W. being the same in both cases, it is not difficult to understand that an error might have been made. I myself was not aware of what had happened until my valet informed me of the mistake, and that Mr Westerham – he is a Senator, and a man for whom I have a great admiration – had sent round for his bag and returned mine.'

'Then I don't see –'

'But you will see. That's only the beginning of the story. Yesterday, as it chanced, I ran up against Senator Westerham, and I happened to mention the matter to him jestingly. To my great surprise, he did not seem to know what I was talking about, and when I explained, he denied the story absolutely. He had not taken my bag off the ship in mistake for his own – in fact, he had not travelled with such an article amongst his luggage.'

'What an extraordinary thing!'

'Mr Blunt, it *is* an extraordinary thing. There seems no rhyme or reason in it. Why, if any one wanted to steal my kitbag, he could do so easily enough without resorting to all this round-about business. And anyway, it was *not* stolen, but returned to me. On the other hand, if it were taken by mistake, why use Senator Westerham's name? It's a crazy business – but just for curiosity I mean to get to the bottom of it. I hope the case is not too trivial for you to undertake?'

'Not at all. It is a very intriguing little problem, capable as you say, of many simple explanations, but nevertheless baffling on the face of it. The first thing, of course, is the *reason* of the substitution, if substitution it was. You say nothing was missing from your bag when it came back into your possession?'

'My man says not. He would know.'

'What was in it, if I may ask?'

'Mostly boots.'

'Boots,' said Tommy, discouraged.

'Yes,' said Mr Wilmott. 'Boots. Odd, isn't it?'

'You'll forgive my asking you,' said Tommy, 'but you didn't carry any secret papers, or anything of that sort sewn in the lining of a boot or screwed into a false heel?'

The Ambassador seemed amused by the question.

'Secret diplomacy hasn't got to that pitch, I hope.'

'Only in fiction,' said Tommy with an answering smile, and a slightly apologetic manner. 'But you see, we've got to account for the thing somehow. Who came for the bag – the other bag, I mean?'

'Supposed to be one of Westerham's servants. Quite a quiet, ordinary man, so I understand. My valet saw nothing wrong with him.'

'Had it been unpacked, do you know?'

'That I can't say. I presume not. But perhaps you'd like to ask the valet a few questions? He can tell you more than I can about the business.'

'I think that would be the best plan, Mr Wilmott.'

The Ambassador scribbled a few words on a card and handed it to Tommy.

'I opine that you would prefer to go round to the Embassy and make your inquiries there? If not, I will have the man, his name is Richards, by the way – sent round here.'

'No, thank you, Mr Wilmott. I should prefer to go to the Embassy.'

The Ambassador rose, glancing at his watch.

'Dear me, I shall be late for an appointment. Well, goodbye, Mr Blunt. I leave the matter in your hands.'

He hurried away. Tommy looked at Tuppence, who had been scribbling demurely on her pad in the character of the efficient Miss Robinson.

'What about it, old thing?' he asked. 'Do you see, as the old bird put it, any rhyme or reason in the proceedings?'

'None whatever,' replied Tuppence cheerily.

'Well, that's a start, anyway! It shows that there is really something very deep at the back of it.'

'You think so?'

'It's a generally accepted hypothesis. Remember Sherlock Holmes and the depth the butter had sunk into the parsley – I mean the other way round. I've always had a devouring wish to know all about that case. Perhaps Watson will disinter it from his notebook one of these days. Then I shall die happy. But we must get busy.'

'Quite so,' said Tuppence. 'Not a quick man, the esteemed Wilmott, but sure.'

'She knows men,' said Tommy. 'Or do I say *he* knows men. It is so confusing when you assume the character of a male detective.'

'Oh, my dear fellow, my dear fellow!'

'A little more action, Tuppence, and a little less repetition.'

'A classic phrase cannot be repeated too often,' said Tuppence with dignity.

'Have a muffin,' said Tommy kindly.

'Not at eleven o'clock in the morning, thank you. Silly case, this. Boots – you know. Why boots?'

'Well,' said Tommy. 'Why not?'

'It doesn't fit. Boots.' She shook her head. 'All wrong. Who wants other people's boots? The whole thing's mad.'

'Possibly they got hold of the wrong bag,' suggested Tommy.

'That's possible. But if they were after papers, a despatch case would be more likely. Papers are the only things one thinks of in connection with ambassadors.'

'Boots suggest footprints,' said Tommy thoughtfully. 'Do you think they wanted to lay a trail of Wilmott's footsteps somewhere?'

Tuppence considered the suggestion, abandoning her role, then shook her head.

'It seems wildly impossible,' she said. 'No, I believe we shall have to resign ourselves to the fact that the boots have nothing to do with it.'

'Well,' said Tommy with a sigh, 'the next step is to interview friend Richards. He may be able to throw some light on the mystery.'

On production of the Ambassador's card, Tommy was admitted to the Embassy, and presently a pale young man, with a respectful manner and a subdued voice, presented himself to undergo examination.

'I am Richards, sir. Mr Wilmott's valet. I understood you wished to see me?'

'Yes, Richards. Mr Wilmott called on me this morning, and suggested that I should come round and ask you a few questions. It is this matter of the kitbag.'

'Mr Wilmott was rather upset over the affair, I know, sir. I can hardly see why, since no harm was done. I certainly understood from the man who called for the other bag that it belonged to Senator Westerham, but of course, I may have been mistaken.'

'What kind of man was he?'

'Middle-aged. Grey hair. Very good class, I should say – most respectable. I understood he was Senator Westerham's valet. He left Mr Wilmott's bag and took away the other.'

'Had it been unpacked at all?'

'Which one, sir?'

'Well, I meant the one you brought from the boat. But I should like to know about the other as well – Mr Wilmott's own. Had that been unpacked, do you fancy?'

'I should say not, sir. It was just as I strapped it up on the boat. I should say the gentleman – whoever he was – just opened it – realized it wasn't his, and shut it up again.'

'Nothing missing? No small article?'

'I don't think so, sir. In fact, I'm quite sure.'

'And now the other one. Had you started to unpack that?'

'As a matter of fact, sir, I was just opening it at the very moment Senator Westerham's man arrived. I'd just undone the straps.'

'Did you open it at all?'

'We just unfastened it together, sir, to be sure no mistake had been made this time. The man said it was all right, and he strapped it up again and took it away.'

'What was inside? Boots also?'

'No, sir, mostly toilet things, I fancy. I know I saw a tin of bath salts.'

Tommy abandoned that line of research.

'You never saw anyone tampering with anything in your master's cabin on board ship, I suppose?'

'Oh, no, sir.'

'Never anything suspicious of any kind?'

'And what do I mean by that, I wonder,' he thought to himself with a trace of amusement. 'Anything suspicious – just words!'

But the man in front of him hesitated.

'Now that I remember it –'

'Yes,' said Tommy eagerly. 'What?'

'I don't think it could have anything to do with it. But there was a young lady.'

'Yes? A young lady, you say, what was she doing?'

'She was taken faint, sir. A very pleasant young lady. Miss Eileen O'Hara, her name was. A dainty looking lady, not tall, with black hair. Just a little foreign looking.'

'Yes?' said Tommy, with even greater eagerness.

'As I was saying, she was taken queer. Just outside Mr Wilmott's cabin. She asked me to fetch the doctor. I helped her to the sofa, and then went off for the doctor. I was some time finding him, and when I found him and brought him back, the young lady was nearly all right again.'

'Oh!' said Tommy.

'You don't think, sir –'

'It's difficult to know what to think,' said Tommy noncommittally. 'Was this Miss O'Hara travelling alone?'

'Yes, I think so, sir.'

'You haven't seen her since you landed?'

'No, sir.'

'Well,' said Tommy, after a minute or two spent in reflection. 'I think that's all. Thank you, Richards.'

'Thank *you*, sir.'

Back at the office of the Detective Agency, Tommy retailed his conversation with Richards to Tuppence, who listened attentively.

'What do you think of it, Tuppence?'

'Oh, my dear fellow, we doctors are always sceptical of a sudden faintness! So very convenient. And Eileen as well as O'Hara. Almost too impossibly Irish, don't you think?'

'It's something to go upon at last. Do you know what I am going to do, Tuppence? Advertise for the lady.'

'What?'

'Yes, any information respecting Miss Eileen O'Hara known to have travelled such and such a ship and such and such a date. Either she'll answer it herself if she's genuine, or someone may come forward to give us information about her. So far, it's the only hope of a clue.'

'You'll also put her on her guard, remember.'

'Well,' said Tommy, 'one's got to risk something.'

'I still can't see any sense in the thing,' said Tuppence, frowning. 'If a gang of crooks get hold of the Ambassador's bag for an hour or two, and then send it back, what possible good can it do them. Unless there are papers in it they want to copy, and Mr Wilmott swears there was nothing of the kind.'

Tommy stared at her thoughtfully.

'You put these things rather well, Tuppence,' he said at last. 'You've given me an idea.'

* * *

It was two days later. Tuppence was out to lunch. Tommy, alone in the austere office of Mr Theodore Blunt, was improving his mind by reading the latest sensational thriller.

The door of the office opened and Albert appeared.

'A young lady to see you, sir. Miss Cicely March. She says she has called in answer to an advertisement.'

'Show her in at once,' cried Tommy, thrusting his novel into a convenient drawer.

In another minute, Albert had ushered in the young lady. Tommy had just time to see that she was fair haired and extremely pretty, when the amazing occurrence happened.

The door through which Albert had just passed out was rudely burst open. In the doorway stood a picturesque figure – a big dark man, Spanish in appearance, with a flaming red tie. His features were distorted with rage, and in his hand was a gleaming pistol.

'So this is the office of Mr Busybody Blunt,' he said in perfect English. His voice was low and venomous. 'Hands up at once – or I shoot.'

It sounded no idle threat. Tommy's hands went up obediently. The girl, crouched against the wall, gave a gasp of terror.

'This young lady will come with me,' said the man. 'Yes, you will, my dear. You have never seen me before, but that doesn't matter. I can't have my plans ruined by a silly little chit like you. I seem to remember that you were one of the passengers on the *Nomadic.* You must have been peering into things that didn't concern you – but I've no intention of letting you blab any secrets to Mr Blunt here. A very clever gentleman, Mr Blunt, with his fancy advertisements. But as it happens, I keep an eye on the advertisement columns. That's how I got wise to his little game.'

'You interest me exceedingly,' said Tommy. 'Won't you go on?'

'Cheek won't help you, Mr Blunt. From now on, you're a marked man. Give up this investigation, and we'll leave you alone. Otherwise – God help you! Death comes swiftly to those who thwart our plans.'

Tommy did not reply. He was staring over the intruder's shoulder as though he saw a ghost.

As a matter of fact he was seeing something that caused him far more apprehension than any ghost could have done. Up to now, he had not given a thought to Albert as a factor in the game. He had taken for granted that Albert had already been dealt with by the mysterious stranger. If he had thought of him at all, it was as one lying stunned on the carpet in the outer office.

He now saw that Albert had miraculously escaped the stranger's attention. But instead of rushing out to fetch a police-man in good sound British fashion, Albert had elected to play a lone hand. The door behind the stranger had opened noise-lessly, and Albert stood in the aperture enveloped in a coil of rope.

An agonized yelp of protest burst from Tommy, but too late. Fired with enthusiasm, Albert flung a loop of rope over the intruder's head, and jerked him backwards off his feet.

The inevitable happened. The pistol went off with a roar and Tommy felt the bullet scorch his ear in passing, ere it buried itself in the plaster behind him.

'I've got him, sir,' cried Albert, flushed with triumph. 'I've lassoed him. I've been practising with a lasso in my spare time, sir. Can you give me a hand? He's very violent.'

Tommy hastened to his faithful henchman's assistance, men-tally determining that Albert should have no further spare time.

'You damned idiot,' he said. 'Why didn't you go for a police-man? Owing to this fool's play of yours, he as near as anything plugged me through the head. Whew! I've never had such a near escape.'

'Lassoed him in the nick of time, I did,' said Albert, his ardour quite undamped. 'It's wonderful what those chaps can do on the prairies, sir.'

'Quite so,' said Tommy, 'but we're not on the prairies. We happen to be in a highly civilized city. And now, my dear sir,' he added to his prostrate foe. 'What are we going to do with you?'

A stream of oaths in a foreign language was his only reply.

'Hush,' said Tommy. 'I don't understand a word of what you're saying, but I've got a shrewd idea it's not the kind of language to use before a lady. You'll excuse him, won't you, Miss – do you know, in the excitement of this little upset, I've quite forgotten your name?'

'March,' said the girl. She was still white and shaken. But she came forward now and stood by Tommy looking down on the recumbent figure of the discomfited stranger. 'What are you going to do with him?'

'I could fetch a bobby now,' said Albert helpfully.

But Tommy, looking up, caught a very faint negative movement of the girl's head, and took his cue accordingly.

'We'll let him off this time,' he remarked. 'Nevertheless I shall give myself the pleasure of kicking him downstairs – if it's only to teach him manners to a lady.'

He removed the rope, hauled the victim to his feet, and propelled him briskly through the outer office.

A series of shrill yelps was heard and then a thud. Tommy came back, flushed but smiling.

The girl was staring at him with round eyes.

'Did you – hurt him?'

'I hope so,' said Tommy. 'But these dagoes make a practice of crying out before they're hurt – so I can't be quite sure about it. Shall we come back into my office, Miss March, and resume our interrupted conversation? I don't think we shall be interrupted again.'

'I'll have my lasso ready, sir, in case,' said the helpful Albert.

'Put it away,' ordered Tommy sternly.

He followed the girl into the inner office and sat down at his desk, whilst she took a chair facing him.

'I don't quite know where to begin,' said the girl. 'As you heard that man say, I was a passenger on the *Nomadic*. The lady you advertised about, Miss O'Hara, was also on board.'

'Exactly,' said Tommy. 'That we know already but I suspect you must know something about her doings on board that boat, or else that picturesque gentleman would not have been in such a hurry to intervene.'

'I will tell you everything. The American Ambassador was on board. One day, as I was passing his cabin, I saw this woman inside, and she was doing something so extraordinary that I stopped to watch. She had a man's boot in her hand –'

'A boot?' cried Tommy excitedly. 'I'm sorry, Miss March, go on.'

'With a little pair of scissors, she was slitting up the lining. Then she seemed to push something inside. Just at that minute the doctor and another man came down the passage, and immediately she dropped back on the couch and groaned. I waited, and I gathered from what was being said that she had pretended to feel faint. I say *pretended* – because when I first caught sight of her, she was obviously feeling nothing of the kind.'

Tommy nodded.

'Well?'

'I rather hate to tell you the next part. I was – curious. And also, I'd been reading silly books, and I wondered if she'd put a bomb or a poisoned needle or something like that in Mr Wilmott's boot. I know it's absurd – but I did think so. Anyway, next time I passed the empty cabin, I slipped in and examined the boot. I drew out from the lining a slip of paper. Just as I had it in my hand, I heard the steward coming, and I hurried out so as not to be caught. The folded paper was still in my hand. When I got into my own cabin I examined it. Mr Blunt, it was nothing but some verses from the Bible.'

'Verses from the Bible?' said Tommy, very much intrigued.

'At least I thought so at the time. I couldn't understand it, but I thought perhaps it was the work of a religious maniac. Anyway, I didn't feel it was worth while replacing it. I kept it without thinking much about it until yesterday when I used it to make into a boat for my little nephew to sail in his bath. As the paper got wet, I saw a queer kind of design coming out all over it. I hastily took it out of the bath, and smoothed it out flat again. The water had brought out the hidden message. It was a kind of tracing – and looked like the mouth of a harbour. Immediately after that I read your advertisement.'

Tommy sprang from his chair.

'But this is most important. I see it all now. That tracing is probably the plan of some important harbour defences. It had been stolen by this woman. She feared someone was on her track, and not daring to conceal it amongst her own belongings, she contrived this hiding-place. Later, she obtained possession of the bag in which the boot was packed – only to discover that the paper had vanished. Tell me, Miss March, you have brought this paper with you?'

The girl shook her head.

'It's at my place of business. I run a beauty parlour in Bond Street. I am really an agent for the "Cyclamen" preparations in New York. That is why I had been over there. I thought the paper might be important, so I locked it up in the safe before coming out. Ought not Scotland Yard to know about it?'

'Yes, indeed.'

'Then shall we go there now, get it out, and take it straight to Scotland Yard?'

'I am very busy this afternoon,' said Tommy, adopting his professional manner and consulting his watch. 'The Bishop of London wants me to take up a case for him. A very curious problem, concerning some vestments and two curates.'

'Then in that case,' said Miss March, rising, 'I will go alone.'

Tommy raised a hand in protest.

'As I was about to say,' he said, 'the Bishop must wait. I will leave a few words with Albert. I am convinced, Miss March, that until that paper has been safely deposited with Scotland Yard you are in active danger.'

'Do you think so?' said the girl doubtfully.

'I don't think so, I'm sure. Excuse me.' He scribbled some words on the pad in front of him, then tore off the leaf and folded it.

Taking his hat and stick, he intimated to the girl that he was ready to accompany her. In the outer office he handed the folded paper to Albert with an air of importance.

'I am called out on an urgent case. Explain that to his lordship if he comes. Here are my notes on the case for Miss Robinson.'

'Very good, sir,' said Albert, playing up. 'And what about the Duchess's pearls?'

Tommy waved his hand irritably.

'That must wait also.'

He and Miss March hurried out. Half-way down the stairs they encountered Tuppence coming up. Tommy passed her with a brusque: 'Late again, Miss Robinson. I am called out on an important case.'

Tuppence stood still on the stairs and stared after them. Then, with raised eyebrows, she went on up to the office.

As they reached the street, a taxi came sailing up to them. Tommy, on the point of hailing it, changed his mind.

'Are you a good walker, Miss March?' he asked seriously.

'Yes, why? Hadn't we better take that taxi? It will be quicker.'

'Perhaps you did not notice. That taxi driver has just refused a fare a little lower down the street. He was waiting for us. Your enemies are on the look-out. If you feel equal to it, it would be better for us to walk to Bond Street. In the crowded streets they will not be able to attempt much against us.'

'Very well,' said the girl, rather doubtfully.

They walked westwards. The streets, as Tommy had said, were crowded, and progress was slow. Tommy kept a sharp look out. Occasionally he drew the girl to one side with a quick gesture, though she herself had seen nothing suspicious.

Suddenly glancing at her, he was seized with compunction.

'I say, you look awfully done up. The shock of that man. Come into this place and have a good cup of strong coffee. I suppose you wouldn't hear of a nip of brandy.'

The girl shook her head, with a faint smile.

'Coffee be it then,' said Tommy. 'I think we can safely risk its being poisoned.'

They lingered some time over their coffee, and finally set off at a brisker pace.

'We've thrown them off, I think,' said Tommy, looking over his shoulder.

Cyclamen Ltd was a small establishment in Bond Street, with

pale pink taffeta curtains, and one or two jars of face cream and a cake of soap decorating the window.

Cicely March entered, and Tommy followed. The place inside was tiny. On the left was a glass counter with toilet preparations. Behind this counter was a middle-aged woman with grey hair and an exquisite complexion, who acknowledged Cicely March's entrance with a faint inclination of the head before continuing to talk to the customer she was serving.

This customer was a small dark woman. Her back was to them and they could not see her face. She was speaking in slow difficult English. On the right was a sofa and a couple of chairs with some magazines on a table. Here sat two men – apparently bored husbands waiting for their wives.

Cicely March passed straight on through a door at the end which she held ajar for Tommy to follow her. As he did so, the woman customer exclaimed, 'Ah, but I think that is an *amico* of mine,' and rushed after them, inserting her foot in the door just in time to prevent its closing. At the same time the two men rose to their feet. One followed her through the door, the other advanced to the shop attendant and clapped his hand over her mouth to drown the scream rising to her lips.

In the meantime, things were happening rather quickly beyond the swing door. As Tommy passed through a cloth was flung over his head, and a sickly odour assailed his nostrils. Almost as soon however, it was jerked off again, and a woman's scream rang out.

Tommy blinked a little and coughed as he took in the scene in front of him. On his right was the mysterious stranger of a few hours ago, and busily fitting handcuffs upon him was one of the bored men from the shop parlour. Just in front of him was Cicely March wrestling vainly to free herself, whilst the woman customer from the shop held her firmly pinioned. As the latter turned her head, and the veil she wore unfastened itself and fell off, the well-known features of Tuppence were revealed.

'Well done, Tuppence,' said Tommy, moving forward. 'Let me give you a hand. I shouldn't struggle if I were you, Miss O'Hara – or do you prefer to be called Miss March?'

'This is Inspector Grace, Tommy,' said Tuppence. 'As soon as I read the note you left I rang up Scotland Yard, and Inspector Grace and another man met me outside here.'

'Very glad to get hold of this gentleman,' said the Inspector, indicating his prisoner. 'He's wanted badly. But we've never had cause to suspect this place – thought it was a genuine beauty shop.'

'You see,' explained Tommy gently, 'we do have to be so very careful! Why should anyone want the Ambassador's bag for an hour or so? I put the question the other way round. Supposing it was the other bag that was the important one. Someone wanted that bag to be in the Ambassador's possession for an hour or so. Much more illuminating! Diplomatic luggage is not subjected to the indignities of a Customs examination. Clearly smuggling. But smuggling of what? Nothing too bulky. At once I thought of drugs. Then that picturesque comedy was enacted in my office. They'd seen my advertisement and wanted to put me off the scent – or failing that, out of the way altogether. But I happened to notice an expression of blank dismay in the charming lady's eyes when Albert did his lasso act. That didn't fit in very well with her supposed part. The stranger's attack was meant to assure my confidence in her. I played the part of the credulous sleuth with all my might – swallowed her rather impossible story and permitted her to lure me here, carefully leaving behind full instructions for dealing with the situation. Under various pretexts I delayed our arrival, so as to give you all plenty of time.'

Cicely March was looking at him with a stony expression.

'You are mad. What do you expect to find here?'

'Remembering that Richards saw a tin of bath salts, what do you say about beginning with the bath salts, eh, Inspector?'

'A very sound idea, sir.'

He picked up one of the dainty pink tins, and emptied it on the table. The girl laughed.

'Genuine crystals, eh?' said Tommy. 'Nothing more deadly than carbonate of soda?'

'Try the safe,' suggested Tuppence.

There was a small wall safe in the corner. The key was in the lock. Tommy swung it open and gave a shout of satisfaction. The back of the safe opened out into a big recess in the wall, and that recess was stacked with the same elegant tins of bath salts. Rows and rows of them. He took one out and prised up the lid. The top showed the same pink crystals, but underneath was a fine white powder.

The Inspector uttered an ejaculation.

'You've got it, sir. Ten to one, that tin's full of pure cocaine. We knew there was a distributing area somewhere round here, handy to the West End, but we haven't been able to get a clue to it. This is a fine coup of yours, sir.'

'Rather a triumph for Blunt's Brilliant Detectives,' said Tommy to Tuppence, as they emerged into the street together. 'It's a great thing to be a married man. Your persistent schooling has at last taught me to recognize peroxide when I see it. Golden hair has got to be the genuine article to take me in. We will concoct a businesslike letter to the Ambassador, informing him that the matter has been dealt with satisfactorily. And now, my dear fellow, what about tea, and lots of hot buttered muffins?'

CHAPTER XXIII

The Man Who Was No. 16

Tommy and Tuppence were closeted with the Chief in his private room. His commendation had been warm and sincere.

'You have succeeded admirably. Thanks to you we have laid our hands on no less than five very interesting personages, and from them we have received much valuable information. Meanwhile I learn from a creditable source that headquarters in Moscow have taken alarm at the failure of their agents to report. I think that in spite of all our precautions they have begun to suspect that all is not well at what I may call the distributing centre – the office of Mr Theodore Blunt – the International Detective Bureau.'

'Well,' said Tommy, 'I suppose they were bound to tumble to it some time or other, sir.'

'As you say, it was only to be expected. But I am a little worried – about Mrs Tommy.'

'I can look after her all right, sir,' said Tommy, at exactly the same minute as Tuppence said, 'I can take care of myself.'

'H'm,' said Mr Carter. 'Excessive self-confidence was always a characteristic of you two. Whether your immunity is entirely due to your own superhuman cleverness, or whether a small percentage of luck creeps in, I'm not prepared to say. But luck changes, you know. However I won't argue the point. From my extensive knowledge of Mrs Tommy, I suppose it's quite useless to ask her to keep out of the limelight for the next week or two?'

Tuppence shook her head very energetically.

'Then all I can do is to give you all the information that I can. We have reason to believe that a special agent has been despatched from Moscow to this country. We don't know what name he is travelling under, we don't know when he will arrive. But we do know something about him. He is a man who gave us great trouble in the war, an ubiquitous kind of fellow who turned up all over the place where we least wanted him. He is a Russian by birth, and an accomplished linguist – so much so that he can pass as half a dozen other nationalities, including our own. He is also a past-master in the art of disguise. And he has brains. It was he who devised the No. 16 code.

'When and how he will turn up, I do not know. But I am fairly certain that he *will* turn up. We do know this – he was not personally acquainted with the real Mr Theodore Blunt. I think that he will turn up at your office, on the pretext of a case which he will wish you to take up, and will try you with the pass words. The first, as you know, is the mention of the number sixteen – which is replied to by a sentence containing the same number. The second, which we have only just learnt, is an inquiry as to whether you have ever crossed the Channel. The answer to that is: "I was in Berlin on the 13th of last month." As far as we know that is all. I would suggest that you reply correctly, and so endeavour to gain his confidence. Sustain the fiction if you possibly can. But even if he appears to be completely deceived, remain on your guard. Our friend is particularly astute, and can play a double game as well, or better, than you can. But in either case I hope to get him through you. From this day forward I am adopting special precautions. A dictaphone was installed last night in your office, so that one of my men in the room below will be able to hear everything that passes in your office. In this way I shall be immediately informed if anything arises, and can take the necessary steps to safeguard you and your wife whilst securing the man I am after.'

After a few more instructions, and a general discussion of tactics, the two young people departed and made their way as rapidly as possible to the offices of Blunt's Brilliant Detectives.

'It's late,' said Tommy, looking at his watch. 'Just on twelve o'clock. We've been a long time with the Chief. I hope we haven't missed a particularly spicy case.'

'On the whole,' said Tuppence, 'we've not done badly. I

was tabulating results the other day. We've solved four baffling murder mysteries, rounded up a gang of counterfeiters, ditto gang of smugglers –'

'Actually two gangs,' interpolated Tommy. 'So we have! I'm glad of that. "Gangs" sounds so professional.'

Tuppence continued, ticking off the items on her fingers.

'One jewel robbery, two escapes from violent death, one case of missing lady reducing her figure, one young girl befriended, an alibi successfully exploded, and alas! one case where we made utter fools of ourselves. On the whole, jolly good! We're *very* clever, I think.'

'You would think so,' said Tommy. 'You always do. Now I have a secret feeling that once or twice we've been rather lucky.'

'Nonsense,' said Tuppence. 'All done by the little grey cells.'

'Well, I was damned lucky once,' said Tommy. 'The day that Albert did his lasso act! But you speak, Tuppence, as though it was all over?'

'So it is,' said Tuppence. She lowered her voice impressively. 'This is our last case. When they have laid the super spy by the heels, the great detectives intend to retire and take to bee keeping or vegetable marrow growing. It's always done.'

'Tired of it, eh?'

'Ye-es, I think I am. Besides, we're so successful now – the luck might change.'

'Who's talking about luck now?' asked Tommy triumphantly.

At that moment they turned in at the doorway of the block of buildings in which the International Detective Bureau had its offices, and Tuppence did not reply.

Albert was on duty in the outer office, employing his leisure in balancing, or endeavouring to balance, the office ruler upon his nose.

With a stern frown of reproof, the great Mr Blunt passed into his own private office. Divesting himself of his overcoat and hat, he opened the cupboard, on the shelves of which reposed his classic library of the great detectives of fiction.

'The choice narrows,' murmured Tommy. 'On whom shall I model myself today?'

Tuppence's voice, with an unusual note in it, made him turn sharply.

'Tommy,' she said, 'what day of the month is it?'

'Let me see – the eleventh – why?'

'Look at the calendar.'

Hanging on the wall was one of those calendars from which you tear a leaf every day. It bore the legend of Sunday the 16th. Today was Monday.

'By Jove, that's odd. Albert must have torn off too many. Careless little devil.'

'I don't believe he did,' said Tuppence. 'But we'll ask him.'

Albert, summoned and questioned, seemed very astonished. He swore he had only torn off two leaves, those of Saturday and Sunday. His statement was presently supported, for whereas the two leaves torn off by Albert were found in the grate, the succeeding ones were lying neatly in the wastepaper basket.

'A neat and methodical criminal,' said Tommy. 'Who's been here this morning, Albert? A client of any kind?'

'Just one, sir.'

'What was he like?'

'It was a she. A hospital nurse. Very upset and anxious to see you. Said she'd wait until you came. I put her in "Clerks" because it was warmer.'

'And from there she could walk in here, of course, without your seeing her. How long has she been gone?'

'About half an hour, sir. Said she'd call again this afternoon. A nice motherly-looking body.'

'A nice motherly – oh, get out, Albert.'

Albert withdrew, injured.

'Queer start, that,' said Tommy. 'It seems a little purposeless. Puts us on our guard. I suppose there isn't a bomb concealed in the fireplace or anything of that kind?'

He reassured himself on that point, then he seated himself at the desk and addressed Tuppence.

'*Mon ami,*' he said, 'we are here faced with a matter of the utmost gravity. You recall, do you not, the man who was No. 4. Him whom I crushed like an egg shell in the Dolomites – with the aid of high explosives, *bien entendu.* But he was not really dead – ah, no, they are never really dead, these super-criminals. This is the man – but even more so, if I may put it. He is the 4 squared – in other words, he is now the No. 16. You comprehend, my friend?'

'Perfectly,' said Tuppence. 'You are the great Hercule Poirot.'

'Exactly. No moustaches, but lots of grey cells.'

'I've a feeling,' said Tuppence, 'that this particular adventure will be called the "Triumph of Hastings".'

'Never,' said Tommy. 'It isn't done. Once the idiot friend, always the idiot friend. There's an etiquette in these matters. By the way, *mon ami*, can you not part your hair in the middle instead of one side? The present effect is unsymmetrical and deplorable.'

The buzzer rang sharply on Tommy's desk. He returned the signal, and Albert appeared bearing a card.

'Prince Vladiroffsky,' read Tommy, in a low voice. He looked at Tuppence. 'I wonder – Show him in, Albert.'

The man who entered was of middle height, graceful in bearing, with a fair beard, and apparently about thirty-five years of age.

'Mr Blunt?' he inquired. His English was perfect. 'You have been most highly recommended to me. Will you take up a case for me?'

'If you will give me the details –?'

'Certainly. It concerns the daughter of a friend of mine – a girl of sixteen. We are anxious for no scandal – you understand.'

'My dear sir,' said Tommy, 'this business has been running successfully for sixteen years owing to our strict attention to that particular principle.'

He fancied he saw a sudden gleam in the other's eye. If so, it passed as quickly as it came.

'You have branches, I believe, on the other side of the Channel?'

'Oh, yes. As a matter of fact,' he brought out the word with great deliberation. 'I myself was in Berlin on the 13th of last month.'

'In that case,' said the stranger, 'it is hardly necessary to keep up the little fiction. The daughter of my friend can be conveniently dismissed. You know who I am – at any rate I see you have had warning of my coming.'

He nodded towards the calendar on the wall.

'Quite so,' said Tommy.

'My friends – I have come over here to investigate matters. What has been happening?'

'Treachery,' said Tuppence, no longer able to remain quiescent.

The Russian shifted his attention to her, and raised his eyebrows.

'Ah ha, that is so, is it? I thought as much. Was it Sergius?'

'We think so,' said Tuppence unblushingly.

'It would not surprise me. But you yourselves, you are under no suspicion?'

'I do not think so. We handle a good deal of *bona fide* business, you see,' explained Tommy.

The Russian nodded.

'That is wise. All the same, I think it would be better if I did not come here again. For the moment I am staying at the Blitz. I will take Marise – this is Marise, I suppose?'

Tuppence nodded.

'What is she known as here?'

'Oh, Miss Robinson.'

'Very well, Miss Robinson, you will return with me to the Blitz and lunch with me there. We will all meet at headquarters at three o'clock. Is that clear?' He looked at Tommy.

'Perfectly clear,' replied Tommy, wondering where on earth headquarters might be.

But he guessed that it was just those headquarters that Mr Carter was so anxious to discover.

Tuppence rose and slipped on her long black coat with its leopardskin collar. Then, demurely, she declared herself ready to accompany the Prince.

They went out together, and Tommy was left behind, a prey to conflicting emotions.

Supposing something had gone wrong with the dictaphone? Supposing the mysterious hospital nurse had somehow or other learnt of its installation, and had rendered it useless.

He seized the telephone and called a certain number. There was a moment's delay, and then a well-known voice spoke.

'Quite O.K. Come round to the Blitz at once.'

Five minutes later Tommy and Mr Carter met in the Palm Court of the Blitz. The latter was crisp and reassuring.

'You've done excellently. The Prince and the little lady are at lunch in the restaurant. I've got two of my men in there as waiters. Whether he suspects, or whether he doesn't – and I'm fairly sure he doesn't – we've got him on toast. There are two men posted upstairs to watch his suite, and more outside ready to follow wherever they go. Don't be worried about your wife. She'll be kept in sight the whole time. I'm not going to run any risks.'

Occasionally one of the Secret Service men came to report progress. The first time it was a waiter, who took their orders for cocktails, the second time it was a fashionable vacant-faced young man.

'They're coming out,' said Mr Carter. 'We'll retire behind this pillar in case they sit down here, but I fancy he'll take her up to his suite. Ah, yes, I thought so.'

From their post of vantage, Tommy saw the Russian and Tuppence cross the hall and enter the lift.

The minutes passed, and Tommy began to fidget.

'Do you think, sir. I mean, alone in that suite –'

'One of my men's inside – behind the sofa. Don't worry, man.'

A waiter crossed the hall and came up to Mr Carter.

'Got the signal they were coming up, sir – but they haven't come. Is it all right?'

'What?' Mr Carter spun round. 'I saw them go into the lift myself. Just,' he glanced up at the clock – 'four and a half minutes ago. And they haven't shown up . . .'

He hurried across to the lift which had just at that minute come down again, and spoke to the uniformed attendant.

'You took up a gentleman with a fair beard and a young lady a few minutes ago to the second floor.'

'Not the second floor, sir. Third floor the gentleman asked for.'

'Oh!' The Chief jumped in, motioning Tommy to accompany him. 'Take us up to the third floor, please.'

'I don't understand this,' he murmured in a low voice. 'But keep calm. Every exit from the hotel is watched, and I've got a man on the third floor as well – on every floor, in fact. I was taking no chances.'

The lift door opened on the third floor and they sprang out, hurrying down the corridor. Half-way along it, a man dressed as a waiter came to meet them.

'It's all right, Chief. They're in No. 318.'

Carter breathed a sigh of relief.

'That's all right. No other exit?'

'It's a suite, but there are only these two doors into the corridor, and to get out from any of these rooms, they'd have to pass us to get to the staircase or the lifts.'

'That's all right then. Just telephone down and find out who is supposed to occupy this suite.'

The waiter returned in a minute or two.

'Mrs Cortlandt Van Snyder of Detroit.'

Mr Carter became very thoughtful.

'I wonder now. Is this Mrs Van Snyder an accomplice, or is she –'

He left the sentence unfinished.

'Hear any noise from inside?' he asked abruptly.

'Not a thing. But the doors fit well. One couldn't hope to hear much.'

Mr Carter made up his mind suddenly.

'I don't like this business. We're going in. Got the master key?'

'Of course, sir.'

'Call up Evans and Clydesly.'

Reinforced by the other two men, they advanced towards the door of the suite. It opened noiselessly when the first man inserted his key.

They found themselves in a small hall. To the right was the open door of a bathroom, and in front of them was the sitting-room. On the left was a closed door and from behind it a faint sound – rather like an asthmatic pug – could be heard. Mr Carter pushed the door open and entered.

The room was a bedroom, with a big double bed, ornately covered with a bedspread of rose and gold. On it, bound hand and foot, with her mouth secured by a gag and her eyes almost starting out of her head with pain and rage, was a middle-aged fashionably-dressed woman.

On a brief order from Mr Carter, the other men had covered the whole suite. Only Tommy and his Chief had entered the bedroom. As he leant over the bed and strove to unfasten the knots, Carter's eyes went roving round the room in perplexity. Save for an immense quantity of truly American luggage, the room was empty. There was no sign of the Russian or Tuppence.

In another minute the waiter came hurrying in, and reported that the other rooms were also empty. Tommy went to the window, only to draw back and shake his head. There was no balcony – nothing but a sheer drop to the street below.

'Certain it was this room they entered?' asked Carter peremptorily.

'Sure. Besides –' The man indicated the woman on the bed.

With the aid of a pen-knife, Carter parted the scarf that was half choking her and it was at once clear that whatever her sufferings they had not deprived Mrs Cortlandt Van Snyder of the use of her tongue.

When she had exhausted her first indignation, Mr Carter spoke mildly.

'Would you mind telling me exactly what happened – from the beginning?'

'I guess I'll sue the hotel for this. It's a perfect outrage. I was just looking for my bottle of "Killagrippe", when a man sprung on me from behind and broke a little glass bottle right under my nose, and before I could get my breath I was all in. When I came to I was lying here, all trussed up, and goodness knows what's happened to my jewels. He's gotten the lot, I guess.'

'Your jewels are quite safe, I fancy,' said Mr Carter drily. He wheeled round and picked up something from the floor. 'You were standing just where I am when he sprang upon you?'

'That's so,' assented Mrs Van Snyder.

It was a fragment of thin glass that Mr Carter had picked up. He sniffed it and handed it to Tommy.

'Ethyl chloride,' he murmured. 'Instant anaesthetic. But it only keeps one under for a moment or two. Surely he must still have been in the room when you came to, Mrs Van Snyder?'

'Isn't that just what I'm telling you? Oh! it drove me half crazy to see him getting away and me not able to move or do anything at all.'

'Getting away?' said Mr Carter sharply. 'Which way?'

'Through that door.' She pointed to one in the opposite wall. 'He had a girl with him, but she seemed kind of limp as though she'd had a dose of the same dope.'

Carter looked a question at his henchman.

'Leads into the next suite, sir. But double doors – supposed to be bolted on each side.'

Mr Carter examined the door carefully. Then he straightened himself up and turned towards the bed.

'Mrs Van Snyder,' he said quietly, 'do you still persist in your assertion that the man went out this way?'

'Why, certainly he did. Why shouldn't he?'

'Because the door happens to be bolted on this side,' said Mr Carter dryly. He rattled the handle as he spoke.

A look of the utmost astonishment spread over Mrs Van Snyder's face.

'Unless someone bolted the door behind him,' said Mr Carter, 'he cannot have gone out that way.'

He turned to Evans, who had just entered the room.

'Sure they're not anywhere in this suite? Any other communicating doors?'

'No, sir, and I'm quite sure.'

Carter turned his gaze this way and that about the room. He opened the big hanging-wardrobe, looked under the bed, up the chimney and behind all the curtains. Finally, struck by a sudden idea, and disregarding Mrs Van Snyder's shrill protests, he opened the large wardrobe trunk and rummaged swiftly in the interior.

Suddenly Tommy, who had been examining the communicating door, gave an exclamation.

'Come here, sir, look at this. They did go this way.'

The bolt had been very cleverly filed through, so close to the socket that the join was hardly perceptible.

'The door won't open because it's locked on the other side,' explained Tommy.

In another minute they were out in the corridor again and the waiter was opening the door of the adjoining suite with his pass key. This suite was untenanted. When they came to the communicating door, they saw that the same plan had been adopted. The bolt had been filed through, and the door was locked, the key having been removed. But nowhere in the suite was there any sign of Tuppence or the fair-bearded Russian and there was no other communicating door, only the one on the corridor.

'But I'd have seen them come out,' protested the waiter. 'I couldn't have helped seeing them. I can take my oath they never did.'

'Damn it all,' cried Tommy. 'They can't have vanished into thin air!'

Carter was calm again now, his keen brain working.

'Telephone down and find out who had this suite last and when.'

Evans who had come with them, leaving Clydesly on guard in the other suite, obeyed. Presently he raised his head from the telephone.

'An invalid French lad, M. Paul de Vareze. He had a hospital nurse with him. They left this morning.'

An exclamation burst from the other Secret Service man, the waiter. He had gone deathly pale.

'The invalid boy – the hospital nurse,' he stammered. 'I – they passed me in the passage. I never dreamed – I had seen them so often before.'

'Are you sure they were the same?' cried Mr Carter. 'Are you sure, man? You looked at them well?'

The man shook his head.

'I hardly glanced at them. I was waiting, you understand, on the alert for the others, the man with the fair beard and the girl.'

'Of course,' said Mr Carter, with a groan. 'They counted on that.'

With a sudden exclamation, Tommy stooped down and pulled something from under the sofa. It was a small rolled-up bundle of black. Tommy unrolled it and several articles fell out. The outside wrapper was the long black coat Tuppence had worn that day. Inside was her walking dress, her hat and a long fair beard.'

'It's clear enough now,' he said bitterly. 'They've got her – got Tuppence. That Russian devil has given us the slip. The hospital nurse and the boy were accomplices. They stayed here for a day or two to get the hotel people accustomed to their presence. The man must have realized at lunch that he was trapped and proceeded to carry out his plan. Probably he counted on the room next door being empty since it was when he fixed the bolts. Anyway he managed to silence both the woman next door and Tuppence, brought her in here, dressed her in boy's clothes, altered his own appearance, and walked out bold as brass. The clothes must have been hidden ready. But I don't quite see how he managed Tuppence's acquiescence.'

'I can see,' said Mr Carter. He picked up a little shining piece of steel from the carpet. 'That's a fragment of a hypodermic needle. She was doped.'

'My God!' groaned Tommy. 'And he's got clear away.'

'We don't know that,' said Carter quickly. 'Remember every exit is watched.'

'For a man and a girl. Not for a hospital nurse and an invalid boy. They'll have left the hotel by now.'

Such, on inquiry, proved to be the case. The nurse and her patient had driven away in a taxi some five minutes earlier.

'Look here, Beresford,' said Mr Carter, 'for God's sake pull yourself together. You know that I won't leave a stone unturned to find that girl. I'm going back to my office at once and in less than five minutes every resource of the department will be at work. We'll get them yet.'

'Will you, sir? He's a clever devil, that Russian. Look at the cunning of this coup of his. But I know you'll do your best. Only – pray God it's not too late. They've got it in for us badly.'

He left the Blitz Hotel and walked blindly along the street, hardly knowing where he was going. He felt completely paralysed. Where to search? What to do?

He went into the Green Park, and dropped down upon a seat. He hardly noticed when someone else sat down at the opposite end, and was quite startled to hear a well-known voice.

'If you please, sir, if I might make so bold –'

Tommy looked up.

'Hullo, Albert,' he said dully.

'I know all about it, sir – but don't take on so.'

'Don't take on –' He gave a short laugh. 'Easily said, isn't it?'

'Ah, but think, sir. Blunt's Brilliant Detectives! Never beaten. And if you'll excuse my saying so I happened to overhear what you and the Missus was ragging about this morning. Mr Poirot, and his little grey cells. Well, sir, why not use your little grey cells, and see what you can do.'

'It's easier to use your little grey cells in fiction than it is in fact, my boy.'

'Well,' said Albert stoutly, 'I don't believe anybody could put the Missus out, for good and all. You know what she is, sir, just like one of those rubber bones you buy for little dorgs – guaranteed indestructible.'

'Albert,' said Tommy, 'you cheer me.'

'Then what about using your little grey cells, sir?'

'You're a persistent lad, Albert. Playing the fool has served us pretty well up to now. We'll try it again. Let us arrange our facts neatly, and with method. At ten minutes past two exactly, our quarry enters the lift. Five minutes later we speak to the lift man, and having heard what he says we also go up to the third floor. At say, nineteen minutes past two we enter the suite of

Mrs Van Snyder. And now, what significant fact strikes us?'

There was a pause, no significant fact striking either of them.

'There wasn't such a thing as a trunk in the room, was there?' asked Albert, his eyes lighting suddenly.

'*Mon ami*,' said Tommy, 'you do not understand the psychology of an American woman who has just returned from Paris. There were, I should say, about nineteen trunks in the room.'

'What I meantersay is, a trunk's a handy thing if you've got a dead body about you want to get rid of – not that she *is* dead, for a minute.'

'We searched the only two there were big enough to contain a body. What is the next fact in chronological order?'

'You've missed one out – when the Missus and the bloke dressed up as a hospital nurse passed the waiter in the passage.'

'It must have been just before we came up in the lift,' said Tommy. 'They must have had a narrow escape of meeting us face to face. Pretty quick work, that. I –'

He stopped.

'What is it, sir?'

'Be silent, *mon ami*. I have the kind of little idea – colossal, stupendous – that always comes sooner or later to Hercule Poirot. But if so – if that's it – Oh, Lord, I hope I'm in time.'

He raced out of the Park, Albert hard on his heels, inquiring breathlessly as he ran, 'What's up, sir? I don't understand.'

'That's all right,' said Tommy. 'You're not supposed to. Hastings never did. If your grey cells weren't of a very inferior order to mine, what fun do you think I should get out of this game? I'm talking damned rot – but I can't help it. You're a good lad, Albert. You know what Tuppence is worth – she's worth a dozen of you and me.'

Thus talking breathlessly as he ran, Tommy re-entered the portals of the Blitz. He caught sight of Evans, and drew him aside with a few hurried words. The two men entered the lift, Albert with them.

'Third floor,' said Tommy.

At the door of No. 318 they paused. Evans had a pass key,

and used it forthwith. Without a word of warning, they walked straight into Mrs Van Snyder's bedroom. The lady was still lying on the bed, but was now arrayed in a becoming negligee. She stared at them in surprise.

'Pardon my failure to knock,' said Tommy pleasantly. 'But I want my wife. Do you mind getting off that bed?'

'I guess you've gone plumb crazy,' cried Mrs Van Snyder.

Tommy surveyed her thoughtfully, his head on one side.

'Very artistic,' he pronounced, 'but it won't do. We looked *under* the bed – but not *in* it. I remember using that hiding-place myself when young. Horizontally across the bed, underneath the bolster. And that nice wardrobe trunk all ready to take away the body in later. But we were a bit too quick for you just now. You'd had time to dope Tuppence, put her under the bolster, and be gagged and bound by your accomplices next door, and I'll admit we swallowed your story all right for the moment. But when one came to think it out – with order and method – impossible to drug a girl, dress her in boy's clothes, gag and bind another woman, and change one's own appearance – all in five minutes. Simply a physical impossibility. The hospital nurse and the boy were to be a decoy. We were to follow that trail, and Mrs Van Snyder was to be pitied as a victim. Just help the lady off the bed, will you, Evans? You have your automatic? Good.'

Protesting shrilly, Mrs Van Snyder was hauled from her place of repose. Tommy tore off the coverings and the bolster.

There, lying horizontally across the top of the bed was Tuppence, her eyes closed, and her face waxen. For a moment Tommy felt a sudden dread, then he saw the slight rise and fall of her breast. She was drugged – not dead.

He turned to Albert and Evans.

'And now, Messieurs,' he said dramatically, 'the final *coup*!'

With a swift, unexpected gesture he seized Mrs Van Snyder by her elaborately dressed hair. It came off in his hand.

'As I thought,' said Tommy. '*No.* 16!'

* * *

It was about half an hour later when Tuppence opened her eyes and found a doctor and Tommy bending over her.

Over the events of the next quarter of an hour a decent veil had better be drawn, but after that period the doctor departed with the assurance that all was now well.

'*Mon ami*, Hastings,' said Tommy fondly. 'How I rejoice that you are still alive.'

'Have we got No. 16?'

'Once more I have crushed him like an egg-shell – in other words, Carter's got him. The little grey cells! By the way, I'm raising Albert's wages.'

'Tell me all about it.'

Tommy gave her a spirited narrative, with certain omissions.

'Weren't you half frantic about me?' asked Tuppence faintly.

'Not particularly. One must keep calm, you know.'

'Liar!' said Tuppence. 'You look quite haggard still.'

'Well, perhaps, I was just a little worried, darling. I say – we're going to give it up now, aren't we?'

'Certainly we are.'

Tommy gave a sigh of relief.

'I hoped you'd be sensible. After a shock like this –'

'It's not the shock. You know I never mind shocks.'

'A rubber bone – indestructible,' murmured Tommy.

'I've got something better to do,' continued Tuppence. 'Something ever so much more exciting. Something I've never done before.'

Tommy looked at her with lively apprehension.

'I forbid it, Tuppence.'

'You can't,' said Tuppence. 'It's a law of nature.'

'What are you talking about, Tuppence?'

'I'm talking,' said Tuppence, 'of Our Baby. Wives don't whisper nowadays. They shout. OUR BABY! Tommy, isn't everything marvellous?'

Postscript

1929 was a very busy year for Agatha Christie, for she had not just one book published but two. Her bad patch was over, personal stability was coming back, and the crisis, as distressing as it must have been, was finished.

Agatha Christie had recovered her sense of humour. The best proof of that is in Partners in Crime *in which she amused herself by parodying detectives who at that time enjoyed success with their readers.*

'Each story here was written in the manner of some particular detective of the time. Some of them by now I cannot even recognize. I remember Thornley Colton, the blind detective – Austin Freeman, of course; Freeman Wills Crofts with his wonderful timetables; and inevitably Sherlock Holmes . . . some are household names, others have more or less perished in oblivion. They all seemed to me at the time to write well and entertainingly in their different fashions,' she declared in her autobiography.

In fact, Partners in Crime *is more than a simple collection of short stories. Agatha Christie conceived it as a whole, with an introductory chapter which sets the scene, allowing the characters to live thirteen times 'in the style of . . .' The thirteenth text is a self-parody and takes the narrative full circle back to the first chapter. This is without doubt the reason why these were not published beforehand in magazines, unlike Agatha Christie's other short stories.*

For this occasion, Agatha Christie rediscovered the two heroes of her first 'thriller', The Secret Adversary. *Tommy and Tuppence Beresford, married and happy were it not for the thrilling adventures they had had six years previously. Life seemed to them, according to Tuppence's words, 'satisfactory, but dull'. Agatha Christie furnishes them with the great thrill of danger and action that Tuppence summons with all her wishes by the device of the 'International Detective Agency, Theodore Blunt, Manager', of which Tommy becomes the Director for some months, seconded by his wife and young Albert, the assistant porter met in* The Secret Adversary.

   Each of the agency's cases gives them the occasion to imitate a different detective of crime fiction, and for Agatha Christie an opportunity to write a kind of pastiche – sometimes with respect – of some of her fellow masters. Though some of them are still famous today, others have not been remembered by posterity.

The Affair of the Pink Pearl
The detective parodied is Dr John Thorndyke, forensic scientist with rigorous and scientific methods of investigation, created by R. Austin Freeman in 1907 in The Red Thumbmark. *He is the hero of the majority of his novels and stories.*

The Adventure of the Sinister Stranger
In the case of Dr Bowers, Tommy and Tuppence adopt the style and the methods of brothers Francis and Desmond Okewood, heroes of a famous thriller The Secret Hand: Some further adventures by Desmond Okewood of the British Secret Service, *published in 1918 by Douglas Valentine. In the course of the story, allusion is also made to another king of the thriller, Sapper, and to her hero Bulldog Drummond.*

The Gentleman Dressed in Newspaper
Reference is made in this short story to two detectives created by Isabel Ostrander (1885–1924): Timothy McCarthy and Riordan, in the story McCarthy, Incog. (1923). *Isabel Ostrander is an American author who wrote about twenty detective stories which appeared in the 1920s. Several of them had McCarthy as the hero:* Annihilation, The Clue in the Air, How Many Cards, The Twenty-Six Clues. *Her stories were published in Britain a short time after their appearance in the USA.*

The Case of the Missing Lady
Tommy plays Sherlock Holmes and Tuppence plays Watson. For once, the penpusher behaves more brilliantly than the investigator. Christie's revenge, perhaps . . . ?

Blindman's Buff
Agatha Christie took a risk in imitating Thornley Colton, the blind
detective who uses his other senses to resolve criminal affairs, created by
Clinton Holland Stagg (*1890–1916*) *in* Thornley Colton, Blind
Detective *(1923) and* Thornley Colton, Blind Reader of the
Hearts *(1915).*

The Man in the Mist
Complete with cassock and battered umbrella, Tommy imitates Father
Brown, the detective of the good Lord created by Gilbert Keith Chesterton
(*1874–1936*), one of the giants of detective literature.

The Crackler
Tommy and Tuppence are involved in an affair which presents all the
characteristics of plots conceived by the king of thriller Edgar Wallace
(*1875–1932*).

The Sunningdale Mystery
Here, it is Baroness Orczy and her 'old man in the corner', the prototype
'armchair detective', who are the objects of the pastiche. She who made
the adventures of the Scarlet Pimpernel famous throughout the world
was also an excellent author of detective stories, and her old man in
the corner was the hero of three very interesting collections: The Case
of Miss Elliott (*1905*), The Old Man in the Corner (*1909*), and
Unravelled Knots (*1925*). The old man in the corner solved criminal
affairs which the young journalist of the Evening Observer, Polly
Burton, subjected him to, without moving from his regular place in a
tea room: here Tommy plays the old man and Tuppence plays Polly.

The House of Lurking Death
The Beresfords use the methods of Inspector Hanaud of the Sûreté here.
Gabriel Hanaud, the head of the French police, was created by Alfred
Edward Woodley Mason in 1910 in At the Villa Rose. He returned
to service four times in The House of Arrow (*1924*), The Prisoner
of the Opal (*1928*), They Wouldn't Be Chessmen (1935), and
The House in Lorship Lane (*1946*). Tuppence naturally plays the
role of Hanaud's associate, Ricardo.

460 Agatha Christie 1920s – Volume Four

The Unbreakable Alibi
Agatha Christie attacked the specialist of apparently irrefutable alibis
here: Inspector Joseph French, created by Freeman Wills Crofts (1879–
1957) in Inspector French's Greatest Case (1925) and who figured
in about thirty stories.

The Clergyman's Daughter
The detective parodied here is a specialist of complex affairs, which have
to be approached in the way of a puzzle: Roger Sheringham, created in
1925 by Anthony Berkeley (1893–1971) in The Layton Court Mystery, and in whom he entrusted further inquiries in a good ten or so
stories.

The Ambassador's Boots
The detective parodied is the very snobbish Reggie Fortune, whom Scotland Yard calls upon from time to time as a scientific counsellor. Fortune
was created by Henry Christopher Bailey (1878–1961) and figured in
numerous short stories (Call Mr Fortune, the first anthology, dating
from 1920) before graduating in 1934 to the novel Shadow on the
Wall. He then came back on the scene several times in further collections
of short stories and novels.

The Man Who Was Number 16
In this final short story, Agatha Christie is gently mocking herself.
Tommy embodies a Hercule Poirot who has no moustache but is equipped
with 'myriads of grey cells' and Tuppence is his Hastings who announces
victory – but perhaps rather too quickly!

THE MYSTERIOUS
MR QUIN

CONTENTS

CHAPTER I

The Coming of Mr Quin

It was New Year's Eve.

The elder members of the house party at Royston were assembled in the big hall.

Mr Satterthwaite was glad that the young people had gone to bed. He was not fond of young people in herds. He thought them uninteresting and crude. They lacked subtlety and as life went on he had become increasingly fond of subtleties.

Mr Satterthwaite was sixty-two – a little bent, dried-up man with a peering face oddly elflike, and an intense and inordinate interest in other people's lives. All his life, so to speak, he had sat in the front row of the stalls watching various dramas of human nature unfold before him. His role had always been that of the onlooker. Only now, with old age holding him in its clutch, he found himself increasingly critical of the drama submitted to him. He demanded now something a little out of the common.

There was no doubt that he had a flair for these things. He knew instinctively when the elements of drama were at hand. Like a war horse, he sniffed the scent. Since his arrival at Royston this afternoon, that strange inner sense of his had stirred and bid him be ready. Something interesting was happening or going to happen.

The house party was not a large one. There was Tom Evesham, their genial good-humoured host, and his serious political wife who had been before her marriage Lady Laura Keene. There was Sir Richard Conway, soldier, traveller and sportsman, there were six or seven young people whose names Mr Satterthwaite had not grasped and there were the Portals.

It was the Portals who interested Mr Satterthwaite.

He had never met Alex Portal before, but he knew all about him. Had known his father and his grandfather. Alex Portal ran pretty true to type. He was a man of close on forty, fair-haired, and blue-eyed like all the Portals, fond of sport, good at games, devoid of imagination. Nothing unusual about Alex Portal. The usual good sound English stock.

But his wife was different. She was, Mr Satterthwaite knew, an Australian. Portal had been out in Australia two years ago, had met her out there and had married her and brought her home. She had never been to England previous to her marriage. All the same, she wasn't at all like any other Australian woman Mr Satterthwaite had met.

He observed her now, covertly. Interesting woman – very. So still, and yet so – alive. Alive! That was just it! Not exactly beautiful – no, you wouldn't call her beautiful, but there was a kind of calamitous magic about her that you couldn't miss – that no man could miss. The masculine side of Mr Satterthwaite spoke there, but the feminine side (for Mr Satterthwaite had a large share of femininity) was equally interested in another question. *Why did Mrs Portal dye her hair?*

No other man would probably have known that she dyed her hair, but Mr Satterthwaite knew. He knew all those things. And it puzzled him. Many dark women dye their hair blonde; he had never before come across a fair woman who dyed her hair black.

Everything about her intrigued him. In a queer intuitive way, he felt certain that she was either very happy or very unhappy – but he didn't know which, and it annoyed him not to know. Furthermore there was the curious effect she had upon her husband.

'He adores her,' said Mr Satterthwaite to himself, 'but sometimes he's – yes, afraid of her! That's very interesting. That's uncommonly interesting.'

Portal drank too much. That was certain. And he had a curious way of watching his wife when she wasn't looking.

'Nerves,' said Mr Satterthwaite. 'The fellow's all nerves. She knows it too, but she won't do anything about it.'

He felt very curious about the pair of them. Something was going on that he couldn't fathom.

He was roused from his meditations on the subject by the solemn chiming of the big clock in the corner.

'Twelve o'clock,' said Evesham. 'New Year's Day. Happy New Year – everybody. As a matter of fact that clock's five minutes fast ... I don't know why the children wouldn't wait up and see the New Year in?'

'I don't suppose for a minute they've really gone to bed,' said his wife placidly. 'They're probably putting hairbrushes or something in our beds. That sort of thing does so amuse them. I can't think why. We should never have been allowed to do such a thing in my young days.'

'*Autre temps, autres moeurs*,' said Conway, smiling.

He was a tall soldierly-looking man. Both he and Evesham were much of the same type – honest upright kindly men with no great pretensions to brains.

'In my young days we all joined hands in a circle and sang Auld Lang Syne,' continued Lady Laura. 'Should auld acquaintance be forgot – so touching, I always think the words are.'

Evesham moved uneasily.

'Oh! drop it, Laura,' he muttered. '*Not here.*'

He strode across the wide hall where they were sitting, and switched on an extra light.

'Very stupid of me,' said Lady Laura, *sotto voce*. 'Reminds him of poor Mr Capel, of course. My dear, is the fire too hot for you?'

Eleanor Portal made a brusque movement.

'Thank you. I'll move my chair back a little.'

What a lovely voice she had – one of those low murmuring echoing voices that stay in your memory, thought Mr Satterthwaite. Her face was in shadow now. What a pity.

From her place in the shadow she spoke again.

'Mr – Capel?'

'Yes. The man who originally owned this house. He shot himself you know – oh! very well, Tom dear, I won't speak of it unless you like. It was a great shock for Tom, of course, because he was here when it happened. So were you, weren't you, Sir Richard?'

'Yes, Lady Laura.'

An old grandfather clock in the corner groaned, wheezed, snorted asthmatically, and then struck twelve.

'Happy New Year, Tom,' grunted Evesham perfunctorily.

Lady Laura wound up her knitting with some deliberation.

'Well, we've seen the New Year in,' she observed, and added, looking towards Mrs Portal, 'What do you think, my dear?'

Eleanor Portal rose quickly to her feet.

'Bed, by all means,' she said lightly.

'She's very pale,' thought Mr Satterthwaite, as he too rose, and began busying himself with candlesticks. 'She's not usually as pale as that.'

He lighted her candle and handed it to her with a funny little old-fashioned bow. She took it from him with a word of acknowledgment and went slowly up the stairs.

Suddenly a very odd impulse swept over Mr Satterthwaite. He wanted to go after her – to reassure her – he had the strangest feeling that she was in danger of some kind. The impulse died down, and he felt ashamed. *He* was getting nervy too.

She hadn't looked at her husband as she went up the stairs, but now she turned her head over her shoulder and gave him a long searching glance which had a queer intensity in it. It affected Mr Satterthwaite very oddly.

He found himself saying good night to his hostess in quite a flustered manner.

'I'm sure I hope it *will* be a happy New Year,' Lady Laura was saying. 'But the political situation seems to me to be fraught with grave uncertainty.'

'I'm sure it is,' said Mr Satterthwaite earnestly. 'I'm sure it is.'

'I only hope,' continued Lady Laura, without the least change of manner, 'that it will be a dark man who first crosses the threshold. You know that superstition, I suppose, Mr Satterthwaite? No? You surprise me. To bring luck to the house it must be a dark man who first steps over the door step on New Year's

Day. Dear me, I hope I shan't find anything *very* unpleasant in my bed. I never trust the children. They have such very high spirits.'

Shaking her head in sad foreboding, Lady Laura moved majestically up the staircase.

With the departure of the women, chairs were pulled in closer round the blazing logs on the big open hearth.

'Say when,' said Evesham, hospitably, as he held up the whisky decanter.

When everybody had said when, the talk reverted to the subject which had been tabooed before.

'You knew Derek Capel, didn't you, Satterthwaite?' asked Conway.

'Slightly – yes.'

'And you, Portal?'

'No, I never met him.'

So fiercely and defensively did he say it, that Mr Satterthwaite looked up in surprise.

'I always hate it when Laura brings up the subject,' said Evesham slowly. 'After the tragedy, you know, this place was sold to a big manufacturer fellow. He cleared out after a year – didn't suit him or something. A lot of tommy rot was talked about the place being haunted of course, and it gave the house a bad name. Then, when Laura got me to stand for West Kidleby, of course it meant living up in these parts, and it wasn't so easy to find a suitable house. Royston was going cheap, and – well, in the end I bought it. Ghosts are all tommy rot, but all the same one doesn't exactly care to be reminded that you're living in a house where one of your own friends shot himself. Poor old Derek – we shall never know why he did it.'

'He won't be the first or the last fellow who's shot himself without being able to give a reason,' said Alex Portal heavily.

He rose and poured himself out another drink, splashing the whisky in with a liberal hand.

'There's something very wrong with him,' said Mr Satterthwaite, to himself. 'Very wrong indeed. I wish I knew what it was all about.'

'Gad!' said Conway. 'Listen to the wind. It's a wild night.'

'A good night for ghosts to walk,' said Portal with a reckless laugh. 'All the devils in Hell are abroad tonight.'

'According to Lady Laura, even the blackest of them would bring us luck,' observed Conway, with a laugh. 'Hark to that!'

The wind rose in another terrific wail, and as it died away there came three loud knocks on the big nailed doorway.

Everyone started.

'Who on earth can that be at this time of night?' cried Evesham.

They stared at each other.

'I will open it,' said Evesham. 'The servants have gone to bed.'

He strode across to the door, fumbled a little over the heavy bars, and finally flung it open. An icy blast of wind came sweeping into the hall.

Framed in the doorway stood a man's figure, tall and slender. To Mr Satterthwaite, watching, he appeared by some curious effect of the stained glass above the door, to be dressed in every colour of the rainbow. Then, as he stepped forward, he showed himself to be a thin dark man dressed in motoring clothes.

'I must really apologize for this intrusion,' said the stranger, in a pleasant level voice. 'But my car broke down. Nothing much, my chauffeur is putting it to rights, but it will take half an hour or so, and it is so confoundedly cold outside –'

He broke off, and Evesham took up the thread quickly.

'I should think it was. Come in and have a drink. We can't give you any assistance about the car, can we?'

'No, thanks. My man knows what to do. By the way, my name is Quin – Harley Quin.'

'Sit down, Mr Quin,' said Evesham. 'Sir Richard Conway, Mr Satterthwaite. My name is Evesham.'

Mr Quin acknowledged the introductions, and dropped into the chair that Evesham had hospitably pulled forward. As he sat, some effect of the firelight threw a bar of shadow across his face which gave almost the impression of a mask.

Evesham threw a couple more logs on the fire.

'A drink?'

'Thanks.'

Evesham brought it to him and asked as he did so:

'So you know this part of the world well, Mr Quin?'

'I passed through it some years ago.'

'Really?'

'Yes. This house belonged then to a man called Capel.'

'Ah! yes,' said Evesham. 'Poor Derek Capel. You knew him?'

'Yes, I knew him.'

Evesham's manner underwent a faint change, almost imperceptible to one who had not studied the English character. Before, it had contained a subtle reserve, now this was laid aside. Mr Quin had known Derek Capel. He was the friend of a friend, and, as such, was vouched for and fully accredited.

'Astounding affair, that,' he said confidentially. 'We were just talking about it. I can tell you, it went against the grain, buying this place. If there had been anything else suitable, but there wasn't you see. I was in the house the night he shot himself – so was Conway, and upon my word, I've always expected his ghost to walk.'

'A very inexplicable business,' said Mr Quin, slowly and deliberately, and he paused with the air of an actor who has just spoken an important cue.

'You may well say inexplicable,' burst in Conway. 'The thing's a black mystery – always will be.'

'I wonder,' said Mr Quin, non-committally. 'Yes, Sir Richard, you were saying?'

'Astounding – that's what it was. Here's a man in the prime of life, gay, light-hearted, without a care in the world. Five or six old pals staying with him. Top of his spirits at dinner, full of plans for the future. And from the dinner table he goes straight upstairs to his room, takes a revolver from a drawer and shoots himself. Why? Nobody ever knew. Nobody ever will know.'

'Isn't that rather a sweeping statement, Sir Richard?' asked Mr Quin, smiling.

Conway stared at him.

'What d'you mean? I don't understand.'

'A problem is not necessarily unsolvable because it has remained unsolved.'

'Oh! Come, man, if nothing came out at the time, it's not likely to come out now – ten years afterwards?'

Mr Quin shook his head gently.

'I disagree with you. The evidence of history is against you. The contemporary historian never writes such a true history as the historian of a later generation. It is a question of getting the true perspective, of seeing things in proportion. If you like to call it so, it is, like everything else, a question of relativity.'

Alex Portal leant forward, his face twitching painfully.

'You are right, Mr Quin,' he cried, 'you are right. Time does not dispose of a question – it only presents it anew in a different guise.'

Evesham was smiling tolerantly.

'Then you mean to say, Mr Quin, that if we were to hold, let us say, a Court of Inquiry tonight, into the circumstances of Derek Capel's death, we are as likely to arrive at the truth as we should have been at the time?'

'*More* likely, Mr Evesham. The personal equation has largely dropped out, and you will remember facts as facts without seeking to put your own interpretation upon them.'

Evesham frowned doubtfully.

'One must have a starting point, of course,' said Mr Quin in his quiet level voice. 'A starting point is usually a theory. One of you must have a theory, I am sure. How about you, Sir Richard?'

Conway frowned thoughtfully.

'Well, of course,' he said apologetically, 'we thought – naturally we all thought – that there must be a woman in it somewhere. It's usually either that or money, isn't it? And it certainly wasn't money. No trouble of that description. So – what else could it have been?'

Mr Satterthwaite started. He had leant forward to contribute a small remark of his own and in the act of doing so, he had caught sight of a woman's figure crouched against the balustrade of the gallery above. She was huddled down against it, invisible from everywhere but where he himself sat, and she was evidently listening with strained attention to what was going on below. So immovable was she that he hardly believed the evidence of his own eyes.

But he recognized the pattern of the dress easily enough – an old-world brocade. It was Eleanor Portal.

And suddenly all the events of the night seemed to fall into pattern – Mr Quin's arrival, no fortuitous chance, but the appearance of an actor when his cue was given. There was a drama being played in the big hall at Royston tonight – a drama none the less real in that one of the actors was dead. Oh! yes, Derek Capel had a part in the play. Mr Satterthwaite was sure of that.

And, again suddenly, a new illumination came to him. This was Mr Quin's doing. It was he who was staging the play – was giving the actors their cues. He was at the heart of the mystery pulling the strings, making the puppets work. He knew everything, even to the presence of the woman crouched against the woodwork upstairs. Yes, he knew.

Sitting well back in his chair, secure in his role of audience, Mr Satterthwaite watched the drama unfold before his eyes. Quietly and naturally, Mr Quin was pulling the strings, setting his puppets in motion.

'A woman – yes,' he murmured thoughtfully. 'There was no mention of any woman at dinner?'

'Why, of course,' cried Evesham. 'He announced his engagement. That's just what made it seem so absolutely mad. Very bucked about it he was. Said it wasn't to be announced just yet – but gave us the hint that he was in the running for the Benedick stakes.'

'Of course we all guessed who the lady was,' said Conway. 'Marjorie Dilke. Nice girl.'

It seemed to be Mr Quin's turn to speak, but he did not do so, and something about his silence seemed oddly provocative. It was as though he challenged the last statement. It had the effect of putting Conway in a defensive position.

'Who else could it have been? Eh, Evesham?'

'I don't know,' said Tom Evesham slowly. 'What did he say exactly now? Something about being in the running for the Benedick stakes – that he couldn't tell us the lady's name till he had her permission – it wasn't to be announced yet. He said, I remember, that he was a damned lucky fellow. That he wanted his two old friends to know that by that time next year he'd be a happy married man. Of course, we assumed it was Marjorie. They were great friends and he'd been about with her a lot.'

'The only thing –' began Conway and stopped.

'What were you going to say, Dick?'

'Well, I mean, it was odd in a way, if it were Marjorie, that the engagement shouldn't be announced at once. I mean, why the secrecy? Sounds more as though it were a married woman – you know, someone whose husband had just died, or who was divorcing him.'

'That's true,' said Evesham. 'If that were the case, of course, the engagement couldn't be announced at once. And you know, thinking back about it, I don't believe he had been seeing much of Marjorie. All that was the year before. I remember thinking things seemed to have cooled off between them.'

'Curious,' said Mr Quin.

'Yes – looked almost as though someone had come between them.'

'Another woman,' said Conway thoughtfully.

'By jove,' said Evesham. 'You know, there was something almost indecently hilarious about old Derek that night. He looked almost drunk with happiness. And yet – I can't quite explain what I mean – but he looked oddly defiant too.'

'Like a man defying Fate,' said Alex Portal heavily.

Was it of Derek Capel he was speaking – or was it of himself? Mr Satterthwaite, looking at him, inclined to the latter view. Yes, that was what Alex Portal represented – a man defying Fate.

His imagination, muddled by drink, responded suddenly to that note in the story which recalled his own secret preoccupation.

Mr Satterthwaite looked up. She was still there. Watching, listening – still motionless, frozen – like a dead woman.

'Perfectly true,' said Conway. 'Capel *was* excited – curiously so. I'd describe him as a man who had staked heavily and won against well nigh overwhelming odds.'

'Getting up courage, perhaps, for what he's made up his mind to do?' suggested Portal.

And as though moved by an association of ideas, he got up and helped himself to another drink.

'Not a bit of it,' said Evesham sharply. 'I'd almost swear nothing of that kind was in his mind. Conway's right. A successful gambler who has brought off a long shot and can hardly believe in his own good fortune. That was the attitude.'

Conway gave a gesture of discouragement.

'And yet,' he said. 'Ten minutes later –'

They sat in silence. Evesham brought his hand down with a bang on the table.

'Something must have happened in that ten minutes,' he cried. 'It must! But what? Let's go over it carefully. We were all talking. In the middle of it Capel got up suddenly and left the room –'

'Why?' said Mr Quin.

The interruption seemed to disconcert Evesham.

'I beg your pardon?'

'I only said: Why?' said Mr Quin.

Evesham frowned in an effort of memory.

'It didn't seem vital – at the time – Oh! of course – the Post. Don't you remember that jangling bell, and how excited we were. We'd been snowed up for three days, remember. Biggest snowstorm for years and years. All the roads were impassable. No newspapers, no letters. Capel went out to see if something had come through at last, and got a great pile of things. Newspapers and letters. He opened the paper to see if there was any news, and then went upstairs with his letters. Three minutes afterwards, we heard a shot . . . Inexplicable – absolutely inexplicable.'

'That's not inexplicable,' said Portal. 'Of course the fellow got some unexpected news in a letter. Obvious, I should have said.'

'Oh! Don't think we missed anything so obvious as that. It was one of the Coroner's first questions. *But Capel never opened one of his letters.* The whole pile lay unopened on his dressing-table.'

Portal looked crestfallen.

'You're sure he didn't open just one of them? He might have destroyed it after reading it?'

'No, I'm quite positive. Of course, that would have been the natural solution. No, every one of the letters was unopened. Nothing burnt – nothing torn up – There was no fire in the room.'

Portal shook his head.

'Extraordinary.'

'It was a ghastly business altogether,' said Evesham in a low voice. 'Conway and I went up when we heard the shot, and found him – It gave me a shock, I can tell you.'

'Nothing to be done but telephone for the police, I suppose?' said Mr Quin.

'Royston wasn't on the telephone then. I had it put in when I bought the place. No, luckily enough, the local constable happened to be in the kitchen at the time. One of the dogs – you remember poor old Rover, Conway? – had strayed the day before. A passing carter had found it half buried in a snowdrift and had taken it to the police station. They recognized it as Capel's, and a dog he was particularly fond of, and the constable came up with it. He'd just arrived a minute before the shot was fired. It saved us some trouble.'

'Gad, that was a snowstorm,' said Conway reminiscently. 'About this time of year, wasn't it? Early January.'

'February, I think. Let me see, we went abroad soon afterwards.'

'I'm pretty sure it was January. My hunter Ned – you remember Ned? – lamed himself the end of January. That was just after this business.'

'It must have been quite the end of January then. Funny how difficult it is to recall dates after a lapse of years.'

'One of the most difficult things in the world,' said Mr Quin, conversationally. 'Unless you can find a landmark in some big public event – an assassination of a crowned head, or a big murder trial.'

'Why, of course,' cried Conway, 'it was just before the Appleton case.'

'Just after, wasn't it?'

'No, no, don't you remember – Capel knew the Appletons – he'd stayed with the old man the previous Spring – just a week before he died. He was talking of him one night – what an old curmudgeon he was, and how awful it must have been for a young and beautiful woman like Mrs Appleton to be tied to him. There was no suspicion then that she had done away with him.'

'By jove, you're right. I remember reading the paragraph in the paper saying an exhumation order had been granted. It would have been that same day – I remember only seeing it with half my mind, you know, the other half wondering about poor old Derek lying dead upstairs.'

'A common, but very curious phenomenon, that,' observed Mr Quin. 'In moments of great stress, the mind focuses itself upon some quite unimportant matter which is remembered long afterwards with the utmost fidelity, driven in, as it were, by the mental stress of the moment. It may be some quite irrelevant detail, like the pattern of a wallpaper, but it will never be forgotten.'

'Rather extraordinary, your saying that, Mr Quin,' said Conway. 'Just as you were speaking, I suddenly felt myself back in Derek Capel's room – with Derek lying dead on the floor – I saw as plainly as possible the big tree outside the window, and the shadow it threw upon the snow outside. Yes, the moonlight, the snow, and the shadow of the tree – I can see them again this minute. By Gad, I believe I could draw them, and yet I never realized I was looking at them at the time.'

'His room was the big one over the porch, was it not?' asked Mr Quin.

'Yes, and the tree was the big beech, just at the angle of the drive.'

Mr Quin nodded, as though satisfied. Mr Satterthwaite was curiously thrilled. He was convinced that every word, every inflection of Mr Quin's voice, was pregnant with purpose. He was driving at something – exactly what Mr Satterthwaite did not know, but he was quite convinced as to whose was the master hand.

There was a momentary pause, and then Evesham reverted to the preceding topic.

'That Appleton case, I remember it very well now. What a sensation it made. She got off, didn't she? Pretty woman, very fair – remarkably fair.'

Almost against his will, Mr Satterthwaite's eyes sought the kneeling figure up above. Was it his fancy, or did he see it shrink a little as though at a blow. Did he see a hand slide upwards to the table cloth – and then pause.

There was a crash of falling glass. Alex Portal, helping himself to whisky, had let the decanter slip.

'I say – sir, damn' sorry. Can't think what came over me.'

Evesham cut short his apologies.

'Quite all right. Quite all right, my dear fellow. Curious – That smash reminded me. That's what she did, didn't she? Mrs Appleton? Smashed the port decanter?'

'Yes. Old Appleton had his glass of port – only one – each night. The day after his death, one of the servants saw her take the decanter out and smash it deliberately. That set them talking, of course. They all knew she had been perfectly wretched with him. Rumour grew and grew, and in the end, months later, some of his relatives applied for an exhumation order. And sure enough, the old fellow had been poisoned. Arsenic, wasn't it?'

'No – strychnine, I think. It doesn't much matter. Well, of course, there it was. Only one person was likely to have done it. Mrs Appleton stood her trial. She was acquitted more through lack of evidence against her than from any overwhelming proof of innocence. In other words, she was lucky. Yes, I don't suppose there's much doubt she did it right enough. What happened to her afterwards?'

'Went out to Canada, I believe. Or was it Australia? She had an uncle or something of the sort out there who offered her a home. Best thing she could do under the circumstances.'

Mr Satterthwaite was fascinated by Alex Portal's right hand as it clasped his glass. How tightly he was gripping it.

'You'll smash that in a minute or two, if you're not careful,' thought Mr Satterthwaite. 'Dear me, how interesting all this is.'

Evesham rose and helped himself to a drink.

'Well, we're not much nearer to knowing why poor Derek Capel shot himself,' he remarked. 'The Court of Inquiry hasn't been a great success, has it, Mr Quin?'

Mr Quin laughed . . .

It was a strange laugh, mocking – yet sad. It made everyone jump.

'I beg your pardon,' he said. 'You are still living in the past, Mr Evesham. You are still hampered by your preconceived notion. But I – the man from outside, the stranger passing by, see only – facts!'

'Facts?'

'Yes – facts.'

'What do you mean?' said Evesham.

'I see a clear sequence of facts, outlined by yourselves but of which you have not seen the significance. Let us go back ten years and look at what we see – untrammelled by ideas or sentiment.'

Mr Quin had risen. He looked very tall. The fire leaped fitfully behind him. He spoke in a low compelling voice.

'You are at dinner. Derek Capel announces his engagement. You think then it was to Marjorie Dilke. You are not so sure now. He has the restlessly excited manner of a man who has successfully defied Fate – who, in your own words, has pulled off a big coup against overwhelming odds. Then comes the clanging of the bell. He goes out to get the long overdue mail. He doesn't open his letters, but you mention yourselves that *he opened the paper to glance at the news*. It is ten years ago – so we cannot know what the news was that day – a far-off earthquake, a near at hand political crisis? The only thing we do know about the contents of that paper is that it contained one small paragraph – *a paragraph stating that the Home Office had given permission to exhume* the body of Mr Appleton three days ago.'

'What?'

Mr Quin went on.

'Derek Capel goes up to his room, and there he sees something out of the window. Sir Richard Conway has told us that the curtain was not drawn across it and further that it gave on to the drive. What did he see? What could he have seen that forced him to take his life?'

'What do you mean? What did he see?'

'I think,' said Mr Quin, 'that he saw a policeman. A policeman who had come about a dog – But Derek Capel didn't know that – he just saw – a policeman.'

There was a long silence – as though it took some time to drive the inference home.

'My God!' whispered Evesham at last. 'You can't mean that? Appleton? But he wasn't there at the time Appleton died. The old man was alone with his wife –'

'But he may have been there a week earlier. Strychnine is not very soluble unless it is in the form of hydrochloride. The greater part of it, put into the port, would be taken in the last glass, perhaps a week after he left.'

Portal sprung forward. His voice was hoarse, his eyes bloodshot.

'Why did she break the decanter?' he cried. 'Why did she break the decanter? Tell me that!'

For the first time that evening, Mr Quin addressed himself to Mr Satterthwaite.

'You have a wide experience of life, Mr Satterthwaite. Perhaps you can tell us that.'

Mr Satterthwaite's voice trembled a little. His cue had come at last. He was to speak some of the most important lines in the play. He was an actor now – not a looker-on.

'As I see it,' he murmured modestly, 'she – cared for Derek Capel. She was, I think, a good woman – and she had sent him away. When her husband – died, she suspected the truth. And so, to save the man she loved, she tried to destroy the evidence against him. Later, I think, he persuaded her that her suspicions were unfounded, and she consented to marry him. But even then, she hung back – women, I fancy, have a lot of instinct.'

Mr Satterthwaite had spoken his part.

Suddenly a long trembling sigh filled the air.

'My God!' cried Evesham, starting, 'what was that?'

Mr Satterthwaite could have told him that it was Eleanor Portal in the gallery above, but he was too artistic to spoil a good effect.

Mr Quin was smiling.

'My car will be ready by now. Thank you for your hospitality, Mr Evesham. I have, I hope, done something for my friend.'

They stared at him in blank amazement.

'That aspect of the matter has not struck you? He loved this woman, you know. Loved her enough to commit murder for her sake. When retribution overtook him, as he mistakenly thought, he took his own life. But unwittingly, he left her to face the music.'

'She was acquitted,' muttered Evesham.

'Because the case against her could not be proved. I fancy – it may be only a fancy – that she is still – facing the music.'

Portal had sunk into a chair, his face buried in his hands.

Quin turned to Satterthwaite.

'Goodbye, Mr Satterthwaite. You are interested in the drama, are you not?'

Mr Satterthwaite nodded – surprised.

'I must recommend the Harlequinade to your attention. It is dying out nowadays – but it repays attention, I assure you. Its symbolism is a little difficult to follow – but the immortals are always immortal, you know. I wish you all goodnight.'

They saw him stride out into the dark. As before, the coloured glass gave the effect of motley . . .

Mr Satterthwaite went upstairs. He went to draw down his window, for the air was cold. The figure of Mr Quin moved down the drive, and from a side door came a woman's figure, running. For a moment they spoke together, then she retraced

her steps to the house. She passed just below the window, and
Mr Satterthwaite was struck anew by the vitality of her face. She
moved now like a woman in a happy dream.

'Eleanor!'

Alex Portal had joined her.

'Eleanor, forgive me – forgive me – You told me the truth,
but God forgive me – I did not quite believe . . .'

Mr Satterthwaite was intensely interested in other people's
affairs, but he was also a gentleman. It was borne in upon him
that he must shut the window. He did so.

But he shut it very slowly.

He heard her voice, exquisite and indescribable.

'I know – I know. You have been in hell. So was I once. Loving
– yet alternately believing and suspecting – thrusting aside one's
doubts and having them spring up again with leering faces . . .
I know, Alex, I know . . . But there is a worse hell than that, the
hell I have lived in with you. I have seen your doubt – your fear
of me . . . poisoning all our love. That man – that chance passer
by, saved me. I could bear it no longer, you understand. Tonight
– tonight I was going to kill myself . . . Alex . . . Alex . . .'

CHAPTER II

The Shadow on the Glass

'Listen to this,' said Lady Cynthia Drage.

She read aloud from the journal she held in her hand.

'Mr and Mrs Unkerton are entertaining a party at Greenways House this week. Amongst the guests are Lady Cynthia Drage, Mr and Mrs Richard Scott, Major Porter, D.S.O., Mrs Staverton, Captain Allenson and Mr Satterthwaite.'

'It's as well,' remarked Lady Cynthia, casting away the paper, to know what we're in for. But they *have* made a mess of things!'

Her companion, that same Mr Satterthwaite whose name figured at the end of the list of guests, looked at her interrogatively. It had been said that if Mr Satterthwaite were found at the houses of those rich who had newly arrived, it was a sign either that the cooking was unusually good, or that a drama of human life was to be enacted there. Mr Satterthwaite was abnormally interested in the comedies and tragedies of his fellow men.

Lady Cynthia, who was a middle-aged woman, with a hard face and a liberal allowance of make-up, tapped him smartly with the newest thing in parasols which lay rakishly across her knee.

'Don't pretend you don't understand me. You do perfectly. What's more I believe you're here on purpose to see the fur fly!'

Mr Satterthwaite protested vigorously. He didn't know what she was talking about.

'I'm talking about Richard Scott. Do you pretend you've never heard of him?'

'No, of course not. He's the Big Game man, isn't he?'

'That's it – "Great big bears and tigers, etc." as the song says.

Of course, he's a great lion himself just now – the Unkertons
would naturally be mad to get hold of him – *and* the bride! A
charming child – oh! quite a charming child – but so naïve,
only twenty, you know, and he must be at least forty-five.'

'Mrs Scott seems to be very charming,' said Mr Satterthwaite
sedately.

'Yes, poor child.'

'Why poor child?'

Lady Cynthia cast him a look of reproach, and went on
approaching the point at issue in her own manner.

'Porter's all right – a dull dog, though – another of these
African hunters, all sunburnt and silent. Second fiddle to
Richard Scott and always has been – life-long friends and all
that sort of thing. When I come to think of it, I believe they
were together on that trip –'

'Which trip?'

'*The* trip. The Mrs Staverton trip. You'll be saying next you've
never heard of Mrs Staverton.'

'I *have* heard of Mrs Staverton,' said Mr Satterthwaite, almost
with unwillingness.

And he and Lady Cynthia exchanged glances.

'It's so exactly like the Unkertons,' wailed the latter, 'they are
absolutely hopeless – socially, I mean. The idea of asking those
two together! Of course they'd heard that Mrs Staverton was a
sportswoman and a traveller and all that, and about her book.
People like the Unkertons don't even begin to realize what
pitfalls there are! I've been running them, myself, for the last
year, and what I've gone through nobody knows. One has to
be constantly at their elbow. "Don't do that! You can't do this!"
Thank goodness, I'm through with it now. Not that we've quarrelled – oh! no, I never quarrel, but somebody else can take on
the job. As I've always said, I can put up with vulgarity, but I
can't stand meanness!'

After this somewhat cryptic utterance, Lady Cynthia was silent
for a moment, ruminating on the Unkertons' meanness as displayed to herself.

'If I'd still been running the show for them,' she went on

presently, 'I should have said quite firmly and plainly: "You can't ask Mrs Staverton with the Richard Scotts. She and he were once – "'

She stopped eloquently.

'But were they once?' asked Mr Satterthwaite.

'My dear man! It's well known. That trip into the Interior! I'm surprised the woman had the face to accept the invitation.'

'Perhaps she didn't know the others were coming?' suggested Mr Satterthwaite.

'Perhaps she did. That's far more likely.'

'You think –?'

'She's what I call a dangerous woman – the sort of woman who'd stick at nothing. I wouldn't be in Richard Scott's shoes this week-end.'

'And his wife knows nothing, you think?'

'I'm certain of it. But I suppose some kind friend will enlighten her sooner or later. Here's Jimmy Allenson. Such a nice boy. He saved my life in Egypt last winter – I was so bored, you know. Hullo, Jimmy, come here at once.'

Captain Allenson obeyed, dropping down on the turf beside her. He was a handsome young fellow of thirty, with white teeth and an infectious smile.

'I'm glad somebody wants me,' he observed. 'The Scotts are doing the turtle dove stunt, two required, not three, Porter's devouring the *Field*, and I've been in mortal danger of being entertained by my hostess.'

He laughed. Lady Cynthia laughed with him. Mr Satterthwaite, who was in some ways a little old-fashioned, so much so that he seldom made fun of his host and hostess until after he had left their house, remained grave.

'Poor Jimmy,' said Lady Cynthia.

'Mine not to reason why, mine but to swiftly fly. I had a narrow escape of being told the family ghost story.'

'An Unkerton ghost,' said Lady Cynthia. 'How screaming.'

'Not an Unkerton ghost,' said Mr Satterthwaite. 'A Greenways ghost. They bought it with the house.'

'Of course,' said Lady Cynthia, 'I remember now. But it

doesn't clank chains, does it? It's only something to do with a window.'

Jimmy Allenson looked up quickly.

'A window?'

But for the moment Mr Satterthwaite did not answer. He was looking over Jimmy's head at three figures approaching from the direction of the house – a slim girl between two men. There was a superficial resemblance between the men, both were tall and dark with bronzed faces and quick eyes, but looked at more closely the resemblance vanished. Richard Scott, hunter and explorer, was a man of extraordinarily vivid personality. He had a manner that radiated magnetism. John Porter, his friend and fellow hunter, was a man of squarer build with an impassive, rather wooden face, and very thoughtful grey eyes. He was a quiet man, content always to play second fiddle to his friend.

And between these two walked Moira Scott who, until three months ago, had been Moira O'Connell. A slender figure, big wistful brown eyes, and golden red hair that stood out round her small face like a saint's halo.

'That child mustn't be hurt,' said Mr Satterthwaite to himself. 'It would be abominable that a child like that should be hurt.'

Lady Cynthia greeted the newcomers with a wave of the latest thing in parasols.

'Sit down, and don't interrupt,' she said. 'Mr Satterthwaite is telling us a ghost story.'

'I love ghost stories,' said Moira Scott. She dropped down on the grass.

'The ghost of Greenways House?' asked Richard Scott.

'Yes. You know about it?'

Scott nodded.

'I used to stay here in the old days,' he explained. 'Before the Elliots had to sell up. The Watching Cavalier, that's it, isn't it?'

'The Watching Cavalier,' said his wife softly. 'I like that. It sounds interesting. Please go on.'

But Mr Satterthwaite seemed somewhat loath to do so. He assured her that it was not really interesting at all.

'Now you've done it, Satterthwaite,' said Richard Scott sardonically. 'That hint of reluctance clinches it.'

In response to popular clamour, Mr Satterthwaite was forced to speak.

'It's really very uninteresting,' he said apologetically. 'I believe the original story centres round a Cavalier ancestor of the Elliot family. His wife had a Roundhead lover. The husband was killed by the lover in an upstairs room, and the guilty pair fled, but as they fled, they looked back at the house, and saw the face of the dead husband at the window, watching them. That is the legend, but the ghost story is only concerned with a pane of glass in the window of that particular room on which is an irregular stain, almost imperceptible from near at hand, but which from far away certainly gives the effect of a man's face looking out.'

'Which window is it?' asked Mrs Scott, looking up at the house.

'You can't see it from here,' said Mr Satterthwaite. 'It is round the other side but was boarded up from the inside some years ago – forty years ago, I think, to be accurate.'

'What did they do that for? I thought you said the ghost didn't walk.'

'It doesn't,' Mr Satterthwaite assured her. 'I suppose – well, I suppose there grew to be a superstitious feeling about it, that's all.'

Then, deftly enough, he succeeded in turning the conversation. Jimmy Allenson was perfectly ready to hold forth upon Egyptian sand diviners.

'Frauds, most of them. Ready enough to tell you vague things about the past, but won't commit themselves as to the future.'

'I should have thought it was usually the other way about,' remarked John Porter.

'It's illegal to tell the future in this country, isn't it?' said Richard Scott. 'Moira persuaded a gypsy into telling her fortune, but the woman gave her her shilling back, and said there was nothing doing, or words to that effect.'

'Perhaps she saw something so frightful that she didn't like to tell it me,' said Moira.

'Don't pile on the agony, Mrs Scott,' said Allenson lightly. 'I, for one, refuse to believe that an unlucky fate is hanging over you.'

'I wonder,' thought Mr Satterthwaite to himself. 'I wonder . . .'

Then he looked up sharply. Two women were coming from the house, a short stout woman with black hair, inappropriately dressed in jade green, and a tall slim figure in creamy white. The first woman was his hostess, Mrs Unkerton, the second was a woman he had often heard of, but never met.

'Here's Mrs Staverton,' announced Mrs Unkerton, in a tone of great satisfaction. 'All friends here, I think.'

'These people have an uncanny gift for saying just the most awful things they can,' murmured Lady Cynthia, but Mr Satterthwaite was not listening. He was watching Mrs Staverton.

Very easy – very natural. Her careless 'Hullo! Richard, ages since we met. Sorry I couldn't come to the wedding. Is this your wife? You must be tired of meeting all your husband's weather-beaten old friends.' Moira's response – suitable, rather shy. The elder woman's swift appraising glance that went on lightly to another old friend.

'Hullo, John!' The same easy tone, but with a subtle difference in it – a warming quality that had been absent before.

And then that sudden smile. It transformed her. Lady Cynthia had been quite right. A dangerous woman! Very fair – deep blue eyes – not the traditional colouring of the siren – a face almost haggard in repose. A woman with a slow dragging voice and a sudden dazzling smile.

Iris Staverton sat down. She became naturally and inevitably the centre of the group. So you felt it would always be.

Mr Satterthwaite was recalled from his thoughts by Major Porter's suggesting a stroll. Mr Satterthwaite, who was not as a general rule much given to strolling, acquiesced. The two men sauntered off together across the lawn.

'Very interesting story of yours just now,' said the Major.

'I will show you the window,' said Mr Satterthwaite.

He led the way round to the west side of the house. Here there was a small formal garden – the Privy Garden, it was always called, and there was some point in the name, for it was surrounded by high holly hedges, and even the entrance to it ran zigzag between the same high prickly hedges.

Once inside, it was very charming with an old-world charm of formal flower beds, flagged paths and a low stone seat, exquisitely carved. When they had reached the centre of the garden, Mr Satterthwaite turned and pointed up at the house. The length of Greenways House ran north and south. In this narrow west wall there was only one window, a window on the first floor, almost overgrown by ivy, with grimy panes, and which you could just see was boarded up on the inside.

'There you are,' said Mr Satterthwaite.

Craning his neck a little, Porter looked up.

'H'm I can see a kind of discolouration on one of the panes, nothing more.'

'We're too near,' said Mr Satterthwaite. 'There's a clearing higher up in the woods where you get a really good view.'

He led the way out of the Privy Garden, and turning sharply to the left, struck into the woods. A certain enthusiasm of showmanship possessed him, and he hardly noticed that the man at his side was absent and inattentive.

'They had, of course, to make another window, when they boarded up this one,' he explained. 'The new one faces south overlooking the lawn where we were sitting just now. I rather fancy the Scotts have the room in question. That is why I didn't want to pursue the subject. Mrs Scott might have felt nervous if she had realized that she was sleeping in what might be called the haunted room.'

'Yes. I see,' said Porter.

Mr Satterthwaite looked at him sharply, and realized that the other had not heard a word of what he was saying.

'Very interesting,' said Porter. He slashed with his stick at some tall foxgloves, and, frowning, he said, 'She ought not to have come. She ought never to have come.'

People often spoke after this fashion to Mr Satterthwaite. He seemed to matter so little, to have so negative a personality. He was merely a glorified listener.

'No,' said Porter, 'she ought never to have come.'

Mr Satterthwaite knew instinctively that it was not of Mrs Scott he spoke.

'You think not?' he asked.

Porter shook his head as though in foreboding.

'I was on that trip,' he said abruptly. 'The three of us went. Scott and I and Iris. She's a wonderful woman – and a damned fine shot.' He paused. 'What made them ask her?' he finished abruptly.

Mr Satterthwaite shrugged his shoulders.

'Ignorance,' he said.

'There's going to be trouble,' said the other. 'We must stand by – and do what we can.'

'But surely Mrs Staverton –?'

'I'm talking of Scott.' He paused. 'You see – there's Mrs Scott to consider.'

Mr Satterthwaite had been considering her all along, but he did not think it necessary to say so, since the other man had so clearly forgotten her until this minute.

'How did Scott meet his wife?' he asked.

'Last winter, in Cairo. A quick business. They were engaged in three weeks, and married in six.'

'She seems to me very charming.'

'She is, no doubt about it. And he adores her – but that will make no difference.' And again Major Porter repeated to himself, using the pronoun that meant to him one person only: 'Hang it all, she shouldn't have come . . .'

Just then they stepped out upon a high grassy knoll at some little distance from the house. With again something of the pride of the showman, Mr Satterthwaite stretched out his arm.

'Look,' he said.

It was fast growing dusk. The window could still be plainly descried, and apparently pressed against one of the panes was a man's face surmounted by a plumed cavalier's hat.

'Very curious,' said Porter. 'Really very curious. What will happen when that pane of glass gets smashed some day?'

Mr Satterthwaite smiled.

'That is one of the most interesting parts of the story. That pane of glass has been replaced to my certain knowledge at least eleven times, perhaps oftener. The last time was twelve years ago when the then owner of the house determined to destroy the myth. But it's always the same. *The stain reappears* – not all at once, the discolouration spreads gradually. It takes a month or two as a rule.'

For the first time, Porter showed signs of real interest. He gave a sudden quick shiver.

'Damned odd, these things. No accounting for them. What's the real reason of having the room boarded up inside?'

'Well, an idea got about that the room was – unlucky. The Eveshams were in it just before the divorce. Then Stanley and his wife were staying here, and had that room when he ran off with his chorus girl.'

Porter raised his eyebrows.

'I see. Danger, not to life, but to morals.'

'And now,' thought Mr Satterthwaite to himself, 'the Scotts have it . . . I wonder . . .'

They retraced their steps in silence to the house. Walking almost noiselessly on the soft turf, each absorbed in his own thoughts, they became unwittingly eavesdroppers.

They were rounding the corner of the holly hedge when they heard Iris Staverton's voice raised fierce and clear from the depths of the Privy Garden.

'You shall be sorry – sorry – for this!'

Scott's voice answered low and uncertain, so that the words could not be distinguished, and then the woman's voice rose again, speaking words that they were to remember later.

'Jealousy – it drives one to the Devil – it *is* the Devil! It can drive one to black murder. Be careful, Richard, for God's sake, be careful!'

And then on that she had come out of the Privy Garden ahead of them, and on round the corner of the house without seeing them, walking swiftly, almost running, like a woman hag-ridden and pursued.

Mr Satterthwaite thought again of Lady Cynthia's words. A dangerous woman. For the first time, he had a premonition of tragedy, coming swift and inexorable, not to be gainsaid.

Yet that evening he felt ashamed of his fears. Everything seemed normal and pleasant. Mrs Staverton, with her easy insouciance, showed no sign of strain. Moira Scott was her charming, unaffected self. The two women appeared to be get-ting on very well. Richard Scott himself seemed to be in boister-ous spirits.

The most worried looking person was stout Mrs Unkerton. She confided at length in Mr Satterthwaite.

'Think it silly or not, as you like, there's something giving me the creeps. And I'll tell you frankly, I've sent for the glazier unbeknown to Ned.'

'The glazier?'

'To put a new pane of glass in that window. It's all very well. Ned's proud of it – says it gives the house a tone. I don't like it. I tell you flat. We'll have a nice plain modern pane of glass, with no nasty stories attached to it.'

'You forget,' said Mr Satterthwaite, 'or perhaps you don't know. The stain comes back.'

'That's as it may be,' said Mrs Unkerton. 'All I can say is if it does, it's against nature!'

Mr Satterthwaite raised his eyebrows, but did not reply.

'And what if it does?' pursued Mrs Unkerton defiantly. 'We're not so bankrupt, Ned and I, that we can't afford a new pane of glass every month – or every week if need be for the matter of that.'

Mr Satterthwaite did not meet the challenge. He had seen too many things crumple and fall before the power of money to believe that even a Cavalier ghost could put up a successful fight. Nevertheless, he was interested by Mrs Unkerton's mani-fest uneasiness. Even she was not exempt from the tension in the atmosphere – only she attributed it to an attenuated ghost story, not to the clash of personalities amongst her guests.

Mr Satterthwaite was fated to hear yet another scrap of conversation which threw light upon the situation. He was going up the wide staircase to bed, John Porter and Mrs Staverton were sitting together in an alcove of the big hall. She was speaking with a faint irritation in her golden voice.

'I hadn't the least idea the Scotts were going to be here. I daresay, if I had known, I shouldn't have come, but I can assure you, my dear John, that now I am here, I'm not going to run away –'

Mr Satterthwaite passed on up the staircase out of earshot. He thought to himself: 'I wonder now – How much of that is true? Did she know? I wonder – what's going to come of it?'

He shook his head.

In the clear light of the morning he felt that he had perhaps been a little melodramatic in his imaginings of the evening before. A moment of strain – yes, certainly – inevitable under the circumstances – but nothing more. People adjusted themselves. His fancy that some great catastrophe was pending was nerves – pure nerves – or possibly liver. Yes, that was it, liver. He was due at Carlsbad in another fortnight.

On his own account he proposed a little stroll that evening just as it was growing dusk. He suggested to Major Porter that they should go up to the clearing and see if Mrs Unkerton had been as good as her word, and had a new pane of glass put in. To himself, he said: 'Exercise, that's what I need. Exercise.'

The two men walked slowly through the woods. Porter, as usual, was taciturn.

'I can't help feeling,' said Mr Satterthwaite loquaciously, 'that we were a little foolish in our imaginings yesterday. Expecting – er – trouble, you know. After all, people have to behave themselves – swallow their feelings and that sort of thing.'

'Perhaps,' said Porter. After a minute or two he added: 'Civilized people.'

'You mean –?'

'People who've lived outside civilization a good deal sometimes go back. Revert. Whatever you call it.'

They emerged on to the grassy knoll. Mr Satterthwaite was breathing rather fast. He never enjoyed going up hill.

He looked towards the window. The face was still there, more life-like than ever.

'Our hostess has repented, I see.'

Porter threw it only a cursory glance.

'Unkerton cut up rough, I expect,' he said indifferently. 'He's the sort of man who is willing to be proud of another family's ghost, and who isn't going to run the risk of having it driven away when he's paid spot cash for it.'

He was silent a minute or two, staring, not at the house, but at the thick undergrowth by which they were surrounded.

'Has it ever struck you,' he said, 'that civilization's damned dangerous?'

'Dangerous?' Such a revolutionary remark shocked Mr Satterthwaite to the core.

'Yes. There are no safety valves, you see.'

He turned abruptly, and they descended the path by which they had come.

'I really am quite at a loss to understand you,' said Mr Satterthwaite, pattering along with nimble steps to keep up with the other's strides. 'Reasonable people –'

Porter laughed. A short disconcerting laugh. Then he looked at the correct little gentleman by his side.

'You think it's all bunkum on my part, Mr Satterthwaite? But there are people, you know, who can tell you when a storm's coming. They feel it beforehand in the air. And other people can foretell trouble. There's trouble coming now, Mr Satterthwaite, big trouble. It may come any minute. It may –'

He stopped dead, clutching Mr Satterthwaite's arm. And in that tense minute of silence it came – the sound of two shots and following them a cry – a cry in a woman's voice.

'My God!' cried Porter, 'it's come.'

He raced down the path, Mr Satterthwaite panting behind him. In a minute they came out on to the lawn, close by the hedge of the Privy Garden. At the same time, Richard Scott and Mr Unkerton came round the opposite corner of the house.

They halted, facing each other, to left and right of the entrance to the Privy Garden.

'It – it came from in there,' said Unkerton, pointing with a flabby hand.

'We must see,' said Porter. He led the way into the enclosure. As he rounded the last bend of the holly hedge, he stopped dead. Mr Satterthwaite peered over his shoulder. A loud cry burst from Richard Scott.

There were three people in the Privy Garden. Two of them lay on the grass near the stone seat, a man and a woman. The third was Mrs Staverton. She was standing quite close to them by the holly hedge, gazing with horror-stricken eyes, and holding something in her right hand.

'Iris,' cried Porter. 'Iris. For God's sake! What's that you've got in your hand?'

She looked down at it then – with a kind of wonder, an unbelievable indifference.

'It's a pistol,' she said wonderingly. And then – after what seemed an interminable time, but was in reality only a few seconds, 'I – picked it up.'

Mr Satterthwaite had gone forward to where Unkerton and Scott were kneeling on the turf.

'A doctor,' the latter was murmuring. 'We must have a doctor.'

But it was too late for any doctor. Jimmy Allenson who had complained that the sand diviners hedged about the future, and Moira Scott to whom the gypsy had returned a shilling, lay there in the last great stillness.

It was Richard Scott who completed a brief examination. The iron nerve of the man showed in this crisis. After the first cry of agony, he was himself again.

He laid his wife gently down again.

'Shot from behind,' he said briefly. 'The bullet has passed right through her.'

Then he handled Jimmy Allenson. The wound here was in the breast and the bullet was lodged in the body.

John Porter came towards them.

'Nothing should be touched,' he said sternly. 'The police must see it all exactly as it is now.'

'The police,' said Richard Scott. His eyes lit up with a sudden flame as he looked at the woman standing by the holly hedge. He made a step in that direction, but at the same time John Porter also moved, so as to bar his way. For a moment it seemed as though there was a duel of eyes between the two friends.

Porter very quietly shook his head.

'No, Richard,' he said. 'It looks like it – but you're wrong.'

Richard Scott spoke with difficulty, moistening his dry lips.

'Then why – has she got that in her hand?'

And again Iris Staverton said in the same lifeless tone: 'I – picked it up.'

'The police,' said Unkerton rising. 'We must send for the police – at once. You will telephone perhaps, Scott? Someone should stay here – yes, I am sure someone should stay here.'

In his quiet gentlemanly manner, Mr Satterthwaite offered to do so. His host accepted the offer with manifest relief.

'The ladies,' he explained. 'I must break the news to the ladies, Lady Cynthia and my dear wife.'

Mr Satterthwaite stayed in the Privy Garden looking down on the body of that which had once been Moira Scott.

'Poor child,' he said to himself. 'Poor child . . .'

He quoted to himself the tag about the evil men do living after them. For was not Richard Scott in a way responsible for his innocent wife's death? They would hang Iris Staverton, he supposed, not that he liked to think of it, but was not it at least a part of the blame he laid at the man's door? The evil that men do –

And the girl, the innocent girl, had paid.

He looked down at her with a very deep pity. Her small face, so white and wistful, a half smile on the lips still. The ruffled golden hair, the delicate ear. There was a spot of blood on the lobe of it. With an inner feeling of being something of a detective, Mr Satterthwaite deduced an ear-ring, torn away in her fall. He craned his neck forward. Yes, he was right, there was a small pearl drop hanging from the other ear.

Poor child, poor child.

'And now, sir,' said Inspector Winkfield.

They were in the library. The Inspector, a shrewd-looking forceful man of forty odd, was concluding his investigations. He had questioned most of the guests, and had by now pretty well made up his mind on the case. He was listening to what Major Porter and Mr Satterthwaite had to say. Mr Unkerton sat heavily in a chair, staring with protruding eyes at the opposite wall.

'As I understand it, gentlemen,' said the Inspector, 'you'd been for a walk. You were returning to the house by a path that winds round the left side of what they call the Privy Garden. Is that correct?'

'Quite correct, Inspector.'

'You heard two shots, and a woman's scream?'

'Yes.'

'You then ran as fast as you could, emerged from the woods and made your way to the entrance of the Privy Garden. If anybody had left that garden, they could only do so by one entrance. The holly bushes are impassable. If anyone had run out of the garden and turned to the right, he would have been met by Mr Unkerton and Mr Scott. If he had turned to the left, he could not have done so without being seen by you. Is that right?'

'That is so,' said Major Porter. His face was very white.

'That seems to settle it,' said the Inspector. 'Mr and Mrs Unkerton and Lady Cynthia Drage were sitting on the lawn, Mr Scott was in the Billiard Room which opens on to that lawn. At ten minutes past six, Mrs Staverton came out of the house, spoke a word or two to those sitting there, and went round the corner of the house towards the Privy Garden. Two minutes later the shots were heard. Mr Scott rushed out of the house and together with Mr Unkerton ran to the Privy Garden. At the same time you and Mr – er – Satterthwaite arrived from the opposite direction. Mrs Staverton was in the Privy Garden with a pistol in her hand from which two shots had been fired. As I see it, she shot the lady first from behind as she was sitting on the bench. Then Captain Allenson sprang up and went for her, and she shot him in the chest as he came towards her. I understand that there had been a – er – previous attachment between her and Mr Richard Scott –'

'That's a damned lie,' said Porter.

His voice rang out hoarse and defiant. The Inspector said nothing, merely shook his head.

'What is her own story?' asked Mr Satterthwaite.

'She says that she went into the Privy Garden to be quiet for a little. Just before she rounded the last hedge, she heard the shots. She came round the corner, saw the pistol lying at her feet, and picked it up. No one passed her, and she saw no one in the garden but the two victims.' The Inspector gave an eloquent pause. 'That's what she says – and although I cautioned her, she insisted on making a statement.'

'If she said that,' said Major Porter, and his face was still deadly white, 'she was speaking the truth. I know Iris Staverton.'

'Well, sir,' said the Inspector, 'there'll be plenty of time to go into all that later. In the meantime, I've got my duty to do.'

With an abrupt movement, Porter turned to Mr Satterthwaite. 'You! Can't you help? Can't *you* do something?'

Mr Satterthwaite could not help feeling immensely flattered. He had been appealed to, he, most insignificant of men, and by a man like John Porter.

He was just about to flutter out a regretful reply, when the butler, Thompson, entered, with a card upon a salver which he took to his master with an apologetic cough. Mr Unkerton was still sitting huddled up in a chair, taking no part in the proceedings.

'I told the gentleman you would probably not be able to see him, sir,' said Thompson. 'But he insisted that he had an appointment and that it was most urgent.'

Unkerton took the card.

'Mr Harley Quin,' he read. 'I remember, he was to see me

about a picture. I did make an appointment, but as things are –'

But Mr Satterthwaite had started forward.

'Mr Harley Quin, did you say?' he cried. 'How extraordinary, how very extraordinary. Major Porter, you asked me if I could help you. I think I can. This Mr Quin is a friend – or I should say, an acquaintance of mine. He is a most remarkable man.'

'One of these amateur solvers of crime, I suppose,' remarked the Inspector disparagingly.

'No,' said Mr Satterthwaite. 'He is not that kind of man at all. But he has a power – an almost uncanny power – of showing you what you have seen with your own eyes, of making clear to you what you have heard with your own ears. Let us, at any rate, give him an outline of the case, and hear what he has to say.'

Mr Unkerton glanced at the Inspector, who merely snorted and looked at the ceiling. Then the former gave a short nod to Thompson, who left the room and returned ushering in a tall, slim stranger.

'Mr Unkerton?' The stranger shook him by the hand. 'I am sorry to intrude upon you at such a time. We must leave our little picture chat until another time. Ah! my friend, Mr Satterthwaite. Still as fond of the drama as ever?'

A faint smile played for a minute round the stranger's lips as he said these last words.

'Mr Quin,' said Mr Satterthwaite impressively, 'we have a drama here, we are in the midst of one, I should like, and my friend, Major Porter, would like, to have your opinion of it.'

Mr Quin sat down. The red-shaded lamp threw a broad band of coloured light over the checked pattern of his overcoat, and left his face in shadow almost as though he wore a mask.

Succinctly, Mr Satterthwaite recited the main points of the tragedy. Then he paused, breathlessly awaiting the words of the oracle.

But Mr Quin merely shook his head.

'A sad story,' he said. 'A very sad and shocking tragedy. The lack of motive makes it very intriguing.'

Unkerton stared at him.

'You don't understand,' he said. 'Mrs Staverton was heard

to threaten Richard Scott. She was bitterly jealous of his wife. Jealousy –'

'I agree,' said Mr Quin. 'Jealousy or Demoniac Possession. It's all the same. But you misunderstand me. I was not referring to the murder of Mrs Scott, but to that of Captain Allenson.'

'You're right,' cried Porter, springing forward. 'There's a flaw there. If Iris had ever contemplated shooting Mrs Scott, she'd have got her alone somewhere. No, we're on the wrong tack. And I think I see another solution. Only those three people went into the Privy Garden. That is indisputable and I don't intend to dispute it. But I reconstruct the tragedy differently. Supposing Jimmy Allenson shoots first Mrs Scott and then himself. That's possible, isn't it? He flings the pistol from him as he falls – Mrs Staverton finds it lying on the ground and picks it up just as she said. How's that?'

The Inspector shook his head.

'Won't wash, Major Porter. If Captain Allenson had fired that shot close to his body, the cloth would have been singed.'

'He might have held the pistol at arm's length.'

'Why should he? No sense in it. Besides, there's no motive.'

'Might have gone off his head suddenly,' muttered Porter, but without any great conviction. He fell to silence again, suddenly rousing himself to say defiantly: 'Well, Mr Quin?'

The latter shook his head.

'I'm not a magician. I'm not even a criminologist. But I will tell you one thing – I believe in the value of impressions. In any time of crisis, there is always one moment that stands out from all the others, one picture that remains when all else has faded. Mr Satterthwaite is, I think, likely to have been the most unprejudiced observer of those present. Will you cast your mind back, Mr Satterthwaite, and tell us the moment that made the strongest impression on you? Was it when you heard the shots? Was it when you first saw the dead bodies? Was it when you first observed the pistol in Mrs Staverton's hand? Clear your mind of any preconceived standard of values, and tell us.'

Mr Satterthwaite fixed his eyes on Mr Quin's face, rather as a schoolboy might repeat a lesson of which he was not sure.

'No,' he said slowly. 'It was not any of those. The moment that I shall always remember was when I stood alone by the bodies – afterwards – looking down on Mrs Scott. She was lying on her side. Her hair was ruffled. There was a spot of blood on her little ear.'

And instantly, as he said it, he felt that he had said a terrific, a significant thing.

'Blood on her ear? Yes, I remember,' said Unkerton slowly.

'Her ear-ring must have been torn out when she fell,' explained Mr Satterthwaite.

But it sounded a little improbable as he said it.

'She was lying on her left side,' said Porter. 'I suppose it was that ear?'

'No,' said Mr Satterthwaite quickly. 'It was her right ear.'

The Inspector coughed.

'I found this in the grass,' he vouchsafed. He held up a loop of gold wire.

'But my God, man,' cried Porter. 'The thing can't have been wrenched to pieces by a mere fall. It's more as though it had been shot away by a bullet.'

'So it was,' cried Mr Satterthwaite. 'It was a bullet. It must have been.'

'There were only two shots,' said the Inspector. 'A shot can't have grazed her ear and shot her in the back as well. And if one shot carried away the ear-ring, and the second shot killed her, it can't have killed Captain Allenson as well – not unless he was standing close in front of her – very close – facing her as it might be. Oh! no, not even then, unless, that is –'

'Unless she was in his arms, you were going to say,' said Mr Quin, with a queer little smile. 'Well, why not?'

Everyone stared at each other. The idea was so vitally strange to them – Allenson and Mrs Scott – Mr Unkerton voiced the same feeling.

'But they hardly knew each other,' he said.

'I don't know,' said Mr Satterthwaite thoughtfully. 'They might have known each other better than we thought. Lady Cynthia said he saved her from being bored in Egypt last winter, and you' – he turned to Porter – 'you told me that Richard Scott met his wife in Cairo last winter. They might have known each other very well indeed out there . . .'

'They didn't seem to be together much,' said Unkerton.

'No – they rather avoided each other. It was almost unnatural, now I come to think of it –'

They all looked at Mr Quin, as if a little startled at the conclusions at which they had arrived so unexpectedly.

Mr Quin rose to his feet.

'You see,' he said, 'what Mr Satterthwaite's impression has done for us.' He turned to Unkerton. 'It is your turn now.'

'Eh? I don't understand you.'

'You were very thoughtful when I came into this room. I should like to know exactly what thought it was that obsessed you. Never mind if it has nothing to do with the tragedy. Never mind if it seems to you – superstitious –' Mr Unkerton started, ever so slightly. 'Tell us.'

'I don't mind telling you,' said Unkerton. 'Though it's nothing to do with the business, and you'll probably laugh at me into the bargain. I was wishing that my Missus had left well alone and not replaced that pane of glass in the haunted window. I feel as though doing that has maybe brought a curse upon us.'

He was unable to understand why the two men opposite him stared so.

'But she hasn't replaced it yet,' said Mr Satterthwaite at last.

'Yes, she has. Man came first thing this morning.'

'My God!' said Porter, 'I begin to understand. That room, it's panelled, I supposed, not papered?'

'Yes, but what does that –?'

But Porter had swung out of the room. The others followed him. He went straight upstairs to the Scotts' bedroom. It was a charming room, panelled in cream with two windows facing south. Porter felt with his hands along the panels on the western wall.

'There's a spring somewhere – must be. Ah!' There was a click, and a section of the panelling rolled back. It disclosed the grimy panes of the haunted window. One pane of glass was clean and new. Porter stooped quickly and picked up something. He held it out on the palm of his hand. It was a fragment of ostrich feather. Then he looked at Mr Quin. Mr Quin nodded.

He went across to the hat cupboard in the bedroom. There were several hats in it – the dead woman's hats. He took out one with a large brim and curling feathers – an elaborate Ascot hat.

Mr Quin began speaking in a gentle, reflective voice.

'Let us suppose,' said Mr Quin, 'a man who is by nature intensely jealous. A man who has stayed here in bygone years and knows the secret of the spring in the panelling. To amuse himself he opens it one day, and looks out over the Privy Garden. There, secure as they think from being overlooked, he sees his wife and another man. There can be no possible doubt in his mind as to the relations between them. He is mad with rage. What shall he do? An idea comes to him. He goes to the cupboard and puts on the hat with the brim and feathers. It is growing dusk, and he remembers the story of the stain on the glass. Anyone looking up at the window will see as they think the Watching Cavalier. Thus secure he watches them, and at the moment they are clasped in each other's arms, he shoots. He is a good shot – a wonderful shot. As they fall, he fires once more – that shot carries away the ear-ring. He flings the pistol out of the window into the Privy Garden, rushes downstairs and out through the Billiard Room.'

Porter took a step towards him.

'But he let her be accused!' he cried. 'He stood by and let her be accused. Why? Why?'

'I think I know why,' said Mr Quin. 'I should guess – it's only guess-work on my part, mind – that Richard Scott was once madly in love with Iris Staverton – so madly that even meeting her years afterwards stirred up the embers of jealousy again. I should say that Iris Staverton once fancied that she might love him, that she went on a hunting trip with him and another – and that she came back in love with the better man.'

'The better man,' muttered Porter, dazed. 'You mean –?'

'Yes,' said Mr Quin, with a faint smile. 'I mean you.' He paused a minute, and then said: 'If I were you – I should go to her now.'

'I will,' said Porter.

He turned and left the room.

CHAPTER III

At the 'Bells and Motley'

Mr Satterthwaite was annoyed. Altogether it had been an unfortunate day. They had started late, there had been two punctures already, finally they had taken the wrong turning and lost themselves amidst the wilds of Salisbury Plain. Now it was close on eight o'clock, they were still a matter of forty miles from Marswick Manor whither they were bound, and a third puncture had supervened to render matters still more trying.

Mr Satterthwaite, looking like some small bird whose plumage had been ruffled, walked up and down in front of the village garage whilst his chauffeur conversed in hoarse undertones with the local expert.

'Half an hour at *least*,' said that worthy pronouncing judgment.

'And lucky at that,' supplemented Masters, the chauffeur. 'More like three quarters if you ask me.'

'What is this – place, anyway?' demanded Mr Satterthwaite fretfully. Being a little gentleman considerate of the feelings of others, he substituted the word 'place' for 'God-forsaken hole' which had first risen to his lips.

'Kirtlington Mallet.'

Mr Satterthwaite was not much wiser, and yet a faint familiarity seemed to linger round the name. He looked round him disparagingly. Kirtlington Mallet seemed to consist of one straggling street, the garage and the post office on one side of it balanced by three indeterminate shops on the other side. Farther down the road, however, Mr Satterthwaite perceived something that creaked and swung in the wind, and his spirits rose ever so slightly.

'There's an Inn here, I see,' he remarked.

' "Bells and Motley," ' said the garage man. 'That's it – yonder.'

'If I might make a suggestion, sir,' said Masters, 'why not try it? They would be able to give you some sort of a meal, no doubt – not, of course, what you are accustomed to.' He paused apologetically, for Mr Satterthwaite was accustomed to the best cooking of continental chefs, and had in his own service a *cordon bleu* to whom he paid a fabulous salary.

'We shan't be able to take the road again for another three quarters of an hour, sir. I'm sure of that. And it's already past eight o'clock. You could ring up Sir George Foster, sir, from the Inn, and acquaint him with the cause of our delay.'

'You seem to think you can arrange everything, Masters,' said Mr Satterthwaite snappily.

Masters, who did think so, maintained a respectful silence.

Mr Satterthwaite, in spite of his earnest wish to discountenance any suggestion that might possibly be made to him – he was in that mood – nevertheless looked down the road towards the creaking Inn sign with faint inward approval. He was a man of birdlike appetite, an epicure, but even such men can be hungry.

'The "Bells and Motley," ' he said thoughtfully. 'That's an odd name for an Inn. I don't know that I ever heard it before.'

'There's odd folks come to it by all account,' said the local man.

He was bending over the wheel, and his voice came muffled and indistinct.

'Odd folks?' queried Mr Satterthwaite. 'Now what do you mean by that?'

The other hardly seemed to know what he meant.

'Folks that come and go. That kind,' he said vaguely.

Mr Satterthwaite reflected that people who come to an Inn are almost of necessity those who 'come and go.' The definition seemed to him to lack precision. But nevertheless his curiosity was stimulated. Somehow or other he had got to put in three quarters of an hour. The 'Bells and Motley' would be as good as anywhere else.

With his usual small mincing steps he walked away down the road. From afar there came a rumble of thunder. The mechanic looked up and spoke to Masters.

'There's a storm coming over. Thought I could feel it in the air.'

'Crikey,' said Masters. 'And forty miles to go.'

'Ah!' said the other. 'There's no need to be hurrying over this job. You'll not be wanting to take the road till the storm's passed over. That little boss of yours doesn't look as though he'd relish being out in thunder and lightning.'

'Hope they'll do him well at that place,' muttered the chauffeur. 'I'll be pushing along there for a bite myself presently.'

'Billy Jones is all right,' said the garage man. 'Keeps a good table.'

Mr William Jones, a big burly man of fifty and landlord of the 'Bells and Motley,' was at this minute beaming ingratiatingly down on little Mr Satterthwaite.

'Can do you a nice steak, sir – *and* fried potatoes, and as good a cheese as any gentleman could wish for. This way, sir, in the coffee-room. We're not very full at present, the last of the fishing gentlemen just gone. A little later we'll be full again for the hunting. Only one gentleman here at present, name of Quin –'

Mr Satterthwaite stopped dead.

'Quin?' he said excitedly. 'Did you say Quin?'

'That's the name, sir. Friend of yours perhaps?'

'Yes, indeed. Oh! yes, most certainly.' Twittering with excitement, Mr Satterthwaite hardly realized that the world might contain more than one man of that name. He had no doubts at all. In an odd way, the information fitted in with what the man at the garage had said. 'Folks that come and go . . .' a very apt description of Mr Quin. And the name of the Inn, too, seemed a peculiarly fitting and appropriate one.

'Dear me, dear me,' said Mr Satterthwaite. 'What a *very* odd thing. That we should meet like this! Mr Harley Quin, is it not?'

'That's right, sir. This is the coffee-room, sir. Ah! here is the gentleman.'

Tall, dark, smiling, the familiar figure of Mr Quin rose from

the table at which he was sitting, and the well-remembered voice
spoke.

'Ah! Mr Satterthwaite, we meet again. An unexpected
meeting!'

Mr Satterthwaite was shaking him warmly by the hand.

'Delighted. Delighted, I'm sure. A lucky breakdown for me.
My car, you know. And you are staying here? For long?'

'One night only.'

'Then I am indeed fortunate.'

Mr Satterthwaite sat down opposite his friend with a little
sigh of satisfaction, and regarded the dark, smiling face opposite
him with a pleasurable expectancy.

The other man shook his head gently.

'I assure you,' he said, 'that I have not a bowl of goldfish or
a rabbit to produce from my sleeve.'

'Too bad,' cried Mr Satterthwaite, a little taken aback. 'Yes,
I must confess – I do rather adopt that attitude towards you. A
man of magic. Ha, ha. That is how I regard you. A man of
magic.'

'And yet,' said Mr Quin, 'it is you who do the conjuring tricks,
not I.'

'Ah!' said Mr Satterthwaite eagerly. 'But I cannot do them
without you. I lack – shall we say – inspiration?'

Mr Quin smilingly shook his head.

'That is too big a word. I speak the cue, that is all.'

The landlord came in at that minute with bread and a slab
of yellow butter. As he set the things on the table there was a
vivid flash of lightning, and a clap of thunder almost overhead.

'A wild night, gentlemen.'

'On such a night –' began Mr Satterthwaite, and stopped.

'Funny now,' said the landlord, unconscious of the question,
'if those weren't just the words I was going to use myself. It was
just such a night as this when Captain Harwell brought his bride
home, the very day before he disappeared for ever.'

'Ah!' cried Mr Satterthwaite suddenly. 'Of course!'

He had got the clue. He knew now why the name Kirtlington
Mallet was familiar. Three months before he had read every

detail of the astonishing disappearance of Captain Richard Harwell. Like other newspaper readers all over Great Britain he had puzzled over the details of the disappearance, and, also like every other Briton, had evolved his own theories.

'Of course,' he repeated. 'It was at Kirtlington Mallet it happened.'

'It was at this house he stayed for the hunting last winter,' said the landlord. 'Oh! I knew him well. A main handsome young gentleman and not one that you'd think had a care on his mind. He was done away with – that's my belief. Many's the time I've seen them come riding home together – he and Miss Le Couteau, and all the village saying there'd be a match come of it – and sure enough, so it did. A very beautiful young lady, and well thought of, for all she was a Canadian and a stranger. Ah! there's some dark mystery there. We'll never know the rights of it. It broke her heart, it did, sure enough. You've heard as she's sold the place up and gone abroad, couldn't bear to go on here with everyone staring and pointing after her – through no fault of her own, poor young dear! A black mystery, that's what it is.'

He shook his head, then suddenly recollecting his duties, hurried from the room.

'A black mystery,' said Mr Quin softly.

His voice was provocative in Mr Satterthwaite's ears.

'Are you pretending that we can solve the mystery where Scotland Yard failed?' he asked sharply.

The other made a characteristic gesture.

'Why not? Time has passed. Three months. That makes a difference.'

'That is a curious idea of yours,' said Mr Satterthwaite slowly. 'That one sees things better afterwards than at the time.'

'The longer the time that has elapsed, the more things fall into proportion. One sees them in their true relationship to one another.'

There was a silence which lasted for some minutes.

'I am not sure,' said Mr Satterthwaite, in a hesitating voice, 'that I remember the facts clearly by now.'

'I think you do,' said Mr Quin quietly.

It was all the encouragement Mr Satterthwaite needed. His general role in life was that of listener and looker-on. Only in the company of Mr Quin was the position reversed. There Mr Quin was the appreciative listener, and Mr Satterthwaite took the centre of the stage.

'It was just over a year ago,' he said, 'that Ashley Grange passed into the possession of Miss Eleanor Le Couteau. It is a beautiful old house, but it had been neglected and allowed to remain empty for many years. It could not have found a better chatelaine. Miss Le Couteau was a French Canadian, her fore-bears were *émigrés* from the French Revolution, and had handed down to her a collection of almost priceless French relics and antiques. She was a buyer and a collector also, with a very fine and discriminating taste. So much so, that when she decided to sell Ashley Grange and everything it contained after the tra-gedy, Mr Cyrus G. Bradburn, the American millionaire, made no bones about paying the fancy price of sixty thousand pounds for the Grange as it stood.'

Mr Satterthwaite paused.

'I mention these things,' he said apologetically, 'not because they are relevant to the story – strictly speaking, they are not – but to convey an atmosphere, the atmosphere of young Mrs Harwell.'

Mr Quin nodded.

'Atmosphere is always valuable,' he said gravely.

'So we get a picture of this girl,' continued the other. 'Just twenty-three, dark, beautiful, accomplished, nothing crude and unfinished about her. And rich – we must not forget that. She was an orphan. A Mrs St Clair, a lady of unimpeachable breeding and social standing, lived with her as duenna. But Eleanor Le Couteau had complete control of her own fortune. And fortune-hunters are never hard to seek. At least a dozen impecunious young men were to be found dangling round her on all occasions, in the hunting field, in the ballroom, wherever she went. Young Lord Leccan, the most eligible *parti* in the country, is reported to have asked her to marry him, but she remained heart free. That is, until the coming of Captain Richard Harwell.

'Captain Harwell had put up at the local Inn for the hunting. He was a dashing rider to hounds. A handsome, laughing dare-devil of a fellow. You remember the old saying, Mr Quin? "Happy the wooing that's not long doing." The adage was carried out at least in part. At the end of two months, Richard Harwell and Eleanor Le Couteau were engaged.

'The marriage followed three months afterwards. The happy pair went abroad for a two weeks' honeymoon, and then returned to take up their residence at Ashley Grange. The land-lord has just told us that it was on a night of storm such as this that they returned to their home. An omen, I wonder? Who can tell? Be that as it may, the following morning very early – about half-past seven, Captain Harwell was seen walking in the garden by one of the gardeners, John Mathias. He was bare-headed, and was whistling. We have a picture there, a picture of light-heartedness, of careless happiness. And yet from that minute, as far as we know, no one ever set eyes on Captain Richard Harwell again.'

Mr Satterthwaite paused, pleasantly conscious of a dramatic moment. The admiring glance of Mr Quin gave him the tribute he needed, and he went on.

'The disappearance was remarkable – unaccountable. It was not till the following day that the distracted wife called in the police. As you know, they have not succeeded in solving the mystery.'

'There have, I suppose, been theories?' asked Mr Quin.

'Oh! theories, I grant you. Theory No. 1, that Captain Harwell had been murdered, done away with. But if so, where was the body? It could hardly have been spirited away. And besides, what motive was there? As far as was known, Captain Harwell had not an enemy in the world.'

He paused abruptly, as though uncertain. Mr Quin leaned forward.

'You are thinking,' he said softly, 'of young Stephen Grant.'

'I am,' admitted Mr Satterthwaite. 'Stephen Grant, if I remem-ber rightly, had been in charge of Captain Harwell's horses, and had been discharged by his master for some trifling offence. On the morning after the homecoming, very early, Stephen Grant was seen in the vicinity of Ashley Grange, and could give no good account of his presence there. He was detained by the police as being concerned in the disappearance of Captain Harwell, but nothing could be proved against him, and he was eventually discharged. It is true that he might be supposed to bear a grudge against Captain Harwell for his summary dismissal, but the motive was undeniably of the flimsiest. I suppose the police felt they must do something. You see, as I said just now, Captain Harwell had not an enemy in the world.'

'As far as was known,' said Mr Quin reflectively.

Mr Satterthwaite nodded appreciatively.

'We are coming to that. What, after all, *was* known of Captain Harwell? When the police came to look into his antecedents they were confronted with a singular paucity of material. Who was Richard Harwell? Where did he come from? He had appeared, literally out of the blue as it seemed. He was a magnificent rider, and apparently well off. Nobody in Kirtlington Mallet had bothered to inquire further. Miss Le Couteau had had no parents or guardians to make inquiries into the prospects and standing of her fiancé. She was her own mistress. The police theory at this point was clear enough. A rich girl and an impudent impostor. The old story!

'But it was not quite that. True, Miss Le Couteau had no parents or guardians, but she had an excellent firm of solicitors in London who acted for her. Their evidence made the mystery deeper. Eleanor Le Couteau had wished to settle a sum outright upon her prospective husband, but he had refused. He himself was well off, he declared. It was proved conclusively that Harwell never had a penny of his wife's money. Her fortune was absolutely intact.

'He was, therefore, no common swindler, but was his object a refinement of the art? Did he propose blackmail at some future date if Eleanor Harwell should wish to marry some other man? I will admit that something of that kind seemed to me the most likely solution. It had always seemed so to me – until tonight.'

Mr Quin leaned forward, prompting him.

'Tonight?'

'Tonight. I am not satisfied with that. How did he manage to disappear so suddenly and completely – at that hour in the morning, with every labourer bestirring himself and tramping to work? Bareheaded, too.'

'There is no doubt about the latter point – since the gardener saw him?'

'Yes – the gardener – John Mathias. Was there anything there, I wonder?'

'The police would not overlook him,' said Mr Quin.

'They questioned him closely. He never wavered in his statement. His wife bore him out. He left his cottage at seven to attend to the greenhouses, he returned at twenty minutes to eight. The servants in the house heard the front door slam at about a quarter after seven. That fixes the time when Captain Harwell left the house. Ah! yes, I know what you are thinking.'

'Do you, I wonder?' said Mr Quin.

'I fancy so. Time enough for Mathias to have made away with his master. But why, man, why? And if so, where did he hide the body?'

The landlord came in bearing a tray.

'Sorry to have kept you so long, gentlemen.'

He set upon the table a mammoth steak and beside it a dish filled to overflowing with crisp brown potatoes. The odour from the dishes was pleasant to Mr Satterthwaite's nostrils. He felt gracious.

'This looks excellent,' he said. 'Most excellent. We have been discussing the disappearance of Captain Harwell. What became of the gardener, Mathias?'

'Took a place in Essex, I believe. Didn't care to stay hereabouts. There were some as looked askance at him, you understand. Not that I ever believe he had anything to do with it.'

Mr Satterthwaite helped himself to steak. Mr Quin followed

suit. The landlord seemed disposed to linger and chat. Mr Satterthwaite had no objection, on the contrary.

'This Mathias now,' he said. 'What kind of a man was he?'

'Middle-aged chap, must have been a powerful fellow once but bent and crippled with rheumatism. He had that mortal bad, was laid up many a time with it, unable to do any work. For my part, I think it was sheer kindness on Miss Eleanor's part to keep him on. He'd outgrown his usefulness as a gardener, though his wife managed to make herself useful up at the house. Been a cook she had, and always willing to lend a hand.'

'What sort of a woman was she?' asked Mr Satterthwaite, quickly.

The landlord's answer disappointed him.

'A plain body. Middle-aged, and dour like in manner. Deaf, too. Not that I ever knew much of them. They'd only been here a month, you understand, when the thing happened. They say he'd been a rare good gardener in his time, though. Wonderful testimonials Miss Eleanor had with him.'

'Was she interested in gardening?' asked Mr Quin, softly.

'No, sir, I couldn't say that she was, not like some of the ladies round here who pay good money to gardeners and spend the whole of their time grubbing about on their knees as well. Foolishness I call it. You see, Miss Le Couteau wasn't here very much except in the winter for hunting. The rest of the time she was up in London and away in those foreign seaside places where they say the French ladies don't so much as put a toe into the water for fear of spoiling their costumes, or so I've heard.'

Mr Satterthwaite smiled.

'There was no – er – woman of any kind mixed up with Captain Harwell?' he asked.

Though his first theory was disposed of, he nevertheless clung to his idea.

Mr William Jones shook his head.

'Nothing of that sort. Never a whisper of it. No, it's a dark mystery, that's what it is.'

'And your theory? What do you yourself think?' persisted Mr Satterthwaite.

'What do I think?'

'Yes.'

'Don't know what to think. It's my belief as how he was done in, but who by I can't say. I'll fetch you gentlemen the cheese.'

He stumped from the room bearing empty dishes. The storm, which had been quitening down, suddenly broke out with redoubled vigour. A flash of forked lightning and a great clap of thunder close upon each other made little Mr Satterthwaite jump, and before the last echoes of the thunder had died away, a girl came into the room carrying the advertised cheese.

She was tall and dark, and handsome in a sullen fashion of her own. Her likeness to the landlord of the 'Bells and Motley' was apparent enough to proclaim her his daughter.

'Good evening, Mary,' said Mr Quin. 'A stormy night.'

She nodded.

'I hate these stormy nights,' she muttered.

'You are afraid of thunder, perhaps?' said Mr Satterthwaite kindly.

'Afraid of thunder? Not me! There's little that I'm afraid of. No, but the storm sets them off. Talking, talking, the same thing over and over again, like a lot of parrots. Father begins it. "It reminds me, this does, of the night poor Captain Harwell . . ." And so on, and so on.' She turned on Mr Quin. 'You've heard how he goes on. What's the sense of it? Can't anyone let past things be?'

'A thing is only past when it is done with,' said Mr Quin.

'Isn't this done with? Suppose he wanted to disappear? These fine gentlemen do sometimes.'

'You think he disappeared of his own free will?'

'Why not? It would make better sense than to suppose a kind-hearted creature like Stephen Grant murdered him. What should he murder him for, I should like to know? Stephen had had a drop too much one day and spoke to him saucy like, and got the sack for it. But what of it? He got another place just as good. Is that a reason to murder a man in cold blood?'

'But surely,' said Mr Satterthwaite, 'the police were quite satisfied of his innocence?'

'The police! What do the police matter? When Stephen comes into the bar of an evening, every man looks at him queer like. They don't really believe he murdered Harwell, but they're not sure, and so they look at him sideways and edge away. Nice life for a man, to see people shrink away from you, as though you were something different from the rest of folks. Why won't Father hear of our getting married, Stephen and I? "You can take your pigs to a better market, my girl. I've nothing against Stephen, but – well, we don't know, do we?"'

She stopped, her breast heaving with the violence of her resentment.

'It's cruel, cruel, that's what it is,' she burst out. 'Stephen, that wouldn't hurt a fly! And all through life there'll be people who'll think he did. It's turning him queer and bitter like. I don't wonder, I'm sure. And the more he's like that, the more people think there must have been something in it.'

Again she stopped. Her eyes were fixed on Mr Quin's face, as though something in it was drawing this outburst from her.

'Can nothing be done?' said Mr Satterthwaite.

He was genuinely distressed. The thing was, he saw, inevitable. The very vagueness and unsatisfactoriness of the evidence against Stephen Grant made it the more difficult for him to disprove the accusation.

The girl whirled round on him.

'Nothing but the truth can help him,' she cried. 'If Captain Harwell were to be found, if he was to come back. If the true rights of it were only known –'

She broke off with something very like a sob, and hurried quickly from the room.

'A fine-looking girl,' said Mr Satterthwaite. 'A sad case altogether. I wish – I very much wish that something could be done about it.'

His kind heart was troubled.

'We are doing what we can,' said Mr Quin. 'There is still nearly half an hour before your car can be ready.'

Mr Satterthwaite stared at him.

'You think we can come at the truth just by – talking it over like this?'

'You have seen much of life,' said Mr Quin gravely. 'More than most people.'

'Life has passed me by,' said Mr Satterthwaite bitterly.

'But in so doing has sharpened your vision. Where others are blind you can see.'

'It is true,' said Mr Satterthwaite. 'I am a great observer.'

He plumed himself complacently. The moment of bitterness was passed.

'I look at it like this,' he said after a minute or two. 'To get at the cause for a thing, we must study the effect.'

'Very good,' said Mr Quin approvingly.

'The effect in this case is that Miss Le Couteau – Mrs Harwell, I mean, is a wife and yet not a wife. She is not free – she cannot marry again. And look at it as we will, we see Richard Harwell as a sinister figure, a man from nowhere with a mysterious past.'

'I agree,' said Mr Quin. 'You see what all are bound to see, what cannot be missed, Captain Harwell in the limelight, a suspicious figure.'

Mr Satterthwaite looked at him doubtfully. The words seemed somehow to suggest a faintly different picture to his mind.

'We have studied the effect,' he said. 'Or call it the *result*. We can now pass –'

Mr Quin interrupted him.

'You have not touched on the result on the strictly material side.'

'You are right,' said Mr Satterthwaite, after a moment or two for consideration. 'One should do the thing thoroughly. Let us say then that the result of the tragedy is that Mrs Harwell is a wife and not a wife, unable to marry again, that Mr Cyrus Bradburn has been able to buy Ashley Grange and its contents for – sixty thousand pounds, was it? – and that somebody in Essex has been able to secure John Mathias as a gardener! For all that we do not suspect "somebody in Essex" or Mr Cyrus Bradburn of having engineered the disappearance of Captain Harwell.'

'You are sarcastic,' said Mr Quin.

Mr Satterthwaite looked sharply at him.

'But surely you agree –?'

'Oh! I agree,' said Mr Quin. 'The idea is absurd. What next?'

'Let us imagine ourselves back on the fatal day. The disappearance has taken place, let us say, this very morning.'

'No, no,' said Mr Quin, smiling. 'Since, in our imagination, at least, we have power over time, let us turn it the other way. Let us say the disappearance of Captain Harwell took place a hundred years ago. That we, in the year two thousand twenty-five are looking back.'

'You are a strange man,' said Mr Satterthwaite slowly. 'You believe in the past, not the present. Why?'

'You used, not long ago, the word atmosphere. There is no atmosphere in the present.'

'That is true, perhaps,' said Mr Satterthwaite thoughtfully. 'Yes, it is true. The present is apt to be – parochial.'

'A good word,' said Mr Quin.

Mr Satterthwaite gave a funny little bow.

'You are too kind,' he said.

'Let us take – not this present year, that would be too difficult, but say – last year,' continued the other. 'Sum it up for me, you who have the gift of the neat phrase.'

Mr Satterthwaite thought for a minute. He was jealous of his reputation.

'A hundred years ago we have the age of powder and patches,' he said. 'Shall we say that 1924 was the age of Crossword Puzzles and Cat Burglars?'

'Very good,' approved Mr Quin. 'You mean that nationally, not internationally, I presume?'

'As to Crossword Puzzles, I must confess that I do not know,' said Mr Satterthwaite. 'But the Cat Burglar had a great innings on the Continent. You remember that series of famous thefts from French châteaux? It is surmised that one man alone could not have done it. The most miraculous feats were performed to gain admission. There was a theory that a troupe of acrobats were concerned – the Clondinis. I once saw their performance

– truly masterly. A mother, son and daughter. They vanished from the stage in a rather mysterious fashion. But we are wandering from our subject.'

'Not very far,' said Mr Quin. 'Only across the Channel.'

'Where the French ladies will not wet their toes, according to our worthy host,' said Mr Satterthwaite, laughing.

There was a pause. It seemed somehow significant.

'Why did he disappear?' cried Mr Satterthwaite. 'Why? Why? It is incredible, a kind of conjuring trick.'

'Yes,' said Mr Quin. 'A conjuring trick. That describes it exactly. Atmosphere again, you see. And wherein does the essence of a conjuring trick lie?'

'The quickness of the hand deceives the eye,' quoted Mr Satterthwaite glibly.

'That is everything, is it not? To deceive the eye? Sometimes by the quickness of the hand, sometimes – by other means. There are many devices, the pistol shot, the waving of a red handkerchief, something that seems important, but in reality is not. The eye is diverted from the real business, it is caught by the spectacular action that means nothing – nothing at all.'

Mr Satterthwaite leant forward, his eyes shining.

'There is something in that. It is an idea.'

He went on softly. 'The pistol shot. What was the pistol shot in the conjuring trick we were discussing? What is the spectacular moment that holds the imagination?'

He drew in his breath sharply.

'The disappearance,' breathed Mr Satterthwaite. 'Take that away, and it leaves nothing.'

'Nothing? Suppose things took the same course without that dramatic gesture?'

'You mean – supposing Miss Le Couteau were still to sell Ashley Grange and leave – for no reason?'

'Well.'

'Well, why not? It would have aroused talk, I suppose, there would have been a lot of interest displayed in the value of the contents in – Ah! Wait!'

He was silent a minute, then burst out.

'You are right, there is too much limelight, the limelight on Captain Harwell. And because of that, *she* has been in shadow. *Miss Le Couteau*! Everyone asking "Who was Captain Harwell? Where did he come from?" But because she is the injured party, no one makes inquiries about her. Was she really a French Canadian? Were those wonderful heirlooms really handed down to her? You were right when you said just now that we had not wandered far from our subject – *only across the Channel.* Those so-called heirlooms were stolen from the French châteaux, most of them valuable *objets d'art*, and in consequence difficult to dispose of. She buys the house – for a mere song, probably. Settles down there and pays a good sum to an irreproachable English woman to chaperone her. Then *he* comes. The plot is laid beforehand. The marriage, the disappearance and the nine days' wonder! What more natural than that a broken-hearted woman should want to sell everything that reminds her of her past happiness. The American is a connoisseur, the things are genuine and beautiful, some of them beyond price. He makes an offer, she accepts it. She leaves the neighbourhood, a sad and tragic figure. The great *coup* has come off. The eye of the public has been deceived by the quickness of the hand and the spectacular nature of the trick.'

Mr Satterthwaite paused, flushed with triumph.

'But for you, I should never have seen it,' he said with sudden humility. 'You have a most curious effect upon me. One says things so often without even seeing what they really mean. You have the knack of showing one. But it is still not quite clear to me. It must have been most difficult for Harwell to disappear as he did. After all, the police all over England were looking for him.

'It would have been simplest to remain hidden at the Grange,' mused Mr Satterthwaite. 'If it could be managed.'

'He was, I think, very near the Grange,' said Mr Quin.

His look of significance was not lost on Mr Satterthwaite.

'Mathias' cottage?' he exclaimed. 'But the police must have searched it?'

'Repeatedly, I should imagine,' said Mr Quin.

'Mathias,' said Mr Satterthwaite, frowning.

'And Mrs Mathias,' said Mr Quin.

Mr Satterthwaite stared hard at him.

'If that gang was really the Clondinis,' he said dreamily, 'there were three of them in it. The two young ones were Harwell and Eleanor Le Couteau. The mother now, was she Mrs Mathias? But in that case . . .'

'Mathias suffered from rheumatism, did he not?' said Mr Quin innocently.

'Oh!' cried Mr Satterthwaite. 'I have it. But could it be done? I believe it could. Listen. Mathias was there a month. During that time, Harwell and Eleanor were away for a fortnight on a honeymoon. For the fortnight before the wedding, they were supposedly in town. A clever man could have doubled the parts of Harwell and Mathias. When Harwell was at Kirtlington Mallet, Mathias was conveniently laid up with rheumatism, with Mrs Mathias to sustain the fiction. Her part was very necessary. Without her, someone might have suspected the truth. As you say, Harwell was hidden in Mathias' cottage. He *was* Mathias. When at last the plans matured, and Ashley Grange was sold, he and his wife gave out they were taking a place in Essex. Exit John Mathias and his wife – for ever.'

There was a knock at the coffee-room door, and Masters entered. 'The car is at the door, sir,' he said.

Mr Satterthwaite rose. So did Mr Quin, who went across to the window, pulling the curtains. A beam of moonlight streamed into the room.

'The storm is over,' he said.

Mr Satterthwaite was pulling on his gloves.

'The Commissioner is dining with me next week,' he said importantly. 'I shall put my theory – ah! – before him.'

'It will be easily proved or disproved,' said Mr Quin. 'A comparison of the objects at Ashley Grange with a list supplied by the French police –!'

'Just so,' said Mr Satterthwaite. 'Rather hard luck on Mr Bradburn, but – well –'

'He can, I believe, stand the loss,' said Mr Quin.

Mr Satterthwaite held out his hand.

'Goodbye,' he said. 'I cannot tell you how much I have appreciated this unexpected meeting. You are leaving here tomorrow, I think you said?'

'Possibly tonight. My business here is done ... I come and go, you know.'

Mr Satterthwaite remembered hearing those same words earlier in the evening. Rather curious.

He went out to the car and the waiting Masters. From the open door into the bar the landlord's voice floated out, rich and complacent.

'A dark mystery,' he was saying. 'A dark mystery, that's what it is.'

But he did not use the word 'dark.' The word he used suggested quite a different colour. Mr William Jones was a man of discrimination who suited his adjectives to his company. The company in the bar liked their adjectives full flavoured.

Mr Satterthwaite reclined luxuriously in the comfortable limousine. His breast was swelled with triumph. He saw the girl Mary come out on the steps and stand under the creaking Inn sign.

'She little knows,' said Mr Satterthwaite to himself. 'She little knows what *I* am going to do!'

The sign of the 'Bells and Motley' swayed gently in the wind.

CHAPTER IV

The Sign in the Sky

The Judge was finishing his charge to the jury.

'Now, gentlemen, I have almost finished what I want to say to you. There is evidence for you to consider as to whether this case is plainly made out against this man so that you may say he is guilty of the murder of Vivien Barnaby. You have had the evidence of the servants as to the time the shot was fired. They have one and all agreed upon it. You have had the evidence of the letter written to the defendant by Vivien Barnaby on the morning of that same day, Friday, September 13th – a letter which the defence has not attempted to deny. You have had evidence that the prisoner first denied having been at Deering Hill, and later, after evidence had been given by the police, admitted he had. You will draw your own conclusions from that denial. This is not a case of direct evidence. You will have to come to your own conclusions on the subject of motive – of means, of opportunity. The contention of the defence is that some person unknown entered the music room after the defendant had left it, and shot Vivien Barnaby with the gun which, by strange forgetfulness, the defendant had left behind him. You have heard the defendant's story of the reason it took him half an hour to get home. If you disbelieve the defendant's story and are satisfied, beyond any reasonable doubt, that the defendant did, upon Friday, September 13th, discharge his gun at close quarters to Vivien Barnaby's head with intent to kill her, then, gentlemen, your verdict must be Guilty. If, on the other hand, you have any reasonable doubt, it is your duty to acquit the prisoner. I will now ask you to retire to your room and consider and let me know when you have arrived at a conclusion.'

The jury were absent a little under half an hour. They returned the verdict that to everyone had seemed a foregone conclusion, the verdict of 'Guilty.'

Mr Satterthwaite left the court after hearing the verdict, with a thoughtful frown on his face.

A mere murder trial as such did not attract him. He was of too fastidious a temperament to find interest in the sordid details of the average crime. But the Wylde case had been different. Young Martin Wylde was what is termed a gentleman – and the victim, Sir George Barnaby's young wife, had been personally known to the elderly gentleman.

He was thinking of all this as he walked up Holborn, and then plunged into a tangle of mean streets leading in the direction of Soho. In one of these streets there was a small restaurant, known only to the few, of whom Mr Satterthwaite was one. It was not cheap – it was, on the contrary, exceedingly expensive, since it catered exclusively for the palate of the jaded *gourmet*. It was quiet – no strains of jazz were allowed to disturb the hushed atmosphere – it was rather dark, waiters appeared soft-footed out of the twilight, bearing silver dishes with the air of participating in some holy rite. The name of the restaurant was Arlecchino.

Still thoughtful, Mr Satterthwaite turned into the Arlecchino and made for his favourite table in a recess in the far corner. Owing to the twilight before mentioned, it was not until he was quite close to it that he saw it was already occupied by a tall dark man who sat with his face in shadow, and with a play of colour from a stained window turning his sober garb into a kind of riotous motley.

Mr Satterthwaite would have turned back, but just at that moment the stranger moved slightly and the other recognized him.

'God bless my soul,' said Mr Satterthwaite, who was given to old-fashioned expressions. 'Why, it's Mr Quin!'

Three times before he had met Mr Quin, and each time the meeting had resulted in something a little out of the ordinary. A strange person, this Mr Quin, with a knack of showing you the things you had known all along in a totally different light.

At once Mr Satterthwaite felt excited – pleasurably excited. His role was that of the looker-on, and he knew it, but sometimes when in the company of Mr Quin he had the illusion of being an actor – and the principal actor at that.

'This is very pleasant,' he said, beaming all over his dried-up little face. 'Very pleasant indeed. You've no objection to my joining you, I hope?'

'I shall be delighted,' said Mr Quin. 'As you see, I have not yet begun my meal.'

A deferential head waiter hovered up out of the shadows. Mr Satterthwaite, as befitted a man with a seasoned palate, gave his whole mind to the task of selection. In a few minutes, the head waiter, a slight smile of approbation on his lips, retired, and a young satellite began his ministrations. Mr Satterthwaite turned to Mr Quin.

'I have just come from the Old Bailey,' he began. 'A sad business, I thought.'

'He was found guilty?' said Mr Quin.

'Yes, the jury were out only half an hour.'

Mr Quin bowed his head.

'An inevitable result – on the evidence,' he said.

'And yet,' began Mr Satterthwaite – and stopped.

Mr Quin finished the sentence for him.

'And yet your sympathies were with the accused? Is that what you were going to say?'

'I suppose it was. Martin Wylde is a nice-looking young fellow – one can hardly believe it of him. All the same, there have been a good many nice-looking young fellows lately who have turned out to be murderers of a particularly cold-blooded and repellent type.'

'Too many,' said Mr Quin quietly.

'I beg your pardon?' said Mr Satterthwaite, slightly startled.

'Too many for Martin Wylde. There has been a tendency from the beginning to regard this as just one more of a series of the same type of crime – a man seeking to free himself from one woman in order to marry another.'

'Well,' said Mr Satterthwaite doubtfully. 'On the evidence –'

'Ah!' said Mr Quin quickly. 'I am afraid I have not followed all the evidence.'

Mr Satterthwaite's self-confidence came back to him with a rush. He felt a sudden sense of power. He was tempted to be consciously dramatic.

'Let me try and show it to you. I have met the Barnabys, you understand. I know the peculiar circumstances. With me, you will come behind the scenes – you will see the thing from inside.'

Mr Quin leant forward with his quick encouraging smile.

'If anyone can show me that, it will be Mr Satterthwaite,' he murmured.

Mr Satterthwaite gripped the table with both hands. He was uplifted, carried out of himself. For the moment, he was an artist pure and simple – an artist whose medium was words.

Swiftly, with a dozen broad strokes, he etched in the picture of life at Deering Hill. Sir George Barnaby, elderly, obese, purse-proud. A man perpetually fussing over the little things of life. A man who wound up his clocks every Friday afternoon, and who paid his own house-keeping books every Tuesday morning, and who always saw to the locking of his own front door every night. A careful man.

And from Sir George he went on to Lady Barnaby. Here his touch was gentler, but none the less sure. He had seen her but once, but his impression of her was definite and lasting. A vivid defiant creature – pitifully young. A trapped child, that was how he described her.

'She hated him, you understand? She had married him before she knew what she was doing. And now –'

She was desperate – that was how he put it. Turning this way and that. She had no money of her own, she was entirely dependent on this elderly husband. But all the same she was a creature at bay – still unsure of her own powers, with a beauty that was as yet more promise than actuality. And she was greedy. Mr Satterthwaite affirmed that definitely. Side by side with defiance there ran a greedy streak – a clasping and a clutching at life.

'I never met Martin Wylde,' continued Mr Satterthwaite. 'But I heard of him. He lived less than a mile away. Farming, that was his line. And she took an interest in farming – or pretended to. If you ask me, it was pretending. I think that she saw in him her only way of escape – and she grabbed at him, greedily, like a child might have done. Well, there could only be one end to that. We know what that end was, because the letters were read out in court. He kept her letters – she didn't keep his, but from the text of hers one can see that he was cooling off. He admits as much. There was the other girl. She also lived in the village of Deering Vale. Her father was the doctor there. You saw her in court, perhaps? No, I remember, you were not there, you said. I shall have to describe her to you. A fair girl – very fair. Gentle. Perhaps – yes, perhaps a tiny bit stupid. But very restful, you know. And loyal. Above all, loyal.'

He looked at Mr Quin for encouragement, and Mr Quin gave it him by a slow appreciative smile. Mr Satterthwaite went on.

'You heard that last letter read – you must have seen it, in the papers, I mean. The one written on the morning of Friday, September 13th. It was full of desperate reproaches and vague threats, and it ended by begging Martin Wylde to come to Deering Hill that same evening at six o'clock. "*I will leave the side door open for you, so that no one need know you have been here. I shall be in the music room.*" It was sent by hand.'

Mr Satterthwaite paused for a minute or two.

'When he was first arrested, you remember, Martin Wylde denied that he had been to the house at all that evening. His statement was that he had taken his gun and gone out shooting in the woods. But when the police brought forward their evidence, that statement broke down. They had found his fingerprints, you remember, both on the wood of the side door and on one of the two cocktail glasses on the table in the music room. He admitted then that he had come to see Lady Barnaby, that they had had a stormy interview, but that it had ended in his having managed to soothe her down. He swore that he left his gun outside leaning against the wall near the door, and that he left Lady Barnaby alive and well, the time being then a minute or two after a quarter past six. He went straight home, he says. But evidence was called to show that he did not reach his farm until a quarter to seven, and as I have just mentioned, it is barely a mile away. It would not take half an hour to get there. He forgot all about his gun, he declares. Not a very likely statement – and yet –'

'And yet?' queried Mr Quin.

'Well,' said Mr Satterthwaite slowly, 'it's a possible one, isn't it? Counsel ridiculed the supposition, of course, but I think he was wrong. You see, I've known a good many young men, and these emotional scenes upset them very much – especially the dark, nervous type like Martin Wylde. Women now, can go through a scene like that and feel positively better for it after-wards, with all their wits about them. It acts like a safety valve for them, steadies their nerves down and all that. But I can see Martin Wylde going away with his head in a whirl, sick and miserable, and without a thought of the gun he had left leaning up against the wall.'

He was silent for some minutes before he went on.

'Not that it matters. For the next part is only too clear, unfor-tunately. It was exactly twenty minutes past six when the shot was heard. All the servants heard it, the cook, the kitchen maid, the butler, the housemaid and Lady Barnaby's own maid. They came rushing to the music room. She was lying huddled over the arm of her chair. The gun had been discharged close to the back of her head, so that the shot hadn't a chance to scatter. At least two of them penetrated the brain.'

He paused again and Mr Quin asked casually:

'The servants gave evidence, I suppose?'

Mr Satterthwaite nodded.

'Yes. The butler got there a second or two before the others, but their evidence was practically a repetition of each other's.'

'So they *all* gave evidence,' said Mr Quin musingly. 'There were no exceptions?'

'Now I remember it,' said Mr Satterthwaite, 'the housemaid was only called at the inquest. She's gone to Canada since, I believe.'

'I see,' said Mr Quin.

There was a silence, and somehow the air of the little restaurant seemed to be charged with an uneasy feeling. Mr Satterthwaite felt suddenly as though he were on the defensive.

'Why shouldn't she?' he said abruptly.

'Why should she?' said Mr Quin with a very slight shrug of the shoulders.

Somehow, the question annoyed Mr Satterthwaite. He wanted to shy away from it – to get back on familiar ground.

'There couldn't be much doubt who fired the shot. As a matter of fact the servants seemed to have lost their heads a bit. There was no one in the house to take charge. It was some minutes before anyone thought of ringing up the police, and when they did so they found that the telephone was out of order.'

'Oh!' said Mr Quin. 'The telephone was out of order.'

'It was,' said Mr Satterthwaite – and was struck suddenly by the feeling that he had said something tremendously important. 'It might, of course, have been done on purpose,' he said slowly. 'But there seems no point in that. Death was practically instantaneous.'

Mr Quin said nothing, and Mr Satterthwaite felt that his explanation was unsatisfactory.

'There was absolutely no one to suspect but young Wylde,' he went on. 'By his own account, even, he was only out of the house three minutes before the shot was fired. And who else could have fired it? Sir George was at a bridge party a few houses away. He left there at half-past six and was met just outside the gate by a servant bringing him the news. The last rubber finished at half-past six exactly – no doubt about that. Then there was Sir George's secretary, Henry Thompson. He was in London that day, and actually at a business meeting at the moment the shot was fired. Finally, there is Sylvia Dale, who after all, had a perfectly good motive, impossible as it seems that she should have had anything to do with such a crime. She was at the station of Deering Vale seeing a friend off by the 6.28 train. That lets her out. Then the servants. What earthly motive could any one of them have? Besides they all arrived on the spot practically simultaneously. No, it must have been Martin Wylde.'

But he said it in a dissatisfied kind of voice.

They went on with their lunch. Mr Quin was not in a talkative mood, and Mr Satterthwaite had said all he had to say. But the silence was not a barren one. It was filled with the growing dissatisfaction of Mr Satterthwaite, heightened and fostered in some strange way by the mere acquiescence of the other man.

Mr Satterthwaite suddenly put down his knife and fork with a clatter.

'Supposing that that young man is really innocent,' he said. 'He's going to be hanged.'

He looked very startled and upset about it. And still Mr Quin said nothing.

'It's not as though –' began Mr Satterthwaite, and stopped. 'Why shouldn't the woman go to Canada?' he ended inconsequently.

Mr Quin shook his head.

'I don't even know what part of Canada she went to,' continued Mr Satterthwaite peevishly.

'Could you find out?' suggested the other.

'I suppose I could. The butler, now. He'd know. Or possibly Thompson, the secretary.'

He paused again. When he resumed speech, his voice sounded almost pleading.

'It's not as though it were anything to do with me?'

'That a young man is going to be hanged in a little over three weeks?'

'Well, yes – if you put it that way, I suppose. Yes, I see what you mean. Life and death. And that poor girl, too. It's not that I'm hard-headed – but, after all – what good will it do? Isn't the whole thing rather fantastic? Even if I found out where the woman's gone in Canada – why, it would probably mean that I should have to go out there myself.'

Mr Satterthwaite looked seriously upset.

'And I was thinking of going to the Riviera next week,' he said pathetically.

And his glance towards Mr Quin said as plainly as it could
be said, 'Do let me off, won't you?'

'You have never been to Canada?'

'Never.'

'A very interesting country.'

Mr Satterthwaite looked at him undecidedly.

'You think I ought to go?'

Mr Quin leaned back in his chair and lighted a cigarette.
Between puffs of smoke, he spoke deliberately.

'You are, I believe, a rich man, Mr Satterthwaite. Not a millionaire, but a man able to indulge a hobby without counting the
expense. You have looked on at the dramas of other people.
Have you never contemplated stepping in and playing a part?
Have you never seen yourself for a minute as the arbiter of
other people's destinies – standing in the centre of the stage
with life and death in your hands?'

Mr Satterthwaite leant forward. The old eagerness surged
over him.

'You mean – if I go on this wild-goose chase to Canada –?'

Mr Quin smiled.

'Oh! it was your suggestion, going to Canada, not mine,' he
said lightly.

'You can't put me off like that,' said Mr Satterthwaite earnestly. 'Whenever I have come across you –' He stopped.

'Well?'

'There is something about you I do not understand. Perhaps
I never shall. The last time I met you –'

'On Midsummer's Eve.'

Mr Satterthwaite was startled, as though the words held a clue
that he did not quite understand.

'Was it Midsummer's Eve?' he asked confusedly.

'Yes. But let us not dwell on that. It is unimportant, is it not?'

'Since you say so,' said Mr Satterthwaite courteously. He felt
that elusive clue slipping through his fingers. 'When I come
back from Canada' – he paused a littsle awkwardly – 'I – I –
should much like to see you again.'

'I am afraid I have no fixed address for the moment,' said

Mr Quin regretfully. 'But I often come to this place. If you also frequent it, we shall no doubt meet before very long.'

They parted pleasantly.

Mr Satterthwaite was very excited. He hurried round to Cook's and inquired about boat sailings. Then he rang up Deering Hill. The voice of a butler, suave and deferential, answered him.

'My name is Satterthwaite. I am speaking for a – er – firm of solicitors. I wished to make a few inquiries about a young woman who was recently housemaid in your establishment.'

'Would that be Louisa, sir? Louisa Bullard?'

'That is the name,' said Mr Satterthwaite, very pleased to be told it.

'I regret she is not in this country, sir. She went to Canada six months ago.'

'Can you give me her present address?'

The butler was afraid he couldn't. It was a place in the mountains she had gone to – a Scotch name – ah! Banff, that was it. Some of the other young women in the house had been expecting to hear from her, but she had never written or given them any address.

Mr Satterthwaite thanked him and rang off. He was still undaunted. The adventurous spirit was strong in his breast. He would go to Banff. If this Louisa Bullard was there, he would track her down somehow or other.

To his own surprise, he enjoyed the trip greatly. It was many years since he had taken a long sea voyage. The Riviera, Le Touquet and Deauville, and Scotland had been his usual round. The feeling that he was setting off on an impossible mission added a secret zest to his journey. What an utter fool these fellow travellers of his would think him did they but know the object of his quest! But then – they were not acquainted with Mr Quin.

In Banff he found his objective easily attained. Louisa Bullard was employed in the large Hotel there. Twelve hours after his arrival he was standing face to face with her.

She was a woman of about thirty-five, anaemic looking, but

with a strong frame. She had pale brown hair inclined to curl, and a pair of honest brown eyes. She was, he thought, slightly stupid, but very trustworthy.

She accepted quite readily his statement that he had been asked to collect a few further facts from her about the tragedy at Deering Hill.

'I saw in the paper that Mr Martin Wylde had been convicted, sir. Very sad, it is, too.'

She seemed, however, to have no doubt as to his guilt.

'A nice young gentleman gone wrong. But though I wouldn't speak ill of the dead, it was her ladyship what led him on. Wouldn't leave him alone, she wouldn't. Well, they've both got their punishment. There's a text used to hang on my wall when I was a child, "God is not mocked," and it's very true. I knew something was going to happen that very evening – and sure enough it did.'

'How was that?' said Mr Satterthwaite.

'I was in my room, sir, changing my dress, and I happened to glance out of the window. There was a train going along, and the white smoke of it rose up in the air, and if you'll believe me it formed itself into the sign of a gigantic hand. A great white hand against the crimson of the sky. The fingers were crooked like, as though they were reaching out for something. It fair gave me a turn. "Did you ever now?" I said to myself. "That's a sign of something coming" – and sure enough at that very minute I heard the shot. "It's come," I said to myself, and I rushed downstairs and joined Carrie and the others who were in the hall, and we went into the music room and there she was, shot through the head – and the blood and everything. Horrible! I spoke up, I did, and told Sir George how I'd seen the sign beforehand, but he didn't seem to think much of it. An unlucky day, that was, I'd felt it in my bones from early in the morning. Friday, and the 13th – what could you expect?'

She rambled on. Mr Satterthwaite was patient. Again and again he took her back to the crime, questioning her closely. In the end he was forced to confess defeat. Louisa Bullard had told all she knew, and her story was perfectly simple and straightforward.

Yet he did discover one fact of importance. The post in question had been suggested to her by Mr Thompson, Sir George's secretary. The wages attached were so large that she was tempted, and accepted the job, although it involved her leaving England very hurriedly. A Mr Denman had made all the arrangements this end and had also warned her not to write to her fellow-servants in England, as this might 'get her into trouble with the immigration authorities,' which statement she had accepted in blind faith.

The amount of wages, casually mentioned by her, was indeed so large that Mr Satterthwaite was startled. After some hesitation he made up his mind to approach this Mr Denman.

He found very little difficulty in inducing Mr Denman to tell all he knew. The latter had come across Thompson in London and Thompson had done him a good turn. The secretary had written to him in September saying that for personal reasons Sir George was anxious to get this girl out of England. Could he find her a job? A sum of money had been sent to raise the wages to a high figure.

'Usual trouble, I guess,' said Mr Denman, leaning back nonchalantly in his chair. 'Seems a nice quiet girl, too.'

Mr Satterthwaite did not agree that this was the usual trouble. Louisa Bullard, he was sure, was not a cast-off fancy of Sir George Barnaby's. For some reason it had been vital to get her out of England. But why? And who was at the bottom of it? Sir George himself, working through Thompson? Or the latter working on his own initiative, and dragging in his employer's name?

Still pondering over these questions, Mr Satterthwaite made the return journey. He was cast down and despondent. His journey had done no good.

Smarting under a sense of failure, he made his way to the *Arlecchino* the day after his return. He hardly expected to be successful the first time, but to his satisfaction the familiar figure was sitting at the table in the recess, and the dark face of Mr Harley Quin smiled a welcome.

'Well,' said Mr Satterthwaite as he helped himself to a pat of butter, 'you sent me on a nice wild-goose chase.'

Mr Quin raised his eyebrows.

'I sent you?' he objected. 'It was your own idea entirely.'

'Whosever idea it was, it's not succeeded. Louisa Bullard has nothing to tell.'

Thereupon Mr Satterthwaite related the details of his conversation with the housemaid and then went on to his interview with Mr Denman. Mr Quin listened in silence.

'In one sense, I was justified,' continued Mr Satterthwaite. 'She was deliberately got out of the way. But why? I can't see it.'

'No?' said Mr Quin, and his voice was, as ever, provocative.

Mr Satterthwaite flushed.

'I daresay you think I might have questioned her more adroitly. I can assure you that I took her over the story again and again. It was not my fault that I did not get what we want.'

'Are you sure,' said Mr Quin, 'that you did not get what you want?'

Mr Satterthwaite looked up at him in astonishment, and met that sad, mocking gaze he knew so well.

The little man shook his head, slightly bewildered.

There was a silence, and then Mr Quin said, with a total change of manner:

'You gave me a wonderful picture the other day of the people in this business. In a few words you made them stand out as clearly as though they were etched. I wish you would do something of that kind for the place – you left that in shadow.'

Mr Satterthwaite was flattered.

'The place? Deering Hill? Well, it's a very ordinary sort of house nowadays. Red brick, you know, and bay windows. Quite hideous outside, but very comfortable inside. Not a very large house. About two acres of ground. They're all much the same, those houses round the links. Built for rich men to live in. The inside of the house is reminiscent of a hotel – the bedrooms are like hotel suites. Baths and hot and cold basins in all the bedrooms and a good many gilded electric-light fittings. All wonderfully comfortable, but not very country-like. You can tell that Deering Vale is only nineteen miles from London.'

Mr Quin listened attentively.

'The train service is bad, I have heard,' he remarked.

'Oh! I don't know about that,' said Mr Satterthwaite, warming to his subject. 'I was down there for a bit last summer. I found it quite convenient for town. Of course the trains only go every hour. 48 minutes past the hour from Waterloo – up to 10.48.'

'And how long does it take to Deering Vale?'

'Just about three quarters of an hour. 28 minutes past the hour at Deering Vale.'

'Of course,' said Mr Quin with a gesture of vexation. 'I should have remembered. Miss Dale saw someone off by the 6.28 that evening, didn't she?'

Mr Satterthwaite did not reply for a minute or two. His mind had gone back with a rush to his unsolved problem. Presently he said:

'I wish you would tell me what you meant just now when you asked me if I was sure I had not got what I wanted?'

It sounded rather complicated, put that way, but Mr Quin made no pretence of not understanding.

'I just wondered if you weren't being a little too exacting. After all, you found out that Louisa Bullard was deliberately got out of the country. That being so, there must be a reason. And the reason must lie in what she said to you.'

'Well,' said Mr Satterthwaite argumentatively. 'What did she say? If she'd given evidence at the trial, what could she have said?'

'She might have told what she saw,' said Mr Quin.

'What did she see?'

'A sign in the sky.'

Mr Satterthwaite stared at him.

'Are you thinking of *that* nonsense? That superstitious notion of its being the hand of God?'

'Perhaps,' said Mr Quin, 'for all you and I know it may have been the hand of God, you know.'

The other was clearly puzzled at the gravity of his manner.

'Nonsense,' he said. 'She said herself it was the smoke of the train.'

'An up train or a down train, I wonder?' murmured Mr Quin.

'Hardly an up train. They go at ten minutes to the hour. It must have been a down train – the 6.28 – no, that won't do. She said the shot came immediately afterwards, and we know the shot was fired at twenty minutes past six. The train couldn't have been ten minutes early.'

'Hardly, on that line,' agreed Mr Quin.

Mr Satterthwaite was staring ahead of him.

'Perhaps a goods train,' he murmured. 'But surely, if so –'

'There would have been no need to get her out of England. I agree,' said Mr Quin.

Mr Satterthwaite gazed at him, fascinated.

'The 6.28,' he said slowly. 'But if so, if the shot was fired then, why did everyone say it was earlier?'

'Obvious,' said Mr Quin. 'The clocks must have been wrong.'

'All of them?' said Mr Satterthwaite doubtfully. 'That's a pretty tall coincidence, you know.'

'I wasn't thinking of it as a coincidence,' said the other. 'I was thinking it was Friday.'

'Friday?' said Mr Satterthwaite.

'You did tell me, you know, that Sir George always wound the clocks on a Friday afternoon,' said Mr Quin apologetically.

'He put them back ten minutes,' said Mr Satterthwaite, almost in a whisper, so awed was he by the discoveries he was making. 'Then he went out to bridge. I think he must have opened the note from his wife to Martin Wylde that morning – yes, decidedly he opened it. He left his bridge party at 6.30, found Martin's gun standing by the side door, and went in and shot her from behind. Then he went out again, threw the gun into the bushes where it was found later, and was apparently just coming out of the neighbour's gate when someone came running to fetch him. But the telephone – what about the telephone? Ah! yes, I see. He disconnected it so that a summons could not be sent to the police that way – they might have noted the time it was received. And Wylde's story works out now. The real time he left was five and twenty minutes past six. Walking slowly, he would reach home about a quarter to seven. Yes, I see it all. Louisa was the only danger with her endless talk about her superstitious fancies. Someone might realize the significance of the train and then – goodbye to that excellent *alibi*.'

'Wonderful,' commented Mr Quin.

Mr Satterthwaite turned to him, flushed with success.

'The only thing is – how to proceed now?'

'I should suggest Sylvia Dale,' said Mr Quin.

Mr Satterthwaite looked doubtful.

'I mentioned to you,' he said, 'she seemed to me a little – er – stupid.'

'She has a father and brothers who will take the necessary steps.'

'That is true,' said Mr Satterthwaite, relieved.

A very short time afterwards he was sitting with the girl telling her the story. She listened attentively. She put no questions to him but when he had done she rose.

'I must have a taxi – at once.'

'My dear child, what are you going to do?'

'I am going to Sir George Barnaby.'

'Impossible. Absolutely the wrong procedure. Allow me to –'

He twittered on by her side. But he produced no impression. Sylvia Dale was intent on her own plans. She allowed him to go with her in the taxi, but to all his remonstrances she addressed a deaf ear. She left him in the taxi while she went into Sir George's city office.

It was half an hour later when she came out. She looked exhausted, her fair beauty drooping like a waterless flower. Mr Satterthwaite received her with concern.

'I've won,' she murmured, as she leant back with half-closed eyes.

'What?' He was startled. 'What did you do? What did you say?'

She sat up a little.

'I told him that Louisa Bullard had been to the police with her story. I told him that the police had made inquiries and that he had been seen going into his own grounds and out again a few minutes after half-past six. I told him that the game was up. He – he went to pieces. I told him that there was still time for him to get away, that the police weren't coming for another hour to arrest him. I told him that if he'd sign a confession that he'd killed Vivien I'd do nothing, but that if he didn't I'd scream and tell the whole building the truth. He was so panicky that he didn't know what he was doing. He signed the paper without realizing what he was doing.'

She thrust it into his hands.

'Take it – take it. You know what to do with it so that they'll set Martin free.'

'He actually signed it,' cried Mr Satterthwaite, amazed.

'He is a little stupid, you know,' said Sylvia Dale. 'So am I,' she added as an afterthought. 'That's why I know how stupid people behave. We get rattled, you know, and then we do the wrong thing and are sorry afterwards.'

She shivered and Mr Satterthwaite patted her hand.

'You need something to pull you together,' he said. 'Come, we are close to a very favourite resort of mine – the *Arlecchino*. Have you ever been there?'

She shook her head.

Mr Satterthwaite stopped the taxi and took the girl into the little restaurant. He made his way to the table in the recess, his heart beating hopefully. But the table was empty.

Sylvia Dale saw the disappointment in his face.

'What is it?' she asked.

'Nothing,' said Mr Satterthwaite. 'That is, I half expected to see a friend of mine here. It doesn't matter. Some day, I expect, I shall see him again . . .'

CHAPTER V

The Soul of the Croupier

Mr Satterthwaite was enjoying the sunshine on the terrace at Monte Carlo.

Every year regularly on the second Sunday in January, Mr Satterthwaite left England for the Riviera. He was far more punctual than any swallow. In the month of April he returned to England, May and June he spent in London, and had never been known to miss Ascot. He left town after the Eton and Harrow match, paying a few country house visits before repairing to Deauville or Le Touquet. Shooting parties occupied most of September and October, and he usually spent a couple of months in town to wind up the year. He knew everybody and it may safely be said that everybody knew him.

This morning he was frowning. The blue of the sea was admirable, the gardens were, as always, a delight, but the people disappointed him – he thought them an ill-dressed, shoddy crowd. Some, of course, were gamblers, doomed souls who could not keep away. Those Mr Satterthwaite tolerated. They were a necessary background. But he missed the usual leaven of the *élite* – his own people.

'It's the exchange,' said Mr Satterthwaite gloomily. 'All sort of people come here now who could never have afforded it before. And then, of course, I'm getting old . . . All the young people – the people coming on – they go to these Swiss places.'

But there were others that he missed, the well-dressed Barons and Counts of foreign diplomacy, the Grand Dukes and the Royal Princes. The only Royal Prince he had seen so far was working a lift in one of the less well-known hotels. He missed, too, the beautiful and expensive ladies. There was still a few of them, but not nearly as many as there used to be.

Mr Satterthwaite was an earnest student of the drama called Life, but he liked his material to be highly coloured. He felt discouragement sweep over him. Values were changing – and he – was too old to change.

It was at that moment that he observed the Countess Czarnova coming towards him.

Mr Satterthwaite had seen the Countess at Monte Carlo for many seasons now. The first time he had seen her she had been in the company of a Grand Duke. On the next occasion she was with an Austrian Baron. In successive years her friends had been of Hebraic extraction, sallow men with hooked noses, wearing rather flamboyant jewellery. For the last year or two she was much seen with very young men, almost boys.

She was walking with a very young man now. Mr Satterthwaite happened to know him, and he was sorry. Franklin Rudge was a young American, a typical product of one of the Middle West States, eager to register impression, crude, but loveable, a curious mixture of native shrewdness and idealism. He was in Monte Carlo with a party of other young Americans of both sexes, all much of the same type. It was their first glimpse of the Old World and they were outspoken in criticism and in appreciation.

On the whole they disliked the English people in the hotel, and the English people disliked them. Mr Satterthwaite, who prided himself on being a cosmopolitan, rather liked them. Their directness and vigour appealed to him, though their occasional solecisms made him shudder.

It occurred to him that the Countess Czarnova was a most unsuitable friend for young Franklin Rudge.

He took off his hat politely as they came abreast of him, and the Countess gave him a charming bow and smile.

She was a very tall woman, superbly made. Her hair was black, so were her eyes, and her eyelashes and eyebrows were more superbly black than any Nature had ever fashioned.

Mr Satterthwaite, who knew far more of feminine secrets than it is good for any man to know, rendered immediate homage to the art with which she was made up. Her complexion appeared to be flawless, of a uniform creamy white.

The very faint bistre shadows under her eyes were most effective. Her mouth was neither crimson nor scarlet, but a subdued wine colour. She was dressed in a very daring creation of black and white and carried a parasol of the shade of pinky red which is most helpful to the complexion.

Franklin Rudge was looking happy and important.

'There goes a young fool,' said Mr Satterthwaite to himself. 'But I suppose it's no business of mine and anyway he wouldn't listen to me. Well, well, I've bought experience myself in my time.'

But he still felt rather worried, because there was a very attractive little American girl in the party, and he was sure that she would not like Franklin Rudge's friendship with the Countess at all.

He was just about to retrace his steps in the opposite direction when he caught sight of the girl in question coming up one of the paths towards him. She wore a well-cut tailor-made 'suit' with a white muslin shirt waist, she had on good, sensible walking shoes, and carried a guide-book. There are some Americans who pass through Paris and emerge clothed as the Queen of Sheba, but Elizabeth Martin was not one of them. She was 'doing Europe' in a stern, conscientious spirit. She had high ideas of culture and art and she was anxious to get as much as possible for her limited store of money.

It is doubtful if Mr Satterthwaite thought of her as either cultured or artistic. To him she merely appeared very young.

'Good morning, Mr Satterthwaite,' said Elizabeth. 'Have you seen Franklin – Mr Rudge – anywhere about?'

'I saw him just a few minutes ago.'

'With his friend the Countess, I suppose,' said the girl sharply.

'Er – with the Countess, yes,' admitted Mr Satterthwaite.

'That Countess of his doesn't cut any ice with me,' said the girl in a rather high, shrill voice. 'Franklin's just crazy about her. *Why* I can't think.'

'She's got a very charming manner, I believe,' said Mr Satterthwaite cautiously.

'Do you know her?'

'Slightly.'

'I'm right down worried about Franklin,' said Miss Martin. 'That boy's got a lot of sense as a rule. You'd never think he'd fall for this sort of siren stuff. And he won't hear a thing, he gets madder than a hornet if anyone tries to say a word to him. Tell me, anyway – is she a real Countess?'

'I shouldn't like to say,' said Mr Satterthwaite. 'She may be.'

'That's the real Ha Ha English manner,' said Elizabeth with signs of displeasure. 'All I can say is that in Sargon Springs – that's our home town, Mr Satterthwaite – that Countess would look a mighty queer bird.'

Mr Satterthwaite thought it possible. He forebore to point out that they were not in Sargon Springs but in the principality of Monaco, where the Countess happened to synchronize with her environment a great deal better than Miss Martin did.

He made no answer and Elizabeth went on towards the Casino. Mr Satterthwaite sat on a seat in the sun, and was presently joined by Franklin Rudge.

Rudge was full of enthusiasm.

'I'm enjoying myself,' he announced with naïve enthusiasm. 'Yes, sir! This is what I call seeing life – rather a different kind of life from what we have in the States.'

The elder man turned a thoughtful face to him.

'Life is lived very much the same everywhere,' he said rather wearily. 'It wears different clothes – that's all.'

Franklin Rudge stared.

'I don't get you.'

'No,' said Mr Satterthwaite. 'That's because you've got a long way to travel yet. But I apologize. No elderly man should permit himself to get into the habit of preaching.'

'Oh! that's all right.' Rudge laughed, displaying the beautiful teeth of all his countrymen. 'I don't say, mind you, that I'm not disappointed in the Casino. I thought the gambling would be different – something much more feverish. It seems just rather dull and sordid to me.'

'Gambling is life and death to the gambler, but it has no great spectacular value,' said Mr Satterthwaite. 'It is more exciting to read about than to see.'

The young man nodded his agreement.

'You're by way of being rather a big bug socially, aren't you?' he asked with a diffident candour that made it impossible to take offence. 'I mean, you know all the Duchesses and Earls and Countesses and things.'

'A good many of them,' said Mr Satterthwaite. 'And also the Jews and the Portuguese and the Greeks and the Argentines.'

'Eh?' said Mr Rudge.

'I was just explaining,' said Mr Satterthwaite, 'that I move in English society.'

Franklin Rudge meditated for a moment or two.

'You know the Countess Czarnova, don't you?' he said at length.

'Slightly,' said Mr Satterthwaite, making the same answer he had made to Elizabeth.

'Now there's a woman whom it's been very interesting to meet. One's inclined to think that the aristocracy of Europe is played out and effete. That may be true of the men, but the women are different. Isn't it a pleasure to meet an exquisite creature like the Countess? Witty, charming, intelligent, generations of civilization behind her, an aristocrat to her finger-tips!'

'Is she?' asked Mr Satterthwaite.

'Well, isn't she? You know what her family are?'

'No,' said Mr Satterthwaite. 'I'm afraid I know very little about her.'

'She was a Radzynski,' explained Franklin Rudge. 'One of the oldest families in Hungary. She's had the most extraordinary life. You know that great rope of pearls she wears?'

Mr Satterthwaite nodded.

'That was given her by the King of Bosnia. She smuggled some secret papers out of the kingdom for him.'

'I heard,' said Mr Satterthwaite, 'that the pearls had been given her by the King of Bosnia.'

The fact was indeed a matter of common gossip, it being

reported that the lady had been a *chère amie* of His Majesty's in days gone by.

'Now I'll tell you something more.'

Mr Satterthwaite listened, and the more he listened the more he admired the fertile imagination of the Countess Czarnova. No vulgar 'siren stuff' (as Elizabeth Martin had put it) for her. The young man was shrewd enough in that way, clean living and idealistic. No, the Countess moved austerely through a labyrinth of diplomatic intrigues. She had enemies, detractors – naturally! It was a glimpse, so the young American was made to feel, into the life of the old régime with the Countess as the central figure, aloof, aristocratic, the friend of counsellors and princes, a figure to inspire romantic devotion.

'And she's had any amount to contend against,' ended the young man warmly. 'It's an extraordinary thing but she's never found a woman who would be a real friend to her. Women have been against her all her life.'

'Probably,' said Mr Satterthwaite.

'Don't you call it a scandalous thing?' demanded Rudge hotly.

'N – no,' said Mr Satterthwaite thoughtfully. 'I don't know that I do. Women have got their own standards, you know. It's no good our mixing ourselves up in their affairs. They must run their own show.'

'I don't agree with you,' said Rudge earnestly. 'It's one of the worst things in the world today, the unkindness of woman to woman. You know Elizabeth Martin? Now she agrees with me in theory absolutely. We've often discussed it together. She's only a kid, but her ideas are all right. But the moment it comes to a practical test – why, she's as bad as any of them. Got a real down on the Countess without knowing a darned thing about her, and won't listen when I try to tell her things. It's all *wrong*, Mr Satterthwaite. I believe in democracy – and – what's that but brotherhood between men and sisterhood between women?'

He paused earnestly. Mr Satterthwaite tried to think of any circumstances in which a sisterly feeling might arise between the Countess and Elizabeth Martin and failed.

'Now the Countess, on the other hand,' went on Rudge,

'admires Elizabeth immensely, and thinks her charming in every way. Now what does that show?'

'It shows,' said Mr Satterthwaite dryly, 'that the Countess has lived a considerable time longer than Miss Martin has.'

Franklin Rudge went off unexpectedly at a tangent.

'Do you know how old she is? She told me. Rather sporting of her. I should have guessed her to be twenty-nine, but she told me of her own accord that she was thirty-five. She doesn't look it, does she?' Mr Satterthwaite, whose private estimate of the lady's age was between forty-five and forty-nine, merely raised his eyebrows.

'I should caution you against believing all you are told at Monte Carlo,' he murmured.

He had enough experience to know the futility of arguing with the lad. Franklin Rudge was at a pitch of white hot chivalry when he would have disbelieved any statement that was not backed with authoritative proof.

'Here is the Countess,' said the boy, rising.

She came up to them with the languid grace that so became her. Presently they all three sat down together. She was very charming to Mr Satterthwaite, but in rather an aloof manner. She deferred to him prettily, asking his opinion, and treating him as an authority on the Riviera.

The whole thing was cleverly managed. Very few minutes had elapsed before Franklin Rudge found himself gracefully but unmistakably dismissed, and the Countess and Mr Satterthwaite were left *tête-à-tête*.

She put down her parasol and began drawing patterns with it in the dust.

'You are interested in that nice American boy, Mr Satterthwaite, are you not?'

Her voice was low with a caressing note in it.

'He's a nice young fellow,' said Mr Satterthwaite, non-committally.

'I find him sympathetic, yes,' said the Countess reflectively. 'I have told him much of my life.'

'Indeed,' said Mr Satterthwaite.

'Details such as I have told to few others,' she continued dreamily. 'I have had an extraordinary life, Mr Satterthwaite. Few would credit the amazing things that have happened to me.'

Mr Satterthwaite was shrewd enough to penetrate her meaning. After all, the stories that she had told to Franklin Rudge *might* be the truth. It was extremely unlikely, and in the last degree improbable, but it was *possible* . . . No one could definitely say: 'That is not so –'

He did not reply, and the Countess continued to look out dreamily across the bay.

And suddenly Mr Satterthwaite had a strange and new impression of her. He saw her no longer as a harpy, but as a desperate creature at bay, fighting tooth and nail. He stole a sideways glance at her. The parasol was down, he could see the little haggard lines at the corners of her eyes. In one temple a pulse was beating.

It flowed through him again and again – that increasing certitude. She was a creature desperate and driven. She would be merciless to him or to anyone who stood between her and Franklin Rudge. But he still felt he hadn't got the hang of the situation. Clearly she had plenty of money. She was always beautifully dressed, and her jewels were marvellous. There could be no real urgency of that kind. Was it love? Women of her age did, he well knew, fall in love with boys. It might be that. There was, he felt sure, something out of the common about the situation.

Her *tête-à-tête* with him was, he recognized, a throwing down of the gauntlet. She had singled him out as her chief enemy. He felt sure that she hoped to goad him into speaking slightingly of her to Franklin Rudge. Mr Satterthwaite smiled to himself. He was too old a bird for that. He knew when it was wise to hold one's tongue.

He watched her that night in the Cercle Privé, as she tried her fortunes at roulette.

Again and again she staked, only to see her stake swept away. She bore her losses well, with the stoical *sang froid* of the old *habitué.* She staked *en plein* once or twice, put the maximum on red, won a little on the middle dozen and then lost it again, finally she backed *manque* six times and lost every time. Then with a little graceful shrug of the shoulders she turned away.

She was looking unusually striking in a dress of gold tissue with an underlying note of green. The famous Bosnian pearls were looped round her neck and long pearl ear-rings hung from her ears.

Mr Satterthwaite heard two men near him appraise her.

'The Czarnova,' said one, 'she wears well, does she not? The Crown jewels of Bosnia look fine on her.'

The other, a small Jewish-looking man, stared curiously after her.

'So those are the pearls of Bosnia, are they?' he asked. '*En vérité.* That is odd.'

He chuckled softly to himself.

Mr Satterthwaite missed hearing more, for at the moment he turned his head and was overjoyed to recognize an old friend.

'My dear Mr Quin.' He shook him warmly by the hand. 'The last place I should ever have dreamed of seeing you.'

Mr Quin smiled, his dark attractive face lighting up.

'It should not surprise you,' he said. 'It is Carnival time. I am often here in Carnival time.'

'Really? Well, this is a great pleasure. Are you anxious to remain in the rooms? I find them rather warm.'

'It will be pleasanter outside,' agreed the other. 'We will walk in the gardens.'

The air outside was sharp, but not chill. Both men drew deep breaths.

'That is better,' said Mr Satterthwaite.

'Much better,' agreed Mr Quin. 'And we can talk freely. I am sure that there is much that you want to tell me.'

'There is indeed.'

Speaking eagerly, Mr Satterthwaite unfolded his perplexities. As usual he took pride in his power of conveying atmosphere. The Countess, young Franklin, uncompromising Elizabeth – he sketched them all in with a deft touch.

'You have changed since I first knew you,' said Mr Quin, smiling, when the recital was over.

'In what way?'

'You were content then to look on at the drama that life offered. Now – you want to take part – to act.'

'It is true,' confessed Mr Satterthwaite. 'But in this case I do not know what to do. It is all very perplexing. Perhaps –' He hesitated. 'Perhaps you will help me?'

'With pleasure,' said Mr Quin. 'We will see what we can do.'

Mr Satterthwaite had an odd sense of comfort and reliance.

The following day he introduced Franklin Rudge and Elizabeth Martin to his friend Mr Harley Quin. He was pleased to see that they got on together. The Countess was not mentioned, but at lunch time he heard news that aroused his attention.

'Mirabelle is arriving in Monte this evening,' he confided excitedly to Mr Quin.

'The Parisian stage favourite?'

'Yes. I daresay you know – it's common property – she is the King of Bosnia's latest craze. He has showered jewels on her, I believe. They say she is the most exacting and extravagant woman in Paris.'

'It should be interesting to see her and the Countess Czarnova meet tonight.'

'Exactly what I thought.'

Mirabelle was a tall, thin creature with a wonderful head of dyed fair hair. Her complexion was a pale mauve with orange lips. She was amazingly chic. She was dressed in something that looked like a glorified bird of paradise, and she wore chains of jewels hanging down her bare back. A heavy bracelet set with immense diamonds clasped her left ankle.

She created a sensation when she appeared in the Casino.

'Your friend the Countess will have a difficulty in outdoing this,' murmured Mr Quin in Mr Satterthwaite's ear.

The latter nodded. He was curious to see how the Countess comported herself.

She came late, and a low murmur ran round as she walked unconcernedly to one of the centre roulette tables.

She was dressed in white – a mere straight slip of marocain such as a débutante might have worn and her gleaming white neck and arms were unadorned. She wore not a single jewel.

'It is clever, that,' said Mr Satterthwaite with instant approval. 'She disdains rivalry and turns the tables on her adversary.'

He himself walked over and stood by the table. From time to time he amused himself by placing a stake. Sometimes he won, more often he lost.

There was a terrific run on the last dozen. The numbers 31 and 34 turned up again and again. Stakes flocked to the bottom of the cloth.

With a smile Mr Satterthwaite made his last stake for the evening, and placed the maximum on Number 5.

The Countess in her turn leant forward and placed the maximum on Number 6.

'*Faites vos jeux,*' called the croupier hoarsely. '*Rien ne va plus. Plus rien.*'

The ball span, humming merrily. Mr Satterthwaite thought to himself: '*This means something different to each of us. Agonies of hope and despair, boredom, idle amusement, life and death.*'

Click!

The croupier bent forward to see.

'*Numéro cinque, rouge, impair et manque.*'

Mr Satterthwaite had won!

The croupier, having raked in the other stakes, pushed forward Mr Satterthwaite's winnings. He put out his hand to take them. The Countess did the same. The croupier looked from one to the other of them.

'*A Madame,*' he said brusquely.

The Countess picked up the money. Mr Satterthwaite drew back. He remained a gentleman. The Countess looked him full in the face and he returned her glance. One or two of the people round pointed out to the croupier that he had made a mistake, but the man shook his head impatiently. He had decided. That was the end. He raised his raucous cry:

'*Faites vos jeux, Messieurs et Mesdames.*'

Mr Satterthwaite rejoined Mr Quin. Beneath his impeccable

demeanour, he was feeling extremely indignant. Mr Quin
listened sympathetically.

'Too bad,' he said, 'but these things happen.

'We are to meet your friend Franklin Rudge later. I am giving
a little supper party.'

The three met at midnight, and Mr Quin explained his plan.

'It is what is called a "Hedges and Highways" party,' he
explained. 'We choose our meeting place, then each one goes
out and is bound in honour to invite the first person he meets.'

Franklin Rudge was amused by the idea.

'Say, what happens if they won't accept?'

'You must use your utmost powers of persuasion.'

'Good. And where's the meeting place?'

'A somewhat Bohemian café – where one can take strange
guests. It is called Le Caveau.'

He explained its whereabouts, and the three parted. Mr Satterthwaite was so fortunate as to run straight into Elizabeth
Martin and he claimed her joyfully. They reached Le Caveau
and descended into a kind of cellar where they found a table
spread for supper and lit by old-fashioned candles in candlesticks.

'We are the first,' said Mr Satterthwaite. 'Ah! here comes
Franklin –'

He stopped abruptly. With Franklin was the Countess. It was
an awkward moment. Elizabeth displayed less graciousness than
she might have done. The Countess, as a woman of the world,
retained the honours.

Last of all came Mr Quin. With him was a small, dark man,
neatly dressed, whose face seemed familiar to Mr Satterthwaite.
A moment later he recognized him. It was the croupier who
earlier in the evening had made such a lamentable mistake.

'Let me introduce you to the company, M. Pierre Vaucher,'
said Mr Quin.

The little man seemed confused. Mr Quin performed the
necessary introductions easily and lightly. Supper was brought
– an excellent supper. Wine came – very excellent wine. Some
of the frigidity went out of the atmosphere. The Countess was

very silent, so was Elizabeth. Franklin Rudge became talkative. He told various stories – not humorous stories, but serious ones. And quietly and assiduously Mr Quin passed round the wine.

'I'll tell you – and this is a true story – about a man who made good,' said Franklin Rudge impressively.

For one coming from a Prohibition country he had shown no lack of appreciation of champagne.

He told his story – perhaps at somewhat unnecessary length. It was, like many true stories, greatly inferior to fiction.

As he uttered the last word, Pierre Vaucher, opposite him, seemed to wake up. He also had done justice to the champagne. He leaned forward across the table.

'I, too, will tell you a story,' he said thickly. 'But mine is the story of a man who did not make good. It is the story of a man who went, not up, but down the hill. And, like yours, it is a true story.'

'Pray tell it to us, monsieur,' said Mr Satterthwaite courteously.

Pierre Vaucher leant back in his chair and looked at the ceiling.

'It is in Paris that the story begins. There was a man there, a working jeweller. He was young and light-hearted and industrious in his profession. They said there was a future before him. A good marriage was already arranged for him, the bride not too bad-looking, the dowry most satisfactory. And then, what do you think? One morning he sees a girl. Such a miserable little wisp of a girl, messieurs. Beautiful? Yes, perhaps, if she were not half starved. But anyway, for this young man, she has a magic that he cannot resist. She has been struggling to find work, she is virtuous – or at least that is what she tells him. I do not know if it is true.'

The Countess's voice came suddenly out of the semi-darkness.

'Why should it not be true? There are many like that.'

'Well, as I say, the young man believed her. And he married her – an act of folly! His family would have no more to say to him. He had outraged their feelings. He married – I will call her Jeanne – it was a good action. He told her so. He felt that she should be very grateful to him. He had sacrificed much for her sake.'

'A charming beginning for the poor girl,' observed the Countess sarcastically.

'He loved her, yes, but from the beginning she maddened him. She had moods – tantrums – she would be cold to him one day, passionate the next. At last he saw the truth. She had never loved him. She had married him so as to keep body and soul together. That truth hurt him, it hurt him horribly, but he tried his utmost to let nothing appear on the surface. And he still felt he deserved gratitude and obedience to his wishes. They quarrelled. She reproached him – Mon Dieu, what did she not reproach him with?

'You can see the next step, can you not? The thing that was bound to come. She left him. For two years he was alone, working in his little shop with no news of her. He had one friend – absinthe. The business did not prosper so well.

'And then one day he came into the shop to find her sitting there. She was beautifully dressed. She had rings on her hands. He stood considering her. His heart was beating – but beating! He was at a loss what to do. He would have liked to have beaten her, to have clasped her in his arms, to have thrown her down on the floor and trampled on her, to have thrown himself at her feet. He did none of those things. He took up his pincers and went on with his work. "Madame desires?" he asked formally.

'That upset her. She did not look for that, see you. "Pierre," she said. "I have come back." He laid aside his pincers and looked at her. "You wish to be forgiven?" he said. "You want me to take you back? You are sincerely repentant?" "Do you want me back?" she murmured. Oh! very softly she said it.

'He knew she was laying a trap for him. He longed to seize her in his arms, but he was too clever for that. He pretended indifference.

'"I am a Christian man," he said. "I try to do what the Church directs." "Ah!" he thought, "I will humble her, humble her to her knees."

'But Jeanne, that is what I will call her, flung back her head and laughed. Evil laughter it was. "I mock myself at you, little Pierre," she said. "Look at these rich clothes, these rings and bracelets. I came to show myself to you. I thought I would make you take me in your arms and when you did so, then – *then* I would spit in your face and tell you how I hated you!"'

'And on that she went out of the shop. Can you believe, messieurs, that a woman could be as evil as all that – to come back only to torment me?'

'No,' said the Countess. 'I would not believe it, and any man who was not a fool would not believe it either. But all men are blind fools.'

Pierre Vaucher took no notice of her. He went on.

'And so that young man of whom I tell you sank lower and lower. He drank more absinthe. The little shop was sold over his head. He became of the dregs, of the gutter. Then came the war. Ah! it was good, the war. It took that man out of the gutter and taught him to be a brute beast no longer. It drilled him – and sobered him. He endured cold and pain and the fear of death – but he did not die and when the war ended, he was a man again.

'It was then, messieurs, that he came South. His lungs had been affected by the gas, they said he must find work in the South. I will not weary you with all the things he did. Suffice it to say that he ended up as a croupier, and there – there in the Casino one evening, he saw her again – the woman who had ruined his life. She did not recognize him, but he recognized her. She appeared to be rich and to lack for nothing – but messieurs, the eyes of a croupier are sharp. There came an evening when she placed her last stake in the world on the table. Ask me not how I know – I do know – one feels these things. Others might not believe. She still had rich clothes – why not pawn them, one would say? But to do that – pah! your credit is gone at once. Her jewels? Ah no! Was I not a jeweller in my time? Long ago the real jewels have gone. The pearls of a King are sold one by one, are replaced with false. And meantime one must eat and pay one's hotel bill. Yes, and the rich men – well, they have seen one about for many years. Bah! they say – she is over fifty. A younger chicken for my money.'

A long shuddering sigh came out of the windows where the Countess leant back.

'Yes. It was a great moment, that. Two nights I have watched her. Lose, lose, and lose again. And now the end. She put all on one number. Beside her, an English milord stakes the maximum also – on the next number. The ball rolls . . . The moment has come, she has lost . . .

'Her eyes meet mine. What do I do? I jeopardize my place in the Casino. I rob the English milord. "*A Madame*" I say, and pay over the money.'

'Ah!' There was a crash, as the Countess sprang to her feet and leant across the table, sweeping her glass on to the floor.

'Why?' she cried. 'That's what I want to know, *why* did you do it?'

There was a long pause, a pause that seemed interminable, and still those two facing each other across the table looked and looked . . . It was like a duel.

A mean little smile crept across Pierre Vaucher's face. He raised his hands.

'Madame,' he said, 'there is such a thing as pity . . .'

'Ah!'

She sank down again.

'I see.'

She was calm, smiling, herself again.

'An interesting story, M. Vaucher, is it not? Permit me to give you a light for your cigarette.'

She deftly rolled up a spill, and lighted it at the candle and held it towards him. He leaned forward till the flame caught the tip of the cigarette he held between his lips.

Then she rose unexpectedly to her feet.

'And now I must leave you all. Please – I need no one to escort me.'

Before one could realize it she was gone. Mr Satterthwaite would have hurried out after her, but he was arrested by a startled oath from the Frenchman.

'*A thousand thunders!*'

He was staring at the half-burned spill which the Countess had dropped on the table. He unrolled it.

'*Mon Dieu!*' he muttered. 'A fifty thousand franc bank note. You understand? Her winnings tonight. All that she had in the world. And she lighted my cigarette with it! Because she was too proud to accept – pity. Ah! proud, she was always proud as the Devil. She is unique – wonderful.'

He sprang up from his seat and darted out. Mr Satterthwaite and Mr Quin had also risen. The waiter approached Franklin Rudge.

'*La note, monsieur,*' he observed unemotionally.

Mr Quin rescued it from him quickly.

'I feel kind of lonesome, Elizabeth,' remarked Franklin Rudge. 'These foreigners – they beat the band! I don't understand them. What's it all mean, anyhow?'

He looked across at her.

'Gee, it's good to look at anything so hundred per cent American as you.' His voice took on the plaintive note of a small child. 'These foreigners are so *odd.*'

They thanked Mr Quin and went out into the night together. Mr Quin picked up his change and smiled across at Mr Satterthwaite, who was preening himself like a contented bird.

'Well,' said the latter. 'That's all gone off splendidly. Our pair of love birds will be all right now.'

'Which ones?' asked Mr Quin.

'Oh!' said Mr Satterthwaite, taken aback. 'Oh! yes, well, I suppose you are right, allowing for the Latin point of view and all that –'

He looked dubious.

Mr Quin smiled, and a stained glass panel behind him invested him for just a moment in a motley garment of coloured light.

CHAPTER VI

The Man from the Sea

Mr Satterthwaite was feeling old. That might not have been surprising since in the estimation of many people he *was* old. Careless youths said to their partners: 'Old Satterthwaite? Oh! he must be a hundred – or at any rate about eighty.' And even the kindest of girls said indulgently, 'Oh! Satterthwaite. Yes, he's quite old. He *must* be sixty.' Which was almost worse, since he was sixty-nine.

In his own view, however, he was not old. Sixty-nine was an interesting age – an age of infinite possibilities – an age when at last the experience of a lifetime was beginning to tell. But to feel old – that was different, a tired discouraged state of mind when one was inclined to ask oneself depressing questions. What was he after all? A little dried-up elderly man, with neither chick nor child, with no human belongings, only a valuable Art collection which seemed at the moment strangely unsatisfying. No one to care whether he lived or died . . .

At this point in his meditations Mr Satterthwaite pulled himself up short. What he was thinking was morbid and unprofitable. He knew well enough, who better, that the chances were that a wife would have hated him or alternatively that he would have hated her, that children would have been a constant source of worry and anxiety, and that demands upon his time and affection would have worried him considerably.

'To be safe and comfortable,' said Mr Satterthwaite firmly – that was the thing.

The last thought reminded him of a letter he had received that morning. He drew it from his pocket and re-read it, savouring its contents pleasurably. To begin with, it was from a Duchess, and Mr Satterthwaite liked hearing from Duchesses. It is true that the letter began by demanding a large subscription for charity and but for that would probably never have been written, but the terms in which it was couched were so agreeable that Mr Satterthwaite was able to gloss over the first fact.

So you've deserted the Riviera, wrote the Duchess. *What is this island of yours like? Cheap? Cannotti put up his prices shamefully this year, and I shan't go to the Riviera again. I might try your island next year if you report favourably, though I should hate five days on a boat. Still anywhere you recommend is sure to be pretty comfortable – too much so. You'll get to be one of those people who do nothing but coddle themselves and think of their comfort. There's only one thing that will save you, Satterthwaite, and that is your inordinate interest in other people's affairs . . .*

As Mr Satterthwaite folded the letter, a vision came up vividly before him of the Duchess. Her meanness, her unexpected and alarming kindness, her caustic tongue, her indomitable spirit.

Spirit! Everyone needed spirit. He drew out another letter with a German stamp upon it – written by a young singer in whom he had interested himself. It was a grateful affectionate letter.

'*How can I thank you, dear Mr Satterthwaite? It seems too wonderful to think that in a few days I shall be singing Isolde . . .*'

A pity that she had to make her *début* as Isolde. A charming, hardworking child, Olga, with a beautiful voice but no temperament. He hummed to himself. '*Nay order him! Pray understand it! I command it. I, Isolde.*' No, the child hadn't got it in her – the spirit – the indomitable will – all expressed in that final 'Ich Isoldé!'

Well, at any rate he had done something for somebody. This island depressed him – why, oh! why had he deserted the Riviera which he knew so well and where he was so well known? Nobody here took any interest in him. Nobody seemed to realize that here was *the* Mr Satterthwaite – the friend of Duchesses and Countesses and singers and writers. No one in the island was of any social importance or of any artistic importance either. Most people had been there seven, fourteen, or twenty-one years running and valued themselves and were valued accordingly.

With a deep sigh Mr Satterthwaite proceeded down from the Hotel to the small straggling harbour below. His way lay between an avenue of bougainvillaea – a vivid mass of flaunting scarlet, that made him feel older and greyer than ever.

'I'm getting old,' he murmured. 'I'm getting old and tired.'

He was glad when he had passed the bougainvillaea and was walking down the white street with the blue sea at the end of it. A disreputable dog was standing in the middle of the road, yawning and stretching himself in the sun. Having prolonged his stretch to the utmost limits of ecstasy, he sat down and treated himself to a really good scratch. He then rose, shook himself, and looked round for any other good things that life might have to offer.

There was a dump of rubbish by the side of the road and to this he went sniffing in pleasurable anticipation. True enough, his nose had not deceived him! A smell of such rich putrescence that surpassed even his anticipations! He sniffed with growing appreciation, then suddenly abandoning himself, he lay on his back and rolled frenziedly on the delicious dump. Clearly the world this morning was a dog paradise!

Tiring at last, he regained his feet and strolled out once more into the middle of the road. And then, without the least warning, a ramshackle car careered wildly round the corner, caught him full square and passed on unheeding.

The dog rose to his feet, stood a minute regarding Mr Satterthwaite, a vague dumb reproach in his eyes, then fell over. Mr Satterthwaite went up to him and bent down. The dog was dead. He went on his way, wondering at the sadness and cruelty of life. What a queer dumb look of reproach had been in the dog's eyes. 'Oh! World,' they seemed to say. 'Oh! Wonderful World in which I have trusted. Why have you done this to me?'

Mr Satterthwaite went on, past the palm trees and the straggling white houses, past the black lava beach where the surf thundered and where once, long ago, a well-known English swimmer had been carried out to sea and drowned, past the rock pools where children and elderly ladies bobbed up and down and called it bathing, along the steep road that winds upwards to the top of the cliff. For there on the edge of the cliff was a house, appropriately named La Paz. A white house with faded green shutters tightly closed, a tangled beautiful garden, and a walk between cypress trees that led to a plateau on the edge of the cliff where you looked down – down – down – to the deep blue sea below.

It was to this spot that Mr Satterthwaite was bound. He had developed a great love for the garden of La Paz. He had never entered the villa. It seemed always to be empty. Manuel, the Spanish gardener, wished one good-morning with a flourish and gallantly presented ladies with a bouquet and gentlemen with a single flower as a buttonhole, his dark face wreathed in smiles.

Sometimes Mr Satterthwaite made up stories in his own mind about the owner of the villa. His favourite was a Spanish dancer, once world-famed for her beauty, who hid herself here so that the world should never know that she was no longer beautiful.

He pictured her coming out of the house at dusk and walking through the garden. Sometimes he was tempted to ask Manuel for the truth, but he resisted the temptation. He preferred his fancies.

After exchanging a few words with Manuel and graciously accepting an orange rosebud, Mr Satterthwaite passed on down the cypress walk to the sea. It was rather wonderful sitting there – on the edge of nothing – with that sheer drop below one. It made him think of Tristan and Isolde, of the beginning of the third act with Tristan and Kurwenal – that lonely waiting and of Isolde rushing up from the sea and Tristan dying in her arms. (No, little Olga would never make an Isolde. Isolde of Cornwall, that Royal hater and Royal lover . . .) He shivered. He felt old, chilly, alone . . . What had he had out of life? Nothing – nothing. Not as much as that dog in the street . . .

It was an unexpected sound that roused him from his reverie. Footsteps coming along the cypress walk were inaudible, the first he knew of somebody's presence was the English monosyllable 'Damn.'

He looked round to find a young man staring at him in

obvious surprise and disappointment. Mr Satterthwaite recognized him at once as an arrival of the day before who had more or less intrigued him. Mr Satterthwaite called him a young man – because in comparison to most of the die-hards in the Hotel he *was* a young man, but he would certainly never see forty again and was probably drawing appreciably near to his half century. Yet in spite of that, the term young man fitted him – Mr Satterthwaite was usually right about such things – there was an impression of immaturity about him. As there is a touch of puppyhood about many a full grown dog so it was with the stranger.

Mr Satterthwaite thought: 'This chap has really never grown up – not properly, that is.'

And yet there was nothing Peter Pannish about him. He was sleek – almost plump, he had the air of one who has always done himself exceedingly well in the material sense and denied himself no pleasure or satisfaction. He had brown eyes – rather round – fair hair turning grey – a little moustache and rather florid face.

The thing that puzzled Mr Satterthwaite was what had brought him to the island. He could imagine him shooting things, hunting things, playing polo or golf or tennis, making love to pretty women. But in the Island there was nothing to hunt or shoot, no games except Golf-Croquet, and the nearest approach to a pretty woman was represented by elderly Miss Baba Kindersley. There were, of course, artists, to whom the beauty of the scenery made appeal, but Mr Satterthwaite was quite certain that the young man was not an artist. He was clearly marked with the stamp of the Philistine.

While he was resolving these things in his mind, the other spoke, realizing somewhat belatedly that his single ejaculation so far might be open to criticism.

'I beg your pardon,' he said with some embarrassment. 'As a matter of fact, I was – well, startled. I didn't expect anyone to be here.'

He smiled disarmingly. He had a charming smile – friendly – appealing.

'It is rather a lonely spot,' agreed Mr Satterthwaite, as he moved politely a little further up the bench. The other accepted the mute invitation and sat down.

'I don't know about lonely,' he said. 'There always seems to be *someone* here.'

There was a tinge of latent resentment in his voice. Mr Satterthwaite wondered why. He read the other as a friendly soul. Why this insistence on solitude? A rendezvous, perhaps? No – not that. He looked again with carefully veiled scrutiny at his companion. Where had he seen that particular expression before quite lately? That look of dumb bewildered resentment.

'You've been up here before then?' said Mr Satterthwaite, more for the sake of saying something than for anything else.

'I was up here last night – after dinner.'

'Really? I thought the gates were always locked.'

There was a moment's pause and then, almost sullenly, the young man said:

'I climbed over the wall.'

Mr Satterthwaite looked at him with real attention now. He had a sleuthlike habit of mind and he was aware that his companion had only arrived on the preceding afternoon. He had had little time to discover the beauty of the villa by daylight and he had so far spoken to nobody. Yet after dark he had made straight for La Paz. Why? Almost involuntarily Mr Satterthwaite turned his head to look at the green-shuttered villa, but it was as ever serenely lifeless, close shuttered. No, the solution of the mystery was not there.

'And you actually found someone here then?'

The other nodded.

'Yes. Must have been from the other Hotel. He had on fancy dress.'

'Fancy dress?'

'Yes. A kind of Harlequin rig.'

'What?'

The query fairly burst from Mr Satterthwaite's lips. His companion turned to stare at him in surprise.

'They often do have fancy dress shows at the Hotels, I suppose?'

'Oh! quite,' said Mr Satterthwaite. 'Quite, quite, quite.'

He paused breathlessly, then added:

'You must excuse my excitement. Do you happen to know anything about catalysis?'

The young man stared at him.

'Never heard of it. What is it?'

Mr Satterthwaite quoted gravely: '*A chemical reaction depending for its success on the presence of a certain substance which itself remains unchanged.*'

'Oh,' said the young man uncertainly.

'I have a certain friend – his name is Mr Quin, and he can best be described in the terms of catalysis. His presence is a sign that things are going to happen, because when he is there strange revelations come to light, discoveries are made. And yet – he himself takes no part in the proceedings. I have a feeling that it was my friend you met here last night.'

'He's a very sudden sort of chap then. He gave me quite a shock. One minute he wasn't there and the next minute he was! Almost as though he came up out of the sea.'

Mr Satterthwaite looked along the little plateau and down the sheer drop below.

'That's nonsense, of course,' said the other. 'But it's the feeling he gave me. Of course, really, there isn't the foothold for a fly.' He looked over the edge. 'A straight clear drop. If you went over – well, that would be the end right enough.'

'An ideal spot for a murder, in fact,' said Mr Satterthwaite pleasantly.

The other stared at him, almost as though for the moment he did not follow. Then he said vaguely: 'Oh! yes – of course . . .'

He sat there, making little dabs at the ground with his stick and frowning. Suddenly Mr Satterthwaite got the resemblance he had been seeking. That dumb bewildered questioning. *So had the dog looked who was run over.* His eyes and this young man's eyes asked the same pathetic question with the same reproach. '*Oh! world that I have trusted – what have you done to me?*'

He saw other points of resemblance between the two, the same pleasure-loving easy-going existence, the same joyous abandon to the delights of life, the same absence of intellectual questioning. Enough for both to live in the moment – the world was a good place, a place of carnal delights – sun, sea, sky – a discreet garbage heap. And then – what? A car had hit the dog. What had hit the man?

The subject of these cogitations broke in at this point, speaking, however, more to himself than to Mr Satterthwaite.

'One wonders,' he said, 'what it's All For?'

Familiar words – words that usually brought a smile to Mr Satterthwaite's lips, with their unconscious betrayal of the innate egoism of humanity which insists on regarding every manifestation of life as directly designed for its delight or its torment. He did not answer and presently the stranger said with a slight, rather apologetic laugh:

'I've heard it said that every man should build a house, plant a tree and have a son.' He paused and then added: 'I believe I planted an acorn once . . .'

Mr Satterthwaite stirred slightly. His curiosity was aroused – that ever-present interest in the affairs of other people of which the Duchess had accused him was roused. It was not difficult. Mr Satterthwaite had a very feminine side to his nature, he was as good a listener as any woman, and he knew the right moment to put in a prompting word. Presently he was hearing the whole story.

Anthony Cosden, that was the stranger's name, and his life had been much as Mr Satterthwaite had imagined it. He was a bad hand at telling a story but his listener supplied the gaps easily enough. A very ordinary life – an average income, a little soldiering, a good deal of sport whenever sport offered, plenty of friends, plenty of pleasant things to do, a sufficiency of women. The kind of life that practically inhibits thought of any description and substitutes sensation. To speak frankly, an animal's life. 'But there are worse things than that,' thought **Mr Satterthwaite** from the depths of his experience. 'Oh! many worse things than that . . .' This world had seemed a very good place to Anthony Cosden. He had grumbled because everyone always grumbled but it had never been a serious grumble. And then – *this*.

He came to it at last – rather vaguely and incoherently. Hadn't felt quite the thing – nothing much. Saw his doctor, and the doctor had persuaded him to go to a Harley Street man. And then – the incredible truth. They'd tried to hedge about it – spoke of great care – a quiet life, but they hadn't been able to disguise that that was all eyewash – letting him down lightly. It boiled down to this – six months. That's what they gave him. Six months.

He turned those bewildered brown eyes on Mr Satterthwaite. It was, of course, rather a shock to a fellow. One didn't – one didn't somehow, know what to *do*.

Mr Satterthwaite nodded gravely and understandingly.

It was a bit difficult to take in all at once, Anthony Cosden went on. How to put in the time. Rather a rotten business waiting about to get pipped. He didn't feel really ill – not yet. Though that might come later, so the specialist had said – in fact, it was bound to. It seemed such nonsense to be going to die when one didn't in the least want to. The best thing, he had thought, would be to carry on as usual. But somehow that hadn't worked.

Here Mr Satterthwaite interrupted him. Wasn't there, he hinted delicately, any woman?

But apparently there wasn't. There were women, of course, but not that kind. His crowd was a very cheery crowd. They didn't, so he implied, like corpses. He didn't wish to make a kind of walking funeral of himself. It would have been embarrassing for everybody. So he had come abroad.

'You came to see these islands? But why?' Mr Satterthwaite was hunting for something, something intangible but delicate that eluded him and yet which he was sure was there. 'You've been here before, perhaps?'

'Yes.' He admitted it almost unwillingly. 'Years ago when I was a youngster.'

And suddenly, almost unconsciously so it seemed, he shot a quick glance backward over his shoulder in the direction of the villa.

'I remembered this place,' he said, nodding at the sea. '*One step to eternity*!'

'And that is why you came up here last night,' finished Mr Satterthwaite calmly.

Anthony Cosden shot him a dismayed glance.

'Oh! I say – really –' he protested.

'Last night you found someone here. This afternoon you have found me. Your life has been saved – twice.'

'You may put it that way if you like – but damn it all, it's *my* life. I've a right to do what I like with it.'

'That is a cliché,' said Mr Satterthwaite wearily.

'Of course I see your point,' said Anthony Cosden generously. 'Naturally you've got to say what you can. I'd try to dissuade a fellow myself, even though I knew deep down that he was right. And you know that I'm right. A clean quick end is better than a lingering one – causing trouble and expense and bother to all. In any case it's not as though I had anyone in the world belonging to me . . .'

'If you had –?' said Mr Satterthwaite sharply.

Cosden drew a deep breath.

'I don't know. Even then, I think, this way would be best. But anyway – I haven't . . .'

He stopped abruptly. Mr Satterthwaite eyed him curiously. Incurably romantic, he suggested again that there was, somewhere, some woman. But Cosden negatived it. He oughtn't, he said, to complain. He had had, on the whole, a very good life. It was a pity it was going to be over so soon, that was all. But at any rate he had had, he supposed, everything worth having. Except a son. He would have liked a son. He would like to know now that he had a son living after him. Still, he reiterated the fact, he had had a very good life –

It was at this point that Mr Satterthwaite lost patience. Nobody, he pointed out, who was still in the larval stage, could claim to know anything of life at all. Since the words *larval stage*

clearly meant nothing at all to Cosden, he proceeded to make
his meaning clearer.

'You have not begun to live yet. You are still at the beginning
of life.'

Cosden laughed.

'Why, my hair's grey. I'm forty –'

Mr Satterthwaite interrupted him.

'That has nothing to do with it. Life is a compound of physical
and mental experiences. I, for instance, am sixty-nine, and I am
really sixty-nine. I have known, either at first or second hand,
nearly all the experiences life has to offer. You are like a man
who talks of a full year and has seen nothing but snow and ice!
The flowers of Spring, the languorous days of Summer, the
falling leaves of Autumn – he knows nothing of them – not
even that there are such things. And you are going to turn your
back on even this opportunity of knowing them.'

'You seem to forget,' said Anthony Cosden dryly, 'that, in any
case, I have only six months.'

'Time, like everything else, is relative,' said Mr Satterthwaite.
'That six months might be the longest and most varied experience of your whole life.'

Cosden looked unconvinced.

'In my place,' he said, 'you would do the same.'

Mr Satterthwaite shook his head.

'No,' he said simply. 'In the first place, I doubt if I should
have the courage. It needs courage and I am not at all a brave
individual. And in the second place –'

'Well?'

'I always want to know what is going to happen tomorrow.'

Cosden rose suddenly with a laugh.

'Well, sir, you've been very good in letting me talk to you. I
hardly know why – anyway, there it is. I've said a lot too much.
Forget it.'

'And tomorrow, when an accident is reported, I am to leave
it at that? To make no suggestion of suicide?'

'That's as you like. I'm glad you realize one thing – that you
can't prevent me.'

'My dear young man,' said Mr Satterthwaite placidly, 'I can hardly attach myself to you like the proverbial limpet. Sooner or later you would give me the slip and accomplish your purpose. But you are frustrated at any rate for this afternoon. You would hardly like to go to your death leaving me under the possible imputation of having pushed you over.'

'That is true,' said Cosden. 'If you insist on remaining here –'

'I do,' said Mr Satterthwaite firmly.

Cosden laughed good-humouredly.

'Then the plan must be deferred for the moment. In which case I will go back to the hotel. See you later perhaps.'

Mr Satterthwaite was left looking at the sea.

'And now,' he said to himself softly, 'what next? There must be a next. I wonder . . .'

He got up. For a while he stood at the edge of the plateau looking down on the dancing water beneath. But he found no inspiration there, and turning slowly he walked back along the path between the cypresses and into the quiet garden. He looked at the shuttered, peaceful house and he wondered, as he had often wondered before, who had lived there and what had taken place within those placid walls. On a sudden impulse he walked up some crumbling stone steps and laid a hand on one of the faded green shutters.

To his surprise it swung back at his touch. He hesitated a moment, then pushed it boldly open. The next minute he stepped back with a little exclamation of dismay. A woman stood in the window facing him. She wore black and had a black lace mantilla draped over her head.

Mr Satterthwaite floundered wildly in Italian interspersed with German – the nearest he could get in the hurry of the moment to Spanish. He was desolated and ashamed, he explained haltingly. The Signora must forgive. He thereupon retreated hastily, the woman not having spoken one word.

He was halfway across the courtyard when she spoke – two sharp words like a pistol crack.

'Come back!'

It was a barked-out command such as might have been addressed to a dog, yet so absolute was the authority it conveyed, that Mr Satterthwaite had swung round hurriedly and trotted back to the window almost automatically before it occurred to him to feel any resentment. He obeyed like a dog. The woman was still standing motionless at the window. She looked him up and down appraising him with perfect calmness.

'You are English,' she said. 'I thought so.'

Mr Satterthwaite started off on a second apology.

'If I had known you were English,' he said, 'I could have expressed myself better just now. I offer my most sincere apologies for my rudeness in trying the shutter. I am afraid I can plead no excuse save curiosity. I had a great wish to see what the inside of this charming house was like.'

She laughed suddenly, a deep, rich laugh.

'If you really want to see it,' she said, 'you had better come in.'

She stood aside, and Mr Satterthwaite, feeling pleasurably excited, stepped into the room. It was dark, since the shutters of the other windows were closed, but he could see that it was scantily and rather shabbily furnished and that the dust lay thick everywhere.

'Not here,' she said. 'I do not use this room.'

She led the way and he followed her, out of the room across a passage and into a room the other side. Here the windows gave on the sea and the sun streamed in. The furniture, like that of the other room, was poor in quality, but there were some worn rugs that had been good in their time, a large screen of Spanish leather and bowls of fresh flowers.

'You will have tea with me,' said Mr Satterthwaite's hostess. She added reassuringly: 'It is perfectly good tea and will be made with boiling water.'

She went out of the door and called out something in Spanish, then she returned and sat down on a sofa opposite her guest. For the first time, Mr Satterthwaite was able to study her appearance.

The first effect she had upon him was to make him feel even

more grey and shrivelled and elderly than usual by contrast with her own forceful personality. She was a tall woman, very sunburnt, dark and handsome though no longer young. When she was in the room the sun seemed to be shining twice as brightly as when she was out of it, and presently a curious feeling of warmth and aliveness began to steal over Mr Satterthwaite. It was as though he stretched out thin, shrivelled hands to a reassuring flame. He thought, 'She's so much vitality herself that she's got a lot left over for other people.'

He recalled the command in her voice when she had stopped him, and wished that his protégée, Olga, could be imbued with a little of that force. He thought: 'What an Isolde she'd make! And yet she probably hasn't got the ghost of a singing voice. Life is badly arranged.' He was, all the same, a little afraid of her. He did not like domineering women.

She had clearly been considering him as she sat with her chin in her hands, making no pretence about it. At last she nodded as though she had made up her mind.

'I am glad you came,' she said at last. 'I needed someone very badly to talk to this afternoon. And you are used to that, aren't you?'

'I don't quite understand.'

'I meant people tell you things. You knew what I meant! Why pretend?'

'Well – perhaps –'

She swept on, regardless of anything he had been going to say.

'One could say anything to you. That is because you are half a woman. You know what we feel – what we think – the queer, queer things we do.'

Her voice died away. Tea was brought by a large, smiling Spanish girl. It was good tea – China – Mr Satterthwaite sipped it appreciatively.

'You live here?' he inquired conversationally.

'Yes.'

'But not altogether. The house is usually shut up, is it not? At least so I have been told.'

'I am here a good deal, more than anyone knows. I only use these rooms.'

'You have had the house long?'

'It has belonged to me for twenty-two years – and I lived here for a year before that.'

Mr Satterthwaite said rather inanely (or so he felt): 'That is a very long time.'

'The year? Or the twenty-two years?'

His interest stirred, Mr Satterthwaite said gravely: 'That depends.'

She nodded.

'Yes, it depends. They are two separate periods. They have nothing to do with each other. Which is long? Which is short? Even now I cannot say.'

She was silent for a minute, brooding. Then she said with a little smile:

'It is such a long time since I have talked with anyone – such a long time! I do not apologize. You came to my shutter. You wished to look through my window. And that is what you are always doing, is it not? Pushing aside the shutter and looking through the window into the truth of people's lives. If they will let you. And often if they will not let you! It would be difficult to hide anything from you. You would guess – and guess right.'

Mr Satterthwaite had an odd impulse to be perfectly sincere.

'I am sixty-nine,' he said. 'Everything I know of life I know at second hand. Sometimes that is very bitter to me. And yet, because of it, I know a good deal.'

She nodded thoughtfully.

'I know. Life is very strange. I cannot imagine what it must be like to be that – always a looker-on.'

Her tone was wondering. Mr Satterthwaite smiled.

'No, you would not know. Your place is in the centre of the stage. You will always be the Prima Donna.'

'What a curious thing to say.'

'But I am right. Things have happened to you – will always happen to you. Sometimes, I think, there have been tragic things. Is that so?'

Her eyes narrowed. She looked across at him.

'If you are here long, somebody will tell you of the English swimmer who was drowned at the foot of this cliff. They will tell you how young and strong he was, how handsome, and they will tell you that his young wife looked down from the top of the cliff and saw him drowning.'

'Yes, I have already heard that story.'

'That man was my husband. This was his villa. He brought me out here with him when I was eighteen, and a year later he died – driven by the surf on the black rocks, cut and bruised and mutilated, battered to death.'

Mr Satterthwaite gave a shocked exclamation. She leant forward, her burning eyes focused on his face.

'You spoke of tragedy. Can you imagine a greater tragedy than that? For a young wife, only a year married, to stand helpless while the man she loved fought for his life – and lost it – horribly.'

'Terrible,' said Mr Satterthwaite. He spoke with real emotion. 'Terrible. I agree with you. Nothing in life could be so dreadful.'

Suddenly she laughed. Her head went back.

'You are wrong,' she said. 'There is something more terrible. And that is for a young wife to stand there and hope and long for her husband to drown . . .'

'But good God,' cried Mr Satterthwaite, 'you don't mean –?'

'Yes, I do. That's what it was really. I knelt there – knelt down on the cliff and prayed. The Spanish servants thought I was praying for his life to be saved. I wasn't. I was praying that I might wish him to be spared. I was saying one thing over and over again, "God, help me not to wish him dead. God, help me not to wish him dead." But it wasn't any good. All the time I hoped – hoped – and my hope came true.'

She was silent for a minute or two and then she said very gently in quite a different voice:

'That is a terrible thing, isn't it? It's the sort of thing one can't forget. I was terribly happy when I knew he was really dead and couldn't come back to torture me any more.'

'My child,' said Mr Satterthwaite, shocked.

'I know. I was too young to have that happen to me. Those things should happen to one when one is older – when one is more prepared for – for beastliness. Nobody knew, you know, what he was really like. I thought he was wonderful when I first met him and was so happy and proud when he asked me to marry him. But things went wrong almost at once. He was angry with me – nothing I could do pleased him – and yet I tried so hard. And then he began to like hurting me. And above all to terrify me. That's what he enjoyed most. He thought out all sorts of things . . . dreadful things. I won't tell you. I suppose, really, he must have been a little mad. I was alone here, in his power, and cruelty began to be his hobby.' Her eyes widened and darkened. 'The worst was my baby. I was going to have a baby. Because of some of the things he did to me – it was born dead. My little baby. I nearly died, too – but I didn't. I wish I had.'

Mr Satterthwaite made an inarticulate sound.

'And then I was delivered – in the way I've told you. Some girls who were staying at the hotel dared him. That's how it happened. All the Spaniards told him it was madness to risk the sea just there. But he was very vain – he wanted to show off. And I – I saw him drown – and was glad. God oughtn't to let such things happen.'

Mr Satterthwaite stretched out his little dry hand and took hers. She squeezed it hard as a child might have done. The maturity had fallen away from her face. He saw her without difficulty as she had been at nineteen.

'At first it seemed too good to be true. The house was mine and I could live in it. And no one could hurt me any more! I was an orphan, you know, I had no near relations, no one to care what became of me. That simplified things. I lived on here – in this villa – and it seemed like Heaven. Yes, like Heaven. I've never been so happy since, and never shall again. Just to wake up and know that everything was all right – no pain, no terror, no wondering what he was going to do to me next. Yes, it was Heaven.'

She paused a long time, and Mr Satterthwaite said at last:

'And then?'

'I suppose human beings aren't ever satisfied. At first, just being free was enough. But after a while I began to get – well, lonely, I suppose. I began to think about my baby that died. If only I had had my baby! I wanted it as a baby, and also as a plaything. I wanted dreadfully something or someone to play with. It sounds silly and childish, but there it was.'

'I understand,' said Mr Satterthwaite gravely.

'It's difficult to explain the next bit. It just – well, happened, you see. There was a young Englishman staying at the hotel. He strayed in the garden by mistake. I was wearing Spanish dress and he took me for a Spanish girl. I thought it would be rather fun to pretend I was one, so I played up. His Spanish was very bad but he could just manage a little. I told him the villa belonged to an English lady who was away. I said she had taught me a little English and I pretended to speak broken English. It was such fun – such fun – even now I can remember what fun it was. He began to make love to me. We agreed to pretend that the villa was our home, that we were just married and coming to live there. I suggested that we should try one of the shutters – the one you tried this evening. It was open and inside the room was dusty and uncared for. We crept in. It was exciting and wonderful. We pretended it was our own house.'

She broke off suddenly, looked appealingly at Mr Satterthwaite.

'It all seemed lovely – like a fairy tale. And the lovely thing about it, to me, was that it wasn't true. It wasn't real.'

Mr Satterthwaite nodded. He saw her, perhaps more clearly than she saw herself – that frightened, lonely child entranced with her make believe that was so safe because it wasn't real.

'He was, I suppose, a very ordinary young man. Out for adventure, but quite sweet about it. We went on pretending.'

She stopped, looked at Mr Satterthwaite and said again:

'You understand? We went on pretending . . .'

She went on again in a minute.

'He came up again the next morning to the villa. I saw him from my bedroom through the shutter. Of course he didn't dream I was inside. He still thought I was a little Spanish peasant girl. He stood there looking about him. He'd asked me to meet him. I'd said I would but I never meant to.

'He just stood there looking worried. I think he was worried about me. It was nice of him to be worried about me. He *was* nice . . .'

She paused again.

'The next day he left. I've never seen him again.

'My baby was born nine months later. I was wonderfully happy all the time. To be able to have a baby so peacefully, with no one to hurt you or make you miserable. I wished I'd remembered to ask my English boy his Christian name. I would have called the baby after him. It seemed unkind not to. It seemed rather unfair. He'd given me the thing I wanted most in the world, and he would never even know about it! But of course I told myself that he wouldn't look at it that way – that to know would probably only worry and annoy him. I had been just a passing amusement for him, that was all.'

'And the baby?' asked Mr Satterthwaite.

'He was splendid. I called him John. Splendid. I wish you could see him now. He's twenty. He's going to be a mining engineer. He's been the best and dearest son in the world to me. I told him his father had died before he was born.'

Mr Satterthwaite stared at her. A curious story. And somehow, a story that was not completely told. There was, he felt sure, something else.

'Twenty years is a long time,' he said thoughtfully. 'You've never contemplated marrying again?'

She shook her head. A slow, burning blush spread over her tanned cheeks.

'The child was enough for you – always?'

She looked at him. Her eyes were softer than he had yet seen them.

'Such queer things happen!' she murmured. 'Such queer things . . . You wouldn't believe them – no, I'm wrong, *you* might, perhaps. I didn't love John's father, not at the time. I don't think I even knew what love was. I assumed, as a matter of course, that the child would be like me. But he wasn't. He mightn't have been my child at all. He was like his father – he was like no one but his father. I learnt to know that man – through his child. Through the child, I learnt to love him. I love him now. I always shall love him. You may say that it's imagination, that I've built up an ideal, but it isn't so. I love the man, the real, human man. I'd know him if I saw him tomorrow – even though it's over twenty years since we met. Loving him has made me into a woman. I love him as a woman loves a man. For twenty years I've lived loving him. I shall die loving him.'

She stopped abruptly – then challenged her listener.

'Do you think I'm mad – to say these strange things?'

'Oh! my dear,' said Mr Satterthwaite. He took her hand again.

'You do understand?'

'I think I do. But there's something more, isn't there? Something that you haven't yet told me?'

Her brow clouded over.

'Yes, there's something. It was clever of you to guess. I knew at once you weren't the sort one can hide things from. But I don't want to tell you – and the reason I don't want to tell you is because it's best for you not to know.'

He looked at her. Her eyes met his bravely and defiantly.

He said to himself: 'This is the test. All the clues are in my hand. I ought to be able to know. If I reason rightly I shall know.'

There was a pause, then he said slowly:

'Something's gone wrong.' He saw her eyelids give the faintest quiver and knew himself to be on the right track.

'Something's gone wrong – suddenly – after all these years.' He felt himself groping – groping – in the dark recesses of her mind where she was trying to hide her secret from him.

'The boy – it's got to do with him. You wouldn't mind about anything else.'

He heard the very faint gasp she gave and knew he had probed correctly. A cruel business but necessary. It was her will against his. She had got a dominant, ruthless will, but he too had a will hidden beneath his meek manners. And he had behind him the Heaven-sent assurance of a man who is doing his proper job. He felt a passing contemptuous pity for men whose business it was to track down such crudities as crime. This detective business of the mind, this assembling of clues, this delving for the truth, this wild joy as one drew nearer to the goal ... Her very passion to keep the truth from him helped her. He felt her stiffen defiantly as he drew nearer and nearer.

'It is better for me not to know, you say. Better for *me*? But you are not a very considerate woman. You would not shrink from putting a stranger to a little temporary inconvenience. It is more than that, then? If you tell me you make me an accomplice before the fact. That sounds like crime. Fantastic! I could not associate crime with you. Or only one sort of crime. A crime against yourself.'

Her lids drooped in spite of herself, veiled her eyes. He leaned forward and caught her wrist.

'It *is* that, then! You are thinking of taking your life.'

She gave a low cry.

'How did you know? How did you know?'

'But why? You are not tired of life. I never saw a woman less tired of it – more radiantly alive.'

She got up, went to the window, pushing back a strand of her dark hair as she did so.

'Since you have guessed so much I might as well tell you the truth. I should not have let you in this evening. I might have known that you would see too much. You are that kind of man. You were right about the cause. It's the boy. He knows nothing. But last time he was home, he spoke tragically of a friend of his, and I discovered something. If he finds out that he is illegitimate it will break his heart. He is proud – horribly proud! There is a girl. Oh! I won't go into details. But he is coming very soon – and he wants to know all about his father – he wants details. The girl's parents, naturally, want to know. When he discovers the truth, he will break with her, exile himself, ruin his life. Oh! I know the things you would say. He is young, foolish, wrong-headed to take it like that! All true, perhaps. But does it matter what people ought to be? They are what they are. *It will break his heart* . . . But if, before he comes, there has been an accident, everything will be swallowed up in grief for me. He will look through my papers, find nothing, and be annoyed that I told him so little. But he will not suspect the truth. It is the best way. One must pay for happiness, and I have had so much – oh! so much happiness. And in reality the price will be easy, too. A little courage – to take the leap – perhaps a moment or so of anguish.'

'But, my dear child –'

'Don't argue with me.' She flared round on him. 'I won't listen to conventional arguments. My life is my own. Up to now, it has been needed – for John. But he needs it no longer. He wants a mate – a companion – he will turn to her all the more willingly because I am no longer there. My life is useless, but my death will be of use. And I have the right to do what I like with my own life.'

'Are you sure?'

The sternness of his tone surprised her. She stammered slightly.

'If it is no good to anyone – and I am the best judge of that –'

He interrupted her again.

'Not necessarily.'

'What do you mean?'

'Listen. I will put a case to you. A man comes to a certain place – to commit suicide, shall we say? But by chance he finds another man there, so he fails in his purpose and goes away – to live. The second man has saved the first man's life, not by being necessary to him or prominent in his life, but just by the mere physical fact of having been in a certain place at a certain moment. You take your life today and perhaps, some five, six, seven years hence, someone will go to death or disaster simply for lack of your presence in a given spot or place. It may be a runaway horse coming down a street that swerved aside at sight of you and so fails to trample a child that is playing in the gutter. That child may live to grow up and be a great musician, or discover a cure for cancer. Or it may be less melodramatic than that. He may just grow up to ordinary everyday happiness . . .'

She stared at him.

'You are a strange man. These things you say – I have never thought of them . . .'

'You say your life is your own,' went on Mr Satterthwaite. 'But can you dare to ignore the chance that you are taking part in a gigantic drama under the orders of a divine Producer? Your cue may not come till the end of the play – it may be totally unimportant, a mere walking-on part, but upon it may hang the issues of the play if you do not give the cue to another player. The whole edifice may crumple. You as you, may not matter to anyone in the world, but you as a person in a particular place may matter unimaginably.'

She sat down, still staring.

'What do you want me to do?' she said simply.

It was Mr Satterthwaite's moment of triumph. He issued orders.

'I want you at least to promise me one thing – to do nothing rash for twenty-four hours.'

She was silent for a moment or two and then she said: 'I promise.'

'There is one other thing – a favour.'

'Yes?'

'Leave the shutter of the room I came in by unfastened, and keep vigil there tonight.'

She looked at him curiously, but nodded assent.

'And now,' said Mr Satterthwaite, slightly conscious of anticlimax, 'I really must be going. God bless you, my dear.'

He made a rather embarrassed exit. The stalwart Spanish girl met him in the passage and opened a side door for him, staring curiously at him the while.

It was just growing dark as he reached the hotel. There was a solitary figure sitting on the terrace. Mr Satterthwaite made straight for it. He was excited and his heart was beating quite fast. He felt that tremendous issues lay in his hands. One false move –

But he tried to conceal his agitation and to speak naturally and casually to Anthony Cosden.

'A warm evening,' he observed. 'I quite lost count of time sitting up there on the cliff.'

'Have you been up there all this time?'

Mr Satterthwaite nodded. The swing door into the hotel opened to let someone through, and a beam of light fell suddenly on the other's face, illuminating its look of dull suffering, of uncomprehending dumb endurance.

Mr Satterthwaite thought to himself: 'It's worse for him than it would be for me. Imagination, conjecture, speculation – they can do a lot for you. You can, as it were, ring the changes upon pain. The uncomprehending blind suffering of an animal – that's terrible . . .'

Cosden spoke suddenly in a harsh voice.

'I'm going for a stroll after dinner. You – you understand? The third time's lucky. For God's sake don't interfere. I know your interference will be well-meaning and all that – but take it from me, it's useless.'

Mr Satterthwaite drew himself up.

'I never interfere,' he said, thereby giving the lie to the whole purpose and object of his existence.

'I know what you think –' went on Cosden, but he was interrupted.

'You must excuse me, but there I beg to differ from you,' said Mr Satterthwaite. 'Nobody knows what another person is thinking. They may imagine they do, but they are nearly always wrong.'

'Well, perhaps that's so.' Cosden was doubtful, slightly taken aback.

'Thought is yours only,' said his companion. 'Nobody can alter or influence the use you mean to make of it. Let us talk of a less painful subject. That old villa, for instance. It has a curious charm, withdrawn, sheltered from the world, shielding heaven knows what mystery. It tempted me to do a doubtful action. I tried one of the shutters.'

'You did?' Cosden turned his head sharply. 'But it was fastened, of course?'

'No,' said Mr Satterthwaite. 'It was open.' He added gently: 'The third shutter from the end.'

'Why,' Cosden burst out, 'that was the one –'

He broke off suddenly, but Mr Satterthwaite had seen the light that had sprung up in his eyes. He rose – satisfied.

Some slight tinge of anxiety still remained with him. Using his favourite metaphor of a drama, he hoped that he had spoken his few lines correctly. For they were very important lines.

But thinking it over, his artistic judgment was satisfied. On his way up to the cliff, Cosden would try that shutter. It was not in human nature to resist. A memory of twenty odd years ago had brought him to this spot, the same memory would take him to the shutter. And afterwards?

'I shall know in the morning,' said Mr Satterthwaite, and proceeded to change methodically for his evening meal.

It was somewhere round ten o'clock that Mr Satterthwaite set foot once more in the garden of La Paz. Manuel bade him a smiling 'Good morning,' and handed him a single rosebud which Mr Satterthwaite put carefully into his buttonhole. Then he went on to the house. He stood there for some minutes looking up at the peaceful white walls, the trailing orange creeper, and the faded green shutters. So silent, so peaceful. Had the whole thing been a dream?

But at that moment one of the windows opened and the lady who occupied Mr Satterthwaite's thoughts came out. She came straight to him with a buoyant swaying walk, like someone carried on a great wave of exultation. Her eyes were shining, her colour high. She looked like a figure of joy on a frieze. There was no hesitation about her, no doubts or tremors. Straight to Mr Satterthwaite she came, put her hands on his shoulders and kissed him – not once but many times. Large, dark, red roses, very velvety – that is how he thought of it afterwards. Sunshine, summer, birds singing – that was the atmosphere into which he felt himself caught up. Warmth, joy and tremendous vigour.

'I'm so happy,' she said. 'You darling! How did you know? How *could* you know? You're like the good magician in the fairy tales.'

She paused, a sort of breathlessness of happiness upon her.

'We're going over today – to the Consul – to get married. When John comes, his father will be there. We'll tell him there was some misunderstanding in the past. Oh! he won't ask questions. Oh! I'm so happy – so happy – so happy.'

Happiness did indeed surge from her like a tide. It lapped round Mr Satterthwaite in a warm exhilarating flood.

'It's so wonderful to Anthony to find he has a son. I never dreamt he'd mind or care.' She looked confidently into Mr Satterthwaite's eyes. 'Isn't it strange how things come right and end all beautifully?'

He had his clearest vision of her yet. A child – still a child – with her love of make believe – her fairy tales that ended beautifully with two people 'living happily ever afterwards.'

He said gently:

'If you bring this man of yours happiness in these last months, you will indeed have done a very beautiful thing.'

Her eyes opened wide – surprised.

'Oh!' she said. 'You don't think I'd let him die, do you? After all these years – when he's come to me. I've known lots of people whom doctors have given up and who are alive today. Die? Of course he's not going to die!'

He looked at her – her strength, her beauty, her vitality – her indomitable courage and will. He, too, had known doctors to be mistaken . . . The personal factor – you never knew how much and how little it counted.

She said again, with scorn and amusement in her voice:

'You don't think I'd let him die, do you?'

'No,' said Mr Satterthwaite at last very gently. 'Somehow, my dear, I don't think you will . . .'

Then at last he walked down the cypress path to the bench overlooking the sea and found there the person he was expecting to see. Mr Quin rose and greeted him – the same as ever, dark, saturnine, smiling and sad.

'You expected me?' he asked.

And Mr Satterthwaite answered: 'Yes, I expected you.'

They sat together on the bench.

'I have an idea that you have been playing Providence once more, to judge by your expression,' said Mr Quin presently.

Mr Satterthwaite looked at him reproachfully.

'As if you didn't know all about it.'

'You always accuse me of omniscience,' said Mr Quin, smiling.

'If you know nothing, why were you here the night before last – waiting?' countered Mr Satterthwaite.

'Oh, that –?'

'Yes, that.'

'I had a – commission to perform.'

'For whom?'

'You have sometimes fancifully named me an advocate for the dead.'

'The dead?' said Mr Satterthwaite, a little puzzled. 'I don't understand.'

Mr Quin pointed a long, lean finger down at the blue depths below.

'A man was drowned down there twenty-two years ago.'

'I know – but I don't see –'

'Supposing that, after all, that man loved his young wife. Love can make devils of men as well as angels. She had a girlish adoration for him, but he could never touch the womanhood in her – and that drove him mad. He tortured her because he loved her. Such things happen. You know that as well as I do.'

'Yes,' admitted Mr Satterthwaite, 'I have seen such things – but rarely – very rarely . . .'

'And you have also seen, more commonly, that there is such a thing as remorse – the desire to make amends – at all costs to make amends.'

'Yes, but death came too soon . . .'

'Death!' There was contempt in Mr Quin's voice. 'You believe in a life after death, do you not? And who are you to say that the same wishes, the same desires, may not operate in that other life? If the desire is strong enough – a messenger may be found.'

His voice tailed away.

Mr Satterthwaite got up, trembling a little.

'I must get back to the hotel,' he said. 'If you are going that way.'

But Mr Quin shook his head.

'No,' he said. 'I shall go back the way I came.'

When Mr Satterthwaite looked back over his shoulder, he saw his friend walking towards the edge of the cliff.

CHAPTER VII

The Voice in the Dark

I

'I am a little worried about Margery,' said Lady Stranleigh.

'My girl, you know,' she added.

She sighed pensively.

'It makes one feel terribly old to have a grown-up daughter.'

Mr Satterthwaite, who was the recipient of these confidences, rose to the occasion gallantly.

'No one could believe it possible,' he declared with a little bow.

'Flatterer,' said Lady Stranleigh, but she said it vaguely and it was clear that her mind was elsewhere.

Mr Satterthwaite looked at the slender white-clad figure in some admiration. The Cannes sunshine was searching, but Lady Stranleigh came through the test very well. At a distance the youthful effect was really extraordinary. One almost wondered if she were grown-up or not. Mr Satterthwaite, who knew everything, knew that it was perfectly possible for Lady Stranleigh to have grown-up grandchildren. She represented the extreme triumph of art over nature. Her figure was marvellous, her complexion was marvellous. She had enriched many beauty parlours and certainly the results were astounding.

Lady Stranleigh lit a cigarette, crossed her beautiful legs encased in the finest of nude silk stockings and murmured: 'Yes, I really am rather worried about Margery.'

'Dear me,' said Mr Satterthwaite, 'what is the trouble?'

Lady Stranleigh turned her beautiful blue eyes upon him.

'You have never met her, have you? She is Charles' daughter,' she added helpfully.

If entries in 'Who's Who' were strictly truthful, the entries concerning Lady Stranleigh might have ended as follows: *hobbies: getting married.* She had floated through life shedding husbands as she went. She had lost three by divorce and one by death.

'If she had been Rudolph's child I could have understood it,' mused Lady Stranleigh. 'You remember Rudolph? He was always temperamental. Six months after we married I had to apply for those queer things – what do they call them? Conjugal what nots, you know what I mean. Thank goodness it is all much simpler nowadays. I remember I had to write him the silliest kind of letter – my lawyer practically dictated it to me. Asking him to come back, you know, and that I would do all I could, etc., etc., but you never could count on Rudolph, he was so temperamental. He came rushing home at once, which was quite the wrong thing to do, and not at all what the lawyers meant.'

She sighed.

'About Margery?' suggested Mr Satterthwaite, tactfully leading her back to the subject under discussion.

'Of course. I was just going to tell you, wasn't I? Margery has been seeing things, or hearing them. Ghosts, you know, and all that. I should never have thought that Margery could be so imaginative. She is a dear good girl, always has been, but just a shade – dull.'

'Impossible,' murmured Mr Satterthwaite with a confused idea of being complimentary.

'In fact, very dull,' said Lady Stranleigh. 'Doesn't care for dancing, or cocktails or any of the things a young girl ought to care about. She much prefers staying at home to hunt instead of coming out here with me.'

'Dear, dear,' said Mr Satterthwaite, 'she wouldn't come out with you, you say?'

'Well, I didn't exactly press her. Daughters have a depressing effect upon one, I find.'

Mr Satterthwaite tried to think of Lady Stranleigh accompanied by a serious-minded daughter and failed.

'I can't help wondering if Margery is going off her head,' continued Margery's mother in a cheerful voice. 'Hearing voices is a very bad sign, so they tell me. It is not as though Abbot's Mede were haunted. The old building was burnt to the ground in 1836, and they put up a kind of early Victorian château which simply cannot be haunted. It is much too ugly and commonplace.'

Mr Satterthwaite coughed. He was wondering why he was being told all this.

'I thought perhaps,' said Lady Stranleigh, smiling brilliantly upon him, 'that *you* might be able to help me.'

'I?'

'Yes. You are going back to England tomorrow, aren't you?'

'I am. Yes, that is so,' admitted Mr Satterthwaite cautiously.

'And you know all these psychical research people. Of course you do, you know everybody.'

Mr Satterthwaite smiled a little. It was one of his weaknesses to know everybody.

'So what can be simpler?' continued Lady Stranleigh. 'I never get on with that sort of person. You know – earnest men with beards and usually spectacles. They bore me terribly and I am quite at my worst with them.'

Mr Satterthwaite was rather taken aback. Lady Stranleigh continued to smile at him brilliantly.

'So that is all settled, isn't it?' she said brightly. 'You will go down to Abbot's Mede and see Margery, and make all the arrangements. I shall be terribly grateful to you. Of course if Margery is *really* going off her head, I will come home. Ah! here is Bimbo.'

Her smile from being brilliant became dazzling.

A young man in white tennis flannels was approaching them. He was about twenty-five years of age and extremely good-looking.

The young man said simply:

'I have been looking for you everywhere, Babs.'

'What has the tennis been like?'

'Septic.'

Lady Stranleigh rose. She turned her head over her shoulder and murmured in dulcet tones to Mr Satterthwaite: 'It is simply marvellous of you to help me. I shall never forget it.'

Mr Satterthwaite looked after the retreating couple.

'I wonder,' he mused to himself, 'if Bimbo is going to be No. 5.'

II

The conductor of the Train de Luxe was pointing out to Mr Satterthwaite where an accident on the line had occurred a few years previously. As he finished his spirited narrative, the other looked up and saw a well-known face smiling at him over the conductor's shoulder.

'My dear Mr Quin,' said Mr Satterthwaite.

His little withered face broke into smiles.

'What a coincidence! That we should both be returning to England on the same train. You are going there, I suppose.'

'Yes,' said Mr Quin. 'I have business there of rather an important nature. Are you taking the first service of dinner?'

'I always do so. Of course, it is an absurd time – half-past six, but one runs less risk with the cooking.'

Mr Quin nodded comprehendingly.

'I also,' he said. 'We might perhaps arrange to sit together.'

Half-past six found Mr Quin and Mr Satterthwaite established opposite each other at a small table in the dining-car. Mr Satterthwaite gave due attention to the wine list and then turned to his companion.

'I have not seen you since – ah, yes not since Corsica. You left very suddenly that day.'

Mr Quin shrugged his shoulders.

'Not more so than usual. I come and go, you know. I come and go.'

The words seemed to awake some echo of remembrance in

Mr Satterthwaite's mind. A little shiver passed down his spine
– not a disagreeable sensation, quite the contrary. He was conscious of a pleasurable sense of anticipation.

Mr Quin was holding up a bottle of red wine, examining the
label on it. The bottle was between him and the light but for a
minute or two a red glow enveloped his person.

Mr Satterthwaite felt again that sudden stir of excitement.

'I too have a kind of mission in England,' he remarked, smiling broadly at the remembrance. 'You know Lady Stranleigh
perhaps?'

Mr Quin shook his head.

'It is an old title,' said Mr Satterthwaite, 'a very old title. One
of the few that can descend in the female line. She is a Baroness
in her own right. Rather a romantic history really.'

Mr Quin settled himself more comfortably in his chair. A
waiter, flying down the swinging car, deposited cups of soup
before them as if by a miracle. Mr Quin sipped it cautiously.

'You are about to give me one of those wonderful descriptive
portraits of yours,' he murmured, 'that is so, is it not?'

Mr Satterthwaite beamed on him.

'She is really a marvellous woman,' he said. 'Sixty, you know
– yes, I should say at least sixty. I knew them as girls, she and
her sister. Beatrice, that was the name of the elder one, Beatrice
and Barbara. I remember them as the Barron girls. Both good-
looking and in those days very hard up. But that was a great
many years ago – why, dear me, I was a young man myself then.'
Mr Satterthwaite sighed. 'There were several lives then between
them and the title. Old Lord Stranleigh was a first cousin once
removed, I think. Lady Stranleigh's life has been quite a romantic affair. Three unexpected deaths – two of the old man's
brothers and a nephew. Then there was the "Uralia." You
remember the wreck of the "Uralia"? She went down off the
coast of New Zealand. The Barron girls were on board. Beatrice
was drowned. This one, Barbara, was amongst the few survivors.
Six months later, old Stranleigh died and she succeeded to the
title and came into a considerable fortune. Since then she has
lived for one thing only – herself! She has always been the

same, beautiful, unscrupulous, completely callous, interested solely in herself. She has had four husbands, and I have no doubt could get a fifth in a minute.'

He went on to describe the mission with which he had been entrusted by Lady Stranleigh.

'I thought of running down to Abbot's Mede to see the young lady,' he explained. 'I – I feel that something ought to be done about the matter. It is impossible to think of Lady Stranleigh as an ordinary mother.' He stopped, looking across the table at Mr Quin.

'I wish you would come with me,' he said wistfully. 'Would it not be possible?'

'I'm afraid not,' said Mr Quin. 'But let me see, Abbot's Mede is in Wiltshire, is it not?'

Mr Satterthwaite nodded.

'I thought as much. As it happens, I shall be staying not far from Abbot's Mede, at a place you and I both know.' He smiled. 'You remember that little inn, "The Bells and Motley"?'

'Of course,' cried Mr Satterthwaite; 'you will be there?'

Mr Quin nodded. 'For a week or ten days. Possibly longer. If you will come and look me up one day, I shall be delighted to see you.'

And somehow or other Mr Satterthwaite felt strangely comforted by the assurance.

III

'My dear Miss – er – Margery,' said Mr Satterthwaite, 'I assure you that I should not dream of laughing at you.'

Margery Gale frowned a little. They were sitting in the large comfortable hall of Abbot's Mede. Margery Gale was a big squarely built girl. She bore no resemblance to her mother, but took entirely after her father's side of the family, a line of hard-riding country squires. She looked fresh and wholesome and the picture of sanity. Nevertheless, Mr Satterthwaite was reflecting to himself that the Barrons as a family were all inclined to mental instability. Margery might have inherited her physical appearance from her father and at the same time have inherited some mental kink from her mother's side of the family.

'I wish,' said Margery, 'that I could get rid of that Casson woman. I don't believe in spiritualism, and I don't like it. She is one of these silly women that run a craze to death. She is always bothering me to have a medium down here.'

Mr Satterthwaite coughed, fidgeted a little in his chair and then said in a judicial manner:

'Let me be quite sure that I have all the facts. The first of the –er – phenomena occurred two months ago, I understand?'

'About that,' agreed the girl. 'Sometimes it was a whisper and sometimes it was quite a clear voice but it always said much the same thing.'

'Which was?'

'*Give back what is not yours. Give back what you have stolen.* On each occasion I switched on the light, but the room was quite empty and there was no one there. In the end I got so nervous that I got Clayton, mother's maid, to sleep on the sofa in my room.'

'And the voice came just the same?'

'Yes – and this is what frightens me – Clayton did not hear it.'

Mr Satterthwaite reflected for a minute or two.

'Did it come loudly or softly that evening?'

'It was almost a whisper,' admitted Margery. 'If Clayton was sound asleep I suppose she would not really have heard it. She wanted me to see a doctor.' The girl laughed bitterly.

'But since last night even Clayton believes,' she continued.

'What happened last night?'

'I am just going to tell you. I have told no one as yet. I had been out hunting yesterday and we had had a long run. I was dead tired, and slept very heavily. I dreamt – a horrible dream – that I had fallen over some iron railings and that one of the spikes was entering slowly into my throat. I woke to find that it was true – there was some sharp point pressing into the side of my neck, and at the same time a voice was murmuring softly: "*You have stolen what is mine. This is death.*"

'I screamed,' continued Margery, 'and clutched at the air, but there was nothing there. Clayton heard me scream from the room next door where she was sleeping. She came rushing in, and she distinctly felt something brushing past her in the darkness, but she says that whatever that something was, it was not anything human.'

Mr Satterthwaite stared at her. The girl was obviously very shaken and upset. He noticed on the left side of her throat a small square of sticking plaster. She caught the direction of his gaze and nodded.

'Yes,' she said, 'it was not imagination, you see.'

Mr Satterthwaite put a question almost apologetically, it sounded so melodramatic.

'You don't know of anyone – er – who has a grudge against you?' he asked.

'Of course not,' said Margery. 'What an idea!'

Mr Satterthwaite started on another line of attack.

'What visitors have you had during the last two months?'

'You don't mean just people for week-ends, I suppose? Marcia Keane has been with me all along. She is my best friend, and just as keen on horses as I am. Then my cousin Roley Vavasour has been here a good deal.'

Mr Satterthwaite nodded. He suggested that he should see Clayton, the maid.

'She has been with you a long time, I suppose?' he asked.

'Donkey's years,' said Margery. 'She was Mother's and Aunt Beatrice's maid when they were girls. That is why Mother has kept her on, I suppose, although she has got a French maid for herself. Clayton does sewing and pottering little odd jobs.'

She took him upstairs and presently Clayton came to them. She was a tall, thin, old woman, with grey hair neatly parted, and she looked the acme of respectability.

'No, sir,' she said in answer to Mr Satterthwaite's inquiries. 'I have never heard anything of the house being haunted. To tell you the truth, sir, I thought it was all Miss Margery's imagination until last night. But I actually felt something – brushing by me in the darkness. And I can tell you this, sir, *it was not anything human*. And then there is that wound in Miss Margery's neck. She didn't do that herself, poor lamb.'

But her words were suggestive to Mr Satterthwaite. Was it possible that Margery could have inflicted that wound herself? He had heard of strange cases where girls apparently just as sane and well-balanced as Margery had done the most amazing things.

'It will soon heal up,' said Clayton. 'It's not like this scar of mine.'

She pointed to a mark on her own forehead.

'That was done forty years ago, sir; I still bear the mark of it.'

'It was the time the "Uralia" went down,' put in Margery. 'Clayton was hit on the head by a spar, weren't you, Clayton?'

'Yes, Miss.'

'What do you think yourself, Clayton,' asked Mr Satterthwaite, 'what do you think was the meaning of this attack on Miss Margery?'

'I really should not like to say, sir.'

Mr Satterthwaite read this correctly as the reserve of the well-trained servant.

'What do you really think, Clayton?' he said persuasively.

'I think, sir, that something very wicked must have been done in this house, and that until that is wiped out there won't be any peace.'

The woman spoke gravely, and her faded blue eyes met his steadily.

Mr Satterthwaite went downstairs rather disappointed. Clayton evidently held the orthodox view, a deliberate 'haunting' as a consequence of some evil deed in the past. Mr Satterthwaite himself was not so easily satisfied. The phenomena had only taken place in the last two months. Had only taken place since Marcia Keane and Roley Vavasour had been there. He must find out something about these two. It was possible that the whole thing was a practical joke. But he shook his head, dissatisfied with that solution. The thing was more sinister than that. The post had just come in and Margery was opening and reading her letters. Suddenly she gave an exclamation.

'Mother is too absurd,' she said. 'Do read this.' She handed the letter to Mr Satterthwaite.

It was an epistle typical of Lady Stranleigh.

> 'DARLING MARGERY (she wrote),
>
> 'I am so glad you have that nice little Mr Satterthwaite there. He is awfully clever and knows all the big-wig spook people. You must have them all down and investigate things thoroughly. I am sure you will have a perfectly marvellous time, and I only wish I could be there, but I have really been quite ill the last few days. The hotels are so careless about the food they give one. The doctor says it is some kind of food poisoning. I was really *very* ill.
>
> 'Sweet of you to send me the chocolates, darling, but surely just a wee bit silly, wasn't it? I mean, there's such wonderful confectionery out here.
>
> 'Bye-bye, darling, and have a lovely time laying the family ghosts. Bimbo says my tennis is coming on marvellously. Oceans of love.
>
> 'Yours,
> 'BARBARA.'

'Mother always wants me to call her Barbara,' said Margery. 'Simply silly, I think.'

Mr Satterthwaite smiled a little. He realized that the stolid conservatism of her daughter must on occasions be very trying to Lady Stranleigh. The contents of her letter struck him in a way in which obviously they did not strike Margery.

'Did you send your mother a box of chocolates?' he asked.

Margery shook her head. 'No, I didn't, it must have been someone else.'

Mr Satterthwaite looked grave. Two things struck him as of significance. Lady Stranleigh had received a gift of a box of chocolates and she was suffering from a severe attack of poisoning. Apparently she had not connected these two things. Was there a connection? He himself was inclined to think there was.

A tall dark girl lounged out of the morning-room and joined them.

She was introduced to Mr Satterthwaite as Marcia Keane. She smiled on the little man in an easy good-humoured fashion.

'Have you come down to hunt Margery's pet ghost?' she asked in a drawling voice. 'We all rot her about that ghost. Hello, here's Roley.'

A car had just drawn up at the front door. Out of it tumbled a tall young man with fair hair and an eager boyish manner.

'Hello, Margery,' he cried. 'Hello, Marcia! I have brought down reinforcements.' He turned to the two women who were just entering the hall. Mr Satterthwaite recognized in the first one of the two the Mrs Casson of whom Margery had spoken just now.

'You must forgive me, Margery, dear,' she drawled, smiling broadly. 'Mr Vavasour told us that it would be quite all right. It was really his idea that I should bring down Mrs Lloyd with me.'

She indicated her companion with a slight gesture of the hand.

'This is Mrs Lloyd,' she said in a tone of triumph. 'Simply the most wonderful medium that ever existed.'

Mrs Lloyd uttered no modest protest, she bowed and remained with her hands crossed in front of her. She was a highly-coloured young woman of commonplace appearance. Her clothes were unfashionable but rather ornate. She wore a chain of moonstones and several rings.

Margery Gale, as Mr Satterthwaite could see, was not too pleased at this intrusion. She threw an angry look at Roley Vavasour, who seemed quite unconscious of the offence he had caused.

'Lunch is ready, I think,' said Margery.

'Good,' said Mrs Casson. 'We will hold a *séance* immediately afterwards. Have you got some fruit for Mrs Lloyd? She never eats a solid meal before a *séance*.'

They all went into the dining-room. The medium ate two bananas and an apple, and replied cautiously and briefly to the various polite remarks which Margery addressed to her from time to time. Just before they rose from the table, she flung back her head suddenly and sniffed the air.

'There is something very wrong in this house. I feel it.'

'Isn't she wonderful?' said Mrs Casson in a low delighted voice.

'Oh! undoubtedly,' said Mr Satterthwaite dryly.

The *séance* was held in the library. The hostess was, as Mr Satterthwaite could see, very unwilling, only the obvious delight of her guests in the proceedings reconciled her to the ordeal.

The arrangements were made with a good deal of care by Mrs Casson, who was evidently well up in those matters, the chairs were set round in a circle, the curtains were drawn, and presently the medium announced herself ready to begin.

'Six people,' she said, looking round the room. 'That is bad. We must have an uneven number. Seven is ideal. I get my best results out of a circle of seven.'

'One of the servants,' suggested Roley. He rose. 'I will rout out the butler.'

'Let's have Clayton,' said Margery.

Mr Satterthwaite saw a look of annoyance pass over Roley Vavasour's good-looking face.

'But why Clayton?' he demanded.

'You don't like Clayton,' said Margery slowly.

Roley shrugged his shoulders. 'Clayton doesn't like me,' he said whimsically. 'In fact she hates me like poison.' He waited a minute or two, but Margery did not give way. 'All right,' he said, 'have her down.'

The circle was formed.

There was a period of silence broken by the usual coughs and fidgetings. Presently a succession of raps were heard and then the voice of the medium's control, a Red Indian called Cherokee.

'Indian Brave says you Good evening ladies and gentlemen. Someone here very anxious speak. Someone here very anxious give message to young lady. I go now. The spirit say what she come to say.'

A pause and then a new voice, that of a woman, said softly: 'Is Margery here?'

Roley Vavasour took it upon himself to answer.

'Yes,' he said, 'she is. Who is that speaking?'

'I am Beatrice.'

'Beatrice? Who is Beatrice?'

To everyone's annoyance the voice of the Red Indian Cherokee was heard once more.

'I have message for all of you people. Life here very bright and beautiful. We all work very hard. Help those who have not yet passed over.'

Again a silence and then the woman's voice was heard once more.

'This is Beatrice speaking.'

'Beatrice who?'

'Beatrice Barron.'

Mr Satterthwaite leaned forward. He was very excited.

'Beatrice Barron who was drowned in the "Uralia"?'

'Yes, that is right. I remember the "Uralia." I have a message – for this house – *Give back what is not yours.*'

'I don't understand,' said Margery helplessly. 'I – oh, are you really Aunt Beatrice?'

'Yes, I am your aunt.'

'Of course she is,' said Mrs Casson reproachfully. 'How can you be so suspicious? The spirits don't like it.'

And suddenly Mr Satterthwaite thought of a very simple test. His voice quivered as he spoke.

'Do you remember Mr Bottacetti?' he asked.

Immediately there came a ripple of laughter.

'Poor old Boatsupsetty. Of course.'

Mr Satterthwaite was dumbfounded. The test had succeeded. It was an incident of over forty years ago which had happened when he and the Barron girls had found themselves at the same seaside resort. A young Italian acquaintance of theirs had gone out in a boat and capsized, and Beatrice Barron had jestingly named him Boatsupsetty. It seemed impossible that anyone in the room could know of this incident except himself.

The medium stirred and groaned.

'She is coming out,' said Mrs Casson. 'That is all we will get out of her today, I am afraid.'

The daylight shone once more on the room full of people, two of whom at least were badly scared.

Mr Satterthwaite saw by Margery's white face that she was deeply perturbed. When they had got rid of Mrs Casson and the medium, he sought a private interview with his hostess.

'I want to ask you one or two questions, Miss Margery. If you and your mother were to die who succeeds to the title and estates?'

'Roley Vavasour, I suppose. His mother was Mother's first cousin.'

Mr Satterthwaite nodded.

'He seems to have been here a lot this winter,' he said gently. 'You will forgive me asking – but is he – fond of you?'

'He asked me to marry him three weeks ago,' said Margery quietly. 'I said No.'

'Please forgive me, but are you engaged to anyone else?'

He saw the colour sweep over her face.

'I am,' she said emphatically. 'I am going to marry Noel Barton. Mother laughs and says it is absurd. She seems to think it is ridiculous to be engaged to a curate. Why, I should like to know! There are curates and curates! You should see Noel on a horse.'

'Oh, quite so,' said Mr Satterthwaite. 'Oh, undoubtedly.'

A footman entered with a telegram on a salver. Margery tore it open. 'Mother is arriving home tomorrow,' she said. 'Bother. I wish to goodness she would stay away.'

Mr Satterthwaite made no comment on this filial sentiment. Perhaps he thought it justified. 'In that case,' he murmured, 'I think I am returning to London.'

IV

Mr Satterthwaite was not quite pleased with himself. He felt that he had left this particular problem in an unfinished state. True that, on Lady Stranleigh's return, his responsibility was ended, yet he felt assured that he had not heard the last of the Abbot's Mede mystery.

But the next development when it came was so serious in its character that it found him totally unprepared. He learnt of it in the pages of his morning paper. 'Baroness Dies in her Bath,' as the *Daily Megaphone* had it. The other papers were more restrained and delicate in their language, but the fact was the same. Lady Stranleigh had been found dead in her bath and her death was due to drowning. She had, it was assumed, lost consciousness, and whilst in that state her head had slipped below the water.

But Mr Satterthwaite was not satisfied with that explanation. Calling for his valet he made his toilet with less than his usual care, and ten minutes later his big Rolls-Royce was carrying him out of London as fast as it could travel.

But strangely enough it was not for Abbot's Mede he was bound, but for a small inn some fifteen miles distant which bore the rather unusual name of 'The Bells and Motley.' It was with great relief that he heard that Mr Harley Quin was still staying there. In another minute he was face to face with his friend.

Mr Satterthwaite clasped him by the hand and began to speak at once in an agitated manner.

'I am terribly upset. You must help me. Already I have a dreadful feeling that it may be too late – that nice girl may be the next to go, for she is a nice girl, nice through and through.'

'If you will tell me,' said Mr Quin, smiling, 'what it is all about?'

Mr Satterthwaite looked at him reproachfully.

'You know. I am perfectly certain that you know. But I will tell you.'

He poured out the story of his stay at Abbot's Mede and, as

always with Mr Quin, he found himself taking pleasure in his narrative. He was eloquent and subtle and meticulous as to detail.

'So you see,' he ended, 'there must be an explanation.'

He looked hopefully at Mr Quin as a dog looks at his master.

'But it is you who must solve the problem, not I,' said Mr Quin. 'I do not know these people. You do.'

'I knew the Barron girls forty years ago,' said Mr Satterthwaite with pride.

Mr Quin nodded and looked sympathetic, so much so that the other went on dreamily.

'That time at Brighton now, Bottacetti-Boatsupsetty, quite a silly joke but how we laughed. Dear, dear, I was young then. Did a lot of foolish things. I remember the maid they had with them. Alice, her name was, a little bit of a thing – very ingenuous. I kissed her in the passage of the hotel, I remember, and one of the girls nearly caught me doing it. Dear, dear, how long ago that all was.'

He shook his head again and sighed. Then he looked at Mr Quin.

'So you can't help me?' he said wistfully. 'On other occasions –'

'On other occasions you have proved successful owing entirely to your own efforts,' said Mr Quin gravely. 'I think it will be the same this time. If I were you, I should go to Abbot's Mede now.'

'Quite so, quite so,' said Mr Satterthwaite, 'as a matter of fact that is what I thought of doing. I can't persuade you to come with me?'

Mr Quin shook his head.

'No,' he said, 'my work here is done. I am leaving almost immediately.'

At Abbot's Mede, Mr Satterthwaite was taken at once to Margery Gale. She was sitting dry-eyed at a desk in the morning-room on which were strewn various papers. Something in her greeting touched him. She seemed so very pleased to see him.

'Roley and Marcia have just left. Mr Satterthwaite, it is not as the doctors think. I am convinced, absolutely convinced, that Mother was pushed under the water and held there. She was murdered, and whoever murdered her wants to murder me too. I am sure of that. That is why –' she indicated the document in front of her.

'I have been making my will,' she explained. 'A lot of the money and some of the property does not go with the title, and there is my father's money as well. I am leaving everything I can to Noel. I know he will make a good use of it and I do not trust Roley, he has always been out for what he can get. Will you sign it as a witness?'

'My dear young lady,' said Mr Satterthwaite, 'you should sign a will in the presence of two witnesses and they should then sign themselves at the same time.'

Margery brushed aside this legal pronouncement.

'I don't see that it matters in the least,' she declared. 'Clayton saw me sign and then she signed her name. I was going to ring for the butler, but you will do instead.'

Mr Satterthwaite uttered no fresh protest, he unscrewed his fountain pen and then, as he was about to append his signature, he paused suddenly. The name, written just above his own, recalled a flow of memories. Alice Clayton.

Something seemed to be struggling very hard to get through to him. Alice Clayton, there was some significance about that. Something to do with Mr Quin was mixed up with it. Something he had said to Mr Quin only a very short time ago.

Ah, he had it now. Alice Clayton, that was her name. *The little bit of a thing.* People changed – yes, *but not like that.* And the Alice Clayton he knew had had brown eyes. The room seemed whirling round him. He felt for a chair and presently, as though from a great distance, he heard Margery's voice speaking to him anxiously. 'Are you ill? Oh, what is it? I am sure you are ill.'

He was himself again. He took her hand.

'My dear, I see it all now. You must prepare yourself for a great shock. The woman upstairs whom you call Clayton is not

Clayton at all. The real Alice Clayton was drowned on the
"Uralia." '

Margery was staring at him. 'Who – who is she then?'

'I am not mistaken, I cannot be mistaken. The woman you call
Clayton is your mother's sister, Beatrice Barron. You remember
telling me that she was struck on the head by a spar? I should
imagine that that blow destroyed her memory, and that being
the case, your mother saw the chance –'

'Of pinching the title, you mean?' asked Margery bitterly.
'Yes, she would do that. It seems dreadful to say that now she
is dead, but she was like that.'

'Beatrice was the elder sister,' said Mr Satterthwaite. 'By your
uncle's death she would inherit everything and your mother
would get nothing. Your mother claimed the wounded girl as
her *maid*, not as her *sister*. The girl recovered from the blow
and believed, of course, what was told her, that she was Alice
Clayton, your mother's maid. I should imagine that just lately
her memory had begun to return, but that the blow on the
head, given all these years ago, has at last caused mischief on
the brain.'

Margery was looking at him with eyes of horror.

'She killed Mother and she wanted to kill me,' she breathed.

'It seems so,' said Mr Satterthwaite. 'In her brain there was
just one muddled idea – that her inheritance had been stolen
and was being kept from her by you and your mother.'

'But – but Clayton is so old.'

Mr Satterthwaite was silent for a minute as a vision rose up
before him – the faded old woman with grey hair, and the
radiant golden-haired creature sitting in the sunshine at
Cannes. Sisters! Could it really be so? He remembered the Barron girls and their likeness to each other. Just because two lives
had developed on different tracks –

He shook his head sharply, obsessed by the wonder and pity
of life . . .

He turned to Margery and said gently: 'We had better go
upstairs and see her.'

They found Clayton sitting in the little workroom where she

sewed. She did not turn her head as they came in for a reason that Mr Satterthwaite soon found out.

'Heart failure,' he murmured, as he touched the cold rigid shoulder. 'Perhaps it is best that way.'

CHAPTER VIII

The Face of Helen

I

Mr Satterthwaite was at the Opera and sat alone in his big box on the first tier. Outside the door was a printed card bearing his name. An appreciator and a connoisseur of all the arts, Mr Satterthwaite was especially fond of good music, and was a regular subscriber to Covent Garden every year, reserving a box for Tuesdays and Fridays throughout the season.

But it was not often that he sat in it alone. He was a gregarious little gentleman, and he liked filling his box with the élite of the great world to which he belonged, and also with the aristocracy of the artistic world in which he was equally at home. He was alone tonight because a Countess had disappointed him. The Countess, besides being a beautiful and celebrated woman, was also a good mother. Her children had been attacked by that common and distressing disease, the mumps, and the Countess remained at home in tearful confabulation with exquisitely starched nurses. Her husband, who had supplied her with the aforementioned children and a title, but who was otherwise a complete nonentity, had seized at the chance to escape. Nothing bored him more than music.

So Mr Satterthwaite sat alone. *Cavalleria Rusticana* and *Pagliacci* were being given that night, and since the first had never appealed to him, he arrived just after the curtain went down, on Santuzza's death agony, in time to glance round the house with practised eyes, before everyone streamed out, bent on paying visits or fighting for coffee or lemonade. Mr Satterthwaite adjusted his opera glasses, looked round the house, marked down his prey and sallied forth with a well mapped out plan of campaign ahead of him. A plan, however, which he did not put into execution, for just outside his box he cannoned into a tall dark man, and recognized him with a pleasurable thrill of excitement.

'Mr Quin,' cried Mr Satterthwaite.

He seized his friend warmly by the hand, clutching him as though he feared any minute to see him vanish into thin air.

'You must share my box,' said Mr Satterthwaite determinedly. 'You are not with a party?'

'No, I am sitting by myself in the stalls,' responded Mr Quin with a smile.

'Then, that is settled,' said Mr Satterthwaite with a sigh of relief.

His manner was almost comic, had there been anyone to observe it.

'You are very kind,' said Mr Quin.

'Not at all. It is a pleasure. I didn't know you were fond of music?'

'There are reasons why I am attracted to – *Pagliacci*.'

'Ah! of course,' said Mr Satterthwaite, nodding sapiently, though, if put to it, he would have found it hard to explain just why he had used that expression. 'Of course, you would be.'

They went back to the box at the first summons of the bell, and leaning over the front of it, they watched the people returning to the stalls.

'That's a beautiful head,' observed Mr Satterthwaite suddenly.

He indicated with his glasses a spot immediately beneath them in the stalls circle. A girl sat there whose face they could not see – only the pure gold of her hair that fitted with the closeness of a cap till it merged into the white neck.

'A Greek head,' said Mr Satterthwaite reverently. 'Pure Greek.' He sighed happily. 'It's a remarkable thing when you come to think of it – how very few people have hair that *fits* them. It's more noticeable now that everyone is shingled.'

'You are so observant,' said Mr Quin.

'I see things,' admitted Mr Satterthwaite. 'I do see things. For instance, I picked out that head at once. We must have a look at her face sooner or later. But it won't match, I'm sure. That would be a chance in a thousand.'

Almost as the words left his lips, the lights flickered and went down, the sharp rap of the conductor's baton was heard, and the opera began. A new tenor, said to be a second Caruso, was singing that night. He had been referred to by the newspapers as a Jugo Slav, a Czech, an Albanian, a Magyar, and a Bulgarian, with a beautiful impartiality. He had given an extraordinary concert at the Albert Hall, a programme of the folk songs of his native hills, with a specially tuned orchestra. They were in strange half-tones and the would-be musical had pronounced them 'too marvellous.' Real musicians had reserved judgment, realizing that the ear had to be specially trained and attuned before any criticism was possible. It was quite a relief to some people to find this evening that Yoaschbim could sing in ordinary Italian with all the traditional sobs and quivers.

The curtain went down on the first act and applause burst out vociferously. Mr Satterthwaite turned to Mr Quin. He realized that the latter was waiting for him to pronounce judgment, and plumed himself a little. After all, he *knew*. As a critic he was well-nigh infallible.

Very slowly he nodded his head.

'It is the real thing,' he said.

'You think so?'

'As fine a voice as Caruso's. People will not recognize that it is so at first, for his technique is not yet perfect. There are ragged edges, a lack of certainty in the attack. But the voice is there – magnificent.'

'I went to his concert at the Albert Hall,' said Mr Quin.

'Did you? I could not go.'

'He made a wonderful hit with a Shepherd's Song.'

'I read about it,' said Mr Satterthwaite. 'The refrain ends each time with a high note – a kind of cry. A note midway between A and B flat. Very curious.'

Yoaschbim had taken three calls, bowing and smiling. The

lights went up and the people began to file out. Mr Satterthwaite leant over to watch the girl with the golden head. She rose, adjusted her scarf, and turned.

Mr Satterthwaite caught his breath. There were, he knew, such faces in the world – faces that made history.

The girl moved to the gangway, her companion, a young man, beside her. And Mr Satterthwaite noticed how every man in the vicinity looked – and continued to look covertly.

'Beauty!' said Mr Satterthwaite to himself. 'There is such a thing. Not charm, nor attraction, nor magnetism, nor any of the things we talk about so glibly – just sheer beauty. The shape of a face, the line of an eyebrow, the curve of a jaw.' He quoted softly under his breath: '*The face that launched a thousand ships.*' And for the first time he realized the meaning of those words.

He glanced across at Mr Quin, who was watching him in what seemed such perfect comprehension that Mr Satterthwaite felt there was no need for words.

'I've always wondered,' he said simply, 'what such women were really like.'

'You mean?'

'The Helens, the Cleopatras, the Mary Stuarts.'

Mr Quin nodded thoughtfully.

'If we go out,' he suggested, 'we may – see.'

They went out together, and their quest was successful. The pair they were in search of were seated on a lounge half-way up the staircase. For the first time, Mr Satterthwaite noted the girl's companion, a dark young man, not handsome, but with a suggestion of restless fire about him. A face full of strange angles; jutting cheek-bones, a forceful, slightly crooked jaw, deep-set eyes that were curiously light under the dark, over-hanging brows.

'An interesting face,' said Mr Satterthwaite to himself. 'A real face. It means something.'

The young man was leaning forward talking earnestly. The girl was listening. Neither of them belonged to Mr Satterthwaite's world. He took them to be of the 'Arty' class. The girl wore a rather shapeless garment of cheap green silk. Her shoes were of soiled, white satin. The young man wore his evening clothes with an air of being uncomfortable in them.

The two men passed and re-passed several times. The fourth time they did so, the couple had been joined by a third – a fair young man with a suggestion of the clerk about him. With his coming a certain tension had set in. The newcomer was fidgeting with his tie and seemed ill at ease, the girl's beautiful face was turned gravely up towards him, and her companion was scowling furiously.

'The usual story,' said Mr Quin very softly, as they passed.

'Yes,' said Mr Satterthwaite with a sigh. 'It's inevitable, I suppose. The snarling of two dogs over a bone. It always has been, it always will be. And yet, one could wish for something different. Beauty –' he stopped. Beauty, to Mr Satterthwaite, meant something very wonderful. He found it difficult to speak of it. He looked at Mr Quin, who nodded his head gravely in understanding.

They went back to their seats for the second act.

At the close of the performance, Mr Satterthwaite turned eagerly to his friend.

'It is a wet night. My car is here. You must allow me to drive you – er – somewhere.'

The last word was Mr Satterthwaite's delicacy coming into play. 'To drive you home' would, he felt, have savoured of curiosity. Mr Quin had always been singularly reticent. It was extraordinary how little Mr Satterthwaite knew about him.

'But perhaps,' continued the little man, 'you have your own car waiting?'

'No,' said Mr Quin, 'I have no car waiting.'

'Then –'

But Mr Quin shook his head.

'You are most kind,' he said, 'but I prefer to go my own way. Besides,' he said with a rather curious smile, 'if anything should – happen, it will be for you to act. Goodnight, and thank you. Once again we have seen the drama together.'

He had gone so quickly that Mr Satterthwaite had no time to protest, but he was left with a faint uneasiness stirring in his mind. To what drama did Mr Quin refer? *Pagliacci* or another?

Masters, Mr Satterthwaite's chauffeur, was in the habit of waiting in a side street. His master disliked the long delay while the cars drew up in turn before the Opera house. Now, as on previous occasions, he walked rapidly round the corner and along the street towards where he knew he should find Masters awaiting him. Just in front of him were a girl and a man, and even as he recognized them, another man joined them.

It all broke out in a minute. A man's voice, angrily uplifted. Another man's voice in injured protest. And then the scuffle. Blows, angry breathing, more blows, the form of a policeman appearing majestically from nowhere – and in another minute Mr Satterthwaite was beside the girl where she shrank back against the wall.

'Allow me,' he said. 'You must not stay here.'

He took her by the arm and marshalled her swiftly down the street. Once she looked back.

'Oughtn't I –?' she began uncertainly.

Mr Satterthwaite shook his head.

'It would be very unpleasant for you to be mixed up in it. You would probably be asked to go along to the police station with them. I am sure neither of your – friends would wish that.'

He stopped.

'This is my car. If you will allow me to do so, I shall have much pleasure in driving you home.'

The girl looked at him searchingly. The staid respectability of Mr Satterthwaite impressed her favourably. She bent her head.

'Thank you,' she said, and got into the car, the door of which Masters was holding open.

In reply to a question from Mr Satterthwaite, she gave an address in Chelsea, and he got in beside her.

The girl was upset and not in the mood for talking, and Mr Satterthwaite was too tactful to intrude upon her thoughts. Presently, however, she turned to him and spoke of her own accord.

'I wish,' she said pettishly, 'people wouldn't be so silly.'

'It is a nuisance,' agreed Mr Satterthwaite.

His matter-of-fact manner put her at her ease, and she went on as though feeling the need of confiding in someone.

'It wasn't as though – I mean, well, it was like this. Mr Eastney and I have been friends for a long time – ever since I came to London. He's taken no end of trouble about my voice, and got me some very good introductions, and he's been more kind to me than I can say. He's absolutely music mad. It was very good of him to take me tonight. I'm sure he can't really afford it. And then Mr Burns came up and spoke to us – quite nicely, I'm sure, and Phil (Mr Eastney) got sulky about it. I don't know why he should. It's a free country, I'm sure. And Mr Burns is always pleasant, and good-tempered. Then just as we were walking to the Tube, he came up and joined us, and he hadn't so much as said two words before Philip flew out at him like a madman. And – Oh! I don't like it.'

'Don't you?' asked Mr Satterthwaite very softly.

She blushed, but very little. There was none of the conscious siren about her. A certain measure of pleasurable excitement in being fought for there must be – that was only nature, but Mr Satterthwaite decided that a worried perplexity lay uppermost, and he had the clue to it in another moment when she observed inconsequently:

'I do hope he hasn't hurt him.'

'Now which is "him"?' thought Mr Satterthwaite, smiling to himself in the darkness.

He backed his own judgment and said:

'You hope Mr – er – Eastney hasn't hurt Mr Burns?'

She nodded.

'Yes, that's what I said. It seems so dreadful. I wish I knew.'

The car was drawing up.

'Are you on the telephone?' he asked.

'Yes.'

'If you like, I will find out exactly what has happened, and then telephone to you.'

The girl's face brightened.

'Oh, that would be very kind of you. Are you sure it's not too much bother?'

'Not in the least.'

She thanked him again and gave him her telephone number, adding with a touch of shyness: 'My name is Gillian West.'

As he was driven through the night, bound on his errand, a curious smile came to Mr Satterthwaite's lips.

He thought: 'So that is all it is ... *"The shape of a face, the curve of a jaw!"*'

But he fulfilled his promise.

II

The following Sunday afternoon Mr Satterthwaite went to Kew Gardens to admire the rhododendrons. Very long ago (incredibly long ago, it seemed to Mr Satterthwaite) he had driven down to Kew Gardens with a certain young lady to see the bluebells. Mr Satterthwaite had arranged very carefully beforehand in his own mind exactly what he was going to say, and the precise words he would use in asking the young lady for her hand in marriage. He was just conning them over in his mind, and responding to her raptures about the bluebells a little absent-mindedly, when the shock came. The young lady stopped exclaiming at the bluebells and suddenly confided in Mr Satterthwaite (as a true friend) her love for another. Mr Satterthwaite put away the little set speech he had prepared, and hastily rummaged for sympathy and friendship in the bottom drawer of his mind.

Such was Mr Satterthwaite's romance – a rather tepid early Victorian one, but it had left him with a romantic attachment to Kew Gardens, and he would often go there to see the bluebells, or, if he had been abroad later than usual, the rhododendrons, and would sigh to himself, and feel rather sentimental, and really enjoy himself very much indeed in an old-fashioned, romantic way.

This particular afternoon he was strolling back past the tea

houses when he recognized a couple sitting at one of the small
tables on the grass. They were Gillian West and the fair young
man, and at that same moment they recognized him. He saw
the girl flush and speak eagerly to her companion. In another
minute he was shaking hands with them both in his correct,
rather prim fashion, and had accepted the shy invitation prof-
fered him to have tea with them.

'I can't tell you, sir,' said Mr Burns, 'how grateful I am to
you for looking after Gillian the other night. She told me all
about it.'

'Yes, indeed,' said the girl. 'It was ever so kind of you.'

Mr Satterthwaite felt pleased and interested in the pair. Their
naïveté and sincerity touched him. Also, it was to him a peep
into a world with which he was not well acquainted. These
people were of a class unknown to him.

In his little dried-up way, Mr Satterthwaite could be very
sympathetic. Very soon he was hearing all about his new
friends. He noted that Mr Burns had become Charlie, and he
was not unprepared for the statement that the two were
engaged.

'As a matter of fact,' said Mr Burns with refreshing candour,
'it just happened this afternoon, didn't it, Gil?'

Burns was a clerk in a shipping firm. He was making a fair
salary, had a little money of his own, and the two proposed to
be married quite soon.

Mr Satterthwaite listened, and nodded, and congratulated.

'An ordinary young man,' he thought to himself, 'a very ordinary young man. Nice, straightforward young chap, plenty to say
for himself, good opinion of himself without being conceited,
nice-looking without being unduly handsome. Nothing remarkable about him and will never set the Thames on fire. And the
girl loves him . . .'

Aloud he said: 'And Mr Eastney –'

He purposely broke off, but he had said enough to produce
an effect for which he was not unprepared. Charlie Burns's face
darkened, and Gillian looked troubled. More than troubled, he
thought. She looked afraid.

'I don't like it,' she said in a low voice. Her words were addressed to Mr Satterthwaite, as though she knew by instinct that he would understand a feeling incomprehensible to her lover. 'You see – he's done a lot for me. He's encouraged me to take up singing, and – and helped me with it. But I've known all the time that my voice wasn't really good – not first-class. Of course, I've had engagements –'

She stopped.

'You've had a bit of trouble too,' said Burns. 'A girl wants someone to look after her. Gillian's had a lot of unpleasantness, Mr Satterthwaite. Altogether she's had a lot of unpleasantness. She's a good-looker, as you can see, and – well, that often leads to trouble for a girl.'

Between them, Mr Satterthwaite became enlightened as to various happenings which were vaguely classed by Burns under the heading of 'unpleasantness.' A young man who had shot himself, the extraordinary conduct of a Bank Manager (who was a married man!), a violent stranger (who must have been balmy!), the wild behaviour of an elderly artist. A trail of violence and tragedy that Gillian West had left in her wake, recited in the commonplace tones of Charles Burns. 'And it's my opinion,' he ended, 'that this fellow Eastney is a bit cracked. Gillian would have had trouble with him if I hadn't turned up to look after her.'

His laugh sounded a little fatuous to Mr Satterthwaite, and no responsive smile came to the girl's face. She was looking earnestly at Mr Satterthwaite.

'Phil's all right,' she said slowly. 'He cares for me, I know, and I care for him like a friend – but – but not anything more. I don't know how he'll take the news about Charlie, I'm sure. He – I'm so afraid he'll be –'

She stopped, inarticulate in face of the dangers she vaguely sensed.

'If I can help you in any way,' said Mr Satterthwaite warmly, 'pray command me.'

He fancied Charlie Burns looked vaguely resentful, but Gillian said at once: 'Thank you.'

Mr Satterthwaite left his new friends after having promised to take tea with Gillian on the following Thursday.

When Thursday came, Mr Satterthwaite felt a little thrill of pleasurable anticipation. He thought: 'I'm an old man – but not too old to be thrilled by a face. A face . . .' Then he shook his head with a sense of foreboding.

Gillian was alone. Charlie Burns was to come in later. She looked much happier, Mr Satterthwaite thought, as though a load had been lifted from her mind. Indeed, she frankly admitted as much.

'I dreaded telling Phil about Charles. It was silly of me. I ought to have known Phil better. He was upset, of course, but no one could have been sweeter. Really sweet he was. Look what he sent me this morning – a wedding present. Isn't it magnificent?'

It was indeed rather magnificent for a young man in Philip Eastney's circumstances. A four-valve wireless set, of the latest type.

'We both love music so much, you see,' explained the girl. 'Phil said that when I was listening to a concert on this, I should always think of him a little. And I'm sure I shall. Because we have been such friends.'

'You must be proud of your friend,' said Mr Satterthwaite gently. 'He seems to have taken the blow like a true sportsman.'

Gillian nodded. He saw the quick tears come into her eyes.

'He asked me to do one thing for him. Tonight is the anniversary of the day we first met. He asked me if I would stay at home quietly this evening and listen to the wireless programme – not to go out with Charlie anywhere. I said, of course I would, and that I was very touched, and that I would think of him with a lot of gratitude and affection.'

Mr Satterthwaite nodded, but he was puzzled. He was seldom at fault in his delineation of character, and he would have judged Philip Eastney quite incapable of such a sentimental request. The young man must be of a more banal order than he supposed. Gillian evidently thought the idea quite in keeping with her rejected lover's character. Mr Satterthwaite was a little

– just a little – disappointed. He was sentimental himself, and knew it, but he expected better things of the rest of the world. Besides sentiment belonged to his age. It had no part to play in the modern world.

He asked Gillian to sing and she complied. He told her her voice was charming, but he knew quite well in his own mind that it was distinctly second-class. Any success that could have come to her in the profession she had adopted would have been won by her face, not her voice.

He was not particularly anxious to see young Burns again, so presently he rose to go. It was at that moment that his attention was attracted by an ornament on the mantelpiece which stood out among the other rather gimcrack objects like a jewel on a dust heap.

It was a curving beaker of thin green glass, long-stemmed and graceful, and poised on the edge of it was what looked like a gigantic soap-bubble, a ball of iridescent glass. Gillian noticed his absorption.

'That's an extra wedding present from Phil. It's rather pretty, I think. He works in a sort of glass factory.'

'It is a beautiful thing,' said Mr Satterthwaite reverently. 'The glass blowers of Murano might have been proud of that.'

He went away with his interest in Philip Eastney strangely stimulated. An extraordinarily interesting young man. And yet the girl with the wonderful face preferred Charlie Burns. What a strange and inscrutable universe!

It had just occurred to Mr Satterthwaite that, owing to the remarkable beauty of Gillian West, his evening with Mr Quin had somehow missed fire. As a rule, every meeting with that mysterious individual had resulted in some strange and unforeseen happening. It was with the hope of perhaps running against the man of mystery that Mr Satterthwaite bent his steps towards the *Arlecchino* Restaurant where once, in the days gone by, he had met Mr Quin, and which Mr Quin had said he often frequented.

Mr Satterthwaite went from room to room at the *Arlecchino*, looking hopefully about him, but there was no sign of Mr Quin's dark, smiling face. There was, however, somebody else. Sitting at a small table alone was Philip Eastney.

The place was crowded and Mr Satterthwaite took his seat opposite the young man. He felt a sudden strange sense of exultation, as though he were caught up and made part of a shimmering pattern of events. He was in this thing – whatever it was. He knew now what Mr Quin had meant that evening at the Opera. There was a drama going on, and in it was a part, an important part, for Mr Satterthwaite. He must not fail to take his cue and speak his lines.

He sat down opposite Philip Eastney with the sense of accomplishing the inevitable. It was easy enough to get into conversation. Eastney seemed anxious to talk. Mr Satterthwaite was, as always, an encouraging and sympathetic listener. They talked of the war, of explosives, of poison gases. Eastney had a lot to say about these last, for during the greater part of the war he had been engaged in their manufacture. Mr Satterthwaite found him really interesting.

There was one gas, Eastney said, that had never been tried. The Armistice had come too soon. Great things had been hoped for it. One whiff of it was deadly. He warmed to animation as he spoke.

Having broken the ice, Mr Satterthwaite gently turned the conversation to music. Eastney's thin face lit up. He spoke with the passion and abandon of the real music lover. They discussed Yoaschbim, and the young man was enthusiastic. Both he and Mr Satterthwaite agreed that nothing on earth could surpass a really fine tenor voice. Eastney as a boy had heard Caruso and he had never forgotten it.

'Do you know that he could sing to a wine-glass and shatter it?' he demanded.

'I always thought that was a fable,' said Mr Satterthwaite smiling.

'No, it's gospel truth, I believe. The thing's quite possible. It's a question of resonance.'

He went off into technical details. His face was flushed and his eyes shone. The subject seemed to fascinate him, and Mr

Satterthwaite noted that he seemed to have a thorough grasp of what he was talking about. The elder man realized that he was talking to an exceptional brain, a brain that might almost be described as that of a genius. Brilliant, erratic, undecided as yet as to the true channel to give it outlet, but undoubtedly genius.

And he thought of Charlie Burns and wondered at Gillian West.

It was with quite a start that he realized how late it was getting, and he called for his bill. Eastney looked slightly apologetic.

'I'm ashamed of myself – running on so,' he said. 'But it was a lucky chance sent you along here tonight. I – I needed someone to talk to this evening.'

He ended his speech with a curious little laugh. His eyes were still blazing with some subdued excitement. Yet there was something tragic about him.

'It has been quite a pleasure,' said Mr Satterthwaite. 'Our conversation has been most interesting and instructive to me.'

He then made his funny, courteous little bow and passed out of the restaurant. The night was a warm one and as he walked slowly down the street a very odd fancy came to him. He had the feeling that he was not alone – that someone was walking by his side. In vain he told himself that the idea was a delusion – it persisted. Someone was walking beside him down that dark, quiet street, someone whom he could not see. He wondered what it was that brought the figure of Mr Quin so clearly before his mind. He felt exactly as though Mr Quin were there walking beside him, and yet he had only to use his eyes to assure himself that it was not so, that he was alone.

But the thought of Mr Quin persisted, and with it came something else: a need, an urgency of some kind, an oppressive foreboding of calamity. There was something he must do – and do quickly. There was something very wrong, and it lay in his hands to put it right.

So strong was the feeling that Mr Satterthwaite forebore to fight against it. Instead, he shut his eyes and tried to bring that mental image of Mr Quin nearer. If he could only have asked

Mr Quin – but even as the thought flashed through his mind he knew it was wrong. It was never any use asking Mr Quin anything. 'The threads are all in your hands' – that was the kind of thing Mr Quin would say.

The threads. Threads of what? He analysed his own feeling and impressions carefully. That presentiment of danger, now. Whom did it threaten?

At once a picture rose up before his eyes, the picture of Gillian West sitting alone listening to the wireless.

Mr Satterthwaite flung a penny to a passing newspaper boy, and snatched at a paper. He turned at once to the London Radio programme. Yoaschbim was broadcasting tonight, he noted with interest. He was singing 'Salve Dimora,' from Faust and, afterwards, a selection of his folk songs. 'The Shepherd's Song,' 'The Fish,' 'The Little Deer,' etc.

Mr Satterthwaite crumpled the paper together. The knowledge of what Gillian was listening to seemed to make the picture of her clearer. Sitting there alone . . .

An odd request, that, of Philip Eastney's. Not like the man, not like him at all. There was no sentimentality in Eastney. He was a man of violent feeling, a dangerous man, perhaps –

Again his thought brought up with a jerk. A dangerous man – that meant something. '*The threads are all in your hands.*' That meeting with Philip Eastney tonight – rather odd. A lucky chance, Eastney had said. Was it chance? Or was it part of that interwoven design of which Mr Satterthwaite had once or twice been conscious this evening?

He cast his mind back. There must be *something* in Eastney's conversation, some clue there. There must, or else why this strange feeling of urgency? What had he talked about? Singing, war work, Caruso.

Caruso – Mr Satterthwaite's thoughts went off at a tangent. Yoaschbim's voice was very nearly equal to that of Caruso. Gillian would be sitting listening to it now as it rang out true and powerful, echoing round the room, setting glasses ringing –

He caught his breath. Glasses ringing! Caruso, singing to a wine-glass and the wine-glass breaking. Yoaschbim singing in the London studio and in a room over a mile away the crash and tinkle of glass – not a wine-glass, a thin, green, glass beaker. A crystal soap bubble falling, a soap bubble that perhaps was not empty . . .

It was at that moment that Mr Satterthwaite, as judged by passers-by, suddenly went mad. He tore open the newspaper once more, took a brief glance at the wireless announcements and then began to run for his life down the quiet street. At the end of it he found a crawling taxi, and jumping into it, he yelled an address to the driver and the information that it was life or death to get there quickly. The driver, judging him mentally afflicted but rich, did his utmost.

Mr Satterthwaite lay back, his head a jumble of fragmentary thoughts, forgotten bits of science learned at school, phrases used by Eastney that night. Resonance – natural periods – if the period of the force coincides with the natural period – there was something about a suspension bridge, soldiers marching over it and the swing of their stride being the same as the period of the bridge. Eastney had studied the subject. Eastney knew. And Eastney was a genius.

At 10.45 Yoaschbim was to broadcast. It was that now. Yes, but the Faust had to come first. It was the 'Shepherd's Song,' with the great shout after the refrain that would – that would – do what?

His mind went whirling round again. Tones, overtones, half-tones. He didn't know much about these things – but Eastney knew. Pray heaven he would be in time!

The taxi stopped. Mr Satterthwaite flung himself out and raced up the stone stairs to a second floor like a young athlete. The door of the flat was ajar. He pushed it open and the great tenor voice welcomed him. The words of the 'Shepherd's Song' were familiar to him in a less unconventional setting.

'Shepherd, see they horse's flowing main –'

He was in time then. He burst open the sitting-room door. Gillian was sitting there in a tall chair by the fireplace.

'*Bayra Mischa's daughter is to wed today:*
To the wedding I must haste away.'

She must have thought him mad. He clutched at her, crying out something incomprehensible, and half pulled, half dragged her out till they stood upon the stairway.

'*To the wedding I must haste away –*
Ya-ha!'

A wonderful high note, full-throated, powerful, hit full in the middle, a note any singer might be proud of. And with it another sound, the faint tinkle of broken glass.

A stray cat darted past them and in through the flat door. Gillian made a movement, but Mr Satterthwaite held her back, speaking incoherently.

'No, no – it's deadly: no smell, nothing to warn you. A mere whiff, and it's all over. Nobody knows quite how deadly it would be. It's unlike anything that's ever been tried before.'

He was repeating the things that Philip Eastney had told him over the table at dinner.

Gillian stared at him uncomprehendingly.

III

Philip Eastney drew out his watch and looked at it. It was just half-past eleven. For the past three-quarters of an hour he had been pacing up and down the Embankment. He looked out over the Thames and then turned – to look into the face of his dinner companion.

'That's odd,' he said, and laughed. 'We seem fated to run into each other tonight.'

'If you call it Fate,' said Mr Satterthwaite.

Philip Eastney looked at him more attentively and his own expression changed.

'Yes?' he said quietly.

Mr Satterthwaite went straight to the point.

'I have just come from Miss West's flat.'

'Yes?'

The same voice, with the same deadly quiet.

'We have – taken a dead cat out of it.'

There was silence, then Eastney said:

'Who are you?'

Mr Satterthwaite spoke for some time. He recited the whole history of events.

'So you see, I was in time,' he ended up. He paused and added quite gently:

'Have you anything – to say?'

He expected something, some outburst, some wild justification. But nothing came.

'No,' said Philip Eastney quietly, and turned on his heel and walked away.

Mr Satterthwaite looked after him till his figure was swallowed up in the gloom. In spite of himself, he had a strange fellow-feeling for Eastney, the feeling of an artist for another artist, of a sentimentalist for a real lover, of a plain man for a genius.

At last he roused himself with a start and began to walk in the same direction as Eastney. A fog was beginning to come up. Presently he met a policeman who looked at him suspiciously.

'Did you hear a kind of splash just now?' asked the policeman.

'No,' said Mr Satterthwaite.

The policeman was peering out over the river.

'Another of these suicides, I expect,' he grunted disconsolately. 'They will do it.'

'I suppose,' said Mr Satterthwaite, 'that they have their reasons.'

'Money, mostly,' said the policeman. 'Sometimes it's a woman,' he said, as he prepared to move away. 'It's not always their fault, but some women cause a lot of trouble.'

'Some women,' agreed Mr Satterthwaite softly.

When the policeman had gone on, he sat down on a seat

with the fog coming up all around him, and thought about Helen of Troy, and wondered if she were a nice, ordinary woman, blessed or cursed with a wonderful face.

CHAPTER IX

The Dead Harlequin

Mr Satterthwaite walked slowly up Bond Street enjoying the sunshine. He was, as usual, carefully and beautifully dressed, and was bound for the Harchester Galleries where there was an exhibition of the paintings of one Frank Bristow, a new and hitherto unknown artist who showed signs of suddenly becoming the rage. Mr Satterthwaite was a patron of the arts.

As Mr Satterthwaite entered the Harchester Galleries, he was greeted at once with a smile of pleased recognition.

'Good morning, Mr Satterthwaite, I thought we should see you before long. You know Bristow's work? Fine – very fine indeed. Quite unique of its kind.'

Mr Satterthwaite purchased a catalogue and stepped through the open archway into the long room where the artist's works were displayed. They were water colours, executed with such extraordinary technique and finish that they resembled coloured etchings. Mr Satterthwaite walked slowly round the walls scrutinizing and, on the whole, approving. He thought that this young man deserved to arrive. Here was originality, vision, and a most severe and exacting technique. There were crudities, of course. That was only to be expected – but there was also something closely allied to genius. Mr Satterthwaite paused before a little masterpiece representing Westminster Bridge with its crowd of buses, trams and hurrying pedestrians. A tiny thing and wonderfully perfect. It was called, he noted, The Ant Heap. He passed on and quite suddenly drew in his breath with a gasp, his imagination held and riveted.

The picture was called The Dead Harlequin. The forefront of it represented a floor of inlaid squares of black and white marble. In the middle of the floor lay Harlequin on his back with his arms outstretched, in his motley of black and red. Behind him was a window and outside that window, gazing in at the figure on the floor, was what appeared to be the same man silhouetted against the red glow of the setting sun.

The picture excited Mr Satterthwaite for two reasons, the first was that he recognized, or thought that he recognized, the face of the man in the picture. It bore a distinct resemblance to a certain Mr Quin, an acquaintance whom Mr Satterthwaite had encountered once or twice under somewhat mystifying circumstances.

'Surely I can't be mistaken,' he murmured. 'If it *is* so – what does it mean?'

For it had been Mr Satterthwaite's experience that every appearance of Mr Quin had some distinct significance attaching to it.

There was, as already mentioned, a second reason for Mr Satterthwaite's interest. He recognized the scene of the picture.

'The Terrace Room at Charnley,' said Mr Satterthwaite. 'Curious – and very interesting.'

He looked with more attention at the picture, wondering what exactly had been in the artist's mind. One Harlequin dead on the floor, another Harlequin looking through the window – or was it the same Harlequin? He moved slowly along the walls gazing at other pictures with unseeing eyes, with his mind always busy on the same subject. He was excited. Life, which had seemed a little drab this morning, was drab no longer. He knew quite certainly that he was on the threshold of exciting and interesting events. He crossed to the table where sat Mr Cobb, a dignitary of the Harchester Galleries, whom he had known for many years.

'I have a fancy for buying no. 39,' he said, 'if it is not already sold.'

Mr Cobb consulted a ledger.

'The pick of the bunch,' he murmured, 'quite a little gem, isn't it? No, it is not sold.' He quoted a price. 'It is a good investment, Mr Satterthwaite. You will have to pay three times as much for it this time next year.'

'That is always said on these occasions,' said Mr Satterthwaite, smiling.

'Well, and haven't I been right?' demanded Mr Cobb. 'I don't believe if you were to sell your collection, Mr Satterthwaite, that a single picture would fetch less than you gave for it.'

'I will buy this picture,' said Mr Satterthwaite. 'I will give you a cheque now.'

'You won't regret it. We believe in Bristow.'

'He is a young man?'

'Twenty-seven or eight, I should say.'

'I should like to meet him,' said Mr Satterthwaite. 'Perhaps he will come and dine with me one night?'

'I can give you his address. I am sure he would leap at the chance. Your name stands for a good deal in the artistic world.'

'You flatter me,' said Mr Satterthwaite, and was going on when Mr Cobb interrupted:

'Here he is now. I will introduce you to him right away.'

He rose from behind his table. Mr Satterthwaite accompanied him to where a big, clumsy young man was leaning against the wall surveying the world at large from behind the barricade of a ferocious scowl.

Mr Cobb made the necessary introductions and Mr Satterthwaite made a formal and gracious little speech.

'I have just had the pleasure of acquiring one of your pictures – The Dead Harlequin.'

'Oh! Well, you won't lose by it,' said Mr Bristow ungraciously. 'It's a bit of damned good work, although I say it.'

'I can see that,' said Mr Satterthwaite. 'Your work interests me very much, Mr Bristow. It is extraordinarily mature for so young a man. I wonder if you would give me the pleasure of dining with me one night? Are you engaged this evening?'

'As a matter of fact, I am not,' said Mr Bristow, still with no overdone appearance of graciousness.

'Then shall we say eight o'clock?' said Mr Satterthwaite. 'Here is my card with the address on it.'

'Oh, all right,' said Mr Bristow. 'Thanks,' he added as a somewhat obvious afterthought.

'A young man who has a poor opinion of himself and is afraid that the world should share it.'

Such was Mr Satterthwaite's summing up as he stepped out into the sunshine of Bond Street, and Mr Satterthwaite's judgment of his fellow men was seldom far astray.

Frank Bristow arrived about five minutes past eight to find his host and a third guest awaiting him. The other guest was introduced as a Colonel Monckton. They went in to dinner almost immediately. There was a fourth place laid at the oval mahogany table and Mr Satterthwaite uttered a word of explanation.

'I half expected my friend, Mr Quin, might drop in,' he said. 'I wonder if you have ever met him. Mr Harley Quin?'

'I never meet people,' growled Bristow.

Colonel Monckton stared at the artist with the detached interest he might have accorded to a new species of jelly fish. Mr Satterthwaite exerted himself to keep the ball of conversation rolling amicably.

'I took a special interest in that picture of yours because I thought I recognized the scene of it as being the Terrace Room at Charnley. Was I right?' As the artist nodded, he went on. 'That is very interesting. I have stayed at Charnley several times myself in the past. Perhaps you know some of the family?'

'No, I don't!' said Bristow. 'That sort of family wouldn't care to know me. I went there in a charabanc.'

'Dear me,' said Colonel Monckton for the sake of saying something. 'In a charabanc! Dear me.'

Frank Bristow scowled at him.

'Why not?' he demanded ferociously.

Poor Colonel Monckton was taken aback. He looked reproachfully at Mr Satterthwaite as though to say:

'These primitive forms of life may be interesting to you as a naturalist, but why drag *me* in?'

'Oh, beastly things, charabancs!' he said. 'They jolt you so going over the bumps.'

'If you can't afford a Rolls Royce you have got to go in charabancs,' said Bristow fiercely.

Colonel Monckton stared at him. Mr Satterthwaite thought:

'Unless I can manage to put this young man at his ease we are going to have a very distressing evening.'

'Charnley always fascinated me,' he said. 'I have been there only once since the tragedy. A grim house – and a ghostly one.'

'That's true,' said Bristow.

'There are actually two authentic ghosts,' said Monckton. 'They say that Charles I walks up and down the terrace with his head under his arm – I have forgotten why, I'm sure. Then there is the Weeping Lady with the Silver Ewer, who is always seen after one of the Charnleys dies.'

'Tosh,' said Bristow scornfully.

'They have certainly been a very ill-fated family,' said Mr Satterthwaite hurriedly. 'Four holders of the title have died a violent death and the late Lord Charnley committed suicide.'

'A ghastly business,' said Monckton gravely. 'I was there when it happened.'

'Let me see, that must be fourteen years ago,' said Mr Satterthwaite, 'the house has been shut up ever since.'

'I don't wonder at that,' said Monckton. 'It must have been a terrible shock for a young girl. They had been married a month, just home from their honeymoon. Big fancy dress ball to celebrate their home-coming. Just as the guests were starting to arrive Charnley locked himself into the Oak Parlour and shot himself. That sort of thing isn't done. I beg your pardon?'

He turned his head sharply to the left and looked across at Mr Satterthwaite with an apologetic laugh.

'I am beginning to get the jimjams, Satterthwaite. I thought for a moment there was someone sitting in that empty chair and that he said something to me.

'Yes,' he went on after a minute or two, 'it was a pretty ghastly shock to Alix Charnley. She was one of the prettiest girls you could see anywhere and cram full of what people call the joy of living, and now they say she is like a ghost herself. Not that I have seen her for years. I believe she lives abroad most of the time.'

'And the boy?'

'The boy is at Eton. What he will do when he comes of age I don't know. I don't think, somehow, that he will reopen the old place.'

'It would make a good People's Pleasure Park,' said Bristow. Colonel Monckton looked at him with cold abhorrence.

'No, no, you don't really mean that,' said Mr Satterthwaite. 'You wouldn't have painted that picture if you did. Tradition and atmosphere are intangible things. They take centuries to build up and if you destroyed them you couldn't rebuild them again in twenty-four hours.'

He rose. 'Let us go into the smoking-room. I have some photographs there of Charnley which I should like to show you.'

One of Mr Satterthwaite's hobbies was amateur photography. He was also the proud author of a book, 'Homes of My Friends.' The friends in question were all rather exalted and the book itself showed Mr Satterthwaite forth in rather a more snobbish light than was really fair to him.

'That is a photograph I took of the Terrace Room last year,' he said. He handed it to Bristow. 'You see it is taken at almost the same angle as is shown in your picture. That is rather a wonderful rug – it is a pity that photographs can't show colouring.'

'I remember it,' said Bristow, 'a marvellous bit of colour. It glowed like a flame. All the same it looked a bit incongruous there. The wrong size for that big room with its black and white squares. There is no rug anywhere else in the room. It spoils the whole effect – it was like a gigantic blood stain.'

'Perhaps that gave you your idea for your picture?' said Mr Satterthwaite.

'Perhaps it did,' said Bristow thoughtfully. 'On the face of it, one would naturally stage a tragedy in the little panelled room leading out of it.'

'The Oak Parlour,' said Monckton. 'Yes, that is the haunted room right enough. There is a Priests' hiding hole there – a movable panel by the fireplace. Tradition has it that Charles I was concealed there once. There were two deaths from duelling in that room. And it was there, as I say, that Reggie Charnley shot himself.'

He took the photograph from Bristow's hand.

'Why, that is the Bokhara rug,' he said, 'worth a couple of thousand pounds, I believe. When I was there it was in the Oak Parlour – the right place for it. It looks silly on that great expanse of marble flags.'

Mr Satterthwaite was looking at the empty chair which he had drawn up beside his. Then he said thoughtfully: 'I wonder when it was moved?'

'It must have been recently. Why, I remember having a conversation about it on the very day of the tragedy. Charnley was saying it really ought to be kept under glass.'

Mr Satterthwaite shook his head. 'The house was shut up immediately after the tragedy and everything was left exactly as it was.'

Bristow broke in with a question. He had laid aside his aggressive manner.

'Why did Lord Charnley shoot himself?' he asked.

Colonel Monckton shifted uncomfortably in his chair.

'No one ever knew,' he said vaguely.

'I suppose,' said Mr Satterthwaite slowly, 'that it *was* suicide.'

The Colonel looked at him in blank astonishment.

'Suicide,' he said, 'why, of course it was suicide. My dear fellow, I was there in the house myself.'

Mr Satterthwaite looked towards the empty chair at his side and, smiling to himself as though at some hidden joke the others could not see, he said quietly:

'Sometimes one sees things more clearly years afterwards than one could possibly at the time.'

'Nonsense,' spluttered Monckton, 'arrant nonsense! How can you possibly see things better when they are vague in your memory instead of clear and sharp?'

But Mr Satterthwaite was reinforced from an unexpected quarter.

'I know what you mean,' said the artist. 'I should say that possibly you were right. It is a question of proportion, isn't it? And more than proportion probably. Relativity and all that sort of thing.'

'If you ask me,' said the Colonel, 'all this Einstein business is a lot of dashed nonsense. So are spiritualists and the spook of one's grandmother!' He glared round fiercely.

'Of course it was suicide,' he went on. 'Didn't I practically see the thing happen with my own eyes?'

'Tell us about it,' said Mr Satterthwaite, 'so that we shall see it with our eyes also.'

With a somewhat mollified grunt the Colonel settled himself more comfortably in his chair.

'The whole thing was extraordinarily unexpected,' he began. 'Charnley had been his usual normal self. There was a big party staying in the house for this ball. No one could ever have guessed he would go and shoot himself just as the guests began arriving.'

'It would have been better taste if he had waited until they had gone,' said Mr Satterthwaite.

'Of course it would. Damned bad taste – to do a thing like that.'

'Uncharacteristic,' said Mr Satterthwaite.

'Yes,' admitted Monckton, 'it wasn't like Charnley.'

'And yet it *was* suicide?'

'Of course it was suicide. Why, there were three or four of us there at the top of the stairs. Myself, the Ostrander girl, Algie Darcy – oh, and one or two others. Charnley passed along the hall below and went into the Oak Parlour. The Ostrander girl said there was a ghastly look on his face and his eyes were staring – but, of course, that is nonsense – she couldn't even see his face from where we were – but he did walk in a hunched way, as if he had the weight of the world on his shoulders. One of the girls called to him – she was somebody's governess, I think, whom Lady Charnley had included in the party out of kindness. She was looking for him with a message. She called out "Lord Charnley, Lady Charnley wants to know –" He paid no attention and went into the Oak Parlour and slammed the door and we heard the key turn in the lock. Then, one minute after, *we heard the shot.*

'We rushed down to the hall. There is another door from the Oak Parlour leading into the Terrace Room. We tried that but it was locked, too. In the end we had to break the door down. Charnley was lying on the floor – dead – with a pistol close beside his right hand. Now, what could that have been but suicide? Accident? Don't tell me. There is only one other possibility – murder – and you can't have murder without a murderer. You admit that, I suppose.'

'The murderer might have escaped,' suggested Mr Satterthwaite.

'That is impossible. If you have a bit of paper and a pencil I will draw you a plan of the place. There are two doors into the Oak Parlour, one into the hall and one into the Terrace Room. Both these doors were locked on the inside *and the keys were in the locks.*'

'The window?'

'Shut, and the shutters fastened across it.'

There was a pause.

'So that is that,' said Colonel Monckton triumphantly.

'It certainly seems to be,' said Mr Satterthwaite sadly.

'Mind you,' said the Colonel, 'although I was laughing just now at the spiritualists, I don't mind admitting that there was a deuced rummy atmosphere about the place – about that room in particular. There are several bullet holes in the panels of the walls, the results of the duels that took place in that room, and there is a queer stain on the floor, that always comes back though they have replaced the wood several times. I suppose there will be another blood stain on the floor now – poor Charnley's blood.'

'Was there much blood?' asked Mr Satterthwaite.

'Very little – curiously little – so the doctor said.'

'Where did he shoot himself, through the head?'

'No, through the heart.'

'That is not the easy way to do it,' said Bristow. 'Frightfully difficult to know where one's heart is. I should never do it that way myself.'

Mr Satterthwaite shook his head. He was vaguely dissatisfied. He had hoped to get at something – he hardly knew what. Colonel Monckton went on.

'It is a spooky place, Charnley. Of course, *I* didn't see anything.'

'You didn't see the Weeping Lady with the Silver Ewer?'

'No, I did not, sir,' said the Colonel emphatically. 'But I expect every servant in the place swore they did.'

'Superstition was the curse of the Middle Ages,' said Bristow. 'There are still traces of it here and there, but thank goodness, we are getting free from it.'

'Superstition,' mused Mr Satterthwaite, his eyes turned again to the empty chair. 'Sometimes, don't you think – it might be useful?'

Bristow stared at him.

'Useful, that's a queer word.'

'Well, I hope you are convinced now, Satterthwaite,' said the Colonel.

'Oh, quite,' said Mr Satterthwaite. 'On the face of it, it seems odd – so purposeless for a newly-married man, young, rich, happy, celebrating his home-coming – curious – but I agree there is no getting away from the facts.' He repeated softly, 'The facts,' and frowned.

'I suppose the interesting thing is a thing we none of us will ever know,' said Monckton, 'the story behind it all. Of course there were rumours – all sorts of rumours. You know the kind of things people say.'

'But no one *knew* anything,' said Mr Satterthwaite thoughtfully.

'It's not a best seller mystery, is it?' remarked Bristow. 'No one gained by the man's death.'

'No one except an unborn child,' said Mr Satterthwaite.

Monckton gave a sharp chuckle. 'Rather a blow to poor Hugo Charnley,' he observed. 'As soon as it was known that there was going to be a child he had the graceful task of sitting tight and waiting to see if it would be a girl or boy. Rather an anxious wait for his creditors, too. In the end a boy it was and a disappointment for the lot of them.'

'Was the widow very disconsolate?' asked Bristow.

'Poor child,' said Monckton, 'I shall never forget her. She didn't cry or break down or anything. She was like something – frozen. As I say, she shut up the house shortly afterwards and, as far as I know, it has never been reopened since.'

'So we are left in the dark as to motive,' said Bristow with a slight laugh. 'Another man or another woman, it must have been one or the other, eh?'

'It seems like it,' said Mr Satterthwaite.

'And the betting is strongly on another woman,' continued Bristow, 'since the fair widow has not married again. I hate women,' he added dispassionately.

Mr Satterthwaite smiled a little and Frank Bristow saw the smile and pounced upon it.

'You may smile,' he said, 'but I do. They upset everything. They interfere. They get between you and your work. They – I only once met a woman who was – well, interesting.'

'I thought there would be one,' said Mr Satterthwaite.

'Not in the way you mean. I – I just met her casually. As a matter of fact – it was in a train. After all,' he added defiantly, 'why shouldn't one meet people in trains?'

'Certainly, certainly,' said Mr Satterthwaite soothingly, 'a train is as good a place as anywhere else.'

'It was coming down from the North. We had the carriage to ourselves. I don't know why, but we began to talk. I don't know her name and I don't suppose I shall ever meet her again. I don't know that I want to. It might be – a pity.' He paused, struggling to express himself. 'She wasn't quite real, you know. Shadowy. Like one of the people who come out of the hills in Gaelic fairy tales.'

Mr Satterthwaite nodded gently. His imagination pictured the scene easily enough. The very positive and realistic Bristow and a figure that was silvery and ghostly – shadowy, as Bristow had said.

'I suppose if something very terrible had happened, so terrible as to be almost unbearable, one might get like that. One might run away from reality into a half world of one's own and then, of course, after a time, one wouldn't be able to get back.'

'Was that what had happened to her?' asked Mr Satterthwaite curiously.

'I don't know,' said Bristow. 'She didn't tell me anything, I am only guessing. One has to guess if one is going to get anywhere.'

'Yes,' said Mr Satterthwaite slowly. 'One has to guess.'

He looked up as the door opened. He looked up quickly and expectantly but the butler's words disappointed him.

'A lady, sir, has called to see you on very urgent business. Miss Aspasia Glen.'

Mr Satterthwaite rose in some astonishment. He knew the name of Aspasia Glen. Who in London did not? First advertised as the Woman with the Scarf, she had given a series of matinées single-handed that had taken London by storm. With the aid of her scarf she had impersonated rapidly various characters. In turn the scarf had been the coif of a nun, the shawl of a mill-worker, the head-dress of a peasant and a hundred other things, and in each impersonation Aspasia Glen had been totally and utterly different. As an artist, Mr Satterthwaite paid full reverence to her. As it happened, he had never made her acquaintance. A call upon him at this unusual hour intrigued him greatly. With a few words of apology to the others he left the room and crossed the hall to the drawing-room.

Miss Glen was sitting in the very centre of a large settee upholstered in gold brocade. So poised she dominated the room. Mr Satterthwaite perceived at once that she meant to dominate the situation. Curiously enough, his first feeling was one of repulsion. He had been a sincere admirer of Aspasia Glen's art. Her personality, as conveyed to him over the footlights, had been appealing and sympathetic. Her effects there had been wistful and suggestive rather than commanding. But now, face to face with the woman herself, he received a totally different impression. There was something hard – bold –

forceful about her. She was tall and dark, possibly about thirty-five years of age. She was undoubtedly very good-looking and she clearly relied upon the fact.

'You must forgive this unconventional call, Mr Satterthwaite,' she said. Her voice was full and rich and seductive.

'I won't say that I have wanted to know you for a long time, but I *am* glad of the excuse. As for coming tonight' – she laughed – 'well, when I want a thing, I simply can't wait. When I want a thing, I simply *must* have it.'

'Any excuse that has brought me such a charming lady guest must be welcomed by me,' said Mr Satterthwaite in an old-fashioned gallant manner.

'How nice you are to me,' said Aspasia Glen.

'My dear lady,' said Mr Satterthwaite, 'may I thank you here and now for the pleasure you have so often given me – in my seat in the stalls.'

She smiled delightfully at him.

'I am coming straight to the point. I was at the Harchester Galleries today. I saw a picture there I simply couldn't live without. I wanted to buy it and I couldn't because you had already bought it. So' – she paused – 'I do want it so,' she went on. 'Dear Mr Satterthwaite, I simply *must* have it. I brought my cheque book.' She looked at him hopefully. 'Everyone tells me you are so frightfully kind. People *are* kind to me, you know. It is very bad for me – but there it is.'

So these were Aspasia Glen's methods. Mr Satterthwaite was inwardly coldly critical of this ultra-femininity and of this spoilt child pose. It ought to appeal to him, he supposed, but it didn't. Aspasia Glen had made a mistake. She had judged him as an elderly dilettante, easily flattered by a pretty woman. But Mr Satterthwaite behind his gallant manner had a shrewd and critical mind. He saw people pretty well as they were, not as they wished to appear to him. He saw before him, not a charming woman pleading for a whim, but a ruthless egoist determined to get her own way for some reason which was obscure to him. And he knew quite certainly that Aspasia Glen was not going to get her own way. He was not going to give up the picture of the Dead Harlequin to her. He sought rapidly in his mind for the best way of circumventing her without overt rudeness.

'I am sure,' he said, 'that everyone gives you your own way as often as they can and is only too delighted to do so.'

'Then you are really going to let me have the picture?'

Mr Satterthwaite shook his head slowly and regretfully. 'I am afraid that is impossible. You see' – he paused – 'I bought that picture for a lady. It is a present.'

'Oh! but surely –'

The telephone on the table rang sharply. With a murmured word of excuse Mr Satterthwaite took up the receiver. A voice spoke to him, a small, cold voice that sounded very far away.

'Can I speak to Mr Satterthwaite, please?'

'It is Mr Satterthwaite speaking.'

'I am Lady Charnley, Alix Charnley. I daresay you don't remember me Mr Satterthwaite, it is a great many years since we met.'

'My dear Alix. Of course, I remember you.'

'There is something I wanted to ask you. I was at the Harchester Galleries at an exhibition of pictures today, there was one called The Dead Harlequin, perhaps you recognized it – it was the Terrace Room at Charnley. I – I want to have that picture. It was sold to you.' She paused. 'Mr Satterthwaite, for reasons of my own I want that picture. Will you resell it to me?'

Mr Satterthwaite thought to himself: 'Why, this is a miracle.' As he spoke into the receiver he was thankful that Aspasia Glen could only hear one side of the conversation. 'If you will accept my gift, dear lady, it will make me very happy.' He heard a sharp exclamation behind him and hurried on. 'I bought it for you. I did indeed. But listen, my dear Alix, I want to ask you to do me a great favour, if you will.'

'Of course. Mr Satterthwaite, I am so *very* grateful.'

He went on. 'I want you to come round now to my house, at once.'

There was a slight pause and then she answered quietly:

'I will come at once.'

Mr Satterthwaite put down the receiver and turned to Miss Glen.

She said quickly and angrily:

'That was the picture you were talking about?'

'Yes,' said Mr Satterthwaite, 'the lady to whom I am presenting it is coming round to this house in a few minutes.'

Suddenly Aspasia Glen's face broke once more into smiles. 'You will give me a chance of persuading her to turn the picture over to me?'

'I will give you a chance of persuading her.'

Inwardly he was strangely excited. He was in the midst of a drama that was shaping itself to some foredoomed end. He, the looker-on, was playing a star part. He turned to Miss Glen.

'Will you come into the other room with me? I should like you to meet some friends of mine.'

He held the door open for her and, crossing the hall, opened the door of the smoking-room.

'Miss Glen,' he said, 'let me introduce you to an old friend of mine, Colonel Monckton. Mr Bristow, the painter of the picture you admire so much.' Then he started as a third figure rose from the chair which he had left empty beside his own.

'I think you expected me this evening,' said Mr Quin. 'During your absence I introduced myself to your friends. I am so glad I was able to drop in.'

'My dear friend,' said Mr Satterthwaite, 'I – I have been carrying on as well as I am able, but –' He stopped before the slightly sardonic glance of Mr Quin's dark eyes. 'Let me introduce you. Mr Harley Quin, Miss Aspasia Glen.'

Was it fancy – or did she shrink back slightly. A curious expression flitted over her face. Suddenly Bristow broke in boisterously. 'I have got it.'

'Got what?'

'Got hold of what was puzzling me. There is a likeness, there is a distinct likeness.' He was staring curiously at Mr Quin. 'You see it?' – he turned to Mr Satterthwaite – 'don't you see a distinct likeness to the Harlequin of my picture – the man looking in through the window?'

It was no fancy this time. He distinctly heard Miss Glen draw in her breath sharply and even saw that she stepped back one pace.

'I told you that I was expecting someone,' said Mr Satterthwaite. He spoke with an air of triumph. 'I must tell you that my friend, Mr Quin, is a most extraordinary person. He can unravel mysteries. He can make you see things.'

'Are you a medium, sir?' demanded Colonel Monckton, eyeing Mr Quin doubtfully.

The latter smiled and slowly shook his head.

'Mr Satterthwaite exaggerates,' he said quietly. 'Once or twice when I have been with him he has done some extraordinarily good deductive work. Why he puts the credit down to me I can't say. His modesty, I suppose.'

'No, no,' said Mr Satterthwaite excitedly. 'It isn't. You make me see things – things that I ought to have seen all along – that I actually have seen – but without knowing that I saw them.'

'It sounds to me deuced complicated,' said Colonel Monckton.

'Not really,' said Mr Quin. 'The trouble is that we are not content just to see things – we will tack the wrong interpretation on to the things we see.'

Aspasia Glen turned to Frank Bristow.

'I want to know,' she said nervously, 'what put the idea of painting that picture into your head?'

Bristow shrugged his shoulders. 'I don't quite know,' he confessed. 'Something about the place – about Charnley, I mean, took hold of my imagination. The big empty room. The terrace outside, the idea of ghosts and things, I suppose. I have just been hearing the tale of the last Lord Charnley, who shot himself. Supposing you are dead, and your spirit lives on? It must be odd, you know. You might stand outside on the terrace looking in at the window at your own dead body, and you would see everything.'

'What do you mean?' said Aspasia Glen. '*See* everything?'

'Well, you would see what happened. You would see –'

The door opened and the butler announced Lady Charnley.

Mr Satterthwaite went to meet her. He had not seen her for nearly thirteen years. He remembered her as she once was, an eager, glowing girl. And now he saw – a Frozen Lady. Very fair, very pale, with an air of drifting rather than walking, a snowflake driven at random by an icy breeze. Something unreal about her. So cold, so far away.

'It was very good of you to come,' said Mr Satterthwaite.

He led her forward. She made a half gesture of recognition towards Miss Glen and then paused as the other made no response.

'I am so sorry,' she murmured, 'but surely I have met you somewhere, haven't I?'

'Over the footlights, perhaps,' said Mr Satterthwaite. 'This is Miss Aspasia Glen, Lady Charnley.'

'I am very pleased to meet you, Lady Charnley,' said Aspasia Glen.

Her voice had suddenly a slight trans-Atlantic tinge to it. Mr Satterthwaite was reminded of one of her various stage impersonations.

'Colonel Monckton you know,' continued Mr Satterthwaite, 'and this is Mr Bristow.'

He saw a sudden faint tinge of colour in her cheeks.

'Mr Bristow and I have met too,' she said, and smiled a little. 'In a train.'

'And Mr Harley Quin.'

He watched her closely, but this time there was no flicker of recognition. He set a chair for her, and then, seating himself, he cleared his throat and spoke a little nervously. 'I – this is rather an unusual little gathering. It centres round this picture. I – I think that if we liked we could – clear things up.'

'You are not going to hold a séance, Satterthwaite?' asked Colonel Monckton. 'You are very odd this evening.'

'No,' said Mr Satterthwaite, 'not exactly a séance. But my friend, Mr Quin, believes, and I agree, that one can, by looking back over the past, see things as they were and not as they appeared to be.'

'The past?' said Lady Charnley.

'I am speaking of your husband's suicide, Alix. I know it hurts you –'

'No,' said Alix Charnley, 'it doesn't hurt me. Nothing hurts me now.'

Mr Satterthwaite thought of Frank Bristow's words. '*She was not quite real you know. Shadowy. Like one of the people who come out of hills in Gaelic fairy tales.*'

'Shadowy,' he had called her. That described her exactly. A shadow, a reflection of something else. Where then was the real Alix, and his mind answered quickly: '*In the past.* Divided from us by fourteen years of time.'

'My dear,' he said, 'you frighten me. You are like the Weeping Lady with the Silver Ewer.'

Crash! The coffee cup on the table by Aspasia's elbow fell shattered to the floor. Mr Satterthwaite waved aside her apologies. He thought: 'We are getting nearer, we are getting nearer every minute – but nearer to what?'

'Let us take our minds back to that night fourteen years ago,' he said. 'Lord Charnley killed himself. For what reason? No one knows.'

Lady Charnley stirred slightly in her chair.

'Lady Charnley knows,' said Frank Bristow abruptly.

'Nonsense,' said Colonel Monckton, then stopped, frowning at her curiously.

She was looking across at the artist. It was as though he drew the words out of her. She spoke, nodding her head slowly, and her voice was like a snowflake, cold and soft.

'Yes, you are quite right. I *know.* That is why as long as I live I can never go back to Charnley. That is why when my boy Dick wants me to open the place up and live there again I tell him it can't be done.'

'Will you tell us the reason, Lady Charnley?' said Mr Quin.

She looked at him. Then, as though hypnotized, she spoke as quietly and naturally as a child.

'I will tell you if you like. Nothing seems to matter very much now. I found a letter among his papers and I destroyed it.'

'What letter?' said Mr Quin.

'The letter from the girl – from that poor child. She was the Merriam's nursery governess. He had – he had made love to her – yes, while he was engaged to me just before we were married. And she – she was going to have a child too. She wrote saying so, and that she was going to tell me about it. So, you see, he shot himself.'

She looked round at them wearily and dreamily like a child who has repeated a lesson it knows too well.

Colonel Monckton blew his nose.

'My God,' he said, 'so that was it. Well, that explains things with a vengeance.'

'Does it?' said Mr Satterthwaite, 'it doesn't explain one thing. *It doesn't explain why Mr Bristow painted that picture.*'

'What do you mean?'

Mr Satterthwaite looked across at Mr Quin as though for encouragement, and apparently got it, for he proceeded:

'Yes, I know I sound mad to all of you, but that picture is the focus of the whole thing. We are all here tonight because of that picture. That picture *had* to be painted – that is what I mean.'

'You mean the uncanny influence of the Oak Parlour?' began Colonel Monckton.

'No,' said Mr Satterthwaite. '*Not* the Oak Parlour. The Terrace Room. That is it! The spirit of the dead man standing outside the window and looking in and seeing his own dead body on the floor.'

'Which he couldn't have done,' said the Colonel, 'because the body was in the Oak Parlour.'

'Supposing it wasn't,' said Mr Satterthwaite, 'supposing it was exactly where Mr Bristow saw it, saw it imaginatively, I mean on the black and white flags in front of the window.'

'You are talking nonsense,' said Colonel Monckton, 'if it was there we shouldn't have found it in the Oak Parlour.'

'Not unless someone carried it there,' said Mr Satterthwaite.

'And in that case how could we have seen Charnley going in at the door of the Oak Parlour?' inquired Colonel Monckton.

'Well, you didn't see his face, did you?' asked Mr Satterthwaite. 'What I mean is, you saw a man going into the Oak Parlour in fancy dress, I suppose.'

'Brocade things and a wig,' said Monckton.

'Just so, and you thought it was Lord Charnley because the girl called out to him as Lord Charnley.'

'And because when we broke in a few minutes later there was only Lord Charnley there dead. You can't get away from that, Satterthwaite.'

'No,' said Mr Satterthwaite, discouraged. 'No – unless there was a hiding-place of some kind.'

'Weren't you saying something about there being a Priests' hole in that room?' put in Frank Bristow.

'Oh!' cried Mr Satterthwaite. 'Supposing –?' He waved a hand for silence and sheltered his forehead with his other hand and then spoke slowly and hesitatingly.

'I have got an idea – it may be just an idea, but I think it hangs together. Supposing someone shot Lord Charnley. Shot him in the Terrace Room. Then he – and another person – dragged the body into the Oak Parlour. They laid it down there with the pistol by its right hand. Now we go on to the next step. It must seem absolutely certain that Lord Charnley has committed suicide. I think that could be done very easily. The man in his brocade and wig passes along the hall by the Oak Parlour door and someone, to make sure of things, calls out to him as Lord Charnley from the top of the stairs. He goes in and locks both doors and fires a shot into the woodwork. There were bullet holes already in that room if you remember, one more wouldn't be noticed. He then hides quietly in the secret chamber. The doors are broken open and people rush in. It seems certain that Lord Charnley has committed suicide. No other hypothesis is even entertained.'

'Well, I think that is balderdash,' said Colonel Monckton. 'You forget that Charnley had a motive right enough for suicide.'

'A letter found afterwards,' said Mr Satterthwaite. 'A lying cruel letter written by a very clever and unscrupulous little actress who meant one day to be Lady Charnley herself.'

'You mean?'

'I mean the girl in league with Hugo Charnley,' said Mr Satterthwaite. 'You know, Monckton, everyone knows, that that man was a blackguard. He thought that he was certain to come into the title.' He turned sharply to Lady Charnley. 'What was the name of the girl who wrote that letter?'

'Monica Ford,' said Lady Charnley.

'Was it Monica Ford, Monckton, who called out to Lord Charnley from the top of the stairs?'

'Yes, now you come to speak of it, I believe it was.'

'Oh, that's impossible,' said Lady Charnley. 'I – I went to her about it. She told me it was all true. I only saw her once afterwards, but surely she couldn't have been acting the whole time.'

Mr Satterthwaite looked across the room at Aspasia Glen.

'I think she could,' he said quietly. 'I think she had in her the makings of a very accomplished actress.'

'There is one thing you haven't got over,' said Frank Bristow, 'there would be blood on the floor of the Terrace Room. Bound to be. They couldn't clear that up in a hurry.'

'No,' admitted Mr Satterthwaite, 'but there is one thing they could do – a thing that would only take a second or two – they could throw over the blood-stains the Bokhara rug. Nobody ever saw the Bokhara rug in the Terrace Room before that night.'

'I believe you are right,' said Monckton, 'but all the same those blood-stains would have to be cleared up some time?'

'Yes,' said Mr Satterthwaite, 'in the middle of the night. A woman with a jug and basin could go down the stairs and clear up the blood-stains quite easily.'

'But supposing someone saw her?'

'It wouldn't matter,' said Mr Satterthwaite. 'I am speaking now of things as they *are*. I said a woman with a jug and basin. But if I had said a Weeping Lady with a Silver Ewer that is what they would have *appeared* to be.' He got up and went across to Aspasia Glen. 'That is what you did, wasn't it?' he said. 'They call you the "Woman with the Scarf" now, but it was that night you played your first part, the "Weeping Lady with the Silver

Ewer." That is why you knocked the coffee cup off that table just now. You were afraid when you saw that picture. You thought someone knew.'

Lady Charnley stretched out a white accusing hand.

'Monica Ford,' she breathed. 'I recognize you now.'

Aspasia Glen sprang to her feet with a cry. She pushed little Mr Satterthwaite aside with a shove of the hand and stood shaking in front of Mr Quin.

'So I was right. Someone *did* know! Oh, I haven't been deceived by this tomfoolery. This pretence of working things out.' She pointed at Mr Quin. '*You* were there. *You* were there outside the window looking in. You saw what we did, Hugo and I. I *knew* there was someone looking in, I felt it all the time. And yet when I looked up, there was nobody there. I knew someone was watching us. I thought once I caught a glimpse of a face at the window. It has frightened me all these years. Why did you break silence now? That is what I want to know?'

'Perhaps so that the dead may rest in peace,' said Mr Quin.

Suddenly Aspasia Glen made a rush for the door and stood there flinging a few defiant words over her shoulder.

'Do what you like. God knows there are witnesses enough to what I have been saying. I don't care, I don't care. I loved Hugo and I helped him with the ghastly business and he chucked me afterwards. He died last year. You can set the police on my tracks if you like, but as that little dried-up fellow there said, I am a pretty good actress. They will find it hard to find me.' She crashed the door behind her, and a moment later they heard the slam of the front door, also.

'Reggie,' cried Lady Charnley, 'Reggie.' The tears were streaming down her face. 'Oh, my dear, my dear, I can go back to Charnley now. I can live there with Dickie. I can tell him what his father was, the finest, the most splendid man in all the world.'

'We must consult very seriously as to what must be done in the matter,' said Colonel Monckton. 'Alix, my dear, if you will let me take you home I shall be glad to have a few words with you on the subject.'

Lady Charnley rose. She came across to Mr Satterthwaite, and laying both hands on his shoulders, she kissed him very gently.

'It is so wonderful to be alive again after being so long dead,' she said. 'It was like being dead, you know. Thank you, dear Mr Satterthwaite.' She went out of the room with Colonel Monckton. Mr Satterthwaite gazed after them. A grunt from Frank Bristow whom he had forgotten made him turn sharply round.

'She is a lovely creature,' said Bristow moodily. 'But she's not nearly so interesting as she was,' he said gloomily.

'There speaks the artist,' said Mr Satterthwaite.

'Well, she isn't,' said Mr Bristow. 'I suppose I should only get the cold shoulder if I ever went butting in at Charnley. I don't want to go where I am not wanted.'

'My dear young man,' said Mr Satterthwaite, 'if you will think a little less of the impression you are making on other people, you will, I think, be wiser and happier. You would also do well to disabuse your mind of some very old-fashioned notions, one of which is that birth has any significance at all in our modern conditions. You are one of those large proportioned young men whom women always consider good-looking, and you have possibly, if not certainly, genius. Just say that over to yourself ten times before you go to bed every night and in three months' time go and call on Lady Charnley at Charnley. That is my advice to you, and I am an old man with considerable experience of the world.'

A very charming smile suddenly spread over the artist's face.

'You have been thunderingly good to me,' he said suddenly. He seized Mr Satterthwaite's hand and wrung it in a powerful grip. 'I am no end grateful. I must be off now. Thanks very much for one of the most extraordinary evenings I have ever spent.'

He looked round as though to say goodbye to someone else and then started.

'I say, sir, your friend has gone. I never saw him go. He is rather a queer bird, isn't he?'

'He goes and comes very suddenly,' said Mr Satterthwaite.

'That is one of his characteristics. One doesn't always see him come and go.'

'Like Harlequin,' said Frank Bristow, 'he is invisible,' and laughed heartily at his own joke.

CHAPTER X

The Bird with
the Broken Wing

Mr Satterthwaite looked out of the window. It was raining steadily. He shivered. Very few country houses, he reflected, were really properly heated. It cheered him to think that in a few hours' time he would be speeding towards London. Once one had passed sixty years of age, London was really much the best place.

He was feeling a little old and pathetic. Most of the members of the house party were so young. Four of them had just gone off into the library to do table turning. They had invited him to accompany them, but he had declined. He failed to derive any amusement from the monotonous counting of the letters of the alphabet and the usual meaningless jumble of letters that resulted.

Yes, London was the best place for him. He was glad that he had declined Madge Keeley's invitation when she had rung up to invite him over to Laidell half an hour ago. An adorable young person, certainly, but London was best.

Mr Satterthwaite shivered again and remembered that the fire in the library was usually a good one. He opened the door and adventured cautiously into the darkened room.

'If I'm not in the way –'

'Was that N or M? We shall have to count again. No, of course not, Mr Satterthwaite. Do you know, the most exciting things have been happening. The spirit says her name is Ada Spiers, and John here is going to marry someone called Gladys Bun almost immediately.'

Mr Satterthwaite sat down in a big easy chair in front of the fire. His eyelids drooped over his eyes and he dozed. From time to time he returned to consciousness, hearing fragments of speech.

'It can't be P A B Z L – not unless he's a Russian. John, you're shoving. I *saw* you. I believe it's a new spirit come.'

Another interval of dozing. Then a name jerked him wide awake.

'Q-U-I-N. Is that right?' 'Yes, it's rapped once for "Yes." Quin. Have you a message for someone here? Yes. For me? For John? For Sarah? For Evelyn? No – but there's no one else. Oh! it's for Mr Satterthwaite, perhaps? It says "Yes." Mr Satterthwaite, it's a message for you.'

'What does it say?'

Mr Satterthwaite was broad awake now, sitting taut and erect in his chair, his eyes shining.

The table rocked and one of the girls counted.

'LAI – it can't be – that doesn't make sense. No word begins LAI.'

'Go on,' said Mr Satterthwaite, and the command in his voice was so sharp that he was obeyed without question.

'LAIDEL? and another L – Oh! that seems to be all.'

'Go on.'

'Tell us some more, please.'

A pause.

'There doesn't seem to be any more. The table's gone quite dead. How silly.'

'No,' said Mr Satterthwaite thoughtfully. 'I don't think it's silly.'

He rose and left the room. He went straight to the telephone. Presently he was through.

'Can I speak to Miss Keeley? Is that you, Madge, my dear? I want to change my mind, if I may, and accept your kind invitation. It is not so urgent as I thought that I should get back to town. Yes – yes – I will arrive in time for dinner.'

He hung up the receiver, a strange flush on his withered cheeks. Mr Quin – the mysterious Mr Harley Quin. Mr Satterthwaite counted over on his fingers the times he had been brought into contact with that man of mystery. Where Mr Quin was concerned – things happened! What had happened or was going to happen – at Laidell?

Whatever it was, there was work for him, Mr Satterthwaite, to do. In some way or other, he would have an active part to play. He was sure of that.

Laidell was a large house. Its owner, David Keeley, was one of those quiet men with indeterminate personalities who seem to count as part of the furniture. Their inconspicuousness has nothing to do with brain power – David Keeley was a most brilliant mathematician, and had written a book totally incomprehensible to ninety-nine hundreds of humanity. But like so many men of brilliant intellect, he radiated no bodily vigour or magnetism. It was a standing joke that David Keeley was a real 'invisible man.' Footmen passed him by with the vegetables, and guests forgot to say how do you do or goodbye.

His daughter Madge was very different. A fine upstanding young woman, bursting with energy and life. Thorough, healthy and normal, and extremely pretty.

It was she who received Mr Satterthwaite when he arrived.

'How nice of you to come – after all.'

'Very delightful of you to let me change my mind. Madge, my dear, you're looking very well.'

'Oh! I'm always well.'

'Yes, I know. But it's more than that. You look – well, blooming is the word I have in mind. Has anything happened, my dear? Anything – well – special?'

She laughed – blushed a little.

'It's too bad, Mr Satterthwaite. You always guess things.'

He took her hand.

'So it's that, is it? Mr Right has come along?'

It was an old-fashioned term, but Madge did not object to it. She rather liked Mr Satterthwaite's old-fashioned ways.

'I suppose so – yes. But nobody's supposed to know. It's a secret. But I don't really mind your knowing, Mr Satterthwaite. You're always so nice and sympathetic.'

Mr Satterthwaite thoroughly enjoyed romance at second hand. He was sentimental and Victorian.

'I mustn't ask who the lucky man is? Well, then all I can say is that I hope he is worthy of the honour you are conferring on him.'

Rather a duck, old Mr Satterthwaite, thought Madge.

'Oh! we shall get on awfully well together, I think,' she said. 'You see, we like doing the same things, and that's so awfully important, isn't it? We've really got a lot in common – and we know all about each other and all that. It's really been coming on for a long time. That gives one such a nice safe feeling, doesn't it?'

'Undoubtedly,' said Mr Satterthwaite. 'But in my experience one can never really know all about anyone else. That is part of the interest and charm of life.'

'Oh! I'll risk it,' said Madge, laughing, and they went up to dress for dinner.

Mr Satterthwaite was late. He had not brought a valet, and having his things unpacked for him by a stranger always flurried him a little. He came down to find everyone assembled, and in the modern style Madge merely said: 'Oh! here's Mr Satterthwaite. I'm starving. Let's go in.'

She led the way with a tall grey-haired woman – a woman of striking personality. She had a very clear rather incisive voice, and her face was clear cut and rather beautiful.

'How d'you do, Satterthwaite,' said Mr Keeley.

Mr Satterthwaite jumped.

'How do you do,' he said. 'I'm afraid I didn't see you.'

'Nobody does,' said Mr Keeley sadly.

They went in. The table was a low oval of mahogany. Mr Satterthwaite was placed between his young hostess and a short dark girl – a very hearty girl with a loud voice and a ringing determined laugh that expressed more the determination to be cheerful at all costs than any real mirth. Her name seemed to be Doris, and she was the type of young woman Mr Satterthwaite most disliked. She had, he considered, no artistic justification for existence.

On Madge's other side was a man of about thirty, whose likeness to the grey-haired woman proclaimed them mother and son.

Next to him –

Mr Satterthwaite caught his breath.

He didn't know what it was exactly. It was not beauty. It was something else – something much more elusive and intangible than beauty.

She was listening to Mr Keeley's rather ponderous dinner-table conversation, her head bent a little sideways. She was there, it seemed to Mr Satterthwaite – and yet she was not there! She was somehow a great deal less substantial than anyone else seated round the oval table. Something in the droop of her body sideways was beautiful – was more than beautiful. She looked up – her eyes met Mr Satterthwaite's for a moment across the table – and the word he wanted leapt to his mind.

Enchantment – that was it. She had the quality of enchantment. She might have been one of those creatures who are only half-human – one of the Hidden People from the Hollow Hills. She made everyone else look rather too real . . .

But at the same time, in a queer way, she stirred his pity. It was as though semi-humanity handicapped her. He sought for a phrase and found it.

'A bird with a broken wing,' said Mr Satterthwaite.

Satisfied, he turned his mind back to the subject of Girl Guides and hoped that the girl Doris had not noticed his abstraction. When she turned to the man on the other side of her – a man Mr Satterthwaite had hardly noticed, he himself turned to Madge.

'Who is the lady sitting next to your father?' he asked in a low voice.

'Mrs Graham? Oh, no! you mean Mabelle. Don't you know her? Mabelle Annesley. She was a Clydesley – one of the ill-fated Clydesleys.'

He started. The ill-fated Clydesleys. He remembered. A brother had shot himself, a sister had been drowned, another had perished in an earthquake. A queer doomed family. This girl must be the youngest of them.

His thoughts were recalled suddenly. Madge's hand touched

his under the table. Everyone else was talking. She gave a faint inclination of her head to her left.

'That's him,' she murmured ungrammatically.

Mr Satterthwaite nodded quickly in comprehension. So this young Graham was the man of Madge's choice. Well, she could hardly have done better as far as appearances went – and Mr Satterthwaite was a shrewd observer. A pleasant, likeable, rather matter-of-fact young fellow. They'd make a nice pair – no nonsense about either of them – good healthy sociable young folk.

Laidell was run on old-fashioned lines. The ladies left the dining-room first. Mr Satterthwaite moved up to Graham and began to talk to him. His estimate of the young man was confirmed, yet there was something that struck him as being not quite true to type. Roger Graham was distrait, his mind seemed far away, his hand shook as he replaced the glass on the table.

'He's got something on his mind,' thought Mr Satterthwaite acutely. 'Not nearly as important as he thinks it is, I dare say. All the same, I wonder what it is.'

Mr Satterthwaite was in the habit of swallowing a couple of digestive pastilles after meals. Having neglected to bring them down with him, he went up to his room to fetch them.

On his way down to the drawing-room, he passed along the long corridor on the ground floor. About half-way along it was a room known as the terrace room. As Mr Satterthwaite looked through the open doorway in passing, he stopped short.

Moonlight was streaming into the room. The latticed panes gave it a queer rhythmic pattern. A figure was sitting on the low window sill, drooping a little sideways and softly twanging the string of a ukelele – not in a jazz rhythm, but in a far older rhythm, the beat of fairy horses riding on fairy hills.

Mr Satterthwaite stood fascinated. She wore a dress of dull dark blue chiffon, ruched and pleated so that it looked like the feathers of a bird. She bent over the instrument crooning to it.

He came into the room – slowly, step by step. He was close to her when she looked up and saw him. She didn't start, he noticed, or seem surprised.

'I hope I'm not intruding,' he began.

'Please – sit down.'

He sat near her on a polished oak chair. She hummed softly under her breath.

'There's a lot of magic about tonight,' she said. 'Don't you think so?'

'Yes, there was a lot of magic about.'

'They wanted me to fetch my uke,' she explained. 'And as I passed here, I thought it would be so lovely to be alone here – in the dark and the moon.'

'Then I –' Mr Satterthwaite half rose, but she stopped him.

'Don't go. You – you fit in, somehow. It's queer, but you do.'

He sat down again.

'It's been a queer sort of evening,' she said. 'I was out in the woods late this afternoon, and I met a man – such a strange sort of man – tall and dark, like a lost soul. The sun was setting, and the light of it through the trees made him look like a kind of Harlequin.'

'Ah!' Mr Satterthwaite leant forward – his interest quickened.

'I wanted to speak to him – he – he looked so like somebody I know. But I lost him in the trees.'

'I think I know him,' said Mr Satterthwaite.

'Do you? He is – interesting, isn't he?'

'Yes, he is interesting.'

There was a pause. Mr Satterthwaite was perplexed. There was something, he felt, that he ought to do – and he didn't know what it was. But surely – surely, it had to do with this girl. He said rather clumsily:

'Sometimes – when one is unhappy – one wants to get away –'

'Yes. That's true.' She broke off suddenly. 'Oh! I see what you mean. But you're wrong. It's just the other way round. I wanted to be alone because I'm happy.'

'Happy?'

'Terribly happy.'

She spoke quite quietly, but Mr Satterthwaite had a sudden sense of shock. What this strange girl meant by being happy wasn't the same as Madge Keeley would have meant by the same words. Happiness, for Mabelle Annesley, meant some kind of intense and vivid ecstasy . . . something that was not only human, but more than human. He shrank back a little.

'I – didn't know,' he said clumsily.

'Of course you couldn't. And it's not – the actual thing – I'm not happy yet – but I'm going to be.' She leaned forward. 'Do you know what it's like to stand in a wood – a big wood with dark shadows and trees very close all round you – a wood you might never get out of – and then, suddenly – just in front of you, you see the country of your dreams – shining and beautiful – you've only got to step out from the trees and the darkness and you've found it . . .'

'So many things look beautiful,' said Mr Satterthwaite, 'before we've reached them. Some of the ugliest things in the world look the most beautiful . . .'

There was a step on the floor. Mr Satterthwaite turned his head. A fair man with a stupid, rather wooden face, stood there. He was the man Mr Satterthwaite had hardly noticed at the dinner-table.

'They're waiting for you, Mabelle,' he said.

She got up, the expression had gone out of her face, her voice was flat and calm.

'I'm coming, Gerard,' she said. 'I've been talking to Mr Satterthwaite.'

She went out of the room, Mr Satterthwaite following. He turned his head over his shoulder as he went and caught the expression on her husband's face. A hungry despairing look.

'Enchantment,' thought Mr Satterthwaite. 'He feels it right enough. Poor fellow – poor fellow.'

The drawing-room was well lighted. Madge and Doris Coles were vociferous in reproaches.

'Mabelle, you little beast – you've been ages.'

She sat on a low stool, turned the ukelele and sang. They all joined in.

'Is it possible,' thought Mr Satterthwaite, 'that so many idiotic songs could have been written about My Baby.'

But he had to admit that the syncopated wailing tunes were

stirring. Though, of course, they weren't a patch on the old-fashioned waltz.

The air got very smoky. The syncopated rhythm went on.

'No conversation,' thought Mr Satterthwaite. 'No good music. No *peace*.' He wished the world had not become definitely so noisy.

Suddenly Mabelle Annesley broke off, smiled across the room at him, and began to sing a song of Grieg's.

'*My swan – my fair one . . .*'

It was a favourite of Mr Satterthwaite's. He liked the note of ingenuous surprise at the end.

'*Wert only a swan then? A swan then?*'

After that, the party broke up. Madge offered drinks whilst her father picked up the discarded ukelele and began twanging it absent-mindedly. The party exchanged goodnights, drifted nearer and nearer to the door. Everyone talked at once. Gerard Annesley slipped away unostentatiously, leaving the others.

Outside the drawing-room door, Mr Satterthwaite bade Mrs Graham a ceremonious goodnight. There were two staircases, one close at hand, the other at the end of a long corridor. It was by the latter that Mr Satterthwaite reached his room. Mrs Graham and her son passed by the stairs near at hand whence the quiet Gerard Annesley had already preceded them.

'You'd better get your ukelele, Mabelle,' said Madge. 'You'll forget it in the morning if you don't. You've got to make such an early start.'

'Come on, Mr Satterthwaite,' said Doris Coles, seizing him boisterously by one arm. 'Early to bed – etcetera.'

Madge took him by the other arm and all three ran down the corridor to peals of Doris's laughter. They paused at the end to wait for David Keeley, who was following at a much more sedate pace, turning out electric lights as he came. The four of them went upstairs together.

Mr Satterthwaite was just preparing to descend to the dining-room for breakfast on the following morning, when there was a light tap on the door and Madge Keeley entered. Her face was dead white, and she was shivering all over.

'Oh, Mr Satterthwaite.'

'My dear child, what's happened?' He took her hand.

'Mabelle – Mabelle Annesley . . .'

'Yes?'

What had happened? What? Something terrible – he knew that. Madge could hardly get the words out.

'She – she hanged herself last night . . . On the back of her door. Oh! it's too horrible.' She broke down – sobbing.

Hanged herself. Impossible. Incomprehensible!

He said a few soothing old-fashioned words to Madge, and hurried downstairs. He found David Keeley looking perplexed and incompetent.

'I've telephoned to the police, Satterthwaite. Apparently that's got to be done. So the doctor said. He's just finished examining the – the – good lord, it's a beastly business. She must have been desperately unhappy – to do it that way – Queer that song last night. Swan song, eh? She looked rather like a swan – a black swan.'

'Yes.'

'Swan Song,' repeated Keeley. 'Shows it was in her mind, eh?'

'It would seem so – yes, certainly it would seem so.'

He hesitated, then asked if he might see – if, that is . . .

His host comprehended the stammering request.

'If you want to – I'd forgotten you have a *penchant* for human tragedies.'

He led the way up the broad staircase. Mr Satterthwaite followed him. At the head of the stairs was the room occupied by Roger Graham and opposite it, on the other side of the passage, his mother's room. The latter door was ajar and a faint wisp of smoke floated through it.

A momentary surprise invaded Mr Satterthwaite's mind. He had not judged Mrs Graham to be a woman who smoked so early in the day. Indeed, he had had the idea that she did not smoke at all.

They went along the passage to the end door but one. David

Keeley entered the room and Mr Satterthwaite followed him.

The room was not a very large one and showed signs of a man's occupation. A door in the wall led into a second room. A bit of cut rope still dangled from a hook high up on the door. On the bed . . .

Mr Satterthwaite stood for a minute looking down on the heap of huddled chiffon. He noticed that it was ruched and pleated like the plumage of a bird. At the face, after one glance, he did not look again.

He glanced from the door with its dangling rope to the communicating door through which they had come.

'Was that open?'

'Yes. At least the maid says so.'

'Annesley slept in there? Did he hear anything?'

'He says – nothing.'

'Almost incredible,' murmured Mr Satterthwaite. He looked back at the form on the bed.

'Where is he?'

'Annesley? He's downstairs with the doctor.'

They went downstairs to find an Inspector of police had arrived. Mr Satterthwaite was agreeably surprised to recognize in him an old acquaintance, Inspector Winkfield. The Inspector went upstairs with the doctor, and a few minutes later a request came that all members of the house party should assemble in the drawing-room.

The blinds had been drawn, and the whole room had a funereal aspect. Doris Coles looked frightened and subdued. Every now and then she dabbed her eyes with a handkerchief. Madge was resolute and alert, her feelings fully under control by now. Mrs Graham was composed, as always, her face grave and impassive. The tragedy seemed to have affected her son more keenly than anyone. He looked a positive wreck this morning. David Keeley, as usual, had subsided into the background.

The bereaved husband sat alone, a little apart from the others. There was a queer dazed look about him, as though he could hardly realize what had taken place.

Mr Satterthwaite, outwardly composed, was inwardly seething with the importance of a duty shortly to be performed.

Inspector Winkfield, followed by Dr Morris, came in and shut the door behind him. He cleared his throat and spoke.

'This is a very sad occurrence – very sad, I'm sure. It's necessary, under the circumstances, that I should ask everybody a few questions. You'll not object, I'm sure. I'll begin with Mr Annesley. You'll forgive my asking, sir, but had your good lady ever threatened to take her life?'

Mr Satterthwaite opened his lips impulsively, then closed them again. There was plenty of time. Better not speak too soon.

'I – no, I don't think so.'

His voice was so hesitating, so peculiar, that everyone shot a covert glance at him.

'You're not sure, sir?'

'Yes – I'm – quite sure. She didn't.'

'Ah! Were you aware that she was unhappy in any way?'

'No. I – no, I wasn't.'

'She said nothing to you. About feeling depressed, for instance?'

'I – no, nothing.'

Whatever the Inspector thought, he said nothing. Instead he proceeded to his next point.

'Will you describe to me briefly the events of last night?'

'We – all went up to bed. I fell asleep immediately and heard nothing. The housemaid's scream aroused me this morning. I rushed into the adjoining room and found my wife – and found her –'

His voice broke. The Inspector nodded.

'Yes, yes, that's quite enough. We needn't go into that. When did you last see your wife the night before?'

'I – downstairs.'

'Downstairs?'

'Yes, we all left the drawing-room together. I went straight up leaving the others talking in the hall.'

'And you didn't see your wife again? Didn't she say goodnight when she came up to bed?'

'I was asleep when she came up.'

'But she only followed you a few minutes later. That's right, isn't it, sir?' He looked at David Keeley, who nodded.

'She hadn't come up half an hour later.'

Annesley spoke stubbornly. The Inspector's eyes strayed gently to Mrs Graham.

'She didn't stay in your room talking, Madam?'

Did Mr Satterthwaite fancy it, or was there a slight pause before Mrs Graham said with her customary quiet decision of manner:

'No, I went straight into my room and closed the door. I heard nothing.'

'And you say, sir' – the Inspector had shifted his attention back to Annesley – 'that you slept and heard nothing. The communicating door was open, was it not?'

'I – I believe so. But my wife would have entered her room by the other door from the corridor.'

'Even so, sir, there would have been certain sounds – a choking noise, a drumming of heels on the door –'

'*No.*'

It was Mr Satterthwaite who spoke, impetuously, unable to stop himself. Every eye turned towards him in surprise. He himself became nervous, stammered, and turned pink.

'I – I beg your pardon, Inspector. But I must speak. You are on the wrong track – the wrong track altogether. Mrs Annesley did not kill herself – I am sure of it. She was murdered.'

There was a dead silence, then Inspector Winkfield said quietly:

'What leads you to say that, sir?'

'I – it is a feeling. A very strong feeling.'

'But I think, sir, there must be more than that to it. There must be some particular reason.'

Well, of course there *was* a particular reason. There was the mysterious message from Mr Quin. But you couldn't tell a police inspector that. Mr Satterthwaite cast about desperately, and found nothing.

'Last night – when we were talking together, she said she was very happy. Very happy – just that. That wasn't like a woman thinking of committing suicide.'

He was triumphant. He added:

'She went back to the drawing-room to fetch her ukelele, so that she wouldn't forget it in the morning. That didn't look like suicide either.'

'No,' admitted the Inspector. 'No, perhaps it didn't.' He turned to David Keeley. 'Did she take the ukelele upstairs with her?'

The mathematician tried to remember.

'I think – yes, she did. She went upstairs carrying it in her hand. I remember seeing it just as she turned the corner of the staircase before I turned off the light down here.'

'Oh!' cried Madge. 'But it's here now.'

She pointed dramatically to where the ukelele lay on a table.

'That's curious,' said the Inspector. He stepped swiftly across and rang the bell.

A brief order sent the butler in search of the housemaid whose business it was to do the rooms in the morning. She came, and was quite positive in her answer. The ukelele had been there first thing that morning when she had dusted.

Inspector Winkfield dismissed her and then said curtly:

'I would like to speak to Mr Satterthwaite in private, please. Everyone may go. But no one is to leave the house.'

Mr Satterthwaite twittered into speech as soon as the door had closed behind the others.

'I – I am sure, Inspector, that you have the case excellently in hand. Excellently. I just felt that – having, as I say, a very strong feeling –'

The Inspector arrested further speech with an upraised hand.

'You're quite right, Mr Satterthwaite. The lady was murdered.'

'You knew it?' Mr Satterthwaite was chagrined.

'There were certain things that puzzled Dr Morris.' He looked across at the doctor, who had remained, and the doctor assented to his statement with a nod of the head. 'We made a thorough examination. The rope that was round her neck wasn't the rope that she was strangled with – it was something much thinner that did the job, something more like a wire. It had cut right into the flesh. The mark of the rope was superimposed on it. She was strangled and then hung up on the door afterwards to make it look like suicide.'

'But who –?'

'Yes,' said the Inspector. 'Who? That's the question. What about the husband sleeping next door, who never said good-night to his wife and who heard nothing? I should say we hadn't far to look. Must find out what terms they were on. That's where you can be useful to us, Mr Satterthwaite. You've the *ongtray* here, and you can get the hang of things in a way we can't. Find out what relations there were between the two.'

'I hardly like –' began Mr Satterthwaite, stiffening.

'It won't be the first murder mystery you've helped us with. I remember the case of Mrs Strangeways. You've got a *flair* for that sort of thing, sir. An absolute *flair*.'

Yes, it was true – he *had a flair*. He said quietly:

'I will do my best, Inspector.'

Had Gerard Annesley killed his wife? Had he? Mr Satterthwaite recalled that look of misery last night. He loved her – and he was suffering. Suffering will drive a man to strange deeds.

But there was something else – some other factor. Mabelle had spoken of herself as coming out of a wood – she was looking forward to happiness – not a quiet rational happiness – but a happiness that was irrational – a wild ecstasy . . .

If Gerard Annesley had spoken the truth, Mabelle had not come to her room till at least half an hour later than he had done. Yet David Keeley had seen her going up those stairs. There were two other rooms occupied in that wing. There was Mrs Graham's, and there was her son's.

Her son's. But he and Madge . . .

Surely Madge would have guessed . . . But Madge wasn't the guessing kind. All the same, no smoke without fire – Smoke!

Ah! he remembered. *A wisp of smoke curling out through Mrs Graham's bedroom door.*

He acted on impulse. Straight up the stairs and into her

room. It was empty. He closed the door behind him and locked it.

He went across to the grate. A heap of charred fragments. Very gingerly he raked them over with his finger. His luck was in. In the very centre were some unburnt fragments – fragments of letters . . .

Very disjointed fragments, but they told him something of value.

'*Life can be wonderful, Roger darling. I never knew . . . all my life has been a dream till I met you, Roger . . .*'

'*. . . Gerard knows, I think . . . I am sorry but what can I do? Nothing is real to me but you, Roger . . . We shall be together, soon.*

'*What are you going to tell him at Laidell, Roger? You write strangely – but I am not afraid . . .*'

Very carefully, Mr Satterthwaite put the fragments into an envelope from the writing-table. He went to the door, unlocked it and opened it to find himself face to face with Mrs Graham.

It was an awkward moment, and Mr Satterthwaite was momentarily out of countenance. He did what was, perhaps, the best thing, attacked the situation with simplicity.

'I have been searching your room, Mrs Graham. I have found something – a packet of letters imperfectly burnt.'

A wave of alarm passed over her face. It was gone in a flash, but it had been there.

'Letters from Mrs Annesley to your son.'

She hesitated for a minute, then said quietly: 'That is so. I thought they would be better burnt.'

'For what reason?'

'My son is engaged to be married. These letters – if they had been brought into publicity through the poor girl's suicide – might have caused much pain and trouble.'

'Your son could burn his own letters.'

She had no answer ready for that. Mr Satterthwaite pursued his advantage.

'You found these letters in his room, brought them into your room and burnt them. Why? You were afraid, Mrs Graham.'

'I am not in the habit of being afraid, Mr Satterthwaite.'

'No – but this was a desperate case.'

'Desperate?'

'Your son might have been in danger of arrest – for murder.'

'Murder!'

He saw her face go white. He went on quickly:

'You heard Mrs Annesley go into your son's room last night. He had told her of his engagement? No, I see he hadn't. He told her then. They quarrelled, and he –'

'That's a lie!'

They had been so absorbed in their duel of words that they had not heard approaching footsteps. Roger Graham had come up behind them unperceived by either.

'It's all right, Mother. Don't – worry. Come into my room, Mr Satterthwaite.'

Mr Satterthwaite followed him into his room. Mrs Graham had turned away and did not attempt to follow them. Roger Graham shut the door.

'Listen, Mr Satterthwaite, you think I killed Mabelle. You think I strangled her – here – and took her along and hung her up on that door – later – when everyone was asleep?'

Mr Satterthwaite stared at him. Then he said surprisingly:

'No, I do not think so.'

'Thank God for that. I couldn't have killed Mabelle. I – I loved her. Or didn't I? I don't know. It's a tangle that I can't explain. I'm fond of Madge – I always have been. And she's such a good sort. We suit each other. But Mabelle was different. It was – I can't explain it – a sort of enchantment. I was, I think – afraid of her.'

Mr Satterthwaite nodded.

'It was madness – a kind of bewildering ecstasy . . . But it was impossible. It wouldn't have worked. That sort of thing – doesn't last. I know what it means now to have a spell cast over you.'

'Yes, it must have been like that,' said Mr Satterthwaite thoughtfully.

'I – I wanted to get out of it all. I was going to tell Mabelle – last night.'

'But you didn't?'

'No, I didn't,' said Graham slowly. 'I swear to you, Mr Satterthwaite, that I never saw her after I said goodnight downstairs.'

'I believe you,' said Mr Satterthwaite.

He got up. It was not Roger Graham who had killed Mabelle Annesley. He could have fled from her, but he could not have killed her. He had been afraid of her, afraid of that wild intangible fairy-like quality of hers. He had known enchantment – and turned his back on it. He had gone for the safe sensible thing that he had known 'would work' and had relinquished the intangible dream that might lead him he knew not where.

He was a sensible young man, and, as such, uninteresting to Mr Satterthwaite, who was an artist and a connoisseur in life.

He left Roger Graham in his room and went downstairs. The drawing-room was empty. Mabelle's ukelele lay on a stool by the window. He took it up and twanged it absent-mindedly. He knew nothing of the instrument, but his ear told him that it was abominably out of tune. He turned a key experimentally.

Doris Coles came into the room. She looked at him reproachfully.

'Poor Mabelle's uke,' she said.

Her clear condemnation made Mr Satterthwaite feel obstinate.

'Tune it for me,' he said, and added: 'If you can.'

'Of course I can,' said Doris, wounded at the suggestion of incompetence in any direction.

She took it from him, twanged a string, turned a key briskly – and the string snapped.

'Well, I never. Oh! I see – but how extraordinary! It's the wrong string – a size too big. It's an A string. How stupid to put that on. Of course it snaps when you try to tune it up. How stupid people are.'

'Yes,' said Mr Satterthwaite. 'They are – even when they try to be clever . . .'

His tone was so odd that she stared at him. He took the ukelele from her and removed the broken string. He went out of the room holding it in his hand. In the library he found David Keeley.

'Here,' he said.

He held out the string. Keeley took it.

'What's this?'

'A broken ukelele string.' He paused and then went on: '*What did you do with the other one?*'

'The other one?'

'*The one you strangled her with.* You were very clever, weren't you? It was done very quickly – just in that moment we were all laughing and talking in the hall.

'Mabelle came back into this room for her ukelele. You had taken the string off as you fiddled with it just before. You caught her round the throat with it and strangled her. Then you came out and locked the door and joined us. Later, in the dead of night, you came down and – and disposed of the body by hanging it on the door of her room. And you put another string on the ukelele – *but it was the wrong string*, that's why you were stupid.'

There was a pause.

'But why did you do it?' said Mr Satterthwaite. 'In God's name, *why*?'

Mr Keeley laughed, a funny giggling little laugh that made Mr Satterthwaite feel rather sick.

'It was so very simple,' he said. 'That's why! And then – nobody ever noticed me. Nobody ever noticed what I was doing. I thought – I thought I'd have the laugh of them . . .'

And again he gave that furtive little giggle and looked at Mr Satterthwaite with mad eyes.

Mr Satterthwaite was glad that at that moment Inspector Winkfield came into the room.

It was twenty-four hours later, on his way to London, that Mr Satterthwaite awoke from a doze to find a tall dark man sitting opposite to him in the railway carriage. He was not altogether surprised.

'My dear Mr Quin!'

'Yes – I am here.'

Mr Satterthwaite said slowly: 'I can hardly face you. I am ashamed – I failed.'

'Are you sure of that?'

'I did not save her.'

'But you discovered the truth?'

'Yes – that is true. One or other of those young men might have been accused – might even have been found guilty. So, at any rate, I saved a man's life. But, she – she – that strange enchanting creature . . .' His voice broke off.

Mr Quin looked at him.

'Is death the greatest evil that can happen to anyone?'

'I – well – perhaps – No . . .'

Mr Satterthwaite remembered . . . Madge and Roger Graham . . . Mabelle's face in the moonlight – its serene unearthly happiness . . .

'No,' he admitted. 'No – perhaps death is not the greatest evil . . .'

He remembered the ruffled blue chiffon of her dress that had seemed to him like the plumage of a bird . . . A bird with a broken wing . . .

When he looked up, he found himself alone. Mr Quin was no longer there.

But he had left something behind.

On the seat was a roughly carved bird fashioned out of some dim blue stone. It had, possibly, no great artistic merit. But it had something else.

It had the vague quality of enchantment.

So said Mr Satterthwaite – and Mr Satterthwaite was a connoisseur.

CHAPTER XI

The World's End

Mr Satterthwaite had come to Corsica because of the Duchess. It was out of his beat. On the Riviera he was sure of his comforts, and to be comfortable meant a lot to Mr Satterthwaite. But though he liked his comfort, he also liked a Duchess. In his way, a harmless, gentlemanly, old-fashioned way, Mr Satterthwaite was a snob. He liked the best people. And the Duchess of Leith was a very authentic Duchess. There were no Chicago pork butchers in her ancestry. She was the daughter of a Duke as well as the wife of one.

For the rest, she was rather a shabby-looking old lady, a good deal given to black bead trimmings on her clothes. She had quantities of diamonds in old-fashioned settings, and she wore them as her mother before her had worn them: pinned all over her indiscriminately. Someone had suggested once that the Duchess stood in the middle of the room whilst her maid flung brooches at her haphazard. She subscribed generously to charities, and looked well after her tenants and dependents, but was extremely mean over small sums. She cadged lifts from her friends, and did her shopping in bargain basements.

The Duchess was seized with a whim for Corsica. Cannes bored her and she had a bitter argument with the hotel proprietor over the price of her rooms.

'And you shall go with me, Satterthwaite,' she said firmly. 'We needn't be afraid of scandal at our time of life.'

Mr Satterthwaite was delicately flattered. No one had ever mentioned scandal in connection with him before. He was far too insignificant. Scandal – and a Duchess – delicious!

'Picturesque you know,' said the Duchess. 'Brigands – all that sort of thing. And extremely cheap, so I've heard. Manuel was positively impudent this morning. These hotel proprietors need putting in their place. They can't expect to get the best people if they go on like this. I told him so plainly.'

'I believe,' said Mr Satterthwaite, 'that one can fly over quite comfortably. From Antibes.'

'They probably charge you a pretty penny for it,' said the Duchess sharply. 'Find out, will you?'

'Certainly, Duchess.'

Mr Satterthwaite was still in a flutter of gratification despite the fact that his role was clearly to be that of a glorified courier.

When she learned the price of a passage by Avion, the Duchess turned it down promptly.

'They needn't think I'm going to pay a ridiculous sum like that to go in one of their nasty dangerous things.'

So they went by boat, and Mr Satterthwaite endured ten hours of acute discomfort. To begin with, as the boat sailed at seven, he took it for granted that there would be dinner on board. But there was no dinner. The boat was small and the sea was rough. Mr Satterthwaite was decanted at Ajaccio in the early hours of the morning more dead than alive.

The Duchess, on the contrary, was perfectly fresh. She never minded discomfort if she could feel she was saving money. She waxed enthusiastic over the scene on the quay, with the palm trees and the rising sun. The whole population seemed to have turned out to watch the arrival of the boat, and the launching of the gangway was attended with excited cries and directions.

'*On dirait*,' said a stout Frenchman who stood beside them, '*que jamais avant on n'a fait cette manoeuvre là!*'

'That maid of mine has been sick all night,' said the Duchess. 'The girl's a perfect fool.'

Mr Satterthwaite smiled in a pallid fashion.

'A waste of good food, I call it,' continued the Duchess robustly.

'Did she get any food?' asked Mr Satterthwaite enviously.

'I happened to bring some biscuits and a stick of chocolate on board with me,' said the Duchess. 'When I found there was no dinner to be got, I gave the lot to her. The lower classes always make such a fuss about going without their meals.'

With a cry of triumph the launching of the gangway was accomplished. A Musical Comedy chorus of brigands rushed aboard and wrested hand-luggage from the passengers by main force.

'Come on, Satterthwaite,' said the Duchess. 'I want a hot bath and some coffee.'

So did Mr Satterthwaite. He was not wholly successful, however. They were received at the hotel by a bowing manager and were shown to their rooms. The Duchess's had a bathroom attached. Mr Satterthwaite, however, was directed to a bath that appeared to be situated in somebody else's bedroom. To expect the water to be hot at that hour in the morning was, perhaps, unreasonable. Later he drank intensely black coffee, served in a pot without a lid. The shutters and the window of his room had been flung open, and the crisp morning air came in fragrantly. A day of dazzling blue and green.

The waiter waved his hand with a flourish to call attention to the view.

'*Ajaccio*,' he said solemnly. '*Le plus beau port du monde!*'

And he departed abruptly.

Looking out over the deep blue of the bay, with the snowy mountains beyond, Mr Satterthwaite was almost inclined to agree with him. He finished his coffee, and lying down on the bed, fell fast asleep.

At *déjeuner* the Duchess was in great spirits.

'This is just what will be good for you, Satterthwaite,' she said. 'Get you out of all those dusty little old-maidish ways of yours.' She swept a lorgnette round the room. 'Upon my word, there's Naomi Carlton Smith.'

She indicated a girl sitting by herself at a table in the window. A round-shouldered girl, who slouched as she sat. Her dress appeared to be made of some kind of brown sacking. She had black hair, untidily bobbed.

'An artist?' asked Mr Satterthwaite.

He was always good at placing people.

'Quite right,' said the Duchess. 'Calls herself one anyway. I knew she was mooching around in some queer quarter of the globe. Poor as a church mouse, proud as Lucifer, and a bee in her bonnet like all the Carlton Smiths. Her mother was my first cousin.'

'She's one of the Knowlton lot then?'

The Duchess nodded.

'Been her own worst enemy,' she volunteered. 'Clever girl too. Mixed herself up with a most undesirable young man. One of that Chelsea crowd. Wrote plays or poems or something unhealthy. Nobody took 'em, of course. Then he stole some-body's jewels and got caught out. I forget what they gave him. Five years, I think. But you must remember? It was last winter.'

'Last winter I was in Egypt,' explained Mr Satterthwaite. 'I had 'flu very badly the end of January, and the doctors insisted on Egypt afterwards. I missed a lot.'

His voice rang with a note of real regret.

'That girl seems to me to be moping,' said the Duchess, raising her lorgnette once more. 'I can't allow that.'

On her way out, she stopped by Miss Carlton Smith's table and tapped the girl on the shoulder.

'Well, Naomi, you don't seem to remember me?'

Naomi rose rather unwillingly to her feet.

'Yes, I do, Duchess. I saw you come in. I thought it was quite likely you mightn't recognize me.'

She drawled the words lazily, with a complete indifference of manner.

'When you've finished your lunch, come and talk to me on the terrace,' ordered the Duchess.

'Very well.'

Naomi yawned.

'Shocking manners,' said the Duchess, to Mr Satterthwaite, as she resumed her progress. 'All the Carlton Smiths have.'

They had their coffee outside in the sunshine. They had been there about six minutes when Naomi Carlton Smith lounged out from the hotel and joined them. She let herself fall slackly on to a chair with her legs stretched out ungracefully in front of her.

An odd face, with its jutting chin and deep-set grey eyes. A clever, unhappy face – a face that only just missed being beautiful.

'Well, Naomi,' said the Duchess briskly. 'And what are you doing with yourself?'

'Oh, I dunno. Just marking time.'

'Been painting?'

'A bit.'

'Show me your things.'

Naomi grinned. She was not cowed by the autocrat. She was amused. She went into the hotel and came out again with a portfolio.

'You won't like 'em, Duchess,' she said warningly. 'Say what you like. You won't hurt my feelings.'

Mr Satterthwaite moved his chair a little nearer. He was interested. In another minute he was more interested still. The Duchess was frankly unsympathetic.

'I can't even see which way the things ought to be,' she complained. 'Good gracious, child, there was never a sky that colour – or a sea either.'

'That's the way I see 'em,' said Naomi placidly.

'Ugh!' said the Duchess, inspecting another. 'This gives me the creeps.'

'It's meant to,' said Naomi. 'You're paying me a compliment without knowing it.'

It was a queer vorticist study of a prickly pear – just recognizable as such. Grey-green with slodges of violent colour where the fruit glittered like jewels. A swirling mass of evil, fleshy – festering. Mr Satterthwaite shuddered and turned his head aside.

He found Naomi looking at him and nodding her head in comprehension.

'I know,' she said. 'But it *is* beastly.'

The Duchess cleared her throat.

'It seems quite easy to be an artist nowadays,' she observed witheringly. 'There's no attempt to copy things. You just shovel on some paint – I don't know what with, not a brush, I'm sure –'

'Palette knife,' interposed Naomi, smiling broadly once more.

'A good deal at a time,' continued the Duchess. 'In lumps. And there you are! Everyone says: "How clever." Well, I've no patience with that sort of thing. Give me –'

'A nice picture of a dog or a horse, by Edwin Landseer.'

'And why not?' demanded the Duchess. 'What's wrong with Landseer?'

'Nothing,' said Naomi. 'He's all right. And you're all right. The tops of things are always nice and shiny and smooth. I respect you, Duchess, you've got force. You've met life fair and square and you've come out on top. But the people who are underneath see the under side of things. And that's interesting in a way.'

The Duchess stared at her.

'I haven't the faintest idea what you're talking about,' she declared.

Mr Satterthwaite was still examining the sketches. He realized, as the Duchess could not, the perfection of technique behind them. He was startled and delighted. He looked up at the girl.

'Will you sell me one of these, Miss Carlton Smith?' he asked.

'You can have any one you like for five guineas,' said the girl indifferently.

Mr Satterthwaite hesitated a minute or two and then he selected a study of prickly pear and aloe. In the foreground was a vivid blur of yellow mimosa, the scarlet of the aloe flower danced in and out of the picture, and inexorable, mathematically underlying the whole, was the oblong pattern of the prickly pear and the sword motif of the aloe.

He made a little bow to the girl.

'I am very happy to have secured this, and I think I have made a bargain. Some day, Miss Carlton Smith, I shall be able to sell this sketch at a very good profit – if I want to!'

The girl leant forward to see which one he had taken. He saw a new look come into her eyes. For the first time she was really aware of his existence, and there was respect in the quick glance she gave him.

'You have chosen the best,' she said. 'I – I am glad.'

'Well, I suppose you know what you're doing,' said the Duchess. 'And I daresay you're right. I've heard that you are quite a connoisseur. But you can't tell me that all this new stuff is art, because it isn't. Still, we needn't go into that. Now I'm only going to be here a few days and I want to see something of the island. You've got a car, I suppose, Naomi?'

The girl nodded.

'Excellent,' said the Duchess. 'We'll make a trip somewhere tomorrow.'

'It's only a two-seater.'

'Nonsense, there's a dickey, I suppose, that will do for Mr Satterthwaite?'

A shuddering sigh went through Mr Satterthwaite. He had observed the Corsican roads that morning. Naomi was regarding him thoughtfully.

'I'm afraid my car would be no good to you,' she said. 'It's a terribly battered old bus. I bought it second-hand for a mere song. It will just get me up the hills – with coaxing. But I can't take passengers. There's quite a good garage, though, in the town. You can hire a car there.'

'Hire a car?' said the Duchess, scandalized. 'What an idea. Who's that nice-looking man, rather yellow, who drove up in a four-seater just before lunch?'

'I expect you mean Mr Tomlinson. He's a retired Indian judge.'

'That accounts for the yellowness,' said the Duchess. 'I was afraid it might be jaundice. He seems quite a decent sort of man. I shall talk to him.'

That evening, on coming down to dinner, Mr Satterthwaite found the Duchess resplendent in black velvet and diamonds, talking earnestly to the owner of the four-seater car. She beckoned authoritatively.

'Come here, Mr Satterthwaite, Mr Tomlinson is telling me the most interesting things, and what do you think? – he is actually going to take us on an expedition tomorrow in his car.'

Mr Satterthwaite regarded her with admiration.

'We must go in to dinner,' said the Duchess. 'Do come and

sit at our table, Mr Tomlinson, and then you can go on with what you were telling me.'

'Quite a decent sort of man,' the Duchess pronounced later.

'With quite a decent sort of car,' retorted Mr Satterthwaite.

'Naughty,' said the Duchess, and gave him a resounding blow on the knuckles with the dingy black fan she always carried. Mr Satterthwaite winced with pain.

'Naomi is coming too,' said the Duchess. 'In her car. That girl wants taking out of herself. She's very selfish. Not exactly self-centred, but totally indifferent to everyone and everything. Don't you agree?'

'I don't think that's possible,' said Mr Satterthwaite, slowly. 'I mean, everyone's interest must go *somewhere*. There are, of course, the people who revolve round themselves – but I agree with you, she's not one of that kind. She's totally uninterested in herself. And yet she's got a strong character – there must be *something*. I thought at first it was her art – but it isn't. I've never met anyone so detached from life. That's dangerous.'

'Dangerous? What do you mean?'

'Well, you see – it must mean an obsession of some kind, and obsessions are always dangerous.'

'Satterthwaite,' said the Duchess, 'don't be a fool. And listen to me. About tomorrow –'

Mr Satterthwaite listened. It was very much his role in life.

They started early the following morning, taking their lunch with them. Naomi, who had been six months in the island, was to be the pioneer. Mr Satterthwaite went over to her as she sat waiting to start.

'You are sure that – I can't come with you?' he said wistfully.

She shook her head.

'You'll be much more comfortable in the back of the other car. Nicely padded seats and all that. This is a regular old rattle trap. You'd leap in the air going over the bumps.'

'And then, of course, the hills.'

Naomi laughed.

'Oh, I only said that to rescue you from the dickey. The Duchess could perfectly well afford to have hired a car. She's the meanest woman in England. All the same, the old thing is rather a sport, and I can't help liking her.'

'Then I could come with you after all?' said Mr Satterthwaite eagerly.

She looked at him curiously.

'Why are you so anxious to come with me?'

'Can you ask?' Mr Satterthwaite made his funny old-fashioned bow.

She smiled, but shook her head.

'That isn't the reason,' she said thoughtfully. 'It's odd . . . But you can't come with me – not today.'

'Another day, perhaps,' suggested Mr Satterthwaite politely.

'Oh, another day!' she laughed suddenly, a very queer laugh, Mr Satterthwaite thought. 'Another day! Well, we'll see.'

They started. They drove through the town, and then round the long curve of the bay, winding inland to cross a river and then back to the coast with its hundreds of little sandy coves. And then they began to climb. In and out, round nerve-shattering curves, upwards, ever upwards on the tortuous winding road. The blue bay was far below them, and on the other side of it Ajaccio sparkled in the sun, white, like a fairy city.

In and out, in and out, with a precipice first one side of them, then the other. Mr Satterthwaite felt slightly giddy, he also felt slightly sick. The road was not very wide. And still they climbed.

It was cold now. The wind came to them straight off the snow peaks. Mr Satterthwaite turned up his coat collar and buttoned it tightly under his chin.

It was very cold. Across the water, Ajaccio was still bathed in sunlight, but up here thick grey clouds came drifting across the face of the sun. Mr Satterthwaite ceased to admire the view. He yearned for a steam-heated hotel and a comfortable arm-chair.

Ahead of them Naomi's little two-seater drove steadily forward. Up, still up. They were on top of the world now. On either side of them were lower hills, hills sloping down to valleys. They looked straight across to the snow peaks. And the wind came tearing over them, sharp, like a knife. Suddenly Naomi's car stopped, and she looked back.

'We've arrived,' she said. 'At the World's End. And I don't think it's an awfully good day for it.'

They all got out. They had arrived in a tiny village, with half a dozen stone cottages. An imposing name was printed in letters a foot high.

'Coti Chiaveeri.'

Naomi shrugged her shoulders.

'That's its official name, but I prefer to call it the World's End.'

She walked on a few steps, and Mr Satterthwaite joined her. They were beyond the houses now. The road stopped. As Naomi had said, this was the end, the back of beyond, the beginning of nowhere. Behind them the white ribbon of the road, in front of them – nothing. Only far, far below, the sea . . .

Mr Satterthwaite drew a deep breath.

'It's an extraordinary place. One feels that anything might happen here, that one might meet – anyone –'

He stopped, for just in front of them a man was sitting on a boulder, his face turned to the sea. They had not seen him till this moment, and his appearance had the suddenness of a conjuring trick. He might have sprung from the surrounding landscape.

'I wonder –' began Mr Satterthwaite.

But at that minute the stranger turned, and Mr Satterthwaite saw his face.

'Why, Mr Quin! How extraordinary. Miss Carlton Smith, I want to introduce my friend Mr Quin to you. He's the most unusual fellow. You are, you know. You always turn up in the nick of time –'

He stopped, with the feeling that he had said something awkwardly significant, and yet for the life of him he could not think what it was.

Naomi had shaken hands with Mr Quin in her usual abrupt style.

'We're here for a picnic,' she said. 'And it seems to me we shall be pretty well frozen to the bone.'

Mr Satterthwaite shivered.

'Perhaps,' he said uncertainly, 'we shall find a sheltered spot?'

'Which this isn't,' agreed Naomi. 'Still, it's worth seeing, isn't it?'

'Yes, indeed.' Mr Satterthwaite turned to Mr Quin. 'Miss Carlton Smith calls this place the world's end. Rather a good name, eh?'

Mr Quin nodded his head slowly several times.

'Yes – a very suggestive name. I suppose one only comes once in one's life to a place like that – a place where one can't go on any longer.'

'What do you mean?' asked Naomi sharply.

He turned to her.

'Well, usually, there's a choice, isn't there? To the right or to the left. Forward or back. Here – there's the road behind you and in front of you – nothing.'

Naomi stared at him. Suddenly she shivered and began to retrace her steps towards the others. The two men fell in beside her. Mr Quin continued to talk, but his tone was now easily conversational.

'Is the small car yours, Miss Carlton Smith?'

'Yes.'

'You drive yourself? One needs, I think, a good deal of nerve to do that round here. The turns are rather appalling. A moment of inattention, a brake that failed to hold, and – over the edge – down – down – down. It would be – very easily done.'

They had now joined the others. Mr Satterthwaite introduced his friend. He felt a tug at his arm. It was Naomi. She drew him apart from the others.

'Who is he?' she demanded fiercely.

Mr Satterthwaite gazed at her in astonishment.

'Well, I hardly know. I mean, I have known him for some years now – we have run across each other from time to time, but in the sense of knowing actually –'

He stopped. These were futilities that he was uttering, and the girl by his side was not listening. She was standing with her head bent down, her hands clenched by her sides.

'He knows things,' she said. 'He knows things . . . How does he know?'

Mr Satterthwaite had no answer. He could only look at her dumbly, unable to comprehend the storm that shook her.

'I'm afraid,' she muttered.

'Afraid of Mr Quin?'

'I'm afraid of his eyes. He sees things . . .'

Something cold and wet fell on Mr Satterthwaite's cheek. He looked up.

'Why, it's snowing,' he exclaimed, in great surprise.

'A nice day to have chosen for a picnic,' said Naomi.

She had regained control of herself with an effort.

What was to be done? A babel of suggestions broke out. The snow came down thick and fast. Mr Quin made a suggestion and everyone welcomed it. There was a little stone Cassecroute at the end of the row of houses. There was a stampede towards it.

'You have your provisions,' said Mr Quin, 'and they will probably be able to make you some coffee.'

It was a tiny place, rather dark, for the one little window did little towards lighting it, but from one end came a grateful glow of warmth. An old Corsican woman was just throwing a handful of branches on the fire. It blazed up, and by its light the newcomers realized that others were before them.

Three people were sitting at the end of a bare wooden table. There was something unreal about the scene to Mr Satterthwaite's eye, there was something even more unreal about the people.

The woman who sat at the end of the table looked like a duchess – that is, she looked more like a popular conception of a duchess. She was the ideal stage *grande dame.* Her aristocratic head was held high, her exquisitely dressed hair was of a snowy white. She was dressed in grey – soft draperies that fell about her in artistic folds. One long white hand supported her chin, the other was holding a roll spread with *pâté de foie gras.* On her right was a man with a very white face, very black hair, and horn-rimmed spectacles. He was marvellously and beautifully dressed. At the moment his head was thrown back, and his left arm was thrown out as though he were about to declaim something.

On the left of the white-haired lady was a jolly-looking little man with a bald head. After the first glance, nobody looked at him.

There was just a moment of uncertainty, and then the Duchess (the authentic Duchess) took charge.

'Isn't this storm too dreadful?' she said pleasantly, coming forward, and smiling a purposeful and efficient smile that she had found very useful when serving on Welfare and other committees. 'I suppose you've been caught in it just like we have? But Corsica is a marvellous place. I only arrived this morning.'

The man with the black hair got up, and the Duchess with a gracious smile slipped into his seat.

The white-haired lady spoke.

'We have been here a week,' she said.

Mr Satterthwaite started. Could anyone who had once heard that voice ever forget it? It echoed round the stone room, charged with emotion – with exquisite melancholy. It seemed to him that she had said something wonderful, memorable, full of meaning. She had spoken from her heart.

He spoke in a hurried aside to Mr Tomlinson.

'The man in spectacles is Mr Vyse – the producer, you know.'

The retired Indian judge was looking at Mr Vyse with a good deal of dislike.

'What does he produce?' he asked. 'Children?'

'Oh, dear me, no,' said Mr Satterthwaite, shocked by the mere mention of anything so crude in connection with Mr Vyse. 'Plays.'

'I think,' said Naomi, 'I'll go out again. It's too hot in here.'

Her voice, strong and harsh, made Mr Satterthwaite jump. She made almost blindly, as it seemed, for the door, brushing Mr Tomlinson aside. But in the doorway itself she came face to face with Mr Quin, and he barred her way.

'Go back and sit down,' he said.

His voice was authoritative. To Mr Satterthwaite's surprise the girl hesitated a minute and then obeyed. She sat down at the foot of the table as far from the others as possible.

Mr Satterthwaite bustled forward and button-holed the producer.

'You may not remember me,' he began, 'my name is Satterthwaite.'

'Of course!' A long bony hand shot out and enveloped the other's in a painful grip. 'My dear man. Fancy meeting you here. You know Miss Nunn, of course?'

Mr Satterthwaite jumped. No wonder that voice had been familiar. Thousands, all over England had thrilled to those wonderful emotion-laden tones. Rosina Nunn! England's greatest emotional actress. Mr Satterthwaite too had lain under her spell. No one like her for interpreting a part – for bringing out the finer shades of meaning. He had thought of her always as an intellectual actress, one who comprehended and got inside the soul of her part.

He might be excused for not recognizing her. Rosina Nunn was volatile in her tastes. For twenty-five years of her life she had been a blonde. After a tour in the States she had returned with the locks of the raven, and she had taken up tragedy in earnest. This 'French Marquise' effect was her latest whim.

'Oh, by the way, Mr Judd – Miss Nunn's husband,' said Vyse, carelessly introducing the man with the bald head.

Rosina Nunn had had several husbands, Mr Satterthwaite knew. Mr Judd was evidently the latest.

Mr Judd was busily unwrapping packages from a hamper at his side. He addressed his wife.

'Some more *pâté*, dearest? That last wasn't as thick as you like it.'

Rosina Nunn surrendered her roll to him, as she murmured simply:

'Henry thinks of the most enchanting meals. I always leave the commissariat to him.'

'Feed the brute,' said Mr Judd, and laughed. He patted his wife on the shoulder.

'Treats her just as though she were a dog,' murmured the

melancholy voice of Mr Vyse in Mr Satterthwaite's ear. 'Cuts up her food for her. Odd creatures, women.'

Mr Satterthwaite and Mr Quin between them unpacked lunch. Hard-boiled eggs, cold ham and gruyère cheese were distributed round the table. The Duchess and Miss Nunn appeared to be deep in murmured confidences. Fragments came along in the actress's deep contralto.

'The bread must be lightly toasted, you understand? Then just a *very* thin layer of marmalade. Rolled up and put in the oven for one minute – not more. Simply delicious.'

'That woman lives for food,' murmured Mr Vyse. 'Simply lives for it. She can't think of anything else. I remember in Riders to the Sea – you know "and it's the fine quiet time I'll be having." I could *not* get the effect I wanted. At last I told her to think of peppermint creams – she's very fond of peppermint creams. I got the effect at once – a sort of far-away look that went to your very soul.'

Mr Satterthwaite was silent. He was remembering.

Mr Tomlinson opposite cleared his throat preparatory to entering into conversation.

'You produce plays, I hear, eh? I'm fond of a good play myself. "Jim the Penman," now, that was a play.'

'My God,' said Mr Vyse, and shivered down all the long length of him.

'A tiny clove of garlic,' said Miss Nunn to the Duchess. 'You tell your cook. It's wonderful.'

She sighed happily and turned to her husband.

'Henry,' she said plaintively, 'I've never even *seen* the caviare.'

'You're as near as nothing to sitting on it,' returned Mr Judd cheerfully. 'You put it behind you on the chair.'

Rosina Nunn retrieved it hurriedly, and beamed round the table.

'Henry is too wonderful. I'm so terribly absent-minded. I never know where I've put anything.'

'Like the day you packed your pearls in your sponge bag,' said Henry jocosely. 'And then left it behind at the hotel. My word, I did a bit of wiring and phoning that day.'

'They were insured,' said Miss Nunn dreamily. 'Not like my opal.'

A spasm of exquisite heartrending grief flitted across her face.

Several times, when in the company of Mr Quin, Mr Satterthwaite had had the feeling of taking part in a play. The illusion was with him very strongly now. This was a dream. Everyone had his part. The words 'my opal' were his own cue. He leant forward.

'Your opal, Miss Nunn?'

'Have you got the butter, Henry? Thank you. Yes, my opal. It was stolen, you know. And I never got it back.'

'Do tell us,' said Mr Satterthwaite.

'Well – I was born in October – so it was lucky for me to wear opals, and because of that I wanted a real beauty. I waited a long time for it. They said it was one of the most perfect ones known. Not very large – about the size of a two-shilling piece – but oh! the colour and the fire.'

She sighed. Mr Satterthwaite observed that the Duchess was fidgeting and seemed uncomfortable, but nothing could stop Miss Nunn now. She went on, and the exquisite inflections of her voice made the story sound like some mournful Saga of old.

'It was stolen by a young man called Alex Gerard. He wrote plays.'

'Very good plays,' put in Mr Vyse professionally. 'Why, I once kept one of his plays for six months.'

'Did you produce it?' asked Mr Tomlinson.

'Oh, *no*,' said Mr Vyse, shocked at the idea. 'But do you know, at one time I actually thought of doing so?'

'It had a wonderful part in it for me,' said Miss Nunn. ' "*Rachel's Children*," it was called – though there wasn't anyone called Rachel in the play. He came to talk to me about it – at the theatre. I liked him. He was nice-looking – and very shy, poor boy. I remember' – a beautiful far-away look stole over her face – 'he bought me some peppermint creams. The opal was lying on the dressing-table. He'd been out in Australia, and he knew something about opals. He took it over to the light to

look at it. I suppose he must have slipped it into his pocket
then. I missed it as soon as he'd gone. There *was* a to-do. You
remember?'

She turned to Mr Vyse.

'Oh, I remember,' said Mr Vyse with a groan.

'They found the empty case in his rooms,' continued the
actress. 'He'd been terribly hard up, but the very next day he
was able to pay large sums into his bank. He pretended to
account for it by saying that a friend of his had put some money
on a horse for him, but he couldn't produce the friend. He
said he must have put the case in his pocket by mistake. I think
that was a terribly weak thing to say, don't you? He might have
thought of something better than that . . . I had to go and give
evidence. There were pictures of me in all the papers. My press
agent said it was very good publicity – but I'd much rather have
had my opal back.'

She shook her head sadly.

'Have some preserved pineapple?' said Mr Judd.

Miss Nunn brightened up.

'Where is it?'

'I gave it to you just now.'

Miss Nunn looked behind her and in front of her, eyed her
grey silk pochette, and then slowly drew up a large purple silk
bag that was reposing on the ground beside her. She began to
turn the contents out slowly on the table, much to Mr Satterthwaite's interest.

There was a powder puff, a lip-stick, a small jewel case, a
skein of wool, another powder puff, two handkerchiefs, a box
of chocolate creams, an enamelled paper knife, a mirror, a little
dark brown wooden box, five letters, a walnut, a small square
of mauve crêpe de chine, a piece of ribbon and the end of a
croissant. Last of all came the preserved pineapple.

'*Eureka*,' murmured Mr Satterthwaite softly.

'I beg your pardon?'

'Nothing,' said Mr Satterthwaite hastily. 'What a charming
paper knife.'

'Yes, isn't it? Somebody gave it to me. I can't remember who.'

'That's an Indian box,' remarked Mr Tomlinson. 'Ingenious little things, aren't they?'

'Somebody gave me that too,' said Miss Nunn. 'I've had it a long time. It used always to stand on my dressing-table at the theatre. I don't think it's very pretty, though, do you?'

The box was of plain dark brown wood. It pushed open from the side. On the top of it were two plain flaps of wood that could be turned round and round.

'Not pretty, perhaps,' said Mr Tomlinson with a chuckle. 'But I'll bet you've never seen one like it.'

Mr Satterthwaite leaned forward. He had an excited feeling.

'Why did you say it was ingenious?' he demanded.

'Well, isn't it?'

The judge appealed to Miss Nunn. She looked at him blankly.

'I suppose I mustn't show them the trick of it – eh?' Miss Nunn still looked blank.

'What trick?' asked Mr Judd.

'God bless my soul, don't you know?'

He looked round the inquiring faces.

'Fancy that now. May I take the box a minute? Thank you.'

He pushed it open.

'Now then, can anyone give me something to put in it – not too big. Here's a small piece of gruyère cheese. That will do capitally. I place it inside, shut the box.'

He fumbled for a minute or two with his hands.

'Now see –'

He opened the box again. It was empty.

'Well, I never,' said Mr Judd. 'How do you do it?'

'It's quite simple. Turn the box upside down, and move the left hand flap half-way round, then shut the right hand flap. Now to bring our piece of cheese back again we must reverse that. The right hand flap half-way round, and the left one closed, still keeping the box upside down. And now – Hey Presto!'

The box slid open. A gasp went round the table. The cheese was there – but so was something else. A round thing that blinked forth every colour of the rainbow.

'*My opal!*'

It was a clarion note. Rosina Nunn stood upright, her hands clasped to her breast.

'My opal! How did it get there?'

Henry Judd cleared his throat.

'I – er – I rather think, Rosy, my girl, you must have put it there yourself.'

Someone got up from the table and blundered out into the air. It was Naomi Carlton Smith. Mr Quin followed her.

'But when? Do you mean –?'

Mr Satterthwaite watched her while the truth dawned on her. It took over two minutes before she got it.

'You mean last year – at the theatre.'

'You know,' said Henry apologetically. 'You *do* fiddle with things, Rosy. Look at you with the caviare today.'

Miss Nunn was painfully following out her mental processes.

'I just slipped it in without thinking, and then I suppose I turned the box about and did the thing by accident, but then – but then –' At last it came. 'But then Alex Gerard didn't steal it after all. Oh!' – a full-throated cry, poignant, moving – 'How dreadful!'

'Well,' said Mr Vyse, 'that can be put right now.'

'Yes, but he's been in prison a year.' And then she startled them. She turned sharp on the Duchess. 'Who is that girl – that girl who has just gone out?'

'Miss Carlton Smith,' said the Duchess, 'was engaged to Mr Gerard. She – took the thing very hard.'

Mr Satterthwaite stole softly away. The snow had stopped, Naomi was sitting on the stone wall. She had a sketch book in her hand, some coloured crayons were scattered around. Mr Quin was standing beside her.

She held out the sketch book to Mr Satterthwaite. It was a very rough affair – but it had genius. A kaleidoscopic whirl of snowflakes with a figure in the centre.

'Very good,' said Mr Satterthwaite.

Mr Quin looked up at the sky.

'The storm is over,' he said. 'The roads will be slippery, but I do not think there will be any accident – now.'

'There will be no accident,' said Naomi. Her voice was charged with some meaning that Mr Satterthwaite did not understand. She turned and smiled at him – a sudden dazzling smile. 'Mr Satterthwaite can drive back with me if he likes.'

He knew then to what length desperation had driven her.

'Well,' said Mr Quin, 'I must bid you goodbye.'

He moved away.

'Where is he going?' said Mr Satterthwaite, staring after him.

'Back where he came from, I suppose,' said Naomi in an odd voice.

'But – but there isn't anything there,' said Mr Satterthwaite, for Mr Quin was making for that spot on the edge of the cliff where they had first seen him. 'You know you said yourself it was the World's End.'

He handed back the sketchbook.

'It's very good,' he said. 'A very good likeness. But why – er – why did you put him in Fancy Dress?'

Her eyes met his for a brief second.

'I see him like that,' said Naomi Carlton Smith.

CHAPTER XII

Harlequin's Lane

Mr Satterthwaite was never quite sure what took him to stay with the Denmans. They were not of his kind – that is to say, they belonged neither to the great world, nor to the more interesting artistic circles. They were Philistines, and dull Philistines at that. Mr Satterthwaite had met them first at Biarritz, had accepted an invitation to stay with them, had come, had been bored, and yet strangely enough had come again and yet again.

Why? He was asking himself that question on this twenty-first of June, as he sped out of London in his Rolls Royce.

John Denman was a man of forty, a solid well-established figure respected in the business world. His friends were not Mr Satterthwaite's friends, his ideas even less so. He was a man clever in his own line but devoid of imagination outside it.

Why am I doing this thing? Mr Satterthwaite asked himself once more – and the only answer that came seemed to him so vague and so inherently preposterous that he almost put it aside. For the only reason that presented itself was the fact that one of the rooms in the house (a comfortable well-appointed house), stirred his curiosity. That room was Mrs Denman's own sitting-room.

It was hardly an expression of her personality because, so far as Mr Satterthwaite could judge, she had no personality. He had never met a woman so completely expressionless. She was, he knew, a Russian by birth. John Denman had been in Russia at the outbreak of the European war, he had fought with the Russian troops, had narrowly escaped with his life on the outbreak of the revolution, and had brought this Russian girl with him, a penniless refugee. In face of strong disapproval from his parents he had married her.

Mrs Denman's room was in no way remarkable. It was well and solidly furnished with good Hepplewhite furniture – a trifle more masculine than feminine in atmosphere. But in it there was one incongruous item: a Chinese lacquer screen – a thing of creamy yellow and pale rose. Any museum might have been glad to own it. It was a collector's piece, rare and beautiful.

It was out of place against that solid English background. It should have been the key-note of the room with everything arranged to harmonize subtly with it. And yet Mr Satterthwaite could not accuse the Denmans of lack of taste. Everything else in the house was in perfectly blended accord.

He shook his head. The thing – trivial though it was – puzzled him. Because of it, so he verily believed, he had come again and again to the house. It was, perhaps, a woman's fantasy – but that solution did not satisfy him as he thought of Mrs Denman – a quiet hard-featured woman, speaking English so correctly that no one would ever have guessed her a foreigner.

The car drew up at his destination and he got out, his mind still dwelling on the problem of the Chinese screen. The name of the Denmans' house was 'Ashmead,' and it occupied some five acres of Melton Heath, which is thirty miles from London, stands five hundred feet above sea level and is, for the most part, inhabited by those who have ample incomes.

The butler received Mr Satterthwaite suavely. Mr and Mrs Denman were both out – at a rehearsal – they hoped Mr Satterthwaite would make himself at home until they returned.

Mr Satterthwaite nodded and proceeded to carry out these injunctions by stepping into the garden. After a cursory examination of the flower beds, he strolled down a shady walk and presently came to a door in the wall. It was unlocked and he passed through it and came out into a narrow lane.

Mr Satterthwaite looked to left and right. A very charming lane, shady and green, with high hedges – a rural lane that twisted and turned in good old-fashioned style. He remembered the stamped address: ASHMEAD, HARLEQUIN'S LANE – remembered too, a local name for it that Mrs Denman had once told him.

'Harlequin's Lane,' he murmured to himself softly. 'I wonder –'

He turned a corner.

Not at the time, but afterwards, he wondered why this time he felt no surprise at meeting that elusive friend of his: Mr Harley Quin. The two men clasped hands.

'So *you're* down here,' said Mr Satterthwaite.

'Yes,' said Mr Quin. 'I'm staying in the same house as you are.'

'Staying there?'

'Yes. Does it surprise you?'

'No,' said Mr Satterthwaite slowly. 'Only – well, you never stay anywhere for long, do you?'

'Only as long as is necessary,' said Mr Quin gravely.

'I see,' said Mr Satterthwaite.

They walked on in silence for some minutes.

'This lane,' began Mr Satterthwaite, and stopped.

'Belongs to me,' said Mr Quin.

'I thought it did,' said Mr Satterthwaite. 'Somehow, I thought it must. There's the other name for it, too, the local name. They call it the "Lovers' Lane." You know that?'

Mr Quin nodded.

'But surely,' he said gently, 'there is a "Lovers' Lane" in every village?'

'I suppose so,' said Mr Satterthwaite, and he sighed a little.

He felt suddenly rather old and out of things, a little dried-up wizened old fogey of a man. Each side of him were the hedges, very green and alive.

'Where does this lane end, I wonder?' he asked suddenly.

'It ends – *here*,' said Mr Quin.

They came round the last bend. The lane ended in a piece of waste ground, and almost at their feet a great pit opened. In it were tin cans gleaming in the sun, and other cans that were too red with rust to gleam, old boots, fragments of newspapers, a hundred and one odds and ends that were no longer of account to anybody.

'A rubbish heap,' exclaimed Mr Satterthwaite, and breathed deeply and indignantly.

'Sometimes there are very wonderful things on a rubbish heap,' said Mr Quin.

'I know, I know,' cried Mr Satterthwaite, and quoted with just a trace of self-consciousness: '*Bring me the two most beautiful things in the city, said God.* You know how it goes, eh?'

Mr Quin nodded.

Mr Satterthwaite looked up at the ruins of a small cottage perched on the brink of the wall of the cliff.

'Hardly a pretty view for a house,' he remarked.

'I fancy this wasn't a rubbish heap in those days,' said Mr Quin. 'I believe the Denmans lived there when they were first married. They moved into the big house when the old people died. The cottage was pulled down when they began to quarry the rock here – but nothing much was done, as you can see.'

They turned and began retracing their steps.

'I suppose,' said Mr Satterthwaite, smiling, 'that many couples come wandering down this lane on these warm summer evenings.'

'Probably.'

'Lovers,' said Mr Satterthwaite. He repeated the word thoughtfully and quite without the normal embarrassment of the Englishman. Mr Quin had that effect upon him. 'Lovers . . . You have done a lot for lovers, Mr Quin.'

The other bowed his head without replying.

'You have saved them from sorrow – from worse than sorrow, from death. You have been an advocate for the dead themselves.'

'You are speaking of yourself – of what *you* have done – not of me.'

'It is the same thing,' said Mr Satterthwaite. 'You know it is,' he urged, as the other did not speak. 'You have acted – through me. For some reason or other you do not act directly – yourself.'

'Sometimes I do,' said Mr Quin.

His voice held a new note. In spite of himself Mr Satterthwaite shivered a little. The afternoon, he thought, must be growing chilly. And yet the sun seemed as bright as ever.

At that moment a girl turned the corner ahead of them and came into sight. She was a very pretty girl, fair-haired and blue-eyed, wearing a pink cotton frock. Mr Satterthwaite recognized her as Molly Stanwell, whom he had met down here before.

She waved a hand to welcome him.

'John and Anna have just gone back,' she cried. 'They thought you must have come, but they simply had to be at the rehearsal.'

'Rehearsal of what?' inquired Mr Satterthwaite.

'This masquerade thing – I don't quite know what you'll call it. There is singing and dancing and all sorts of things in it. Mr Manly, do you remember him down here? He had quite a good tenor voice, is to be pierrot, and I am pierrette. Two professionals are coming down for the dancing – Harlequin and Columbine, you know. And then there is a big chorus of girls. Lady Roscheimer is so keen on training village girls to sing. She's really getting the thing up for that. The music is rather lovely – but very modern – next to no tune anywhere. Claude Wickam. Perhaps you know him?'

Mr Satterthwaite nodded, for, as has been mentioned before, it was his *métier* to know everybody. He knew all about that aspiring genius Claude Wickam, and about Lady Roscheimer who was a fat Jewess with a *penchant* for young men of the artistic persuasion. And he knew all about Sir Leopold Roscheimer who liked his wife to be happy and, most rare among husbands, did not mind her being happy in her own way.

They found Claude Wickam at tea with the Denmans, cramming his mouth indiscriminately with anything handy, talking rapidly, and waving long white hands that had a double-jointed appearance. His short-sighted eyes peered through large horn-rimmed spectacles.

John Denman, upright, slightly florid, with the faintest possible tendency to sleekness, listened with an air of bored attention. On the appearance of Mr Satterthwaite, the musician transferred his remarks to him. Anna Denman sat behind the tea things, quiet and expressionless as usual.

Mr Satterthwaite stole a covert glance at her. Tall, gaunt, very thin, with the skin tightly stretched over high cheek bones, black hair parted in the middle, a skin that was weatherbeaten. An out of door woman who cared nothing for the use of cosmetics. A Dutch Doll of a woman, wooden, lifeless – and yet . . .

He thought: 'There *should* be meaning behind that face, and yet there isn't. That's what's all wrong. Yes, all wrong.' And to Claude Wickam he said: 'I beg your pardon? You were saying?'

Claude Wickam, who liked the sound of his own voice, began all over again. 'Russia,' he said, 'that was the only country in the world worth being interested in. They experimented. With lives, if you like, but still they experimented. Magnificent!' He crammed a sandwich into his mouth with one hand, and added a bite of the chocolate éclair he was waving about in the other. 'Take,' he said (with his mouth full), 'the Russian Ballet.' Remembering his hostess, he turned to her. What did *she* think of the Russian Ballet?

The question was obviously only a prelude to the important point – what Claude Wickam thought of the Russian Ballet, but her answer was unexpected and threw him completely out of his stride.

'I have never seen it.'

'What?' He gazed at her open-mouthed. 'But – surely –'

Her voice went on, level and emotionless.

'Before my marriage, I was a dancer. So now –'

'A busman's holiday,' said her husband.

'Dancing.' She shrugged her shoulders. 'I know all the tricks of it. It does not interest me.'

'Oh!'

It took but a moment for Claude to recover his aplomb. His voice went on.

'Talking of lives,' said Mr Satterthwaite, 'and experimenting in them. The Russian nation made one costly experiment.'

Claude Wickam swung round on him.

'I know what you are going to say,' he cried. 'Kharsanova!

The immortal, the only Kharsanova! You saw her dance?'

'Three times,' said Mr Satterthwaite. 'Twice in Paris, once in London. I shall – not forget it.'

He spoke in an almost reverent voice.

'I saw her, too,' said Claude Wickam. 'I was ten years old. An uncle took me. God! I shall never forget it.'

He threw a piece of bun fiercely into a flower bed.

'There is a statuette of her in a Museum in Berlin,' said Mr Satterthwaite. 'It is marvellous. That impression of fragility – as though you could break her with a flip of the thumb nail. I have seen her as Columbine, in the Swan, as the dying Nymph.' He paused, shaking his head. 'There was genius. It will be long years before such another is born. She was young too. Destroyed ignorantly and wantonly in the first days of the Revolution.'

'Fools! Madmen! Apes!' said Claude Wickam. He choked with a mouthful of tea.

'I studied with Kharsanova,' said Mrs Denman. 'I remember her well.'

'She was wonderful?' said Mr Satterthwaite.

'Yes,' said Mrs Denman quietly. 'She was wonderful.'

Claude Wickam departed and John Denman drew a deep sigh of relief at which his wife laughed.

Mr Satterthwaite nodded. 'I know what you think. But in spite of everything, the music that that boy writes *is* music.'

'I suppose it is,' said Denman.

'Oh, undoubtedly. How long it will be – well, that is different.'

John Denman looked at him curiously.

'You mean?'

'I mean that success has come early. And that is dangerous. Always dangerous.' He looked across at Mr Quin. 'You agree with me?'

'You are always right,' said Mr Quin.

'We will come upstairs to my room,' said Mrs Denman. 'It is pleasant there.'

She led the way, and they followed her. Mr Satterthwaite drew a deep breath as he caught sight of the Chinese screen. He looked up to find Mrs Denman watching him.

'You are the man who is always right,' she said, nodding her head slowly at him. 'What do you make of my screen?'

He felt that in some way the words were a challenge to him, and he answered almost haltingly, stumbling over the words a little.

'Why, it's – it's beautiful. More, it's unique.'

'You're right.' Denman had come up behind him. 'We bought it early in our married life. Got it for about a tenth of its value, but even then – well, it crippled us for over a year. You remember, Anna?'

'Yes,' said Mrs Denman, 'I remember.'

'In fact, we'd no business to buy it at all – not then. Now, of course, it's different. There was some very good lacquer going at Christie's the other day. Just what we need to make this room perfect. All Chinese together. Clear out the other stuff. Would you believe it, Satterthwaite, my wife wouldn't hear of it?'

'I like this room as it is,' said Mrs Denman.

There was a curious look on her face. Again Mr Satterthwaite felt challenged and defeated. He looked round him, and for the first time he noticed the absence of all personal touch. There were no photographs, no flowers, no knick-knacks. It was not like a woman's room at all. Save for that one incongruous factor of the Chinese screen, it might have been a sample room shown at some big furnishing house.

He found her smiling at him.

'Listen,' she said. She bent forward, and for a moment she seemed less English, more definitely foreign. 'I speak to you for you will understand. We bought that screen with more than money – with love. For love of it, because it was beautiful and unique, we went without other things, things we needed and missed. These other Chinese pieces my husband speaks of, those we should buy with money only, we should not pay away anything of ourselves.'

Her husband laughed.

'Oh, have it your own way,' he said, but with a trace of irritation in his voice. 'But it's all wrong against this English background. This other stuff, it's good enough of its kind, genuine solid, no fake about it – but mediocre. Good plain late Hepplewhite.'

She nodded.

'Good, solid, genuine English,' she murmured softly.

Mr Satterthwaite stared at her. He caught a meaning behind these words. The English room – the flaming beauty of the Chinese screen . . . No, it was gone again.

'I met Miss Stanwell in the lane,' he said conversationally. 'She tells me she is going to be pierrette in this show tonight.'

'Yes,' said Denman. 'And she's awfully good, too.'

'She has clumsy feet,' said Anna.

'Nonsense,' said her husband. 'All women are alike, Satterthwaite. Can't bear to hear another woman praised. Molly is a very good-looking girl, and so of course every woman has to have their knife into her.'

'I spoke of dancing,' said Anna Denman. She sounded faintly surprised. 'She is very pretty, yes, but her feet move clumsily. You cannot tell me anything else because I know about dancing.'

Mr Satterthwaite intervened tactfully.

'You have two professional dancers coming down, I understand?'

'Yes. For the ballet proper. Prince Oranoff is bringing them down in his car.'

'Sergius Oranoff?'

The question came from Anna Denman. Her husband turned and looked at her.

'You know him?'

'I used to know him – in Russia.'

Mr Satterthwaite thought that John Denman looked disturbed.

'Will he know you?'

'Yes. He will know me.'

She laughed – a low, almost triumphant laugh. There was nothing of the Dutch Doll about her face now. She nodded reassuringly at her husband.

'Sergius. So he is bringing down the two dancers. He was always interested in dancing.'

'I remember.'

John Denman spoke abruptly, then turned and left the room. Mr Quin followed him. Anna Denman crossed to the telephone and asked for a number. She arrested Mr Satterthwaite with a gesture as he was about to follow the example of the other two men.

'Can I speak to Lady Roscheimer. Oh! it is you. This is Anna Denman speaking. Has Prince Oranoff arrived yet? What? *What?* Oh, my dear! But how ghastly.'

She listened for a few moments longer, then replaced the receiver. She turned to Mr Satterthwaite.

'There has been an accident. There would be with Sergius Ivanovitch driving. Oh, he has not altered in all these years. The girl was not badly hurt, but bruised and shaken, too much to dance tonight. The man's arm is broken. Sergius Ivanovitch himself is unhurt. The devil looks after his own, perhaps.'

'And what about tonight's performance?'

'Exactly, my friend. Something must be done about it.'

She sat thinking. Presently she looked at him.

'I am a bad hostess, Mr Satterthwaite. I do not entertain you.'

'I assure you that it is not necessary. There's one thing though, Mrs Denman, that I would very much like to know.'

'Yes?'

'How did you come across Mr Quin?'

'He is often down here,' she said slowly. 'I think he owns land in this part of the world.'

'He does, he does. He told me so this afternoon,' said Mr Satterthwaite.

'He is –' She paused. Her eyes met Mr Satterthwaite's. 'I think you know what he is better than I do,' she finished.

'I?'

'Is it not so?'

He was troubled. His neat little soul found her disturbing. He felt that she wished to force him further than he was prepared to go, that she wanted him to put into words that which he was not prepared to admit to himself.

'*You* know!' she said. 'I think you know most things, Mr Satterthwaite.'

Here was incense, yet for once it failed to intoxicate him. He shook his head in unwonted humility.

'What can anyone know?' he asked. 'So little – so very little.'

She nodded in assent. Presently she spoke again, in a queer brooding voice, without looking at him.

'Supposing I were to tell you something – you would not laugh? No, I do not think you would laugh. Supposing, then, that to carry on one's' – she paused – 'one's trade, one's profession, one were to make use of a fantasy – one were to pretend to oneself something that did not exist – that one were to imagine a certain person . . . It is a pretence, you understand, a make believe – nothing more. But one day –'

'Yes?' said Mr Satterthwaite.

He was keenly interested.

'The fantasy came true! The thing one imagined – the impossible thing, the thing that could not be – was real! Is that madness? Tell me, Mr Satterthwaite. Is that madness – or do you believe it too?'

'I –' Queer how he could not get the words out. How they seemed to stick somewhere at the back of his throat.

'Folly,' said Anna Denman. 'Folly.'

She swept out of the room and left Mr Satterthwaite with his confession of faith unspoken.

He came down to dinner to find Mrs Denman entertaining a guest, a tall dark man approaching middle age.

'Prince Oranoff – Mr Satterthwaite.'

The two men bowed. Mr Satterthwaite had the feeling that some conversation had been broken off on his entry which would not be resumed. But there was no sense of strain. The Russian conversed easily and naturally on those objects which were nearest to Mr Satterthwaite's heart. He was a man of very fine artistic taste, and they soon found that they had many friends in common. John Denman joined them, and the talk became localized. Oranoff expressed regret for the accident.

'It was not my fault. I like to drive fast – yes, but I am a good driver. It was Fate – chance' – he shrugged his shoulders – 'the masters of all of us.'

'There speaks the Russian in you, Sergius Ivanovitch,' said Mrs Denman.

'And finds an echo in you, Anna Mikalovna,' he threw back quickly.

Mr Satterthwaite looked from one to the other of the three of them. John Denman, fair, aloof, English, and the other two, dark, thin, strangely alike. Something rose in his mind – what was it? Ah! he had it now. The first Act of the Walküre. Siegmund and Sieglinde – so alike – and the alien Hunding. Conjectures began to stir in his brain. Was this the meaning of the presence of Mr Quin? One thing he believed in firmly – wherever Mr Quin showed himself – there lay drama. Was this it here – the old hackneyed three cornered tragedy?

He was vaguely disappointed. He had hoped for better things.

'What has been arranged, Anna?' asked Denman. 'The thing will have to be put off, I suppose. I heard you ringing the Roscheimers up.'

She shook her head.

'No – there is no need to put it off.'

'But you can't do it without the ballet?'

'You certainly couldn't have a Harlequinade without Harlequin and Columbine,' agreed Anna Denman drily. 'I'm going to be Columbine, John.'

'You?' He was astonished – disturbed, Mr Satterthwaite thought.

She nodded composedly.

'You need not be afraid, John. I shall not disgrace you. You forget – it was my profession once.'

Mr Satterthwaite thought: 'What an extraordinary thing a voice is. The things it says – and the things it leaves unsaid and means! I wish I knew . . .'

'Well,' said John Denman grudgingly, 'that solves one half of the problem. What about the other? Where will you find Harlequin?'

'I *have* found him – there!'

She gestured towards the open doorway where Mr Quin had just appeared. He smiled back at her.

'Good lord, Quin,' said John Denman. 'Do you know anything of this game? I should never have imagined it.'

'Mr Quin is vouched for by an expert,' said his wife. 'Mr Satterthwaite will answer for him.'

She smiled at Mr Satterthwaite, and the little man found himself murmuring:

'Oh, yes – I answer for Mr Quin.'

Denman turned his attention elsewhere.

'You know there's to be a fancy dress dance business afterwards. Great nuisance. We'll have to rig you up, Satterthwaite.'

Mr Satterthwaite shook his head very decidedly.

'My years will excuse me.' A brilliant idea struck him. A table napkin under his arm. 'There I am, an elderly waiter who has seen better days.'

He laughed.

'An interesting profession,' said Mr Quin. 'One sees so much.'

'I've got to put on some fool pierrot thing,' said Denman gloomily. 'It's cool anyway, that's one thing. What about you?' He looked at Oranoff.

'I have a Harlequin costume,' said the Russian. His eyes wandered for a minute to his hostess's face.

Mr Satterthwaite wondered if he was mistaken in fancying that there was just a moment of constraint.

'There might have been three of us,' said Denman, with a laugh. 'I've got an old Harlequin costume my wife made me when we were first married for some show or other.' He paused, looking down on his broad shirt front. 'I don't suppose I could get into it now.'

'No,' said his wife. 'You couldn't get into it now.'

And again her voice said something more than mere words. She glanced up at the clock.

'If Molly doesn't turn up soon, we won't wait for her.'

But at that moment the girl was announced. She was already wearing her Pierrette dress of white and green, and very charming she looked in it, so Mr Satterthwaite reflected.

She was full of excitement and enthusiasm over the forth-coming performance.

'I'm getting awfully nervous, though,' she announced, as they drank coffee after dinner. 'I know my voice will wobble, and I shall forget the words.'

'Your voice is very charming,' said Anna. 'I should not worry about it if I were you.'

'Oh, but I do. The other I don't mind about – the dancing, I mean. That's sure to go all right. I mean, you can't go very far wrong with your feet, can you?'

She appealed to Anna, but the older woman did not respond. Instead she said:

'Sing something now to Mr Satterthwaite. You will find that he will reassure you.'

Molly went over to the piano. Her voice rang out, fresh and tuneful, in an old Irish ballad.

> *'Shiela, dark Shiela, what is it that you're seeing?*
> *What is it that you're seeing, that you're seeing in the fire?'*
> *'I see a lad that loves me – and I see a lad that leaves me,*
> *And a third lad, a Shadow Lad – and he's the lad that grieves me.'*

The song went on. At the end, Mr Satterthwaite nodded vigorous approval.

'Mrs Denman is right. Your voice is charming. Not, perhaps, very fully trained, but delightfully natural, and with that unstudied quality of youth in it.'

'That's right,' agreed John Denman. 'You go ahead, Molly, and don't be downed by stage fright. We'd better be getting over to the Roscheimers now.'

The party separated to don cloaks. It was a glorious night and they proposed to walk over, the house being only a few hundred yards down the road.

Mr Satterthwaite found himself by his friend.

'It's an odd thing,' he said, 'but that song made me think of you. *A third lad – a Shadow Lad –* there's mystery there, and wherever there's mystery I – well, think of you.'

'Am I so mysterious?' smiled Mr Quin.

Mr Satterthwaite nodded vigorously.

'Yes, indeed. Do you know, until tonight, I had no idea that you were a professional dancer.'

'Really?' said Mr Quin.

'Listen,' said Mr Satterthwaite. He hummed the love motif from the Walküre. 'That is what has been ringing in my head all through dinner as I looked at those two.'

'Which two?'

'Prince Oranoff and Mrs Denman. Don't you see the difference in her tonight? It's as though – as though a shutter had suddenly been opened and you see the glow within.'

'Yes,' said Mr Quin. 'Perhaps so.'

'The same old drama,' said Mr Satterthwaite. 'I am right, am I not? Those two belong together. They are of the same world, think the same thoughts, dream the same dreams . . . One sees how it has come about. Ten years ago Denman must have been very good-looking, young, dashing, a figure of romance. And he saved her life. All quite natural. But now – what is he, after all? A good fellow – prosperous, successful – but – well, mediocre. Good honest English stuff – very much like that Hepplewhite furniture upstairs. As English – and as ordinary – as that pretty English girl with her fresh untrained voice. Oh, you may smile, Mr Quin, but you cannot deny what I am saying.'

'I deny nothing. In what you see you are always right. And yet – '

'Yet what?'

Mr Quin leaned forward. His dark melancholy eyes searched for those of Mr Satterthwaite.

'Have you learned so little of life?' he breathed.

He left Mr Satterthwaite vaguely disquieted, such a prey to meditation that he found the others had started without him owing to his delay in selecting a scarf for his neck. He went out by the garden, and through the same door as in the afternoon. The lane was bathed in moonlight, and even as he stood in the doorway he saw a couple enlaced in each other's arms.

For a moment he thought –

And then he saw. *John Denman and Molly Stanwell.* Denman's voice came to him, hoarse and anguished.

'I can't live without you. What are we to do?'

Mr Satterthwaite turned to go back the way he had come, but a hand stayed him. Someone else stood in the doorway beside him, someone else whose eyes had also seen.

Mr Satterthwaite had only to catch one glimpse of her face to know how wildly astray all his conclusions had been.

Her anguished hand held him there until those other two had passed up the lane and disappeared from sight. He heard himself speaking to her, saying foolish little things meant to be comforting, and ludicrously inadequate to the agony he had divined. She only spoke once.

'Please,' she said, 'don't leave me.'

He found that oddly touching. He was, then, of use to someone. And he went on saying those things that meant nothing at all, but which were, somehow, better than silence. They went that way to the Roscheimers. Now and then her hand tightened on his shoulder, and he understood that she was glad of his company. She only took it away when they finally came to their destination. She stood very erect, her head held high.

'Now,' she said, 'I shall dance! Do not be afraid for me, my friend. I shall dance.'

She left him abruptly. He was seized upon by Lady Roscheimer, much bediamonded and very full of lamentations. By her he was passed on to Claude Wickam.

'Ruined! Completely ruined. The sort of thing that always happens to me. All these country bumpkins think they can dance. I was never even consulted –' His voice went on – went on interminably. He had found a sympathetic listener, a man who *knew*. He gave himself up to an orgy of self-pity. It only ended when the first strains of music began.

Mr Satterthwaite came out of his dreams. He was alert, once more the critic. Wickam was an unutterable ass, but he could write music – delicate gossamer stuff, intangible as a fairy web – yet with nothing of the pretty pretty about it.

The scenery was good. Lady Roscheimer never spared expense when aiding her protégés. A glade of Arcady with lighting effects that gave it the proper atmosphere of unreality.

Two figures dancing as they had danced through time immemorial. A slender Harlequin flashing spangles in the moonlight with magic wand and masked face . . . A white Columbine pirouetting like some immortal dream . . .

Mr Satterthwaite sat up. He had lived through this before. Yes, surely . . .

Now his body was far away from Lady Roscheimer's drawingroom. It was in a Berlin Museum at a statuette of an immortal Columbine.

Harlequin and Columbine danced on. The wide world was theirs to dance in . . .

Moonlight – and a human figure. Pierrot wandering through the wood, singing to the moon. Pierrot who has seen Columbine and knows no rest. The Immortal two vanish, but Columbine looks back. She has heard the song of a human heart.

Pierrot wandering on through the wood . . . darkness . . . his voice dies away in the distance . . .

The village green – dancing of village girls – pierrots and pierrettes. Molly as Pierrette. No dancer – Anna Denman was right there – but a fresh tuneful voice as she sings her song 'Pierrette dancing on the Green.'

A good tune – Mr Satterthwaite nodded approval. Wickham wasn't above writing a tune when there was a need for it. The majority of the village girls made him shudder, but he realized that Lady Roscheimer was determinedly philanthropical.

They press Pierrot to join the dance. He refuses. With white face he wanders on – the eternal lover seeking his ideal. Evening falls. Harlequin and Columbine, invisible, dance in and out of the unconscious throng. The place is deserted, only Pierrot, weary, falls asleep on a grassy bank. Harlequin and Columbine dance round him. He wakes and sees Columbine. He woos her in vain, pleads, beseeches . . .

She stands uncertain. Harlequin beckons to her to begone. But she sees him no longer. She is listening to Pierrot, to his song of love outpoured once more. She falls into his arms, and the curtain comes down.

The second Act is Pierrot's cottage. Columbine sits on her hearth. She is pale, weary. She listens – for what? Pierrot sings to her – woos her back to thoughts of him once more. The evening darkens. Thunder is heard ... Columbine puts aside her spinning wheel. She is eager, stirred ... She listens no longer to Pierrot. It is her own music that is in the air, the music of Harlequin and Columbine ... She is awake. She remembers.

A crash of thunder! Harlequin stands in the doorway. Pierrot cannot see him, but Columbine springs up with a glad laugh. Children come running, but she pushes them aside. With another crash of thunder the walls fall, and Columbine dances out into the wild night with Harlequin.

Darkness, and through it the tune that Pierrette has sung. Light comes slowly. The cottage once more. Pierrot and Pierrette grown old and grey sit in front of the fire in two arm-chairs. The music is happy, but subdued. Pierrette nods in her chair. Through the window comes a shaft of moonlight, and with it the motif of Pierrot's long-forgotten song. He stirs in his chair.

Faint music – fairy music ... Harlequin and Columbine outside. The door swings open and Columbine dances in. She leans over the sleeping Pierrot, kisses him on the lips ...

Crash! A peal of thunder. She is outside again. In the centre of the stage is the lighted window and through it are seen the two figures of Harlequin and Columbine dancing slowly away, growing fainter and fainter ...

A log falls. Pierrette jumps up angrily, rushes across to the window and pulls the blind. So it ends, on a sudden discord ...

Mr Satterthwaite sat very still among the applause and vociferations. At last he got up and made his way outside. He came upon Molly Stanwell, flushed and eager, receiving compliments. He saw John Denman, pushing and elbowing his way through the throng, his eyes alight with a new flame. Molly came towards him, but, almost unconsciously, he put her aside. It was not her he was seeking.

'My wife? Where is she?'

'I think she went out in the garden.'

It was, however, Mr Satterthwaite who found her, sitting on a stone seat under a cypress tree. When he came up to her, he did an odd thing. He knelt down and raised her hand to his lips.

'Ah!' she said. 'You think I danced well?'

'You danced – as you always danced, Madame Kharsanova.'

She drew in her breath sharply.

'So – you have guessed.'

'There is only one Kharsanova. No one could see you dance and forget. But why – why?'

'What else is possible?'

'You mean?'

She had spoken very simply. She was just as simple now. 'Oh! but you understand. You are of the world. A great dancer – she can have lovers, yes – but a husband, that is different. And he – he did not want the other. He wanted me to belong to him as – as Kharsanova could never have belonged.'

'I see,' said Mr Satterthwaite. 'I see. So you gave it up?'

She nodded.

'You must have loved him very much,' said Mr Satterthwaite gently.

'To make such a sacrifice?' She laughed.

'Not quite that. To make it so light-heartedly.'

'Ah, yes – perhaps – you are right.'

'And now?' asked Mr Satterthwaite.

Her face grew grave.

'Now?' She paused, then raised her voice and spoke into the shadows.

'Is that you, Sergius Ivanovitch?'

Prince Oranoff came out into the moonlight. He took her hand and smiled at Mr Satterthwaite without self-consciousness.

'Ten years ago I mourned the death of Anna Kharsanova,' he said simply. 'She was to me as my other self. Today I have found her again. We shall part no more.'

'At the end of the lane in ten minutes,' said Anna. 'I shall not fail you.'

Oranoff nodded and went off again. The dancer turned to Mr Satterthwaite. A smile played about her lips.

'Well – you are not satisfied, my friend?'

'Do you know,' said Mr Satterthwaite abruptly, 'that your husband is looking for you?'

He saw the tremor that passed over her face, but her voice was steady enough.

'Yes,' she said gravely. 'That may well be.'

'I saw his eyes. They –' he stopped abruptly.

She was still calm.

'Yes, perhaps. For an hour. An hour's magic, born of past memories, of music, of moonlight – That is all.'

'Then there is nothing that I can say?' He felt old, dispirited.

'For ten years I have lived with the man I love,' said Anna Kharsanova. 'Now I am going to the man who for ten years has loved me.'

Mr Satterthwaite said nothing. He had no arguments left. Besides it really seemed the simplest solution. Only – only, somehow, it was not the solution he wanted. He felt her hand on his shoulder.

'I know, my friend, I know. But there is no third way. Always one looks for one thing – the lover, the perfect, the eternal lover . . . It is the music of Harlequin one hears. No lover ever satisfies one, for all lovers are mortal. And Harlequin is only a myth, an invisible presence . . . unless –'

'Yes,' said Mr Satterthwaite. 'Yes?'

'Unless – his name is – Death!'

Mr Satterthwaite shivered. She moved away from him, was swallowed up in the shadows . . .

He never knew quite how long he sat on there, but suddenly he started up with the feeling that he had been wasting valuable time. He hurried away, impelled in a certain direction almost in spite of himself.

As he came out into the lane he had a strange feeling of unreality. Magic – magic and moonlight! And two figures coming towards him . . .

Oranoff in his Harlequin dress. So he thought at first. Then, as they passed him, he knew his mistake. That lithe swaying figure belonged to one person only – Mr Quin . . .

They went on down the lane – their feet light as though they were treading on air. Mr Quin turned his head and looked back, and Mr Satterthwaite had a shock, for it was not the face of Mr Quin as he had ever seen it before. It was the face of a stranger – no, not quite a stranger. Ah! he had it now, it was the face of John Denman as it might have looked before life went too well with him. Eager, adventurous, the face at once of a boy and a lover . . .

Her laugh floated down to him, clear and happy . . . He looked after them and saw in the distance the lights of a little cottage. He gazed after them like a man in a dream.

He was rudely awakened by a hand that fell on his shoulder and he was jerked round to face Sergius Oranoff. The man looked white and distracted.

'Where is she? Where is she? She promised – and she has not come.'

'Madam has just gone up the lane – alone.'

It was Mrs Denman's maid who spoke from the shadow of the door behind them. She had been waiting with her mistress's wraps.

'I was standing here and saw her pass,' she added.

Mr Satterthwaite threw one harsh word at her.

'Alone? Alone, did you say?'

The maid's eyes widened in surprise.

'Yes, sir. Didn't you see her off?'

Mr Satterthwaite clutched at Oranoff.

'Quickly,' he muttered. 'I'm – I'm afraid.'

They hurried down the lane together, the Russian talking in quick disjointed sentences.

'She is a wonderful creature. Ah! how she danced tonight. And that friend of yours. Who is he? Ah! but he is wonderful – unique. In the old days, when she danced the Columbine of Rimsky Korsakoff, she never found the perfect Harlequin. Mordoff, Kassnine – none of them were quite perfect. She had her own little fancy. She told me of it once. Always she danced with a dream Harlequin – a man who was not really there. It was Harlequin himself, she said, who came to dance with her. It was that fancy of hers that made her Columbine so wonderful.'

Mr Satterthwaite nodded. There was only one thought in his head.

'Hurry,' he said. 'We must be in time. Oh! we must be in time.'

They came round the last corner – came to the deep pit and to something lying in it that had not been there before, the body of a woman lying in a wonderful pose, arms flung wide and head thrown back. A dead face and body that were triumphant and beautiful in the moonlight.

Words came back to Mr Satterthwaite dimly – Mr Quin's words: '*wonderful things on a rubbish heap*' . . . He understood them now.

Oranoff was murmuring broken phrases. The tears were streaming down his face.

'I loved her. Always I loved her.' He used almost the same words that had occurred to Mr Satterthwaite earlier in the day. 'We were of the same world, she and I. We had the same thoughts, the same dreams. I would have loved her always . . .'

'How do you know?'

The Russian stared at him – at the fretful peevishness of the tone.

'How do you know?' went on Mr Satterthwaite. 'It is what all lovers think – what all lovers say . . . There is only one lover –'

He turned and almost ran into Mr Quin. In an agitated manner, Mr Satterthwaite caught him by the arm and drew him aside.

'It was *you*,' he said. 'It was *you* who were with her just now?'

Mr Quin waited a minute and then said gently:

'You can put it that way, if you like.'

'And the maid didn't see you?'

'The maid didn't see me.'

'But *I* did. Why was that?'

'Perhaps, as a result of the price you have paid, you see things that other people – do not.'

Mr Satterthwaite looked at him uncomprehendingly for a minute or two. Then he began suddenly to quiver all over like an aspen leaf.

'What is this place?' he whispered. 'What is this place?'

'I told you earlier today. It is *My* lane.'

'A Lovers' Lane,' murmured Mr Satterthwaite. 'And people pass along it.'

'Most people, sooner or later.'

'And at the end of it – what do they find?'

Mr Quin smiled. His voice was very gentle. He pointed at the ruined cottage above them.

'The house of their dreams – or a rubbish heap – who shall say?'

Mr Satterthwaite looked up at him suddenly. A wild rebellion surged over him. He felt cheated, defrauded.

'But *I* –' His voice shook. '*I* have never passed down your lane . . .'

'And do you regret?'

Mr Satterthwaite quailed. Mr Quin seemed to have loomed to enormous proportions . . . Mr Satterthwaite had a vista of something at once menacing and terrifying . . . Joy, Sorrow, Despair.

And his comfortable little soul shrank back appalled.

'Do you regret?' Mr Quin repeated his question. There was something terrible about him.

'No,' Mr Satterthwaite stammered. 'N-no.'

And then suddenly he rallied.

'But I see things,' he cried. 'I may have been only a looker-on at Life – but I see things that other people do not. You said so yourself, Mr Quin . . .'

But Mr Quin had vanished.

Postscript

In March 1930 a new collection of twelve Agatha Christie short stories appeared introducing two new characters: Mr Harley Quin and Mr Satterthwaite. But, unlike the short stories in which Poirot was the hero, these had not been written specifically to make up a single collection.

'These are my favourite. I wrote one, not very often, at intervals perhaps of three or four months, sometimes longer still. Magazines appeared to like them, and I liked them myself, but I refused all offers to do a series for any periodical. I didn't want to do a series of Mr Quin: I only wanted to do one when I felt like it. He was a kind of carry-over for me from my early poems in the Harlequin and Columbine series,' wrote Agatha Christie in her autobiography.

In fact, at around the age of 17/18, deeply impressed by the characters of the commedia dell'arte, *Agatha Christie had written a series of poems inspired by the legend of Arlequin:* The Song of Arlequin, The Song of Colombine, *and* The Song of Pierrot and Pierrette, *which were published in her first collection of poems* The Road of Dreams *(1924). Arlequin's character in particular fascinated Agatha; indeed it is to him that she dedicated* The Mysterious Mr Quin: *'To Arlequin, the invisible'.*

The substitute of Arlequin in this series of almost fairytale, supernatural style detective stories is, of course, Harley Quin who, from his first appearance, finds himself dressed in a curious outfit coloured like a shining stain glass window. 'His mere presence affected human beings. There would be some little fact, some apparently irrelevant phrase, to point him out for what he was: a man shown in a harlequin-coloured light that fell on him through a glass window; a sudden appearance or disappearance. Always he stood for the same thing: he was a friend of lovers, and connected with death' (Agatha Christie's An Autobiography*). Mr Satterthwaite, whom he meets in* The Coming of Mr Quin,* is a gentleman in his sixties, who prides himself on his knowledge of art and photography and escapes from the emptiness of his own life by observing with such interest that of others. Through these short stories, he finds himself mixed up in a whole series of criminal and detective affairs which remain unclear until the apparition and sibylline remarks of Mr Quin open the path of truth to him. Each time Agatha Christie uses Mr Quin as a catalyst.

Apart from the twelve short stories collected together here, Mr Quin and Mr Satterthwaite appear in two other short stories: The Love Detectives, *also written in the 1920s (1927 to be exact) and published in 1950 in the USA in* Three Blind Mice and Other Stories, *and* The Harlequin Tea Set, *written in the 1950s and published in the anthology* Winter's Crimes 3 *in 1971. Both appear in the collection* Problem at Pollensa Bay *(1991). Mr Satterthwaite appeared solo in the short story* Dead Man's Mirror *(in* Murder in the Mews, *1937) and in* Three Act Tragedy *(1935), two Hercule Poirot investigations.*

After its initial appearance in a magazine, The Coming of Mr Quin – *the first story of this collection* – was adapted for the cinema by Leslie Hiscott under the title The Passing of Mr Quin, *produced by Julius Hagne with Stewart Rome, Trilby Clark and Ursula Jeans in the principal roles. Janet Morgan tells us that Agatha Christie did not rate this film much. The script was made into a book by G. Roy McRae and published under the title* The Passing of Mr Quin *by the London Book Company in a cut-price series in 1929. Such practice is clearly not as recent as one might have thought . . .*

All Agatha Christie titles are available from HarperCollins: